WAR OF
HONOR

WAR OF
HONOR

DAVID WEBER

WAR OF HONOR

This is a work of fiction. All the characters and events portrayed in this book are fictional, and any resemblance to real people or incidents is purely coincidental.

A Baen Books Original

Baen Publishing Enterprises
P.O. Box 1403
Riverdale, NY 10471
www.baen.com

ISBN: 0-7434-3545-1

Cover art by David Mattingly
Interior maps by Hunter Peddicord & N.C. Hanger

First printing, October 2002

Library of Congress Cataloging-in-Publication Data

Weber, David, 1952–
     War of honor / David Weber.
        p. cm.
     "A Baen Books original."
     ISBN 0-7434-3545-1
     1. Harrington, Honor (Fictitious character)—Fiction. 2. Space warfare—Fiction.
     I. Title.

PS3573.E217 W375 2002
813'.54—dc21   2002026203

Distributed by Simon & Schuster
1230 Avenue of the Americas
New York, NY 10020

Production by Windhaven Press, Auburn, NH
Printed in the United States of America

10   9   8   7   6   5   4   3   2   1

For every adoptive parent who knows
the true heart-hunger.

God bless.

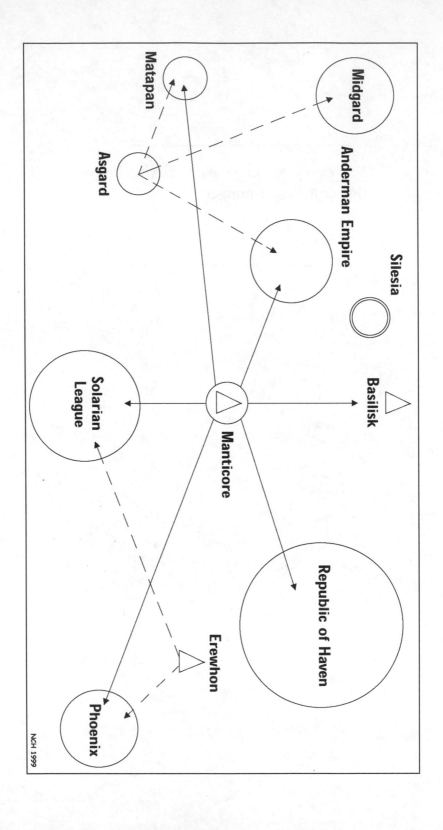

Midgard

Matapan

Asgard

Anderman Empire

Silesia

Basilisk

Solarian
League

Manticore

Republic of Haven

Erewhon

Phoenix

NCH 1999

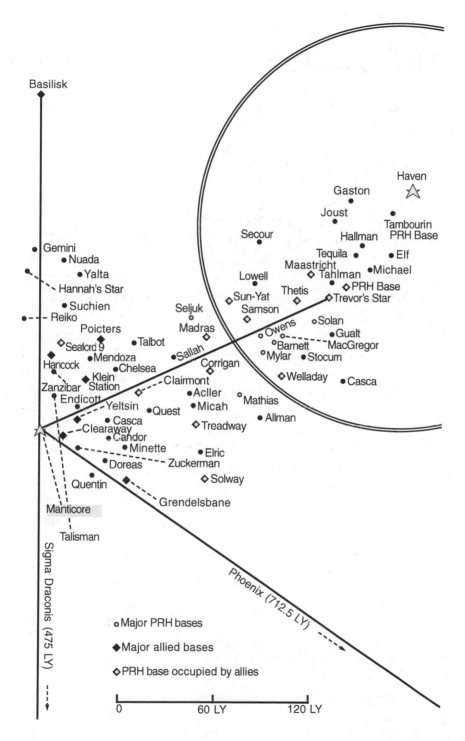

Basilisk

Haven

Gaston

Joust

Secour

Hallman

Tambourin
PRH Base

Gemini

Nuada

Yalta

Tequila

Elf

Maastricht

Hannah's Star

Lowell

Tahlman

Michael

Suchien

Thetis

PRH Base

Reiko

Sun-Yat
Samson

Trevor's Star

Poicters

Seljuk

Madras

Solan

Owens

Gualt

Sealord 9

Talbot

Barnett

MacGregor

Mendoza

Sallah

Mylar

Stocum

Hancock

Chelsea

Corrigan

Welladay

Casca

Zanzibar

Klein
Station

Clairmont

Endicott

Acller

Mathias

Yeltsin

Quest

Micah

Allman

Casca

Clearaway

Treadway

Candor

Minette

Elric

Doreas

Zuckerman

Quentin

Solway

Grendelsbane

Manticore

Talisman

Phoenix (712.5 LY)

Sigma Draconis (475 LY)

○ Major PRH bases

◆ Major allied bases

◇ PRH base occupied by allies

0   60 LY   120 LY

Hunter Peddicord

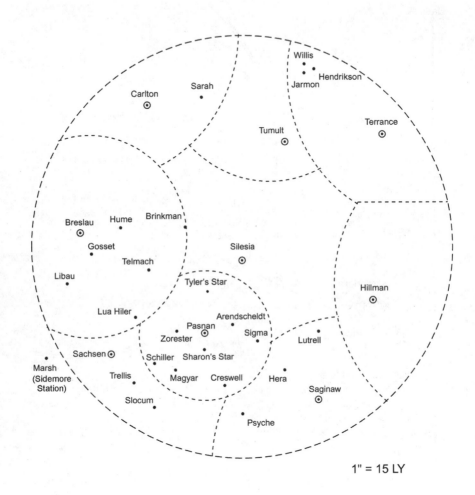

1" = 15 LY

WAR OF HONOR

PROLOGUE

"Com confirms it, Sir." *Korvetten Kapitän* Engelmann sounded as if he couldn't quite believe his own report.

"You're joking." *Kapitän der Sterne* Huang Glockauer, Imperial Andermani Navy, commanding officer of the heavy cruiser IANS *Gangying*, looked at his executive officer in astonishment. "Code Seventeen-Alpha?"

"No question, Sir. Ruihuan's positive. As of thirteen-oh-six hours, that's what they're squawking." Engelmann glanced at the bulkhead date/time display. "That's over six minutes, so I doubt that it's a mistake."

"Then it's got to be a malfunction," Glockauer half-muttered, eyes swinging back to his auxiliary plot and the glittering icon of the four-megaton Andermani-flagged freighter from which *Gangying* had just requested a routine identification. "Nobody could be stupid enough to try to sail right past us squawking a Seventeen-Alpha—much less squawk it in response to a specific challenge!"

"I can't dispute your logic, Skipper," Engelmann replied. He knew Glockauer wasn't actually speaking to him, but one of an executive officer's responsibilities was to play the part of his commanding officer's alter ego. He was responsible for managing the smooth functioning of the captain's ship, of course, but that was only part of his job. He was also responsible for providing a sounding board

1

when the captain needed one, and this situation was so bizarre that Glockauer needed a sounding board badly at the moment.

"On the other hand," the exec continued, "I've seen pirates do some pretty stupid things over the years."

"So have I," Glockauer admitted. "But I've never seen any of them do anything *this* stupid."

"I've been thinking about that, Skip," Engelmann said diffidently, "and I wonder if it's actually so much a case of their being stupid or of someone else's having been sneaky."

"How?"

"Well, every merchant line knows that if one of its ships is taken, whoever grabbed her will want to pull the wool over the eyes of any Navy ships they run into. But most navies have at least their own national shipping list in memory—complete with transponder codes matched to emissions signatures. So pirates also know there's at least some risk an alert plotting and com team will cross check and notice some little flaw any time they use a false transponder code." The exec shrugged. "That's why pirates tend to go on using the original code until they get a prize safely tucked away somewhere, rather than generating a fresh, false one."

"Of course it is," Glockauer said as his second-in-command paused. His comment could have sounded impatient, since Engelmann was busy saying something both of them already knew perfectly well. But he recognized that tone of voice. Binyan was onto something, and Glockauer was willing to give him time to lay out the groundwork for whatever it was.

"The thing I'm wondering, Skipper," the *korvetten kapitän* said, "is whether or not someone at Reichenbach figured out a way to take advantage of that tendency. Suppose they set up the beacon software to tag the transponder with a Seventeen-Alpha if the ship was taken? If they did, then they could also have rigged the rest of their software to strip the tag off when it plays the transponder code back to the bridge crew."

"You're suggesting that someone in the command crew activated a booby trap in the transponder programming when he realized his ship was about to be taken?"

"I'm suggesting that that *might* be what happened," Engelmann agreed. "Think about it. There's no way a normal merchie can hope to stand off a pirate. They're not armed, and the only thing trying to resist boarding parties would accomplish would be to absolutely assure a massacre once they actually got aboard. So if the command crew figured they might be able to pull off something like I'm suggesting may have happened here, it would have to be pretty tempting."

"Um." Glockauer rubbed his upper lip thoughtfully. "You're right about that," he said after moment. "Especially if the pirates decided to keep the original crew alive and force them to work the ship for them. Their best chance of being rescued—their only chance, really—would be for the people who grabbed them to stumble across a warship which somehow managed to realize they'd been taken."

He rubbed his lip some more while he considered the scenario he and Engelmann were discussing. Code Seventeen was a standard, universal merchant ship transponder code, although it was used far more often in bad adventure fiction than in reality. The code's actual meaning was "I am being boarded by pirates," but there wasn't really any point in squawking the code unless there happened to be a friendly warship practically in the merchie's lap when the pirates turned up. In very rare instances, a pirate might break off an attack in the face of a Code Seventeen if he thought there was a warship in range to pick up the signal and intervene. But that happened so seldom that a great many merchant skippers preferred not to squawk Code Seventeen under any circumstances. Pirates had been known to wreak particularly gruesome revenge on merchant spacers who'd attempted to resist . . . or to summon help.

Seventeen-Alpha was even rarer than a straight Code Seventeen, however. Seventeen-Alpha didn't mean "I am being boarded by pirates"; it meant "I have *been* boarded and taken by pirates." Frankly, Glockauer couldn't remember a single instance outside a Fleet training exercise in which he'd ever heard of anyone squawking a Seventeen-Alpha.

"Still," he went on after a moment, putting his thoughts into words, "it'd be risky. If the pirates' prize crew activated the transponder while their own ship was still close enough to pick it up, they'd spot it in a heartbeat, however the merchie's own communications software might have been buggered up. Even if they didn't bring the transponder up while their buddies were still in range, eventually they're going to make port somewhere, and when they do, someone's going to pick up the code. Which would almost certainly entail some seriously unpleasant consequences for whoever activated the booby trap software."

"There's not much question about that," Engelmann acknowledged with a small shrug. "On the other hand, it could be that whoever thought it up figured that between the possibility that the crew would already have been massacred, or that they'd be massacred anyway whenever they reached their final destination, the risk was worth it if it gave any of their people even a tiny chance of being rescued."

"Fair enough," Glockauer conceded. "And I suppose they could have built a few additional precautions into this hypothetical software we're theorizing about. For example, what if the program was designed to delay the activation of the Seventeen-Alpha? If it squawked a clean transponder for, say, twenty-four or thirty-six hours before it added the Code Seventeen, the odds would be pretty good that the original pirate cruiser would be far out of range when it did. And the program could also be set up to terminate the Code Seventeen after a set period, or under specific circumstances—like after the ship translates back out of hyper the first time."

"It could be." Engelmann nodded. "Or, it could be even simpler than that," he pointed out. "The only reason they squawked their beacon at all was because we requested an ID, Skipper. And we identified ourselves as a warship when we did."

"Now that, Binyan, is an excellent thought," Glockauer approved. "If the software's set up to automatically append the Seventeen-Alpha to any ID request from a warship, but not under any other circumstances . . ."

"Exactly," the exec said. "Although, it would have been nice— assuming that there's anything to this entire theory—if Reichenbach had bothered to warn us that they were going to do something like this."

"Might not be a line-wide decision," Glockauer replied. "Mind you, Old Man Reichenbach was born with a poker up his ass, and he runs his company the way he damned well pleases. I wouldn't put it past him to have come up with the idea and ordered it implemented without even discussing it with his skippers. Or, on the other hand, it might be that this was the bright idea of some individual captain. A one-time solo shot, as it were, that Reichenbach himself doesn't know a thing about."

"Or," Engelmann said, reverting to another of a good executive officer's other roles and playing devil's advocate, "it could be that there's nothing spectacular going on here at all. It might just be that some merchie com officer has managed to screw up and accidentally squawk an emergency code without even realizing he's done it."

"Possible," Glockauer said, "but not likely. As you already suggested, their own com equipment ought to be picking up the discrepancy by now . . . unless there's some specific reason why it's not. In any case, we don't have any option but to proceed on the assumption that it's genuine."

"No, Sir," Engelmann agreed, and the two of them returned their attention to the plot.

The green icon of the freighter, still showing the alphanumeric transponder code assigned to AMS *Karawane* and surrounded by the angry scarlet circle of Code Seventeen-Alpha, moved steadily across the display. Glockauer considered the data sidebars carefully, then turned his head to look across at *Gangying*'s tactical officer.

"How's your solution look, Shilan?"

"We've got the overtake on him without any problem, Sir," *Kapitän Leutnant* Shilan Weiss assured him. "And we can pull almost twice his maximum acceleration." She shrugged. "There's no way he could evade us. Even if he turns and runs for it right this second, we can run him down for a zero-zero intercept at least a full light-minute short of the hyper limit."

"Shilan's right, Skipper," Engelmann said. "But just turning and chasing them down would be a brute force solution to the problem." He smiled thinly, and it was not a pleasant expression. "I have to admit that what I'd really prefer would be to come up with some brilliant stratagem that tricked the bastards into letting us close with them without all that effort."

"Not in this universe, Binyan," Glockauer snorted. "Of course, assuming they have someone over there who can run the numbers as well as Shilan, they'll know the moment we go after them that they can't slip away. The only really logical thing for them to do would be to heave to immediately and hope we're inclined to take prisoners rather than just shoot them out of hand. But whether they're inclined to see it that way or not, there's no way to trick any crew of pirates, however stupid they may be, into thinking it would be a good idea to let a heavy cruiser into range of them."

"I'm afraid you're right about that, Skipper," Engelmann admitted. "And there's no way they're going to miss seeing us coming, either."

"Hardly," Glockauer agreed dryly. He gazed at the plot for a few more seconds, then nodded to himself.

"All right, Shilan. If there's no point trying to be cute about it, we might as well be brutally direct. Put us on an intercept heading at five hundred gravities. Ruihuan," he went on, looking at *Kapitän Leutnant* Hoffner, his communications officer, "go ahead and hail them. Tell them who we are, and 'suggest' that they heave to for rendezvous."

"Aye, aye, Sir!" Hoffner acknowledged with a grin.

"And just to give Ruihuan's suggestion a little added point, Shilan," Glockauer continued, "why don't you go ahead and bring up your targeting systems? A few long-range radar and lidar hits should help to convince him we're serious."

"Aye, aye, Sir." Weiss' smile was at least as unpleasant as Engelmann's had been, and she turned back to her console and her tracking party as the heavy cruiser altered course.

Glockauer returned her smile and waved Engelmann towards his own station, then settled back in his command chair to await *Karawane*'s reply to Hoffner's demand that she heave to. His eyes returned to the icon burning in his plot, and his smile faded.

Piracy was always a problem here in the Silesian Confederacy. Silesia had never been anything but a sort of ongoing political meltdown at the best of times, and in this one thousand nine hundred and eighteenth year of mankind's diaspora to the stars, the times were anything but the best. In fact, things had been going steadily downhill even from Silesia's ramshackle norm for the last fifteen T-years.

Little though Glockauer or any other Andermani officer might care to admit it, the Royal Manticoran Navy had been the true mainstay of piracy suppression in the Confederacy for over two centuries. It was only in the last hundred or so T-years that the Andermani Empire's fleet had begun to acquire the size and the numbers to pretend to exercise any meaningful, long-term police power in the area. Glockauer knew that was true, just as he understood that until the last fifty years—seventy-five, at the most—

the Andermani merchant fleet had been too insignificant to justify the expense required to build up the Navy's light forces to a
point which would have permitted it to make any real inroad into
the bloody forays of the Confederacy's pirates and privateers.

Of course, even though piracy suppression was a natural part of
the responsibilities of any naval officer, the Empire's interest in Silesia
had never been limited to, or even primarily focused on, the losses
of its merchant lines. The true Andermani interest in the Confederacy had been unwaveringly focused upon frontier security concerns and the possibility of expansion. It would have been impolitic
(to say the least) to admit that aloud, but no one in the Empire,
the Confederacy, or the Star Kingdom of Manticore with an IQ
above that of a rock could have had any illusions in that regard.
Certainly, the Manties had been quick to depress any Andermani
pretensions to sovereignty in the Confederacy, which they regarded
with depressing arrogance as their own private fishing pond.

The grueling demands of the Manticoran war against the People's
Republic of Haven had distracted the RMN from its traditional
role as the policeman of Silesia, though. That distraction had grown
increasingly pronounced over the last fifty or sixty T-years, during the RMN's build up to face the Peeps, and especially in the
last fourteen or fifteen, after the actual shooting started. Glockauer
wasn't supposed to know about the high-level internal debates in
both the Navy and the Foreign Ministry over how the Empire
ought to have responded to the combination of steadily worsening local conditions and the opportunity the Manties' distraction
offered. Again, however, only an idiot could have been unaware
of them. On the one hand, the Manticoran preoccupation with
the Peeps had been an almost irresistible temptation to satisfy the
Empire's long-standing territorial ambitions while the RMN had
too much on its plate to respond effectively. On the other hand,
the Star Kingdom had been the Empire's buffer against the People's
Republic's insatiable expansionism.

In the end, *real politik* had governed, as it had a tendency to
do in the Empire's foreign policy. Acquiring outright control of
its legitimate sphere of interest in the Confederacy might have been
nice, but joggling Manticore's elbow while the Star Kingdom was
fighting for its life against someone who would just love to gobble
up the Empire, as well, might have been fatal. So the Andermani
Empire had elected to be "neutral" in the Star Kingdom's favor.

But the RMN's abrupt, stunning victory over the People's Navy had been even more complete than anyone had ever anticipated. So far as Glockauer knew, no one in Naval Intelligence had so much as suspected what sort of knockout punch the Manties had been preparing to deliver. Obviously, Intelligence had known at least a little about what Manticoran R&D had been up to. The recent and ongoing additions to the IAN's own hardware were proof enough of that, especially in light of the reports Glockauer had read of the Manties' new weapons and tactics. But he very much doubted that anyone in the Empire had realized the full magnitude of the RMN's qualitative superiority over its foe until Admiral White Haven finally pulled the trigger.

By rights, the RMN should by now have reverted to its pre-war stance throughout the Confederacy. It hadn't, and in some ways, the situation was even worse than it had been before the war. The Manticorans hadn't built their light forces back up to their traditional levels, which meant piracy continued to flourish largely unchecked in much of the Confederacy. Worse, some of the "pirates" out here had acquired rather more capable ships. None of them were bigger than cruisers, but so far the Manties and the IAN between them had destroyed at least three of those which had . . . left the service of the People's Republic of Haven and fled to find greener pastures elsewhere. That meant that not only had the level of lawless activity increased, but so had its scope, with more planetary raids added to run-of-the-mill piracy. Intelligence's most recent estimate was that as many as a quarter million Sillies had been killed in the last year alone. A pinprick against the total population of something the size of the Confederacy, but a horrifying number when it was considered in isolation.

But if the Manties hadn't built their light forces back up, they *had* established a treaty relationship with the Sidemore Republic in the Marsh System. Over the past eight T-years, Sidemore had been built up into a fairly powerful fleet base, despite the Manticorans' need to concentrate most of their effort against the Peeps. The Marsh System's location, just outside the somewhat amorphous borders claimed by the Confederacy and on the flank of the Empire-to-Confederacy leg of the Manties' "Triangle Route," made it an ideal logistics base for the RMN's operations throughout southwestern Silesia.

Other than a certain desire to do it for himself, Glockauer had no objection to watching the Manticorans swat pirates. And their Marsh-based flotillas had enabled them to do a remarkable job of pacifying something like a tenth of the entire Confederacy. But they'd done it by establishing a *Manticoran* presence in an area in which they had persistently refused to countenance an Andermani one. If any star nation had a legitimate interest in controlling the situation in Silesia to protect its own borders and territorial integrity, that nation was the Andermani Empire . . . not the Star Kingdom of Manticore. Worse, the Manties had based an entire task force, two understrength squadrons of the wall, with battlecruiser and cruiser support, at their new Sidemore Station.

Ostensibly, those forces, which were far heavier than would have been required for any legitimate anti-piracy operations, were intended to cover Confederate space against a fresh intrusion of Peep commerce raiding squadrons. The official Manty position— to which the freelance operations of rogue ex-State Security and ex-People's Navy warships lent a certain point—was that covering against any renewal of the Peeps' commerce warfare in the Confederacy was the true (and only) reason for their treaty with Sidemore. No one in the Empire believed that for a moment, and resentment against Manticoran high-handedness had grown steadily over the last five T-years or so. Now that the Peeps had been militarily defeated, whether an actual peace treaty had been finalized or not, that excuse for the RMN's presence in Marsh was growing steadily more threadbare. Resentment over it had increased in direct proportion, and Glockauer suspected that the foreign policy considerations which had mitigated against any confrontation with Manticore were rapidly eroding.

He had no idea of where that might eventually lead. No, that wasn't really true. He had a very good idea of where it *might* lead . . . he only hoped fervently that it wouldn't in the end. Despite the recent and continuing upgrades in his navy's combat power, and despite the obvious idiocy of the new Manticoran First Lord of the Admiralty, he had no desire to face the fleet which had proven its undisputed ability to annihilate the once-mighty People's Navy.

But at the moment, he reminded himself, watching *Karawane*'s icon altering course on his plot, turning futilely away in a wallowing effort to evade his own, fleeter vessel, he didn't have to worry about Manties.

All he had to worry about was what sort of atrocity his boarding parties were likely to discover aboard the fleeing merchantman. Experience suggested that it would not be pleasant.

"Message from Commodore Zrubek, Sir."

Admiral Lester Tourville, who was unabashedly delighted that he was no longer *Citizen* Admiral Tourville, looked up from his plot at Lieutenant Eisenberg's announcement. It still seemed odd to see her on his flag deck, but he supposed Tom Theisman was right. The smoothly functioning staffs he and Javier Giscard had assembled over the last several years had been a major factor in the success of the task forces and fleets under their command. But as valuable as those well-tested command teams had been, they'd also been replaceable. He and Javier had built them once; they could build replacements, if they had to, and in the meantime, those superbly trained staffers were far too valuable for them to hang selfishly onto. And so the subordinates with whom Tourville had fought against the Manties for the better part of ten T-years had moved on to other duties and long- overdue promotions.

On the other hand, his new com officer, Lieutenant Anita Eisenberg, was even newer than most of his replacement staff. She'd been assigned to him less than six T-months ago, and he was still getting accustomed to her rather extreme youthfulness. He had to keep reminding himself that, at a mere twenty-eight T-years, the solidly built blonde wasn't actually the babe in arms she so resembled. The fact that, as a third-generation prolong recipient, she looked as if she were about twelve didn't help, and neither did the fact that she stood only a very little over a meter and a half in height. The truth was that she *was* extremely young for her rank, but that was true of a lot of officers in Haven's navy these days. And, he reminded himself, despite a pronounced predilection for military formality, she possessed a competence and a self-confidence at odds with her undeniable youth.

He brushed the thought aside once more, not without the reflection that perhaps his impression of her youth had something to do with the bone-deep weariness which made him feel every month of his own much greater age, and waved her closer to his command chair. She handed him an electronic memo board, and a dark-haired man looked out of the small screen at him when he pressed the playback button.

"You were right, Sir," Commodore Scott Zrubek told him without preamble. "They were trying to sucker us, just as you suspected they might. So I held the rest of the squadron at extreme range and sent a couple of destroyer divisions in to take a closer look at those 'merchantmen' of theirs. I think there may have been a small change of management when they saw what we were doing."

Zrubek's smile could really be extremely unpleasant, Tourville noted approvingly.

"It looks like they'd stuffed their cargo holds full of missile pods," the commodore continued. "They'd obviously hoped we'd come in close enough for them to roll the pods, but when they realized we weren't going to bring the heavy ships into their range, someone figured out that just killing off the destroyers was only going to really, really piss us off. So since we'd declined to walk into their ambush and there was no way in hell those merchies could run away from us, they decided to own up and surrender while we were in a prisoner-taking mood. Unfortunately, from the preliminary reports, it sounds like their CO had other ideas, so apparently his exec shot him in the back of the head to change his mind."

Tourville grimaced. There'd been a lot of that going around lately, and he supposed he had to consider it a good sign, over all. But that didn't make the scenario Zrubek was describing any less ugly.

"At any rate, Sir," the commodore went on, "we've got the merchantmen, and what looks like the better part of three of the old StateSec intervention battalions that were serving as Marines—more or less, anyway. Some of the StateSec goons may have been conscripts since Saint-Just got the boot, but it looks to me like the bulk of them are pretty hard-core. One or two of them actually wanted to put up a fight when we boarded, and I've got my staff spook running them through the database now. I'm not going to be surprised if some of them turn up on the 'shoot on sight' list.

"In the meantime, we're firmly in control of all six ships, with what I'd estimate to be the equivalent of two or three superdreadnought load-outs worth of missile pods on board. My people are vacuuming the computers now, and the previous owners were too busy bargaining for their lives and surrendering to worry about data dumps. We've got our crypto teams ready for a preliminary run at the secure portions, and I'm having complete downloads prepared to send over to the flagship.

"My present estimate is that Carson sent these poor turkeys out to slow us down because his cupboard is bare of real warships. I wouldn't be surprised if we're able to get our hands on the IFF codes for his minefields, as well. On the other hand, he might be smart enough to plant fake ones on us, so I'm not planning on having any sudden inspirations without clearance from you. I should have the situation here completely squared away within the next five to six hours. I'll put prize crews aboard the merchies and send them back to Haven, and barring anything untoward, I should rendezvous with the rest of the fleet no later than seventeen hundred hours on the twenty-third. The locals seem pretty glad to see us, and I don't think we're going to need much in the way of a garrison to hang onto the planet, so I don't expect anything to delay me.

"Zrubek clear."

The screen blanked, and Tourville nodded in approval. Zrubek was one of the new crop of junior flag officers he and Javier had been grooming for the past three years. The assignment to clear the Montague System of the ragtag remnants of Citizen General Adrian Carson's forces had been the commodore's first real solo operation, and it sounded as if he'd passed his graduation exercise with flying colors. Which was exactly what Tourville had anticipated when he sent the youngster off. In many ways, Montague had been something of a training operation with teeth, but if Zrubek had gotten cocky and strayed into range of the sort of missile firepower which seemed to have been aboard Carson's freighters the outcome could have been very different. That was why Tourville had wanted to be certain Zrubek really was as ready for independent command as he'd thought he was.

Strange, he thought. *All those years under StateSec's thumb, and I thought the worst thing that could happen to me was to get myself shot. Now StateSec is in the crapper, and instead, I have to worry about whether or not the people I send out with task groups are going to bring them back to me in one piece. Funny how much less sleep I lost over the possibility of getting shot.*

He snorted a chuckle at the reflection, then frowned thoughtfully.

With Montague out of the way, Carson was reduced to only two star systems still under his direct control. Citizen Admiral Agnelli, Carson's theoretical ally currently controlled three more, but Agnelli and Carson had been strange bedfellows from the beginning. Both of them were ambitious, but Carson apparently retained at least some genuine loyalty to the New Order created by the Committee of Public Safety. That might have something to do with the high StateSec rank he'd attained under the previous management, and he was a thoroughly unpleasant individual, who remained addicted to brutality and terror as his preferred methods of crowd control. But for all that, there was at least some evidence he was motivated by something other than the possibility of personal gain.

No one would ever be foolish enough to believe anything of that sort where Federico Agnelli was concerned. Tourville reminded himself that he might be prejudiced by the fact that he'd known Agnelli for many years, and detested him for all of them. The reminder was strictly *pro forma*, however, because try as he might, he couldn't think of a single redeeming character-istic Agnelli might have possessed. The man was a marginally competent tactician, with a pronounced belief in his own infal-libility. He'd climbed aboard the Committee's political bandwagon not because of any belief in what Rob Pierre and Oscar Saint-Just had promised the Mob but because it had offered him the opportunity for personal power, and he'd played the political game with a skillfulness which somehow managed to elude him in the field of naval tactics. At least two other flag officers Tourville knew of had been shot because they'd stood in Agnelli's way and he'd convinced StateSec they were "enemies of the People" to get rid of them.

Which meant that if Carson was in as much trouble as Tourville thought he was, especially after the loss of Montague, Agnelli would cut his losses in a heartbeat and abandon his "ally" to his fate. Which was ultimately stupid of him, since it would leave him all alone to face Twelfth Fleet when Tourville got around to him, in turn. But no doubt he believed someone else would turn up for him to play off against the central government. He'd always been able to manage that before, after all, and he'd held off both all internal opposition and the Republican Navy for the better part of three and a half T-years in the process.

Unfortunately for him, that wouldn't be possible much longer, Tourville thought with deep, uncomplicated satisfaction. He,

Giscard, and Thomas Theisman had faced a daunting task when they set about putting down all the Hydra-headed threats to the security of the new government. If he'd had any choice, Tourville would never have accepted any part of the responsibility for dealing with the snake pit of constantly changing alliances and betrayals between everyone who believed he or she had just as much claim to the rulership of the People's Republic of Haven as the people who'd overthrown the Committee. Unfortunately, he hadn't had a choice, any more than Tom Theisman had had one. And the good news was that very few of the warlords and would-be warlords who'd struck out for themselves were still on the board. Which was why Federico Agnelli was about to find himself extremely hard pressed to replace Carson as an ally.

It may just be that we're about to clean up this entire sector, Tourville allowed himself to think. *And if we can do that here, we only have two or three more real trouble spots to deal with. My God. Tom and Eloise were right all along. We really* are *going to win this thing.*

He shook his head, astounded by his own temerity in daring to contemplate anything of the sort, then looked up and handed the memo board back to Eisenberg.

"Thank you, Anita," he said gravely. "See that a copy of the Commodore's dispatch is downloaded to our next report to Nouveau Paris, would you please?"

"Of course, Sir." The com officer clasped the board under her arm, snapped to attention with parade ground precision, turned on her heel, and marched back towards her station.

Tourville watched her go and tried not to smile too broadly.

Admiral Michel Reynaud, Manticore Astro Control Service, missed his old office. Not that anyone seemed about to offer him a great deal of sympathy over its loss, he admitted, and that was probably fair enough. After all, his new, magnificent, huge, luxurious, and all those other superlatives office aboard Her Majesty's Space Station *Hephaestus* was only one of the perks which had come with his recent promotion, so he should undoubtedly stop whining and enjoy it. It was just that splendid though it was, it wasn't the one he'd spent the last fifteen T-years arranging exactly the way he wanted it.

Besides, he'd liked his old job much better than his new one.

Or, no, that wasn't quite true. He'd just liked the people he'd worked for better.

He tipped back in the sinful comfort of his automatically contouring chair and ostentatiously planted the heels of his boots squarely in the middle of his huge desk's blotter. Then he clasped his hands behind his head and gazed up at the deckhead while he contemplated the perversity of success.

When he'd first been sent to the Basilisk System as a relatively junior officer, it hadn't precisely been a plum assignment. As a matter of fact, no one had been certain the Star Kingdom of Manticore was even going to keep the place, and if the Liberals and the Conservative Association had had their way, Manticore wouldn't have. But those ill-matched partners in isolationism hadn't had their way, and over the next half T-century, Basilisk had become an immensely important and valuable possession. The traffic through the Basilisk terminus of the Manticore Wormhole Junction had grown by leaps and bounds, until it accounted for almost a third of all traffic through the Junction, and Lieutenant Reynaud had advanced steadily through Commander Reynaud, to Captain Reynaud, to Admiral Reynaud, commanding officer, Basilisk Astro Control.

And then, of course, the Peeps had blown the entire Basilisk infrastructure to Hell.

Remembered pain twisted Reynaud's face as he recalled the devastating Havenite raid which had utterly demolished a half-century of investment and development. Warehouses, repair facilities, building slips, solar power satellites, orbital farms, transient housing, orbital factories and refineries . . . It had been the single most successful Peep attack of the entire war, and Reynaud had gotten entirely too close a look at it. Indeed, Astro Control had been on the Peep list as well, and only the fact that Eighth Fleet had gotten there in time had saved it. And, he conceded, that was probably the only thing that had saved his own life, as well.

But that had been five T-years ago. Basilisk was rebuilding now, and much more rapidly than anyone—including Reynaud—would have believed possible before the attack. Partly he supposed that was because the original infrastructure had grown only as the demand for it grew, whereas the replacement installations had been designed and constructed to meet an established and clearly understood need. And another factor, he acknowledged unhappily, was that the High Ridge Government had seen the reconstruction of Basilisk as a perfect opportunity to pour vast sums into public projects. Not only did it create jobs, not a minor consideration now that the military was downsizing and demobilized Navy personnel were glutting the job market, but it fitted perfectly with the High Ridge slogan: "Building the Peace."

Damned straight they're "building the peace," Reynaud thought disgustedly. *The idiots certainly couldn't have fought the* war! *But I guess Basilisk is probably less of a scam than some of their other programs.*

And that, he acknowledged, if only to himself, was the real reason he disliked his present job. Not just because it had taken him away from Basilisk while the star system was still climbing back to its feet, but because in his opinion the entire program he'd been tapped to command had been authorized only because High Ridge and his stooges saw it as one more PR-rich boondoggle.

Be fair, he scolded himself. *They may be padding the budget, and they're certainly playing their brainchild for all it's worth politically, but it really is about time someone got behind Kare and pushed. I just hate all the hoopla. And then there's the fact that I don't happen to think the government is the best entity to be doing the pushing. And the fact that I really, really don't like having people like Makris hanging over my shoulder . . . or harassing the people who work for me. And—*

He made himself stop adding to the laundry list of things he didn't much like about the situation. Besides, he admitted very, very privately, a lot of them simply added together and boiled down to how much he hated the fact that Baron High Ridge and his cronies would see to it that they got any credit that came of it.

He glowered at the deckhead for several more seconds, then glanced at his chrono, sighed, returned his feet to their proper place on the decksole, and allowed his chair to come back upright. Speaking of Dr. Kare . . .

The door—it was much too splendid to be called a "hatch," even here aboard *Hephaestus*—opened exactly on schedule. That was not, Reynaud knew, the fault of Dr. Jordin Kare, who seldom got anywhere on schedule. Trixie Hammitt, Reynaud's secretary, on the other hand, was obsessively punctual enough to compensate for an entire regiment of Kares.

The admiral stood behind his desk, smiling and holding out his hand, as Trixie shepherded in the man whose work was at the core of the grandiosely titled Royal Manticoran Astrophysics Investigation Agency's current endeavors. Kare was a man of medium height, with thinning brownish hair and eyes which couldn't seem to make up their mind whether they were gray or blue. He was a good fifteen centimeters shorter than Trixie, and Reynaud's tall, red-haired secretary's compulsively fussy and overabundant energy seemed to bemuse the distinguished astrophysicist. Which was fair enough. It not only bemused Reynaud, it often intimidated him, as well.

"Dr. Kare is here, Sir," she announced with crisp authority, and Reynaud nodded.

"So I see," he observed mildly, and a glint of humor showed in his visitor's eyes as Kare gripped the admiral's hand and shook it firmly. "Could you see about ordering us some refreshments, Trixie?" Reynaud asked.

Hammitt gave him a hard, pointed look, as if to remind him that her duties were clerical, not catering. But then she nodded and withdrew, and he exhaled a deep sigh of relief.

"I don't think we're going to be able to get rid of her that easily much longer," he observed to Kare.

"We're both intelligent, highly motivated men," the physicist replied with a grin. "I'm sure that, given the alternative, between the two of us we'll be able to think of *some* way to . . . divert her."

"I should be ashamed of myself," Reynaud admitted. "I've never had a secretary or an assistant who worked harder or longer hours. I know that, and inside somewhere I appreciate it enormously. But the way she fusses over our meetings drives me stark, staring mad."

"She's only doing her job . . . I think," Kare responded. "Of course, the other possibility that occurred to me is that she's secretly in the pay of one of the Star Kingdom's commercial rivals and that her assignment is to permanently derail the project by pushing its directors over the edge."

"You're being paranoid again, Jordin," Reynaud scolded.

"Not paranoid, just harried," Kare corrected.

"Yeah, right." Reynaud snorted, and waved for his guest to be seated.

It was part of his ambiguous feelings about the entire project that he liked Jordin Kare as much as he did. Of course, the professor was a very likable human being, in his own, absentminded sort of way. He was also one of the more brilliant astrophysicists the Star Kingdom had produced, with at least five academic degrees Reynaud knew about. He suspected there were probably at least two or three others Kare had forgotten to mention to anyone. It was the sort of thing he would have done.

And much as Reynaud hated to admit it, in choosing him to head the scientific side of the RMAIA when they split the agency off from Astro Control, the High Ridge Government had found exactly the right man for the job. Now if they'd only get out of his way and let him get on with it.

"And what wondrous new discoveries do you have for me today, Jordin?" the admiral inquired.

"Actually," Kare said, "there may really be something to report this time."

His smile had vanished, and Reynaud leaned forward in his chair as the physicist's unexpectedly serious tone registered.

"There may?"

"It's too early to be certain, and I hope to God I can keep the bureaucrats out from underfoot while we follow up on it, but I think we may actually be about to crack the locus on the seventh terminus."

"You're joking!"

"No, I'm not." Kare shook his head vigorously. "The numbers are very preliminary, Mike, and we're still a huge distance from nailing down a definitive volume. Even after we do that, of course, we're going to be looking at the better part of a solid T-year, more probably two or three of them, before we get any farther than this end of the string. But unless I'm very mistaken, we've finally correlated enough sensor data to positively state that there actually is a seventh terminus to the Junction."

"My God," Reynaud said quietly. He leaned back once more and shook his head. "I hope you won't take this the wrong way, Jordin, but I never really expected us to find it. It just seemed so unlikely after all these years."

"It's been a bear," Kare agreed, "and I can see at least half a dozen monographs coming out of the hunt for it—probably more. You know the original theoretical math was always highly ambiguous, and it's only been in the last fifteen or twenty T-years that we've had Warshawskies sensitive enough to collect the observational data we needed to confirm it. And we've pushed the boundaries of wormhole theory further than anyone else has done in at least a century, in the process. But it's out there, and for the first time, I'm completely confident we're going to find it."

"Have you mentioned this to anyone else?" Reynaud asked.

"Hardly!" Kare snorted harshly. "After the way those publicity flack idiots went running to the media the last time around?"

"They were just a mite premature," Reynaud conceded.

"A 'mite'?" Kare stared at him incredulously. "They had me sounding like some egotistical, self-seeking crank ready to proclaim he'd discovered the Secrets of the Universe! It took me almost a full T-year to get the record straightened out, and half the delegates to last year's Astrophysics Conference at the Royal Society still seemed to think *I* was the one who'd written those asinine press releases!"

Reynaud started to say something else, then changed his mind. He could hardly tell Kare he was wrong when he was convinced the physicist was exactly right. That was the main reason Reynaud objected so strenuously to the government's involvement in RMAIA. The work itself was important, even vital, and the funding level required for the dozen or so research ships, not to mention the lab and computer time, certainly left it with a price tag very few private concerns could have afforded. But the entire thing was one huge PR opportunity as far as the current Government was concerned. That was the entire reason they'd created the agency in the first place instead of simply increasing the funding for the Astro Control's Survey Command, which had been quietly pursuing the same research for decades. The RMAIA had been launched with huge fanfare as one of the "long-overdue peaceful initiatives" which had been delayed by the war against Haven, but the reality was just a little different from the shiny facade the Government worked so hard to project.

Nothing could have made the calculating reality behind the "peaceful initiative" more obvious than the blatant way the politicos scrambled to make political capital off of the work of the project's scientific staff. Official spokespeople who "forgot" to clear their copy with Kare or Reynaud were bad enough, but at least they could be thumped on for their sins. The project's political overlords, like High Ridge and Lady Descroix, were another matter entirely, and they were the ones who'd really infuriated Kare.

"I agree that we need to keep a lid on this until we have something definite to report," the admiral said after a moment. "I'm guessing that you told your staff people to keep their mouths shut?"

"On the research side, yes," Kare agreed. "The problem is going to come on the funding and administrative side."

Reynaud nodded. The scientists assigned to the project shared Kare's opinions about the PR people almost unanimously. Some of them might even have put it a little stronger than the professor did, in fact. But RMAIA was also awash in paperwork, which was the other main reason Reynaud felt the government would have been better advised to let someone else run it. It had been bad enough in Astro Control, which for all its military rank structure was actually a civil service organization. RMAIA was even worse. Not only did government bureaucrats with perhaps three percent of Dr. Kare's credentials and half that much of his intelligence insist on trying to "direct" his efforts, but they also insisted on exercising a degree of oversight which Reynaud privately estimated had probably doubled the project's time requirements. People who ought to have been attending to research were spending at least fifty percent of their time filling out endless forms, writing and reading memos, and attending administrative conferences that had damn all to do with finding the termini of wormhole junctions. Almost as bad, the project managers were not only scientific ignoramuses; they were also political appointees whose first loyalty was to the politicians who'd given them their prestigious, well-paid jobs. Like Dame Melina Makris, the Exchequer's personal representative on the RMAIA board. Although she was technically in the Countess of New Kiev's department, everyone knew she'd been appointed on the direct nomination of the Prime Minister. Even if there hadn't been any rumors to that effect, Makris herself would have made certain that every soul unfortunate enough to cross her path figured it out. She was officious, overbearing, arrogant, supercilious, and abrasive . . . and those, in Michel Reynaud's opinion, were her good points.

But she also knew precisely how the bureaucratic infighting game was played. Better, in fact, than Reynaud himself did. And she had access to all of the agency's paperwork. Which meant that the moment Kare and his scientific team started requesting additional funds for sensor runs, she was going to go running to the Prime Minister—and the public relations department—with the news that

Dr. Jordin Kare had once again discovered the ultimate secret of the universe.

In which case, that same Dr. Jordin Kare was going to shoot her. And not just in a kneecap.

"Let me think about it for a day or so, Jordin," Reynaud said after a moment. "There has to be a way to lose the funding in the underbrush." He swiveled his chair gently from side to side, tapping his fingers on his blotter while he thought. "I might be able to get Admiral Haynesworth to help us out," he mused aloud. "She doesn't like bureaucratic interference any more than I do, and she still resents the hell out of having the project stripped away from her own people. She's in the middle of a routine Junction beacon survey right now, too. Maybe I can coax her into letting us have a little bit of her budget for the extra sensor runs we're going to need if we collect her data at the same time."

"Good luck." Kare sounded skeptical.

"It's one possibility." Reynaud shrugged. "I may be able to come up with another. Or, much as I hate to admit it, there may not be any way to skate around it. But I promise I'll do my damnedest, because you're right. This is too important for premature release."

"I'd say that was a fairly generous understatement," Kare said seriously. Then he grinned. "On the other hand, and even granting what a tremendous pain in the ass all of this bureaucratic oversight has been, think about it, Mike. We're about to add another terminus to the Junction. And not one of us—especially not me—has the least damned idea where it leads!"

"I know." Reynaud grinned back. "Oh *boy*, do I know!"

CHAPTER ONE

"**S**teeeee-*riiiiike* onnnnne!"

The small white sphere flew past the young man in the green-trimmed, white uniform and smacked into the flat leather glove of the gray-uniformed man crouching behind him. The third man in the tableau—the one who had issued the shouted proclamation—wore an anachronistic black jacket and cap, as well as a face mask and chest protector like the crouching man wore. A rumble of discontent went up at his announcement, sprinkled with a few catcalls, from the crowd which filled the comfortable seats of the stadium to near capacity, and the man in white lowered his long, slender club to glower at the man in black. It didn't do him any good. The black-clad official only returned his glare, and, finally, he turned back towards the playing field while the man who'd caught the ball threw it back to his teammate, standing on the small, raised mound of earth twenty or so meters away.

"Wait a minute," Commodore Lady Michelle Henke, Countess Gold Peak, said, turning in her own seat in the palatial owner's box to look at her hostess. "That's a strike?"

"Of course it is," Lady Dame Honor Harrington, Duchess and Steadholder Harrington, replied gravely.

"I thought you said a 'strike' was when he swung and missed," Henke complained.

"It is," Honor assured her.

"But he *didn't*—swing, I mean."

"It's a strike whether he swings or not, as long as the pitch is in the strike zone."

For just a moment, Henke's expression matched that which the batter had turned upon the umpire, but Honor only looked back with total innocence. When the countess spoke again, it was with the careful patience of one determined not to allow someone else the satisfaction of a petty triumph.

"And the 'strike zone' is?" she asked.

"Anywhere between the knees and the shoulders, as long as the ball also crosses home plate," Honor told her with the competent air of a longtime afficionado.

"You say that like *you* knew the answer a year ago," Henke replied in a pretension-depressing tone.

"That's just the sort of small-minded attitude I might have expected out of you," Honor observed mournfully, and shook her head. "Really, Mike, it's a very simple game."

"Sure it is. That's why this is the only planet in the known universe where they still play it!"

"That's not true," Honor scolded primly while the cream-and-gray treecat stretched across the back of her seat raised his head to twitch his whiskers insufferably at his person's guest. "You know perfectly well that they still play baseball on Old Earth and at least five other planets."

"All right, on seven planets out of the—what? Isn't it something like seventeen *hundred* total inhabited worlds now?"

"As a trained astrogator, you should appreciate the need for precision," Honor said with a crooked grin, just as the pitcher uncorked a nasty, sharp-breaking slider. The wooden bat cracked explosively as it made contact and sent the ball slicing back out over the field. It crossed the short, inner perimeter wall which divided the playing field from the rest of the stadium, and Henke jumped to her feet and opened her mouth to cheer. Then she realized that Honor hadn't moved, and she turned to prop her hands on her hips with an expression halfway between martyred and exasperated.

"I take it that there's some reason that *wasn't* a—whatchamacallit? A 'homerun'?"

"It's not a homerun unless it stays between the foul poles when it crosses the outfield wall, Mike," Honor told her, pointing at the yellow-and-white striped pylons. "That one went foul by at least ten or fifteen feet."

"Feet? *Feet?*" Henke shot back. "My God, woman! Can't you at least keep track of the distances in this silly sport using measurement units civilized people can recognize?"

"*Michelle!*" Honor looked at her with the horror normally reserved for someone who stood up in church to announce she'd decided to take up devil worship and that the entire congregation was invited out to her house for a Black Mass and lemonade.

"What?" Henke demanded in a voice whose severity was only slightly undermined by the twinkle in her eyes.

"I suppose I shouldn't have been as shocked as I was," Honor said, more in sorrow than in anger. "After all, I, too, was once even as you, an infidel lost and unaware of how barren my prebaseball existence had truly been. Fortunately, one who had already seen the truth was there to bring me to the light," she added, and waved to the short, wiry auburn-haired man who stood in his green-on-green uniform directly behind her. "Andrew," she said, "would you be kind enough to tell the Commodore what you said to me when I asked you why it was ninety feet between bases instead of twenty-seven and a half meters?"

"What you actually asked, My Lady," Lieutenant Colonel Andrew LaFollett replied in a gravely meticulous tone, "was why we hadn't converted to meters and rounded up to twenty-eight of them between each pair of bases. Actually, you sounded just a bit put out over it, if I recall correctly."

"Whatever," Honor said with a lordly, dismissive wave. "Just tell her what you told me."

"Of course, My Lady," the commander of her personal security detachment agreed, and turned courteously to Henke. "What I said to the Steadholder, Countess Gold Peak," he said, "was 'This is *baseball*, My Lady!'"

"You see?" Honor said smugly. "There's a perfectly logical reason."

"Somehow, I don't think that adjective means exactly what you think it does," Henke told her with a chuckle. "On the other hand, I have heard it said that Graysons are just a bit on the traditional side, so I suppose there's really no reason to expect them to change anything about a game just because it's over two thousand years old and might need a little updating."

"Updating is only a good idea if it constitutes an improvement, as well, My Lady," LaFollet pointed out. "And it's not quite fair to say we haven't made any changes. If the record books are accurate, there was a time, in at least one league back on Old Earth, when the pitcher didn't even have to bat. Or when a manager could make as many pitching changes in a single game as he wanted to. Saint Austen put an end to that nonsense, at least!"

Henke rolled her eyes and sank back into her seat.

"I hope you won't take this the wrong way, Andrew," she told the colonel, "but somehow the discovery that the founder of your religion was also a baseball fanatic doesn't really surprise me. It certainly explains the careful preservation of some of the . . . archaic aspects of the game, anyway."

"I wouldn't say Saint Austen was a fanatic about baseball, My Lady," LaFollet replied in a considering tone. " 'Fanatic' would probably be much too mild a term, from everything I've ever read."

"I never would have guessed," Henke said dryly, letting her eyes sweep over the stadium once more. The huge sports facility seated at least sixty thousand in its tiers of comfortably upholstered chairs, and she hated to think how much the place must have cost. Especially on a planet like Grayson, where what would normally have been outdoor sports required stadiums with things like air filtration systems just to protect the local population from the heavy metal contents of their own atmosphere.

Not that any expense had been spared on more mundane considerations when James Candless Memorial Field was erected. The immaculately manicured playing field was a green jewel, broken only by white stripes of the traditional powdered lime and the bare, rich brown earth of the base lines. The colors of the field and the even brighter colors of the festively garbed spectators glowed brilliantly in the protective dome's filtered sunlight, and the crowd was liberally festooned with team pennants and banners exhorting the home team to victory. There was even a ventilation system carefully designed to exactly recreate the wind conditions outside the dome, and the Grayson planetary flag, with its crossed swords and open Bible, flew from the top of one of the two foul poles while the Harrington Steading flag flew from the other.

She let her eyes rest balefully on those same foul poles for a moment, then glanced at the huge digital scoreboard projected holographically above the infield, and sighed.

"I know I'm going to regret asking this, but would one of you insufferable know-it-alls care to explain to me where *that*—" she pointed at the scarlet numeral "2" which had appeared in the "STRIKES" column "—came from? I thought it was only strike one."

"That was before the foul ball, Mike," Honor explained brightly.

"But he hit it," Henke protested.

"It doesn't matter. A foul ball counts as a strike."

"But—"

Henke broke off as the pitcher delivered a curveball, which the batter promptly hooked foul over the third base dugout. She looked expectantly at the scoreboard, then drew a deep breath as the count of balls and strikes remained unchanged.

"I thought you said—" she began.

"Foul balls are only strikes until the count has already reached two strikes," Honor said. "After that, they don't count as strikes . . . or balls, either, for that matter. Unless one of them is caught by one of the fielders, of course. Then it counts as an out instead of a dead ball."

Henke regarded her sourly, and Honor grinned back. The countess glowered, then turned an equally disapproving expression upon the armsman.

" 'Simple game,' " she snorted. "Right. Sure!"

The Harrington Treecats lost by a score of eleven to two.

Michelle Henke tried valiantly to project an air of proper commiseration as the luxury air car swept up to the owner's box's private slip to collect her and her hostess' party. Alas, her success was less than total.

"It isn't nice to gloat, Mike," Honor informed her with a certain severity.

"Gloat? Me, gloat? Me, a peer of the Star Kingdom, *gloat* just because your team got waxed while you and your friend the Colonel were so busy pointing out my abysmal ignorance to me? How could you possibly suggest that I'd do such a thing?"

"Possibly because I've known you so long."

"And possibly because it's exactly what you'd be doing if our positions were reversed," Henke suggested.

"All things are possible," Honor agreed. "On the other hand, some are less likely than others, and given the strength of my own character, that one's less likely than most."

"Oh, of course. I keep forgetting what a modest, shy and retiring type you are, Honor," Henke said as they climbed into the air limo, followed by LaFollet, carrying Nimitz's mate Samantha, and the rest of Honor's regular three-man detachment.

"Not shy and retiring. Simply a more mature and responsible individual."

"Not so mature and responsible that you didn't name your team after a certain furry, six-footed celery-thief and his friends," Henke shot back, reaching out to rub the treecat on Honor's shoulder between his ears.

"Nimitz and Samantha had nothing to do with my choice," Honor replied. "Mind you, they approved of it, but I actually picked it as the lesser of two evils." She grimaced. "It was that, or the 'Harrington Salamanders.'"

Henke looked up sharply, then spluttered a half-smothered laugh. "You're joking!"

"I wish I were. As a matter of fact, the Commissioner of Baseball had already assigned the Salamanders name when the Owners' Committee and the Rules Committee agreed to expand the league. I had an awful time changing their minds."

"I think it would've been a marvelous name," Henke told her with an impish grin.

"I'm sure you do," Honor said repressively. "I, on the other hand, don't. Leaving aside the entire question of modesty, can you imagine how High Ridge and his crowd would have reacted? It would have been tailor-made for their op-ed pieces!"

"Um." Henke's grin vanished at the reminder of the unpleasant political realities inherent in the existence of the High Ridge Government. Those realties had become progressively less pleasant and more personal, for Honor at least, over the last three-plus T-years. Which, Henke knew, was the real reason her friend had been so delighted to return briefly to Grayson to attend to her obligations as Steadholder Harrington. It was also one of the reasons Henke herself had shown such alacrity in accepting the invitation to spend her own leave as Honor's guest here.

"You're probably right," she said, after a moment. "Of course, in any properly run universe, High Ridge would never have become Prime Minister in the first place, much less held onto the office for so long. I think I'll complain to the management."

"I do that every Sunday," Honor assured her with very little humor indeed. "And I suspect the Protector has Reverend Sullivan do the same thing, just to put a little more horsepower behind it."

"Horsepower or not, it doesn't seem to be working," Henke observed. She shook her head. "I can't believe they've managed to hang on so long. I mean, Jesus, Honor, most of them *hate* each other! And as for their ideologies—!"

"Of course they hate each other. Unfortunately, at this particular moment they hate your cousin even more. Or feel sufficiently scared of her to hang together, come what may, in opposition to her, at any rate."

"I know," Henke sighed. "I know." She shook her head again. "Beth always has had a temper. It's too bad she still hasn't learned to keep it muzzled."

"That's not quite fair," Honor disagreed, and Henke arched an eyebrow at her.

Michelle Henke, thanks to the assassination which had killed her father, her older brother, the Duke of Cromarty, and the entire crew of the Queen's royal yacht, stood fifth in the line of succession for the Crown of the Star Kingdom of Manticore. Her mother, Caitrin Winton-Henke, Duchess Winton-Henke and Dowager Countess Gold Peak, was Queen Elizabeth III's aunt, the only sibling of the Queen's father, and now Michelle was her mother's only surviving child. Henke had never expected to stand so high in the succession, or to inherit her father's title, for that matter. But she'd known Elizabeth all of her life, and she was only too familiar with the fiery Winton temper which the Queen had inherited in full measure.

Despite that, she had to admit that Honor had actually spent more time with the Queen over the last three T-years than Michelle herself had. Indeed, the visibility of Duchess Harrington as one of the Crown's staunchest supporters in the Lords (and as one of the inner circle of "kitchen advisers" the Queen turned to for advice instead of the members of her official government) was one reason the pro-Government media had spent so much time trying to discredit Honor in any way it could. The subtle (and sometimes not so subtle) vilification which had come her way had been downright ugly at times. But however that might be, she admitted, Honor had not only spent more time working with Elizabeth but also possessed certain advantages others lacked when it came to evaluating people and their emotions. Still . . .

"Honor, I love Beth as my cousin, and I respect her as my monarch," she said after a moment. "But she has the temper of a hexapuma with a broken tooth when something sets her off, and you and I both know it. If she'd just managed to hang onto it when the High Ridge Government was first being formed, she might have been able to split them up instead of driving them together in opposition to her."

"I didn't say she'd handled things perfectly," Honor pointed out, leaning back while Nimitz arranged himself comfortably across her lap. Samantha wiggled down from LaFollet's arms to join him, and Honor gave the female 'cat's ears a welcoming caress. "In fact," she went on, "Elizabeth would be the first to agree that she blew her best opportunity to hang onto control when she lost her temper with them. But while you've been off having adventures in space, I've been sitting on my posterior in the House of Lords, watching High Ridge in action. And from what I've seen there, I don't think it really mattered, in the long run, how she handled them."

"I beg your pardon?" Henke said just a bit uncomfortably. She knew Honor hadn't meant it as a criticism, but she couldn't help feeling at least a little guilty. Her mother held a seat of her own in the Lords as a duchess in her own right, so she and Michelle had seen no reason why she shouldn't hold her daughter's proxy and represent them both. Duchess Winton-Henke had always found politics far more absorbing than Michelle ever had, and the deaths of her husband and son had left her looking for a distraction. Michelle had needed a distraction of her own, which she'd found by throwing herself even more completely into her space-going duties as an officer in the Royal Manticoran Navy.

A distraction Honor had been conspicuously denied.

"Even assuming that there were no ideological fissures within the High Ridge Government, there aren't enough Conservatives, Liberals, and Progressives in the Lords to sustain High Ridge's majority without the support of at least some of the Independents," Honor pointed out. "High Ridge has managed to bring Wallace's New Men on board, as well, of course, but even that's not enough to change the dynamics of the major parties significantly. And however much she might have frightened or angered High Ridge and his cronies, she never said anything threatening to the Independents who've decided to support him, now did she?"

"No," Henke admitted, remembering bits and pieces of

conversations she'd had with her mother and finding herself wishing she'd paid more attention at the time.

"Of course not. He managed to gain their support without her ever losing her temper with them. And even if she had, you would have thought something like the Manpower Scandal would have split a lot of those Independents away from the Government."

"As a matter of fact, that's exactly what I expected to happen when Cathy Montaigne dropped her bomb," Henke agreed, and shrugged. "Personally, I always liked Cathy. I thought she was a little dippy before she went off to Old Earth, maybe, but it was obvious she's always believed in her principles. And, damn, but I like her style."

"I've decided I like her, too," Honor confessed. "I never thought I'd say that about any member of the Liberal Party, either. Of course, aside from the Liberals' anti-genetic slavery stance, I don't know how much she really has in common with the rest of 'her' party." Honor's tone remained almost serene, but her eyes narrowed dangerously. Her bred-in-the-bone hatred for the genetic slave trade was as implacable as a Sphinx winter, probably because of her mother. "I don't believe I've ever heard anyone else express herself so, um . . . eloquently on the topic," she added.

"She does have a way with words, and I'd certainly agree that she suffers from a certain tunnel vision on that particular topic," Henke allowed with a smile. "Not to mention a pronounced need to kick the Establishment in the teeth just on general principles. One of my cousins is married to Cathy's brother-in-law George Larabee, Lord Altamont, and she tells me Lady Altamont, George's mother, is absolutely livid over the way Cathy is openly 'living in sin' with a mere commoner. And not just any commoner! A Gryphon highlander who's on half-pay for his offenses against military discipline!"

Henke chuckled, then sobered.

"This time, though, I thought she had the bastards nailed. God knows how she got her hands on those records—and, personally, I'll be just as happy if He never gets around to explaining it all to me. But from what Mom said, and from everything I read in the 'faxes, it certainly sounded like there wasn't much question that they were genuine."

"No question at all." Honor, who, unlike Henke, had a very good notion of how the Countess of the Tor had come into possession of the damning documentation, agreed. For a moment, she considered explaining her suspicions about Captain Zilwicki and his role in the mysterious intelligence windfall to her friend, then decided against it. They weren't really something Mike needed to know . . . just as she didn't need to know some of the other things Andrew LaFollet had discovered about Anton Zilwicki. Like exactly what it was that the half-pay captain's new private security firm was doing with some of the information which the Countess had *not* turned over to the authorities.

"Unfortunately," she went on instead, "the individuals who were specifically named were all relatively small fish. Socially prominent in some cases, perhaps, and politically important enough to be highly visible in others, but not close enough to the seats of power to be really crippling. The fact that so many of them had connections to the Conservatives and—especially!—to certain members of the Liberal Party, as well, was certainly embarrassing. For that matter, the Ministry of Justice has put a couple of dozen of them away for a long, long time. But there were just enough of them in the other parties or among the Independents—even two among the Centrists, I'm sorry to say—for the apologists to argue that 'everyone did it' and keep any one party from being singled out for blame. And the fact that there were no direct links to the party leaders let the Government defuse the worst possible repercussions by shouting louder than anyone else for the prosecution of the individuals who were named. Like Hendricks, when they recalled him from Old Terra and sent out a new ambassador."

"Or Admiral Young," Henke said grimly, and Honor nodded with a carefully neutral expression. The implacable hostility between her and the Young clan went back for over forty T-years, punctuated by bitter hatred and more than one death. Which was one reason she'd taken great pains to maintain her facade of neutrality when the Navy recalled Admiral Edwin Young from Old Terra, convicted him of violation of the Articles of War before a court-martial, and stripped him of his rank. The civilian courts had been equally harsh, even with his family links to the powerful Earl of North Hollow, whose influence at the highest level of the Prime Minister's own Conservative Association was enormous. He'd managed to escape the death penalty, but despite his exalted birth, he would be spending the next several decades as a guest of the Royal Ministry of Justice.

"Or like Young," she agreed after a moment. "In fact, what happened to him is a pretty fair example of just how ruthlessly the leadership was prepared to cut its losses . . . and exactly who they were prepared to jettison in the process. He was a Young, which made him highly visible, and a Navy flag officer, which made his 'isolated criminal actions' even more satisfyingly visceral. But he was only a fourth cousin of North Hollow, and, frankly, he was a nonentity in terms of the Conservative Association's real power structure. So when North Hollow made no move to save him, he became a highly satisfactory sacrifice to the 'principles' of his noble relative and simultaneously served as 'proof' that North Hollow himself and—by extension—all of the Conservative Association's leadership had never been involved in such heinous offenses. Which was precisely why the Government party leaders turned on *all* the minor fish so violently . . . and publicly. After all, they'd not only broken the law; they'd also betrayed the trust those leaders had reposed in them." It was Honor's turn to shrug. "Much as it stuck in my craw, I have to admit it was a brilliant job of political damage control. Which, however, High Ridge and New Kiev only managed to pull off because a majority of the Lords who weren't involved, including the Independents, decided to look the other way and settle for scapegoats."

"But why?" Henke demanded. "Mom said exactly the same thing to me in one of her letters, but I never understood the logic behind it."

"It all comes down to politics and what you might call the historical imperatives of constitutional evolution," Honor told her as two heavily armed stingships in the markings of the Harrington Steadholder's Guard slid into place on either wing. She and Henke were invited to supper at Protector's Palace, and Honor leaned further back and crossed her legs as the air limo started out on the lengthy flight to Mayhew Steading through a brilliantly blue, cloud-stippled sky, carefully watched over by its escorts.

"Basically," she said, "a majority of the House of Lords are willing to close their eyes to things they don't want to know about, even where something like slavery is concerned, because, however honest they may be themselves, they'd rather have a government like High Ridge's than take a chance on what might replace it. Despite all the corruption and pork barrel vote-buying that involves, they regard High Ridge as a lesser risk than giving Elizabeth and her supporters back control of both houses."

"Mom said something about that—and about how San Martin fitted into the political equation. But she was in a hurry to finish her letter, and I never asked her for a complete explanation," Henke confessed.

"To paraphrase something Admiral Courvoisier once said to me, no captain—or commodore—in the Queen's Navy can afford to be a virgin where politics are concerned, Mike. And especially not when she also stands as close to the Throne as you do."

There was absolutely no condemnation in Honor's tone, but there was a certain sternness in her eyes as her gaze locked ever so briefly with Henke's. The countess looked back almost defiantly for a few heartbeats, but then her eyes fell, and she nodded in unhappy agreement.

"I know," she admitted in a lower voice. "It's just— Well, I suppose when it comes right down to it, I never really liked politics much more than you did. And since Dad and Cal were killed and that slimy bastard managed to steal the premiership from Willie Alexander, the very thought of sitting down in the same chamber as him is enough to turn my stomach."

"And you the one who was just criticizing the Queen for her temper!" Honor scolded gently.

"Guilty as charged," Henke acknowledged. "But you were saying?"

"I was saying that a majority of the House of Lords is backing High Ridge for reasons of its own. Which is probably what your mother meant when she mentioned San Martin. That same majority is afraid of what will happen when the San Martino peers are finally seated."

"Why?" Henke asked with such genuine incomprehension that Honor, despite herself, sighed.

"Mike," she said patiently, "this is basic Political History 101. What's the one thing the Crown has been trying to take away from the Lords ever since there's been a Star Kingdom?"

"The power of the purse," Henke replied.

"Very good," Honor said. "But the Founders, who were otherwise a fairly decent lot, were virtually unanimous in their determination to see to it that they and their descendants hung onto the real political power in the Star Kingdom. That's why the Constitution specifically requires that the Prime Minister come from the House of Lords and specifies that any finance bill must be introduced in the Lords. I happen to think there's something to be said for placing substantial political power in the hands of a legislative chamber which can be . . . insulated from the political and ideological hysteria *du jour,* but the Founders set up too much of a good thing. The fact that they never have to stand for election means that too many of the peers—present company excluded, of course—have . . . questionable contact with reality, let's say. Worse, it's even easier for someone who inherits her title to become an empire builder within the Parliament. Trust me," she added dryly. "I've seen how that works on two different planets now, and with a considerably better vantage point than I ever wanted."

She gazed useeingly out the window at the port escort for several seconds, her long fingers gently caressing both 'cats' soft, silky fur. Nimitz looked up at her speculatively as he tasted her emotions through their empathic link. For a moment, Henke half-expected him to sink his claws, however gently, into Honor's kneecap. He was quite capable of making his displeasure evident when it was time to scold his person for brooding over past events no one could change, anyway. But this time he decided against it, and left Honor alone until she shook herself and turned back to their guest.

"Anyway, I think that over all the Crown would be just as happy to leave the premiership where it is. Much as I like and respect your cousin, honesty compels me to point out that she does have a vested interest in maintaining a hereditary aristocratic system. And I suppose that while I'm in honest mode, I should probably point out that you and I do, too. Now, at least.

"But for generations, the Crown has wanted to see a better balance between the powers of the Commons and the Lords, and the best way to accomplish that would be to give the Commons control of the purse as a counterweight to leaving the premiership permanently lodged in the Lords. Except that the Crown has never been able to assemble the required majority in the Lords to amend the Constitution to transfer that power to the lower house."

"Of course not," Henke snorted with the rich contempt for aristocratic defense of privilege possible only for one born to that same aristocracy. "What? You really think that anyone who has as good a thing going for them as the peers do is going to vote to give half of her power to someone else?"

"Actually," Honor said seriously, "that's exactly what High Ridge is afraid of, and a lot of the Independents agree with him."

"That's what Mom said," Henke said in an exasperated voice, "but I just can't see it happening, somehow."

"High Ridge can. And so can Elizabeth and Willie Alexander. It's all a matter of numbers, Mike, and the San Martino peers could very well shift the balance in the Lords to a point that makes it possible for the Queen to pull it off at last. But the joker in the deck is the combination of the Constitution's limit on the creation of new peerages and the terms of the Act of Annexation which admitted Trevor's Star to the Star Kingdom. The Constitution limits increases in the total membership of the House of Lords to no more than ten percent between any two general elections, and the Act of Annexation specifies that none of the new peers from San Martin will be confirmed or seated until after the *next* general election.

"So what the Government and its supporters in the Lords are trying to do is to postpone that election as long as possible. At the moment, there's not much question that the San Martinos are very solidly behind the Queen and the Centrists. After all, it was our Navy, under Elizabeth and the Cromarty Government, which kicked the Peeps out of the Trevor's Star System and liberated them, and it was Cromarty and your father, as Foreign Secretary, who negotiated the actual terms of their admission to the Star Kingdom. Not only that, but San Martin had no hereditary aristocracy before its annexation, so it's not likely that the San Martinos are going to have the same . . . devoted attachment to the *status quo* in Parliament. Gratitude to the people they see as responsible for their liberation, coupled with that lack of aristocratic tradition, means the new peers would be likely—almost certain, in fact—to support a motion by Lord Alexander, as the leader of the Centrist Party, to transfer that power of the purse to the House of Commons.

"But until they're actually seated, they can't support anything. And what High Ridge and his cronies are up to right now is building a sufficiently strong majority among the members of the existing peerage to resist any such action. According to the latest figures I've seen, the number of current peers opposed to the required constitutional amendment gives them at least a fifteen-percent edge, but that number could erode. And even if it doesn't, two general elections will put enough San Martinos into the Lords to overcome it, assuming their support for the amendment is solid.

"So in addition to trying to increase their own margin of support among the peers, High Ridge and his allies are trying to cut into the Centrist majority in the Commons, as well. Since it's the Commons who vote to confirm the creation of any new peerages, High Ridge hopes that if he can increase his clout in the lower house, he may be able to influence the approval process in a way that confirms peers he figures can be co-opted to support of the continued dominance of the Lords.

"The fact that San Martino MPs are going to be card-carrying Centrists or Crown Loyalists lends that particular concern added point. Technically, San Martin still doesn't have any MPs, either, but their 'special representatives' in the Commons are serving a lot of the same functions, even if they can't actually vote yet. And there's no question where their loyalties lie. Nor have any of the peers failed to take note of that little fact.

"And that, Mike, is why otherwise reasonably decent members of the House of Lords are actively supporting a piece of work like High Ridge and let him get away with his damage control on the Manpower Scandal. None of them really like him, very few of them have any illusions about the 'thoroughness' of his investigation of Countess Tor's charges, and most of them wouldn't trust him or any of his allies to look after their dogs, much less their children. But their general position is that even if the present Constitution is imperfect, the system it's created has served the Star Kingdom well, and at the moment, he's the one defending the *status quo*. I doubt that many of them are blind to the degree of self-interest inherent in their opposition to changing it, but that doesn't make their opposition any less genuine."

"I see." Henke leaned back in her own seat, facing Honor across the passenger compartment of the luxurious vehicle. It still startled her whenever she heard Honor Harrington, of all people, analyzing politics so clearly and concisely. It shouldn't, she supposed, given how acutely Honor had always been able to analyze military problems, but for almost forty T-years, it had always been Henke who understood the Star Kingdom's internal politics better than Honor did. Of course, Henke's understanding had been based on her own family connections. As the Queen's first cousin, she'd absorbed that understanding almost by osmosis, without ever really having to think very much about it. Which, she admitted now, might be part of the reason Honor saw the current situation so much more clearly than she did, for Honor hadn't been born into those rarified circles. She'd come to them with a lack of instinctive insider awareness which had forced her to really think about her new environment.

But the fact that her friend hadn't been born to power and nurtured within the ranks of the Star Kingdom's hereditary elite also created some dangerous blind spots, Henke reflected with carefully hidden anxiety. Blind spots that left her unaware of dangers someone like Henke herself would have recognized instantly, despite any distaste for politics. In spite of all that had happened to place Honor at the very pivot of political power in two separate star nations, she continued to think of herself—and her private life—as the yeoman's daughter she had always been.

Michelle Henke faced her friend and wondered yet again if she should say something to her, remind her of how her private life could and would be used against her by her political foes if she gave them an opening. If she should ask Honor if there were any truth to the rumors beginning to be whispered ever so quietly.

"That sounds like it makes sense," she said instead, after a moment. "It still surprises me to hear it coming from you, though, I guess. May I ask if Lord Alexander shares your analysis?"

"Of course he does. You don't think I haven't discussed it with him—at length—do you?" Honor snorted. "Between my own position in the Lords and my role as Benjamin's friend at court, I've spent more hours than I care to think about in skull sessions with the man who *ought* to be Prime Minister!"

"Yes, I suppose you'd have to," Henke agreed slowly, and cocked her head ever so slightly. "And has Earl White Haven been able to add anything to your perspective, as well?"

"Yes," Honor replied, reaching down to stroke Nimitz's spine. Her eyes, Henke noticed, dropped to watch her own hand on the treecat's silken pelt rather than meet her guest's gaze, and the brevity of her one-word response struck Henke as . . . ominous.

For one moment, the countess considered pressing further, making the question explicit. After all, if she couldn't ask Honor, who could? But the problem was that she couldn't, and so she only leaned back in her own chair and nodded.

"That tallies with what Mom was saying, too," she said then. "And I guess she figured I should have known enough about what was going on to understand it without her drawing a detailed map for me the way you just did." She shrugged. "Sometimes I think she never realized how much I left all that sort of thing to Cal. I was too busy with the Navy."

A fresh memory of sorrow flowed across her face, but she banished it quickly and produced a lopsided smile.

"Now that you *have* explained it, though, I see what you meant about historical imperatives. I still say Beth's temper didn't help things any, though."

"No, it didn't," Honor agreed, looking up from her lapful of 'cat once more with a slight air of what might have been relief. "If nothing else, it made the stakes personal for High Ridge, New Kiev, and Descroix. But from the moment the Duke of Cromarty and your father were killed, it was almost inevitable that we'd wind up where we are. Except, of course, that no one on either side could have realized what was going to happen in the People's Republic while we were tending to our domestic squabbles."

"You can say that again," Henke agreed somberly, and cocked her head. "Do you think Pritchart and Theisman understand what's happening any better than I did?"

"I certainly hope so," Honor said dryly.

CHAPTER TWO

"**W**hat the *hell* do they think they're doing?" Eloise Pritchart half snarled.

The President of the Republic of Haven picked up a chip folio and shook it violently in the direction of Admiral Thomas Theisman as he stepped into her private office. Her expression was so stormy that the Republic's Secretary of War raised an eyebrow in surprise. The platinum-haired, topaz-eyed President was perhaps the most beautiful woman he'd ever personally met. In fact, she was one of those rare human beings on whom even an expression of fury looked good. But others rarely saw her wearing one, because one of her greatest virtues was her ability to remain cool and collected even in the face of the most severe pressure. That virtue had been fundamental to her survival under Oscar Saint-Just's State Security and its reign of terror. It was not much in evidence at the moment, however.

"What's who up to?" he asked mildly, settling into one of the comfortable chairs angled to face her desk while simultaneously providing her visitors with a breathtaking panorama of downtown Nouveau Paris. The work crews were almost finished rebuilding the towers Saint-Just had destroyed when he detonated the nuclear bomb under the Octagon, and Theisman's eyes moved automatically to the gleaming edifice of the New Octagon which had replaced it.

"The damned Manties, that's who!" Pritchart shot back with an undisguised venom that snapped his full attention back to her, and tossed the folio onto the desk. When she put it down, Theisman saw the ID flashes which marked it as an official State Department briefing paper, and he grimaced.

"I take it they haven't responded appropriately to our latest proposals," he observed in that same mild tone.

"They haven't responded to them at all! It's as if we never even presented the position papers."

"It's not like they haven't been dragging their heels for years now, Eloise," Theisman pointed out. "And let's be honest—until recently, we were just as happy they were."

"I know. I know."

Pritchart leaned back in her own chair, drew a deep breath, and waved a hand in a small apologetic gesture. It wasn't an apology for her anger at the Manticorans, only for the way she'd allowed it to show. If anyone in the galaxy had earned the right not to have her snarling at him, it was Thomas Theisman. He and Denis LePic, the People's Commissioner the SS had assigned as his political watchdog, were the ones who'd managed to overthrow the ruthless dictatorship Saint-Just had established as the sole surviving member of the Committee of Public Safety. Saint-Just hadn't survived his removal from office, and Pritchart had no doubt that the rumors about how he'd come to be "killed in the fighting" were accurate. And if those rumors were true—if Theisman had shot him out of hand—then thank God for it. The last thing the People's Republic of Haven had needed was yet another agonizing show trial, followed by the inevitable, highly public purges of the deposed leader's supporters *pour encourager les autres.*

Of course, what the People's Republic of Haven had needed didn't really matter anymore, she reminded herself, because the People's Republic no longer existed. And that, too, had been the work of Admiral Thomas Theisman.

She tipped her chair a bit further back, considering the slightly stocky, brown-haired, utterly unremarkable-looking man on the other side of her desk's gleaming, hand-rubbed Sandoval mahogany. She wondered if the citizens of the Republic of Haven—no longer the *People's* Republic, but simply the Republic—even began to appreciate how much they truly owed him. Disposing of Saint-Just would have been more than enough to earn their eternal gratitude, but he hadn't stopped there. Nor, to the amazement of everyone who hadn't personally known him, had he made even the slightest effort to seize power for himself. The closest he'd come was to combine the resurrected office of Chief of Naval Operations and that of Secretary of War in his own person, insuring that he had firm control of both sides of the Republic's military machine. But once he'd combined them, he'd steadfastly refused to use them for any purely personal end . . . and descended like the wrath of God on any officer who even looked like abusing his own position. That was a restraint the Republic's experience under the previous two regimes had made it flatly impossible for its citizens to believe in.

Of course, Pritchart reminded herself wryly, very few of those citizens could even begin to imagine how desperate Theisman had been to avoid the job which she herself now held.

Much of that desperation had stemmed from his awareness that he lacked many of the qualities a successful politician required. He understood (intellectually) the need for compromise and the necessity of deal-making and horsetrading for advantage, but he would never be comfortable doing either of those things. That didn't keep him from analyzing the process, often with an acuity Pritchart found herself hard pressed to match. It was just that it was something he could understand without being very good at doing, and he was wise enough to recognize that.

He was also remarkably free of personal ambition for someone who'd risen to his rank in the People's Navy, even under the conditions of accelerated promotion which had obtained after the purges of the old officer corps. The gaping holes Rob Pierre's overthrow of the Legislaturalists had left in the ranks of the Navy's senior officers, coupled with the desperate needs of a losing war against the Manticoran Alliance, had required promotions that opened all sorts of opportunities for junior officers who'd been capable . . . or ambitious.

Surviving after being promoted had been a more difficult task. Between State Security's ruthless determination to shoot officers who failed the State as object lessons to their peers and Oscar Saint-Just's near pathological suspicion of any officer who appeared too competent, every flag officer in the People's Navy had known her own life, and all too often the lives of her entire family, had hung by a badly frayed thread. Eloise Pritchart understood how that had worked better than most, for she'd been one of Saint-Just's official spies. Like Denis LePic, she'd been assigned to report directly to Saint-Just's office on the political reliability of one of the People's Republic's senior flag officers. Unfortunately for Saint-Just, her reports had borne no particular relationship to reality.

She'd never really expected that she and Citizen Admiral Javier Giscard, the man she'd been assigned to spy upon and whom she'd found the audacity to fall in love with, instead, would survive. Nor would they have, if Theisman hadn't overthrown Saint-Just before the Secretary for State Security could have Giscard purged.

But they'd done far more than merely survive since then. Pritchart's pre-revolution stature as "Brigade Commander Delta," one of the leading Aprilists, was what had made her so valuable to Saint-Just as one of his people's commissioners. The Aprilists had been widely regarded as the most "respectable" of the various armed revolutionary groups which had opposed the Legislaturalists. They'd also been far and away the most effective, and her Aprilist credentials had lent her an aura of legitimacy which Saint-Just had been eager to co-opt for his new Office of State Security. And, she admitted, like her friend Kevin Usher, she'd permitted herself to be co-opted. Outwardly, at least. She'd had to, if she'd wanted to survive, because she'd known even then that sooner or later any of her old Aprilist comrades who persisted in clinging openly to their ideals would quietly disappear.

They had . . . and she hadn't. There were times she still felt guilty over that, but even on the worst nights, she knew any feeling of guilt was illogical. She'd done what she had not simply to survive, but to place herself in a position which might let her help others, like Giscard, survive as well. Standing up defiantly for her principles would have been noble and gallant . . . and unforgivably stupid. It had been her responsibility to stay alive to *fight* for those principles, however clandestinely, and that was precisely what she and Giscard had done.

In the end, they would have been found out and executed, anyway, if Theisman hadn't gotten to Saint-Just first. And just as Saint-Just had found her reputation as an Aprilist useful for State Security, Theisman had found it equally useful for his own purposes. He'd needed someone—anyone—to whom he could hand the position of head of state. Pritchart doubted that more than half a dozen people in the entire People's Republic had been prepared to believe he truly didn't want that position for himself. In fact, she hadn't believed it herself, at first. But, then, she hadn't really known him before he'd recalled her and Giscard to the Haven System, along with the rest of Twelfth Fleet, to reinforce his own Capital Fleet.

Only the fact that Theisman had always had a reputation within the Navy as a man with no political ambitions had permitted Giscard and Citizen Admiral Lester Tourville—both of whom, unlike her, had known him for years—to convince her to return to Haven. All three of them had been intensely wary anyway, despite the naval officers' acquaintance with him, but Pritchart had been stunned literally speechless when he informed her that he wanted *her* to organize the interim civilian government.

It hadn't been all pure disinterest on his part, of course. She'd recognized immediately how useful she could be to him as a figurehead. After all, she'd had more than sufficient experience in a similar capacity with Saint-Just. And she'd been sufficiently realistic to admit that he had an overwhelming responsibility to reach for anything he might be able to use to prevent the complete fragmentation of the People's Republic. If she was a potentially unifying force, then she had no more choice about accepting the job, figurehead or not, than he had about offering it to her. Or to someone like her, at least.

Ultimately, she felt certain, it had been her relationship with Giscard, with its resonances to his own relationship with LePic, which had made her acceptable to him. He'd known and trusted Giscard; by extension, he'd felt able to trust her because he knew Giscard did. But the thing which had truly astounded her was that when he offered her both the political and the military powers of the head of state, he'd meant it.

There hadn't been any strings, no reservations, no secretly retained authority. The one thing Thomas Theisman would never be was a puppet master. There'd been one, and only one, condition, and that had been that Eloise Pritchart prove to him that she was as committed as he was to the restoration of the old Constitution. Not the Constitution of the People's Republic of Haven, which had created the office of Hereditary President and legally enshrined the dynastic power of the Legislaturalists, but the Constitution of the old Republic. The Republic whose citizens had been expected to be more than mere drones and to vote. The one whose presidents and legislators had served at the will of an electorate which held them responsible for their actions.

Pritchart had felt almost awed when she realized she was in the presence of a true romantic. A man who actually believed in the rule of law, the sanctity of solemn oaths, and the inviolability of personal responsibility.

She wondered if he'd always been so divorced from reality, or if he'd become that way as his own defense mechanism as he watched the star nation of his birth go insane about him. It didn't really matter. What mattered was that he was truly and absolutely committed to the very principles for which the Aprilist Movement had come into existence . . . and that she was almost as hopelessly romantic, in that respect, at least, as he was.

And so, just over eighteen T-months from Oscar Saint-Just's death, Eloise Pritchart, after organizing the transition government and bringing the old Constitution back from the ash heap of history, had become the first elected president of the Republic of Haven in almost two centuries, with Thomas Theisman as her Secretary of War.

There were times when she was highly tempted to shoot him for that.

"You know, Tom," she said, only half-whimsically, "you're a coward."

"Absolutely," he agreed instantly. "It's a survival trait."

"Is that what you call it?" She cocked her head at him. "I'd assumed it was more a combination of laziness and a desire to put someone else in the line of fire."

"A *burning* desire to put someone else there, actually," he corrected affably. Then his smile faded just a bit, and he shrugged.

"There's not quite as much humor in that as I wish there were," he said in a quieter voice. "I think I know my strengths, Eloise. And I hope to hell I know my limitations. There's no way I could've done the job you've done. I know you couldn't have done it, either, if I hadn't been here to do *my* job, but that doesn't change a thing about what you've accomplished."

She waved her hand in midair again, uncomfortable with the sincerity of his tone.

"At any rate," she went on again, after a moment, both her expression and her voice determinedly light, "you managed to arrange things very neatly so that you don't have to deal with the damned Manties. Or, for that matter, the rest of the Cabinet when they hear about the Manties' latest antics."

"And just what do those antics consist of this time?" Theisman asked, accepting her change of mood. "Besides, of course, their failure to accept our most recent proposal?"

"Nothing," she admitted. "But they don't have to do anything else to create enormous problems for us, Tom, and you know it."

"Yes, I suppose I do." He shrugged. "But like I said earlier, the fact that they can't find their ass with both hands has been useful as hell from my perspective. At least I didn't have to worry about them while Javier, Lester, and I ran around pissing on forest fires!"

"There is that," Pritchart agreed with a sober nod.

Not everyone had been prepared to accept Theisman's overthrow of the Committee of Public Safety gracefully. In fact, initially, he'd controlled only the capital system and its fleet. Capital Fleet was the Navy's largest, of course, and two-thirds of the other core systems of the People's Republic had declared for him—or, rather, for Pritchart's interim government—within the first three T-months. The majority of the rest of the People's Navy had also supported him, as well. But a large minority of the Navy had been under the control of other citizen admirals or, even worse, StateSec system commanders, who'd refused to acknowledge the legitimacy of the new government.

It was, as Theisman had just suggested, extremely fortunate that the Manticorans had chosen to continue the negotiations Saint-Just had finessed them into beginning. If they'd decided to resume active military operations, instead, especially with the enormous technological superiority of their new hardware, the entire Republic would have disintegrated—within weeks, probably, but certainly within mere months. As it was, Theisman, with Giscard and Tourville as his primary field commanders, had found himself fighting a vicious, multi-cornered war against a shifting kaleidoscope of enemies. Pritchart had had more than one reason for being unhappy about that. As President, she'd hated the way it had distracted her from concentrating fully on the stalled negotiations with the Star Kingdom. On a more personal level, Giscard's responsibilities as Theisman's senior fleet commander had kept him away from Nouveau Paris—and one Eloise Pritchart's bed—for all but a few weeks out of the last three-plus years. Which, she admitted, she resented even more than the official headaches it created.

Fortunately, she'd never really been concerned (unlike some people) that Theisman might not succeed in his pacification efforts in the end . . . as long as the Manties stayed out of it. The fact that most of his adversaries distrusted one another even more than they distrusted him had given him a powerful advantage, but not even their merry-go-round of mutual betrayal would have been enough to permit the interim government to survive in the face of an active Manticoran resumption of the offensive.

"I know how important it was for you and Javier and Lester to keep the Manties talking while you tended to the shooting," Pritchart went on after a moment. "But the shooting is just about over now, isn't it?"

"Yes, thank God. I expect Javier's next report within another couple of days, and I'll be very surprised if it doesn't tell us that Mikasinovich is ready to call it quits."

"Really?" Pritchart brightened visibly. Citizen General Silas Mikasinovich was the last major StateSec holdout. He'd managed to hammer himself together a six-star vest-pocket empire which had proved a surprisingly tough nut to crack.

"Really," Theisman confirmed, then raised one hand in a brief throwing-away gesture. "I'm afraid you're going to have to amnesty him like the others, and I wish you weren't. But unless I'm badly mistaken, he's enough of a realist to recognize that his only real chance now is to cut the best deal with you that he can."

"I'll give him a lot better deal than he deserves," Pritchart said grimly. "But the bottom line is going to be that he surrenders every one of his capital ships, then gets the hell out of the Republic and stays out."

"I can live with that," Theisman agreed. Especially, he thought, the surrender of his ships. So far, as nearly as Theisman and his staff could tell, not a single Havenite ship above the size of a battlecruiser had managed to simply disappear. He knew damned well that at least some lighter units had elected to set up independent operations as pirates or small-scale warlords safely beyond his own reach, but at least he'd managed to prevent any ships of the wall from doing the same thing, and he intended to keep it that way.

"And now that Lester's moved in and kicked down Carson's

little kingdom," he went on aloud, "all we have left are four or five isolated holdouts like Agnelli and Listerman. Give me another four months—six at the outside—and I'll have all of them out of your hair, as well, Madam President."

"And I will be delighted to see it happen," Pritchart said with a smile, then sobered. "But in some ways, getting Mikasinovich and the others out of the equation is going to make things even worse," she continued. "At least as long as they're still there and their units are still shooting back at yours, I can use him to keep the fire-eaters at bay."

"Giancola and his crowd?" Theisman asked, then snorted harshly at the President's confirming nod. "The man's an idiot!"

"Idiot or not—and much as I dislike him, I don't think he is one, actually—Arnold Giancola is also the Secretary of State," Pritchart pointed out. "I'll admit that the only reason I nominated him for the position was political expediency, despite a less than overwhelming admiration for his stellar intellect, but he does have the job. And the reasons I gave it to him are still in force."

"Which I hope you won't mind my admitting doesn't make me a lot happier," Theisman replied.

"I should think not. It damned well better not, anyway!" Pritchart glowered at the framed copy of the Constitution hanging on the wall opposite her desk.

Arnold Giancola's signature was on it, one of the block of convention delegates who'd solemnly pledged to recreate the ancient glories of the Republic of Haven. Eloise Pritchart's signature was on it, as well, although Thomas Theisman's wasn't . . . which she considered one of the worst miscarriages of historical justice on record.

But the fact that they'd both been at the Constitutional Convention was one of the very few things she and Giancola had in common. Which, unfortunately, hadn't been quite enough, in light of the Republic's current political realities, to keep him out of her cabinet.

Arnold Giancola had been a low mid-level Treasury bureaucrat under Hereditary President Harris. Like hundreds of thousands of other bureaucrats, he'd continued in his precoup position—in his case, administering disbursement of the Basic Living Stipend right here in Nouveau Paris—under the Committee. None of them had been given much choice about that, aside from the very senior Legislaturalist administrators, who'd all been purged by the new management, because someone had to continue to run the day-to-day machinery of the state, and Rob Pierre and Oscar Saint-Just had innumerable ways to make sure they did. But to be completely fair (which Pritchart found difficult in her Secretary of State's case), Giancola had done his job better than most, and with what certainly appeared to have been a genuine concern for the Dolists under his jurisdiction.

His competence had drawn favorable attention from his new superiors, and after four or five T-years, he'd been transferred to the Department of State, which was always in search of capable administrators. He'd done equally well there, rising steadily in seniority, only to be shifted back to Treasury when Rob Pierre nominated Avram Turner to drive through his enormous economic reform package. Giancola's new position had brought him back to his old Nouveau Paris neighborhood, where he'd prospered despite the pain and economic dislocation involved in the Turner Reforms. He was, after all, an effective administrator who possessed an undeniable talent for attracting the loyalty of his subordinates, and he'd done his level best to minimize the reforms' traumas for the citizens for whom he was responsible. As a result, he'd emerged from the Committee's downfall with a base of genuine popular support—quite a large one, actually—on the Republic's capital (and most populous) planet.

He'd capitalized on that support shrewdly. His brother Jason was a senator; his cousin Gerard Younger was a representative; and Arnold himself had played a prominent role in reorganizing the capital following Theisman's overthrow of Saint-Just. He'd obviously had ambitions of his own at the time, but he'd been smart enough, whatever his other failings, to realize Theisman would have squashed him like a bug if he'd acted on them. So instead, he'd settled for building a powerful political machine in Nouveau Paris—still the most important single city in the Republic, although the Mob's heady days of power were a thing of the past. That had not only assured him his slot at the Convention but also allowed him to directly influence the election of a surprising number of representatives and no less than eight senators (including himself), which was not an inconsequential Congressional power base.

It had also made him Pritchart's most significant opposition when she ran for the presidency in the first election under the restored Constitution. Had it come down to a straight contest between the two of them, his candidacy would have been not only significant but a serious challenge, and she knew it. Fortunately, she'd enjoyed two enormous advantages he simply could not overcome: her status as the provisional head of government who'd actually kept her promise and held general elections when she'd said she would, and the endorsement of Thomas Theisman. There had been seven candidates on the ballot, and Pritchart had taken seventy-three percent of the popular vote. Arnold Giancola had taken nineteen percent, and the other five candidates between them had split the remaining eight percent.

The election hadn't even been close, but Giancola had clearly emerged as the second most consequential figure of the restored Republic's youthful political establishment. That was precisely why Pritchart had chosen him for what was technically the number one position in her cabinet. In actual fact, Theisman's combination of the offices of Secretary of War and Chief of Naval Operations made him the *de facto* second-ranking member of the administration, but Giancola was definitely the third. And under the Constitution, it was he who would lead the three-month caretaker administration and supervise the special election to replace Pritchart if something happened to her.

To say she wasn't entirely happy to have him in that position would have been a gross understatement, yet she'd seen no viable alternative. His allies in Congress would have demanded some significant appointment for him even without his showing in the presidential elections, and she'd hoped to bind him to the new administration by giving him a voice in it. Ambitious though he was, he also saw himself as a statesman, and Pritchart was well aware that he truly believed in his own vision for the Republic's future. That genuine patriotism had made no small contribution to his ability to build his political alliances . . . and helped to encourage his personal ambition with a sense of mission. That was precisely what had made him so dangerous, and she'd hoped she could convince his patriotic side to rein in his ambitious side by supporting her in the interests of solidarity during the critical, early years of the restored Republic.

The Constitution had also just coincidentally required him to resign from the Senate to accept a cabinet-level post, and she'd calculated that he would be less dangerous in the cabinet where she could keep an eye on him and demand his loyalty than he would directly controlling a senate seat. But he'd foiled that part of her plans by securing his brother's election in his place in the special election his resignation had set up. Nor had her plans to co-opt him to support her policies proved an unadulterated success. As far as she could tell, he'd simply recognized that he had to work through a different set of rules and priorities in pursuit of his original ambition and policies, and he was building a steadily growing faction in Congress. The fact that he was also busy building support within the Cabinet for at least some of his policies had the potential to turn into a major nightmare, yet she couldn't demand his resignation. It was probably clear to everyone that he was maneuvering to put himself into position to challenge any reelection bid of her own when her term ended in another four T-years, but his alliances in Congress would provoke a bigger fight than ridding herself of him would be worth.

Or more than she thought it would be worth, anyway, she amended.

"That 'idiot' has plans of his own, Tom, and you know it," she said aloud. "I still cherish hopes he'll overstep and give me an excuse to bring the hammer down on him, but he's getting himself well enough entrenched to make it hard. And events are going to play right into his hands if the Manties persist in blowing off the negotiations."

"Why?" Theisman's eyes narrowed. "Giancola's been getting more and more pissed with the Manties for months. What makes that so much more important now?"

"The fact," Pritchart sighed, "that, as I should hardly have to remind you, of all people, Senator *Jason* Giancola became a member of the Naval Affairs Committee last week."

"Oh, *crap*."

"Precisely," the President of the Republic of Haven agreed. "It's obvious that the good senator could hardly wait to spill the beans about Bolthole to his brother."

"After swearing to maintain complete confidentiality!" Theisman snapped.

"Of course he did," Pritchart agreed with a sour chuckle. "Come on, Tom! Half our new legislators are still afraid to sneeze for fear we'll turn out to be another Committee of Public Safety after all, and the other half is trying to pursue 'business as usual' Legislaturalist-style. It's just our bad luck that the Giancolas belong to the second group instead of the first. Kevin warned you there was no way Jason was going to keep his mouth shut if he learned anything Arnold could use, and you know it."

"Yes, I do," Theisman admitted unhappily, and ran his hands through his hair, glaring at nothing in particular for several seconds. Then he sighed and looked back at the President.

"How bad is it?" he asked.

"Not good, I'm afraid. Arnold's been a little more circumspect about dropping hints on me than I would have expected from him, but he's made it pretty clear he knows about the 'black' aspects of the budget, about the existence of the shipyards, and that you sent Shannon Foraker out to take charge of them. Whether or not he knows what's actually going on out there is a bit more problematical, but judging from his attitude, I wouldn't bet against it."

"Crap," Theisman repeated, even more sincerely, and it was his turn to lean back in his chair with a sigh.

There were very few things Rob Pierre and Oscar Saint-Just had done with which Thomas Theisman found himself in complete agreement. Operation Bolthole was one of them, although Theisman was scarcely happy about the circumstances which had made Bolthole necessary.

The thing that most amazed him about Bolthole was that Pierre and Saint-Just had managed to pull it off in near total secrecy. Theisman himself hadn't heard so much as a whisper about it until he'd taken over as commander of Capital Fleet, and virtually no officer outside the project itself below the rank of vice admiral— and damned few senior to that—knew about it even now. Which was a state of affairs Theisman intended to preserve as long as possible.

"Tom," Pritchart said, as if she'd been reading his mind—a possibility he wasn't prepared to discount, after watching her in action for over three years—"we're going to have to take the wraps off of Bolthole sooner or later, anyway, you know."

"Not yet," he replied with spinal-reflex promptness.

"Tom—"

"Not yet," he repeated even more firmly, then made himself pause for a moment.

"You're right," he acknowledged then. "Sooner or later, we'll have to admit Bolthole exists. In fact, I doubt we'll be able to hide the funding for it for more than another year or two, max. But I'm not 'taking the wraps off' until we've produced enough of the new ships and hardware to deter the Manties from a preemptive strike."

"Preemptive strike?" Pritchart arched both eyebrows at him. "Tom, we can't even get them to respond to an offer of a formal peace treaty after better than three full T-years of trying! What in the world makes you think they care enough about what's going on inside the Republic to worry about preemptive strikes?"

"We've been over this before, Eloise," Theisman said, then reminded himself that despite her long Navy association as Giscard's people's commissioner and even her own career as a guerilla commander, the President was essentially a civilian by inclination and orientation alike.

"Right this minute," he went on after a second or so, "the Manties are completely confident that no one poses a significant threat to their naval superiority. Their new missile pods, their new superdreadnoughts, and—especially—their new LACs give them a degree of tactical superiority which would make it suicide for any conventional navy to engage them. Janacek may be an idiot, and he may have brought in other idiots to help him run the Manty Admiralty, but it's obvious that they recognize their technical advantages. That's the only possible explanation for their build-down in conventional hulls. They're actually reducing their fleet to very nearly its prewar size, Eloise. They'd never do that if they weren't so confident of their tech edge that they figured they could hack extremely heavy numerical odds if they had to.

"But look at what that means. Their entire current strategic stance is built on that edge in technology, and their First Lord of the Admiralty is stupid. He's going to be upset enough if he suddenly discovers Pierre and Saint-Just managed to build a shipyard complex even bigger than the one here in the Haven System without anyone in the Star Kingdom so much as suspecting it. But if he figures out what we've had Foraker and her people doing out there for the last couple of T-years, he's not going to be upset—he's going to panic."

"Panic?" Pritchart shook her head. "Tom, this is your area of expertise, not mine. But isn't 'panic' just a little strong? Let's be honest. You and I both know the Manties kicked our butt up one side and down the other. If Saint-Just hadn't managed to snooker them into 'truce talks,' White Haven would have smashed straight through Twelfth Fleet, punched out Capital Fleet, and dictated terms right here on Haven. I was there with Javier and Lester. I *know* there was nothing we could have done to stop him."

"Of course there wasn't . . . then," Theisman agreed. "But that's my very point. We know that, and they know that. Worse, they're depending on it. Which means they have to be certain they maintain that technological edge, especially in light of the reduction in their total tonnage. So if they realize Foraker is busy building us an entire new navy specifically designed to offset their advantages, they're also going to realize they've created a situation which effectively allows us to begin even with them in the new types. Since their entire defensive stance requires them to retain their advantage in those types, one solution would be for them to hit us before we have enough of the new designs available to defend ourselves."

"But that would violate the terms of our truce," Pritchart pointed out.

"Which is just that—a truce," Theisman emphasized. "The war isn't over. Not officially, anyway, which is exactly what Giancola keeps pointing out. Hell, the *Manties* keep pointing it out! I'm sure you saw the same analysis I did on their Prime Minister's most recent speech. They're still 'viewing with alarm' where we're concerned, if only to justify the tax structure they're retaining. So there's no formal treaty to dissuade them from resuming the war any time they choose. And if we openly acknowledge that we're building an entire new fleet capable of standing up to them in combat, the temptation to nip the threat in the bud would have to be intense. Worst of all, Edward Janacek is stupid and arrogant enough to recommend to High Ridge that they do just that."

"I can't help feeling that you're being alarmist," Pritchart told him frankly. "But you're Secretary of War, and I'm not prepared to overrule you on a judgment call like this one. It certainly won't do any harm to exercise a little caution which may turn out to be excessive, and the Manties aren't likely to panic over something they don't know anything about.

"In the meantime, however, your desire to keep the Star Kingdom in the dark may create some domestic problems. To be honest, I'm not entirely comfortable maintaining such a high level of security where Bolthole is concerned, either. Leaving aside the fact that I'm not at all sure burying 'black' funding in the budget is constitutional, whatever the Attorney General may think, it's a little too much like the levels of secrecy Pierre and Saint-Just routinely maintained."

"In some ways, I suppose," Theisman acknowledged. "But I've kept the Naval Affairs Committee informed. That keeps Congress officially in the loop the way the Constitution requires."

"Be honest, Tom," Pritchart chided. "You haven't told them everything about your new toys, now have you?"

"Maybe not everything," he admitted. "But I've kept them fully informed on the purpose of Bolthole, and they know at least a part of what Foraker is doing. If they didn't, the Senator couldn't have 'spilled the beans' to his brother."

"Agreed. And that's precisely the domestic problem that most concerns me. Most of our senators and the members of the Cabinet are still a bit more diffident than I'd really like them to be in a lot of ways. For one thing, if more of them would grow spines and build up other power bases I could use to balance Giancola, it would help a lot when it comes to reining him in. They won't do it any time soon, though, and in the meantime there's still entirely too much of the reflex acceptance of restrictions on information simply because the government says it's 'necessary.' That's the only way we got the budget to keep Bolthole running through without debate in the first place. But if Giancola keeps on pushing more and more strongly for us to take a harder line in the negotiations with the Manties, then sooner or later he's going to start bolstering his arguments by dropping some of the details his brother has obviously fed him. Which is going to bring the Department of State into direct conflict with the Department of War."

"We'll just have to deal with that as it arises," Theisman said. "I realize it can create an awkward situation, and I'll try not to let my paranoia pressure me into maintaining secrecy longer than is actually warranted. But I truly don't think I can overemphasize the importance of building up to a level capable of deterring any Manty temptation towards preemptive action before we go public about the new ships."

"As I said, I'm not prepared—or even tempted—to overrule you in this particular area. I just wish the Manties would stop providing Arnold with fresh grist for his mill. And truth to tell, I think they're up to something, myself. There has to be a reason they keep refusing even to seriously discuss the return of the occupied star systems, and if they're not planning to hang onto them permanently, then what the hell *are* they doing?"

CHAPTER THREE

Ms. Midshipwoman Zilwicki saw the familiar green-on-green uniform before she caught sight of Duchess Harrington. Everyone on Saganami Island knew that uniform, because it was the only non-Navy or Marine uniform allowed on the RMN academy's campus. Helen Zilwicki wasn't supposed to know about the resentment and outrage certain august personages tended to very privately vent behind the scenes over its presence here, but she wasn't her father's daughter for nothing. Anton Zilwicki might have started his naval career as a "techno weenie," but before that career had come to a screeching halt four T-years before, he had more than completed his transition to a full-time intelligence type, and a good one. He wasn't the sort who talked down to anyone, far less to his motherless daughter, and he'd always emphasized how important it was to actually listen to anything she heard.

Of course, his . . . relationship with Lady Catherine Montaigne, Countess of the Tor, also offered Helen a certain insight denied to her fellow midshipmen. Helen never actually tried to eavesdrop on the conversations between her father and Lady Cathy, but the countess was as effervescent and compulsively energetic as Anton Zilwicki was methodical and disciplined. Her exclamation point-punctuated conversations usually seemed as if they were going off in all directions at once, with a sort of high-energy trajectory that left the unwary feeling somewhat as if they'd been run over by a ground lorry . . . or possibly a small fleet of them. In fact, there was always an underlying structure and cohesiveness for anyone who had the wit to stay in shouting distance of Lady Cathy's scalpel-sharp intelligence. And one thing the Countess of the Tor had never possessed was anything like Anton Zilwicki's instinctive respect for authority and tradition. "Irreverent" was far too mild a term to describe her, and her comments on the current Government started at scathing and went rapidly downhill from there.

Which had made it inevitable that Helen would hear Lady Cathy's opinion of the ill-considered attempt Sir Edward Janacek had made to revoke Duchess Harrington's special permission to bring armed personal retainers into the sacred precincts of the Naval Academy.

His efforts had failed ignominiously, exactly (in Helen's opinion) as they deserved to. Fortunately for him, he, or at least his political advisers, had possessed enough sense not to conduct his campaign in a public forum, which had left him room to retreat when he ran into the Queen's unyielding resistance. Since the dispensation which allowed for the presence of the Harrington Steading armsmen on the island in the first place had been granted by the Queen's Bench at the direct request of the Foreign Secretary in light of the fact that Steadholder Harrington and Duchess Harrington were two totally separate legal entities who simply happened to live in the same body as *Admiral* Harrington, the decision to revoke it had not been the purely internal Navy affair Janacek had attempted to make it. The Foreign Secretary who had requested it had also happened to be the Queen's uncle, and the Queen's Bench answered directly to her, not to Edward Janacek or even Prime Minister High Ridge. Given both of those things, only an idiot would have tried to overturn the arrangement out of what was clearly a sense of petty spite.

That, at least, had been the countess' opinion, and nothing Helen had seen or heard elsewhere suggested Lady Cathy had been in error. Not that Helen intended to discuss that observation with any of her classmates. Her father had often admonished her to remember the example of the 'cat, who saw and heard everything but said nothing. Of course, that example had developed a small flaw since the treecats had learned to sign. On the other hand, it was beginning to look as if the 'cats had been doing a lot more hearing and seeing—and thinking—than even her father had ever suspected, so perhaps the analogy was actually even better than she'd thought. Either way, a first-form midshipwoman had no business at all explaining to her fellow students that the civilian head of their service was a small-minded, small-souled, vindictive cretin. Especially not when that was true.

Helen's lips twitched in an almost-smile at the thought, but she banished the expression and stepped out of the way as Colonel LaFollet came through the pistol range door. The armsman's gray eyes swept his surroundings with an attention to detail which had long since become instinctive. He noticed the tall, sturdy young midshipwoman, and his expression suggested that some orderly file in his mind had brought up her image as one of Duchess Harrington's hundreds of students. But recognition or no, those eyes considered her with a cool, analytical detachment which made her suddenly grateful that he was unlikely to consider her a threat to his charge.

She was dressed out for gym at the moment, in the shorts and unitard which were standard issue for midshipwomen. That uniform included no headgear, which excused her from the normal requirement to salute a superior officer, but she braced quickly to attention until he nodded in acknowledgment of the courtesy. Then he stepped past her, and she came to attention once more as Duchess Harrington walked into the range behind him.

"Ms. Zilwicki," the Duchess observed.

"Your Grace," Helen responded respectfully.

The Duchess' immaculate space-black and gold uniform was unique. She was the only RMN officer who properly wore a Grayson Space Navy shoulder flash bearing the flame-enshrouded salamander emblem of the Protector's Own Squadron even in Manticoran uniform, since she was the Protector's Own's official commander. But in addition to that, she was also the only person in history whose uniform tunic carried both the blood-red ribbon of the Star of Grayson and the crimson, blue, and white one of the Parliamentary Medal of Valor. There were persistent rumors that Duchess Harrington had refused the PMV after leading the escape from Cerberus, but even if they were true, she hadn't been able to avoid it after the Cromarty Assassination. Helen suspected that she'd accepted it with very mixed emotions, however, since Baron High Ridge, as the new Prime Minister, had played the media event for all it was worth when he announced she was to receive it.

But Helen had seen those ribbons often before, and neither they nor the treecat who rode on the Duchess' shoulder were what drew her attention this afternoon. That was left to the wooden case in Duchess Harrington's hand. It was the sort of case which was hand-built at an exorbitant price by some skilled craftsman in some tiny shop filled with dusty sunlight and the sweet scent of wood shavings and varnish to wrap around something indecently expensive, and Helen felt a stir of interest. She'd never seen the box before, but she'd spoken to other midshipmen who had, and she knew what was inside it.

Lady Harrington's ".45" was famous—or infamous, depending on one's perspective—throughout the Navy. Those who continued to cling to the notion that she was some sort of loose warhead, a dangerous lunatic unable to recognize the difference between the derring-do of bad historical holo dramas and the reality of a modern officer's duties, saw the archaic hand weapon as proof of their prejudices. Others, like Helen and Anton Zilwicki, regarded it somewhat differently. Perhaps it was because, unlike those who condemned Lady Harrington's "recklessness" and considered her some sort of glory hound, both Helen and her father had spent their own time in a place those critics had never been. It wasn't something Helen ever discussed with any of her classmates, but she sometimes wondered how they would have reacted if she'd ever told them about her adventures on Old Earth. Or mentioned the fact that before she was fifteen T-years old she had killed three men with her bare hands.

No. Helen Zilwicki knew far better than most exactly what had been going through Lady Harrington's mind when she decided to match a piece of technology that was over two millennia old against modern hand weapons in a personal shoot-out with a pirate leader and his bodyguards. But she was also young enough to want very badly to see that piece of technology in action.

Unfortunately, she was already running late for her martial arts class. Although she was rapidly mastering the Academy's preferred *coup de vitesse* style, she was also spending extra time assisting Chief Maddison in teaching the more esoteric *Neue-Stil Handgemenge* developed on New Berlin. It wasn't widely practiced in the Star Kingdom, but she'd had the privilege of studying it under *sensei* Robert Tye, one of Old Earth's two or three most experienced practitioners. Despite her youth, that made her a teaching resource Maddison was determined to put to maximum use. Helen sincerely enjoyed teaching others, but it did put an undeniable squeeze on her time. And even if it hadn't, she'd already finished her own scheduled pistol training for the day. Which meant she couldn't think of an excuse which would justify her in hanging around while Lady Harrington took her .45 to the shooting line.

Damn.

"With your permission, Your Grace?" she said, and Lady Harrington nodded.

"On your way, Ms. Zilwicki," she said with a slight smile, and Helen jogged off towards her waiting instructor.

Honor watched the youthful midshipwoman disappear, and her smile broadened. She approved of Ms. Zilwicki. Not that it was surprising that the young woman should have turned out as well as she had . . . and not just because her mother had been a genuine hero. Few PMVs had been harder earned than that of Captain Helen Zilwicki, but that had been when young Helen was only a child. The father was the place to look for the full flowering of the daughter's strength, and over the last few T-years, Honor had gotten a better chance than most to appreciate just how strong that father was. And the reason Helen never doubted that she could do anything she set her mind to.

In fact, Honor often wished that she'd had a bit more of Helen's confidence, if that was the right word, at the same age. She'd tasted enough of the youngster's emotions through her empathic link with Nimitz to feel quite certain Helen would never have reacted the same way Honor had when Pavel Young had attempted to rape her. Well, *after* Young's rape attempt, anyway, Honor corrected herself. At the actual moment, she would undoubtedly have done precisely what Honor had done, and possibly even more thoroughly than Honor had, judging from her scores in unarmed combat training. But later, when she'd had time to think about it, Helen would never even have considered not telling the Academy commandant what had happened.

If I'd been a bit more like her at her age, Honor reflected, *my life would have been completely different. And Paul would still be alive.* She felt a familiar stir of loss and the echo of grief and inhaled sharply.

Yes, he'd still be alive. But I'd never have met him—not the same way, at least, she reminded herself.

She allowed herself a moment longer to recall all she and Paul Tankersley had been to one another, and then she put the memory gently away once more and followed Andrew towards the range officer's counter to sign in.

Technically, the letter of Grayson law required that she be accompanied by an absolute minimum of two armsmen wherever she went, and she knew LaFollet was far from reconciled to her decision to reduce her normal personal detachment to just himself here on the Island. Truth to tell, she'd been a little surprised when she realized how much she resented that reduction herself, even though it had been her own idea. Of course, her reasons for resenting it weren't quite the same as Andrew's. It was part of his job description to be hyperconscious of any potential threat at all times and in all places, and he was profoundly unhappy at the way it reduced his ability to guarantee her safety. Personally, Honor felt reasonably confident no assassins skulked in the shrubbery of Saganami Island, but she'd long since given up any hope that LaFollet's institutional paranoia would allow them to see eye-to-eye on that particular point.

In addition to his purely practical considerations, however, Honor knew her armsman deeply resented what he saw as a calculated insult to his Steadholder. He knew all about Janacek's efforts to have Honor's personal security detachment entirely barred from the Academy's campus. He'd never said so in so many words, but his firm belief that it was only one more aspect of the petty vindictiveness in which the present Manticoran Government indulged whenever it thought no one could see was painfully obvious to Honor. It would have been even without her link to Nimitz; as it was, he might as well have shouted his disgust aloud.

Unfortunately, and even though she'd been the one who'd suggested the compromise, Honor shared his view of what had inspired Janacek's attempt. Which was why she, too, resented it so bitterly. She hoped her resentment stemmed from the circumstances which had put Janacek into the First Lord's chair once again, not from a sense of her own importance, but she was self-honest enough to admit that she wasn't as certain of that as she would have preferred to be.

She grimaced at the thought and set her pistol case and accessory shoulder bag on the counter as the range officer, an absurdly youthful looking Marine master sergeant whose nameplate read "JOHANNSEN, M.," produced ear protectors for her and LaFollet, along with the proper forms. She signed and thumbprinted the paperwork, then opened the shoulder bag for the special ear protectors she'd had made for Nimitz. The 'cat regarded them with scant favor, but he wasn't about to reject them. Back home on Grayson, her outdoor range allowed him to keep an eye on her while she practiced without bringing him into such proximity as to make the sound of the gunshots a problem. Here at the Academy, with its indoor range, that wasn't a possibility, and she watched patiently while he slipped the protectors into place and adjusted them carefully.

"Ready, Stinker?" she asked. The protectors were advanced developments of devices which had been available even before humanity left Old Earth for the stars. They were fully effective at damping the decibel spikes which could injure someone's hearing, yet normal conversational tones were clearly audible through them, and the 'cat raised one true-hand, closed in the sign for the letter "S," and "nodded" it up and down in affirmation.

"Good," she said, and adjusted her own ear protection. LaFollet had already donned his protectors, and she waited patiently while he stepped through the door to give the firing line itself a careful once over. Satisfied that no desperately determined hired killers had infiltrated it, he opened the door once more and held it courteously for her.

"Thank you, Andrew," she said gravely, and stepped through it.

Colonel LaFollet stood well behind the Steadholder in the noisy range and watched her punch holes in anachronistic paper targets with meticulous precision. Her automatic produced a cloud of sharp-smelling smoke, unlike the pulsers most people came here to fire, but at least there were enough other chemical firearm afficionados in the Navy for the range to have been provided with a highly efficient ventilation system.

It was somehow typical of her that she preferred the ancient, traditional paper to the highly sophisticated, holographically created targets which were used in virtually every combat marksmanship training program. The colonel had often thought that her preference resulted from the way she saw shooting, as much as an art form as a serious form of self-defense. She approached her beloved *coup de vitesse* and her lessons in Grayson-style swordsmanship exactly the same way. Not that she took her training in them any less seriously, as her track record of carnage in all three amply demonstrated. And she did spend at least one session per week working the combat range against realistically programmed holographic opponents.

She was just as good at shooting holes in the bad guys as in the ancient silhouette and bull's-eye paper targets which were her preferred victims, too.

Although he was never likely to pass up the opportunity to tease her, respectfully of course, about her choice of weapons, LaFollet took great comfort from her skill with the antique handgun High Admiral Matthews had presented to her. If he had his way, Lady Harrington would never again have the opportunity to demonstrate her proficiency at self-defense, but his past lack of success in that regard didn't exactly inspire him with confidence for the future. It was scarcely his fault she kept attracting assassination attempts, close personal encounters with bloodthirsty megalomaniac pirates, and transportation to hellhole prison planets, but that didn't change the fact that she did. Which meant Andrew LaFollet was intensely in favor of anything which made her harder to kill.

Nor was the colonel ever likely to underestimate the lethality of her ear-beating, propellant-spewing hand-cannon. It might be big, noisy, and two thousand years out of date, but that didn't make it ineffective. And unlike his Manticoran counterparts, LaFollet had initially been trained using weapons very like the Steadholder's semiauto. Their designs might have been somewhat more sophisticated, and the materials of which they'd been constructed had certainly been more advanced, but the basic operating principles had been virtually identical. He and his security service colleagues had traded them with gleeful jubilation for the pulsers Grayson's alliance with the Star Kingdom had finally made available, yet the twelve T-years he'd spent training with them first left him with a profound respect for their capabilities. Besides, he'd once seen the Steadholder use the very same "antique" .45 to kill two fully prepared opponents armed to the teeth with "modern" weapons.

Not that the hopefully remote possibility that she might someday be required to once again personally wreak effective mayhem against armed opponents was the only reason he was perfectly happy to stand around in a smoky, noisy pistol range while she sent bullet after bullet downrange. No. However comforting he might find her proficiency, the real reason he had no objection to her range visits was much simpler.

They relaxed her. Even more, perhaps, than her *coup de vitesse* katas, her shooting sessions required a complete mental break from all of the host of problems which currently beset her. The need to empty her mind while she concentrated on muscle memory, on breathing, on grip and trigger control, on capturing the sights and sight picture . . . Nothing could have been better designed to distract her, however briefly, from the current political and diplomatic lunacy which had come to focus more and more intensively on her. And that, all by itself, was more than sufficient to win Andrew LaFollet's enthusiastic endorsement.

Which didn't mean he approached her trips to the range without a certain trepidation. For one thing, he wasn't at all in favor of allowing anyone—even fellow naval officers—into the Steadholder's presence with weapons in their hands. He knew better than to raise that particular point with Lady Harrington, however, which was why he'd somehow overlooked reporting to her about the private conversation he'd had with Sergeant Johannsen's predecessor over four T-years ago. The colonel had long since discovered that the easiest way to prevent the Steadholder from complaining about irksome security considerations was simply not to mention them to her. Not even Lady Harrington could get exercised over something she didn't know about, although keeping secrets from her wasn't exactly the easiest thing in the universe.

In this case, though, he was reasonably certain she remained blissfully unaware that Johannsen, like the last range officer, discreetly saw to it that no other shooter was ever admitted to the range while she was at the line. It was certainly possible that sooner or later she would begin wondering why she always seemed to have the range to herself, of course. When she did, she was probably going to ask some extremely pointed questions, and LaFollet wasn't looking forward to answering them. But in the meantime, his if-you-don't-ask, I-won't-tell policy seemed to be working just fine, and tomorrow could look after itself when it got here.

Despite his arrangement with Johannsen, LaFollet's well-trained and carefully honed sense of paranoia prevented him from ever completely relaxing his vigilance. Even as he watched the Steadholder systematically removing the "X" ring from yet another silhouette at a range of fifteen meters, his eyes also constantly scanned the other shooting stations and watched the soundproofed door into the range proper.

Which was why he became aware of the arrival of the tall, broadshouldered, blue-eyed man well before Lady Harrington did.

The colonel recognized the newcomer the instant he stepped through the door, but his professionally expressionless face hid his dismay admirably. Not that LaFollet disliked the new arrival. In point of fact, he admired and respected Admiral Hamish Alexander, Thirteenth Earl of White Haven, almost as much as he admired and respected Lady Harrington, and under other circumstances, he would have been delighted to see him. As it was . . .

The armsman came to attention and saluted, despite the fact that White Haven, unlike the Steadholder, was in civilian dress. That made him stand out like a deacon in a house of joy here on Saganami Island, and LaFollet suspected it was deliberate. The Earl was widely acknowledged as the premier field commander of the entire Manticoran Alliance after his brilliant performance in Operation Buttercup, and the Grayson Space Navy had granted him the rank of Fleet Admiral in its service. He was fully entitled to wear the uniform of his rank—in either navy—whenever he chose, despite the fact that Sir Edward Janacek had seen fit to place him on inactive, half-pay status with indecent speed as one of his first actions as First Lord of the Admiralty. If he could have, Janacek would undoubtedly have attempted to order him not to accept the Grayson promotion, as well. Technically, he had that power, since the Graysons had not made the rank honorary, despite the fact that White Haven was not a Grayson citizen, but not even the High Ridge Government had dared to offer an insult quite that gratuitous to the man who'd won the war. So the First Lord had swallowed the ground glass and accepted it . . . then deprived White Haven of the opportunity to wear *any* uniform on active duty. The fact that White Haven chose not to wear it off-duty, either, even here at the very fountainhead of the Royal Manticoran Navy's officer corps, only emphasized the pettiness and spite of Janacek's action.

The Earl nodded, very much as Lady Harrington would have if she'd been out of uniform, and gestured for the colonel to stand at ease once more. LaFollet relaxed, and White Haven, ears safely covered by his own protectors, crossed to stand beside him and watch Lady Harrington's demolition of her current target. LaFollet was more than a little surprised that Nimitz hadn't alerted the Steadholder to White Haven's arrival via their link. Perhaps she was simply too deeply focused on her shooting to be as fully aware of the 'cat as usual. It certainly wasn't because Nimitz shared LaFollet's sense of dismay. In fact, it was obvious to the armsman that the 'cat not only liked White Haven but actively approved of the Earl's attitude towards his own adopted person.

Which, in LaFollet's opinion, was yet another demonstration of the fact that, despite centuries of association with human society, treecat brains simply didn't work the way human ones did.

The colonel was far too professional—and discreet—to permit his eyes to abandon their systematic scan of his environs. But he watched the Earl, very unobtrusively, from the corner of one eye, and his heart sank as White Haven's unguarded ice-blue gaze clung to the Steadholder and softened warmly.

Lady Harrington fired the final round in her current magazine, and her pistol's slide locked in the open position. She laid it carefully on the shelf at her station, muzzle pointed downrange, and pressed the button to bring her target back to her. She gazed at it thoughtfully for several moments, then pursed her lips in grudging approval of the single large, multi-lobed hole which had replaced the silhouette's "X" ring. She reached up to unhook the target from the carrier, then turned to set it aside and mount a replacement and froze as she saw White Haven.

It was only the briefest of hesitations, so fleeting that anyone who didn't know her as well as LaFollet probably would never have noticed it at all. But LaFollet did know her, and the heart which had sunk at the Earl's expression plummeted.

Against most people, the Steadholder's sharply-carved, high-cheekboned face was an admirable mask for her feelings. Very few of them probably appreciated the years of military discipline and self-discipline which had gone into crafting that mask, but those who truly knew her knew exactly how to read her expression anyway. It was the eyes, of course. Always the eyes. Those huge, chocolate-dark, almond-shaped eyes. The ones she'd inherited from her mother. The ones that mirrored her feelings even more revealingly than Nimitz's body language.

The ones which for no more than two heartbeats, three at the most, glowed with bright, joyful welcome.

Sweet Tester, LaFollet thought almost despairingly, *each of them thinks no one in the world—including each other—can tell what's going on. They actually* believe *that.*

Idiots.

He took himself sternly to task the instant the thought crossed his mind. In the first place, it was no business of his who the Steadholder decided to fall in love with. His job was to protect her, not to tell her what she could or couldn't do with her life. And in the second place, she was obviously as well aware as LaFollet of all the manifold reasons she had no business looking at Earl White Haven that way. If she hadn't been, the two of them would undoubtedly have stopped suffering in such noble silence at least two T-years ago.

And Tester only knew where *that* would have led!

"Hello, Honor," White Haven said, and waved a hand at the perforated target. "I never could shoot that well myself," he went on. "Did you ever consider trying out for the marksmanship team when you were a middy?"

"Hello, Hamish," Lady Harrington responded, and held out her hand. The Earl took it, but rather than shake it in the Manticoran fashion, he raised it and brushed his lips across it as a Grayson might have done. He'd spent long enough on Grayson to make the gesture completely natural looking, but the faintest hint of a blush painted the Steadholder's cheekbones.

"In answer to your question," she went on a moment later, her voice completely normal as she reclaimed her hand, "yes. I did consider trying out for the pistol team. The rifle team never really interested me, I'm afraid, but I've always enjoyed hand weapons. But I was just getting really into the *coup* at that point, and I decided to concentrate on that, instead." She shrugged. "I grew up in the Sphinx bush, you know, so I was already a pretty fair shot when I got here."

"I suppose that's one way to put it," White Haven agreed dryly, picking up the target and raising it to look at her through the hole blown in its center. "My own athletic endeavors were a bit more pacific than yours."

"I know." She nodded and gave him one of the crooked smiles enforced by the artificial nerves in her left cheek. "I understand you and Admiral Caparelli had quite a soccer rivalry during your time on the Island."

"What you understand is that Tom Caparelli kicked my aristocratic backside up one side of the field and down the other," the Earl corrected, and she chuckled.

"That might be true, but I've become far too diplomatic to put it quite so frankly," she told him.

"I see." He lowered the target, and the humor in his expression faded just a bit. "Speaking about being diplomatic, I'm afraid I didn't hunt you up here in your hidey hole just to enjoy your company. Not," he added, "that your company isn't always a pleasure."

"You're not too shabby as a diplomat yourself," she observed, and anyone but Andrew LaFollet might not even have noticed the very slight edge which had crept into her voice.

"Decades spent as the brother of an ambitious politician do that to you," White Haven assured her easily. "In fact, the reason I came looking for you was that the aforesaid ambitious politician and I spent most of the morning together."

"Ah?" Lady Harrington cocked an eyebrow at him.

"I had to fly into Landing on business anyway," the Earl explained, "so I dropped by to see Willie . . . who happened to have just returned from Mount Royal Palace."

"I see." The Steadholder's tone had suddenly become far more neutral, and she ejected the magazine from her pistol, released the slide, and tucked the weapon into the fitted recess in its case.

"Should I assume he asked you to drop by to see me?" she went on.

"Not specifically. But Elizabeth had invited him to the Palace as the Leader of the Opposition to hear the official briefing on the latest inspirations to strike High Ridge and his flunkies." Lady Harrington looked up from the gun case to dart a sharp glance at the Earl, but he either failed to notice or pretended that he had. "The official message inviting the Opposition Leader to the briefing had somehow gone astray. Again."

"I see," she repeated, and closed the gun case with a snap. She reached for her accessory bag, but White Haven's hand got to it before hers, and smiling, he slung it over his own shoulder.

She smiled back, but her eyes were troubled. LaFollet wasn't surprised. The Steadholder had come an enormous distance from the politically unsophisticated naval officer she'd been when LaFollet first became her armsman. Which meant she was unaware neither of the fresh contempt in White Haven's voice when he spoke of the Prime Minister, nor of the pettiness of High Ridge's obviously intentional failure to advise Lord Alexander of the briefing.

Like the Steadholder, although to a lesser degree, the colonel had become better informed on Manticoran political processes than he'd ever really wanted to be. Because of that, he knew there was no specific constitutional requirement for the Prime Minister to invite the leader of his opposition in Parliament to the Queen's official weekly briefings. By long tradition, however, he was supposed to invite the Opposition Leader to the regular briefings, both as a matter of common courtesy and to ensure that if there were a sudden change of government, the individual who would almost certainly replace him as Prime Minister was as fully up to speed as possible.

No one expected any politician, even the Prime Minister of the Star Kingdom of Manticore, to invite his main political rival to Cabinet meetings, or to special Crown briefings. That would have been both unreasonable and foolish. But the twice-a-week general briefings were another matter entirely, and LaFollet knew Duke Cromarty had been scrupulous even at the height of the war against the Peeps about inviting High Ridge, who'd led the Opposition at the time, to attend them. It was typical of High Ridge to "forget" to extend the same courtesy to the man who'd been Cromarty's political second-in-command.

"Was it your impression there was a specific reason this particular invitation might have 'gone astray'?" the Steadholder went on after a moment.

"Not really," White Haven admitted, "although I doubt very much that he was overjoyed to see Willie, given the nature and content of the briefing. On the other hand, he might have been better off because Willie was there anyway." Lady Harrington tilted her head inquiringly, and the Earl chuckled. "My impression is that Her Majesty actually behaves herself a bit better when Willie's present to act as a buffer between her and her Prime Minister," he said dryly.

"I'm afraid that's probably true," Lady Harrington observed, both her voice and her expression rather more serious than the Earl's. "I wish it weren't," she went on, turning away to reach for Nimitz. The 'cat leapt into her arms and swarmed up into his proper position on her right shoulder. He perched there, with the tips of his true-feet's claws digging into the special fabric of her uniform tunic just below her shoulder blade while one true-hand removed his ear protectors, and she turned back to White Haven. "Lord knows I sympathize with her, but showing her contempt for him so obviously, even in private, doesn't help the situation at all."

"No, it doesn't," the Earl agreed, his own tone less amused than it had been a moment before. "On the other hand, Elizabeth and High Ridge are like oil and water. And say what you will about her tactfulness, or lack thereof, no one could ever accuse her of deceitfulness."

"There's deceitfulness, and there's guile," the Steadholder replied. "And then there's the recognition that grinding someone's face in the fact that you loathe and despise him, even if you only do it in private, can only make things worse."

"It's hardly fair to say she 'grinds' it into his face, Honor," White Haven protested mildly.

"Yes, it is," she contradicted firmly. "Face it, Hamish. Elizabeth doesn't handle people she despises well. I know, because in my own way, I have the same weakness." She did not, LaFollet noticed, say anything about the famous White Haven temper. "But I've had to learn there are some situations I just can't solve by simply reaching for a bigger hammer when someone irritates me. Elizabeth recognizes that intellectually, but once her emotions become involved, it's almost impossible for her to mask her feelings except in the most official settings."

She held the Earl's gaze until, finally, he nodded almost unwillingly; then she shrugged.

"Elizabeth has enormous strengths," she said then, "but there are times I wish she had a little more of Benjamin's . . . interpersonal skills. She can *lead* in a way very few people could possibly match, but she's the wrong woman in the wrong place when it comes to manipulating people who don't already want to be led into following her. And that's doubly true when the people she ought to be convincing to do what she wants want to do exactly the opposite for reasons of their own."

"I know," White Haven sighed. "I know. But," he added in a

stronger, more cheerful voice, "that's what she has people like you and Willie for—to advise her when she's headed into trouble."

"Willie, maybe," Lady Harrington said with another shrug.

"And you," the Earl insisted. "She's come to rely on you for a lot more than your insight into Grayson politics, and you know it."

"Maybe," she repeated, obviously more than a little uncomfortable with the thought, and he changed the subject.

"At any rate, I decided that since I was in the area, and since Willie had bent my ear about what High Ridge—and Janacek—had to say at the briefing, I'd stop by and see about bringing you up to speed, as well."

Of course you did, LaFollet thought dryly. *After all, it was obviously your bounden duty to get this critical information to her as rapidly as possible . . . in person.*

Nimitz glanced at the armsman over White Haven's shoulder, and his ears flicked in obvious amusement as he tasted the colonel's emotions. LaFollet stuck out a mental tongue at the 'cat, and Nimitz's grass-green eyes danced devilishly, but he declined to do anything more overt.

"Thank you," Lady Harrington told the Earl, and her tone was just as casually serious as his was, as if she were totally oblivious to the shared amusement of her 'cat and her henchman. Which she most certainly wasn't, LaFollet reminded himself, and forced his unruly thoughts back under control. Fortunately, the only thing she could sense through her link to Nimitz was emotions, not the thoughts which had produced them. Under most circumstances, she was capable of deducing approximately what those thoughts must have been with almost frightening accuracy, but in this instance, that ability seemed to have deserted her. Which, the colonel reflected with much less amusement, probably reflected the intensity with which she refused to face what was actually happening between her and White Haven.

"It may take a while," the Earl warned her. "What does your schedule look like for the rest of the afternoon?"

"I have an evening guest lecture over at the Crusher, but that's not until after dinner, and I've already finish-polished my notes for it. Until then, I'm free. I have a small clutch of papers I really ought to be reading and grading, but they're all extra-credit electives, and I can probably afford to let them slide for a single afternoon."

"Good." White Haven glanced at his chrono. "I hadn't thought about it until you mentioned dinner, but it's just about lunchtime. Could I buy you lunch somewhere?"

"No, but I'll buy *you* lunch," she countered, and LaFollet felt a fresh sinking sensation as he saw the way her eyes suddenly danced even more devilishly than Nimitz's had. White Haven arched a questioning eyebrow, and she chuckled. "You're here on the Island, Hamish, and whether Janacek likes it or not, you are a flag officer. Why not let me com ahead to Casey and reserve one of the flag dining rooms for lunch?"

"Oh, Honor, that's *evil*," White Haven said with a sudden huge grin, and LaFollet closed his eyes in profound agreement. Casey Hall was the enormous cafeteria right off the Quadrangle. Its main dining hall was capable of seating almost a third of Saganami Island's entire student body simultaneously, but it also boasted smaller, much more palatial dining rooms for more senior officers. Including fifteen or twenty small, private rooms reserved for admirals and very senior captains of the list and their guests on a first-come, first-served basis.

"Janacek will fall down in a frothing fit when he hears you and I had lunch together in the very heart of what he'd like to consider his own private domain," the Earl continued. "Especially when he figures out I came straight from Willie's after discussing what he and High Ridge had to say at the briefing this morning."

"I doubt we'll be quite that lucky," Lady Harrington disagreed, "but we can at least hope his blood pressure will kick up a few points."

"I like it," White Haven announced cheerfully, and waved for her to precede him towards the door.

For the tiniest sliver of a moment, Andrew LaFollet hovered on the brink of the unthinkable. But the instant passed, and as he stepped around the Steadholder to open the door for her, he pressed his lips firmly together against the words he had no business saying.

They really don't have a clue, he thought. *That's why they don't realize I'm not the only person—the only two-footed person, anyway— who's begun to notice the way the two of them look at each other. The last thing they need is to go traipsing off to a private lunch in such a public place, but they don't even realize it.*

He opened the door, glanced through it in a quick, automatic search, then stood aside to allow the Steadholder and her guest through it. He watched them heading for Johannsen's desk to sign off the range sheet, and shook his head mentally.

Father Church says You look after children and fools, he told the Comforter. *I hope You're looking after both of them now.*

CHAPTER FOUR

Captain Thomas Bachfisch, owner and master of the armed merchant ship *Pirates' Bane*, was a lean, spare man with a thin, lined face. He was more than a little stoop-shouldered, and despite his immaculately tailored blue civilian uniform, he did not cut an impressive figure. Nor, for that matter, did *Pirates' Bane*. At around five million tons, the freighter was of little more than average size for most regions of space, although she did tend towards the upper end of the tonnage range here in Silesia. But although she was obviously well maintained, she was not—despite her defiantly aggressive name—much to look at. To an experienced eye, it was apparent that she was at least half a T-century old, and probably a product of the now-defunct Gopfert Yard in the New Berlin System. Gopfert had once been one of the busiest shipyards in the entire Andermani Empire, supplying not only the Empire's great merchant houses but also building warships and auxiliaries for the Imperial Navy. But that had been a long time ago, and nowadays *Pirates' Bane*'s lines were clearly dated, a bit antique. Indeed, her brand spanking new paint made her look like an over-aged dowager after an unsuccessful make-over, and anything less like her war-like name would have been difficult to imagine. Which was just fine with Captain Bachfisch. There were times, especially for a merchant spacer here in the Silesian Confederacy, when being underestimated was the very best thing that could happen.

As his present occupation demonstrated.

He stood in his freighter's boat bay, hands clasped loosely behind him, and watched with grim satisfaction as the latest group of Silesians to underestimate his vessel shuffled towards the waiting shuttle from the Andermani cruiser *Todfeind*. They were more than merely subdued as they filed between the row of waiting Andermani Marines and the armed crewmen Bachfisch had detailed to deliver them to their new jailers.

"We'll send your handcuffs back across as soon as we get these . . . people properly brigged, Captain," the Andy *oberleutnant der Sterne* in charge of the Marine detail promised him.

"I appreciate that, *Oberleutnant*." Bachfisch's tenor voice was just a bit on the nasal side, and its clipped Manticoran enunciation contrasted sharply with the Andermani officer's harsher accent.

"Believe me, Sir, the pleasure is all ours." The *oberleutnant* finished his count as the last prisoner marched droopingly past him. "I make that thirty-seven, *Kapitän*," he announced, and Bachfisch nodded.

The *oberleutnant* punched an entry into his memo board, then shook his head and gave the blue-coated man beside him a much more admiring look than naval officers were wont to waste on mere merchant captains.

"I hope you'll pardon me for asking, *Kapitän*," he said with a marked air of diffidence, "but just how did you manage to capture them?" Bachfisch cocked his head at him, and the *oberleutnant* shook his own head quickly. "That may not have sounded exactly the way I meant it, Sir. It's just that, usually, pirates are more likely to capture merchant crews than the other way around. It's always a pleasant surprise when someone manages to turn the tables on them, instead. And I have to admit that when the *Kapitän* told me to come across and take them off your hands I did a little research. This isn't the first time you've handed us a batch of pirates."

Bachfisch regarded the youthful officer, the equivalent of an RMN lieutenant (junior grade), thoughtfully for a moment. He'd already transmitted his complete report to *Todfeind*'s captain, and the cruiser's legal officer had taken sworn statements from all of his officers and most of his senior ratings. That was SOP here in the Confederacy, where witnesses to acts of piracy were frequently unable to attend the eventual trials of the pirates in question. But it was obvious from the *oberleutnant's* earnest expression that his seniors hadn't chosen to share that information with him . . . and that curiosity was eating him alive.

"I prefer handing any batch of pirates over to you rather than to the Sillies," Bachfisch said after a moment. "At least when I hand them over to the Empire, I can be reasonably certain I won't be seeing them again. They know it, too. They were an unhappy lot when I told them who'd be taking them into custody from us.

"As to how we came to turn the tables on them . . ." He shrugged. "The *Bane* may not look it, *Oberleutnant*, but she's as heavily armed as a lot of heavy cruisers. Most merchies can't afford the tonnage penalty and structural modifications to mount a worthwhile armament, but the *Bane* isn't like most merchies." He chuckled dryly. "As a matter of fact, she started life as a *Vogel*-class armed collier for your own Navy something like seventy T-years ago. I picked her up cheap when she was finally listed for disposal about ten T-years ago because her inertial compensator was pretty much shot. Aside from that, she was in fairly good shape, though, so it wasn't too hard to get her back on-line. I replaced and updated her original armament at the same time, and I put a good bit of thought into how to camouflage the weapon ports while I was at it." Another shrug. "So most pirates don't have a clue that the 'helpless merchant ship' they're about to close with and board is actually several times as heavily armed as they are.

"Not until we open the ports and blow them to Hell, anyway," he said, and his tenor voice was suddenly harsh and very, very cold. Then he shook himself. "As for the clowns we just handed over to you," he went on in a more conversational tone which never warmed his eyes at all, "they were already in their boarding shuttles on the way across to us when their ship and the rest of their crewmates turned into plasma behind them. So they really didn't have much choice but to leave their weapons behind, come through the personnel lock one at a time, and surrender, exactly the way we told them to. They certainly didn't want to piss off our gunners by trying to do anything else."

The *oberleutnant* looked at the lined face and those icy eyes and decided not to ask any more of the multitude of questions still hovering in his mind. He felt reasonably confident Bachfisch would have answered them courteously enough, but there was something about the merchant skipper which discouraged too much familiarity.

The young Andermani officer looked around the boat bay gallery. Like everything else about *Pirates' Bane*, the bay was perfectly maintained. It was also spotless, with freshly painted bulkheads and a deck which looked literally clean enough to eat off of. One look at the freighter's captain would have been sufficient to warn anyone that he ran an extraordinarily taut ship, especially for a trader here in Silesia, but this went beyond mere tautness. *Pirates' Bane* looked far more like a warship, or the naval auxiliary as which she had begun life, than she looked like any "normal" merchant-man the lieutenant had ever boarded.

He returned his eyes to *Pirates' Bane*'s captain and came briefly to attention. He wasn't in the habit of expending military courtesy on mere merchant spacers, but this one was different. And despite the *oberleutnant's* own awareness of the steadily escalating tension between his own navy and that of the Star Kingdom of Manticore, he recognized that difference.

"Well, *Kapitän*," he said, "let me repeat my *Kapitän's* expression of admiration. And I'd like to add my own to it."

"Thank you, *Oberleutnant*," Bachfisch replied gravely.

"And," the Andy assured him with a thin smile, "I believe you can be confident that you won't be seeing this particular batch of pirates again."

Todfeind accelerated steadily away from *Pirates' Bane*, and Bachfisch stood on his command deck, watching the visual imagery of the departing heavy cruiser. For just a moment, his eyes filled with a deep, naked longing, but it vanished as quickly as it had come, and he turned to his bridge crew.

"Well, we've wasted enough time doing our civil duty," he remarked dryly, and most of the people on the bridge grinned at him. Bachfisch might never lose his Manticoran accent, but he'd spent the last forty T-years in Silesia, and like most crews in Silesia, the one he'd assembled aboard the *Bane* was drawn from every imaginable source. It included Silesians, Andies, other Manticorans, Sollies, even one or two men and women who obviously sprang from the People's Republic of Haven. But the one thing every one of them had in common was that, like the crew of the *Bane*'s sister ship *Ambuscade*, they'd signed on with the express assurance that their ships would never be surrendered to the raiders who plagued Silesia. It might be a bit much to call any of them crusaders, and certainly if they were knights at all, most of them were at best a murky shade of gray, but every one of them took a profound satisfaction in knowing any pirate who went after the *Bane* or *Ambuscade* would never make another mistake.

None of them were quite certain precisely what it was which had motivated their skipper to spend the past four decades amassing the financial resources to purchase, arm, and maintain what amounted to a pair of Q-ships of his very own. For that matter, no one—with the possible exceptions of Captain Laurel Malachi, *Ambuscade*'s skipper, and Jinchu Gruber, the *Bane*'s exec—had the least idea how the Captain had gotten his hands on the warrant as a naval auxiliary which let him evade the Confederacy's prohibition against privately owned armed vessels. Not that any of them cared. However curious they might occasionally be, what mattered was that unlike most merchant spacers in the Confederacy, they could be relatively certain when they set out on a run that they would reach the other end safely even if they did happen across a pirate cruiser or two in the process.

The fact that most of them had their own axes to grind where the brutal freebooters who terrorized Silesian merchant shipping were concerned only added to their willingness to follow Bachfisch wherever he led without any carping little questions. His demand that they submit to military-style discipline and weapons training, both shipboard and small arms—and the short shrift he gave anyone who came up short against the high standards he required—was perfectly all right with them. Indeed, they regarded it as a trifling price to pay for the combination of security and the opportunity to pick off the occasional pirate. And every one of them knew it was the fact that Bachfisch's ships always reached their destinations with their cargoes intact which allowed him to charge the premium freight rates which also allowed him to pay them extraordinarily well by Silesian standards.

Thomas Bachfisch was perfectly well aware that most naval officers would have been appalled at the thought of accepting some of the personnel who served aboard his ships. There'd been a time when he would have experienced profound second thoughts about allowing some of them aboard, himself. But that had been a long time ago, and what he felt today was a deep pride in how well his disparate people had come together. Indeed, he would have backed either of his crews against most regular warships of up to battlecruiser tonnage, not just against the typical pirate scum they usually encountered.

He looked back at the visual display for a moment, then glanced at his tac officer's plot and frowned. In keeping with her armed status, *Pirates' Bane* boasted a sensor outfit and weapons control stations superior to those aboard most official Confederate Navy warships, and his frown deepened as he noted the data sidebar on the plot.

He stepped closer and looked over the tac officer's shoulder. She sensed his presence and turned to look up at him with a questioning expression.

"Can I help you, Skipper?" she asked.

"Um." Bachfisch rested his left hand lightly on her right shoulder and leaned forward to tap a query on her data pad. The computer considered his inquiry for a nanosecond or two, then obediently reported *Todfeind*'s tonnage. Lieutenant Hairston looked down at the fresh numbers blinking on her own display, compared them to the acceleration sidebar, and pursed her lips.

"They'd appear to be in a bit of a hurry, wouldn't they?" she observed.

"I suppose that's one way to put it, Roberta," Bachfisch murmured.

He straightened and rubbed his chin gently while he gazed intently at the plot. *Todfeind* wasn't the very newest ship in the Andy inventory, but her class had been designed less than ten T-years ago, and she massed right on four hundred thousand tons. At that tonnage, her normal maximum acceleration should have been around five hundred gravities. Since the Andermani Navy, like every other navy in space, normally restricted its skippers to less than the maximum acceleration available to them under full military power, she should have been accelerating at no more than four hundred or so. But according to the tac officer's sensors, she was pulling just over four-seventy-five.

"They're right on the edge of their compensator's max performance," Hairston observed, and Bachfisch glanced at her. He started to say something, then shrugged, smiled at her, patted her shoulder once more, and turned to the exec.

"I know the contract specifically allows for delays in transit occasioned by piratical activity, Jinchu," he said. "But we've lost a bit more time than I'd wanted to, even to swat another pirate. I think we can make it up if we can talk Santerro into letting us jump the transshipment queue in Broadhurst, but I don't want to dawdle on the way there."

"Understood, Skipper," Gruber replied, and nodded sideways at *Pirates' Bane*'s astrogator. "I've had Larry working an updated course ever since we diverted to deliver our 'guests.' "

"That's what I like to see," Bachfisch observed with a smile. "Conscientious subordinates with their noses pressed firmly to the grindstone!" Gruber chuckled, and Bachfisch waved at the main maneuvering plot.

"We've got a long way to go," he observed. "So let's be about it, Jinchu."

"Yes, Sir," the exec said, and turned to the astrogator. "You heard the Captain, Larry. Let's take her out of orbit."

"Aye, aye, Sir," the astrogator replied formally, and Bachfisch listened to the familiar, comforting efficiency of his bridge crew as he walked slowly across the deck and settled into his own command chair. No one could have guessed from his demeanor that he was barely aware of his officers' well-drilled smoothness as he leaned back and crossed his legs, but most of his attention was someplace else entirely as he considered *Todfeind*'s acceleration numbers.

It was always possible Hairston's explanation was the right one. High as that acceleration rate might be, it was still within the safe operating envelope of most navies' inertial compensators. But not by very much, and the Andies were just as insistent about avoiding unnecessary risks or wear on their compensators and impeller nodes as the Royal Manticoran Navy. So if *Todfeind*'s captain had elected to push the envelope that hard, then logically he must be in a very great hurry, indeed.

But what Bachfisch knew that Hairston didn't was that the Andermani captain had invited Bachfisch and his senior officers to supper aboard his ship. The IAN didn't extend that sort of invitation to mere merchant spacers every day of the week, and Bachfisch had been sorely tempted to accept it. Unfortunately, as he'd just finished remarking to Gruber, the detour to deliver the captured pirates had put *Pirates' Bane* well behind schedule, so he'd been forced to decline the invitation. But if *Kapitän der Sterne* Schweikert had seen fit to issue one in the first place, then he'd obviously planned on hanging around long enough for the meal to be served.

Which suggested that he *wasn't* in any particular hurry. Which, in turn, suggested that he wasn't pushing the envelope on his compensator.

Which suggested that the Andermani Navy had cracked the secret of the improved compensator efficiency which had been one of the RMN's major tactical advantages over the Peeps for years.

Thomas Bachfisch had visited his native star nation no more than half a dozen times over the past forty T-years. Most of his old friends and associates in the Star Kingdom had given up on him decades ago, sadly writing him off as someone who had "gone native" in Silesia, of all places. And, he admitted, there was at least some truth to that verdict. But that didn't mean he'd failed to stay abreast of the news from Manticore, and he had a shrewd notion that the Queen's Navy would not be happy to discover that the increasingly resentful Imperial Andermani Navy's ships were now just as fast as its own.

Assuming anyone at the current Admiralty was prepared to believe it, at any rate.

CHAPTER FIVE

Admiral Sir Edward Janacek (retired), Royal Manticoran Navy, looked up from the report on his desk terminal and hid a frown as his yeoman secretary ushered Reginald Houseman into his office. He hid it because the First Lord of the Admiralty of the Star Kingdom of Manticore wasn't supposed to greet one of his fellow lords with a grimace. But despite almost thirty T-years as a civilian, he continued to think of himself as a naval officer, and any naval officer would have regarded Houseman with distaste. Houseman rarely even attempted to conceal his own deep and abiding contempt for the Star Kingdom's military, and when he did make the attempt, he failed. Worse, Houseman and his entire family were hopelessly inept and politically naive in Janacek's view . . . to put it mildly. The fact that they were exactly the sort of Liberal Party idiots Janacek had left the Navy in order to oppose more effectively made the current situation more ironic than he cared to contemplate, but there it was. Houseman and his allies among the Liberals were absolutely essential at the moment, which was what made it politically impossible for Janacek to allow his distaste to show.

"The Second Lord is here, Sir," the secretary announced unnecessarily, in the obsequious voice he kept on tap especially for Houseman's visits. Like many who not so secretly despised the military, Houseman reveled in any opportunity to extract subservience from it.

"Thank you, Christopher." Janacek nodded dismissal to the secretary, then stood and extended his hand to Houseman. "It's always good to see you, Reginald," he lied smoothly. "Should I assume you have those projections for me?"

"Edward," Houseman replied, shaking the proffered hand with a smile Janacek felt certain was at least as false as his own. The First Lord waved for his visitor to seat himself, and Houseman settled into one of the comfortable chairs facing Janacek's desk.

"I do, indeed, have the numbers you requested," he went on, and produced a chip folio. He leaned forward to place the folio on the corner of Janacek's blotter, then leaned back once again. "And they support your conclusions rather well, actually."

"Good." Janacek managed to conceal his irritation at the edge of condescension in Houseman's tone. It wasn't easy, even for someone with his decades of political experience, but he made it look that way. And it wasn't as if Houseman's attitude was a surprise. Even though Janacek was now a civilian, the fact that he'd ever been a naval officer was sufficient to contaminate him—in Houseman's eyes—with the automatic ineptitude and stupidity of all officers. Which made any evidence of competence or imagination on the First Lord's part perpetually surprising and unexpected.

Of course, Janacek reflected, *the fact that the Navy's officers in general—and one of them in particular—have made their opinion of him crystal clear probably has a little something to do with the strength of his feelings. Pity it's the only thing I'll ever agree with that lunatic Harrington about.*

"Assuming that we freeze construction on all units not at least sixty-five percent completed, scrap about twelve percent of our older ships of the wall still in commission, mothball another sixteen percent of the wall to go with them, and put the yard space we won't need anymore into inactive controlled storage, we can implement your plans and still reduce naval spending by approximately fourteen percent of the currently budgeted funds," Houseman continued, and this time there was a pronounced note of approval in his voice. "That amounts to the better part of two trillion dollars we can divert to far more useful ends."

"I'm glad to hear it," Janacek replied, and he was. Not, perhaps, for the same reasons which had produced Houseman's obvious pleasure, but he'd long since accepted that politics made strange bedfellows. His toleration of Houseman as Second Lord, the civilian lord in charge of the Admiralty's fiscal policy, was certainly proof of that! On the grander scale, the liberation of so much cash for the Government to use primarily on projects of which Janacek himself heartily disapproved was yet another. He understood the logic behind the strategy, and intellectually he approved of it, but that made it only marginally more palatable.

He extracted Houseman's datachip from its folio and plugged it into his own console, then brought up the file header. He advanced to the first page of the report summary and scanned the first few paragraphs while Houseman adjusted his own memo pad in his lap and keyed its display.

"As you'll note in paragraph two," the Second Lord began, "we can begin by listing the entire *King William*-class for disposal. After that . . ."

"So you agree we can safely reduce military spending," Lady Elaine Descroix observed in that bright, cheerful tone which always set Baron High Ridge's teeth on edge. Descroix was a small, sweet-faced woman who took great pains to project the image of everyone's favorite aunt, and he reminded himself yet again not to forget the armor-plated pseudocroc behind her smile.

"Within limits, Elaine," the Prime Minister of Manticore cut in smoothly before the First Lord could respond to his Foreign Secretary. "And that assumes the situation in the People's Republic—excuse me, the *Republic* of Haven—remains effectively what it currently is."

High Ridge made himself return her smile with one of his own. One with a carefully gauged edge of steel. Pseudocroc or not, Descroix wasn't in charge of this meeting. He was, and the sun-bright spaciousness of his luxurious woodpaneled office was the outward sign and confirmation of his ascendancy. The antique clocks which had cluttered its shelves, coffee tables, and credenzas during the Duke of Cromarty's tenure had disappeared, replaced by his own knickknacks and memorabilia, but this was the same office from which four T-centuries of prime ministers had governed the Star Kingdom, and his smile reminded her of the power he represented.

"Oh, I think we can assume the situation will remain

unchanged," Descroix assured him. Her eyes acknowledged his expression's message, but even as they did, her own smile showed a decided complacency. "We can keep them talking for as long as we need to. After all, what else can they do?"

"I'm still not convinced we should have completely ignored their last proposals," another voice said, and High Ridge turned to consider the third member of the quartet which had assembled in his office to await Janacek's arrival. Marisa Turner, Countess of New Kiev and Chancellor of the Exchequer since the last Cabinet reorganization, looked troubled. Then again, she often looked troubled. It wasn't that she didn't understand political necessity when it looked her right in the eye, but she sometimes found pursuing that necessity . . . distasteful.

Which has never prevented her from pursuing it anyway, he reminded himself cynically.

"We didn't have much choice, Marisa," Descroix assured her, and shrugged when New Kiev looked at her. "If we're going to be completely honest," the Foreign Secretary continued, "on the surface, their proposal was much too reasonable. If we'd accepted it, certain elements in Parliament would probably have insisted that we seriously consider using it as the basis for a formal treaty. Which would have opened the door to the territorial concessions from us which were also part of their new proposals. And which, of course, would have required us to give up far too much of all that our courageous Navy won for us."

New Kiev's expression flickered for an instant, but High Ridge noticed that she raised no objection to Descroix's explanation. Which underscored her willingness to do what pragmatism required, however unpleasant she might find that, because she understood the subtext of the explanation as well as anyone else in the office.

In the final analysis, everyone in the present Government understood all the reasons not to bring the war against the Peeps to a formal conclusion. There was no real need, given the Star Kingdom's overwhelming technical superiority. The Havenite Secretary of War, Theisman, obviously understood just how helpless his forces were in the face of that superiority. Even if he hadn't, in High Ridge's private opinion, he'd never have the nerve to resort once more to open military action against a star nation which had so decisively defeated his own. If he'd come equipped with that sort of testosterone supply, he would never have supinely surrendered the absolute power which had lain in his grasp to someone like Pritchart!

No. If operations were ever resumed, the People's Navy—or the *Republican* Navy, as it now chose to style itself—would be quickly annihilated, and it knew it. Which meant that until the Star Kingdom deigned to propose the terms of a formal treaty of peace, the new Havenite government had no choice but to continue to talk. Which, he conceded, was a most fortunate state of affairs, given the domestic threats he and his political allies faced.

The Constitution required a general election no less than once every four Manticoran years, except under certain carefully specified extraordinary circumstances . . . yet the last election had been over five Manticoran years ago. One of the circumstances which permitted electoral delays was the existence of a declared state of emergency, proclaimed by the Crown and confirmed by a two-thirds majority of both houses. Any state of emergency, however, had to be reconfirmed each year, both by the Crown and by the same majority in each house, or it automatically lapsed.

The other circumstance which permitted the postponement of a general election was the existence of a state of war. The Constitution didn't *require* that elections be postponed in either case; it merely provided that they could be, at the discretion of the current government. Unlike High Ridge, the Duke of Cromarty's primary base of support had been found in the Commons, and despite occasional sags in the public's morale, it had remained essentially firm. Cromarty had timed the elections carefully, but he'd also called two of them during the course of the war, and his majority in the lower house had increased after each.

High Ridge's primary support base, however, lay in the *Lords*, which meant that the last thing he wanted, for many reasons, was to call a general election. And since sustaining a state of emergency required a majority in *both* houses—not to mention the concurrence of the Crown, which he was most unlikely to get—only the official state of war against Haven allowed him to hold off the election which, under current conditions, would almost certainly have proved a disaster.

But that state of war was useful in other ways, as well. High Ridge had not only managed to postpone confirmation of the San Martino peers and an almost certain embarrassing electoral defeat for both the Liberals and Progressives (his own Conservative Association's representation in the lower house was already so tiny that no conceivable popular vote could have had much impact upon it), but also to maintain the "wartime only" tax measures which had been instigated by the Cromarty Government. Those taxes were unpopular, to say the very least, but their passage was firmly associated in the public mind with Cromarty—and thus with the Centrist Party.

The Star Kingdom's Constitution had been drafted by people determined to restrict the power of the state by restricting the power to tax, and the Founders had crafted a fiscal system in which the government's income was intended to depend primarily on import and export duties and property and sales taxes. The Constitution specifically required that any *income* tax be flat-rated and limited to a maximum of eight percent of gross income except in time of emergency. To make their position crystal clear, the Founders had also specified that even in emergency conditions, any graduated income tax could be enacted only with the approval of a super-majority in both houses and automatically lapsed (unless confirmed by the same super-majority) in five T-years or at the next general election.

Those restrictions had made it very difficult for the Cromarty Government to pass the income tax (with a top rate of almost forty percent in the uppermost brackets) and special import duties required to finance the war. The public had accepted the immense financial burden of that tax structure with glum resignation only because Cromarty had successfully made the case for its necessity . . . and because the voters had expected it to lapse as soon as the war ended. Unfortunately for their expectations, the war hadn't ended (not officially, at any rate), and so the taxes remained in effect.

Naturally, High Ridge and his allies deeply (and publicly) regretted the fact that the Havenite refusal to conclude a formal peace required them to maintain the tax burden the Centrists had enacted. But their duty to ensure the Star Kingdom's security would not allow them in good conscience to reduce taxes until they could be positive the military theat had been ended once and for all in a formal treaty. In the meantime, that same tax structure provided an enormous influx of funds they could divert to other programs now that the shooting had stopped. Which was, of course, a simple, unanticipated consequence of the unsettled international situation.

Quite a bit of that largess had gone very quietly to certain political action organizations, union leaders, industrialists, and financiers. Siphoning those funds discreetly into the intended hands had been relatively easy, although it had been necessary to dress up the transfers with justifications like "research grants," "employment conditions studies," "educational subsidies," or "industrial expansion incentives." The new Royal Manticoran Astrophysics Investigation Agency had been one of the most successful of those sorts of ploys. No doubt some practical good would come of it, but its real value was that it had engaged the public imagination. It was the poster child for the "Building the Peace" campaign New Kiev had devised, and with excellent reason. After all, something like three quarters of the Star Kingdom's prosperity rested on its carrying trade and the mammoth through traffic the Manticoran Wormhole Junction serviced. Discovering additional destinations the Junction could serve could only enhance that wealth.

Of course, it was also a hideously expensive undertaking ... rather more so than its administrators fully realized, High Ridge devoutly hoped. Almost ten full percent of its budget could be neatly skimmed off the top and passed directly to various ship builders and consulting firms without ever being wasted on something useful, and it had become such a popular icon no one dared question its expenditures.

Here and there, a few more odd forty- or fifty-million-dollar transfers had disappeared completely even without benefit of the RMAIA's cloak of respectability. Most of them had gone through discretionary funds or payments whose recipients could be concealed under a claim of national security endorsed by obliging members of the intelligence community, but very little of that sort of thing had actually been required.

By far the largest expenditures, however, had gone into long-cherished Progressive and Liberal social programs. High Ridge himself regarded them as nothing more than vote-buying boon-doggles, and he was certain Descroix shared his view, whatever she might say for public consumption. But New Kiev was another matter. She truly believed that the "poor" of the Star Kingdom were destitute ... despite the fact that the poorest of them enjoyed an effective income at least four times that of the average citizen of their Grayson allies, and somewhere around seven or eight times that of the average Havenite living in the financially ravaged

Republic. She and her fellow Liberals were determined to build a new "fairer and more equitable Star Kingdom" in which the "indecent wealth of the monied classes" would be redistributed by government fiat, since the normal operation of the marketplace seemed incapable of doing so.

If pressed, High Ridge would have admitted that, as a matter of principle, he ought to have found the Liberals far more threatening than he ever could the Centrists. The impassioned rhetoric of New Kiev's more vociferous cohorts carried an ugly echo of the thinking which had led to the collapse of the original Republic of Haven and the creation of the People's Republic, after all. Fortunately, there was very little chance of their ever achieving their proclaimed goals in the Star Kingdom. And in the meantime, by giving both the Exchequer and the Home Office to the Liberals and strongly and publicly supporting New Kiev's domestic programs, he was able to blunt at least the sharper edges of the electorate's traditional view of the Conservative Association as the purely reactionary defender of aristocratic privilege at the expense of all other classes.

That had taken on additional importance following that damned Montaigne woman's hysterical slavery charges and the scandal they'd spawned. For that matter, the reorganization which had given the Liberals such a disproportionate share of ministerial power had been dictated by the same scandal. Support for the Government's handling of the resultant witch hunt had been reasonably solid in the Lords, although it had proven unfortunately necessary to sacrifice a few individuals to the moral outrage of the proles. The Commons had been a different matter, however, and Alexander's efforts to initiate a special inquiry—separate from and in addition to the official Government investigation—had been dangerous. In fact, it had been extremely dangerous, because although there'd been one or two names from the Centrists and a single Crown Loyalist in the files Montaigne and her common-born lover had turned over, there'd been many more Conservatives and Progressives.

And Liberals.

That had been the most dangerous aspect of the entire scandal, given the size of the Liberal Party's representation in the lower house. Not so much because of the convictions Alexander and his cronies might have secured, though those would have been bad enough, as because of the Liberals' internal revulsion at the mere possibility that any of their own could have been involved in something like genetic slave trading. That was the problem with people who insisted on defining themselves in terms of their principles and holier-than-thou morality. When something offended those principles (or at least threatened to draw the public's eye to their public violation), they tended to attack the offenders without any consideration at all of pragmatic strategy. High Ridge himself deplored the very existence of something like genetic slavery, of course, although he frankly doubted it was carried on on anything like the scale that hysterics like Montaigne insisted it was. But much as he deplored it, there were other matters to be considered, and he could scarcely be expected to throw away his one opportunity to prevent the Crown from destroying the fundamental balance of power mandated by the Constitution over a single issue, however much public agitation that issue might generate.

Unfortunately, it was impossible to explain that to a Liberal. Or, at least, to a Liberal member of the House of Commons who thought his constituents or the press might be listening in on the explanation. There'd been a dangerous groundswell of Liberal support for Alexander's demand for a separate inquiry, and High Ridge had managed to defuse it only by shifting things around to give New Kiev the Cabinet's second-ranking position and make Sir Harrison MacIntosh Home Secretary. In his new post, MacIntosh had been the member of the Government responsible for overseeing the investigation, and he had a well-established reputation as a jurist. He was also a member of the Commons, not a peer, which had allowed the Liberal MPs to argue that he would never be a party to any "aristocratic coverup." And just as importantly, certain indiscretions in his past, coupled with a personality that was far more pragmatic in private than his public persona might have suggested, had helped provide the Prime Minister with a certain additional leverage even New Kiev wasn't aware existed.

The existence of that leverage had been another excellent reason to shuffle New Kiev from the Home Office to the Exchequer, as well. There was absolutely no way of predicting what she might have done if she'd been running the slavery investigation and it had taken her to places she didn't want to know existed. It was entirely possible, however, that such a journey would have led her to publicly break with the Government's handling of the case as a matter of principle, which would have been disastrous. As it was, with her good friend MacIntosh in charge of the affair, she'd been able to look the other way, confident he would get to the bottom of things . . . and safely insulated from confronting such ugly possibilities (and hard political decisions) herself.

All in all, High Ridge was rather pleased with how neatly he'd managed to turn a potential liability into an advantage and, at the same time, cover himself and his own party against charges of collusion with the accused. If it became necessary, he could always point out that it was his coalition partners, the Liberals, who'd dropped the ball. And the fact that the Liberal Party enjoyed such a towering reputation for moral rectitude, at least among its own voters and a certain segment of the news media, also provided an additional layer of cover. After all, if anything had been allowed to slip past during the course of the investigation, it had to have been an honest mistake on the part of such upright investigators.

Nor, for that matter, did it hurt to have New Kiev and her coeterie of Liberal advisers—like the Housemans—to hide behind if any awkward questions were asked about fiscal and monetary policy, ether.

That point might become particularly critical in the next few months, since the time limit on the graduated income tax was rapidly running out. The other tax increases could be legally maintained until the next general election, but not the income tax, and the disappearance of that huge fiscal surplus (which the Centrist-controlled House of Commons would never vote to renew) was the real reason Janacek and Houseman had been instructed to cut naval spending still further. Without those cuts, non-military spending would have to be reduced, instead, which was tactically unacceptable to any of the Government's parties. High Ridge devoutly hoped they could finesse the cuts through without having to admit their true motives, but if they couldn't, he firmly intended to lay the blame off on New Kiev. After all, everyone knew Liberals were the "tax and spend" party, and it was remotely possible that he could hang onto enough Independents in the Lords to sustain his majority there even if he was forced to cut New Kiev adrift. Possible, but highly unlikely, which was the reason it was so vital to get the cuts and new budget approved as quietly and expeditiously as possible.

Assuming all went well and they got away with that, it would still be useful to have New Kiev at the head of the Exchequer. If nothing else, the fact that she held such a powerful post in the Cabinet was a potent argument to bolster the claim that the current Government was, in fact, a broad-based coalition which embraced all political viewpoints and perspectives.

Perhaps even more importantly, High Ridge knew that when it came down to it, he and New Kiev agreed absolutely on one principle which was anathema to the Centrists: both of them believed in using the power of the state to accomplish their ideological goals. They differed intensely on what those goals should be, but both were perfectly prepared to embrace a degree of intrusiveness into public policy and private lives (or, at least, other people's private lives) which Alexander's Centrists would bitterly have opposed . . . and to make tactical compromises with one another along the way. And the Prime Minister had to admit that New Kiev's plethora of spending initiatives and government programs was having an effect. Quite a few of them provided funding for projects and services—like RMAIA—which even a Centrist had to admit were beneficial, however much he might have disputed the notion that it was appropriate for government to provide them. Others were less universally regarded as beneficial, but created a strong sense of loyalty among those who actually benefitted from them. And all of them capitalized on the very natural and human desire to turn from the sacrifices, death, and destruction of war and embrace something positive and life affirming.

Which was why the polls showed a slow but steady erosion of electoral support for the Centrists. Conditions were still far from ripe for the carefully timed election he intended to call, and it was unlikely anything could cut deeply enough into their support to deprive the Centrists of their position as the single largest party in the Commons. Especially not since any general election would also transform the San Martin "observers" into full-fledged members of Parliament. But if the projected trend lines continued, they would almost certainly lose their position as the *majority* party, even with the San Martinos. The Liberals, in particular, were gaining ground steadily, and that was another reason New Kiev was hardly likely to rock the boat. Not to mention yet another reason it was so crucial to sneak the new cuts past the Opposition.

Nonetheless, High Ridge reminded himself—again—not to underestimate the countess' distaste for the tactics pragmatic expediency forced upon her. Nor could he afford to forget that anything which smacked of imperialism and territorial expansion was complete heresy to any good Liberal, whatever a Progressive might think. It was time to smooth the waters a bit, he decided, and gave Descroix a quelling glance before he turned to face New Kiev squarely.

"None of us have any imperial ambitions, Marisa," he told her earnestly. "Despite that, however, and especially in light of the security problems the Cromarty Government committed us to in the annexation of Trevor's Star, we're going to have to insist on *some* Havenite concessions. And it's about time they were the ones who gave a little ground, too. We already made a major gesture towards meeting them more than halfway by agreeing to the general repatriation of POWs when we didn't have anything but a truce agreement, you know."

New Kiev gazed at the Prime Minister for several seconds, then nodded thoughtfully. Descroix, on the other hand, confident that New Kiev was looking elsewhere, rolled her eyes cynically. "Repatriating prisoners of war" sounded very generous, but New Kiev ought to realize as well as she did that the Star Kingdom hadn't proposed it out of the goodness of High Ridge's heart or to demonstrate its willingness to be accommodating. Just getting out from under the expense of feeding and caring for the far more numerous Peep prisoners held by the Manticoran Alliance would have been worthwhile in its own right, and as for the enormous PR advantages in being the Government which had "brought our men and women home" . . .

"Surely they know as well as we do that the next major concession has to come from their side," High Ridge continued earnestly. "And they must be aware that territorial adjustments to address our new security issues are inevitable. Yet every proposal Secretary Giancola has so far put forward has been based on the return of all occupied systems as a very first step. There's no way any Manticoran government could accede to that sort of demand when our military personnel paid so high a price to occupy them in the first place."

That wasn't quite accurate, of course, though he had no intention of pointing that out. The Havenite position did, indeed, insist on the return of all occupied planets, but everyone in the Foreign Office recognized that as little more than the staking out of a bargaining position from which concessions could later be made. And High Ridge, unlike New Kiev, knew Descroix's reports to the Cabinet had carefully not mentioned Giancola's latest suggestion that perhaps plebiscites—overseen by the Republic, of course— might allow individual star systems to choose which side should retain control of them.

It was probably as well he hadn't brought that up, he thought, watching New Kiev's lips tighten ever so slightly at the words "military personnel." She might not share the contempt which a Reginald Houseman felt for the Star Kingdom's military, but like most of the Liberal leaders, she was at best ambivalent whenever it came to the use of military force. The fact that the Star King-dom occupied any foreign star systems, regardless of how or why that had come about, offended every anti-imperialist bone in her body, and knowing political expediency forced her to actually support such an occupation, publically at least, only made it worse.

The fact that she was the only person in the office who felt that way became obvious a moment later, however.

"I agree, of course," Stefan Young, Earl North Hollow, said. North Hollow had received the Office of Trade as the price of bringing the enormously potent secret files his father had assembled to the Government's support. The power of those files was also the reason he was the fifth and final person present for this high-level strategy session despite his ministry's relatively junior rank in the official Cabinet hierarchy. After all, they were what had provided the crucial leverage which had made High Ridge confident he could . . . constructively direct MacIntosh's slavery investigation if that became 47necessary.

"We can't possibly contemplate the return of any Peep systems until our own security needs have been properly addressed," North Hollow continued. "All the same, Michael, I do feel a little con-cern over how the Opposition is likely to react to Edward's rec-ommendation that we build down our capital ships still further."

Janacek frowned at him, and the earl waved his hand languidly.

"Oh, *I'm* not questioning them," he assured the First Lord. "And speaking both in a personal sense and as Trade Secretary, I cer-tainly support transferring that funding from the maintenance and crewing of obsolescent warships to more productive ends! Nor," he added a bit more grimly, "am I about to lose any sleep worrying about admirals throwing tantrums because someone took their toys away from them. But we are proposing a substantial shift in the present stance and composition of the Fleet, and I think we have to be careful about the potential openings we give the Opposition if we move too boldly."

Translated, High Ridge thought sardonically, *my* wife *thinks we have to be careful.*

Stefan Young was much smarter than his older brother, Pavel, had been before Honor Harrington killed him on the Landing City dueling grounds. Not that being smarter than Pavel would exactly have required a genius IQ, but at least Stefan could usually zip his own shoes without assistance. Neither of them, however, would ever amount to more than a pale shadow of their father, and High Ridge was just as glad of it. No leader of the Conservative Association could have crossed Dimitri and survived, and all of them had known it, for his extensive, painstakingly assembled files had contained far too many devastating political secrets.

When Dimitri died, his eldest son had shown disturbing signs of an ambition which would inevitably have challenged High Ridge's own position. Fortunately, Harrington had eliminated that threat along with Pavel, and Stefan, although ambitious enough and possessed of the same deadly files, was also wise enough to be guided by his wife. Lady North Hollow was a most astute tactician and strategist, and she clearly recognized that Stefan was not the material of which charismatic political leaders were made. Before her marriage to him, Georgia Young—the former Georgia Sakristos—had been a senior aide to both Dmitri and Pavel, however. Officially, she'd been their security chief, but it was common knowledge, though never openly discussed, that she'd actually been the "dirty tricks" specialist for both of them, which was the reason High Ridge had selected her to chair the Conservative Association's Policy Coordination Committee. The fact that placing her at the head of the PCC might also help bind her loyalties to the Association's current leadership had played a not insignificant part in his decision, and while he was never likely to forget she was a two-edged sword, it had worked out well so far.

Which was why recognizing that the concern North Hollow had just raised actually came from his wife suggested that it was at least potentially a valid one, the Prime Minister reflected.

"Edward?" he invited.

"I fully recognize that the Admiralty is proposing a not inconsiderable change in priorities," Janacek said a touch pompously. "But the realities of the current situation require a systematic reconsideration of our previous posture."

He did not, High Ridge noted, specify even here exactly why that was. No one else seemed to notice that minor fact, and the First Lord continued in the same measured tones.

"The deployment policies and force mix we inherited from the Cromarty Government might have made sense as the basis for prosecuting the war against Haven. Mind you, I believe our force mix was badly skewed in favor of the older, less effective capital ship types. Like certain other officers, I'd wanted to change that mix for years, even before the war broke out, but it was probably too much to expect any Admiralty to recognize the validity of such new and radical concepts."

He let his eyes circle the conference table, but no one chose to comment. All of them knew he was referring to Admiral Sonja Hemphill. It was a habit of his to give Hemphill and her so-called *jeune école* full credit for the enormous changes in the Royal Navy's hardware, since, after all, she was his cousin. Of course, that overlooked the fact that the success of the new ship types which had revolutionized combat had resulted at least as much from people who'd managed to restrain Hemphill's enthusiasm by opposing her most radical suggestions. And the fact that she'd all but publicly disassociated herself from the Janacek Admiralty because of her fundamental disagreement with the Government's policies. That disagreement was probably the only reason he didn't mention her by name. It might also have been an unwonted exercise in tact, however. It was an open secret that it was Hemphill who'd cast the decisive vote at the court-martial leading to Pavel Young's dismissal from the Queen's service, which probably wasn't something to remind Pavel's brother of just at the moment.

"But whatever might have been the case before the war began, or even as recently as four or five T-years ago," Janacek resumed, "the Cromarty military posture is hopelessly out of date in light of the new realities of naval warfare and our current fiscal constraints. Our plan will hold the number of battle squadrons up to approximately ninety percent of the current totals."

By, he did not add, reducing each squadron from eight ships

to six. Which meant that a ten percent reduction in squadrons represented a *thirty-three* percent reduction in hulls.

"As for the ships we're talking about taking out of commission, whether by scrapping or mothballing," he continued, "the truth is that they would be no more than obsolete deathtraps if they were committed to combat against the new missile pod super-dreadnoughts or LAC carriers. Not only would it be unconscionable for us to send our men and women out to die in ships which were little more than targets, but every dollar we spend on manning or maintaining those ships is a dollar not spent on the new types which have proven their combat superiority so decisively. From every perspective, including that of maintaining a lean, efficient fighting force, the inventory of useless older types has to be reduced."

"But in favor of what?" North Hollow pressed. However bright he might not have been, he was extremely good at projecting the attitude he wanted, and at the moment, he was earnestly questioning, certainly not criticizing.

"The Navy has been badly in need of lighter units for years," Janacek replied. "For the most part, the relative drawdown in those types was unavoidable, especially in the early years of the war. The need to build the largest and most powerful wall of battle we possibly could diverted us from the construction and maintenance of the light cruisers and cruisers required for things like commerce protection. Those we did build were never sufficient to meet the scouting and screening requirements of our main battle fleets, let alone police commerce in places like Silesia. As a consequence, pirate activity everywhere in the Confederacy beyond the immediate reach of Sidemore Station is entirely out of hand."

"So you intend to concentrate on building up the forces we need to protect our shipping," North Hollow said, nodding sagely. "As Secretary of Trade, I can only approve of that objective, and I do. But I'm afraid of what some so-called 'expert' working for the Opposition might be able to make of it. Especially given the decision to suspend work on the SD(P)s which haven't yet been completed."

He cocked an eyebrow at the First Lord, and Janacek made a sound which the less charitable might have described as an irritated grunt.

"No other navy in space has so far commissioned *any* pod

superdreadnoughts," he pronounced with the infallibility of God. "Admiral Jurgensen and his analysts at ONI have amply confirmed that! We, on the other hand, have a solid core of over sixty. That's more than sufficient to defeat any conventional navy, especially with the CLACs to support and scout for them."

"No other navy?" North Hollow repeated. "What about the Graysons?"

"I meant, no potentially hostile navy, of course," Janacek corrected somewhat testily. "And while no one but a planet full of lunatic religious fanatics would be idiotic enough to pour so huge a percentage of their gross planetary product into their naval budgets at a time like this, at least they're our lunatics. Exactly why they think they need such an out-sized navy is open to different interpretations, of course, and I, for one, don't happen to believe their official explanations are the whole truth."

In fact, as all of his colleagues knew, Janacek nursed more than a few dark suspicions about Grayson. Their religious ardor made them automatically suspect, and he did not find their argument that the lack of a formal peace treaty required them to continue to build up their defenses convincing. It was entirely too convenient a pretext . . . as he and the rest of the Cabinet had already discovered. Besides, Graysons were uppity, without the proper respect and deference such a planet full of hayseed neobarbs ought to show the Alliance's senior navy. He'd already had three venomously polite exchanges with their High Admiral Matthews—who'd only been a *commodore*, for God's sake, when Grayson signed the Alliance—that amply demonstrated Grayson's overinflated opinion of its interstellar significance.

One confrontation had been over the long-overdue security restrictions he'd found it necessary to institute at ONI after getting rid of Givens. The previous Second Space Lord's "open door" policy with second-rate navies like Grayson's had been a standing invitation to disastrous security breaches. In fact, the risk had been even greater with Grayson than any of the Alliance's other minor navies, given Benjamin Mayhew's willingness to trust ex-Peep officers like Admiral Alfredo Yu, the *de facto* commander of his grandiosely titled "Protector's Own." A man who would turn his coat once was always capable of turning it again if it seemed advantageous, and the restoration of the old Havenite constitution would actually provide a moral pretext for doing so.

Yet the Graysons had steadfastly refused to cut such officers out of the information loop. They'd actually had the effrontery to dismiss the Admiralty's entirely legitimate security concerns on the basis that the officers in question had "proven" their loyalty. Of course they had! And the ones most likely to go running home to Haven were the ones who would have taken the greatest care to be sure they'd proved they wouldn't. No doubt they could even justify their deceit on the basis of patriotism, now that the StateSec regime they'd fled had been demolished!

Well, Janacek had put a stop to that nonsense, and if the "High Admiral" had a problem with the closing of the open door he'd so willfully abused, that was his lookout.

The second confrontation had been over the First Lord's decision to shut down the joint Manticore-Grayson R&D programs. There'd been no need to continue funding them—not when what they'd already produced would provide at least twenty T-years worth of development work under peacetime budgetary constraints. Besides, it was obvious to Janacek that what the "joint programs" really amounted to was little more than a way for Grayson to siphon off technology from Manticore without footing the bill for developing it on its own. It was hardly surprising Matthews had been miffed when he cut off access to the trough . . . especially after the way the Cromarty Government and Mourncreek Admiralty had coddled and cosseted their Grayson pets.

And as for the third one . . . There was no way Matthews could have been unaware of the insult to the First Lord involved in granting that asshole White Haven the rank of a full admiral in their precious Navy. And it would be a cold day in Hell before Janacek forgot it, either.

"Whatever it is they think they're doing, though," he went on after a moment, "not even Graysons are stupid enough to think they could hope to accomplish anything significant on an interstellar scale without our support. Whether they want to be or not, they're as much in our pocket as the Erewhonese, and they know it. So their navy—even assuming both that they could find some way to sustain it at its present size for more than a year or two without bankrupting themselves and that they knew what the hell they were doing with it without us to hold their hands—is really a non-factor in our security considerations. Except inasmuch as it actually increases 'our' modern warship strength, that is."

It never occurred to anyone in the room to question that assessment of their ally, and the Trade Secretary shrugged.

"I only raised the point because someone on the other side is likely to contrast it with our own building policies," North Haven said. "But what about the argument that our current superiority in that class could be challenged by someone else? The Peeps, for instance. They've certainly seen them in action, and they have a powerful incentive to acquire the same sorts of capabilities, especially since we don't have a formal peace treaty with them."

Janacek glared at him, and North Hollow shrugged again, this time half-apologetically.

"I'm only trying to play devil's advocate, Edward," he said mildly. "You know if I don't ask you these questions now, the Opposition will certainly ask them later. And someone on the other side is just as certain to point out that even though we have a monopoly on the new types, the numbers of them we have are relatively low in comparison to our total ship list. They're going to suggest that if another navy launched a concerted effort to overcome our lead in the new classes, we don't have a sufficient numerical advantage to guarantee someone like the Peeps couldn't succeed in the attempt."

"You're probably right," Janacek conceded sourly. "But in answer to your question, our only conceivable enemy for the immediate future would be the Peeps. As you say, they undoubtedly have an incentive to match our capabilities, but, frankly, their tech base is much too far behind ours for them to duplicate our hardware any time within the next ten years or so, by ONI's most conservative estimate. I've discussed this very question with Admiral Jurgensen, and he assures me his analysts are virtually unanimous in that opinion.

"Furthermore, even if they had the technical ability to build matching ships, they'd still have to lay down the hulls, build them, crew them, and then train them up to an operational standard before they could pose any threat to us. As all of you are aware from the ONI reports I've shared with you, Theisman, Tourville, and Giscard are still busy fighting their own dissident elements with exactly the same obsolescent ships they used against us. We've seen absolutely no sign of any enhancement in their capabilities. Even better, from our perspective as a potential adversary, the way they're continuing to kill one another off is not only continuing to cost them their more experienced officers and crews but producing a steady drain even on the ships they do have."

He shook his head.

"No, Stefan. Only the Peeps have any reason to threaten us, and they simply don't have the capability. By the time they could begin to produce a fleet which could threaten us, we'd have plenty of lead time to increase our own SD(P) and CLAC strength. In the meantime, sixty-four of the new superdreadnoughts are more than sufficient."

"I don't doubt it," North Hollow said. "But those sixty-four ships can only be in one place at a time, or that's what an Opposition analyst might argue, anyway. So what argument do we use to justify not completing all the other SD(P)s already under construction?"

"They don't have to be in more than one place at a time," Janacek told him. "Eighth Fleet was essentially an offensive instrument, a means to project force against an enemy. Now that we've folded its modern units over into Third Fleet, of course, it also serves a powerful defensive purpose as a deterrent at Trevor's Star, but it remains an offensive asset. Third Fleet's superiority to anything it might face is so pronounced that it would be able to cut its way directly through any opposition to the capital system of any opponent, much as Eighth Fleet was in the course of doing to the Peeps when the current truce was arranged."

He unaccountably failed, High Ridge noted, to mention the name of the officer who'd been in command of Eighth Fleet at the time.

"Given that capability, what we really need to be concerned about is the protection of our own territory and the defense of the Havenite star systems we currently control against the purely obsolescent ship types any potential adversary might be able to bring to bear against them. The most cost-effective and efficient way to do that is to use the new light attack craft. We can build and man LACs in enormous numbers compared to superdreadnoughts, and enough of them will be able to hold any star system that needs to be held. In the meantime, the ships which we're not currently completing will still be available if we need them later. We're not scrapping them, after all. We're merely halting construction. The hulls will remain in their building slips and docks, and all of the materials already acquired for their completion will be kept in orbital storage, as well. The money we save in the meantime can be used to build up the force of LACs we require for system defense and also to support the construction of our anti-piracy forces, not to mention the many vital domestic programs which urgently require funding," Janacek added, glancing sideways at New Kiev.

"And," Descroix murmured, also flicking a glance at the Chancellor of the Exchequer, "suspending construction will be a demonstration of our own desire for peace. Superdreadnoughts, as Edward so rightly points out, are used to *project* power. They're offensive weapons systems, unlike the cruisers he wants to build as an anti-piracy measure. And LACs are even less suitable for aggression against our neighbors, because they're not even hyper-capable without a carrier."

"An excellent point," New Kiev said, nodding vigorously as her anti-imperialism reflex triggered.

"I see." North Hollow frowned thoughtfully for a long moment, then nodded himself, slowly. "I see," he repeated more briskly, "and I completely agree, of course. Nonetheless, I continue to have some concerns about the way in which an alarmist jingoist might try to attack the new policies. In particular, I'm concerned about White Haven and Harrington."

The effect of those two names was remarkable. Every other face in the room tightened with expressions which ranged from hostility through revulsion and contempt to just a trace of outright fear. North Hollow alone seemed unaffected, although all of them knew that was a lie, for he had even more reason than any of the others to hate and loath Honor Harrington. Nor was he likely to have forgotten that Hamish Alexander had been president of the court-martial which had ended his dead brother's military career in bitter disgrace.

"The two of them have been troublesome and obstructionist enough over other issues," the earl continued levelly. "Given their stature in the public mind as great wartime leaders, they could prove even more troublesome over an issue this directly related to the Navy."

"Harrington," Janacek grated, "is a maniac. Oh, I suppose she's charismatic enough, but she has yet to demonstrate anything approaching true strategic insight. And my God, the casualty figures she's run up!" He snorted harshly. "'*Salamander*,' indeed! Too bad the fire seems to burn everyone *else* to a crisp!"

"But she does enjoy immense popularity," North Hollow pointed out calmly.

"Of course she does!" Janacek growled. "The Opposition media's seen to that, and the general public is too ignorant of military realities and too besotted with her public image of derring-do to question it."

For just a moment, North Hollow seemed to hover on the brink of asking the First Lord if Admiral White Haven's reputation was equally undeserved, but not even he was foolish enough to do that. The savagely caustic (and highly public) tongue-lashing White Haven had administered to Janacek when they'd both been serving officers was legendary.

"We all realize Harrington's reputation is grossly overinflated, Edward," High Ridge said soothingly instead, "but that doesn't invalidate Stefan's point. Particularly given how critical the enactment of our new budget and spending priorities has become. However she acquired that reputation, she possesses it, and she's learned to use it effectively when she launches her attacks against our policies."

"She and White Haven together," Descroix amplified.

"I know." Janacek drew a deep breath and made himself sit back in his chair. "In fact, I might as well admit that not offering Harrington a space-going command was a mistake. I wanted to keep her off any flag bridges, especially since she's obviously totally out of her depth as a flag officer, despite the promotions the previous Admiralty administration so unwisely showered upon her. The last thing I wanted was her anywhere near the Havenite front while we were in the process of negotiations, because God only knew what sort of unilateral lunatic action she might have committed us to. That's why I approved her request to return to the Saganami Island faculty; I thought we could keep her safely shelved teaching, instead. Failing that, I'd hoped the Graysons would be foolish enough to call her home and offer her a command, since they so obviously worship the ground she walks on. I never expected her to turn into a permanent fixture at Saganami, but she has, and now I can't justify removing the damned 'Salamander' from the faculty without opening a tremendous can of worms." He shrugged unhappily. "I hadn't considered that she might realize that by keeping her here on Manticore I'd also keep her handy to Parliament as well as keeping her in the public eye."

"And none of us realized she and White Haven would make such an effective team." Descroix's voice was sour, and for a few seconds her benign, harmless mask slipped as her eyes went flint-hard.

"Precisely the point I wished to raise," North Hollow said. "Either of them alone would be bad enough; together, they're the greatest single obstacle we face in the Lords. Would anyone disagree with that?"

"You're probably right," New Kiev said after a moment. "William Alexander is bad enough, but he was always a team player, completely loyal to Cromarty. He stayed in the background, so the public saw him as the nuts-and-bolts member of Cromarty's team—a technician and strategist, and an excellent one, but not a leader. Not with the sort of charisma Harrington has or the reputation for command his brother enjoys. And the same thing's true for James Webster and Sebastian D'Orville on the Navy side. They're both respected, but neither of them ever captured the public's eye the way Harrington and White Haven did. And, of course, neither of them holds a seat in Parliament, however influential they may be as Opposition 'analysts.'"

"So I think we're all in agreement," North Hollow said, "that anything which could, um, decrease White Haven's and Harrington's popularity, especially at this particular moment, would be . . . advantageous?"

He looked around the conference table with bright, speculative eyes, and one by one, the others nodded. New Kiev's nod was smaller and less enthusiastic than the others, almost uncomfortable, but it was a nod nonetheless.

"The question which comes to mind, My Lord," Descroix remarked, "is precisely how we could go about decreasing the popularity either of them enjoys, much less both of them. Goodness knows they've proved remarkably resistant to previous efforts in that direction."

"Ah, but that was because our efforts were directed at . . . disarming each of them. Not *both* of them," North Hollow said with a most unpleasant smile.

CHAPTER SIX

" **S**o the contracts should be in our hands by the end of
♦ ♦ ♦ the week, Your Grace."

Richard Maxwell, Honor's personal Manticoran attorney and
acting solicitor general for the Duchy of Harrington, punched the
forward button on his memo pad. A new page displayed itself, and
he studied it for a moment, then gave a small, satisfied nod.

"That's just about it, Your Grace," he said.

"An excellent brief, Richard," Honor approved. "I'm particularly
pleased with the progress on the lodge agreements."

"I'm still not as good at contract law as Willard," Maxwell
pointed out, "but that wasn't really a problem in this case. That
whole area is absolutely prime ski territory, and the access to the
coast offers a year-round recreational possibility for the operators.
They were eager to close, and they were willing to pay a considerably higher premium for the rights to build there than we'd
anticipated, especially now that the cessation of hostilities has given
the civilian economy a push forward again. Willard was right about
Odom, too; he's almost as sharp a negotiator as Willard himself.
He knew exactly when to push at the final session, and at the
expense of possible immodesty, I think I've been getting better at
this whole commercial law business, too. And I have to admit that
having Clarise Childers available as backup hasn't hurt a bit."

"I've been very satisfied with Merlin," Honor agreed. "And I've noticed Clarise always lends a certain . . . presence to any meeting. Whether she's actually there or not."

She smiled at Maxwell, and he grinned back at the studied understatement of her remark.

Merlin Odom was Willard Neufsteiller's handpicked deputy on Manticore, managing the operations of the steadily growing Harrington financial empire in the Star Kingdom in accordance with Neufsteiller's general directives from Grayson. At forty-two, he was much younger than Willard, and even less inclined to get out of the office in the name of heathen exercise. But the heavy-set lawyer with the brown hair, blue eyes, and startlingly red goatee was already demonstrating similar instincts. With a few more decades of experience, he would be more than ready to take over when Willard finally retired, which was a very high compliment indeed.

As for Childers, the mere fact that everyone knew her services were available to Honor at need was an asset beyond price. Not only was she one of the most capable attorneys in the Star Kingdom in her own right, but her firm's short—very short—client list loomed large in the mind of any commercial negotiator. Honor herself had become one of the richest individuals in the Star Kingdom over the past decade and a half, and her Sky Domes of Grayson was firmly established among the Kingdom Five Hundred list of top corporations. But Childers worked directly for Klaus Hauptman, whose personal and corporate wealth was at least equal to the combined assets of his half dozen closest competitors. Clarise Childers was the president and senior partner of the enormous law firm of Childers, Strauslund, Goldman, and Wu, whose sole clients were the Hauptman Cartel (which *headed* the Kingdom Five Hundred by a wide margin), the Hauptman family . . . and, on occasion, Honor Harrington.

"With the commercial side of things under control for the moment, Your Grace," Maxwell went on, his pleasantly ugly face thoughtful, "what I'd like to do next would be to spend some time setting up the Harrington judiciary."

"Do we really have to do that this quickly?" Honor asked with a small grimace. "It's not like we have anything approaching a true population in the duchy yet!"

"Your Grace," Maxwell said a bit sternly, "if anyone in the Star Kingdom should know better than that, it's you. You've already been through setting up a new steading on Grayson, after all."

"But I left most of that to Howard Clinkscales," Honor pointed out. "All I really did was sign off on the decisions he'd already reached."

"I happen to know from private correspondence with Lord Clinkscales that you were considerably more involved in the process than that, Your Grace," Maxwell disagreed respectfully. "And even if you hadn't been, you've had plenty of time to see how badly a well-organized infrastructure is needed in situations like this."

"The cases aren't parallel," Honor objected. "As a steadholder, I hold the powers of high, middle, and low justice in Harrington. I don't want them, mind you, and any steadholder's power of arbitrary decision has been steadily reduced by precedents over the last few centuries. Not to mention what the Sword's done to subordinate steading law codes to the planetary Constitution since the 'Mayhew Restoration.' But Steadholder Harrington is still a head of state in her own right, with all of the legal prerogatives and responsibilities that entails. *Duchess* Harrington is only an administrator—a Crown governor, basically."

"And, like a governor, the Duchess holds the powers of judicial review and commutation," Maxwell pointed out in turn. "And, like a governor, she's effectively the chief magistrate of her duchy. Which means she needs a functioning system of courts and law enforcement in place."

"To enforce it against whom?" Honor asked plaintively. "The total population of the duchy is—what? Clear up to two thousand now? Scattered over how many thousands of square kilometers?"

"The actual number is a bit higher than that," Maxwell told her. "Not a lot, I'll admit, but higher. And it's about to get a lot higher than it is, for another reason with which your Grayson experience with Sky Domes should make you familiar. Once the survey and construction crews for the ski lodges move in, the current population is going to go up by at least a factor of five. And once the lodges and resorts start attracting tourists and the permanent population to service them, the number will skyrocket."

"All right, all right," Honor sighed. "I surrender. Pull together a proposal for me by next Wednesday, and I promise to get back to you on it as soon as I can."

"Hear that, Nimitz?" the attorney said over his shoulder, to the cream-and-gray 'cat sprawled comfortably on the custom-made perch beside his smaller, dappled brown-and-cream mate. Nimitz pricked up his ears, and Maxwell chuckled. "I expect you to keep an eye on her and see to it that she really does pay attention to my memos," he said.

Nimitz considered him for a moment, then rose to a half-sitting position on the perch, and raised his true-hands. He placed the right true-hand, fingers together and palm facing to the left, on the upturned palm of his left true-hand, which pointed away from his body. The right true-hand slid out along the left palm, over the left fingers, and stopped with its heel resting on the left fingertips.

"Traitor," Honor muttered darkly as she read the sign for "Okay," and Nimitz bleeked a laugh and started signing again.

· <Not my fault you need a keeper,> the flashing fingers said. <Besides, he brings celery.>

"To think your loyalty can be bought so cheaply," Honor told him, shaking her head sorrowfully.

<Not loyalty,> Nimitz's true-hands replied. <Just cooperation.>

"Right," Honor snorted. Then she looked back at Maxwell. "Well, now that you've recruited your furry minion, I suppose I really don't have any choice but to read your memo. Although, exactly where you expect me to fit it into my schedule is beyond me."

"I'm sure that between them Mac and Miranda can find somewhere to steal an hour or two for you to spend reading. I promise I'll make it as concise as I can, too. But before you approve any plans, you really do need to read more than just the digest and the section heads, Your Grace. I'm flattered that you trust me, but the ultimate decisions and the consequences they may have are up to you."

"I know," she said more seriously, and tapped a command into the terminal at her desk. She studied the display for a few seconds, and then entered a brief note.

"I just picked Wednesday out of a hat," she admitted, "but it looks like it will actually work anyway. And it's a good thing, too, because I've got an exam at Saganami Island that afternoon. I'm going to be swamped grading papers in my copious free time at least through the weekend. So if you can get it to me by Wednesday morning, or even better, by Tuesday evening, I'll fit it in somehow before I get buried under papers."

"I'm glad to hear it, Your Grace," Maxwell told her, "but don't you have a session in the Lords Wednesday, as well? I thought I saw a notice that the Government intended to move its new budget this week, and even though this is important, I wouldn't want it to interfere with any preparations for that."

"No," Honor said with another, more heartfelt grimace. "It's been moved to next Wednesday. I'm not sure why, but the Government notified us day before yesterday that they were moving the debate back a week. And there won't be a lot of preparation to do, either. High Ridge will say exactly the same things he's been saying for the last three T-years, and Earl White Haven and I will say exactly the same things *we've* been saying for the last three years. Then the House will vote—narrowly, of course—to draft the budget the Government wants, the Commons will move amendments to change it, the Lords will strip them back out again, and absolutely nothing will change."

Maxwell looked at her, wondering if she realized just how bitter (and exhausted) she sounded at that instant. Not that he was surprised to hear it.

The House of Lords' power to initiate finance bills was only part of its advantage in controlling the power of the purse in the Star Kingdom. In addition, any bill which actually passed had to pass in the final form approved by the Lords. That meant that, as Honor had just complained, the Lords could effectively strip out any Commons-sponsored amendment of which it disapproved and require a straight up-or-down vote on its own version of any financial bill. Under normal circumstances, the Commons still had quite a lot of say-so, since it could always refuse to approve the Lords' final version and—especially—refuse approval for any extraordinary funding measures required to support the Lords' budgets. But these circumstances weren't normal. The "extraordinary funding measures" were already in place, and the authority the Lords also enjoyed to pass special financial enabling authority for core government services on an emergency basis even without the Commons' approval in the event of a budgetary standoff was the icing on the cake.

Of course, prudent prime ministers were usually careful not to overstrain their weapons. For the Lords to ride roughshod over the Commons required a situation in which a sufficiently sizable piece of the electorate would be prepared to blame the *Commons* for failure to achieve compromise. Under those circumstances, the house which had to stand for reelection faced a fatal disadvantage, but if the Lords had been foolish enough to court situations in which they would be blamed for the ensuing shutdown of most government services, the long-term resentment might have allowed the Crown to strip the senior house of the power of the purse long ago.

That was precisely why the High Ridge Government had been so assiduously attempting to buy public support . . . and what had made Duchess Harrington and Earl White Haven so valuable as the Opposition's spokespeople in the House of Lords. Where the naval budgets, in particular, were concerned, their voices carried a great deal of weight with the electorate.

And it was also why High Ridge and his allies wanted so desperately to reduce their effectiveness by any means possible,

The members of the Government themselves had to be extremely careful about seeming to pick personal quarrels with the two most famous heroes of the war against the Peeps. But that only required them to be more inventive and delegate attacks to suitably distanced henchmen. Nor did it do a thing to restrain the Government-sponsored "commentators" and 'faxes or the idiots who actually believed them, and Lady Harrington's cumulative exhaustion was beginning to show.

Of course, it wasn't as if she hadn't had more than her fair share of experience with partisan press coverage, both in the Star Kingdom and on Grayson, and she handled it with a degree of outward calm Maxwell was privately certain was mostly mask. He'd come to know her well enough over the past few T-years to recognize that for all her ability to project serenity and calm, her temper was probably at least as dangerous as that of the Queen herself. It seemed to be more difficult to make her lose it, but he would have been very hesitant to suggest that anything at all was beyond her once she did . . . as the ghosts of Pavel Young and Denver Summervale could have attested.

In a way, it was even worse for her than for either of the Alexander brothers, Maxwell reflected. At least High Ridge and his cronies regarded them as representing only a single dangerous opponent, whereas it was no secret at all that Lady Harrington's contributions to debates in the Lords represented the views of Protector Benjamin, as well as those of Elizabeth III.

Neither of whom gave a thimble of spit in a blast furnace for Baron High Ridge and his ministerial colleagues.

The attorney started to say something, then changed his mind. He could hardly tell her anything she didn't already know. And even if he could have, it really wasn't his place to offer her unsolicited political advice or confidences, whatever rumors he might have been picking up.

Besides, he reflected, *there's a better way to do it . . . assuming I decide I have any business sticking my oar into her private life, that is. I won't have to tell her a thing; I'll just have to have a word with Miranda or Mac. Let* them *figure out how to bring it up with her.*

"Lord Alexander and Earl White Haven have arrived, Your Grace."

"Thank you, Mac. Ask them to come straight in, would you please?"

"Of course, Your Grace."

Honor put her reader on hold, freezing it on the third page of Midshipwoman Zilwicki's analysis of the Battle of Cape St. Vincent, and looked up with a smile. James MacGuiness, the only steward in the entire Royal Manticoran Navy who wasn't actually *in* the Navy, smiled back at her, and then bent his head in an almost-bow before he withdrew from her study. She watched him go fondly, fully aware of how critical to the smooth functioning of her life he'd become over the past twenty T-years.

She glanced across at Nimitz, draped in splendid isolation across the double perch he normally shared with his mate. It was Thursday, and Samantha was absent, accompanying Miranda and Farragut to the Andreas Venizelos Academy, the orphanage and private school Honor had endowed for the children of war dead, Manticoran and Grayson alike. AVA had campuses in both the Star Kingdom and Yeltsin, and Miranda, as Honor's chief of staff, deputized for her regularly, since the press of other duties consumed more and more of her own time. The kids idolized Nimitz, Samantha, Farragut, and treecats in general, and all 'cats loved to spend time with children, whether they had four limbs or six. It was a treat all of the 'cats looked forward to, and Nimitz often went with the others even when Honor couldn't. But not when something like today's meeting was on his person's schedule.

She looked past the 'cat and caught a glimpse of LaFollet, outside the study door standing his post even here, before it closed behind MacGuiness. Then she pushed herself up out of her chair and crossed to stand in the enlarged bay window that overhung her mansion's landscaped grounds like a sort of hanging turret. The window's outer, floor-to-ceiling crystoplast wall looked out over the bright blue beauty of Jason Bay, and she allowed herself a moment to enjoy the view afresh, then turned back to face the door once more and twitched her Grayson-style gown and vest straight.

Over the years, she'd become completely accustomed to the traditional Grayson garments. She still considered them thoroughly useless for anything except looking ornamental, but she'd been forced to admit that looking ornamental wasn't necessarily a bad thing. And there was another reason to wear them almost constantly here in the Star Kingdom, when she wasn't in uniform, at least. They helped remind everyone, including herself, of who else she was ... and of how much the Star Kingdom and the entire Manticoran Alliance owed the people of her adoptive planet.

Yet another point that ass High Ridge seems able to effortlessly ignore ... or worse, she thought bitterly, then brushed the familiar surge of anger aside. This wasn't the time for her to be storing up still more mental reasons to go for the Prime Minister's throat.

MacGuiness returned a very few moments later with Hamish and William Alexander.

"Earl White Haven and Lord Alexander, Your Grace," Honor's steward and majordomo murmured, and withdrew, closing the polished wooden doors quietly behind him.

"Hamish. Willie."

Honor crossed the room to them, holding out her hand in welcome, and it no longer seemed odd to her to greet them so informally. Every once in a while she experienced a sudden sense of unreality when she heard herself addressing her Queen or Benjamin Mayhew by their given names, but even those moments were becoming fewer and further between. In an odd sort of way, she remained fully aware of who she was and where she'd come from even as she found herself moving more and more naturally at the very pinnacle of political power in two separate star nations. She seldom thought consciously about it, but when the realization crossed her awareness, she recognized the way in which her belated admission to the innermost councils of her two nations shaped her perspective.

She was an outsider who'd been elevated to the status of one of the most powerful of all insiders. Because of that, she saw things through different eyes, from what she knew her allies sometimes regarded as an almost ingenuous viewpoint. The degree of sophisticated, vicious, endlessly polite (outwardly, at least) political infighting they took so much for granted, even when they deplored it, was alien to her both by nature and by experience. In some ways, her Grayson and Manticoran friends understood one another far better than she understood either of them, yet she'd come to realize that her very sense of detachment from the partisan bloodletting about her was a sort of armor. Her adversaries and allies alike regarded her as deplorably unsophisticated and direct, unwilling—or unable—to "play the game" by the rules they all understood so well. And that made her an unknown, unpredictable quantity, especially for her opponents. They knew all about the subtle shadings of position, of advantage and opportunity, which guided their own decisions and tactical maneuvers, but they found the simplicity and directness of her positions curiously baffling. It was as if they couldn't quite believe she was exactly who she said she was, that she truly believed exactly the things she said she did, because they were so unlike that themselves. So they persisted in regarding her with nervous wariness, perpetually waiting for the instant in which she finally revealed her "true" nature.

That could be a useful thing where enemies were concerned, but it had its downside, as well. Even her closest allies—particularly the aristocratic ones, she reflected, tasting the emotions of her guests—sometimes failed to realize there was nothing to reveal. They might have come to recognize that intellectually, but the Star Kingdom's peers were too much a part of the world to which they'd been born to be able to truly divorce themselves from it, even if they'd wanted to. They didn't, of course, and why should they? It *was* their world, and Honor was honest enough to admit that it had at least as many positive aspects as negative ones. But even the best of them—even a man like Hamish Alexander, who'd spent seven or eight decades as a Queen's officer—could never quite free themselves from the dance whose measures they'd trod since childhood.

She brushed the thought aside as she shook hands with each

of the Alexanders in turn, and then waved them towards their customary chairs with a smile. It was a warm, welcoming smile, and she was no longer aware of how much warmer it became when her eyes met White Haven's.

William Alexander, on the other hand, certainly was aware of it. He'd been aware of the habitual warmth with which she greeted his brother for quite some time, actually, although he hadn't realized he was. Just as he hadn't noticed all the private, intimate little conversations, or the way Hamish inevitably seemed to find some reason to remain behind for some last-minute private discussion of the details with her after one of their three-cornered strategy sessions. Now he uneasily watched her smile, and his uneasiness grew as Hamish returned it.

"Thank you for inviting us over, Honor," White Haven said, holding onto her hand for perhaps a heartbeat longer than simple courtesy required.

"As if I haven't been inviting both of you over before each of High Ridge's little soirees for years now," Honor replied with a snort.

"Yes, you have," White Haven agreed. "But I wouldn't want you to think we were starting to take you for granted, Your Grace," he added with a lurking smile.

"Hardly," Honor said dryly. "The three of us have made ourselves sufficiently unpopular with the Government for me to doubt that any of us is likely to take either of the other two 'for granted.'"

"Not unless we want to prove the validity of that fellow from Old Earth," William put in. "You know, what's his name. Hancock? Arnold?" He shook his head. "One of those ancient American guys." He looked at his brother. "You're the historian of the family, Hamish. Who am I thinking of?"

"Unless I'm very much mistaken," White Haven replied, "the man whose name you're fumbling so ineptly for was Benjamin Franklin. He was the one who advised his fellow rebels that they must all hang together unless they wanted to be hanged separately, although it astonishes me that a historical illiterate like yourself could even dredge up the reference."

"Given the number of years that have flowed under the bridge since your precious Franklin, I think anyone who doesn't have more than a trace of anal retentiveness in his nature is doing remarkably well to remember him at all," William told him. "Of course,

I was quite confident that you'd be able to give me chapter and verse on him."

"Before you pursue that thought any further, Willie," Honor warned him, "I should probably mention that I'm fairly familiar with Franklin and his period myself."

"Oh. Well, in that case, of course, my exquisite natural courtesy precludes any further consideration of— Well, you know."

"I do, indeed," Honor told him ominously, and they both chuckled.

A soft knock sounded from the direction of the study door, and then it opened once again to readmit MacGuiness. He wheeled in a cart of refreshments prepared by Mistress Thorne, Honor's Grayson cook, and parked it at the end of her desk. It was no longer necessary for him to ask her guests what they preferred, and he poured a stein of Old Tillman for White Haven before he drew the cork from a bottle of Sphinx burgundy and offered it for Lord Alexander's inspection. Honor and Hamish grinned at onc another as William carefully examined the cork and sniffed delicately before nodding his gracious approval of the offering. Then MacGuiness poured a second Old Tillman for Honor. She took it and smiled at him as he withdrew, and then she and Hamish raised their foamy, condensation-dewed steins to one another in a beer-drinkers' salute, pointedly excluding the hopelessly effete wine-snob in their midst.

"I must say, Honor," Hamish said with a sigh of pleasure as he lowered his stein once more, "that I'm much more partial to your taste in refreshments than I ever was to the sorts of things you encounter at most of Willie's political get-togethers."

"That's because you're attending the wrong sorts of get-togethers," Honor suggested with a twinkle. "Far be it from me to suggest that blue-blooded, natural born aristocrats like your honorable brother are a bit isolated from the simpler pleasures of life, but one thing I was always delighted about on Grayson is that even the snobbiest of steadholders isn't ashamed to admit he likes an occasional beer."

"The supposed virtues of a taste for beer are grossly exaggerated by those unfortunate souls blind to the superior virtues of a decent vintage," William informed them both. "I don't mind an *occasional* beer, myself. It certainly beats water. But why settle for second-best when a superior alternative is available?"

"We didn't," his brother replied. "We were wondering why you did."

"Behave yourselves, children," Honor scolded, feeling briefly more like their nanny than their political colleague, despite the fact that even the younger Alexander was well over twenty T-years older than she. "We have other things to discuss before we settle down to letting you two insult one another properly."

"Aye, aye, Ma'am," White Haven said with a broad grin, and she shook her head fondly at him.

"Actually," William said, his tone suddenly much more serious, "you're quite right, Honor. We do have several things to discuss, including one concern I really wish didn't have to be brought up."

Honor sat back in her chair, eyes narrowing as she tasted his emotions. Despite the customary banter between the brothers, both of them radiated an underlying sense of tension frosted with anger. That much she was accustomed to; it was an inevitable consequence of the political situation they'd come to discuss. But she'd never before sensed anything quite like the level of . . . anxiety she was picking up from William at the moment. There was something new and especially pointed about his emotions, a sense of focused urgency. More than that, he seemed to be trying to suppress whatever it was—or at least to feel a hesitance about admitting its source which surprised her after all of the crises they'd weathered together by now.

"And what would that be?" she asked cautiously.

"Well . . ." William looked at her for a moment, then glanced at his brother and visibly drew a steadying breath.

"According to my sources," he said in the voice of a man determined to get through difficult ground and setting up the groundwork for the journey, "we're about to be hit with fresh naval reductions in the new budget. The new estimates are in, and it's pretty clear that the termination of the Emergency Income Tax Act is about to start cutting into their slush funds and pork barrel pretty badly. They don't like that one bit, but they're not stupid enough to try to renew it. Not when they know we'll kill it in the Commons and use the opportunity to both advertise their real spending priorities and simultaneously deprive them of the ability to go on blaming *us* for all of the Kingdom's fiscal woes. So instead, Janacek is going to recommend cutting our active duty ships of the wall by about twenty percent to free up funds from the other 'wartime taxes.' He's also planning to suspend construction on virtually all the incomplete SD(P)s for the same reason, and High Ridge thinks he's found a way to neutralize you and Hamish when the new cuts are debated in the Lords."

"Fresh reductions?!" Hamish repeated, then muttered something vicious under his breath which Honor was just as happy not to have heard clearly.

"How can they possibly justify cutting the Fleet even further?" she asked William, and she was more than a little surprised that she sounded so calm herself. "We're already down to a lower number of hulls than we had before the war started," she pointed out. "And as they're fond of reminding people, the war still isn't over."

"Not officially, anyway," Hamish growled.

"They plan to justify it exactly the way they've justified all the other reductions," William replied to Honor's question. "By pointing to how much of the naval budget they can save through the increased effectiveness and combat power of the new types. They don't need all those 'obsolescent' older ships getting in the way of the new, lean, efficient Navy Janacek has single-handedly created."

Despite her own total agreement with William's opinion of High Ridge and Sir Edward Janacek, Honor winced at the ferocious sarcasm in his bitter voice. His brother, on the other hand, was too furious to pay it much attention.

"That's the biggest load of bullshit I've heard in months," Hamish grated. "Even for them, it sets some new record!"

"It's a logical progression from everything else they've done, Hamish," Honor observed. Her voice was by far the most serene one in the room, but there was nothing particularly serene about her agate-hard eyes. "Still, I'm a bit surprised at the size of this reduction. They've already cut away every bit of fat and muscle; now they're working on the bones."

"That's a depressingly accurate analysis," William agreed. "And you're right, this is a direct, straight-line extension of the same justification they've used every step of the way. The new ship types are more powerful, more survivable, and less manpower intensive, and with the demise of the income tax, their budget is suddenly so tight something has to give."

" '*Give*,' is it?" Hamish repeated savagely. "I'll *give* that lying, conniving, pigheaded idiot Janacek something! In fact, I'll—"

"Calm down, Hamish," Honor said, never looking away from William . . . and not even thinking about how casually she'd addressed White Haven. "We already knew they regard the Navy budget as some kind of piggy bank they can keep raiding forever for their precious 'peace dividend.' Losing our tempers and frothing at the mouth while we chew pieces off of them in debate the way they deserve is only going to make us look like we're overreacting. Which will only make them look more reasonable. However stupid their policy may be, we have to stick together and sound calm and rational when we oppose it. That's especially true for the two of us, and you know it."

"You're right," he said, after another brief, fulminating pause. Then he drew a deep breath. "So they're going to reduce our combat power even further, are they?" he said. His brother nodded, and Hamish snorted. "And I suppose Jurgensen and his pet analysts at ONI are going to back Janacek up?"

"Of course they are," William replied, and it was Honor's turn to snort bitterly.

It hadn't surprised anyone when Janacek began his second tenure as First Lord of the Admiralty by placing Hamish Alexander on inactive, half-pay status. The Earl of White Haven's war record had been brilliant, but the combined reincarnation of Horatio Nelson, Togo Heimachoro, Raymond Spruance, Gustav Anderman, and Edward Saganami couldn't have been brilliant enough to outweigh the bitter, personal animosity between himself and Sir Edward Janacek.

That much, at least, had been expected, however petty and vindictive it might have been. But Honor suspected that the rest of the Navy had been as surprised and dismayed as she had when Janacek decided Sir Thomas Caparelli and Patricia Givens also "deserved a rest."

Actually, she reflected, Caparelli might truly have needed the break, after the massive strain of acting as the Star Kingdom's senior uniformed commander for over a decade. Unfortunately, that hadn't been the real reason for his relief. She'd come to know the former First Space Lord fairly well following her return from Cerberus, and one thing Thomas Caparelli would never be was any political appointee's yes-man. His integrity would never have permitted him to assist in Janacek's downsizing of the Navy when the Government had simultaneously declined to bring the war against the Peeps to a true conclusion. And so, like White Haven, although for different reasons, he'd had to go.

Admiral Givens had gone for largely the same reasons as Caparelli, despite her phenomenally successful record as Director of the Office of Naval Intelligence. Her loyalty to and close working relationship with Caparelli would probably have required her dismissal in Janacek's eyes as part of his "clean broom" theory of personnel management under any circumstances. There were also rumors about fundamental disagreements between her and Janacek over his plans to restructure the Navy's intelligence priorities, but her greatest sin had been her refusal to slant her analyses at ONI to say what her civilian superiors wanted them to say. So, she too had found herself on half-pay as her reward for helping to preserve the Star Kingdom.

One thing of which no one would ever be able to accuse her replacement was excessive independence. Admiral Francis Jurgensen had become something of an anachronism in the war-fighting Royal Navy: a flag officer who owed his exalted rank far more to political patronage than to any personal ability. Such officers had been depressingly common before the war, although they'd been weeded out ruthlessly since, usually by Caparelli, but far too often (and painfully) by enemy action. Unfortunately, they were making a comeback under the Admiralty's new management. However disgusting she might find that, Honor supposed it was inevitable. After all, Sir Edward Janacek had been exactly that sort of officer throughout his own career.

What mattered in Jurgensen's case, however, was that he understood precisely what Janacek and his political superiors wanted to hear. Honor wasn't prepared to accuse him of actually falsifying evidence, although she was far from certain he would refuse to do so. But it was widely known within the Service, and especially within the Intelligence community, that Jurgensen had a long history of *interpreting* evidence to suit his superiors' requirements.

"Well, I suppose it was inevitable," White Haven said, frowning at his brother. "They have to free up the cash to pay for their vote-buying schemes somehow."

"No," William agreed, "something like it probably was inevitable, and to be candid, it doesn't really surprise me. In fact, to be completely honest, what did surprise—and dismay me—was the other thing my sources have reported to me."

"Other thing?" Honor looked at him sharply, puzzled once again by the curious spikes of uncertainty and unhappiness radiating from him. One of the frustrating things about her ability to sense emotions was her *in*ability to sense the thoughts behind them. As in this case. She was reasonably certain that the unmistakable anger threaded through William's emotions wasn't directed specifically at her, yet she was obviously a factor in his distress, and whatever had angered him was tied directly up with her somehow.

"Yes." William looked away for a moment, gazing at the life-sized portrait of Paul Tankersley Michelle Henke had commissioned for Honor's last birthday. It hung facing Honor's desk and work station, and he let his eyes rest on that smiling face for just a second. Then he drew a deep breath, squared his shoulders, and turned to look at both Honor and White Haven simultaneously.

"According to my sources, High Ridge and his allies feel confident that they've found a way to severely damage your and Hamish's credibility, Honor. It's as obvious to them as it is to us that you two would be our most effective spokesmen against this insanity, but they believe they've come up with a way to largely neutralize you by . . . diverting you from the topic."

"It'll be a cold day in Hell first!" White Haven snarled, but Honor felt her belly tighten as the emotions behind William's blue eyes washed through her.

"Drop the shoe, Willie," she told him quietly, and he sighed.

"Tomorrow morning," he told her in a flattened voice, "Solomon Hayes' column will carry a report that you and Hamish are lovers."

Honor felt the blood drain from her face, but even her own shock paled beside the sudden, white-hot spike of fury she tasted from White Haven. William lacked her own empathic sense, but he didn't need it, and his face was a mask and his voice flatter than ever as he continued.

"You both know how Hayes works. He won't come right out and say so unequivocally or name names to support his allegations, but the message will be completely clear. He's going to suggest that you've been lovers for over two T-years now . . . and High Ridge's pet columnists are already drafting op-ed pieces designed to fan the flames. That's apparently the real reason High Ridge rescheduled the opening debate in the Lords—to give the lynch mob time to get a good start. They'll be careful to project an image of fair-mindedness and insist your personal lives should have absolutely no bearing on matters of public policy, but they know exactly how crippling such charges will be to both of you. And the public's admiration for you both, as individuals as well as naval heroes, will make the backlash even worse, especially since there won't be any way to disprove Hayes' story."

He barked a laugh which contained no humor at all.

"At best," he went on harshly, "it will be your word against his . . . and a carefully orchestrated background chorus designed to drown out anything you say. And to be honest, the two of you have spent so much time together, both publicly and in private, and worked so closely with one another that it's going to be impossible to refute the inevitable allegations that you obviously had ample opportunity for it!"

"*Refute?*" White Haven sounded strangled, but Honor could only sit in paralyzed shock. Behind her, she heard the soft thud as Nimitz leapt from his perch to her desk. She felt the 'cat reaching out to her, felt him trying to insert himself between her and her pain as he'd done so often before, even before he vaulted over her shoulder and landed in her lap. She scooped him into her arms without even turning her chair and held him tightly, pressing her face into his silky fur while he crooned to her, but this time no one could protect her from the pain. Not even Nimitz.

For the most part, Manticoran social mores were far more relaxed than those of Grayson. Indeed, those of the capital planet itself were more liberal than those of Honor's native Sphinx. Normally, the idea that an affair between two consenting adults was the business of anyone besides the two adults concerned would have been laughable. Normally.

But not in this case. Not for Steadholder Harrington, who also had to concern herself with the sensibilities of her Grayson subjects and how Grayson public opinion would rebound against her. And through her, against Protector Benjamin and his beleaguered efforts to maintain Grayson's military preparedness in the face of the Star Kingdom's effective abandonment of the Manticoran Alliance. Her earlier relationship with Paul had been hard enough for Grayson to swallow, but at least if they'd never married, neither of them had been married to someone else, either.

White Haven was, and that was the second prong of the threat, for Lady Emily Alexander, Countess White Haven, was one of the most beloved public figures in the entire Star Kingdom.

Once one of Manticore's most beautiful and talented HD actresses, she'd been confined to a life-support chair following an air car accident since before Honor's third standard birthday, yet Emily Alexander had refused to let her life end. The accident had crippled her physically, but the damage hadn't affected the brilliance of mind and strength of will which had propelled her to the very top of her vocation. The surgeons had managed to salvage enough of her motor control centers to give her almost full use of one hand and arm and almost normal speech, although the regulation of her involuntary muscles depended entirely upon her life-support chair. It wasn't much. Indeed, it was pathetically little, but small as it was, she had made it enough.

Unable to take the stage again, she'd become a producer and writer, a poet who was also a brilliant historian and the semi-official biographer of the House of Winton. And along with her stature as the great tragic heroine of Manticore, the beloved example who challenged and inspired an entire kingdom with the proof of how much could be overcome by sheer, dauntless courage, had come the great romantic story of her marriage to Hamish Alexander. Of the devotion and love which had survived almost six T-decades of confinement to her chair. Many men would have sought the dissolution of their marriages, however gently and on however generous terms, so that they could remarry, but Hamish had rejected any suggestion that he might have done so.

There'd been whispers of occasional discreet liaisons between him and registered courtesans, over the years, but such relationships were fully accepted—even regarded as therapeutic—on Manticore. Gryphon and Sphinx were less convinced of that, each for its own reasons, but the capital planet was far more . . . sophisticated in that regard.

Yet there was a universe of difference between occasionally patronizing a registered professional courtesan, particularly when one's spouse was a complete invalid, and entering upon an affair with a nonprofessional. And that was especially true for Hamish and Emily Alexander, who were Second Reformation Roman Catholics and who'd married monogamously, for better or for worse, until death parted them. Both of them took their marriage vows seriously, and even if they hadn't, the depth of Hamish Alexander's love for his wife was something not even his most bitter personal or political enemy would have dared to doubt.

Until now. Until Honor.

She raised her face from Nimitz's fur and stared at William, unable even to look at Hamish, and her pain only grew as she realized at last what William had been thinking. He'd been wondering if the story Hayes was about to publish might be true, and she knew why.

Because it should have been. Because if she'd had the courage to tell Hamish what she felt, they *would* have become lovers. Whether that would have constituted a betrayal in Lady Emily's eyes or not, Honor didn't know . . . and it wouldn't have mattered. And that, she realized, was the true reason she'd politely declined every invitation to visit the Alexander family seat at White Haven, despite the closeness of their working political relationship. Because that was Emily's place, the home she never left. The place where she belonged with Hamish, and which Honor's very presence would somehow have violated. And because as long as she'd never herself met Emily, Honor could pretend she had never transgressed against her, even in her heart of hearts.

And that was the most bitter irony of all. She had no idea if the people who'd fed Hayes the story for his savage gossip column in the *Landing Tattler* believed their allegations. But while there'd been no physical violation of Hamish's marriage to Emily, she knew both of them had wanted there to be one. Neither would ever have admitted it to the other, but now they would stand accused of the very thing both had been determined would never happen, and any effort to refute the allegations would only make it worse.

It was absurd, a tiny corner of her brain told her. Every right of privacy should have protected her and Hamish, even if they had been lovers. And it didn't matter. Even here in the Star Kingdom, no more damaging scandal could have been devised, not given the iconic stature of Lady Emily and her husband, because William was right. The very people most likely to share Honor's personal values and support her political views would be the ones most revolted by her "betrayal" of such a beloved public figure, and what made it damaging in Manticore would make it devastating on Grayson.

The fact that their personal lives had nothing to do with their accomplishments or judgment as naval officers would mean nothing. The idea that their feelings for one another did somehow prejudice their thinking would be suggested, however indirectly, by someone. She knew it would. And ridiculous as the charge would be, it would stick. But that wasn't the real purpose of the attack. The real purpose was to divert the debate from a discussion of the dangers of Janacek's proposals to the personal character of the man and woman who had become his most effective naval critics. The Government wouldn't have to refute their arguments this time. Not if it could force them to expend all of their energy and moral capital defending themselves against such sensational charges.

And if High Ridge and his cronies could discredit them on this issue, they could be discredited on *any* issue. . . .

"Who passed the rumors to Hayes?" she asked, and the levelness of her voice astonished her.

"Does it matter?" William replied.

"Yes," she said, but her voice was no longer merely level and the soft, sibilant snarl of Nimitz's fury sounded behind it. "It does."

William looked at her in alarm, and what he saw in her chocolate-dark eyes turned alarm to fear.

"I don't know for certain," he told her after a moment. "And if I did, I don't think I'd tell you."

"I can find out for myself." Her tone was a soprano dagger, and she felt an icy purpose sweep through her. "I found out who bought Paul Tankersley's murder," she told the brother of the man she loved. "And I can find the scum responsible for this."

"No, you can't," William said urgently, then shook his head sharply. "I mean, of course you can, but what good would it do?" He stared at her in raw appeal. "Your duel with Young almost destroyed you, Honor! If you found out who was behind this, and you challenged him, it would be ten times worse—far more destructive than the rumors themselves! You'd be finished as a political figure here in the Star Kingdom, whatever happened. And that doesn't even consider the question of how many people would believe the stories had to be true for you to take such action."

"He's right." Hamish Alexander's voice was grating iron, and she turned to look at him at last. He made himself meet her eyes levelly, and she realized that for the first time he knew. He knew what a part of him must have suspected with growing strength for years now—that she'd always known what he felt for her, and that she'd felt the same thing.

"He's right," White Haven repeated. "Neither one of us can afford to give the story that much credibility. Especially," he turned to glare at his brother, "when there isn't a shred of truth in it."

William returned his ferocious glare levelly, as aware as Honor that most of that fury was directed somewhere else.

"I believe you," he said with quiet sincerity. "But the problem is proving it."

"*Proving* it!" White Haven snarled.

"I know. I know!" William shook his head again, his expression almost as angry as his brother's. "You shouldn't have to prove a damned thing, either of you! But you know as well as I do that that isn't how it works against character assassination like this, and there isn't any way to prove a negative. Particularly not when the two of you have worked so closely together. We—all of us—have overspent the political capital your accomplishments have generated. We've deliberately thrown you together, focused the public's perception on the two of you as a team. That's the way the voters think of you now, and that's actually going to make it easier for them to believe this crap. Especially when someone starts talking about how much time you've spent alone with each other."

"Alone?" Both Alexanders turned back to Honor at her one-word question. "I'm a *steadholder*, Willie. I never go anywhere without my armsmen—I can't, under Grayson law! When have the two of us ever really had a chance to be 'alone' together?"

"You know better than that, Honor," William said almost compassionately. "First, no one would believe you couldn't have slipped away, even from Andrew, if you truly wanted to. And they wouldn't believe it because you know as well as I do that they'd be right; you could have. And second, even if that weren't true, do you think anyone would doubt for a moment that every one of your armsmen would lie the Devil out of Hell if you asked him to?"

It was her turn to glare back at him, but then she felt her shoulders sag, because he was right. Of course he was, and she'd known it before she even opened her mouth. It was only a drowning woman searching frantically for any straw to grasp.

"So what do we do now?" she asked bitterly. "Can they really get away with reducing the fight for political control of the entire Star Kingdom to something as petty and poisonous as an invented rumor of infidelity?"

"No," William replied. "They can't reduce the entire fight to something like that, Honor. But that isn't really what you were asking, and the truth is that you and Hamish have been two of our most potent weapons . . . and they *can* destroy our ability to use either of you against them effectively. It's stupid and vicious and small-minded, but that doesn't mean it won't work. At the very least, it's almost certain to cripple you two while they drive through the naval cuts and the budget, but I'm sure they're hoping for a much longer-term effect, as well. And the beauty of it, from their perspective, is that the more vehemently you or any of your friends and allies deny it, the more surely a certain percentage of the electorate will believe it must be true."

Honor stared at him, then looked back at Hamish and saw the matching anguish in his eyes. His emotions were too painful for her to endure, and so she closed her empathic sense down until she felt only Nimitz, only his love and concern . . . and his help-less inability to fight this foe for her. She pulled her eyes away from Hamish, returning them to William, and fought to keep her shoulders from sagging still further.

"So what do we do?" she asked him softly.

"I don't know, Honor," he told her. "I just don't know."

CHAPTER SEVEN

"What do you think they're really up to, Guns?"

"Sir?" Lieutenant Commander Anna Zahn, Sidemore Navy, HMS *LaFroye*'s tactical officer, looked up from her plot in some surprise. Captain Ackenheil wasn't much addicted to formalities, including the punctilious announcement of his presence whenever he arrived on the bridge, and she hadn't realized he was there.

"I asked what you think they're really up to," the Manticoran said, and gestured at her display. It was set to astrography mode and interstellar scale at the moment, and over a dozen stars were tagged with red, flashing icons.

"I don't really know, Sir," Zahn replied after a moment. She was one of the relatively few Sidemore officers serving aboard Royal Navy ships in senior positions. It wasn't because of any prejudice against Sidemorians, so much as it was the fact that there weren't all that many senior Sidemore officers serving *anywhere*. The entire Sidemore Navy was barely eight T-years old, which meant that Zahn was incredibly junior for her rank by Manticoran standards. She also happened to be extremely good at her job, which was how she'd come to be assigned as the tactical officer aboard the senior ship of CruDiv 237. Intellectually, she knew she wouldn't have been here if the Manties didn't believe she would be able to pull her own weight. It had been Manticoran policy since the beginning of Sidemore's alliance with the Star Kingdom to cross-assign officers whenever possible as one way to be sure both navies were familiar with RMN doctrine and procedures and also as a way to build the SN's experience base as rapidly as possible. Which didn't mean they were about to put anyone whose competence they doubted into a position as sensitive as that of a heavy cruiser's tactical officer. But whatever her brain might know, her emotions remained stubbornly unconvinced.

Maybe it wasn't just her. Maybe the entire Sidemore Navy—such as it was, and what there was of it—wasn't quite able to believe that anyone else would take it seriously at its young and tender age. She couldn't really speak for the rest of her home world's officer corps, but there were enough times she still felt like the new kid in class herself when she measured her own meager seven T-years of naval experience against the professional resume of someone like Ackenheil, who was very nearly three times her own age and a highly decorated combat veteran, to boot. Which made her a bit hesitant about offering an opinion, even when it was asked for. Particularly since she was the current officer of the watch, and she really should have been keeping her eye on the entire command deck rather than puzzling over reports she wasn't officially supposed to be worrying her head over, anyway. *LaFroye* was in a standard parking orbit, with her wedge down and little more than a skeleton watch, and she'd turned the con over to Lieutenant Turner, the astrogator (who was eleven T-years older than she was and had nine more T-years of experience), so it wasn't exactly as if she were neglecting her duties, but still . . .

Ackenheil's firm lips seemed to quiver, as if a smile threatened to take them over for just a moment, and she felt herself blush. She *hated* it when she blushed. It made her feel even more like a schoolgirl pretending to be a naval officer.

Jason Ackenheil managed—with difficulty—not to smile as Lieutenant Commander Zahn's cheekbones turned a delicate pink, and he scolded himself for wanting to. Well, not really wanting to, perhaps. It was just that the young Sidemore officer was so determined to get it right and so convinced that the Royal Manticoran Navy had made special allowances to put her into her present slot. The fact that she was an extraordinarily talented young woman, with one of the best sets of tactical instincts he'd ever seen, seemed to escape her somehow.

But perhaps he shouldn't blame her for that. The truth was that despite her ability, the Navy had indeed gone out of its way to assign SN officers to responsible slots aboard the RMN ships deployed to Sidemore Station, and some of them—no, be honest, *all* of them—were extremely short on experience, by Manticoran standards, for the positions they held. There was no way to avoid that. Unless they wanted the Sidemorians to have an entire navy which contained no officer above the rank of lieutenant, then the locals had no choice but to promote at a ridiculously rapid rate. Like the prewar Grayson Navy, the Sidemorians had acquired a skeletal core of Manticoran "loaners," but the bulk of their officer corps was being built from within, and assigning as many as possible of their more promising home-grown officers to Royal Navy ships was one way to transfer some of the much greater Manticoran experience to them.

Everyone knew that, and he'd been prepared to discover that Zahn was . . . less than totally qualified when he was first informed that she would be assigned to *LaFroye.* As it turned out, his worries had been unnecessary, as he'd realized within the first week after her arrival. That had been over six T-months ago, and his initial favorable impression of her had been amply confirmed over that period. Still, he had to admit that there were times when he felt rather more like her uncle than her CO. It was just that she was so damned *young.* He was more accustomed to junior-grade lieutenants her age than he was to lieutenant commanders, and it was difficult, sometimes, to keep that from showing, however competent the lieutenant commander in question might be. Which, he reminded himself a bit sternly, probably didn't do a thing to bolster her belief that she'd earned her position. Besides, he genuinely wanted to hear what she had to say. Young she might be, but he'd learned to respect her analytical abilities almost as much as her tactical skills, and he walked over to stand beside her station chair.

"No one really *knows* what they're planning, Commander," he said as he leaned over her shoulder to study the incidents displayed on her plot. "Certainly no one from ONI seems to have a clue! Nor, to be devastatingly honest about it, do I. Which is why I'd be interested in any hypotheses you might care to offer. You certainly couldn't do any worse job of reading their minds than the rest of us have been doing."

Zahn felt herself relax just a bit at the very slight twinkle in the captain's brown eyes. Then she glanced back at the data on her plot and frowned, this time thoughtfully.

"I suppose, Sir," she said slowly, "that it's possible they really are engaged in normal piracy-suppression operations."

"But you don't think they are," Ackenheil encouraged when she paused.

"No, Sir." She looked back up at him and shook her head. "Of course, I don't think anyone else really believes that's what's going on either, do they?"

"Hardly," Ackenheil agreed dryly.

There were two more incidents than there'd been the last time he checked, he noticed, and rubbed his chin while he considered them. He supposed he should be grateful the Imperial Andermani Navy had chosen to make a substantial effort to squash the operations of pirates in and around the region the RMN patrolled from its base in the Marsh System. God knew there'd been enough times he'd felt as if he needed to be in two or three places simultaneously to deal with the vermin. Ever since Honor Harrington had destroyed Andre Warnecke's "privateer" squadron in Marsh, no pirate in his right mind was going to come anywhere near Sidemore, but that hadn't prevented the run-of-the-mill attacks, murders, and general atrocities which were standard for Silesia along the fringe of Sidemore Station's area of responsibility. So whatever else he might think, he had to admit to feeling an undeniable relief as he watched the steady drop in pirate attacks, on planets, as well as merchant shipping, which the Andies' efforts had produced.

But welcome as that might be, it was also disturbing. The Andermani had been careful to tread lightly in the region after the Admiralty announced its intention to establish a fleet base in Marsh. A few Andermani officers Ackenheil had met hadn't bothered to disguise the resentment they'd felt over the Star Kingdom's treaty with the Republic of Sidemore. They'd obviously regarded it as one more example of Manticoran interference in an area they felt properly belonged to the Andermani Empire's sphere of interest. But whatever they might have felt, the Empire had made no formal protest, and the official Andie position was that anything which reduced lawlessness in Silesia was welcome.

The diplomats who said that lied in their teeth, and everyone knew it, but that had been the official position for almost nine

T-years. And during those same nine T-years, the Andie Navy had restricted its presence in and around the Marsh System to port visits by destroyers, interspersed occasionally with the odd division of light cruisers, and very rarely by individual heavy cruisers or battlecruisers. It had been enough to remind the Star Kingdom that the Empire also had an interest in the region without using forces heavy enough to be seen as some sort of provocative challenge to Manticore's presence.

But over the past few months, that seemed to be changing. There'd been only three Andie port calls during those months, and aside from one heavy cruiser of the new *Verfechter* class, only destroyers had actually visited Sidemore. But if the situation remained unchanged in the Marsh System itself, that was certainly not true elsewhere. It seemed that everywhere Ackenheil looked, Andermani patrols were suddenly picking off pirates, privateers, and other low-lifes, and they weren't using destroyers or light cruisers to do it with, either.

He leaned a bit closer to Zahn's plot and frowned as he read the data codes beside the two incidents he'd been unaware of.

"A battlecruiser division here at Sandhill?" he asked, crooking one eyebrow in surprise as he indicated a star in the Confederacy's Breslau Sector.

"Yes, Sir," Zahn confirmed, and pointed to the second new incident, in the Tyler System, near the northeastern border of the Posnan Sector. "And this one was apparently an entire squadron of heavy cruisers," she said.

"I didn't know they had this many cruisers in their entire navy," Ackenheil said ironically, waving at the widely scattered crimson icons. Three of them represented pirate interceptions by forces containing nothing heavier than a destroyer; all the rest marked operations which had involved cruisers or *battle*cruisers.

"They do seem to be turning up everywhere we look, Sir," Zahn agreed, and pulled at the lobe of her left ear in an "I'm thinking" gesture Ackenheil was pretty sure she didn't know she used.

"Which suggests what to you?" he pressed, returning to his original question.

"Which suggests, at an absolute minimum," she said in a crisper voice, lowering her hand from her ear and forgetting her diffidence as she grappled with the problem, "a very substantial redeployment of their available assets. I think sometimes we forget that the only Andermani ships we're hearing about are the ones which actually intercept someone, Sir. There are probably half a dozen ships, or even more, out there that we aren't hearing about for every one someone does tell us about."

"An excellent point," Ackenheil murmured.

"As to why they should redeploy this way just to catch pirates, though," Zahn went on with a tiny shrug, her dark eyes distant, "I can't think of any compelling operational reason for it, Skipper. It's not as if they'd suddenly started suffering particularly heavy losses among their merchies—or not that we've heard anything about, anyway. I checked the Intelligence reports to confirm that. And even if they have developed some sudden concern about pirates or privateers, why use battlecruisers?"

"Why not use them, if they've got them?" Ackenheil asked, slipping smoothly into the Devil's advocate role. "After all, they have to blood and train their ships somehow, and it's not as if they had any major wars to do it in. That's one of the reasons the RMN deployed some of its best crews and skippers out here before the war—to use anti-pirate operations as a tactical finishing school."

"That might make some sense, Sir," Zahn agreed. "But it doesn't fit their previous operational patterns. And I asked Tim to do some research for me."

She looked a question at Ackenheil, and he nodded. Her husband was a civilian analyst employed in Fleet Operations' Records Division in Marsh, and he was very highly thought of by Commodore Tharwan, who headed RecDiv. Which was one reason the captain was so interested in the lieutenant commander's opinion, he admitted to himself.

"He says that as far as ONI's database is aware, they've never committed anything as heavy as a battlecruiser division to routine anti-piracy ops," Zahn went on. "Records says that the only times they've used forces that heavy were when someone had managed to put together a force of pirates or privateers capable of carrying out at least squadron-level strikes, like Warnecke did." She shook her head and waved a hand at the red icons on her plot. "Nothing like that has been going on anywhere in the region they're operating across now, Skipper."

"So if they're operating outside their normal parameters, using heavier forces, despite the fact that threat levels have remained basically unchanged, that brings me back to my original question," Ackenheil said. "What *do* you think they're really up to?"

Zahn gazed at the plot for several silent seconds. The captain didn't think she even saw it, and he could almost physically feel the intensity with which she pondered. Whether she was thinking about the raw data or considering whether or not to tell him what she really thought was more than he could say, but he made himself wait patiently until she turned her head to look back up at him.

"If you want my honest opinion, Sir," she said quietly, "I think they want us to know they're transferring steadily heavier forces into Silesia. And I think they want us to know that they're conducting active operations—against pirates . . . for the moment— all along the periphery of our own patrol areas."

"And they want us to know that because—?" Ackenheil arched one eyebrow as he gazed down at her somber expression, and she drew a deep breath.

"It's only a gut feeling, Skipper, and I don't have a single bit of hard evidence I could use to support it, but I think they've decided it's time to press their own claims in the Confederacy."

Ackenheil's other eyebrow rose to join its fellow. Not in rejection of her theory, but in surprise that so junior an officer, even one whose ability he thought so highly of, should have come up with it. He'd considered the same possibility himself, and he wished he'd been able to dismiss it out of hand.

"Why do you think that? And why should they decide to push it at this particular moment?" he asked, curious about her reasoning.

"I guess one reason the thought has crossed my mind is that I'm from Sidemore," Zahn admitted, turning her gaze back to her plot. "We were never directly in the Andies' path, but before Duchess Harrington came through and rescued us from Warnecke and his butchers, the Empire was the only real interstellar power in our neck of the galaxy. We sort of got used to looking over our shoulders and wondering when the Emperor was going to make his move in Silesia's direction." She shrugged again. "It didn't really threaten us directly, because we didn't have anything anyone wanted badly enough to make it worth the Andies' while to take us over. But even as far off the beaten path as we were, we heard enough to know that the Empire has wanted to bite off chunks of the Confederacy for as long as anyone could remember."

"I can't argue with you there," Ackenheil said after a moment, remembering the intelligence reports he'd studied both before *LaFroye* deployed to Sidemore and since arriving. No one had officially suggested that the Andies might be contemplating making a move, however long-standing their ambitions in Silesia might have been, but he supposed it made sense for Zahn to consider the possibility very seriously. As she'd just pointed out, she was from the region herself, with a sensitivity to the nuances of its power structure, such as it was, that any outsider—even an outsider who served in the Royal Manticoran Navy—would have to work long and hard to match.

"As to why they might have decided that this was the right time to do something about it, Skipper," Zahn went on, "I can think of a couple of factors. The biggest one, though, is probably the way the Alliance has kicked the Peeps' butts. They don't think they have to worry about Haven coming through Manticore at them, anymore, and if they don't need a buffer zone any longer, they might not see any reason to go on being 'neutral' in our favor. And—"

She stopped speaking abruptly, and Ackenheil looked sharply down at the crown of her head. He started to prompt her to continue, then paused as he suddenly realized what she'd probably been about to say.

And now that we're downsizing the Fleet—like idiots—and we've gotten ourselves a Prime Minister who wouldn't recognize a principle if it bit him on the ass and a Foreign Secretary with a spine about as stiff as warm butter, they probably can't believe the opportunity we've handed them, he told himself sourly. *True enough, but* not *the sort of thing a Sidemorian exactly wants to say to her Manticoran skipper.*

"I see what you're getting at," he said aloud, after a few seconds. "I wish I could find some reason to disagree with you. Unfortunately, I can't."

Zahn looked back up at him, her expression anxious, and he shrugged.

"ONI hasn't gotten around to putting the pieces together as well as you have, Anna. Not yet. But I think they're going to."

"And what do we do about it, Sir?" the lieutenant commander asked softly.

"I don't know," Ackenheil admitted. He started to say something more, then shook his head with a small smile and turned away.

Zahn watched him go, and just as he had recognized what she'd left unsaid, she knew what he hadn't said. Any Sidemorian would have known, although no one she knew would have been tactless enough to say so to any of their Manticoran allies. All of them knew precisely what the Cromarty Government's policy would have been in the face of any Andermani effort to expand its territory into Silesia.

No one had a clue how the *High Ridge* Government might react . . . but they didn't expect it to be good.

CHAPTER EIGHT

Lady Catherine Montaigne, Countess of the Tor, stalked around her sitting room with all of her characteristic energy . . . and very little of her characteristic cheerfulness.

"*Damn* the lot of them!" she snarled over her shoulder to the slab-sided, broad-shouldered man seated motionlessly in his favorite armchair. In every way, they might have been expressly designed as physical opposites. She was at least fifteen centimeters taller than he was, and so slender she looked even taller than she actually was, while he was so broad that he appeared almost squat. She was golden-haired and blue-eyed; his hair was black, his eyes dark. She literally could not sit still, while his ability to sit motionless in thought frequently reminded an observer of a boulder of his own Gryphon granite. Her staccato speech patterns and blindingly fast changes of subject often bewildered those unprepared to keep pace with the speed of her thoughts; he was deliberate and disciplined to a fault in his own. And where she held one of the Star Kingdom's thirty oldest peerages, he was a Gryphon highlander, with all of the bred-in-the-bone hostility towards all things aristocratic which that implied.

And they were also lovers. Among other things.

"Don't tell me that you're surprised by their tactics, Cathy," he rumbled in a voice so deep it appeared to come from somewhere just south of his toenails. It was a remarkably mild voice, given

135

the speaker's obvious distaste for what it was saying. "Against someone like *Harrington*?" He laughed with absolutely no humor at all. "She's probably the one person they hate more than they hate you right now!"

"But this is so *despicable*, even for them, Anton," Lady Cathy shot back. "No, I'm not surprised—I'm just pissed off. No, not pissed off. I'm ready to go out and start removing body parts from the assholes. Preferably ones they're particularly fond of. Painfully. With a very dull knife."

"And if you can figure out a way to do it, I'll be delighted to help," he replied. "In the meantime, Harrington and White Haven are just going to have to fight their own battles. And it's not exactly as if they don't have anyone they can call on for support while they do."

"You're right," she admitted unhappily. "Besides, our track record isn't all that good, is it?" She grimaced. "I know damned well that Jeremy expected us to do better than we did, given what you managed to hack out of those idiots' files. I hate disappointing him—disappointing all of them. And I don't much like failing at anything, myself."

"You want me to believe that you expected them to just roll over?" he asked, and there was a hint of a twinkle in the dark eyes.

"No," she half-snarled at him. "But I did hope that we'd get more of the bastards nailed!"

"I understand what you're saying. But we did get convictions for over seventy percent of the names on my list. Given the timing, that's actually better than we had any right to expect."

"And if I'd come straight home by way of the Junction the way you'd wanted to, the timing wouldn't have mattered," she grated.

"Woman, we've been over this," Anton Zilwicki said in a voice as patient as his beloved mountains. "Neither one of us could have foreseen the Cromarty Assassination. If it hadn't been for that, we'd have been fine, and you were perfectly right about the need to get Jeremy off Old Earth." He shrugged. "I admit that I haven't spent as many years as deeply committed to the Anti-Slavery League as you have, but it's grossly unfair of you to blame yourself for spending three extra weeks getting home."

"I know." She stopped her pacing and stood gazing out the window for several taut moments, then drew a deep breath, straightened her shoulders, and turned to face him.

"I know," she repeated more briskly. "And you're right. Given the fact that that asshole High Ridge was in charge of the Government by the time we got home, we did do very well to get as many convictions as we did. Even Isaac admits that."

She grimaced again, and Zilwicki nodded. Isaac Douglas, somewhat to Zilwicki's surprise, appeared to have attached himself permanently to the countess. Zilwicki had more than half-expected Isaac to accompany Jeremy X, but he remained in Lady Cathy's service as combination butler and bodyguard. And, Zilwicki knew, as the countess' clandestine pipeline to the thoroughly proscribed organization known as "the Ballroom" and its escaped slave "terrorists."

He was also the favorite uncle, preceptor, and assistant protector of Berry and Lars, the two children Zilwicki had formally adopted after Helen rescued them on Old Earth. And a very reassuring presence for them Isaac was, too. And for Zilwicki, come to that.

"Of course," the countess continued, "he hasn't exactly told me so in so many words, but he would have told me if he'd thought otherwise. So I suppose he's probably about as satisfied as we could reasonably expect. Not that I think for a minute that he and the Ballroom—or Jeremy—are prepared to call it quits. Especially not since they know who was on the list and wasn't convicted."

She looked acutely unhappy as she finished her last sentence, and Zilwicki shrugged.

"You don't like killing." His rumbling bass was gentle yet implacable. "Neither do I. But I'm not going to lose any sleep over the sick bastards involved in the genetic slave trade—and neither should you."

"And neither *do* I," she said with a wan smile. "Not in the intellectual sense. Not in the philosophical sense, either. But much as I hate slavery and anyone who participates in it, there's still something deep down inside me that hates the administration of 'justice' without benefit of due process." Her smile turned even more wry. "You'd think that after all these years hanging around with bloodthirsty terrorists I'd've gotten over my squeamishness."

"Not squeamishness," Zilwicki corrected. "An excess of principle, perhaps, but principles are good things to have, by and large."

"Maybe. But let's be honest. Jeremy and I—and the Ballroom and I—have been allies for too many years for me to pretend I don't know exactly what he and his fellow 'terrorists' do. Or that

I haven't tacitly condoned it by working with them. So I can't quite escape the suspicion that at least part of my present . . . unhappiness stems from the fact that this time I'm afraid it's going to be happening on my own doorstep. Which seems more than a little hypocritical to me."

"That's not hypocrisy," he disagreed. "It's human nature. And Jeremy knows you feel that way."

"So what?" she asked when he paused.

"So I doubt he's going to do anything quite as drastic here in the Star Kingdom as you're afraid he might. Jeremy X isn't the sort to let anything stand between him and genetic slave peddlers or their customers. But he's also your friend, and even though we didn't get everyone on the list, the Star Kingdom is still a paragon of virtue where genetic slavery is concerned compared to places like the Silesian Confederacy and the Solarian League. I feel quite confident that he'll be able to keep himself busy for years with the Sillies and the Sollies who were also on the list without extending his hunt to Manticore. Especially if you and I manage to keep the pressure turned up on our domestic piglets without him turning all of them into ground sausage."

"You may have a point," she said after a thoughtful moment. "Mind you, you wouldn't have one if he didn't have a shopping list for those other places. And I'm not sure how successful we're going to be at keeping the pressure on now that High Ridge and that unmitigated asshole MacIntosh have managed to 'damage control' everything right under the carpet."

"Let's not forget New Kiev," Zilwicki replied, and this time the shifting plate tectonics of anger rumbled in his deep voice. The countess looked a question at him, and he growled bitterly. "Whatever anyone else might think, High Ridge and MacIntosh couldn't have pulled it off if she hadn't let them." Lady Cathy started to open her mouth, but his waving hand stopped whatever she'd meant to say. "I'm not saying they were stupid enough to actively involve her in any coverups or damage control strategy sessions. All I'm saying is that like every other fucking aristocrat supporting High Ridge, she's not about to do one single goddamned thing that might risk rocking the boat and letting Alexander form a government. Not if all she has to do is close her eyes to something as unimportant as genetic slavery!"

"You're right," the countess admitted after a moment, her

expression manifestly unhappy. Then she began to stalk around the apartment once again.

"I know people think I suffer from tunnel vision—those who don't call it monomania—where slavery is concerned," she said. "They're probably even right. But anyone who isn't outraged by it fails the litmus test for basic humanity. Besides, how can anyone talk about their support for civil rights, legal protections, social betterment, and all those other noble causes Marisa Turner preaches about so learnedly if they're willing to shut their eyes to a trade in human beings—in specifically designed and conditioned human beings—that violates all of those pious principles?"

Her blue eyes flashed, her fair cheeks glowed with outrage that was not at all feigned, and Anton Zilwicki leaned back in his chair to admire her afresh. "Lady Prancer." That was her friends' teasing nickname for her, and it was apt. There was certainly something of the highbred filly about her restless movements and explosive temperament. But behind the filly there was something else, something uncomfortably akin to the hunting hunger of a Sphinx hexapuma. Zilwicki was one of the very few people who'd been allowed to see both of them, and he found both equally attractive in their own very different ways.

"So you don't exactly see New Kiev as the ideal leader for the Liberal Party?" he inquired ironically, and she snorted bitterly in reply.

"If I'd ever had any doubts about it, they disappeared the instant she agreed to climb into bed with High Ridge," the countess declared roundly. "Whatever the short-term tactical advantages might be, the long-term consequences are going to be disastrous. For her and for the party both."

"You agree with me that sooner or later the wheels are bound to come off the High Ridge Government, then?"

"Of course they are!" She glowered at him. "What is this? Twenty Questions? I know you're a lot more interested in interstellar power politics than I am—at least where the slavery issue isn't a factor— but even I can see that those idiots are heading us right back into some stupid fucking confrontation with the Havenites. And that they're in the process of wrecking the Alliance before they do it. *And* that they're too goddamned blind even to see it coming! Or to realize the electorate isn't nearly as stupid as they think it is. When the shit does hit the fan, and the public finds out just how right White Haven and Harrington have been about our naval preparedness all along, there's going to be Hell to pay. And even the rank-and-file Liberals are going to realize that New Kiev's been High Ridge's willing political whore. They're going to look at all of the 'Building the Peace' social spending she's so busy congratulating herself over right now, and they're going to recognize it for exactly what it was. And they're going to understand how funneling all that money into her pet projects took it away from the Navy. And while we're on the subject of stupid, shitty political maneuvers, let's not overlook what she—and the rest of the Liberal leadership right along with her—are perfectly prepared to help High Ridge do to Harrington and White Haven. You think there's not going to be a backlash against *that* when everyone finally figures out what a put-up job it was? Please!"

She rolled her eyes in exasperation and folded her arms.

"There! Did I pass your little quiz?" she demanded.

Zilwicki chuckled as she bestowed one of her patented glares upon him. Then he nodded.

"With flying colors," he agreed. "But I wasn't really trying to find out whether or not you already knew water was wet. What I was doing was laying the groundwork for another question."

"Which is?" she asked.

"Which is," he said, and every bit of humor had vanished from his crumbling granite voice, "why the *fuck* you're letting her take your party down with her?"

"*I'm* letting her?! My God, Anton! I've been hammering away with everything I've got ever since I got back from Sol. Not that it's done any damned good. Maybe I could've accomplished more if High Ridge hadn't replaced Cromarty and I'd gotten my seat in the Lords back, but I've certainly done everything I can from outside Parliament! And," she added moodily, "made myself almost as unpopular again as I was the day they first excluded me, to boot."

"Excuses," Zilwicki said flatly, and she stared at him in disbelief. "Excuses," he repeated. "Damn it, Cathy, haven't you learned *anything* from all you managed to accomplish working with Jeremy and the rest of the Anti-Slavery League?"

"What the hell you talking about?" she demanded.

"I'm talking about your inability to separate yourself from the Countess of the Tor now that you're back home." She gazed at him in obvious incomprehension, and he sighed. "You're trying to play the game by their rules," he explained in a more patient voice. "You're letting who you are dictate the avenues available to you. Maybe that's inevitable given your title and family connections."

She started to interrupt, but he shook his head quickly.

"No, that wasn't a highlander's slam at all things aristocratic. And I certainly wasn't accusing you of being the sort of overbred cretin High Ridge or even New Kiev are. I'm only saying that you have an inherited position of power. The fact that you do is obviously going to shape the way you approach problems and issues, in that you're going to attack them from the powerbase you already have. Fair?"

"So far," she said slowly, studying his expression with intense speculation of her own. "And this is going someplace?"

"Of course it is. Just not to someplace an aristocrat might naturally think of," he amended with a slight smile.

"Like where?"

"Let me put it this way. We're both in agreement that the current Government is in a position to continue to exclude you from the House of Lords, effectively indefinitely, which means that your position as a peer actually doesn't give you any advantage at all. Put another way, the powerbase you have is all but useless under the current political circumstances. Yes?"

"That might be putting it a bit dramatically, but it's essentially accurate," she conceded, gazing at him in fascinated speculation.

One of the things she most loved about him was the depth of insight and analytical contemplation his controlled exterior hid from so many casual observers. He lacked her own darting quickness, her ability to isolate the critical elements of most problems almost by instinct. But by the same token, there were times that ability deserted or failed her, and when it did, she tended to try to substitute energy and enthusiasm for analysis. To batter her way through a problem, instead of taking it apart and reasoning out the best approach to it. That was one mistake Anton never made, and he often prevented her from making it, either.

"In that case, what you need is a *new* powerbase," he said. "One that your current base helps you acquire, perhaps, but one completely separate from it."

"Such as?" she asked.

"Such as a seat in the Commons," he told her simply.

"What?!" She blinked. "I can't hold a seat in the Commons—I'm a peer! And even if I weren't, the one thing High Ridge isn't going to allow is a general election, so I couldn't run for a seat even if I were eligible for one!"

"The Countess of the Tor can't hold a seat in the House of Commons," Zilwicki agreed. "But Catherine Montaigne could . . . if she weren't the Countess of the Tor anymore."

"I—" She started a quick response, then froze, staring at him in shock.

"That's what I meant about letting your inherited position of power stand in your way," he said gently. "I know you don't have any greater instinctive veneration for aristocratic privilege than I do—probably less, in your own way, because that's the background you come from and you know how often anything like veneration is completely undeserved. But sometimes I think you're still blinkered by the social stratum you grew up in. Hasn't it ever occurred to you that since they managed to emasculate your position as a peer by excluding you from the Lords, your title's actually been a hindrance rather than a help?"

"I—" She shook herself. "Actually, it never has," she said slowly. "I mean, in a way, it's just . . ."

"It's just who you are," he finished for her. "But it isn't, really, you know. Maybe it was before you left for Old Terra, but you've grown a lot since then. How important is it to you to be a peer of the realm?"

"More important than I'd like to admit," she confessed frankly after a long moment of thought, and shook her head. "Damn. Until you actually asked that question, I'd've said it didn't matter a good goddamn to me. But it does."

"I'm not surprised," he told her gently. "But let me ask you this. Is being Countess of the Tor as important to you as your principles?"

"No way in Hell," she said instantly, with a fierce certainty which startled even her just a bit.

"Then consider this scenario," he suggested, crossing his legs and settling even more comfortably into his chair. "A fiery noblewoman, consumed with the passion of her convictions, renounces her claim to one of the most respected and venerated titles of nobility in the entire Star Kingdom. Determined to fight for her principles, she sacrifices the privileged status of her birth in order to seek election—*election*, mind you—to the House of Commons because she's been excluded from the House of Lords because of those same convictions. And once elected, of course, she has a moral imprimatur she would never have enjoyed as the holder of an inherited title. She's paid an obvious price for her principles, given up of her own volition something no one could have taken from her, because it's the only way she can fight effectively for what she believes in. And unlike her aristocratic opponents, who are obviously fighting at least in part to maintain their own privileged positions under the *status quo*, she's started out by *giving up* her special privileges. Not to mention the fact that her successful election campaign demonstrates that she commands the popular support to get herself into Parliament on her own merits in the first place. Which none of them do. Or, at least, which none of them is prepared to risk finding out whether or not they do."

"I don't believe I quite recognize the self-sacrificing heroine of your little morality tale." She spoke dryly, but her blue eyes glowed. "And even if I did resign my title, I'd hardly be swearing some sort of self-sacrificing vow of poverty. I'd have to talk to my accountants to be sure, but right off the top of my head, I'd guess that less than twenty-five percent of the total Tor fortune is actually entailed. To be honest, well over half of the current family fortune came from Mother's side and has nothing at all to do with the title."

"I realize that, but somehow I wouldn't expect your brother to complain if you suddenly dumped the title on him," he said, even more dryly then she had, and she snorted. If Henry Montaigne suddenly found himself Earl of the Tor, he would equally suddenly find himself among the top ten percent of the Star Kingdom of Manticore's wealthiest subjects. Of course, *Cathy* Montaigne would still be among the top three or four percent, but that was another matter entirely.

"But even though giving up the title wouldn't exactly consign you to poverty and leave you living in the gutter," he continued, "it wouldn't be a purely symbolic sacrifice, either. People would recognize that. And it would let you turn what High Ridge and his kind have made a liability—your exclusion from the Lords—into an asset."

"Do you actually think I'd be able to accomplish more as a very junior MP than I can from where I am right now?"

"Yes," he said simply.

"But I wouldn't have any seniority, wouldn't qualify for any of the choice committee chairmanships."

"And precisely which committees in the Lords are you sitting on at this moment?" he asked sardonically, and chuckled when she made a face at him. "Seriously, Cathy," he went on more earnestly, "you could scarcely accomplish less politically sitting in the Commons than you can as a peer who's been denied her seat in the Lords. And the house you sit in won't have any effect one way or the other on the types of influence you have outside official government channels. Besides, the Commons' seniority rules are a lot less ironclad. You might be surprised at the access to useful committee assignments which could be open to you. Especially if the Centrists decide to look for common ground with you."

"And they probably would, wouldn't they?" she mused aloud, her expression thoughtful. "If nothing else, they'd see me as a potential wedge to split New Kiev and the party leadership further away from the malcontents like me."

"At the very least," he agreed. "And let's be honest here. One reason that they'd see you as a potential wedge is because that's precisely what you would be. In fact, it's the reason you'd be there in the first place."

She glanced at him sharply, and he chuckled without humor.

"Come on, Cathy! We both know Jeremy taught you to be honest with yourself where your objectives and tactics are concerned. Don't you want to remove New Kiev and her cronies from control of the party?"

"And aren't you a Crown Loyalist who'd love to see the Liberals cripple themselves in internecine internal warfare?" she shot back.

"It wouldn't exactly break my heart," he acknowledged cheerfully enough. "But by the same token, since I've come to know you, I've actually been forced to admit that not all Liberals are goddamned idiots. Which, I might add, was not an easy thing for me to accept. I suppose present company is responsible for seducing me—you should pardon the expression—into recognizing the possibility that not all of them have overaged oatmeal for brains.

"However that may be," he went on with a slight smile as she stuck out her tongue at him, "I've come to the conclusion that I can live with a lot of the sorts of things you and Liberals like you believe in. We'll probably never agree on everything, but there's a lot to be said for a society where merit trumps bloodlines. I don't have a lot of use for most of the social-interventionist, lack-of-reality economic crap that comes along as part of the package with most Liberals, but then, neither do you, do you?"

"You know I don't."

"Well then." He shrugged. "As I see it, if you're able to influence the party into pursuing goals compatible with the ones I favor anyway, then there's no reason I shouldn't work with you—or even other Liberals. But as you suggested a few minutes ago, there's not much chance of New Kiev and her bunch climbing out of bed with that unmitigated bastard High Ridge anytime soon. So if I want to work with *any* Liberals, I have to try to put someone like you in charge of them." He grinned at her. "You see? Nothing but pure, unadulterated, calculating self-interest on my part."

"Sure it is." She snorted, then stood in uncharacteristic stillness for several heartbeats while she thought it over.

"This is all very fascinating, Anton," she said finally. "But even if this entire ambitious scenario you've mapped out for me were workable, it would still depend on High Ridge calling elections. Which means that however interesting the possibilities are, I can't do anything about them. Probably not for years, the way things are going right now."

"I agree that there's not much chance High Ridge is going to call a general election any sooner than he has to," Zilwicki agreed calmly. "But I've been doing a little quiet research. And it seems that the Member of Parliament for the Borough of High Threadmore right here in Landing has just been offered a very lucrative position with one of the major Solarian banking houses. If he accepts it, he'll have to relocate to the League. The only reason he hasn't already said yes is that he takes his responsibilities as a member of the old Liberal Party seriously, and he's extremely unhappy with the way New Kiev and the party leadership have decided to play fast and loose with their principles in the name of political advantage. According to my sources, which include the gentleman in question, he and his family could certainly use the additional income the new position would provide, but he feels he has a moral responsibility to himself and to his constituents to stay where he is and try to prevent things from getting still worse.

"Now, if he were to accept the banking job, he'd be required to resign his seat in Parliament. High Threadmore wouldn't like that, because a majority of the borough's voters are also members of the old Liberal Party, and they're no happier with their present party leadership than he is. But under the Constitution, his resignation would automatically trigger a special election to refill his seat within a maximum of two months. That's an absolute requirement, one not even High Ridge could prevent or defer, time of war or no time of war. And if you were to register as a candidate for his seat, and if he were to give you his enthusiastic endorsement and actively campaign for you, and if your campaign strategy emphasized the fact that you've renounced one of the most prestigious peerages in the entire Star Kingdom in order to seek election as a mere commoner as a matter of principle . . ."

He shrugged, and her eyes slowly widened as she stared at him.

CHAPTER NINE

"**N**o."

Queen Elizabeth III looked into Honor's eyes and shook her head fiercely.

"Please, Elizabeth," Honor began. "Right now my presence is doing more harm than good. If I go home to—"

"You *are* home," Elizabeth interrupted sharply, her warm mahogany face hard, and the treecat on her shoulder flattened his ears in reaction to his person's anger. That anger wasn't directed at Honor, but that made it no weaker. Worse, Honor could taste it almost as clearly as Ariel could, and for just an instant she wished she had matching ears that she could flatten in response. The whimsical thought flickered briefly through her brain, then vanished, and she drew a lung-stretching breath before she spoke again, as calmly as she could.

"That wasn't what I meant," she said, then closed her mouth once more as Elizabeth waved one hand in a chopping-off gesture.

"I know it wasn't." The Queen grimaced and shook her head. "I didn't mean for it to sound that way, either," she went on a bit contritely. "But I don't apologize for the thought behind it. You're a Manticoran, Honor, and a peer of the realm, and you deserve one *hell* of a lot better than this!"

She gestured at the wall-mounted HD, and against her will,

Honor followed the gesture to where Patrick DuCain and Minerva Prince, hosts of the weekly syndicated political talk show *Into the Fire* were grilling a panel of journalists in front of huge holograms of Honor's face . . . and White Haven's.

The sound was switched off, a small mercy for which Honor was profoundly grateful, but she didn't really have to hear it. She tried to remember who it was back on Old Terra who was supposed to have said that something was "*déjà vu* all over again." She couldn't, but that didn't matter either. She didn't have to recall names to know precisely how whoever had rendered that masterpiece of redundancy must have felt, because watching DuCain and Prince brought back agonizing memories of the vicious partisan confrontations which had followed the First Battle of Hancock. She'd been one of the focuses for those bruising exchanges, too, so she supposed she should be used to it by now. But she wasn't. No one could grow accustomed to it, she thought bitterly.

"What I may or may not deserve has very little bearing on what's actually happening, Elizabeth," she said, her voice still calm and level even as she felt the stiff tension in Nimitz's long, wiry body on her own shoulder. "Nor does it have any bearing on the damage being done while this goes on."

"Perhaps not," Elizabeth conceded. "But if you retire to Grayson now, they win. Worse, everyone will know they won. And besides," her voice dropped and her ramrod-straight spine seemed to sag ever so slightly, "it probably wouldn't make any difference, anyway."

Honor opened her mouth again, then closed it. Not because she was prepared to give up the argument, but because she was afraid Elizabeth was right.

Every insider in Parliament, Lords and Commons alike, recognized exactly what had been done to her, and it didn't matter at all. Hayes' initial column had been followed quickly by the first op-ed piece, and that first "respectable" commentary had been the polished, meticulously crafted opening salvo in a carefully planned campaign. It was the first picador's dart, placed with impeccable skill, and the fact that the High Ridge Government was an alliance of so many parties gave a disastrously broad base to the orchestrated attack. The Manticoran public was accustomed to vociferous exchanges between party organs and spokespeople, but this time the party lines were blurred. No, not blurred. The real problem was that the divisions were even clearer than usual . . . and that this time every single major party except the Centrists and Crown Loyalists was on the other side. The condemnation came from across the entire traditional political spectrum, and that gave it a dangerous degree of legitimacy in all too much of the public's eyes. Surely so many people of such diverse views would never agree on anything which wasn't self-evidently true!

That first column had appeared in the *Landing Guardian*, the flagship newsfax of the Manticoran Liberal Party, under the byline of Regina Clausel. Clausel had been a newsy for almost fifty T-years . . . and an operative of the Liberal Party for over thirty-five. She maintained her credentials as a reporter and ostensibly independent-minded political commentator, but she was recognized in professional media circles as one of the Liberals' primary front people. She was also widely respected in those same circles for her ability, despite the way she'd subordinated it to the requirements of her ideology. Effectiveness was far more important than intellectual integrity, after all, Honor thought bitterly.

What mattered in this case, however, was her sheer visibility. She was a regular on four different issue-oriented HD programs, her column appeared in eighteen major and scores of lesser 'faxes, and her informal, comfortable prose and calm affability before the cameras had captured a broad readership and viewership. Many of her readers weren't Liberals—indeed, a fair percentage were actually Centrists, who read her columns or watched her on HD because she seemed reassuring evidence that even someone one disagreed with politically could have a brain. Her well-crafted and presented arguments made even readers who disagreed with her think, and if one was inclined to agree with her already, they often seemed to sparkle with their own brand of brilliance.

She was also one of the very few political columnists outside the Centrist party who had not savaged Honor over her duels with Denver Summervale and Pavel Young. Honor wasn't certain why, since the Liberal Party was officially dedicated to stamping out the custom of dueling. That was one of the few planks of their formal platform with which she found herself in agreement, whatever her bloodthirsty reputation might be. The suppression of the genetic slave trade was another, but she felt even more strongly—on a personal level—about the Code Duello. If duels had

never been legal, Paul would never have been killed . . . and Honor
wouldn't have been forced to use the same custom as the only way
she could punish the men who'd planned his death. The fact that
she knew a predator part of her personality might find the code
all too apt to her needs under certain circumstances was another
reason she would have preferred to see it stamped out. She didn't
like wondering if she could trust herself in that regard.

According to William Alexander's sources, the most probable
reason for Clausel's silence on that occasion was actually quite
simple: she'd hated the Young clan for decades. Much of that hatred
apparently sprang from ideological antipathy, but there also seemed
to be an intensely personal element to it. That must make her
present alliance with the Conservative Association even more
awkward for her than for most Liberals, but no one could have
guessed it from how skillfully she'd played her assigned role.

She never once openly condemned either Honor or White
Haven. Indeed, she spent over a third of her total word count
castigating *Hayes* for the customary sleaziness of his regular
"Tattler's Tidbits" column and another third pleading with their
fellows of the press not to leap to judgment on the basis of such
a suspect source. And then, having established her own professionalism, integrity, skepticism, and total sympathy for the sacrificial victims, she spent the final third of the column giving
Hayes' sleaze the deadly tang of legitimacy.

Honor could remember the closing paragraphs of that dagger-
edged column word for word, even now.

> "It goes without saying that the private lives of any
> of this Kingdom's citizens, however prominent, ought to
> be just that: private. What transpires between two con-
> senting adults is their business, and no one else's, and
> it would be well for all of us of the press to remember
> that as this story unfolds. Just as it is incumbent upon
> all of us to remember the highly questionable source of
> these initial, completely unconfirmed allegations.
>
> "Yet at the same time, distasteful as any of us must
> find it, there are questions which must be asked.
> Unpleasant conjectures which must be examined, if only
> to refute them. We have made icons of our heroes. We
> have elevated them to the highest levels of our respect

and admiration for their amply demonstrated courage and skill in the crucible of combat against the enemies of all we believe in and value. Whatever the final outcome of this story, it cannot in any way diminish the tremendous contributions made to the war against Havenite aggression by the man who commanded Eighth Fleet and brought the People's Navy to its knees, or by the woman whose superb courage and tactical skill have won her the nickname of 'the Salamander.'

"Yet true though that is, are courage and skill enough? What demands are appropriate for us to place upon heroes whom we have also made political leaders and statesmen? Does the ability to excel in one arena transfer to excellence in another, completely different type of struggle? And when it comes to matters as fundamental as character, fidelity to one's sworn word, and loyalty to the important people in one's life, does heroism in war transfer to heroic stature as a human being?

"Most troubling, of course, will be those who insist that we may see the greater in the lesser. That in the personal choices and decisions of our lives, we see the true reflection of our public choices and positions. That as we succeed—or fail—against the measure of our inner, personal codes and values, so we reveal our ability to successfully bear—or falter under—the weight of our public responsibilities.

"And what of the question of judgment? What of the charges, which will inevitably be made, that any public figure, any statesman, who might have placed himself or herself in such a false position by such indiscretions has demonstrated a woeful lack of judgment which cannot be overlooked in one responsible for charting the policies and future of the Star Kingdom of Manticore? It is very early—far too early—for us to rush to decision on any of those troubling questions. Indeed, one is tempted to point out that it is really far too early even to ask such questions, for there is as yet no confirmation that the ugly rumors contain any shred of truth.

"And yet those questions *are* being asked, however quietly, however discreetly, in the backs of our minds. And at the end of the day, fair or not, reasonable or not, we must find some answer for them, if only the conclusion that they should never have been asked in the first place. For we are speaking of our leaders, of a man and woman venerated by all of us in time of war, whose judgment and whose ability to lead us in time of peace we have made critical to the prosperity and security of our Kingdom.

"Perhaps there is a lesson here. None of us is perfect, all of us have made mistakes, and even our heroes are but human. It is neither fair nor just to insist that anyone excel in *all* areas of human endeavor. That anyone be as capable in matters of state as he or she is in the harsh furnace of war. In the end, perhaps we have elevated our heroes too high, raised them to a pinnacle no mere mortal should be expected to scale. And if, in the end, they have fallen from the heights like the Icarus of ancient legend, is the fault theirs, or is it ours?"

Clausel's column had been devastating less for what it said than for the ground it had prepared, and the columns which followed— written by Conservatives, by Progressives, by other Liberals, and by Independents personally committed to the Government for whatever reason—drove their roots deep into that well-tilled soil with a damning nonpartisan aura that was as convincing as it was false.

Honor had released her own statement, of course, and she knew William Alexander had used his own press contacts to do as much preemptive spadework as he could before the story broke, as well. She'd done some of her own, for that matter, and even appeared, not without a certain carefully concealed trepidation, on *Into the Fire* herself. The experience had not been one of the most enjoyable of her life.

Neither Prince, a lifelong Liberal, nor DuCain, a card-carrying Crown Loyalist, had ever attempted to conceal their own political affiliations. That was one of the things which made their program so widely watched. But for all their political differences, they respected one another, and they made a conscientious effort to extend that same respect to their guests and reserve their own polemics for their closing segment. But that didn't mean they refrained from hardhitting questions.

"I read your statement of the fifteenth with considerable interest, Your Grace," Prince had observed on camera. "I noted that you acknowledge a 'close personal and professional relationship' with Earl White Haven."

"Actually," Honor had corrected calmly, fingers stroking Nimitz' ears as he lay in her lap and looked far calmer than he was, "I didn't 'acknowledge' anything, Minerva. I *explained* that I have a close personal and professional relationship with both Earl White Haven and his brother, Lord Alexander."

"Yes, you did." Prince had accepted the correction gracefully. "Would you care to take this opportunity to explain that a bit more fully for our viewers?"

"Of course, Minerva." Honor had looked directly at the live camera and smiled with the ease she had learned to project. "Both the Earl and I support the Centrist Party, and Lord Alexander, since Duke Cromarty's death, has been the leader of that party. Given the Centrists' majority in the Commons and the dominance of the current Government's parties in the Lords, it was inevitable that the three of us should become close political allies. In fact, that relationship has been the subject of speeches and debates in the Lords for almost three T-years now . . . as has the strength of our opposition to the High Ridge Government's policies."

"But the thrust of the present controversy, Your Grace," DuCain had observed, "is that your relationship with Earl White Haven goes beyond a purely political alliance."

"And it does," Honor had admitted calmly. "Earl White Haven and I have known one another for over fifteen T-years now, ever since the Battle of Yeltsin. I've always had the deepest professional respect for him. As, I believe, just about anyone not blinded by petty jealousy and personal animosity must."

DuCain's eyes had flickered with amusement at her none-too-veiled reference to Sir Edward Janacek, and she'd continued in the same calm tone.

"I'm pleased to say that after our initial meeting at Yeltsin's Star, and particularly in the three or four years preceding my capture by the People's Navy, professional respect had the opportunity to turn into personal friendship, as well. A friendship which has only been deepened by how closely we've worked on a political basis in the Lords since my return from Hades. I regard him not simply as a colleague but as a close personal friend, and neither of us has ever attempted to suggest otherwise. Nor will we."

"I see." DuCain had glanced at Prince, handing the focus smoothly back to her, and she'd nodded understanding of her own.

"Your statement also denied that you were anything more than friends and colleagues, Your Grace. Would you care to expand on that?"

"There isn't a great deal to expand upon, Minerva." Honor had shrugged. "The entire present furor amounts to no more than the repetition and endless analysis of unsubstantiated allegations from a completely unreliable source. A man, not to put too fine a point upon it, who makes his living from sensationalism and is none too shy about creating it out of whole cloth when reality doesn't offer him a sufficient supply. And who refuses—out of 'journalistic ethics'—to 'compromise his integrity' by naming his sources, since, of course, they spoke to him only on conditions of confidentiality."

Her soprano voice had been completely level. The fingers caressing Nimitz's ears had never strayed from their gentle rhythm. But her eyes had been very, very cold, and Prince had seemed to recoil ever so slightly.

"That may be the case, Your Grace," she'd said after a moment, "but the strength of the controversy seems to be growing, not ebbing. Why do you think that is?"

"I suspect that it's partly human nature," Honor had replied. What she'd wanted to say was: *Because the High Ridge Government—with your precious New Kiev's connivance—is deliberately orchestrating it as a smear campaign, you idiot!* But, of course, she couldn't. Charges of deliberately falsified smear campaigns had been the first refuge of the guilty for so long that resorting to them now would only have convinced a huge chunk of the public that the accusations must, in fact, be true. After all, if they weren't, the accused would simply have produced the proof instead of resorting to that tired old tactic, wouldn't they?

"There's an inevitable, and probably healthy, tendency to continuously test the character of those in positions of political power or influence," Honor had said instead. "A tendency to assume the worst because it's so important that we not allow ourselves to be taken in by manipulators and cretins who deceive us into believing they're better than they are.

"That, unfortunately, can have its downside when reckless, unsubstantiated charges are flung about, because no one can prove a negative. I've made my own position as clear as I possibly can. I have no intention of belaboring the point, nor do I feel that endless protestations of innocence on my part—or Earl White Haven's, for that matter—would be appropriate or serve any useful purpose. We can both insist endlessly that there's no shred of truth to the allegations that we've ever been physically intimate, but we can't *prove* it. At the same time, however, I would point out that my statement also invited anyone who has evidence to prove anything to the contrary to bring that evidence forward. No one has."

"But according to Mr. Hayes," DuCain had pointed out in return, "that's because Earl White Haven's security and—especially—your own is too efficient at . . . suppressing unpleasant evidence."

"My armsmen are extremely efficient at protecting me from physical threats, as they demonstrated right here in Landing, at Regiano's, several years ago," Honor had replied. "And they do serve my security functions as Steadholder Harrington, both on Grayson and here on Manticore, as well. I suppose that if I really wanted them to, they could be quite effective in suppressing or concealing evidence. But Mr. Hayes claims to have spoken to people who say they have firsthand knowledge of the alleged improprieties. Unless he's prepared to accuse me of resorting to threats of physical violence to silence those witnesses, I fail to see how my armsmen could prevent him from bringing them forward. And if I were prepared to resort to threats of violence, why in the world wouldn't I have started with him instead of these supposed witnesses of his?"

Her smile had been thin, but no one had been likely to miss its implications . . . or forget the ghosts of Denver Summervale and Pavel Young.

"The fact is, of course, that there have been no threats," she had continued with another shrug. "Nor will there be, although Mr. Hayes will undoubtedly continue to use the 'threat' of my armsmen to explain his failure to produce witnesses. In the meantime, however, I believe we've dealt with the matter as thoroughly as it deserves, and, as I say, I have no intention of belaboring my denial of the allegations."

"Of course, Your Grace," Prince had murmured. "In that case,

I wonder if you'd care to comment on the proposed naval budgets? For example . . ."

The rest of the interview had dealt exclusively with legitimate questions of politics and policy, and Honor felt confident she'd handled that portion of it well. She was less confident that anyone had bothered to notice. All of the post-interview analysis—including, unfortunately, the "Point-Counterpoint" commentary with which DuCain and Prince always closed their program—had completely ignored it to concentrate once again on the far more interesting scandal. According to William Alexander's pollsters and analysts, she'd scored a few points with the interview—even won a slight opinion swing in her favor. But it hadn't been enough to stem the tide in the long run, and the other side had attacked with redoubled fury.

They didn't have it all their own way, of course. Indeed, Honor was surprised to find half a dozen prominent Liberals and even one or two Conservative commentators who genuinely sought to disassociate themselves from the witch hunt. A part of her was ashamed when she recognized her surprise for what it was. Realized she'd become so cynical about the supporters of the High Ridge Government that the very thought that any of them might possess true integrity was astonishing to her. But only a part of her felt that, and as the tempo increased those voices of reason simply disappeared—not silenced, but drowned out and pounded under by the carefully conducted orchestra of innuendo and accusation.

Nor had she been devoid of other defenders. Catherine Montaigne, in the midst of a campaign which pitted her against her own party's leadership, had come out swinging. Her scathing denunciation of the tactics being employed had been downright vicious, nor had she shrunk from identifying New Kiev and other senior members of the Liberal Party as accomplices in what she openly defined as a smear campaign. Ironically, even as the party leadership turned on her in fury for her temerity, it was actually helping her with the voters of High Threadmore. But that was one isolated borough, where people were actually listening to what was said in the course of a fiercely contested election, and not simply the sound and fury frothing on the surface.

Klaus and Stacey Hauptman had also come out strongly in her support, although there'd been little they could actually do. Stacey had made it clear the Hauptman resources were prepared to stand behind her, but to be honest, the Hauptman fortune, vast as it was, would not have added materially to the political war chest Honor could produce out of her own resources. Their private investigators (and also, though she had no intention of mentioning it to anyone, including William Alexander, Anton Zilwicki), however, had delved as deeply as the law permitted—and perhaps even a little deeper, in some instances—into Hayes' background and his files. That was one way they *could* help, because it allowed Honor to keep her own security people scrupulously away from the scandalmonger. But whoever was orchestrating Hayes' security was obviously very good at her job and had money to burn. Zilwicki's theory, which Elijah Sennett, the Hauptman Cartel's chief of security, shared was that the person doing that job was Countess North Hollow. Somehow, that didn't surprise Honor a bit.

Unfortunately, Manticoran slander and libel laws, while harder hitting than many, had their own loopholes. The most important one was that the law recognized a journalist's right to maintain the confidentiality of her sources and set a very high hurdle for plaintiff demands that those sources' identities be revealed. As long as Hayes restricted himself to reporting that his "sources" suggested that Honor and Hamish were lovers and never once said that he himself claimed they were, he stayed one thin millimeter on the safe side of the libel laws. Honor had done her dead level best to goad him into making that fatal assertion, but he'd refused to be drawn into that error. She could still sue for slander and, probably, win, but the trial would stretch out for years (at least), and however monumental the damages awarded might be in the end, it would have no impact on the current political situation . . . except to convince people that she was desperate to shut his mouth any way she could.

Fortunately, perhaps, the Code Duello also specifically exempted journalists from being challenged on the basis of published reporting or commentary. It would have been possible to contrive some other basis for a duel, perhaps, but she had to agree with William; in the end, it would only make the damage even worse. Besides, Hayes had obviously taken careful note of what had happened to Pavel Young. There was no way in the universe he was going to place himself in any position where Honor might possibly challenge him.

So there was simply no practical way to staunch the flow of

rumors which fueled the corrosive speculation of the Government commentators and their supporters.

The Centrist columnists, many of them just as fiercely partisan as any Liberal or Conservative, fired back desperately. But the assaults came from too many directions, were conducted with too much skill, and here and there individual defenders began to fall silent. One or two who'd been expected to defend her and White Haven never really seemed to make a serious attempt, and she knew William was noting who those silent voices belonged to. Not simply to punish them for their lack of support later, but because he wondered why they were silent. Over the decades, there had been persistent rumors about the Earls of North Hollow and their ability to manipulate allies and opponents alike by judicious use of the secrets contained within their files. Which was why Alexander wondered if perhaps there was something he should know about those who were silent so conveniently to Stefan Young's advantage.

Yet in the end, all of the Centrist efforts, and even the direct support of the Queen herself, had proved insufficient. The crippling darts had been placed too skillfully. Honor knew she and White Haven continued to enjoy a solid core of support among Manticoran voters, but she also knew that support had eroded heavily. It couldn't affect their seats in the Lords, but the storm of public criticism over their alleged infidelities was reflected in a significant drop in voter support for their party allies in the Commons. They had been transformed from assets in both houses into liabilities in the house where it really mattered, the one High Ridge and his allies didn't already control.

Bad as it was for White Haven, it was even worse for Honor. For all his continuing vigor, Hamish Alexander was one hundred and three T-years old, almost fifty T-years older than she was. In a society with prolong, where life spans would be as much as three T-centuries, that gap meant very little. But Hamish was from the very first generation of Manticoran prolong recipients. Most first- and second-generation prolong recipients had grown to at least young adulthood surrounded by pre-prolong parents and grandparents, uncles and aunts. Their fundamental attitudes towards what age meant, and particularly towards the significance of differences in age, had been formed in a society which had not yet developed a true acceptance for how long people, themselves included, were now likely to live.

Worse, perhaps, the earlier, less advanced generations of the prolong therapies stopped the physical aging process at a later stage, cosmetically, at least. So, as a first-generation recipient, Hamish's black hair was liberally threaded with silver, his face more deeply graven by character lines and crows feet. In a pre-prolong society, he might have been taken for a vigorous man in his mid-forties or very early fifties. But Honor was a third-generation recipient. Physically, she was no more than into her late twenties, and so for many of those following the story, she was the "younger woman." The Jezebel. In their eyes, his "betrayal" of Lady White Haven after so many years of unwavering fidelity could only have resulted from the way she had tempted and systematically pursued him.

The one thing for which she was truly grateful at the moment was that she'd managed to convince both her parents to stay safely on Grayson. It would have been bad enough if her father had been in the Star Kingdom, because as gentle and compassionate a man as Alfred Harrington was, Honor knew perfectly well from whom she had inherited her own temper. Very few people had ever seen her father actually lose his temper; of those who had, not all had survived the experience, although that had been in his own days of naval service, and he seldom discussed it even with her.

But her mother would have been worse. *Far* worse. On Allison Chou Harrington's birth world of Beowulf, public opinion would have laughed itself silly at the hysterical thought that matters of the heart were the business of anyone except the individuals actually involved. The nature of the Alexanders' marriage vows would have weighed heavily in the scale of Beowulf opinion, but the Beowulfers would have concluded, with healthy rationality, that if the individuals in question—*all* the individuals in question—were prepared to modify those vows, that was their own affair. In any case, the notion that any of it could have any impact on Honor's public responsibilities would have been ludicrous.

Allison Harrington, despite almost a T-century as a citizen of the Star Kingdom, remained very much a Beowulfer in that respect. And Honor's mother. Her recent letters to Honor radiated a bare-clawed ferocity which was almost frightening, and Honor shuddered every time she thought of Allison loose on something like *Into the Fire*. Or, even worse, in the same room as Regina Clausel. Her mother might be tiny, but so were treecats.

✧   ✧   ✧

That thought brought her back to the present, and she looked up at her Queen and sighed.

"I don't know, Elizabeth," she said, and her own voice sounded flat and defeated to her. Her shoulders sagged, and she scrubbed her eyes wearily with her right hand. "I just don't know *what* might help anymore. Maybe going to Grayson would be a mistake, but all I know for certain is that every day I stay here and appear in the House of Lords seems to make it worse."

"It's my fault," Elizabeth told her sadly. "I should have managed this whole thing better. Willie tried to tell me, but I was too angry, too badly hurt to listen. I needed Allen Summervale to shake some sense into me, and he was dead."

"Elizabeth—" Honor began, but the Queen shook her head.

"I should have held onto my temper," she said. "Should have tried sweet reason until I could find the issue to split them up instead of declaring war against them and driving them together!"

"Whatever you should or shouldn't have done is beside the point now," Honor said gently. "Personally, I don't think there ever was any 'wedge issue' you could have used to break them up. Not with the threat of the San Martino peers hanging over them."

"Then I should have gone the whole nine meters," Elizabeth said bitterly. "I should have said damn the constitutional crisis and refused to accept High Ridge as my Prime Minister. Let them try to govern without the Crown's support!"

"That would have flown in the face of every constitutional precedent we have," Honor shot back in her defense.

"So what? Precedents can be modified or replaced!"

"In the middle of a war?" Honor challenged.

"A war we were winning . . . until I let those unmitigated *bastards* accept Saint-Just's 'truce'!" Elizabeth snapped.

"Stop it, Elizabeth!" Honor half-glared at her monarch. "You can second-guess yourself forever, and it won't change a thing. You were like a captain in the middle of a battle. She has to decide what to do *now*, while the missiles and the beams are still flying. Anyone can sit down after the fact and see exactly what she ought to have done. But she had to make her choices *then*, with what she knew and felt at the time, and you didn't know how the war was going to end. And you certainly didn't know a High Ridge Government would use the truce talks to avoid a general election!

"Of course you could have provoked a showdown. But you can't foretell the future and you're not a mind reader. So you chose not to risk completely paralyzing our government when you didn't know how the war would end, and then High Ridge mousetrapped us all with these unending truce talks of his. No one's ever said he and Descroix and New Kiev don't understand how domestic politics work, especially the dirty variety."

"No. No, they haven't," Elizabeth agreed finally, and sighed. "I wish the Constitution gave me the authority to dissolve Parliament and call new elections myself."

"So do I," Honor said. "But it doesn't, so you can't. Which brings us back to me. Because unlike you, High Ridge can call for new elections whenever he decides to, and if he can use Hamish and me to keep this bloodfest alive long enough, he may be able to push the public opinion polls far enough in his favor to decide the time is right."

"Maybe you're right," Elizabeth conceded, obviously against her will. "But even if you are, I don't think going 'home' to Grayson is the answer, either, Honor. Bad enough that it would look like they'd run you out of town, but domestic politics aren't all we have to worry about here, are they?"

"No." Honor shook her head, because this time, the Queen had a point.

The Star Kingdom's mores were essentially liberal, and Honor and Hamish's "crime" in Manticoran eyes was that any affair between them would have violated the sanctity of a personal oath White Haven had chosen to swear in a particular sacrament of marriage. Other religions and denominations accepted other, less restrictive versions of marriage, and each of them was just as legally binding and just as morally acceptable in the eyes of society as a whole. In many ways, that made his alleged offense even worse, because he had voluntarily bound himself to a particular, intensely personal union with his wife when there'd been no social or legal requirement that he do so. If he'd now chosen to offer his love to another woman, then he had evaded a personal responsibility he'd chosen freely to accept. That was bad enough, but on Grayson, where there actually was—or had until very recently been—a universal religious and social code and a single institution of marriage, the damage was even worse.

What surprised Honor about the Graysons' reaction wasn't its strength, but the fact that such a small percentage of them put any stock at all in the allegations. She'd thought, especially after her relationship with Paul, that most of the population would be ready to believe the worst and to condemn her for it. But the reverse was true, and it had taken her a while to realize why that was.

White Haven enjoyed immense public respect on Grayson in his own right, yet that was almost beside the point. It was Honor who mattered, and they knew her. It was really that simple. They actually knew her there, and they remembered that she'd never denied she and Paul had been lovers, never tried to pretend she was anyone but who she was. Even those who continued to hate her for who she was knew she would have refused to deny the truth, and because of that, they recognized the lie when they heard it.

Which was precisely why the damage was even worse. The Graysons weren't angry at her over any allegations of impropriety which they knew were false; they were furious at Manticore for allowing those allegations to be made. They saw the entire agonizing ordeal as a public insult and humiliation to the woman who had twice saved their world from conquest, and at least once from nuclear bombardment by religious fanatics. Honor had always felt horribly embarrassed by the Graysons' unabashed hero worship of her, not least because she felt it denigrated the sacrifices made by so many others in the battles she'd fought at Yeltsin's Star. But her worst nightmares had never envisioned anything like this.

Grayson's attitude towards the Star Kingdom had shifted dangerously over the last three T-years. There were still immense reservoirs of gratitude, admiration, and respect for the Royal Navy, for the Centrists, and—especially—for Queen Elizabeth, herself. But there was also a deep, seething rage directed at the Kingdom's current government and the arrogant fashion in which it had arbitrarily and unilaterally accepted Oscar Saint-Just's truce offer when unequivocal victory had been within the Alliance's grasp. That decision was widely regarded as a betrayal of all of the Star Kingdom's allies, and especially of Grayson, which had made by far the greatest contribution—and sacrifices—of all those allies.

Nor had High Ridge's subsequent policy mitigated that outrage in any way. It was as obvious to Grayson as it was to the Havenites themselves that High Ridge and Descroix had no intention of negotiating in good faith. There might be different interpretations of the reasons for that, but recognition of their duplicity was virtually universal. High Ridge hadn't made things any better by continuing as he had begun, simply announcing his decisions to those who were supposed to be his treaty partners rather than consulting with them and acting in concert. Partly, Honor suspected, that insensitivity resulted from his intense focus on his purely domestic concerns, but it was also an inescapable reflection of his own personality. He considered Manticoran yeomen and commoners his infinite inferiors, and *foreign* commoners, by definition, were even less worthy of the expenditure of his precious time.

Benjamin IX and his Council, as well as a working majority of the Grayson Keys, recognized the unique and dangerous balance of political power within the Star Kingdom. They knew what was happening, and they were no strangers to complex internal political battles of their own. Yet even with that knowledge, it was difficult for them to restrain their anger and to remember to direct it against High Ridge and his cronies, rather than at the Star Kingdom as a whole. For the elected members of the Conclave of Steaders—and especially for the vast bulk of the Grayson population, who were not only less "sophisticated" but also less fully informed about the ramifications of which Benjamin was only too well aware—it was even more difficult.

And now the same people who'd already infuriated Grayson public opinion had falsely and publicly attacked their greatest planetary hero, who was also the second ranking officer of their navy, the Protector's Champion, only the second person in history to have received the Star of Grayson not merely once, but twice, *and* one of their eighty-two steadholders.

And a woman. Even now, the surviving strictures of Grayson's pre-Alliance social code absolutely precluded public insult to a woman. Any woman. And especially this woman.

Which meant that the very tactics which had so thoroughly neutralized Honor in the domestic Manticoran political calculus had produced exactly the opposite effect on Grayson. Public opinion and support there had rallied about her even more fiercely than before, but it was an angry public opinion. A rising sea of infuriated outrage which had turned her into a symbol which threatened the outright disruption of an alliance Benjamin was already holding together by his fingernails.

She had nowhere to go. She could accomplish nothing on Manticore, and her very presence here, combined with the High Ridge Government's determination to keep her neutralized, only kept the scandal alive and fanned the furnace of Grayson anger. Yet if she fled to Grayson, she would only make it worse, because the Graysons would undoubtedly decide (with justification) that she'd been hounded out of the Star Kingdom. The damage which had already been done would be multiplied, and her presence on Grayson would keep the planet's rage alive by keeping her very much in the public eye, and so she drew a deep, unhappy breath, and shook her head.

"No," she repeated to her monarch, "domestic politics aren't all we have to worry about."

"I don't like what we're hearing about Silesia." Sir Edward Janacek tilted back in his chair while he regarded the two men sitting on the far side of the magnificent desk he'd had moved into his office to replace the smaller, plainer one which had served Baroness Mourncreek.

Admiral Francis Jurgensen, Second Space Lord of the Admiralty, was a small, neat man. His uniform, as always, was impeccable, and his brown eyes were open and guileless. Admiral Sir Simon Chakrabarti was much taller and broad-shouldered. His complexion was almost as dark as Elizabeth Winton's, but aside from that he actually reminded people a great deal of Sir Thomas Caparelli— physically, at least, and at first glance. Any similarity was illusory, however. Chakrabarti had managed to attain his present very senior rank without ever commanding in combat. He'd last seen action as Lieutenant Commander Chakrabarti, executive officer in the heavy cruiser *Invincible,* against Silesian pirates, over thirty-five T-years before. Since that time, his career had been devoted primarily to administration, with a detour for a brief stint at BuWeaps.

Some might have questioned how that sort of career qualified a man to be First Space Lord, but as Janacek saw it, at this moment the Navy had less need of some grizzled veteran of a warrior than it did of a superior administrator. Anyone could win battles when his wall of battle held such a decisive qualitative edge, but it required someone who understood the ins and outs of administrative decisions and budgetary realities to balance the requirements of the Service against the need to downsize the Fleet. Chakrabarti

had that understanding, not to mention exemplary political connections. His brother-in-law was Adam Damakos, the Liberal MP
who was the ranking member of the Naval Affairs Committee of
the House of Commons, but he was also the cousin of Akahito
Fitzpatrick, the Duke of Gray Water, one of Baron High Ridge's
closest allies in the Conservative Association. That would have made
him the perfect choice for such an important position even without
any other recommendations. And at least Janacek had been able
to pick the man himself, instead of having someone foisted off
on him the way that idiot Houseman had been chosen as Second
Lord!

"I don't like it at all," he went on. "What the hell do the Andies
think they're doing?" He looked pointedly at Jurgensen, and the
admiral shrugged.

"The information we've been able to put together so far is still
pretty self-contradictory," he said. "In the absence of any official
explanations—or demands—from their foreign minister, all we can
do is guess about their final intentions."

"I realize that, Francis." Janacek spoke mildly, but his eyes
narrowed. "On the other hand, you are the head of the Office of
Naval Intelligence. Doesn't that mean you're sort of in charge of
guessing about these things?"

"Yes, it does," Jurgensen replied calmly. "I simply wanted it on
the record that our analysts are scarcely in possession of the sort
of hard information which would allow us to make definite projections of the Andermanis' intentions."

He regarded the First Lord levelly, with the confidence of decades
of experience in seeing to it that his posterior was safely covered
before sticking his neck out. He waited until Janacek nodded
understanding of the qualification, then shrugged again.

"Bearing that proviso in mind," he said then, "it does appear
that the Andies are engaged in a systematic redeployment intended
to encircle Sidemore Station from the north and northeast, interposing between the station and the rest of the Confederacy. We
have no indications as yet that Emperor Gustav is contemplating
any sort of operations against us, although that possibility can
never be completely discounted. It seems more likely, however, that
what he has in mind—so far, at least—is basically to put on a show
of force."

"A show of force to accomplish what?" Chakrabarti asked.

"There's a lot of debate about that," Jurgensen told him. "The majority opinion at the moment is that the Andies will probably be approaching us sometime soon through diplomatic channels to put forward territorial claims in Silesia."

"Bastards," Janacek said conversationally, and grimaced. "Still, I suppose it makes sense. They've had their eye on Silesia for as long as I can remember. I can't say I'm surprised to hear that the opportunistic sons-of-bitches think the time has come to start carving off the choicer bits."

"We've made our position on that quite clear, historically speaking," Chakrabarti observed, and cocked his head at the First Lord.

"And that position hasn't changed—yet," Janacek replied.

"Will it?" Chakrabarti asked with atypical bluntness, and it was Janacek's turn to shrug.

"I don't know," he admitted. "That decision would have to be made at the Cabinet level. At this point, however, and absent any instructions to the contrary, our policy remains unchanged. Her Majesty's Government—" he used the phrase without even a flicker of irony "—is not prepared to accept any acquisition of territory, by the Andermani Empire or anyone else, at the expense of the present government of the Silesian Confederacy."

"In that case," Chakrabarti said pragmatically, "we probably ought to reinforce Sidemore to offset this 'show of force' of Francis'."

"It's not *my* show of force, Simon," Jurgensen calmly corrected.

"Whatever." Chakrabarti waved a dismissive hand. "We still ought to consider deploying at least a couple of more battle squadrons to Sidemore, whoever's show of force it is."

"Um." Janacek rubbed an index finger in slow circles on his desktop and frowned down at it. "I can follow your thinking, Simon, but coming up with that much tonnage isn't going to be easy."

Chakrabarti looked at him for a moment, but decided against pointing out that finding the necessary ships of the wall might have been easier if the Government hadn't just decided to scrap so many of them. For all his bureaucratic career track, he'd spent too many decades as a naval officer not to recognize the bitter irony of the situation. He was also too experienced as a uniformed politician to make the point.

"Easy or not, Sir Edward," he said instead, his voice just a tiny bit more formal, "if we're going to stand by our current policy to discourage Andie adventurism, then we need to beef up Sidemore. We don't have to use the new pod superdreadnoughts, but we have to deploy something that would at least be more than purely symbolic. If we don't, we're effectively telling them we're not prepared to go to the mat."

Janacek looked up, and the First Space Lord met his gaze levelly. Then Jurgensen cleared his throat.

"Actually," he said carefully, "it might be wiser to send some of the SD(P)s, after all."

"Oh?" Chakrabarti looked at the Second Space Lord and frowned.

"Yes," Jurgensen said. "I've been conducting a general review of our intelligence on the Andermani over the last week or two, and I've come across a few . . . disturbing reports."

"Disturbing reports about what, Francis?" Janacek asked, joining Chakrabarti in frowning at him.

"They're not very specific," Jurgensen replied. "That's the main reason they haven't already been passed along to you, Edward. I know you prefer hard data to vague speculation, so we've been trying to confirm them first. Under the circumstances, however, even though they're still unconfirmed, I think we have to take them into account when we consider what sort of reinforcements Sidemore might require."

"Which would be much easier to do if you'd tell us what they say," Chakrabarti pointed out.

"I'll have a *precis* to you by the end of the day," Jurgensen promised. "Essentially, though, we've had some indications—none of them, as I say, confirmed—that the Andies may recently have begun deploying some new weapons systems of their own. Unfortunately, we don't have very many details about just what sort of hardware we may be talking about."

"And you didn't see fit to bring this information to our attention?" Janacek inquired ominously.

"I wasn't even aware of its existence until two weeks ago," Jurgensen said. "And prior to this meeting, the possibility of deploying additional forces to deter the Andies hadn't even been discussed. Under the previously existing circumstances, I felt that it would be advisable to attempt to confirm the information one way or another before bringing it to your attention."

Janacek frowned at him for several seconds, then shrugged.

"Either way, there wouldn't have been much we could have done until you did confirm it," he conceded, and Jurgensen nodded calmly. "But I can't say I'm happy to hear about it, whether it's confirmed or not," the First Lord continued. "The Andies' hardware was almost as good as ours before the war; if they've improved theirs since, we may have to seriously reconsider force levels in Silesia. The Prime Minister isn't going to like hearing about that less than four months after we finished telling Parliament we're making further reductions in our wall."

Jurgensen and Chakrabarti nodded solemnly, secure in the knowledge that they had proposed nothing of the sort, whatever the civilian lords of the Admiralty might have had to say about it. Of course, neither of them had protested the reductions, but that was entirely different from bearing responsibility for them.

"What sort of details *do* you have?" Chakrabarti asked after a moment.

"Almost none, actually," Jurgensen admitted. "A Sidemorian analyst claims that visual imagery of one of the IAN's new *Thor*-class battlecruisers shows fewer missile ports than the class is supposed to have. Exactly what that might mean, we currently have no idea, and we haven't yet confirmed his claim with an independent analysis of the imagery. The raw visual take is on its way here, but we won't see it for another week or two.

"In addition, we have two reports from merchant skippers suggesting that the Andies may have managed at least some improvement in their inertial compensators. The evidence is extremely sketchy, but both of the captains involved report observing Andermani ships pulling accelerations considerably higher than they should have been."

"Merchant skippers!" Chakrabarti snorted, but Jurgensen shook his head.

"That was my own initial reaction, Simon, which is one reason I wanted to get confirmation before reporting it. But one of the merchant captains involved is a half-pay admiral."

"What?" Janacek eyes sharpened. "Which half-pay admiral?"

"An Admiral Bachfisch," Jurgensen replied.

"Oh, him!" Janacek snorted. "I remember now. A fuck-up who almost got his ship blown out of space!"

"Not, perhaps, the best possible reference for someone's resume,"

Jurgensen agreed. "But he is an experienced man, with over thirty T-years on active duty before he, um, left active naval service."

Janacek snorted again, although with a bit less panache this time. Chakrabarti, on the other hand, suddenly looked more thoughtful, and Jurgensen twitched one shoulder.

"There are a half dozen other reports, most of them from independent stringers run by our naval attaches in the Empire, that indicate the Andies have at least been experimenting with longer-ranged missiles, and we've known for years now that they've been developing their own pods. What we don't know, and what I haven't found a way to confirm one way or the other yet, is whether or not they've begun laying down SD(P)s of their own."

"Find a way to confirm it, one way or the other." There was an edge in Janacek's voice. His estimates of necessary force levels had been predicated upon maintaining the RMN's monopoly on the new superdreadnought types. His reports to the Cabinet hadn't even considered the possibility that the Andermani might already be beginning construction of their own SD(P)s.

There wasn't any reason to bring it up, he told himself defensively. *It's the* Peeps *we have to worry about; not the Andies. If we had to, we could survive letting them have the entire Confederacy, in the short term, at least. Besides, Francis hadn't said a word to me about it then.*

"In the meantime," he continued, turning back to Chakrabarti, "I need firm proposals from you on the exact strength we need to transfer to Sidemore."

"Do you want me to use worst-case assumptions?" the First Space Lord asked, and Janacek shook his head.

"Not worst-case. We don't need to frighten ourselves into overreacting when none of this has even been confirmed by Intelligence. Assume some improvements in their capabilities, but let's not get carried away."

"That still leaves a lot of uncertainty, Ed," Chakrabarti pointed out, and Janacek frowned. "I just want to be certain I base my proposals on what you want them based on," the admiral said.

"All right," Janacek said, "assume their present capabilities are approximately equal to what ours were, say, six T-years ago. No SD(P)s, no Ghost Rider, and no CLACs, but otherwise assume that they have everything we had, including the new compensators."

"Fine," Chakrabarti agreed with a satisfied nod. Then he cocked his head. "On the basis of those assumptions, though, I can already tell you that 'a couple of battle squadrons' isn't going to be enough. Not playing so close to the Andies' backyard."

"There are limits to our resources," Janacek told him.

"I understand. But we may be looking at a situation where we have no choice but to rob Peter if we're going to pay Paul."

"It's highly probable that the Government will be able to control the situation through diplomatic measures," Janacek said. "If it turns out that we're going to require a more concrete proof of our commitment, we'll just have to do whatever is necessary to come up with it."

"Yes, Sir. But if we're going to reinforce Sidemore on the scale I think the threat levels we'll be assuming are going to require, then we'll also have to pick somebody to command those reinforcements. Rear Admiral Hewitt, the station's present commander, is actually on the junior side for what's already assigned to it. He's much too junior to command what's about to become one of our three largest fleet commands, whether we call it a 'fleet' formally or not."

"Um," Janacek said again, frowning down at his desk in thought. Chakrabarti had a point, but picking a new station CO wasn't going to be easy. Sidemore had proved fairly useful, but scarcely essential or vital even during the war. Now that the war had been effectively won, Sidemore would become increasingly less relevant to the Star Kingdom's strategic needs, which meant no ambitious officer was going to appreciate being shuffled off to command it. And that didn't even consider the potential mousetraps built into the assignment.

Despite his words to Jurgensen and Chakrabarti, Janacek was privately certain the Government would much prefer to avoid any distracting confrontation with the Andermani, and rightly so. The First Lord had never been in favor of the expansionist pressures he'd often sensed in both the Navy and Parliament, anyway. That was why he'd done his best to disengage from Basilisk during his first tenure at the Admiralty, before that maniac Harrington almost got them into a shooting war with the Peeps five T-years early.

If it came down to it, he would certainly recommend to the Cabinet that reasonable territorial concessions be made to the Andermani. It wasn't as if the territories in question belonged to the Star Kingdom, anyway, and nothing inside Silesia struck him as being worth the risk of a shooting incident, much less an actual war. But that meant whoever was sent out to Sidemore would find himself in the unenviable position of attempting to deter the Andermani in the full knowledge that no additional reinforcements would be forthcoming. And if the Andermani declined to be deterred and there was an incident of any sort, the Government would almost certainly disavow the station commander's actions. Even in a best-case situation, whoever wound up in command would be remembered as the officer on whose watch the Empire had moved in on Silesia. It wouldn't have been his fault, of course, but that wouldn't prevent his peers—and his superiors—from associating it with his assumption of command.

So where did he find someone who could make bricks without straw if he had to, convince the Andermani he would fight to the death before he let them have Silesia (until, at least, he got the inevitable order to hand it over to them), and be expendable if it became necessary for the Government to disavow him? Right off the top of his head, he couldn't think of anyone, but he was sure something would come to him.

CHAPTER TEN

Vice Admiral Shannon Foraker stood in the boat bay gallery with her hands clasped loosely behind her and gazed out through the bay's clear vacuum at the unwinking stars as she watched the incoming pinnace settle into the docking buffers. The service umbilicals ran out to it, followed by the boarding tube, and she straightened her shoulders and stood a bit straighter as the side party came to attention.

The telltales on the gallery end of the tube blinked from red to the amber of standby, and then to the bright green that indicated a tight seal and good atmosphere. Then the hatch opened, and the bosun's pipes began to squeal in the high, shrill voices she'd never been able to develop a taste for.

"Secretary of War, arriving!" the intercom announced as a slightly stocky, brown-haired man in an admiral's uniform stepped through the hatch and into the sound of the pipes, and the side party snapped instantly to attention. So did Admiral Foraker as she watched the newcomer salute RHNS *Sovereign of Space*'s captain.

Captain Patrick M. Reumann returned the salute sharply. At just over a hundred and ninety centimeters, Reumann was half a head taller than the visitor, and Foraker supposed he was the physically more imposing of the two, despite his receding hairline. But somehow that didn't seem to matter. It wasn't because of any weakness in the captain; the man picked as the skipper of the lead ship of the newest, most powerful superdreadnought class in the Republican Navy wasn't exactly likely to be a weakling in anyone's book. It was just that for the Navy generally, and for everyone connected to Operation Bolthole in particular, Thomas Theisman had become a larger than life figure, almost an icon.

That wasn't something Shannon Foraker would have spent much thought on six or seven T-years ago. She'd been amazingly oblivious to the harsh realities of naval service under Rob Pierre and State Security. Until she'd been brought face-to-face with the ugly truth, at least. The humiliation and shame of being forced to become an unwilling accomplice to StateSec's brutality had changed Foraker's universe forever. The talented, apolitical "techno nerd" who'd wanted no more than to do her job with patriotism and honor had recognized that she couldn't—not under StateSec. She'd seen an admiral she trusted and respected driven to the brink of mutiny, seen an ex-skipper she'd respected even more actually driven into willing treason because his own sense of honor could take no more violation, and been sent all too closely to the brink of imprisonment or execution herself.

In the wake of those experiences, the same qualities which had made her an outstanding tactical officer in the People's Navy had been brought to bear on other problems . . . which was why she— and Admiral Tourville and Admiral Giscard—were still alive. But it was unlikely that anything she'd done would have prevented the same ultimate outcome if not for Thomas Theisman.

She hadn't known Theisman before Oscar Saint-Just's overthrow, but she'd come to know him since, and somehow he just kept on getting more impressive. He'd joined a select handful of other senior officers in Foraker's estimation, one of the dedicated cadre which had somehow kept the concepts of duty and honor alive in their own lives, no matter what their political masters had demanded of them. More important, he was also the man who'd restored the *Navy's* honor. Lester Tourville and Javier Giscard might exercise command of the Republic's fleets, but it was Thomas Theisman who'd made it possible for them to do so. Just as he was the man who'd invited the Navy's officers and ratings to rediscover their self-respect. To remember that they'd chosen to wear the uniforms they wore because they believed in something, not because a reign of terror would shoot them if they declined to become willing agents of terror themselves.

He had restored the Navy to itself, made it his ally in the defense of the restored Constitution, both out of its own sense of honor and obligation and as a means to cleanse its shield of the filth with which StateSec had spattered it. And because he'd given it back that sense of mission, of commitment, of standing *for* something, the Navy would have followed him unflinchingly through the gates of Hell itself.

Just as Shannon Foraker would have.

"Permission to come aboard, Sir?" the Secretary of War requested formally as the twittering pipes finally fell silent, and Captain Reumann nodded sharply.

"Welcome aboard the *Sovereign*, Sir!" he replied in a carrying voice. "It's a pleasure to see you back aboard again," he added in a lower, more conversational tone, and held out his right hand.

"It's a pleasure to *be* back, Pat," Theisman replied, gripping the proffered hand and shaking it firmly. "I only wish Bolthole were close enough to Nouveau Paris that I could get out here more than three or four times a year."

"So do we, Sir," Reumann assured him.

"Well," the Secretary said, glancing approvingly around the orderly, disciplined boat bay, "maybe we'll be doing a little something about that."

"Excuse me?" The captain cocked his head, and Theisman grinned, although there was a faint edge of something besides humor—possibly even a trace of worry—in his expression.

"Don't worry about it, Pat. I promise I'll explain everything before I head back to the capital. In the meantime, however, Admiral Foraker and I have a few things we need to discuss."

"Of course, Sir," Reumann acknowledged, and stepped back as Theisman turned to offer his hand to Shannon.

"Admiral," the Secretary of War said, and Shannon smiled.

"Admiral," she repeated, fully aware of how much he preferred to think of himself in his persona as Chief of Naval Operations, someone who was still a serving officer and not merely a political animal. His eyes twinkled as he squeezed her hand firmly, then she cocked her head.

"I'd tentatively scheduled welcoming cocktails in the officers' mess," she said, "but none of our plans were set in ceramacrete. Should I assume from what you just said to Pat that I should reschedule the festivities until after you've had a chance to tell me just what brings you clear out here?"

"Actually, I think I'd prefer for you to do that, if it won't inconvenience people," Theisman said, and she shrugged.

"As I said, none of our plans were really definite, Sir. We didn't have enough of an idea of what was on your agenda for this trip to make any hard and fast arrangements." She turned to a chunky captain at her right elbow. "Five, I seem to have forgotten my com again. Would you screen Paulette for me? Ask her to see to it that everyone knows we're going to Plan Beta."

"Of course, Ma'am," Captain William Anders replied with a slight grin. One thing about the old Shannon Foraker which remained the same was a degree of . . . absentmindedness where the minutiae of day-to-day life was involved. It took a certain talent to "forget" her wrist com, but she managed to do it at least twice a week.

The hirsute captain activated his own com and punched in the combination for Lieutenant Paulette Baker, Foraker's flag lieutenant, and she turned her own attention back to Theisman.

"Do we need to speak in private, Sir? Or should I assemble my staff, as well?"

"I'll want to bring all of them up to speed while I'm out here," he said, "but I think I'd prefer to brief you individually before that."

"Of course. In that case, would you care to accompany me to my day cabin?"

"I think that would be an excellent idea," he agreed, and she glanced back at Anders.

"Did you catch that, Five?" she asked.

"I did. And I'll pass it on to Paulette, as well."

"Thank you." She smiled at him with a warmth which transfigured her narrow, severely attractive face, and then gestured respectfully for Theisman to proceed her to the lifts.

"After you, Sir," she invited.

It took several minutes to reach Foraker's day cabin, despite the fact that the architects had deliberately placed it close to the lift shaft core. Of course, "close" was a relative term aboard something the size of *Sovereign of Space*. The superdreadnought was the next best thing to nine million tons of battle steel and armor. She was also the first unit of the biggest and most powerful class of warships the Republic of Haven had ever built, although it probably wouldn't hold that distinction for long. The plans for the follow-on *Temeraire* class were well into the final approval stage, and if things stayed on schedule, the first *Temeraire* would be laid down here at Bolthole within the next three or four months, for completion in another thirty-six. Which might have been a considerably longer building time than someone like the Manties would have required, but still represented an enormous decrease in construction times for Haven . . . much of which was the work of one Vice Admiral Shannon Foraker and her staff.

Still, they got to their destination eventually, and Foraker removed her cap and tossed it to Chief Callahan, her steward, as she and Theisman stepped past the Marine sentry and through the hatch into her cabin.

Chief Petty Officer Sylvester Callahan caught the airborne headgear with the ease of much practice and only a hint of a long-suffering sigh. Foraker was well aware that she owed that restraint to Theisman's presence, and she grinned smugly at the steward. Not that she'd been quite so comfortable with him when he was first assigned to her. It had taken her months to get used to the very notion of having a "steward" of her own, admiral or no admiral, because such "elitist" institutions had been among the first casualties of Rob Pierre's systematic efforts to eradicate all traces of the old Legislaturalist officer corps. A part of Foraker had rebelled against the restoration of the old officer corps' privileges, and she was just as happy Theisman had refused to reinstate at least half of them. But she'd also been forced to admit that assigning stewards to commanding officers and flag officers actually made an awful lot of sense. Any CO had vastly more productive things to do with her time than to tidy up her own quarters or polish her own boots. Perhaps even more importantly, senior officers needed keepers who they could count on to keep their lives functioning smoothly while they dealt with the unending series of decisions and judgment calls which came with their own jobs.

And those of them who tended to be just a tad on the absent-minded side needed keepers more than most, she admitted.

"The Admiral and I have some things we need to discuss, Sly," she told Callahan. "Do you think you could scare up a few munchies for us while we do?"

"I'm sure I can, Ma'am," Callahan replied. "How heavy did you have in mind?" She cocked an eyebrow at him, and he shrugged. "Lieutenant Baker already commed about the change in plans," he explained. "As I understand it, dinner is being moved back by about an hour and cocktails are being moved around behind it. So I simply wondered whether you and the Admiral would require a light snack, or something a little more substantial to carry you."

"Um." Foraker frowned, then glanced at Theisman. "Admiral?"

"I'm still on Nouveau Paris time," the Secretary told her. "Which means I'm about two hours overdue for lunch right this minute. So I think 'a little more substantial' is a pretty fair description of what I'd like."

"Hear that, Sly?"

"I did, Ma'am."

"Then make it so," she told him with a grin, and he bowed slightly and withdrew in the general direction of his pantry.

She watched him go, then turned back to Theisman once more, and waved at one of the comfortable chairs.

"Please, Admiral. Have a seat," she invited.

"Thank you."

Theisman settled into the indicated chair and gazed about himself thoughtfully. This was his first visit to Foraker's shipboard quarters, and he was impressed by the simplicity of the furnishings with which she'd surrounded herself. She seemed to have overcome her aversion to "pampering" herself at least to the extent of acquiring proper powered chairs, and the wet bar and liquor cabinet in one corner of the spacious compartment looked promising. But aside from that, she seemed to have settled for standard Navy-issue furniture and carpet, and the handful of art pieces on the bulkheads, while pleasant to the eye, were hardly high-ticket items. Which was pretty much in keeping with the woman he'd selected to head Project Bolthole for him, and he was pleased to see that she was still with him, despite the power and authority Shannon Foraker had come to wield.

A few of his initial appointees had disappointed him in that respect, succumbing to the temptation to regard themselves as the new masters of the Republican Navy, and not as its stewards and servants. Some of them had responded to his subtle promptings and gotten themselves reorganized. Those who hadn't had been quietly but firmly shunted aside into duties which still let him make use of their undeniable talents but took them out of any position to put their imprint on his Navy.

"Tell me," he said, bringing his gaze back to Foraker as she sat in a facing chair, "why do you call Captain Anders 'Five'?"

"Haven't the foggiest," Foraker replied. "I started out calling him William, and he politely but firmly informed me that he preferred 'Five.' I'm not sure where the nickname came from, but I'm guessing it was some disreputable event in his lower-deck past. On the other hand, I don't really care what he wants to be called as long as he goes on doing his job as well as he does."

"I can live with that," Theisman told her with a chuckle. Then he sobered slightly. "You know, much as I loathed and despised the Committee of Public Safety, I have to admit Pierre and his cronies actually accomplished some good. Like the way they eventually managed to turn the economy around for one, and the way they broke the Legislaturalists' stranglehold on the officer corps, for another. Under the old regime, someone like Anders would never have gotten a commission. Which would have been an enormous loss."

Foraker nodded in complete agreement. Anders had been a petty officer with over thirty-five T-years of service when Rob Pierre overthrew the Legislaturalists, but that was as high as he ever would have gone under the old regime, and that truly would have been a loss for the entire Navy. Like Foraker, his childhood experience with the old Legislaturalist educational system had taught him that he was going to have to teach himself anything he really wanted to learn, and that was precisely what he'd done. Unfortunately, he hadn't been a Legislaturalist. In fact, his family had been Dolists, which had made his attainment even of petty officer's rank quite an achievement.

But the destruction of the old Legislaturalist order, coupled with the People's Navy's desperate need for competence, regardless of its sources, had changed all of that. By the time Thomas Theisman shot Saint-Just (assuming that the rumors about the mechanics of the ex-Chairman's demise were as accurate as Foraker strongly suspected they were), PO Anders had become Lieutenant Commander Anders. He might not have gone a lot higher even under Pierre and Saint-Just, though. In fact, he might well have found himself shot by the Committee, instead, because he had a contrary streak at least a meter wide. Somehow, he seemed to lack the admiration for the "People" which had been the magic key to promotion in the brave new world created by people like Rob Pierre and Cordelia Ransom. Personally, Foraker suspected that his contrariness stemmed from the fact that he knew *he* had overcome the limitations of his childhood and the People's Republic's ramshackle excuse for an educational system to make something out of himself and had nothing but contempt for people who hadn't even made the same attempt.

However that might have been, she was delighted to have him as her chief of staff, and his promotion since the fall of the Committee was amply deserved. In some ways, she regretted pulling him out of his original slot in R&D, because he was one of the best practical engineers in the Navy, if not the entire Republic. Unhappily, she needed him even more where he was, interpreting for the engineers who had to communicate with those less gifted individuals who happened, in this less than perfect universe, to be their superior officers. And, she admitted, she needed him to do the same interpreting for her when she spoke to those engineers' superiors.

Now, if the only people I had to communicate with were the engineering types themselves, she thought, *maybe I could get Five back where he belongs. Unfortunately, this is the real world.*

"I don't know about the rest of the Navy, Sir," she said after a moment, "but I, for one, am delighted to have him out here."

"I'm delighted to have both of you out here," Theisman told her with simple sincerity. "Lester Tourville told me you were the right woman for Bolthole, and the job you've done only reconfirms my faith in his judgment."

Foraker felt her cheekbones heat, but she managed to meet his regard steadily enough, then glanced up with a hint of relief as Callahan returned with a tray of sandwiches and raw vegetables. He positioned it on a small table between their chairs, poured each of them a cup of coffee, set the coffee carafe beside the sandwiches, and disappeared once more.

"That's someone else I'm delighted to have out here," Foraker said wryly, contemplating the food and drink which had so magically appeared.

"I can't imagine why," Theisman murmured with a small smile, and reached happily for one of the sandwiches. "Ummm . . . delicious!" he sighed.

"He has a way about him," Foraker agreed, and selected a carrot. She sat back, nibbling politely to keep the Secretary company while he ate, and waited.

It wasn't a long wait. Theisman finished one sandwich and ate half of a second one, then built himself a small plate of celery and carrot sticks with just a little more of the rich bleu cheese dip than he really ought to be eating, and leaned back in his own chair.

"Now that the pangs of starvation have been blunted, I suppose I should get down to the reason for my visit," he said, and his eyes gleamed as Foraker sat up straighter, her expression intent.

"To be perfectly honest," he continued, "one of the reasons I'm here is to do a personal eyeball check of your reports. Not that I have any concerns about their accuracy, but because a part of me just has to see the reality behind them." He shook his head. "I sometimes wonder if you really realize all you've managed to accomplish out here, Shannon."

"I think you can safely assume all of us realize that, Sir," she told him dryly. "At least, we all know we've spent the better part of four T-years—some of us over five—more or less in exile while we did it!"

"I know you have, and I expect the entire Navy is going to appreciate it just as much as I do when we finally tell them what you've been doing," he said seriously. "And although I have rather mixed feelings about the timing, it's possible that the rest of the Service is going to begin finding out just a bit sooner than we thought."

"It is?" Foraker's eyes narrowed, and he nodded.

"I know you've been working to my original timetable. And to be candid, I'd really prefer to stick to that timetable. Unfortunately, that may not be possible. And if it isn't, at least you and Captain Anders and the rest of your people have gotten more done in less time than I'd believed would be possible when I first sent you here."

"I'm happy to hear that . . . mostly, Sir," she said cautiously when he paused. "At the same time, and as much as all of my people deserve to be recognized, we're still well short of the deployment levels you specified when you assigned me here. And while I've gotten the number of building slips up to target levels, we've only laid the first keels in a third of them within the last six months or so."

"Believe me, Shannon, you can't be more aware of that than I am. On the other hand, there are things going on back at Nouveau Paris that may not leave me much choice about accelerating the deployment schedule."

"May I ask what sort of things, Sir?" she inquired even more cautiously, and he snorted.

"Nothing catastrophic!" he reassured her. "Probably not even anything serious . . . yet, at least. But basically, and for your private information, the President and I are finding ourselves more and more likely to be locking horns with Secretary Giancola. That," his eyes narrowed and his voice turned just a bit crisper, "doesn't leave this day cabin, Shannon."

"Of course not, Sir," she reassured him, and inwardly she felt an undeniable glow of pleasure that he trusted her enough to share what he obviously considered sensitive information with her.

"I don't know that anything is actually going to come of it," he went on after a moment. "In fact, it's entirely possible that the President and I are worrying unduly. But the Secretary of State is becoming more and more impatient with the Manties, and it looks to us as if he's in the process of building a block of support for his position in Congress. As a part of his efforts, we believe he's been dropping a few hints here and there about Bolthole."

Foraker's expression tightened indignantly, and he gave her a crooked smile.

"I know. I know! He's not supposed to be doing that, and if he is, then he's in violation of the Classified Information Act. But even if he is, we can't whack him the way we would some underling. Or, rather, we could, but the President feels that the political cost might be extremely high. Both because of the support he's managed to build in Congress and because if we acted to punish him for violating the Information Act, at least some people would see our charges as no more than a justification for purging a political opponent. We'd have every legal right to proceed against him—assuming he's guilty of what we think he is—but the practical consequences of doing so might very well be to undermine the legitimacy we've worked so hard to earn."

"I understand that, I suppose, Sir," Foraker said. "I don't much like it, but I can see what you're saying."

"I don't much like it either," Theisman told her with massive understatement. "But whether we like it or not, we still have to decide how we're going to respond. Obviously, my original concerns about coming out into the open too soon and panicking the Manties into doing something hasty still apply. On the other hand, you've done much better than I'd hoped at tweaking the production queue. How many *Sovereigns* are you projecting by the end of this quarter?"

"Assuming we don't hit any more bottlenecks, I believe we'll be looking at right on sixty-six of them, Sir," she told him with simple, well-justified pride. "We have thirty-eight currently in full commission, with another sixteen in various stages of working up, and the yard is supposed to hand a dozen more over to us next month."

"And the *Astra* class?"

"As you know, we haven't assigned them quite the same priority the superdreadnoughts have had, Sir. And Commander Clapp came up with a few LAC modifications we decided were worth retrofitting to the completed birds as well as incorporating in those still on the production line, which has slowed things still further. We have about thirty of the *Astras* either in commission or working up, but we don't have complete LAC groups to put aboard them. And the same shortage of LACs is putting a crimp into our training schedule, as well. I don't think we could deploy more than twenty, or possibly two dozen, by the end of the quarter."

"I understand." Theisman leaned back in his chair and gazed up at the deckhead, lips pursed in thought. He stayed that way for quite some time, then shrugged.

"You're still enormously far ahead of where I expected you to be," he told her. "What I'm hoping is that we can keep you and Bolthole under wraps for at least one additional quarter, possibly two, but I don't think we can hope for much more than that. And, in a worst-case scenario, we may have to go public *this* quarter."

He saw her slightly puzzled expression and waved one hand.

"If Secretary Giancola creates a situation in which he and the President and the rest of the Cabinet end up on opposite sides of a public debate, I don't want him dropping any bombshells about our new and improved military posture. Not out of the blue, anyway. I can't be positive, but I suspect that he's at least considering the advantages of suddenly revealing the capabilities of the ships you've been building and working up out here.

"The Manties clearly don't have any serious interest in

negotiating a treaty which would return any of our occupied planets. There's some disagreement as to why that should be true. I personally tend to agree with General Usher over at FIA—that they could care less about hanging onto our territory except for the political advantages it secures the High Ridge crowd domestically—but other people have different theories. Including, I'm afraid, quite a few of the analysts at FIS . . . and at NavInt, for that matter."

Foraker nodded. General Kevin Usher had been President Pritchart's personal choice to head the new Federal Investigation Agency when Oscar Saint-Just's repressive StateSec machine was demolished. The old organization had been split into two new ones—Usher's FIA, and the Federal Intelligence Service, specifically charged with foreign intelligence at the federal level. The new agencies' carefully chosen names had the advantage of a complete break with names like Internal Security and State Security, but they performed many of the same intelligence functions. With Usher in command, Pritchart could be confident that the FIA would *not* perform the old suppressive functions, and there were rumors that the President had wanted him in charge of the functions now assigned to both agencies. But many members of Congress had balked at the notion of creating yet another single intelligence/security umbrella organization. And, much as Foraker respected President Pritchart, she agreed with their disinclination. Not just because she, too, feared the potential for such an agency to become a new StateSec under a President other than Eloise Pritchart and a director other than Kevin Usher, either. She'd been less impressed with Wilhelm Trajan, the FIS's new director, than she was with Usher, but she'd been delighted when Theisman resurrected Naval Intelligence as an independent agency within the Navy, as well. There were simply some questions civilian analysts wouldn't think to ask, much less know how to answer.

Unfortunately, it sounded as if the old turf wars between competing intelligence outfits were rearing their ugly heads once more. Which, she reflected, was probably inevitable, given that each set of analysts would come at the raw data with its own institutional priorities and preconceptions. And to be completely fair-minded, Usher was supposed to be concerning himself with domestic matters and *counter*-intelligence, not with analyzing foreign intelligence data. Not that having several competing analyses might not offer its own advantages, since a rigorous debate was probably the best way to get at the actual truth.

"The people who disagree with General Usher tend to fall into two main camps," Theisman told her. "One group, which agrees with Secretary Giancola's position and probably represents the largest number of dissidents, believes the Manticoran government intends to hang onto the occupied planets indefinitely. Their view is that Descroix's refusal to respond to any of our proposals or to make any serious offers of her own is simply a ploy to waste time until they've properly prepared public opinion in the Star Kingdom to accept outright annexation of at least some of the occupied planets. For the most part, they point to Trevor's Star as their example, although at least some of them will admit that the junction terminus makes that system a special case. A much smaller percentage will even admit that the way the Legislaturalists and StateSec treated the San Martinos made the system even more of a special case. I personally can't see any Manticoran government pursuing any sort of territory-grabbing policy across the board, but I suppose it would be stupid to completely rule out the possibility. Especially if there were to be some sort of drastic change in the Manties' internal political dynamics.

"The second group who disagrees with General Usher's analysis doesn't bother its head with imputing any deep, conspiratorial machinations to the Manties. They're still locked into the mindset that the Manties are our natural and inevitable enemies. I don't know how much of that is left over from old Public Information propaganda and how much of it's simply the result of how long we've been at war with the Star Kingdom. Whatever the origin of their beliefs, though, they're either unwilling or unable to consider the possibility of a lasting peace with the Manties. So in their view, of course the Star Kingdom has no interest in negotiating seriously with us. All that High Ridge and Descroix are doing is killing time before the war between us inevitably breaks out again."

"I hope you'll pardon my saying this, Sir, but that's bullshit," Foraker said, and Theisman looked at her. His raised eyebrows invited her to continue, and she gave her head a little toss and obeyed.

"I've met some of the Manties," she reminded him. "Both after I was captured by Admiral Harrington in Silesia, and after Admiral

Tourville captured her. Certainly some of them hate us, if only because we've been fighting each other for so long, but most of the people I've met on the other side didn't have any more desire to conquer the Republic than *I* had to conquer the Star Kingdom. I realize naval officers are expected to follow orders, and that if their government decided to continue the war against us, they would. Even admitting that, though, I don't think any Manticoran government is going to be able to ignore public opinion against fighting a war that doesn't have to be fought.

"But leaving all of that aside, if they really expected to be going back to war any time soon, I can't believe that even the High Ridge Government would be building down their navy to the extent all of our intelligence reports seem to indicate."

It was Theisman's turn to nod. Given her position in command of Bolthole, Foraker was in the pipeline for any scraps of intelligence about Manticoran building policies and technology.

"If they seriously anticipated resuming combat operations," she pointed out, "they certainly wouldn't be delaying construction of the ships they'd need to fight the war. They may not realize that by doing so they're giving us an opportunity to build up a counterweight, but even assuming our security has held as well as we hope, they'd want as great a margin of superiority as they could get. Remember, their Eighth Fleet was the only real spearhead they had, and now that they've deactivated it and reassigned its wall to Third Fleet—not to mention scrapping and mothballing their pre-pod wall of battle so enthusiastically—their "spearhead" is a lot shorter than it was. As I see it, the fact that they're busy systematically reducing their margin of superiority even over the wall of battle we hope they think is all we have is the best possible indication that they think the war is effectively over."

"I see." Theisman regarded her for a moment. "And I think I generally agree with you, as well. But tell me, Shannon—if the Manties did plan on retaining all of the occupied planets and systems, would you be in favor of resuming operations against them if what you've been building out here really does level the tactical balance?"

"Do you mean me, personally, Sir? Or are you asking what I think the government's policy should be?"

"Either—or both."

She thought about it very carefully, taking her time, and her expression was almost surprised when she decided how to reply.

"Do you know, Sir, I never really thought that hard about it. But now that you ask, I think probably I *would* be in favor." She shook her head, obviously bemused by her own conclusion. "I never thought I'd say that, but it's true. Maybe part of it's patriotism, and maybe part of it's a desire for revenge—to get some of our own back after how completely they kicked our butts. And much as I hate to admit it, maybe part of it's a desire to see how my new hardware would actually perform."

"I'm afraid you're not alone, whatever the reason you feel that way," he told her somberly. "Personally, I think it would be insane for us to go back to war with the Star Kingdom under almost any circumstances I can imagine. Even if Bolthole lets us meet them with something like technical parity, our experience over the last fifteen years should certainly indicate to anyone with the brains of an amoeba that the cost—for both sides—would be enormous. But one of the things the President and I have to be aware of is that there's a huge residual anger at the 'enemy' we've been fighting for so long, not only in the Navy but in the electorate, as well. That's why Giancola scares us. We're afraid his demand for a more confrontational foreign policy will resonate with that anger and hatred. That it could actually, God help us all, create a fresh public support for resuming the war. And if we can't get the stupid Manties to at least put some sort of serious, permanent peace proposal on the table, they're playing directly into the hands of the idiots on our side of the line who want to go back to war with them.

"That's why I need you to be aware that the moment at which we reveal the existence of Bolthole and the ships you've been building out here is going to be a matter of very careful political consideration. Both the President and I, on one side, and the confrontationalists, on the other, will want to announce the new fleet at the moment which would be most advantageous for us. The President and I need to find a time when we can be confident the Manties won't be tempted into some sort of preemptive action, which means holding off for as long as we can to build up the most powerful deterrent possible. The confrontationalists will be looking for a time when the fact that we now have the capability to match the Manty advantages—

or to offset them, at least—will generate the most push behind their own policies.

"The decision will be made at a higher level than yours, of course. But we need you to be ready, and you need to understand that the amount of notice you're likely to get will be slight. And," he smiled wryly, "we also need you to go right on working your miracles and exceeding our expectations, because whenever Bolthole gets announced to the rest of thc galaxy, we're going to need to have all of the available muscle we can."

Chapter Eleven

Hamish Alexander followed James MacGuiness through the door to the private gymnasium under Honor's Jason Bay mansion and stopped.

Honor was on the mat at the center of the large, brightly lit and well-appointed gym. She wore a traditional white *gi*, with the black belt which now bore eight braided rank knots. That didn't surprise him, because he'd known she'd gained the eighth one just over a T-year ago. *Coup de vitesse* wasn't his sport—he'd put his time into soccer and fencing—but he knew that there remained only a single formally recognized grade for her to attain. Given her tenacity where things which mattered to her were concerned, that ninth knot was as good as on her belt; it was only a question of when.

But somehow he didn't think that was what she had on her mind this afternoon. She wasn't running through her practice *katas*, nor was she working out against a human partner. No, she was going all out in a full-contact bout against the humanoid training remote she'd had specially built, and it was pushing her hard.

Just how hard became evident as the remote executed a devastating attack. White Haven knew too little about *coup de vitesse* to understand what he'd seen. It was like fencing, where the untrained eye could see the action but never hope to understand its nuances and complexity. All he knew was that he'd seen the remote's hands move with blurring speed. One of those hands locked onto Honor's right arm and carried it high, while the other shot out in a fist-thrust that slammed into her belly, and then it turned, twisting her captive arm, throwing hips and shoulders into her torso, and she went flying through the air to slam down on the mats with bone-bruising force.

White Haven's surprise turned into alarm as the remote charged after her with—literally—inhuman speed. But she hit the mat rolling, came up on her knees in one, fluid motion, and her own hands were waiting by the time the remote reached her. She reached up, seized the front of its *gi*, and rolled backwards, as if to pull it down atop herself. But even as she rolled and her shoulders touched the mat, her knees came up into the remote's belly. They lifted powerfully, her legs straightened, and suddenly it was the remote which went hurtling through the air.

It hit the mat with an earthquake shock, and promptly started to come upright, but Honor had continued her own motion through a backwards somersault. Before the remote could regain its balance and come to its feet, she was upon it from behind. Her right arm snaked forward, locking itself around the remote's neck, squeezing its throat in the crook of her elbow, and then the heel of her other hand smashed into the back of its head like a sledge-hammer.

White Haven winced in sympathetic anguish. For all its savage power, that ferocious, left-handed blow was delivered with lethal precision, and the fact that it was her left hand made its precision even more remarkable, because that hand was no longer human. He suspected that no one, outside her therapists (and probably Andrew LaFollet), would ever know how hard she'd had to work to master the replacement for the arm she'd lost on Cerberus. But he knew few people ever learned how to use a powered prosthesis as naturally as the organic limb it had replaced or to regain the true full range of motion, and the process took many years for those who did manage it.

Honor had done it in little more than three . . . and done it well enough to not merely regain her old form at *coup de vitesse*, but to actually attain the next rank of mastery.

Of course, the prosthesis did provide a few unusual advantages. For one thing, it was several times more powerful than natural flesh and bone. There were limits to what she could do with that strength, because her shoulder had been undamaged when she lost her arm, and the natural limitations of that joint dictated how much stress she could exert. But the fact that "her" left arm was far stronger than any arm had any business being was dramatically— one might almost have said gruesomely—evident when the back of the training remote's "skull" deformed under the force of her blow and the entire head flopped forward in a disturbingly realistic representation of a snapped neck.

The remote collapsed onto its front, and Honor slumped across it, her breathing harsh and ragged in the suddenly silent gym. No one moved, and White Haven glanced across to where Andrew LaFollet and Simon Mattingly had stood watching their Steadholder.

Their expressions were not reassuring. Remotes like Honor's were rare. That was primarily due to their expense, but it also reflected the fact that they could be dangerous. In fact, they could be deadly. Like Honor's prosthetic arm, their maximum strength was far greater than that of any human, even a genetically-modified heavy-worlder like Honor Harrington, and their reflexes were much faster. Any training remote came equipped with governors and software inhibitors intended to protect the user, but it was ultimately the responsibility of the person training against one of them to determine its actual settings. More than one human being had been seriously injured, or even killed, as a consequence. No remote had ever "gone berserk," but they performed precisely as their owners instructed them to, and sometimes those owners made mistakes when they specified performance levels.

It was obvious from LaFollet's worried expression that the Grayson thought Honor was approaching precisely that mistake. Given the fact that, unlike White Haven, LaFollet was also a practitioner of *coup de vitesse*—that he regularly sparred with Honor, in fact—the armsman was certainly in a position to judge, and the earl swallowed a bitter mental curse as he watched Honor push herself pantingly back up on her knees, and then stand.

He'd known for years, since the day they first met at Yeltsin's Star, that Honor Harrington's temper was lethal. People seldom saw it, and he also knew that the calm and serenity she normally projected were just as real as her temper. Yet it was there, chained and subordinated by duty and compassion, perhaps, but without losing one bit of its power. And sometimes it frayed its leash. There were stories about the times it had almost slipped free, part of the legend which had grown up around "the Salamander," but that temper was almost never a match for the discipline and strength of will which restrained it.

Almost . . . but not always. He'd known that, too, but this was the first time he'd ever seen her deliberately free it. That was why LaFollet was worried, and why the "sparring bout" had ended only in the "death" of the remote, and the earl winced again at the recognition of how much pain it must have taken to drive her to that state.

She stood gazing down at the crumpled remote for several seconds, then drew a deep breath, straightened her shoulders, and looked up at LaFollet. She peeled off her sparring gloves, removed her protective mouthpiece, and nodded to him, and the armsman nodded back, obviously trying to conceal his relief, as he pressed buttons on a hand unit. The training remote stirred, then rose and walked off the mat with mechanical calm, completely unaffected by its recent demise, and Honor watched it go. Then she turned and looked at White Haven.

She showed no surprise at seeing him. She must have known he was there, sensed his emotions, from the moment he entered the gym. He smiled at her, but it was a crooked, half-bitter smile, wise with the knowledge of how badly they'd hurt one another without ever meaning to.

He hadn't realized for a long time that she could actually feel the emotions of those around her. It wasn't really his fault he hadn't, because so far as he was aware, no other human had ever shared the treecats' empathic sense. But once he'd begun to guess the truth, preposterous though that truth had seemed, he'd wondered how he'd ever failed to realize. It explained so much about her uncanny ability to "read" people . . . and about the way she reached out so naturally to those about her, constantly soothing someone else's pain or healing someone else's hurt.

And who can do that for her? *Who can give back even a little of all she gives to everyone else?* he wondered bitterly. *Not me. All I can do is make it still worse by sitting here radiating how much I love her when that's the very thing ripping both of us apart.*

Somehow, even after he'd begun to suspect the truth, he'd managed to avoid facing its inevitable implications. Of course she knew how he felt about her. She'd always known, and it had been

that knowledge which had driven her away to the squadron command which had landed her on Hades as a POW and nearly killed
her. And now he knew the complete reason she'd run away. Because
she'd not only sensed his emotions but shared them. And so while
he'd thought he was suffering in such noble, splendid isolation by
concealing his love for her, she'd been bearing the burden of
knowing exactly how they *both* felt.

Her expression wavered for just a moment before she smiled
at him, and he kicked himself mentally. Beating himself up for
feeling what he felt and for "inflicting" it upon her did neither
of them any good. Nor was it his fault. He knew both those things,
yet the knowing changed neither his emotions nor his guilt and
frustration for inundating her with them . . . which only made all
of them worse.

"Hamish," she said, and her soprano was husky. A large, dark
bruise was rising on her right cheek, and her upper lip was swollen.
He didn't much care for the way she favored her right side, either,
but she only held out her flesh and blood hand to him, and he
took it in his and kissed it. It was no longer the simple, adopted
Grayson courtesy it had been, and both of them knew it, and he
wondered miserably what they were going to do.

"Honor," he said in reply as he released her hand.

Nimitz and Samantha leapt down from their perches and came
pattering across the gym towards them, but he scarcely noticed.
His attention was fixed on Honor.

"To what do I owe the pleasure of your company?" she asked
in a very nearly normal voice, and he produced a smile which he
knew fooled neither of them.

*And would I really want it to? Hard as this is, painful as I know
it is for her, there's still something wonderful about it. About knowing
that she knows* exactly *how much I love her, no matter how much
it's cost us both. And how much it's cost Emily.*

The thought of his wife reminded him why he was here . . . and
why he'd come in person, rather than screening her. Why he'd
deliberately arranged to *make* her feel his emotions. Something
flickered in her eyes, and his mouth quirked with wry bitterness
as he saw her recognition. At least it was only emotions, and not
thoughts, he reminded himself.

"I come bearing an invitation," he said, much more lightly than
he felt. Nimitz and Samantha arrived while he was speaking, and

Honor bent to scoop Nimitz up without ever taking her eyes from White Haven's face. She straightened, cradling the 'cat in her arms.

"An invitation?" she repeated, and he felt a fresh flicker of pain at the wariness in her voice.

"Not from me," he hastened to reassure her, and then chuckled humorlessly. "The last thing you and I need right now is to give the scandalmongers more ammunition!"

"True," she agreed, and smiled with a flash of what might have been genuine amusement. But the smile disappeared almost as quickly as it had come, and she cocked her head at him. "If not from you, then from whom?" she asked, and he drew a deep breath.

"From my wife," he said very, very softly.

Honor never moved, yet in that instant it was as if he could feel *her* emotions, sense the way she flinched inside as if from an unexpected blow. She stared at him, and he wanted to reach out and take her in his arms. But he couldn't, of course.

"I know it sounds bizarre," he went on, instead, "but I promise I haven't lost my mind. In fact, the invitation was Emily's idea. Very few people realize it, but the truth is that she's probably even better at picking political problems apart and finding answers than Willie is. And right this minute, Honor, you and I need all the help we can get. She knows that . . . and she wants to offer it."

Honor couldn't take her eyes from his face. She felt as if the training remote had just punched her in the belly all over again. The totally unexpected "invitation" had hit her like a pulser dart, and behind the shock was another emotion: fear. No, not fear—panic. He couldn't be serious! Surely he must realize by now why she'd so persistently avoided ever meeting his wife, and that had been before the Government 'faxes began their systematic demolition of her life. How could he even ask her to face Emily Alexander now? When his own emotions shouted at her that he knew exactly how she felt about him? And that she knew exactly how he felt about her? The countless layers of betrayal inherent in their love and all the pain and devastation the press accounts had heaped upon them wrapped themselves about her, clinging to her like some strangling shroud, and yet underneath it all she could taste his need for her to accept his "invitation."

She was drowning, crushed under the intensity radiating from them both, and she closed her eyes and fought for some fragile semblance of calm. It was impossible. This time, she couldn't step away, couldn't throttle back her sensitivity and awareness, couldn't close the circuit down. The uncontrolled cataract of their emotions crashed back and forth, doubling and redoubling, almost like some bizarre feedback effect, and her thoughts were coated in ceramacrete. She felt Nimitz, swept along with her like some ancient whaler from Old Earth, careening on a "Nantucket sleigh ride" as her emotional turmoil dragged him after her like a sounding whale, seeking escape from the harpoon's anguish in the depths, and there was nothing she could do about that, either.

And at the bottom of that tide race, there was Hamish. There was always Hamish, the source of so much pain because of what should have been so wonderful. The man who'd finally accepted the knowledge that she could feel exactly what he felt, know precisely how deeply he loved her. And who knew she also knew precisely how deeply he still loved his wife, how exquisitely his own sense of having betrayed both Honor and Emily by letting himself love them both tormented him. And how desperately he wanted her to accept his impossible suggestion.

She wavered, unable to reach out to him—too terrified by what he proposed to accept it, yet equally unable to refuse. And as she hung there, she suddenly felt something else. Something she'd never felt before.

Her eyes snapped open, and her head turned as they locked on Samantha. Nimitz's mate crouched beside her, and now the 'cat's emotions came roaring through her like yet another hurricane. She'd felt Samantha's presence—the "mind-glow," the 'cats had called it after they learned to sign—countless times before, but never like this. Never so intensely and powerfully. It crashed and roared with Samantha's own sense of shock and discovery . . . and a terrible, singing joy and astonished recognition.

There was too much going on, too many pressures and impossible demands, for Honor to sort out what was happening, but she felt Samantha reaching out. Stretching. There was no word in any human language for what the 'cat was doing in that instant, and Honor knew she would never be able to truly explain it even to herself, yet she had an instant of warning, a brief flash of awareness. Just long enough for her to cry out, although she would never know whether it was in protesting horror or in shared joy.

It didn't really matter which it was. She could no more have stopped what was happening than she could have halted Manticore in its orbit. Nothing could have stopped it, and she watched through three sets of eyes—hers, Nimitz's, and above all, Samantha's—as Hamish Alexander's head turned towards the 'cat. As astonishment and disbelief flared in those ice-blue eyes and he reached out a hand just as Samantha hurled herself from the floor into his arms with a high, ringing bleek of joy.

CHAPTER TWELVE

"How could it have happened?"

It was the first coherent sentence Hamish Alexander had strung together in almost ten minutes. He cradled the wildly purring treecat in his arms, as if she were the most precious thing in the universe, and his blue eyes glowed with disbelief and soaring welcome as he stared down at her. He knew what had happened. No one could have spent as much time as he had with Honor and Nimitz—and Samantha—or, for that matter, with Elizabeth and Ariel, and not recognize an adoption bonding when he saw it. But knowing what had happened and understanding it were two different things.

Honor stared at him while the echoes of her own shocked disbelief rippled back and forth within her. Unlike White Haven, she was one of the greatest living human authorities on treecats. More members of the Harrington clan had been adopted over the centuries than any other single Sphinxian family, and she'd spent much of her childhood, especially after her own adoption, reading the private journals of those earlier adopted Harringtons. Some of them had contained speculations and theories which had never been publicly discussed, not to mention an absolutely unrivaled store of first-hand observations. On top of that, Nimitz and Samantha had been the very first treecats ever to learn to sign, and she'd spent endless hours since then "listening" to their fascinating explanations of the treecat society and customs even her ancestors had been able to observe only from the outside.

And that was one reason—of all too many—for her shock. To the best of her knowledge, nothing like this had ever happened before. Except in very special cases, like that of Prince Consort Justin and Monroe, the 'cat who had previously adopted Elizabeth's father, treecats recognized "their" people within seconds, minutes at the outside, of first meeting. Monroe had been all but comatose, shattered and almost totally destroyed by King Roger's death, the first time Justin entered his proximity after the assassination. He'd been truly aware of nothing, not even the grieving family of his murdered person, until the traitor responsible for the King's death came foolishly within his reach, intent on murdering Justin, as well. The intense emotional shock he and the future Prince Consort had shared in fighting off the killer's attack had dragged Monroe back from the brink of extinction and forged the adoption bond between them.

But unless the 'cat half of a bond was literally at death's door, he always recognized the unfulfilled . . . polarity of the human meant to become his other half. Only Samantha hadn't. She'd met Hamish scores of times, without so much as twitching a whisker in any sort of recognition.

"I don't know how," Honor told Hamish, and realized it was the first thing she'd said since that initial paralyzing moment of shock.

The earl raised his eyes from Samantha at last, and even without her ability to taste his emotions, Honor would have recognized the consternation woven through the texture of his joy.

"Honor, I—"

He broke off, his expression mingling chagrin and apology, joy and dismay and a dark understanding of at least some of the frightening implications. It was obvious that the words he wanted hovered just out of reach, eluding his ability to explain his emotional whirlwind to her. But he didn't have to, and she shook her head, hoping her own expression concealed the depths of her astonishment . . . and dread.

"I know it wasn't your idea," she told him. "It wasn't Sam's either, but . . ."

She looked down at Nimitz. He was staring at his mate, his long, sinuous body stiff with a shock as deep as Honor's own, but he turned his head and looked up at her when he felt her gaze.

She wanted to scream at him, and at Samantha. If someone had given her ten years to think about it, she couldn't possibly have come up with something better calculated to make everything immeasurably worse. When the newsies heard about this, any trace of momentum the attacks upon her and White Haven might have lost would return tenfold.

Even now, after the 'cats had been "talking" for almost four T-years, much of the Manticoran public continued to regard them as little more than pets, or, at most, very young children. The notion that they were a fully sentient species with an ancient, sophisticated society, might have been accepted intellectually, but it would be decades yet before that acceptance replaced the earlier general view of treecats as adorable, fluffy animals.

Which meant it would be all too easy for the character assassins to convince people that the only reason Samantha was with White Haven was because Honor had given her to him. Efforts to explain what had really happened would be dismissed with a knowing, leering wink as nothing more than a clumsy pretext, a maneuver the seductress Harrington had concocted as a cover to let her stay close to the object of her adulterous affair.

Yet bad as that was, there was worse. Nimitz and Samantha were mates, even more deeply fused in many ways than Nimitz and Honor. They could be parted for a time by things like military necessity, as wedded human warriors had been over the millennia, but they couldn't be separated permanently. It would have been cruel even to try, and it would also have been wrong—wrong on the deepest level of morality. Which meant there was no way Honor could justify even asking them not to be together when they were on the same planet. But they could no more be separated from their adopted humans than they could from each other, and so they couldn't be together, either . . . unless Honor and Hamish were.

And that was the one thing, above all, which she and White Haven dared not be.

It was insane. There was no way High Ridge and North Hollow could have begun to conceive all the ramifications of the sleazy political maneuver they'd embraced. But even if they'd been able to, it wouldn't have stopped them, because aside from the potential to complete the rupture between Grayson and the Star

Kingdom, it was working perfectly for them. And if they ever spared a single thought for the Alliance, which Honor doubted, they undoubtedly continued to think of Manticore as the dominant benefactress and Grayson as the grateful suppliant. Whatever infantile tantrums the Graysons might pitch, they would return to the fold like obedient little children when Manticore spoke firmly to them.

They truly didn't have a clue, not a suspicion of how severely they'd wounded the special relationship Elizabeth and Benjamin had created with one another, or how deeply they'd offended the common steaders of Grayson. And so they would gleefully exploit this latest disastrous turn, completely oblivious to its consequences beyond the narrow confines of the domestic arena.

Which meant that the adoption of a single human by a silken-furred being who weighed barely eight kilos could topple an alliance which had cost literally trillions of dollars and thousands of lives to forge.

"I don't know how it happened," she repeated, "and I don't have any idea at all where we go from here."

Where they went was White Haven, the seat of the Earls of White Haven for four hundred and forty-seven T-years. It was the last place in the universe Honor Harrington wanted to go, but she was too exhausted to fight any longer.

She stared without speaking out the window of the air limo at the stingships flying escort, and White Haven was wise enough to leave her to her silence. There was nothing more either of them could have said, anyway, and even though he shared her dismay at what had happened, he couldn't damp the bright sparkles of joy still flickering through him as he contemplated the warm, silken weight in his lap. Honor understood that perfectly, but it didn't make things any easier on her, and so she sat at the eye of a magic circle of stillness, feeling White Haven beside her and Andrew LaFollet and Armsman 1/c Spencer Hawke behind her, and watched the stingships.

On Grayson they would have been Harrington Steading aircraft. Here on Manticore, they wore the blue-and-silver colors of the House of Winton, and Colonel Ellen Shemais, second-in-command of the Queen's Own Regiment and Elizabeth's personal bodyguard, had personally explained to the pilots of those escorts that both of them had better already be fireballs on the ground before anyone got into range to shoot at Duchess Harrington.

Usually, Honor's mouth quirked in a wry smile at that thought, but not today. Today, all she could do was gaze out the window at the cobalt blue sky, watching the stingships glow in the reddening light of late, barely substratospheric afternoon, while she hugged Nimitz to her breasts and tried very hard not to think at all.

She failed, of course.

She knew she shouldn't be doing this, that White Haven was the one place she must not go, yet the knowledge was useless. The maelstrom of emotions which had battered her in the gymnasium had joined with the exhaustion of months under bitter attack and her growing grief and sense of utter helplessness as she watched herself being used as the wedge to drive two star nations she loved apart. She'd given all she had to the struggle, held her head up publicly in defiance of her enemies, spent her strength and her political capital like a wastrel, and nothing she or any of her allies could do had changed a single thing.

She was tired. Not physically, but with a soul-deep heart sickness that had driven her spirit to its knees, and she could no longer fight the inevitable. Not when Hamish wanted her to make this trip so badly. And not when some tiny inner part of her needed to face the woman she had wronged in her heart even if she'd never committed a single overt act of betrayal.

The limo sped on into the north while the sun sank lower and lower in the west, and Honor Harrington sat silently in her seat, empty as the thin, icy air beyond the crystoplast, and waited.

White Haven was much smaller than she'd expected.

Oh, it covered more ground than Harrington House did on Grayson, but that was because it had been built on a planet friendly to humans, not one where humanity's most deadly enemy was the planetary environment itself. It could afford to sprawl comfortably over the gently rolling slopes of its grounds, and its low wings, none of them more than two stories tall, seemed to invite visitors to join it. It was made of native stone, with the immensely thick walls the first-wave colonists had used as insulation against the harsh winter climate of these northern latitudes, and it possessed a certain imposing presence, despite the fact that its oldest, central block had obviously been designed and built before its owners realized they were about to become nobles. It was only a little more ostentatious than an extremely large and rambling, extended farmhouse, but it didn't really need to be anything more impressive than that, and subsequent generations had been wise enough to insist that their architects coordinate the centuries of expansion with the original, simple structure. Other noble families had possessed less wisdom, and all too many of their family seats had become hodgepodges of architectural cacophony as a result.

White Haven hadn't. It had grown much larger over the years, yet it was what it was. It refused to be anything else, and if at first glance it might seem that newer, more modern estates—like Harrington House—were grander and more magnificent, that was *only* at first glance. Because White Haven had what those new and splendid homes' owners simply couldn't buy, however hard they tried. It had history. It had lawns of ankle-deep sod, pampered by generations of gardeners, and Old Terran oak trees a meter and a half through at the base, which had made the journey from Old Earth herself aboard the sublight colony ship *Jason* four centuries earlier. It had thick, soft Terran moss and immensely dense hedges and thickets of crown blossom and flame seed that draped around stone picnic tables, gazebos, and half-hidden, stone-flagged patios, and it sat there, whispering that it had always been here and always would be.

There were places on Grayson, like Protector's Palace, which were even older and possessed that same sense of ancientness. But Protector's Palace, like every other Grayson building, was a fortress against its world. Part of that world, and yet forever separate from it. Like Honor's own parents' house on Sphinx, though on a far larger scale, White Haven wore its age like a comfortable garment. That made it something she understood, and if White Haven was a fortress in its own way, its defenses were raised against the maddening pressure of human affairs, and not against its planet.

Despite all that had happened to finally drive her to this place, Honor sensed the living, welcoming presence of Hamish Alexander's home, and a part of her reached out to it. Yet even as she yearned towards its shelter, she knew it could never be hers, and a fresher, bleaker wave of resignation washed through her as Simon Mattingly landed the limo gently on the pad.

Hamish climbed out of his seat, cradling Samantha in his arms, and his slightly strained smile invited her to follow him from the limo. She was grateful to him for sparing her pleasantries which neither of them needed, and she managed to return his smile with one of her own.

Like him, she carried Nimitz in her arms, not in his usual place on her shoulder. She needed that extra contact, that sense of additional connection, and she clung to it as she walked towards a side door with White Haven while LaFollet, Mattingly, and Hawke followed at her heels.

The door opened at their approach, and a man who radiated a subtle kinship to James MacGuiness looked out with a small bow of greeting.

"Welcome home, My Lord," he said to White Haven.

"Thank you, Nico." White Haven acknowledged his greeting with a smile. "This is Duchess Harrington. Is Lady Emily in the atrium?"

"She is, My Lord," Nico replied, and bestowed another, more formal bow on Honor. His emotions were complex, compounded of his deep loyalty to the Alexander family, and to Hamish and Emily Alexander in particular, and an awareness that there was no truth to the vicious stories about Hamish and Honor. She tasted his sympathy for her, but there was also a sharp edge of resentment. Not for anything she'd done, but for the pain others had brought to people for whom he cared, using her as the weapon.

"Welcome to White Haven, Your Grace," he said, and to his credit, not a trace of his ambivalence at seeing her there colored his voice or his manner.

"Thank you," she said, smiling at him as warmly as her emotionally battered state allowed.

"Should I announce you to Her Ladyship, My Lord?" Nico asked the earl.

"No, thank you. She's . . . expecting us. We'll find our own way, but ask Cook to put together a light supper for three, please. No, make that for five," he corrected, nodding at the two treecats. "And make sure there's plenty of celery."

"Of course, My Lord."

"And see to it that Her Grace's armsmen get fed, as well."

"Of course," Nico repeated as he stood aside, then closed the door behind them, and Honor turned to LaFollet.

"I think Earl White Haven, Lady White Haven, and I need to

discuss things in private, Andrew," she said quietly. "You and Simon and Spencer stay here."

"I—" LaFollet began an immediate protest, then clamped his jaws tight.

He should be used to this by now, he told himself. The Steadholder had made great strides in accepting that it was his job to keep her alive whether she liked it or not, but the old stubbornness still reasserted itself at times. At least if it had to do it right now, White Haven was probably about as safe a place as she could be. And even if it hadn't been, he thought, looking at her exhausted face, he wasn't about to argue with her. Not now.

"Of course, My Lady," he said.

"Thank you," Honor said softly, and looked at Nico.

"Take care of them for me, please," she asked, and the retainer bowed more deeply still.

"I'd be honored to, Your Grace," he assured her, and she smiled one last time at her armsmen and then turned to follow White Haven down a wide, stone-floored hallway.

She had a vague impression of deeply bayed windows set in the immensely thick walls—of tasteful paintings, bright area rugs and throws, and furniture which managed to merge expense and age with comfort and utility—but none of it really registered. And then White Haven opened another door, and ushered her through it into a crystoplast-roofed atrium which must have been twenty or thirty meters on a side. That wasn't very large for Grayson, where the need to seal "outdoor gardens" against the local environment created enormous greenhouse domes, but it was the largest atrium she'd ever seen in a private home in the Star Kingdom.

It also seemed younger than much of the rest of the estate, and she looked sharply at White Haven as a spike in his emotions told her why that was so.

He'd built it for Emily. This was *her* place, and Honor felt a sudden, wrenching sense of wrongness. She was an intruder, an invader. She had no business in this peaceful, plant-smelling space. But she was here, now, and it was too late to run, and so she followed White Haven across the atrium to the splashing fountain and koi pond at its heart.

A woman sat waiting there. Her life-support chair hovered a half-meter off the atrium floor, and it turned smoothly and silently on its counter grav to face them.

Honor felt her spine stiffen and her shoulders straighten. Not in hostility or defensiveness, but in acknowledgment and . . . respect. Her chin rose, and she returned Lady Emily Alexander's regard levelly.

Lady Emily was taller than Honor had expected, or would have been, if she'd ever stood on her two feet again. She was also frail, the antithesis of Honor's slimly solid, broad-shouldered, well-muscled physique. Where Honor was dark-haired and dark-eyed, Lady Emily's hair was as golden blond as Alice Truman's, and her eyes were a deep and brilliant green. She looked as if a kiss of breeze would lift her out of her chair and carry her away, for she could not have weighed over forty kilos, and her long-fingered hands were thin and fragile-looking.

And she was still one of the most beautiful women in the entire Star Kingdom.

It wasn't just her face, or her eyes, or her hair or bone structure. Anyone with her wealth could have had those things, in these days of biosculpt and cosmetic gene therapy. It was something else. Some inner quality she'd been able to transmit to the camera during her actress days, yet one which was infinitely stronger in person than it could have been through any electronic medium. It reached out to anyone who came near her, and as Honor felt it, magnified and multiplied through her link to Nimitz, she understood precisely why Nico was so devoted to his Countess.

"Emily," White Haven's deep voice was deeper even than usual, "allow me to introduce Duchess Harrington."

"Welcome to White Haven, Your Grace." The voice was a husky shadow of the warm, almost purring contralto which had reached out to so many HD viewers, but it retained more than a ghost of its old power. The countess held out one delicate hand—the only one she could move, Honor realized, and stepped forward to take it.

"Thank you, Lady White Haven," she said softly, and her thanks were deep-felt and genuine, for there was no anger, no hatred in Lady Emily's greeting. Sadness, yes—a vast, bottomless sorrow, and a weariness which almost matched Honor's own. But not anger. Not at Honor. There *was* anger, a deep, seething rage, but it was directed at another target. At the men and women who had callously used her, just as surely as they'd used Honor or Hamish, for political advantage.

"You're not as tall as I expected from the talk show circuit and news reports," Lady Emily observed, with a faint smile. "I expected you to be at least three meters tall, and here you are, scarcely two and a half."

"I think we all look taller on HD, Your Grace."

"So we do." Lady Emily's smile grew broader. "I always did, at any rate," she went on, and her tone and emotions alike were barren of any self-pity for those vanished days. She cocked her head— the only thing, besides her right arm, that she could move—and gazed up at Honor thoughtfully.

"You look as if this has been even uglier for you than I was afraid it had," she said calmly. "I regret that, just as I regret that you and I must meet under these circumstances. But the more I've thought about it, the more it's become clear to me that it's essential for the three of us to decide how we will all respond to these . . . people."

Honor looked down into those brilliantly green, understanding eyes, and felt something deep within her begin to yield as she tasted the genuine compassion at Emily Alexander's core. There was resentment, as well. There had to be, for however special Lady Emily might be, she remained a human being, and no mere mortal confined forever to a life-support chair could look at Honor, standing beside her husband, and not resent the younger woman's physical health and vitality. Yet that resentment was only a part of what she felt when she looked at Honor, and her understanding, her refusal to prejudge or to condemn, reached out to her guest like a comforting embrace.

Lady Emily's eyes narrowed slightly, and she pursed her lips. Then she glanced at Hamish, and one graceful eyebrow rose as she saw the treecat in his arms. She started to speak, then paused and visibly changed what she'd been about to say.

"I see we have even more to talk about than I'd expected," she said instead, gazing speculatively at Samantha. "But that should probably wait. Hamish, I think Her Grace and I need to get to know one another. Go find something to do."

A whimsical smile took the possible sting from the final sentence, and Honor surprised herself by smiling back. It was a fragile, weary smile, but genuine, and White Haven actually chuckled.

"I will," he agreed. "But I've already told Nico to ask Cook to put together something for dinner, so don't take too long."

"If we take too long, it won't be the first time dinner's gotten cold," his wife replied serenely. "Now go away."

He chuckled again, swept a deep bow to both women, and then, suddenly, they were alone.

"Please, Your Grace," Lady Emily said. "Have a seat."

She waved her mobile arm once more, indicating a bench of natural stone with a thick, woven seat cushion built into a natural rock wall beside the splashing fountain. A miniature Old Earth willow's drooping branches framed it welcomingly, and built-in stone planters spilled Manticoran cloud flowers to either side of it. It was as if the plants surrounded the bench in a protective, earthy-smelling shield of brilliant blue and red and yellow petals, and Lady Emily's life-support chair turned silently in a half-circle until she faced it, as well. She'd maneuvered the chair without manipulating a single control with her good hand, Honor realized. Obviously, the doctors had managed to provide at least limited neural interfacing, despite the catastrophic damage to her motor centers, and Honor was glad.

"Thank you, Lady White Haven," she replied, and crossed to the bench and seated herself. She settled Nimitz into her lap, where he lay alert and watchful but without the quivering tension he might have exhibited under other circumstances.

Lady Emily's lips quirked in another wry smile, and she shook her head.

"Your Grace, I think that whatever else happens, the two of us are going to come to know one another much too well to continue with all these formalities. Unless you object, I shall call you Honor, and you shall call me Emily."

"Of course . . . Emily," Honor agreed. It was odd, she thought. Emily was older than her own mother, and a tiny part of Honor recognized that seniority and responded to it. But only a tiny part. And that, she realized, was because although she could taste Emily's awareness of her own relative youth, the countess radiated no sense of superiority. She was aware of her own age and experience, but she was also aware of Honor's, and her sense of sureness, of being the one who knew how to proceed in this painful instance, arose from the fact that her experience was different from Honor's, not greater.

"Thank you," Emily said, and her chair tilted slightly backwards in mid-air while she gazed thoughtfully at her guest.

"You realize that Hamish asked you here at my suggestion," she said after a moment, more as someone observing an unexpected truth than as if she were asking a question or making a statement, and Honor nodded.

"I'd hoped you would, just as I'd hoped you'd come," Emily continued. "I meant it when I said I regret meeting under these circumstances, but I've been curious about you for years now. So in a way, I'm happy to finally meet you, although I could certainly wish it hadn't come about this way."

She paused for a moment, then gave her head a small toss and continued more briskly.

"You and Hamish—and I—have been made the victims of a concerted, vicious attack. One that depends for success on innuendo and hypocrisy in the service of the belief that the end justifies any means whatsoever. And ugly as it may be, and for all the potential for public opinion to recoil on the accusers in disgust, it's unfortunately effective. Because it relies on the knife in the back rather than open confrontation, it can never be answered by reasoned argument or proof of innocence, however genuine and however convincingly presented. Even if you and Hamish were having an affair, which I don't for a moment believe you are, it ought to be your business. And mine, perhaps, but no one else's. Yet even though almost anyone in the Star Kingdom would agree with that statement in the abstract, by now it's completely useless as a defense. You realize that, don't you?"

"Yes." Honor nodded again, stroking Nimitz's silky pelt.

"I don't know that there *is* a defense, really," Emily said frankly. "It's always harder to prove a negative, and the more you two or your surrogates deny the lies being told about you, the more a certain portion of the electorate will believe them. Worse, all of the Government newsfaxes and commentators are beginning to take it as a given that you're guilty as charged. Very soon now, they won't even bother to argue the case any longer. The assumption of guilt will simply be there, in everything they write or say, and the taint will cling despite anything you can do."

Honor felt her shoulders hunching once more as Emily calmly spelled out what she'd already realized for herself.

"The most damning point of their 'indictment'—and the one I find the most personally infuriating—is the allegation that you and Hamish have betrayed *me*," Emily continued, and although her voice remained as level and thoughtful as before, she couldn't hide her own seething anger. It was an anger Honor understood only too well, the fury of someone who knew she had been cynically used as a weapon against all she believed in and stood for.

"If they choose to involve me in their games and machinations," Emily told her, "then I think it's only fitting that I respond. I realize neither you nor Hamish have asked me to become involved. I even understand why."

She looked very steadily into Honor's eyes for a moment, her own eyes very dark and still, and Honor felt the fusion of fury and compassion at her core.

"To an extent, Honor, I was willing to stay out of the fray if that was what the two of you wished. In part, I'm ashamed to admit, because I was . . . afraid to do otherwise. Or perhaps not afraid. Perhaps I was simply too tired. My health has been particularly poor for the past year or so, which is undoubtedly one reason Hamish has tried so hard to keep me out of this. And that ill health may also explain why something inside me quailed every time I thought about becoming involved, anyway. And there may have been . . . other reasons."

Again, their eyes met, and again Honor felt the complex freight of emotions hanging between them.

"But that was cowardice on my part," Lady Emily continued quietly. "An abandonment of my own responsibility to stand and fight against anyone who wants to destroy my life. And certainly of my responsibility to prevent moral pygmies with the ideology and ethics of back-alley rats from raping the political processes of the Star Kingdom."

She paused for a moment, jaw clamped, and this time Honor tasted something else in her emotions. A scathing self-condemnation. Anger at herself for having evaded her obligations. And not, Honor realized, solely because of weariness or ill health—or even Hamish's desire to shield her. This was a woman who had looked into her mirror and faced her own resentment, her sense of hurt and shame, and her perfectly natural anger at the younger woman whose name had been so publicly linked with her husband's. She'd faced those things and overcome them, yet a part of her could not forgive herself for taking so long to do it.

"One reason I asked Hamish to invite you here," Lady Emily told her unflinchingly, "was to tell you that whatever he—or you—

may wish, this is not simply your fight. It's also mine, and I intend to take the battle to the enemy. These . . . *people* have seen fit to drag me and people I care about into their tawdry, vicious games, and I won't have it."

There was, Honor reflected, something frightening about the complete calm with which Lady Emily delivered that final sentence.

"The only possible reply I can see," White Haven's wife continued "is to turn the hook for their entire attack against them. Not to mount a defense so much as to take the war to them, for a change."

Honor sat up straighter on the bench, leaning forward with the first faint flickers of hope as she tasted Emily's resolution.

"I don't wish to sound vain," the countess said, "but it would be foolish for me to pretend not to know that, like you and Hamish, although for different reasons, I enjoy a unique status with the Manticoran public. I've seen enough of you on HD, and heard enough about you from others, to know you sometimes find your public stature more than a little embarrassing and exaggerated. Mine often strikes me the same way, but it exists, and it's the reason High Ridge and his flunkies have been able to attack you and Hamish so effectively.

"But the key to their entire position is to portray me as a 'wronged woman' as the result of your alleged actions. The public's anger has been generated not because you and Hamish might have had an affair, but because Hamish and I married in the Church, in a sacrament we've never renounced or altered which pledged us to honor a monogamous marriage. And because you're a naval officer, not a registered courtesan. If you were an RC, the public might resent any relationship between you and Hamish on my behalf, but no one would consider that either of you had 'betrayed' me or our marriage. But you aren't an RC, and that lets them portray any affair between the two of you as a direct attack upon me. You and he have already issued statements of denial, and you were wise to let those initial statements stand without the sort of repeated denials which so many people would consider little more than sure proof of guilt. You were also wise to avoid the rather disgusting tactic of claiming that even if you'd been guilty, 'everyone' does it. I know some of your advisors must have suggested that approach as a way to brush off the seriousness of your alleged offense, but any move in that direction would have been tantamount to admitting that the charges were justified. Yet even though you've issued your denials with dignity and as calmly and effectively as you possibly could have, they haven't been enough. So I believe it's time to move to the next level of counterattack."

"Counterattack?" Honor asked.

"Precisely." Emily nodded firmly. "As you may know, I virtually never leave White Haven these days. I doubt that I've been off the grounds more than three times in the last T-year, because I love it here. And, frankly, because I find the rest of the world entirely too fatiguing.

"But that's about to change. The Government hacks who have been so busily raping you and Hamish in their columns have used me to do it. So I've already informed Willie that I'll be in Landing next week. I'll be staying at our house in the capital for a month or two, and I shall be entertaining for the first time in decades, albeit on a small scale. And I will make it my personal business to be certain everyone knows that *I* know there isn't a shred of truth to the allegations that you and Hamish have ever slept together. I'll also make it my business to inform anyone who asks—and, for that matter, anyone who doesn't ask—that I consider you a personal friend in my own right and a close political colleague of my husband. I imagine it will become at least a little more difficult for those assassins to spread their poison if the 'wronged woman' announces to the entire galaxy that she isn't wronged and never has been."

Honor stared at her, heart rising in the first true hope she'd felt in weeks. She was neither so naive nor so foolish as to believe Emily could wave some sort of magic wand and make all of it go away. But Emily was certainly correct about one aspect of it. The portion of the Government press which had been shedding such huge crocodile tears over how dreadfully Lady White Haven had been betrayed, and how terribly her husband's infidelity must have hurt her, could hardly continue to weep for her if she were busy publicly laughing at the absurdity of their allegations.

"I think . . . I think that would help enormously, Emily," she said after a moment, and the slight quaver around the edges of her voice surprised her.

"No doubt it will," Emily replied, but Honor felt a fresh tremor of anxiety at the taste of the other woman's emotions. The countess wasn't done yet. There was something more—and worse—to come, and she watched the older woman draw a deep breath.

"No doubt it will," she repeated, "but there's one other point I think we must discuss, Honor."

"Another point?" Honor asked tautly.

"Yes. I said that I know you and Hamish aren't lovers, and I do. I know because, frankly, I've known that he has had lovers. Not many of them, of course, but a few."

She looked away from her guest, at something only she could see, and the deep, bittersweet longing at her center pricked Honor's eyes with tears. It wasn't anger, or a sense of betrayal. It was regret. It was loss. It was sorrow for the one thing she and the man who loved her—and whom she loved, with all her heart—could never share again. She didn't blame him for seeking that one thing with others; but she bled inside with the knowledge that she could never give it to him herself.

"All of them, with one single exception he deeply regrets, have been registered courtesans," she went on softly, "but he's also respected and liked them. If he hadn't, he would never have taken them to bed. He isn't the sort of man to have casual affairs, or to 'sleep around.' He has too much integrity for that." She smiled sadly. "I suppose it must sound odd for a wife to speak about her husband's integrity when he chooses his lovers, but it's really the only word that fits. If he'd asked me, I would've told him that, yes, it hurts, but not because he's being 'unfaithful' to me. It hurts because I can no longer give him the one thing they can . . . and that he can no longer give it to me. Which is why he's never asked me, because he already knows what I'd say. And that's also why he's been so utterly discreet. He knows that no one in our circles would have faulted him for patronizing an RC under the circumstances, and that most other Manticorans would understand, as well. But he's always been determined to avoid putting that to the test. Not to shield his own reputation, but to protect me, to avoid underscoring the fact that I'll never again leave this chair. He doesn't want to humiliate me by even suggesting that I might be somehow . . . inadequate. A cripple.

"And he refuses to do that," she went on, turning to look at Honor once more, "because he loves me. I truly believe that he loves me as much today as he did the day he proposed to me. The day we married. The day they pulled me from that air car and told him I would never walk or breathe again unassisted."

She drew another deep breath, the muscles of her diaphragm controlled by the life-support chair interfaces because she could no longer directly control them herself.

"And that's been the difference between me and all of his lovers, Honor. He cared about them, and he respected them, but he didn't love them. Not the way he loves me.

"Or the way he loves you."

Honor jerked back on the bench, as if Emily had just thrust a dagger into her heart. Her eyes flew to meet Emily's, and saw the brimming tears, the knowledge . . . and the compassion.

"He hasn't told me he does," the countess said quietly. "But he hasn't had to. I know him too well, you see. If he didn't, he would have had you out here to meet me years ago, given how closely the two of you have worked together in the Lords. And he would have turned to me the instant this whole affair hit, instead of trying so desperately to keep me out of it. To protect me. I'm his chief analyst and adviser, though very few people realize it, and there's no way he would have failed to introduce us to one another, especially after High Ridge's cronies launched these attacks on the two of you . . . unless there were some reason he couldn't. And that reason—the reason he was willing to see his own name and reputation ruined by false charges and the Opposition's ability to fight High Ridge effectively undermined rather than enlist my aid to defeat them—is that he was afraid I'd see the truth and be wounded by his 'betrayal.' And just as it's the reason he's kept me from meeting you, it's the fact that he loves you which has prevented him from even trying to become anything more than your friend and colleague. You're not a professional, and even if you were, he knows it wouldn't be a brief affair. Not this time. And deep inside, he's afraid that for the first time he might truly betray me."

"I— How did—?"

Honor tried desperately to get a grip on herself, but she couldn't. Emily Alexander had just given her the final clue she'd needed, the final puzzle piece. Everything she'd ever felt from Hamish snapped suddenly into place, and she wondered how Emily, without her own link to Nimitz, had been able to grasp the core truth so completely.

"Honor, I've been married to Hamish for over seventy T-years. I *know* him, and I love him, and I see how this is tearing him apart. It was already there before this smear campaign was launched, but it wasn't destroying him the way it is now. I think . . . I think that what happened is that the lies and the false accusations forced him to look closely at things he'd held at a distance, somehow. They made him admit the truth to himself on some deeper level, and the combination of how much he loves you—loves both of us— and his guilt at having discovered that he can love someone besides me is like a bleeding wound. Worse," she looked directly into Honor's eyes, "he's afraid he's going to tell you openly how he feels. That he *is* going to 'betray me' by taking a lover he truly loves.

"I don't know how I'd react if that happened," she admitted frankly. "I'm afraid to find out. But what I'm even more afraid of is that if the two of you did become lovers, the secret would be impossible to keep. There are too many ways to spy on any-one, and too many people with too much to lose who must want desperately to find proof of his infidelity with you. If they do, that proof will be made public, and any good I may accomplish by telling the world I was never wronged will be instantly undone. In fact, my protestation of his innocence will only make it even worse. And to be totally honest, I'm very much afraid that if the two of you continue to work so closely together, eventually he will act upon his feelings. I don't know what that would do to him, in the long run, any more than I know what it would do to me, but I'm afraid we may both find out. Unless . . ."

"Unless what?" Honor's voice was tight, and her hands tight-ened on Nimitz's softness, as well.

"Unless you do what he can't," Emily said steadily. "As long as both of you are on the same planet, you must work together as political partners. Because you two are—or were, before this all happened—our most effective political weapons, and because if you stop working together, it will be taken as proof of guilt. But for that to be possible, *you* must ensure that nothing else ever happens between you. It isn't fair. I know that. And I'm not tell-ing you this as an anxious wife, fearful that her husband will find someone he loves more than her. I'm telling you because it would be political suicide, and not just for you and Hamish, if the two of you ever became lovers, especially after I come forward and assure the entire Star Kingdom that you never have.

"For more than fifty T-years, my husband has been absolutely faithful to me in every way that truly matters, despite my confinement to this chair. But this time, Honor—this time, I don't think he's strong enough. Or not that, so much, as that I think this time he's up against something too strong *for* him. So you have to be his strength. Fair or not, you have to be the one to maintain the distance and the separation between you."

"I know that," Honor said softly. "I know that. I've known it for years now, Emily. I have to maintain the separation, never let him love me. Never let myself love him."

She looked at her hostess, her face tight with pain.

"I know that . . . and I *can't*," she whispered, and Lady Emily White Haven stared at her in horror as Admiral Lady Dame Honor Harrington, Duchess and Steadholder Harrington, burst into tears.

Chapter Thirteen

Dinner was indeed cold by the time they got to it.

Honor had no idea how the complex, jagged-edged situation was going to resolve itself. For that matter, she didn't even know what she herself felt. She only knew she was afraid to find out.

It was odd, especially for someone with the supportive, loving parents she'd had, not to mention her link to Nimitz, and even more her ability to sense the emotions of those about her. Odd, yet true.

There remained one thing in the universe which could absolutely terrify her: her own heart.

She couldn't understand it—had never been able to understand it. Physical danger, duty, moral responsibility . . . those she could face. Not without fear, but without the crippling sense that somehow her fear would betray her into failure. But not this. This was a different sort of minefield, one she had no idea how to navigate, and one she had no confidence in her ability to face. Yes, she could taste and share the emotions of both Hamish and Emily, but simply knowing what they felt was no magic spell to suddenly make all right.

She knew Hamish Alexander loved her. She knew she loved Hamish Alexander. And she knew Hamish and Emily loved each other, and that all three of them were determined not to hurt the others.

And none of it did a bit of good, because whatever they did, whatever happened, someone was going to be hurt. And looming over that deep immediate and personal dread of pain to come was the chilling knowledge of how many other people would be affected by what ought to be their deeply personal decisions.

Perhaps it would have been different if she'd had more self-confidence, she thought, sipping her wine as she sat across the table from Emily and Hamish. She envied Emily's serenity, especially because she'd felt exactly how dismayed and shaken Emily had been by her own admission in the atrium. The older woman had already known what Hamish felt; the sudden confirmation that Honor returned his love had hit her like a blow. There'd been anger in her reaction. Not a lot, but a sharp, knife-like flicker of fury that Honor should dare to love *her* husband, an automatic response that was built of raw instinct and her awareness of how much more danger Honor's emotions threw all of them into. She'd made herself accept that Hamish's struggle against his feelings was a losing battle; now she'd discovered that the person she'd hoped would be her ally had already lost the same fight. There was enormous potential for jealousy and resentment alike in that moment of realization, and the fact that she'd put her rage aside so quickly and so completely astonished Honor.

But there were a lot of things about Emily Alexander that astonished Honor. She was totally unlike Honor's mother, except in one way: both of them radiated that calm sense of knowing exactly who they were, not just in matters of duty, but in those of the heart, as well. Honor had always envied that in her mother, almost as much as she'd envied—and resented—Allison Harrington's beauty and unabashed sensuality when she herself had been an ugly-duckling, raw-boned, too-tall, gawky adolescent. She'd known even at her most resentful that she was being foolish. Her mother couldn't help her beauty any more than she could help being who she was, and even if she could have been someone else just to make her daughter feel less outclassed and homely, it would have been wrong for her to do so. Wrong for her to be anyone but herself.

She and Honor's father had taught their daughter that, almost without realizing they had. They'd done it by example and by loving her, without limit or qualification. They'd made her whole in all of the ways that mattered most, even while she was wounded in that one secret regard. The quiet place in her heart where she'd been supposed to keep the belief that anyone could truly love her . . . unless they had to.

It had been stupid, stupid, stupid, she told herself. If anyone in the entire galaxy could know that, then certainly with her parents and Nimitz she'd been that one person. But it hadn't helped, and then, at the Academy, had come Pavel Young and Mr. Midshipman Cal Panokulous—the would-be rapist and the man who had hurt her more cruelly still. The damage they'd done had been terrible, yet she'd survived it. Survived and, with Paul Tankersley's help, actually learned to heal. To know that there were people who could—and would—love her. She'd actually, physically felt the love of so many people in her life now, in so many ways. Paul. Her parents, James MacGuiness, Andreas Venizelos, Andrew LaFollet, Alistair McKeon, Jamie Candless, Scotty Tremaine, Miranda LaFollet, Nimitz . . .

Yet deep inside her, somewhere all the healing had failed to reach, there was the fear. No longer the fear that they would not love her, but that they would not be *allowed* to. That the universe would punish them if they dared to, for all too many of those who had loved her had also died because of it.

It wasn't logical, and she knew it, but she'd lost too many lives, and every one of them had torn its own hole in her soul. Officers and ratings who had served with her and paid with their lives for her victories. Armsmen who had died so that their liege lady might live. Friends who had knowingly faced Death—and lost to him— for her sake. It had happened too often, cost too many too much, and the terror that anyone who dared to love her was marked for death mocked her, for logic was a weak weapon when matched against the unreasoning assurance of the heart. She'd made progress in her fight against that irrational certainty. She knew that, too. But if she'd won a few battles, she had yet to win the war, and the tangled weave of emotions and needs, fear and the obligations of honor, that wrapped about her feelings for Hamish Alexander like a shroud threatened to cost her even more ground in the fight.

"So," Hamish said finally, his voice almost startling after their long, mutual silence, "did the two of you decide how we ought to tackle this?"

He kept his tone light, almost droll, but he didn't fool anyone at the table, including himself, and Honor looked at Emily.

"I think we've found a way to at least start getting a handle on it," his wife told him with a serenity Honor was half-surprised, even now, to realize was genuine. "I don't say it will be easy, and I'm not sure it will be quite as effective, under the circumstances, as I would have liked—" she glanced sideways at Honor for a heartbeat "—but I believe we can at least blunt the worst of their attack."

"There's a reason I've always relied on you for the necessary political miracles, Emily," Hamish told her with a smile. "Give me a fleet problem, or a naval battle to fight, and I know exactly what to do. But dealing with scum like High Ridge and Descroix—?" He shook his head. "I just can't wrap my mind around how to handle them."

"Be honest, dear," Emily corrected him gently. "It's not that you really can't do it, and you know it. It's that you get so furious with them that you wind up climbing onto your high moral horse so you can ride them under the hooves of your righteous fury. But when you close your knight errant's helmet, the visibility through that visor is just a little limited, isn't it?"

Her smile took most of the bite from her words, but he winced anyway, and that wince was at least partly genuine.

"I realize any good political analyst has to know when and how to be brutally honest, Emily, but somehow that particular metaphor doesn't do an enormous amount for my self image," he said so dryly Honor chuckled despite herself, and Emily looked at her with a twinkle.

"He does the affronted-but-too-polite-to-admit-it, stiff-necked, aristocratic naval officer quite well, doesn't he?" she remarked.

"I don't think I'll answer that question," Honor replied. "On the other hand, there's something to be said for the . . . directness of a Don Quixote. As long as the windmills don't hit back too hard, at least."

"Granted, granted," Emily conceded. She was eating one-handed with the grace of decades of practice, but now she paused to set down her fork so that she could point with one finger for emphasis. "I'll even grant that the political process needs people willing to shatter themselves on the rocks of conviction rather than countenance deception or deceit. We'd be better off if we had more of them, and the ones we do have have a responsibility to serve as the conscience of our partisan bloodletting. But they can do that effectively in isolation, maintaining our concepts of morality by serving as examples of it whether they ever accomplish anything else or not. But to be *effective* in the political process requires more than personal rectitude, however admirable that may be. You don't have to become the enemy, but you do have to understand her, and that means understanding not simply her motives but her tactics. Because when you understand those two things you can design countertactics. You don't have to descend to the same level; you simply have to recognize what the opposition is up to and allow for it."

"Willie understands that a lot better than I do," Hamish admitted after a moment.

"Yes, he does, and that's why someday he'll be Prime Minister and you won't. Which is probably just as well," Emily said with another, wider smile. "On the other hand, much as I love Willie, he'd make a terrible admiral!"

All three of them laughed, but then Emily cocked her head and looked thoughtfully at Honor.

"I haven't had as long to observe you, Honor," she said, "but I'm a bit surprised by the fact that you seem to be rather more . . . flexible than Hamish. Not that I think you're any more willing to sacrifice your principles on the altar of expediency, but in the sense that you clearly do a better job of putting yourself inside the other person's head."

"Appearances can be deceiving," Honor replied wryly. "I don't begin to understand how a High Ridge or a Janacek thinks. And to be perfectly honest, I don't want to."

"You're wrong, you know," Emily disagreed so firmly that Honor looked at her in some surprise. "You don't understand why they want the things they want, but you can accept that they do. And once you've done that, you also do an excellent job of analyzing how they might go about getting them."

"Not always," Honor said in a darker tone. "I never saw *this*—" she waved one hand around the table in a gesture which encompassed all three of them "—coming."

"No, but now that it's here, you know exactly what it is they're trying to accomplish. That's why it hurts you so much to see them getting away with it," Emily said gently. "No one can fault you for being surprised by gutter tactics so alien to the way your own mind works, Honor, but even at your angriest, you haven't let anger blind you. And from what I've seen of you both in the 'faxes and on HD, as well as here, now that I've had a chance to meet you in person, I think you could turn into a very effective politician, with time."

Honor stared at her in disbelief, and Emily chuckled.

"Oh, you'd never be a natural politician the way Willie is! And, like Hamish, you'd always be most comfortable in the sort of collegial atmosphere the House of Lords is supposed to be. But I've viewed your speeches, and you're much more effective as a public speaker than Hamish is." She smiled at her husband. "That's not an aspersion on him, you understand. But he gets impatient and starts to lecture, and you don't.

"There's more to being politically effective than giving good speeches, Emily," Hamish objected.

"Of course there is. But Honor has already demonstrated her ability to analyze military threat situations and devise strategies to meet them, and just listening to her speak in the Lords, it's evident to me that she can bring that same analytical ability to bear in other arenas, once she learns the conditions which apply there. She still has a lot to learn about politics, especially the cutthroat version practiced here in the Star Kingdom, but it seems to me from watching her over the past few years that her learning curve is steep. She's spent forty T-years learning to be a naval officer; give me half that long in politics, and I'll make her Prime Minister!"

"Oh no you won't!" Honor said roundly. "I'd cut my own throat in less than ten!"

"That seems a bit drastic," Emily observed mildly. "Perhaps there's more of Doña Quixote in you than I'd realized."

Her green eyes flickered for just a moment, and Honor felt her brief flare of regret over her choice of words, but the countess brushed it off quickly.

"No, just more sanity," Hamish observed, oblivious to the quick glances the two women exchanged. He wasn't looking at them, anyway. His attention had strayed back to Samantha, as it had done periodically all evening, and he took another celery stalk from the bowl on the table and offered it to her.

"You're going to make her sick, Hamish," Emily scolded, and he looked up quickly, his expression so much like that of a guilty schoolboy caught in the act that Honor chuckled.

"Not without a lot more celery than that, he's not, Emily," she reassured her hostess. "Mind you," she went on more sternly, transferring her attention to Hamish, "too much celery really is bad for her. She can't digest it, and if she gets too much of it, she'll get constipated."

Samantha turned to give her a dignified look of reproval, and Honor was relieved to feel the female 'cat's amusement. Despite the transcendent joy of having bonded with Hamish, Samantha had been almost instantly aware of the dismay and consternation which had afflicted both Honor and her new person, and that awareness had sent its echoes reverberating through her, as well.

From the feel of her emotions, she still wasn't entirely certain why they were so upset. Which, Honor thought, only served to emphasize that despite all of their centuries of association with humans, treecats remained an alien species. For Nimitz and Samantha—as probably for all of their kind, given their ability to sense one another's emotions—there was absolutely no point in trying to conceal what one felt. Nimitz had accepted over the years that there were times when it was inappropriate, among humans, at least, to show his emotions, especially when they consisted of anger directed at someone senior to Honor in the Navy. But even for him, that was more a matter of good manners (and of making concessions to an inexplicable human code of behavior because it was important to his person) than because he saw any real sense in it. And neither he nor Samantha would have dreamed of attempting to deny how they truly felt about something—especially about something important.

Which explained the growing frustration Honor had received from both of them as the pain of suppressing and denying her feelings for Hamish grew within her. They knew how much she loved him, they knew how much he loved her, and by treecat standards, it was willfully insane for the two of them to subject themselves—and one another—to so much hurt. Which, to make things still worse, was also a hurt the 'cats had no choice but to endure with them.

Intellectually, both Nimitz and Samantha realized that all humans, with the notable exception of Honor herself, were what their own species called "mind-blind." They could even understand that because of that mind-blindness, human society had different imperatives from those of their own. But what they understood intellectually hadn't affected what they *felt*, and what they'd felt was not only frustration but anger at the inexplicable human willfulness which prevented Honor and Hamish from simply admitting the truth which was self-evident to any treecat and getting on with their lives without all this pain and suffering.

But now that the immediate euphoria of recognizing a human partner in Hamish and bonding to him had passed, Samantha was back face-to-face with the realities under which her human friends lived. And because Samantha was extremely intelligent, and an empath, she knew just how badly her adoption choice had disturbed those realities, even if she was still working on fully assimilating all of the reasons why it had.

"If they can't digest it, and if it, um, clogs their systems, then why do they all love it so much?" Emily asked.

"That was something that puzzled every human who ever studied 'cats," Honor said. "So once they learned to sign, we asked them, of course." She shrugged. "Part of their answer was exactly what you might have expected—they love the way it tastes. Think of the most chocolate-addicted human being you've ever met, then cube her craving, and you'll start closing in on just how much they love it. But that's only part of the reason. The other is that there's a trace compound in Sphinxian celery that they need."

"In *Sphinxian* celery?" Emily repeated.

"They love the taste of any celery from anywhere," Honor told her. "But back when humans first came to the Manticore System, we had to make some minor adjustments in our Old Terran flora and fauna before we introduced them into their new environments. As," she added in a dust-dry tone, gesturing briefly at herself, "we've done with human beings themselves, in a few other cases. We didn't do anything really drastic in the case of Sphinx, but a few minor genetic changes were designed into most of the Old Terran food plants to prevent the fixing of elements we didn't need in our diet and to discourage some particularly persistent local parasites and the plant diseases they carry. The basic idea was to get the genegineered plants to manufacture and store a Sphinxian organic compound that's harmless to humans but serves as a natural insect repellant. It worked in all of them, but better in some than in others, and it was most effective of all in celery, of all things. The version in the descendants of the modified Old Terran plants is slightly different from that which occurs in the native flora, sort of a hybrid. But it appears to be either necessary or extremely beneficial to the maintenance of the 'cats' empathic and telepathic senses."

"But where did they get it from before we came along with our celery?" Emily demanded.

"There's a Sphinxian plant that produces the native plants' version of the same compound. They call it 'purple thorn,' and they've known about it forever. But it's scarce and hard to find, and, frankly, they say celery just tastes a whole lot better." Honor shrugged again. "And that, it turns out, is the answer to the Great Celery Theft Mystery which first brought humans and treecats together."

"That's fascinating," Emily said, gazing at Honor raptly, and then moved her gaze to Nimitz and Samantha. She watched them for a moment, and they looked back at her solemnly until she drew a deep breath and turned back to Honor.

"I envy you," she said sincerely. "I would probably have envied you anyway, just for having been adopted in the first place, but to be answering so many questions, finding the answers to so many puzzles after so many centuries . . . That has to be especially wonderful."

"It is," Honor said softly, then surprised both Alexanders—and herself—with a giggle. "On the other hand," she explained half-apologetically as her hosts looked at her in surprise, "watching them sign can be an exhausting experience . . . especially when you get a dozen or so of them in one place! It's like being trapped inside a machine shop or an engine turbine."

"Oh, my!" Emily laughed delightedly. "I never even thought of that side of it."

Nimitz looked back and forth between the smiling humans, then rose in one of the human-style high chairs Nico had managed to dredge up for the treecats and began to sign. His spine was stiff with eloquent dignity, and Honor managed to keep any more laughter out of her voice as she translated for Emily and Hamish.

"He says that if we two-legs think it's hard to keep track of all those signs, then we should try it from the People's side. And that if we'd had the good sense as a species not to limit ourselves to 'mouth-noises' as our sole, miserable means of communication, the People might not have had to learn to wiggle their fingers just to talk to us."

The 'cat finished signing, then twitched his whiskers in disgust as all three humans began to laugh once more. He sniffed audibly, and elevated his nose, but Honor felt his inner delight bubbling up as he made them laugh, and she sent him an answering mental caress of approval.

"That's fascinating, as Emily says," Hamish said, after a moment, "and I can see that I'm going to have to go ahead and learn how to read signs myself. But all levity aside, you and Samantha and Nimitz and I have to face the fact that her decision to adopt me is going to create enormous problems. I'm grateful—awed—that she did it, anyway, but I'd truly like to know how it could have happened. And why she chose to do it at this particular moment."

"You still have a lot to learn about treecats, Hamish," Honor pointed out in a carefully neutral tone. "All of us do, actually. In fact, in some ways, those of us who've been adopted the longest have the most to learn, because we're having to disabuse ourselves of some theories and beliefs we've cherished for quite some time. And one of those beliefs was that a 'cat 'chooses' a human half as some sort of conscious process."

"What do you mean?" Emily asked intently.

"I've spent hours talking with Nimitz and Samantha about it, and I'm not entirely certain I've got it all straight yet," Honor replied. "But to boil it down to its simplest, while all treecats are both telepaths and empaths, some appear to be born with a special ability to reach out to human beings, as well as other members of their own species."

Both Alexanders nodded, but Honor could tell neither of them was fully up to speed on all of the new revelations about treecats. It might not be a bad idea, she decided, to give them a little more background before she tried to answer the question she wasn't at all sure she had an answer for in the first place.

"All 'cats are able to sense both the thoughts and the emotions of other 'cats," she began. "They call thoughts the 'mind-voice' and emotions the 'mind-glow.' Well, to be more accurate, those are the human-style words they've come up with to use when they try to explain things to us. As near as we can tell, Dr. Arif was correct in her original theory that telepaths wouldn't use a spoken language at all. In fact, that was probably the greatest single stumbling block to their ever learning to communicate with us. They knew we communicated using 'mouth-noises,' but the concept of language was so alien to them that it took them literally centuries to learn the meanings of more than a handful of words."

"How did they ever learn at all?" It was Hamish's turn to ask the question, and he reached out to caress Samantha's prick ears gently and tenderly.

"Well, that sort of brings us back to Samantha, in a way," Honor told him, and he looked up from the 'cat sharply.

"It's going to take us years and years to really square away our understanding of treecats," she went on, "but we've already learned an awful lot more than we ever knew before. There are still problems in getting complex concepts across from either side, especially when they're concepts which relate to abilities like telepathy and empathy that humans simply don't have any experiential basis with."

She carefully took no note of the thoughtful glance Hamish gave her over her last sentence.

"One thing which does seem to be clear, however, is that 'cats simply aren't innovators. Their heads don't work that way—or, at least, they haven't in the past. I suppose it's possible that that will change, now that they've begun interacting so much more fully with humans in general. But traditionally, 'cats who're capable of new insights or of conceptualizing new ways to do things have been very, *very* rare. That's one reason treecat society tends to have been extraordinarily stable, and also the reason that it seems to be difficult for them, as a species, to change their minds once they've embarked upon a consensual policy or way to do things."

This was not the time, she decided, to mention the fact that the treecats had spent the better part of four hundred T-years systematically concealing the true extent of their intelligence from the humans who had intruded into and settled upon their planet. Personally, she understood their motives perfectly, and she was confident Hamish and Emily would, as well, but it wouldn't hurt to get the groundwork established before they or the public at large were admitted into the full truth about that little treecat decision.

"But if they produce a limited number of innovators," she continued instead, "they have at least one huge offsetting advantage when it comes to promoting change. Once any 'cat figures out something new, the new knowledge can be very rapidly transmitted to all other treecats."

"Telepathy." White Haven nodded, blue eyes bright. "They just 'tell' each other about it!"

"Not quite," Honor disagreed. "From what Nimitz and Samantha tell me, the level of communication between most treecats is actually fairly analogous to human language, at least where the deliberate exchange of information is concerned. I doubt that most humans will ever be able even to imagine what it must be like to receive all of the emotional 'sideband transmissions' that accompany any treecat conversation. But their ability to explain things to one another on a cognitive level isn't all that much greater than it would be for humans. Faster—*lots* faster, apparently—but not the sort of mind-to-mind, my-mind-is-your-mind, sharing some science-fiction writers have postulated."

"So how do they do it?" the earl asked. "You said they can transmit the new knowledge very rapidly, so obviously something else is happening."

"Exactly. You see, the 'cats' entire society revolves around a particular group called 'memory singers.' They're always female, apparently because females have naturally stronger mind-voices and mind-glows, and they're almost but not quite matriarchs."

Honor frowned thoughtfully.

"The treecat clans are governed by their elders, who are chosen— by a process, I might add, which apparently bears absolutely no relationship to human elections *or* the hereditary transmission of leadership—primarily for their particular abilities in specific activities or crafts which are critical to the clan's survival. But the memory singers form a special craft group, almost a caste, which is treated with enormous deference by the entire clan. In fact, every memory singer is automatically a clan elder, regardless of her actual age. And because of their importance to the clan, they're protected and guarded fanatically and absolutely banned from any activity which might endanger them—sort of like a steadholder."

She grinned with unalloyed cheerfulness for the first time in what seemed to have been years, and both Alexanders chuckled sympathetically.

"The thing that makes them so important is that they're the keepers of the 'cats' history and information base. They're able to form so deep a mental bond with any other 'cat that they actually experience what happened to that other 'cat as if it had happened to them. Not only that, but they can then reproduce

those experiences in precise, exact detail, and share them with other
'cats . . . or pass them on to other memory singers. You might think
of it as sort of the ultimate oral history tradition, except that the
entire experience itself is transmitted, not simply from 'cat to 'cat,
but actually across generations. According to Nimitz and Samantha,
there's a 'memory song' which consists of the actual eyewitness
experience of a 'cat scout who saw the first landing of a survey
crew on Sphinx almost a thousand T-years ago."

Emily and Hamish gazed at the two treecats in something very
like awe, and Nimitz and Samantha returned their looks calmly.

"So what happens," White Haven said slowly, "is that these . . .
'memory singers' are able to share the new concept or the new
ability with whatever 'cat it first occurs to, and then to transmit
it, like a gestalt, to all the others." He shook his head. "My God.
They may be slow to think of new things, but once they do, they're
certainly equipped to spread the good news!"

"Yes, they are," Honor agreed. "But the individuals who are most
important of all to the 'cats are the innovators who are also
memory singers in their own right. Apparently, a sister of Lionheart,
the 'cat who adopted my great-great-great-whatever-grandmother,
was exactly that sort of memory singer, and pretty nearly single-
handedly convinced all of the other 'cats that human-'cat bonds
were a good idea.

"Which brings me to the point of this somewhat long-winded
explanation. You see, none of the 'cats had been able to make heads
or tails out of the way that humans communicate until one of
their memory singers was injured in a fall."

Her expression darkened for a moment. Then she shook it off
and continued levelly.

"As I'm sure you both know, Nimitz was . . . injured when we
were captured, and he lost his mind-voice as a result. He can no
longer 'speak' to any of the other 'cats, which was why my mother
came up with the brilliant idea of teaching him and Samantha to
sign. It had been tried centuries ago without any success, but that
was mostly because at that time the 'cats still didn't understand
how human communication worked. Since they didn't use words
at all, they simply couldn't make the connection between hands
communicating information and thoughts any more than they
could connect 'mouth-noises' to doing the same thing.

"What had changed by the time Nimitz and Sam came along

was that the memory singer the 'cats call Singer From Silence had lost not her mind-voice, but her ability to hear other mind-voices. She could still taste emotions, still sense the mind-glow, but she was deaf to everything else."

She drew a deep breath.

"It must have been devastating, especially for a memory singer. She could still project, still share the memory songs she'd learned before, but she could never learn a new one. For that matter, she could never be entirely certain that anyone else 'heard' her properly, because there was no feedback channel, no way for her to be sure her signal hadn't been garbled.

"So she left her clan, gave up her position as one of its elders, and moved to Bright Water Clan—Nimitz's clan, the same one Lionheart came from. She chose Bright Water because it's always been the clan with the most intimate contact with humans, and she wanted to spend time around the two-legs. She knew we communicated somehow without mind-voices, and she wanted desperately to learn how we did it in the hope that possibly she could learn to do the same thing.

"She couldn't, not in the end, because 'cats simply can't reproduce the sounds of human language. But even though she never learned how to overcome her own mental deafness, she did, after years of listening to humans speak, deduce the rudiments of how spoken language worked. And because she could still transmit memory songs, she was able to pass that knowledge along to all other treecats, which is why they were able to understand us when we spoke to them even before they had a way to speak back with their hands."

"Fascinating," Hamish repeated yet again, his voice soft and his expression rapt. Then he cocked his head and frowned. "But you said all of this relates to Sam somehow."

"Yes, it does. You see, Samantha's treecat name is 'Golden Voice.' She's a memory singer, Hamish."

"She's *what*?" White Haven looked blankly at Honor for a moment, then turned to stare at Samantha, who looked back and gave an unmistakable human-style nod.

"A memory singer," Honor confirmed. "Remember that I said earlier that 'cats who adopt don't really make any choice to do so in the human sense of the word. That extra sensitivity, or ability, or whatever that's part of the ability to taste the mind-glow that makes adoption possible, also drives those of them who have it towards us. They know what it is they're looking for from the memory songs of other 'cats who have adopted, but they don't have any idea *who* they're looking for. It's their choice to seek adoption—or, rather, it's the choice of 'cats for whom adoption is possible to place themselves close enough to humans that it can happen—but the actual moment of adoption is more one of recognition than of seeking someone out. It just sort of . . . happens when they meet the right person.

"Well, Samantha—Golden Voice—was, as far as she or any other treecats know, the first 'cat born with both the mental strength to be a memory singer and the whatever it is that drives 'cats to adopt. From what she's told me, it must have been a dreadful decision to give up either of those possibilities, but she chose to pursue the adoption bond, which is how she met Harold Tschu and adopted him."

"And he was killed serving with you in Silesia, after she and Nimitz had become mates," White Haven said, nodding slowly.

"Which is the only reason she didn't suicide after Harold's death," Honor agreed somberly. The earl's eyes narrowed, and she tossed her head and looked back at him almost defiantly as she sensed his instant flare of denial of any such possibility.

"That's what treecats usually do when they lose their adopted people or their mates, Hamish," she said quietly. "Suicide, or simply . . . shut down and starve themselves to death or die of dehydration. That was the enormous tragedy of adoptions for three T-centuries, until the invention of prolong made it possible for us to live as long as they do. They knew they would almost certainly be giving up decades of life, as much as a century or more, if they adopted . . . and the need for the human mind-glow drove them to it, anyway."

She saw the understanding dawn in his eyes, the shadow of all the centuries of sacrifice which had claimed its victims in the name of joy and love, and she nodded slowly.

"The fusion is so deep and so complete, from their side, at least, that it leaves a huge void deep inside them when they lose their other half. Most of them simply choose not to live after that. King Roger's 'cat Monroe would almost certainly have starved himself to death if—"

She stopped herself abruptly. The fact that Queen Elizabeth's father had been assassinated by Havenite proxies was a secret known only to a handful of her subjects. Honor was one of them, and she knew William Alexander was, too, because they'd both been told at the same time. But they'd also been sworn to secrecy.

"He probably would have starved himself to death if Prince Justin—who wasn't Prince Consort at the time, of course; he and Elizabeth were engaged, but they hadn't married yet—hadn't been attacked by a lunatic while he was trying to get Monroe to eat," she went on instead. "That roused Monroe, and in the ensuing fight against the lunatic, he and Justin adopted one another, which is the only reason Monroe is alive today. Well, the situation was similar with Samantha and Nimitz, because as far as we know, they're the only mated pair ever who have both adopted, and her bond with Nimitz was powerful enough to make her stay with us."

"I see." White Haven gazed at her for a moment, then reached back across to Samantha and stroked the soft, thick fur of her spine.

"Were you lonely?" he asked her quietly. "Was that it?"

The small, slender treecat looked back up at him out of bottomless grass-green eyes, then turned those same eyes to Honor and rose to sit higher on her true-feet so that she could sign.

Her right true-hand's raised thumb tucked under her chin, then drew out and forward in a slight arc. Then both true-hands came up in front of her, little fingers upright and half a centimeter apart before she brought them together and separated them again three or four times. And then her right true-hand positioned itself horizontally below her left, palms facing and fingers curled, and circled in opposite directions.

"She says she was confused, not lonely," Honor translated, but then Samantha's hands moved more urgently.

<Listen before you tell,> the flashing fingers commanded. <You hurt. He hurts. Nimitz and I feel your pain. It hurts us as much as it does you, but understand. This is a two-leg pain, because all but you are mind-blind. Your People can't taste what People taste, and there are reasons you and he can't mate. But that doesn't change what you need to do, and not doing makes you hurt worse. When he came, your pain was very great. Great enough even mind-blind could taste it, and he did. And it made his pain much, much worse. Pain is a terrible thing, but can make the mind-glow even stronger, and did. For the first time, truly tasted him, not just on

own, but through you, as well, and his mind-glow captured. Did not plan it. Did not *want* it. But now, is a wonderful thing. Am sorry it will make hard things harder, but would not—*could* not—change it.>

She stopped signing, hands motionless once more, and gazed trustingly up at Honor.

Strange how all of them have their own "accents," Honor thought almost absently, then gave herself a mental shake, castigating herself for hiding behind extraneous thoughts.

She could see why another human in Samantha's place—assuming any human could have been there—would have hesitated to explain that in such detail to Hamish. Honor herself still had no idea how the hopeless yearning she and Hamish felt could ever be assuaged, how the impossible might somehow be made possible. And if that could never happen, then telling him it was the pain caused by his love for her which had drawn Samantha to him might contaminate the adoption bond with the same hurt and unhappiness. Her ability to taste Samantha's mind-glow and those "emotional sidebands" she'd mentioned to Hamish and Emily told her that the adoption bond was independent of whatever she and Hamish might feel for one another. That it wasn't the specific cause of Hamish's pain which had brought his mind-glow into such acute focus for Samantha, but only the fact of that pain's existence. But Hamish lacked that sensitivity. He would never be able to taste the absolute proof that Samantha's bond to him was completely independent of Nimitz's bond to Honor or the complex emotional tension between himself and Honor, and Samantha knew that. Which was probably only to be expected out of someone who was also a memory singer, Honor knew. Yet even after all these years, she was both surprised and deeply touched by Samantha's sensitivity to humankind's alien codes and concepts and emotions . . . and her determination not to hurt Hamish on their sharp, bitter edges.

Now it was up to Honor to protect him, as well, and she looked up from Samantha to meet his waiting gaze.

"She says," Honor Harrington said, "that the tension you and I have been under made your mind-glow stronger. Strong enough that she really 'saw' it for the first time."

"It did?" White Haven sat back in his chair, surprised, then smiled slowly, and Honor tasted the many levels of bittersweetness inside him.

"I see," he said, looking at her, not aware even then that his very heart was in his eyes for Honor—and Emily—to see. "Well, if it brought us together," he said, "however inconvenient the timing, I can't help feeling at least a little grateful."

CHAPTER FOURTEEN

"**D**amn." The Twelfth Earl of North Hollow said the single word quietly, almost calmly, but there was nothing at all calm about the look in his eyes. He managed not to glare obviously across the huge expanse of Mount Royal Palace's Queen Caitrin's Hall, but only because he knew every eye which wasn't watching the liveried chamberlain by the door prepare to announce the latest arrival was riveted to him.

"Her Grace Admiral Lady Dame Honor Harrington, Duchess and Steadholder Harrington, and Nimitz!"

The huge chamber's advanced sound system carried the announcement to every ear without the need for anything so crass as bellowing, despite the fact that Queen Caitrin's Hall was big enough to have hosted at least two basketball games simultaneously. The chamberlain's voice wasn't intrusive enough to interrupt ongoing conversations, but conversations broke off throughout the Hall anyway. A wave of sudden quiet, almost a hush, rolled outward from the entry as every guest became aware of the tall, slender woman who had just stepped through it.

As always at formal affairs here in the Star Kingdom, she wore her own version of traditional Grayson female attire, but tonight her gown was a deep, jewel-toned blue, not the simple, unadorned white she usually wore. The tabard-like over-vest of the dark, jade green which had become known as "Harrington Green" by clothing designers in two star nations complemented the blue, yet the combination was far more intense than her normal garb, and the Star of Grayson and the Harrington Key flashed golden on her breast. Her hair was straight, gathered at the nape of her neck by a silken ribbon, also of Harrington Green, before it fanned out to spill down her back. The dark brown cascade had been arranged with deceptive simplicity to look natural while it fell gracefully to her left and remained safely out of the way of the treecat on her right shoulder.

She was probably the tallest woman in the whole, vast expanse of Queen Caitrin's Hall. If she wasn't, she was certainly *one* of the tallest, and she moved with the easy, natural grace of a martial artist as she stepped forward into the silence. Andrew LaFollet and Spencer Hawke, both immaculate in Harrington Guard dress uniform, followed at her heels, unannounced by the chamberlain but certainly not unnoticed. Here and there, expressions clouded with disapproval as the two armsmen brought their holstered side arms into the presence of the Queen of Manticore, but no one was going to be foolish enough to comment on it. Not here. Not in front of Elizabeth III.

The Queen had looked up from where she stood engaged in conversation with Lord William Alexander and Theodore Harper, Planetary Grand Duke of Manticore, as Duchess Harrington's arrival was announced. Now, in complete disregard of centuries of protocol, she moved swiftly across the floor with both hands extended and a huge smile of welcome. The duchess smiled back, and swept a deep, graceful Grayson-style curtsey before she took the Queen's proffered hand and shook it firmly.

Something like a silent sigh seemed to roll through the Hall, but if Harrington sensed it, neither she nor the 'cat on her shoulder gave the slightest sign of it. Her expression was calm and attentive as she bent her head to listen to something the Queen had just said, and then she laughed with what certainly appeared to be a completely natural ease. The Queen said something else, touched her lightly on the shoulder, and started to turn back towards the Duke of Manticore, then paused as the chamberlain announced the next arrival.

"Admiral the Earl and Lady White Haven and Samantha!"

If Duchess Harrington's arrival had sent a ripple of quiet throughout the Hall, that announcement produced something much more profound. It was almost as if every one of the scores of guests had simultaneously drawn a deep breath . . . and held it.

The earl was perhaps two centimeters taller than Lady Harrington, and his wife's life-support chair floated silently at his side as the two of them moved forward into the stillness. Neither of them showed the least awareness of all those watching eyes, although the very tip of the tail of the slender, dappled treecat on the earl's shoulder twitched in small, slow arcs. They came through the entry, paused ever so briefly in recognition as they saw the duchess, and then came forward more quickly, with smiles as huge as the Queen's own.

"Honor!" The welcome in Lady White Haven's voice cut clearly through the unnatural stillness, although she certainly hadn't raised it. Then again, she'd learned the actor's tricks for voice projection more than half a century ago. "It's wonderful to see you again!"

"Hello, Emily," Harrington returned the greeting as she and the countess shook hands, then nodded to Earl White Haven. "Hamish," she said, and smiled at the 'cat on his shoulder. "And hello to you, too, Sam!"

"Good evening, Honor," the earl replied, then bowed and kissed the Queen's hand as Elizabeth retraced her steps to greet the newcomers.

"Your Majesty." Conversation had resumed throughout the Hall, but his deep voice carried almost as well as his wife's had.

"My Lord," the Queen replied, then smiled with obvious delight at Lady White Haven. "I'm so glad you decided to come after all, Emily," she said, just loudly enough for those standing close to them to overhear. "We don't see enough of you here in Landing."

"That's because I find Landing a bit on the fatiguing side, I'm afraid, Your Majesty," Emily Alexander said. For all the fairness of her own coloring, there was a similarity—more sensed than seen, yet unmistakable—between her face and the Queen's. Not surprisingly, perhaps, since they were distant cousins. Nor was Elizabeth Emily's only family connection at tonight's gathering, and she cocked her head with another smile of welcome as the Duke of Manticore joined them.

"Hello, Teddy," she greeted him.

"Happy birthday, Aunt Emily," he responded, and bent to kiss her on the cheek. "Wasn't it kind of Her Majesty to arrange things so *I* didn't have to throw a birthday gala for you?" he teased with a twinkle, and she snorted.

"You may have gotten off lightly where parties are concerned," she told him, "but I expect you to make it up when it comes to the gifts!"

"Oh, well. I suppose I can always sell off part of my portfolio to raise the funds," he sighed, and then reached out to shake the earl's hand. "Good to see you, too, Hamish," he said cheerfully. "And I've been looking forward to meeting your new friend," he added, with a small, formal bow all for Samantha.

The 'cat returned the greeting with a regal nod of her own, and he chuckled delightedly.

"I understand you've been learning to sign, Teddy?" Emily inquired, and snorted as he nodded. "Well, in that case, if you behave yourself properly—and bribe her with sufficient celery, of course—you can probably get Sam to help you practice over supper."

"Yes, Auntie," he promised obediently, and she snorted again, then reached up to pat him on the forearm before she returned her attention to the duchess and the Queen.

It was all about timing, Honor thought as the guests filed into the banquet annex to Queen Caitrin's Hall. It was remotely possible that there was someone here tonight who was naive enough to believe Hamish and Emily had just happened to arrive immediately behind her, or that Elizabeth and Emily's nephew had just *happened* to join the three of them—well, five, with Nimitz and Samantha—where every single guest could see them. It was even possible that that same naive someone might think it was pure coincidence that her own title took precedence over every other guest present except the Duke of Manticore. That "coincidence" just happened to seat Honor to the Queen's left and the duke to the Queen's right . . . and the fact that the entire function was officially in honor of Emily's birthday and that Emily was "family" had given Elizabeth the perfect excuse for seating her and her husband at the same table, despite the fact that Hamish was "only" an earl. Which just happened to put Honor and Emily right next to one another where every single guest could see how naturally and cheerfully they spoke with one another.

And where no one could possibly mistake the message the Queen of Manticore had actually arranged this entire evening to communicate.

Timing, she thought again, as she offered Nimitz a fresh stick of celery and she tasted the emotional aura of the banquet. It was always difficult to make definitive judgments about the overwhelming group mind-glow of such a large gathering, but she sensed a definite overall trend which gave her a sense of profound satisfaction. The message had gone home, she decided, and drew a huge, mental breath of relief.

This might actually be going to work after all.

"So much for Plan A," Stefan Young grumbled as he flung his formal frock coat across a chair with childish spitefulness.

"I warned you it could turn around and bite us all on the ass," his wife replied. They'd been home from the ball for half an hour, and she'd already shed her own court costume. Now she sat before the bedroom mirror, considering herself. She stuck out her tongue at her own image and studied it for a moment, then shrugged and moved on to the rest of her appearance. She wore a robe of subtly iridescent Gryphon water silk, one of Gryphon's most prized export goods. That robe had cost more than a low-end air car, and worth every penny of it, she thought with a lazy, hunting-hexapuma smile as she admired the way it clung to every curve. But then the smile faded, and she shrugged and turned to look at him.

"We got over four months of effective use out of it," she pointed out. "That was enough to carry us through the debate on the naval reductions and the vote on the new domestic spending measures."

"I know." The earl had lingered in the study to fortify his frustration with brandy. She could smell it on his breath from where she sat, and she concealed a grimace of distaste as he unbuttoned the old-fashioned studs from his cuffs and tossed them into a jewelry case with a grimace of his own. He hadn't enjoyed the way the Queen had seated Emily Alexander and Duchess Harrington at her own elbow and then monopolized their conversation all through supper.

"I'd just hoped for a longer run," he said after a moment. "Like maybe a permanent one. And I still say we should go ahead and keep pushing to make it work that way."

"No, we shouldn't. Not now that Emily Alexander has spiked our guns so neatly."

"Who cares?" North Hollow demanded, and turned to glower at her. "Of course she's going to cover for him! What else can she do? And so is Elizabeth. And only an idiot would believe that entire charade wasn't set up expressly to do just that! All we have to do is point out the political calculation involved, how cynical they're both being by conniving at covering up a pair of adulterers for pure political advantage, and we can turn the public against them, too!"

"Against *Emily Alexander*?" Georgia Young laughed scornfully. "Two-thirds of the voters in the Star Kingdom think the woman's a saint! Attacking her would be the worst strategic blunder anybody's made since the Peeps started the war early at Hancock Station."

"Um." North Hollow grunted, his expression uglier than ever at the reminder of the battle which had brought about his elder brother's disgrace, then exhaled in an irritated snort. "I just hate to let up on them when we've got them on the run this way," he said almost plaintively.

"That's because you're thinking with your emotions again," Georgia told him. She stood, running her hands across the water silk with a slow, sensual motion that formed a bizarre visual counterpoint for her coldly dispassionate voice. "I know how much you hate Harrington—hate both of them—but when you let hate dictate strategy, it's a recipe for failure."

"I know," Young repeated, his expression still surly. "But I wasn't the one who came up with the idea in the first place, you know."

"No, you weren't. I was," she agreed in that same clinical tone. "On the other hand, you grabbed the concept and ran with it the instant I suggested it, didn't you?"

"Because it sounded like it would work," he replied.

"Because it sounded like it would work . . . and because you wanted to hurt them," she corrected, and shook her head. "Let's be honest, Stefan. It was more important to you personally to make them both suffer than it was for the strategy to work, now wasn't it?"

"I wanted it to work, too!"

"But that was secondary, as far as you were concerned," she said inexorably, and shook her head again. "I'm not saying it was unreasonable of you to want to punish them for what they both did to Pavel. But don't make the same mistake he made. People have a perfectly natural tendency to strike back at anyone who hurts them—the fact that you want to punish Harrington and White Haven is proof enough of that. Unfortunately, Honor Harrington isn't exactly noted for moderation. White Haven is a civilized person. He's going to feel bound to play by the rules, but when *she* strikes back, people have a habit of finding themselves ankle-deep in bodies, and I'd just as soon not be one of the corpses."

"I'm not going to do anything stupid," he growled.

"And I'm not going to *let* you do anything stupid." Her eyes were as cool as her voice. "That's why I asked you to suggest the approach to High Ridge and let him set up the hatchet men. If she decides to come back after anyone, she'll be looking at Hayes first, and then our beloved Prime Minister. Besides," the countess chuckled humorlessly, "not even she can kill off the entire Government. She'd have to stop before she worked her way all the way down to the Office of Trade!"

"I'm not afraid of her," Stefan shot back, and his wife's eyes hardened.

"Then you're an even bigger fool than your brother was," she said in an even, deadly dispassionate tone. His face tightened angrily, but she met his hot glare with an icy calm which shed its heat effortlessly.

"We've had this discussion before, Stefan. And, yes, Pavel was an idiot. I warned him that going after Harrington, especially the way he did it, was like following a wounded hexapuma into the underbrush with a butter knife. But he insisted, and I was only an employee, so I set it up for him. Now he's dead . . . and she isn't. Not only that, but she's enormously more powerful now than she was then, and she's learned how to use that power. Pavel underestimated her then; if you're not afraid of her now, with all the power and allies she's gained since and the evidence of what happened to him in front of you, then you *are* a fool."

"She wouldn't dare come after me," North Hollow protested. "Not after the way she shot Pavel. Public opinion would crucify her!"

"That didn't stop her in Pavel's case. What in the world makes you think it would stop her now? The only two reasons she hasn't gone after you already are that her political allies, like William Alexander, have been restraining her from going after anyone at all and that she doesn't know—not for certain—that you were the one who suggested this particular line of attack to High Ridge. If she were certain of that, I'm not at all certain even Alexander or the Queen herself could stop her, given all the history between her and your family. So be afraid of her, Stefan. Be very afraid, because you're never going to meet a more dangerous person in your life."

"If she's so dangerous, why's she been so meek and mild? There are ways she could have counterattacked without resorting to violence, Georgia! So why hasn't she come out swinging and used all that power you say she's got somehow?" Stefan demanded, but the questions came out petulantly, not challengingly.

"Because we hit her with the kind of attack she's most vulnerable to," the countess told him patiently. "She doesn't have the experience to respond in kind to this sort of assault. She's been mostly on the defensive from the outset, because it's not her sort of battlefield. That's precisely why they went out and recruited Emily Alexander to serve as her general. But if you push her too hard, or make the mistake of coming into the open and hurting someone she cares about when she knows who did it, she won't waste any more time even trying to fight your kind of battle, Stefan. She'll come after you directly, her way, and hang the consequences. Your family should know that better than anyone else."

"Well, we're just going to have to come up with something else, then, aren't we? If Plan A isn't going to put her down for the count after all, what do we suggest to High Ridge for Plan B? Now that Emily Alexander's busted our columnists' balls for daring to suggest that her husband and her 'dear friend' Harrington could be humping each other, how the hell do we get the two of them off our backs? You know they're going to be harder to handle than ever now that we've pissed them off!"

"There's probably something to that," Georgia agreed. "And I'm not sure what to propose as Plan B—not just yet, anyway. I'm confident something will suggest itself to me as the situation clarifies. But whatever it is, Stefan, it's not going to be anything she can trace directly back to you or to me. You may not care if she decides to rip your lungs out, but I like mine just fine where they are, thank you."

"I got the message, Georgia," North Hollow half-snapped. His expression was surlier than ever, but there was fear behind the surliness, and Georgia was relieved to see it. On the other hand . . .

Fear might keep him from doing something outstandingly stupid, but she'd used enough stick for one night, she decided. It was time for the carrot, and she touched the neck of her robe.

It floated down to puddle about her ankles, and suddenly Honor Harrington was the last thing on Stefan's mind.

Honor stood beside the lectern, hands clasped behind her, and gazed up at the huge lecture hall's tiers of seats as they filled.

The Tactical Department's D'Orville Hall home boasted every modern electronic teaching aid known to man. Its simulators could re-create anything from the flight deck of a pinnace to the combat information center of a superdreadnought task force flagship, and reproduce all of the sights and sounds of the most horrific combat. The online teaching interfaces could put an instructor face-to-face with a single student, a group of two or three, or a class literally of hundreds. Those same interfaces made reference works, histories, lecture notes, syllabuses, official after action reports, analyses of past campaigns, and class schedules instantly available to students, as well as delivering student course work and exams equally instantly to instructors.

Saganami Island made full and efficient use of all those capabilities. Yet the Royal Manticoran Navy was a great believer in tradition, as well, and at least once per week, lecture courses met physically in their assigned lecture halls. Honor was perfectly willing to admit that the tradition was scarcely the most modern possible way to transmit knowledge, but that was fine with her. As she herself had discovered as a child, too great a reliance on the electronic classroom could deprive a student of the social interaction which was also a part of the educational process. The electronic format could serve as a shield, a barricade behind which a student could hide or even pretend to be someone else entirely . . . sometimes even to herself. That might not constitute a serious drawback in the education of civilians, but Navy and Marine officers couldn't afford walls of self-deception about who and what they were any more than they could afford to leave their social skills underdeveloped. Their professional responsibilities required them not only to interact with others in a corporate, hierarchical service, but to exude confidence and competence when exercising command in situations in which their ability to lead quite literally might make the difference between life and death. Or, even more importantly sometimes, between success or failure. That was the major reason Saganami Island relentlessly stressed traditions and procedures which forced midshipmen and midshipwomen to deal with one another, and with their superiors and instructors, face-to-face, in the flesh.

Besides, she admitted from behind the serenity of her expression, she enjoyed the opportunity to see the massed faces of her students. The joy of teaching and challenging young minds while simultaneously building the Navy's future was an unalloyed pleasure, the one thing she had unreservedly treasured about her almost five-T-year stay here on the Star Kingdom's capital planet. She even allowed herself to believe that she'd finally made a substantial down payment on the debt she'd owed to her own Saganami Island instructors, and especially to Raoul Courvoisier. And it was at moments like this, when she actually saw one of her classes assembled, all in one place at the same time, that the sense of continuity of past and future and of her own place in that endless chain came to her most strongly.

And at this particular moment, she needed that sense.

Nimitz stirred uneasily on her shoulder, and she tasted his unhappiness, but there wasn't a great deal she could do about that, and they both knew it. Besides, he wasn't unhappy with her; he was—as she herself—unhappy at the situation.

A fresh spasm of pain flickered through her, concealed from her assembling students by the calm mask of her face, and she cursed her own inner weakness.

She ought to have been one of the happiest women in the Star Kingdom, she told herself yet again. Emily Alexander's counterattack had rolled up the High Ridge machine's campaign of slander like a rug, especially when the Queen got behind it and pushed. One or two of the most bitterly partisan 'faxes and commentators continued the attack, but the vast majority had dropped it like a hot rock once Emily's intervention reversed the poll numbers virtually overnight. The abrupt simultaneity with which the campaign had been terminated by almost all participants should have been a flare-lit tipoff to any unbiased observer that it had been carefully coordinated from the beginning, too. Only a command from above could have shut down so many strident voices so instantly. And only people whose deep, principled concern over the "fundamental questions" being beaten to death had been completely artificial from the outset would have abandoned those principles with such alacrity when they became inconvenient.

But if the attack had been beaten back, it hadn't been defeated without leaving scars. The Grayson public, for example, remained furious that it had ever been mounted in the first place. That would have bothered Honor under any circumstances, but the opposition Keys in the Conclave of Steadholders had seized upon it as an additional weapon in their struggle to roll back Benjamin IX's political power. Their persistent attacks on the Manticoran Alliance—or, rather, on the wisdom of Grayson's remaining bound to that Alliance—had been sufficiently unremitting before the allegations of infidelity ever saw the light of day. That opposition to the Alliance had survived even the execution for treason of Steadholder Mueller, who'd first put it forward, and the inexcusable and stupid arrogance with which the High Ridge Government had treated its allies had lent it a dangerous strength since. Now those same steadholders saw the attacks on Honor as yet another weapon with which to bolster their argument, and the fact that so many of them hated her as the symbol of the "Mayhew Restoration" which they loathed with all their hearts only gave them a sense of bitter, ironic satisfaction when they reached for it.

That was bad enough. Benjamin's letters might argue that the furor would die down with time, but Honor knew him too well. He might actually believe it, but he was nowhere near as confident of it as he tried to make himself appear in his messages to her. And whether he believed it or not, she didn't. She'd told herself again and again that her judgment was never at its best when she confronted the possibility of seeing herself used against friends or things she believed in. She'd reminded herself how often Benjamin's analyses of political and social dynamics had proved superior to her own. She'd even spent hours researching past political crises and scandals, some dating back even to Ante Diaspora Earth, and attempting to dissect their long-term consequences and find the parallels to her own situation. And none of it had changed what really mattered. Whatever Benjamin might believe, whatever might actually be true in the long run, in the short run his enemies had done enormous damage to his ability to preserve the Alliance and keep Grayson in it. And it didn't matter how Grayson public opinion might view these events fifteen T-years from now if the planet was split away from the Alliance and its relationship with the Star Kingdom this year, or the next.

But dreadful as that potential disaster was, one almost as dreadful loomed in her personal life, because Emily had been right. Honor's long-standing relationship with Hamish had been a fatal casualty of the attack. The caution—or cowardice—which had kept either of them from ever admitting his or her feelings to the other had been stripped away. Now both of them knew precisely what the other felt, and the pretense that they didn't was becoming more threadbare and fragile by the day.

It was stupid . . . and very human, she supposed, although the observation offered absolutely no comfort. They were both mature, adult human beings. More than that, she knew that however imperfect they often seemed to themselves, both of them possessed a devotion to duty and their own personal honor codes which was stronger than most. They ought to have been able to admit what they felt and to accept that nothing could ever come of it. Perhaps they couldn't simply have walked away from it completely unscathed, but surely they ought to be able to keep it from destroying their lives!

And they couldn't.

She wanted desperately to believe that her own weakness was the direct consequence of her ability to taste Hamish's emotions. There might even be some validity to that. How could anyone expect her to feel the love and desire flooding out from him, however hard he tried to hide it, and not respond to it? For the first time, Honor Harrington truly understood what drew a moth closer and closer to the all-consuming power of a candle flame. Or perhaps what had drawn treecats to bond to humans before prolong, when they knew that to do so would cut their own life spans in half. Perhaps she could have walked away from what she felt for Hamish, but it was literally impossible for her to walk away from what he felt for her.

Then there was Samantha.

The Sphinx Forestry Service had checked its files at Honor's request, and the SFS report confirmed what she'd suspected. There wasn't a single recorded instance of a mated pair of 'cats who had both adopted humans . . . before Nimitz and Samantha. There'd been mated pairs in which one 'cat had adopted and the other hadn't, although even that had been vanishingly rare, but in those cases, at least only one human had been involved. There'd been no need to choose between two-legs who were not or could not be together, and so there'd been no reason for them to face the possibility of permanent separation from either mate or person. The fact that the situation was unique meant there was no precedent to guide any of them, yet in this, as in so much else, Nimitz and Samantha had set their own precedents, with no regard at all for history or tradition.

She wondered sometimes what might have happened if Harold Tschu hadn't been killed in Silesia before Hamish's awareness of her had shifted so radically. Would she and Harry have been drawn inexorably together? It was certainly possible, but even so, she doubted that it would have happened. He'd been a fine man, and she'd respected him, but he'd also been one of her subordinates. Theirs had been a professional relationship, and so far as Honor could tell, the bonds between each of them and their 'cats hadn't carried over to their attitudes towards one another in any way. Certainly the thought that he might ever have been anything more than a friend, the human partner of Nimitz's wife and the human "uncle" of any of the 'cats' children, had never so much as crossed her mind before his death had erased any possibility of it.

Which had absolutely no bearing on her present intolerable position. As Emily had pointed out, she and Hamish had no choice but to continue to work together, cooperating as closely and as . . . intimately as before the attack. And just as political considerations made it impossible for her to avoid Hamish, so did the personal consideration that Nimitz's mate was bonded to him. There was no way she could possibly separate her beloved friend from his wife, yet the very intensity of their bond with one another only made Honor even more exquisitely sensitive to all of the points of resonance between her and Hamish.

No wonder empaths thought it was insane for anyone to attempt to deny what she truly felt!

The lecture hall's seats were almost full, and she glanced at the time display on the wall. Another ninety seconds. Just long enough for one last self-indulgent wallow in her self-pitying misery, she told herself bitingly.

Yet self-pity or not, there was no escape from the grim reality behind it. Emily had bought her a reprieve, nothing more. Friends and allies could defend her from external attack, but they couldn't protect her from her own inner weakness and vulnerability. No one could defend her from that. The only possible answer she could see was to find some way to separate herself from the source of her pain. She might not be able to do that permanently, but perhaps she could do it long enough to at least learn to cope with it better than she could now. And even if she couldn't learn how to do that, she desperately needed some respite, some break in the pressure to let her pause, catch her breath, and regather her strength.

But recognizing that answer did her no good at all when there was no way she *could* separate herself from Hamish and the Star Kingdom's political fray. Not without convincing everyone, friend and foe alike, that she was running away. Perhaps they wouldn't know all of the reasons for her flight, but that wouldn't really matter. The damage would be done, especially on Grayson.

So how, she wondered despairingly, did she find the sheltered haven she needed so desperately without looking as if she had allowed herself to be hounded out of town?

Her wrist chrono beeped softly, and she drew a deep breath and reached forward to rest her hands on the traditional polished wood of the lectern while she gazed out at her respectfully assembled students.

"Good afternoon, Ladies and Gentlemen." Lady Dame Honor Harrington's soprano voice was calm and clear, carrying effortlessly to every listening ear. "This is the last lecture of the term, and before we begin our review for the course final, I want to take this opportunity to tell you all how much I've enjoyed teaching this class. It's been a privilege and a pleasure, as well as a high honor, and the way in which you've responded, the fashion in which you've risen to every challenge, only reaffirms the strength and integrity of our Service and its future. You *are* that future, Ladies and Gentlemen, and it gives me enormous satisfaction to see what good hands the Queen's Navy and all of our allied navies are in."

Silence hovered behind her words, deep and profound, and the wounded corners of her soul relaxed ever so slightly as the answering emotions of her students rolled back through her like an ocean tide. She clung to that sensation from the depths of her battered exhaustion, with the greedy longing of a frozen, starveling waif crouching outside the window of a warm and welcoming kitchen, but no sign of that crossed her serene expression as she gazed back out at them.

"And now," she went on more briskly, "we have a great deal to review and only two hours to review it in. So let's be about it, Ladies and Gentlemen."

"She's like some damned vampire!" Baron High Ridge growled as he slapped the hardcopy of the latest poll numbers down on his blotter.

"Who?" Elaine Descroix asked with an irritatingly winsome little-girl smile. "Emily Alexander or Harrington?"

"Both—*either!*" the Prime Minister snarled. "Damn it! I thought we'd finally put Harrington and White Haven out of our misery, and then along comes White Haven's wife—his *wife*, of all people!—and resurrects both of them. What do we have to do? Cut off their heads and drive stakes through their hearts?"

"Maybe that's exactly what we have to do," Sir Edward Janacek muttered, and Descroix chuckled. Despite her smile, it was not a pleasant sound.

"It might not be a bad idea to wash them both down with holy water and bury them by moonlight, as well," she said, and High Ridge snorted harshly. Then he looked at the other two people present.

"Your suggestion worked even better than I'd hoped it would . . . in the short term," he told Georgia Young, abandoning any pretense that the idea had ever been her husband's. "It took Harrington and White Haven completely out of the equation while we fought through the new budget. But it's beginning to look as if our short-term victory is going to prove a long-term defeat. Unless you've managed to come up with some answer to the rebound in their popularity with the proles, that is."

Almost everyone else in the Prime Minister's paneled office turned to look at Lady North Hollow, but she returned their half-accusing glares with calm composure. Then she waved one graceful hand at the Second Lord of the Admiralty, the single person who wasn't glowering at her at the moment, and smiled at High Ridge.

"As a matter of fact, Prime Minister, I believe Reginald and I may actually have come up with a solution of sorts. It's not a perfect one, but then so few things in this world are truly perfect."

"Solution? What kind of solution?" Janacek demanded. He got the questions in before anyone else could ask, but it was a close run thing.

"I've been doing some additional . . . research on Harrington and White Haven," the countess replied. "It hasn't been easy. In fact, it's been impossible to get anyone inside Harrington's household or inner circle. Her security is provided entirely by her Steadholder's Guard, with backup from the Palace Guard Service, and it's the next best thing to impenetrable. Not to mention the fact that she herself seems to have a damnable ability to 'read' the people around her. I've never seen anything like it.

"Fortunately, White Haven isn't quite that tough a nut. He maintains excellent security on the sensitive materials he receives as a member of the Naval Affairs Committee, and his people are almost as loyal as Harrington's. But they're not as security conscious about, ah . . . household matters as hers are. I wasn't able to put anyone actually inside his or his wife's quarters, but I did manage to get a few listening devices into the *servant's* quarters. And some of his people let much more slip than they thought they did when someone asked them the right questions."

High Ridge and Janacek looked uncomfortable at her deliberate reminder of precisely what it was she did for them. The calm, matter-of-fact way she discussed spying on their political opponents made both of them uneasy, if only because of their awareness of the consequences if they were caught at it. Such privacy violations were illegal for anyone, but the fines and even jail time violators could draw would have been minor considerations beside the devastating public opinion damage awaiting any politician who got caught actually bugging his opponents. And what would have been bad enough for any political figure would be even worse for one of the leaders of the current Government, which was supposed to be in charge of stopping anyone from committing such acts.

However uncomfortable the two Conservatives might have been, Houseman seemed unconcerned, almost as if he were oblivious to any reason why the countess' actions could be considered the least bit improper. Perhaps, High Ridge thought sardonically, because of the way the towering nobility of his intentions justified any act he might choose to commit in order to further them.

As for Descroix, she actually smiled as if she thought the entire thing was some huge, slightly off-color joke.

Lady North Hollow let the silence linger just long enough to make her point. Then, having reminded them of the importance of ensuring the competence of whoever did their dirty work for them, she continued.

"The really ironic thing about it all," she told her audience, "is how close we came to telling the truth about both of them."

High Ridge and Janacek looked at each other in obvious surprise, and she smiled.

"Oh, there's absolutely no evidence that they were ever actually lovers," she assured them. "But apparently it's not for lack of temptation. According to some of the White Haven retainers, Harrington and White Haven are pining over each other like a pair of love-sick teenagers. They may be hiding it from the public—so far—but they're suffering in truly appallingly noble silence."

"Really?" Descroix cocked her head, her eyes calculating. "Are you sure about that, Georgia? I mean, they do spend an inordinate amount of time together. That was what made our original strategy workable. But are you seriously suggesting that there's truly something there?"

"That's what the evidence seems to indicate," the countess replied. "Some of the White Haven servants are quite bitter about it, actually. Apparently their loyalty to Lady White Haven is outraged by the thought that Harrington might be scheming to supplant her. To be honest, that outrage was probably enhanced by our media campaign, and it seems to have faded back somewhat in the last few weeks. But what gave it its original legs was the fact that most of them had already come to the conclusion that whatever Harrington thought, White Haven had been busy falling in love with her for months, if not years. I realize that anything they may have said to my investigators constitutes hearsay evidence, at best, but when it comes right down to it, the servants usually know more about what's going on in any household than their masters do. Besides, the handful of . . . technical assets I managed to get inside White Haven's household pretty much confirm their testimony."

"Well, well, well," Descroix murmured. "Who would ever have thought a stodgy old stick like White Haven would fall so hard after so long? His puppy dog devotion to Saint Emily always made me faintly queasy, you know. So maudlin and lower-class. But this new itch of his rather restores one's faith in human nature, doesn't it?"

"I suppose so," High Ridge said. Descroix seemed oblivious to the distasteful glance he gave her, and he moved his attention back to Lady North Hollow.

"Interesting as all this is, I fail to see precisely how it addresses our current problems, Georgia."

"It doesn't, directly," the countess replied serenely. "But it suggests that we ought to bear it in mind as we examine several other considerations. For example, it's obvious that Harrington is quite concerned at the moment over the domestic Grayson response to all of this. Then there's the fact that her treecat's mate has seen fit to adopt White Haven. The White Haven servants who were already disposed to resent her had an earful to tell my investigators about that—until they dried up completely, that is. It seems that the bond between the 'cats is forcing White Haven and Harrington even closer together. At least some of the servants were convinced that the female's adoption of the Earl had been deliberately contrived by Harrington to let her worm her way into Lady White Haven's position. I don't personally think there was anything to that theory, given how hard the two of them seem to be working at pretending, even to one another, there's nothing between them. Not to mention the fact that Lady White Haven seems to be reacting to all of this extraordinarily calmly, to judge by what my monitors have managed to pick up. But however it happened, that adoption is one more source of tension and unhappiness for both of them. All three of them, really, I suppose.

"To make a long story short, My Lord, both White Haven and Harrington, but especially Harrington, appear to be under enormous emotional and, to some extent at least, political pressure, regardless of the current turnaround in the poll numbers. And I've analyzed both of their records. You can't produce enough pressure to make Harrington flinch from what she believes her duty requires of her under any conceivable set of circumstances . . . except one. You can shoot at her, blow her up, threaten her with assassination, or tell her her principles are political suicide, and she'll spit in your eye. But if you can convince her that something she wants or needs threatens to undermine what she believes her duty requires of her, that's something else entirely. She'll back away from whatever it is, even shut down completely, rather than 'selfishly' pursue her own interests. And once her emotions are fully engaged, once it's become personal for her, all of the 'Salamander's' decisiveness tends to disappear."

"What do you mean?" Descroix asked intently, and the countess shrugged.

"I mean she's not very good at putting herself first," she said bluntly. "In fact, it actually seems to . . . frighten her when her personal needs appear to threaten the things she believes in."

"Frighten?" High Ridge repeated, one eyebrow raised, and Lady North Hollow shrugged.

"'Frighten' probably isn't the best word for it, but I don't know one that would be a better fit. Her record is really remarkably clear in that regard, beginning while she was still a midshipwoman. It's common knowledge that she refused to file charges for attempted rape after a certain incident there." She paused very briefly until her audience nodded understanding of the point they knew she probably wouldn't have made had her husband been present.

Probably.

"There might be some argument over why she kept silent in that particular case," the countess went on. "My own belief is that at least part of it was that she was still too young to have developed enough self-confidence to believe her charges would be believed. But it's also highly probable that she believed any scandal would hurt the Navy, and she wasn't prepared to put what had happened to her personally above the good of the Service. That's certainly been the sort of attitude she's displayed repeatedly since, at any rate. If she can find a way to remove herself from a situation in which what she needs conflicts with her duty or with what someone else needs without transgressing her personal code, she'll take it. She did that before the First Battle of Yeltsin, when she pulled her squadron out of Yeltsin's Star because she thought her presence was undermining Courvoisier's efforts to bring Grayson into the Alliance."

Her tone remained conversational, her expression bland, as she ignored Houseman's sudden grimace. The Second Lord's ugly look of remembered hatred (leavened with more than a little fear) was probably so involuntary he didn't even realize he'd let it show, High Ridge reflected.

"If the bigots who'd been giving her grief had done the same thing to anyone else under her command," the countess continued, "she would have come down on them like the wrath of God. She isn't exactly noted for moderation, you know. But their bigotry and resentment were directed at *her*, and she wasn't prepared to risk blowing Courvoisier's mission by insisting they treat her with the same respect she would have demanded for someone else. So instead, she backed away and took herself out of the equation."

"It sounds almost as if you admire her, Georgia," Descroix observed, and the countess shrugged.

"Admiration doesn't really come into it. But belittling an opponent out of spite when you're trying to formulate a strategy against her is stupid."

This time Houseman actually stirred physically beside her, like a man on the brink of bursting out in protest, but she ignored that, too, and went on speaking directly to Descroix.

"Besides, if you want to look at it from the right angle, what she did in Grayson was to run away from a problem rather than confront it squarely, which is arguably a sign of weakness, not strength. And apparently she did the same thing the first time she realized she and White Haven were straying into forbidden territory. She ran away from the situation—and him—by assuming her squadron command early, which was how the Peeps came to capture her, of course. And she quite clearly did it again on Hades, when she refused to send a courier ship back to the Alliance as soon as she captured one."

"Excuse me?" Janacek blinked at her in surprise. "You're saying she 'ran away' from *Hades*?"

"Not from Hades, Edward," the countess said patiently. "Away from a profoundly painful personal choice she wasn't prepared to make. As Steadholder Harrington, it was clearly and unambiguously her responsibility to return to Grayson and her duties there as soon as humanly possible. What's more, she had to have realized that whether or not the Admiralty could have scraped up the shipping for a mass prisoner evacuation from the Cerberus System, the Graysons damned well would have sent at least one ship. For that matter, they would have dragged her aboard it at gunpoint, if necessary, if they'd known she was alive and where to find her! But if they'd done that, her public duty as Steadholder Harrington would have pulled her away from a *personal* duty to all of the prisoners on the planet. She was not only unprepared to turn her back on that responsibility but literally couldn't force herself to 'abandon' them, whatever she knew she ought to have done. So whether she realized it or not, her decision not to inform anyone in the Alliance of what was happening on Hades while she tried to somehow capture or steal enough personnel lift to pull everyone out was a deliberate evasion of something which was too painful for her even to contemplate."

"I never thought of it that way," Janacek said slowly, and Lady North Hollow shrugged.

"I'm not surprised, Edward. For that matter, I doubt very much that Harrington ever thought of it that way. If she had, she probably wouldn't have been able to do it. Which is the reason she didn't think about it. But the reason this particular character flaw is important to us at this particular moment is that it gives us a possible handle to maneuver her in the way we want."

"How?" High Ridge asked, frowning intensely.

"The key here is that she won't evade *anything* unless there's an 'honorable' way to do it," the countess said. "She may be able to rationalize her way into choosing a way out from among several possible courses of action, but not simply to save herself. There has to be a reason. There has to be something that needs doing, and that she can be convinced—or that she can convince herself—is also her responsibility. Give her an honorable task, a responsibility, especially one that's likely to demand some sacrifice on her part, and the odds are considerably better than even that she'll take it."

"What sort of 'responsibility' did you have in mind?" Descroix arched an eyebrow. "Personally, I can't think of a single thing Harrington would feel compelled to do for any of us—except, perhaps, to pump a little more hydrogen into the furnaces in Hell while we roasted over them!"

"Actually," Reginald Houseman said, speaking up for the first time, "I believe we may have just the job for her. In fact, it's rather like one she was offered once before. She accepted that one, and it almost killed her."

He smiled with an ugly vengefulness he would never have allowed any other audience, and especially not his fellow Liberals, to see.

"Who knows? Maybe this time we'll be luckier."

CHAPTER FIFTEEN

"**I** can't believe you're serious!"

Hamish Alexander shook his head sharply and glared at Honor. They sat in the study of his Landing mansion, with Samantha stretched across the back of his chair, resting her chin on the backs of her true-hands. Nimitz lay across Honor's chair back, and she could taste the cats' unhappiness, their grief at the prospect of a lengthy separation. But she also tasted their acceptance.

There was no trace of that emotion in the Earl of White Haven.

"I'm completely serious, Hamish," she said, far more calmly than she felt. "And before you say it, of course I realize that at the very least this is a political Trojan Horse from High Ridge's perspective. But you and Willie have the situation as well in hand in Parliament as anyone could expect to, under the circumstances, and whatever we may think of Janacek, this is a job that needs doing. And given Sidemore's involvement in it, I feel a certain personal responsibility to do whatever I can to keep Marsh from getting run over in the scrimmage."

"Damn it, Honor, of course you do! And they know exactly how your head works when somebody punches the responsibility button. They're manipulating you into taking this on, and you know it as well as I do!"

"Maybe they are," she agreed evenly. "And certainly I can see a lot of advantages for them in getting me out of the Star Kingdom.

But let's be honest, Hamish. There could be some advantages for *us* in getting me off of Manticore, as well."

"Somehow I don't expect Willie to think that," White Haven said tartly. "And even if he did, I—"

"Willie might surprise you," Honor interrupted. "And I asked you to be honest. When I said 'advantages for us' I wasn't thinking about Parliament."

He closed his mouth abruptly, biting off whatever he'd been about to say, and something inside her flinched from the sudden pain, almost betrayal, that flickered in his ice-blue eyes. But she couldn't afford to show that, and so she made herself return his gaze levelly. Silence crackled between them for several seconds, and then she smiled sadly.

"We need some space between us, Hamish," she said gently. He started to speak again, but her raised hand stopped him. "No. Don't say anything. I didn't come here to argue with you, or even to debate my decision. I came because I've already decided to accept the command, and I needed to tell you that myself. It wasn't an easy decision, and I'm fully aware that Janacek didn't offer it to me out of the goodness of his heart. But that doesn't keep it from being a godsend."

"But—"

"No, I said," she cut him off quietly. "Hamish, we've danced around this for years now, and it's killing both of us. You know it, Nimitz and Samantha know it. So do I . . . and so does Emily."

His face went bone-white, and she felt his instant need to deny her words, to back away, to somehow pretend it wasn't so. But his own honesty was too deep for that, and so he said nothing, and she tasted his shame that it had been left to her to finally openly face the truth for them both.

"I love you," she said very, very softly. "And you love me, and you love Emily. I know that. But I also know that, especially after what High Ridge and his cronies tried to do to us, we don't dare do anything about the way we feel. We *can't*, Hamish, whatever we want, or however desperately we want it. Only I'm not strong enough to stop wanting it." Tears prickled at the backs of her eyes, but she refused to let them spill over. "I don't think I'll ever be that strong. But that doesn't change anything, so I have to find another way. And this is the only one I see that doesn't carry an unacceptable political cost for everyone."

"But they're only offering you the job in the hope that it will blow up in your face," he said.

"I don't know if I'd put it exactly that way myself," she replied. "They've got a genuine problem. They need someone to solve it for them, and whoever that someone is, a solution short of total disaster still has to be their ultimate objective. But you're right that they also need someone to scapegoat if it does turn into a disaster, of course. And to be honest, I'm pretty sure that they wouldn't be thinking that way if they didn't expect it to do just that. They may be right about that, too. But that doesn't change the fact that it's a job someone has to do . . . and that it will let me put some space between us. Please, Hamish. It's important to me for you to understand. I can't be this close to you, not knowing exactly what you feel, and not knowing what I feel. I just can't. It's not your fault; it's not my fault. It's just the way it is."

She felt his pain, and his anger . . . and his shame. But under those emotions, she also tasted his understanding. It wasn't a happy understanding, and it wasn't really agreement, but in its own way, it was more precious to her than either of those things could possibly have been.

"How long will you need space?" he asked, and reached up to stroke Samantha.

"I don't know," she said honestly. "Sometimes I think there isn't enough space in the entire universe. Other times I hope that a break, long enough for both of us to catch our breaths, may be all we really need. But whether it is or not, it's the best I can do. If there's an answer, some sort of solution, I know I can't find it while I'm so busy fighting against letting myself love you."

He closed his eyes, his face tight, and she felt how passionately he longed to find some way to disagree with her. But he couldn't. And so, after an endless moment of silence, he opened his eyes and looked at her once more.

"I don't like it," he told her. "I'll never like it. But that doesn't mean I have any better answer than you do. But for God's sake, be careful, Honor! Don't go jumping into any more furnaces, because God help us all, but you're right. I *do* love you. Put space between us if you have to, but every time you go out and pull one of those 'Salamander' death-rides of yours, something dies inside me. There are limits in all things, love. Including the number of times you can dance on the razor and still come back to me."

She couldn't quite stop the tears now. Not after he'd finally admitted what they both knew. She started to speak, but this time it was his turn to raise one hand and stop her.

"I know you're right," he said. "We can't be together—not really. But I can't lose you, either. I thought I had once, when the Peeps told everyone they'd hanged you, and I can't do that again. So you come back, Honor Harrington. You come back from Silesia, and you come back alive. We'll find some answer, somehow, and you'd damned well better be here when we do!"

"I'm dreadfully sorry, Your Grace, but it simply won't be possible."

Honor leaned back in her chair and crossed her legs, and her chocolate-brown eyes were on the cold side of cool as she gazed at the woman on the other side of the desk. Admiral of the Red Josette Draskovic was a dark-haired, dark-eyed, slender woman about thirty-five T-years older than Honor. She possessed an overabundant supply of nervous energy, and often gave the impression of fidgeting even when she sat completely still. She was also the woman who had replaced Sir Lucien Cortez as Fifth Space Lord, in charge of the Royal Navy's personnel and manpower management, and though she hadn't let a muscle in her face move even a millimeter, Honor felt her smiling in triumph deep down inside.

"Then I suggest that you make it possible," Honor recommended in an even tone.

"I beg your pardon?" Draskovic stiffened, bristling almost visibly, and Honor allowed herself to smile very slightly as she tasted the other woman's emotions. Nimitz was curled neatly in her lap, and the 'cat looked totally relaxed, almost sleepy. But Honor knew better than that; she could feel his seething anger as clearly as she could feel Draskovic's petty sense of power.

Honor and Admiral Draskovic had never met before Sir Edward Janacek returned as First Lord of the Admiralty. Since then, they'd crossed swords twice, and Draskovic had not enjoyed either of her appearances before the House of Lords' Naval Affairs Committee one bit. She owed most of that lack of enjoyment to one Duchess Harrington, who'd turned up for the first one armed with her own analysis of the personnel figures included in the current naval estimates. The bare numbers Draskovic had reported to Parliament hadn't exactly been a lie, but the way she'd presented them had been. And Honor had not only caught her in the act but given the admiral enough rope to hang herself before she produced the actual breakdown between active duty and half-pay personnel.

It had not been Draskovic's best day, and her second appearance had been little better. She hadn't been caught in any lies that time, but Honor's devastating, relentless questions had driven her into near incoherence trying to defend basically indefensible Admiralty policy. She'd looked like a total incompetent—an amateur, competing out of her class—and she'd resented her humiliation even more because, unlike Honor, she'd always been one of the coterie of "political" admirals who'd made their careers out of negotiating the halls of political patronage. Which was undoubtedly the reason she held her present position.

Now it was Draskovic's turn to pay Honor back. As Fifth Space Lord, decisions on personnel assignments were ultimately her responsibility, and those assignments included things like the staff officers and flag captains assigned to fleet and task force commanders. The Royal Navy tradition was that a flag officer being sent out to command one of the Service's fleet stations had broad authority to select her own choices for those positions. The Bureau of Personnel had to sign off on her nominees, but that was only a formality. Traditionally, the only limiting factor was the availability of the officers in question, but Draskovic clearly wasn't a great believer in tradition. Especially not when ignoring it let her get her own back on someone who'd helped her humiliate herself so thoroughly.

Personally, Honor found that the admiral's sense of humiliation left her completely unmoved. Draskovic had made the decision to prostitute herself professionally by agreeing to serve under High Ridge and Janacek, and any embarrassment that brought her was entirely her own fault.

Obviously, Draskovic didn't see it that way, but unfortunately for her, Honor wasn't prepared to acquiesce in the other woman's small-minded vengeance. A fury every bit the equal of Nimitz's blazed behind her hard eyes. She was well aware that that fury owed as much of its strength to her own pain and anger over the wreckage the Government's attacks on her and Hamish had made of her life as to any professional concerns she might have had, and she didn't much care.

No, she thought, *be honest Honor. You* do *care. Because the fact that Draskovic is enough of a political whore to make herself an accomplice of that sort of scum makes her an entirely appropriate target for how mad you are.*

She allowed no trace of her own emotions' blazing power to touch her expression, but her eyes hardened still further, and that thin smile was very, very cold.

"I suggested that you make it possible, Admiral," Honor repeated coolly. "I've given you a list of officers whose services I'll require to discharge my responsibilities as the commander of Sidemore Station. Given the decreased tempo of our operational status against Haven, coupled with the recent drastic downsizing of our wall of battle, I cannot believe that the officers whose services I've requested can't be spared from other duties."

"I realize you consider yourself something of an expert on personnel management, Your Grace," Draskovic said tightly, her tone ugly. "Nonetheless, I suggest to you that I am in a somewhat better position to judge the availability of serving officers in Her Majesty's Navy."

"I have no doubt that you're in a better position to judge . . . should you choose to do so," Honor replied flatly.

"And what, precisely, is the meaning of that, Admiral Harrington?" Draskovic snapped.

"I thought my meaning was quite clear, Admiral. I meant that it's entirely evident to me that you have no intention of considering the actual availability of the officers I've requested. In fact, I very much doubt if you've checked their personnel files at all."

"How *dare* you?" Draskovic sat bolt upright in her chair, and her eyes blazed. "I'm quite well aware that you don't believe the rules of us petty mortals apply to the great '*Salamander,*' Admiral Harrington, but I assure you that they do!"

"I'm quite sure they do," Honor conceded calmly. "That, however, has nothing whatever to do with the topic of our current discussion, Admiral. You're as well aware of that as I am."

"However grossly overinflated your self-image may be, *Admiral,* I remind you that I'm not merely a Space Lord but senior to you by a good fifteen T-years," Draskovic grated. "And I also remind you that neither an admiral's rank nor a peerage nor even the Parliamentary Medal of Valor gives you immunity from charges of insubordination!"

"I don't expect them to . . . normally." Even now, in the grip of her own anger, a small corner of Honor was astonished by her own words. Was it possible that Draskovic's implication that she'd somehow come to see herself as special truly was behind her confrontational attitude? She couldn't completely rule that out, much as she might have liked to, but at the moment it didn't really bother her all that much.

"Meaning what?" Draskovic snarled, leaning forward over her desk to glare at Honor.

"Meaning that I'm as aware as you are—or, as aware as Sir Edward Janacek is, for that matter—that this command wasn't offered to me because of the enormous respect in which the current Admiralty administration holds me. It was given to me in no small part as a deliberate maneuver contrived to remove me from the political equation here in the Star Kingdom."

Draskovic sat abruptly back in her chair, her expression stunned. Clearly, she hadn't anticipated Honor's bareknuckled attitude, and the thinnest possible edge of true humor crept into Honor's smile as she tasted the other woman's astonishment. The fact that Honor had never once played the political game in her own career didn't mean she hadn't known how it was played, though it appeared that possibility had never crossed Draskovic's mind. But if Honor was going to play it at last, she would play it her way—head on, and damn the consequences. Let Draskovic react to it however she wished; they were never going to be anything except enemies, anyway.

"It was also given to me," she continued in that same, chill tone, "because of Silesia's potential to turn into a major catastrophe. You may have believed I was unaware of the fact that this Admiralty is willing to deliberately select a flag officer with the express intention of making her the scapegoat if our relations with the Andermani collapse. If you did, you were in error.

"So under the circumstances, Admiral Draskovic, any violence your sense of authority may have suffered as a consequence of my attitude leaves me completely unmoved. You and I both know that the only reason my personnel requests are 'impossible to meet' is that you chose to deny me the traditional prerogatives of a station commander out of a petty sense of spite. I can't prevent you from abusing your authority in that manner, Admiral. But if you choose to continue to deny my requests, then I'm very much afraid you're going to have to inform the First Lord that it will be impossible for me to accept the command after all."

Draskovic had opened her mouth to snap back, but she closed it with an abrupt click at Honor's last sentence. Her emotions spiked suddenly, and a cold flash of trepidation burned its way through the heart of her fiery anger. Shock was also a part of that spike—disbelief that Honor should so contemptuously drag the cynical political calculation and manipulation at the heart of her assignment to Silesia out into the open. Things simply weren't done that way, and sheer surprise momentarily paralyzed the Fifth Space Lord's speech centers.

Honor tasted every nuance of Draskovic's reaction, and the vicious pleasure it gave her surprised her just a bit, even now. But she allowed no sign of that to cross her face, either. She simply leaned back in her chair, watching Draskovic as the other woman grappled with the fact that she was willing to call the combined bluff of the Government and Admiralty alike.

"I—" Draskovic started to speak, then stopped and cleared her throat.

"I don't care for your tone, Your Grace," she said, after a moment, but her voice was much weaker, almost lame. "Nor do I agree with your so-called analysis of this . . . situation. And I'm not prepared to overlook insubordination and insolence from anyone, regardless of who they are or what their accomplishments may be."

"Fine." Honor stood, lifting Nimitz in her arms. "In that case, Admiral, I'll remove myself from your presence before I give fresh offense. Please be good enough to inform Sir Edward that I must regretfully decline the command of Sidemore Station. I hope you'll be able to find some other competent officer to fill the position. Good day."

She turned and started for the door, and the combination of fury, consternation, and panic blazing up from Draskovic was like a forest fire behind her.

"Wait!"

The single word popped out of Draskovic almost against her will, and Honor paused. She turned in place, looking at the Fifth Space Lord, and arched her eyebrows in polite question. Muscles bunched in Draskovic's jaw as she clenched her teeth so tightly

Honor could almost hear them grinding from five meters away, but Honor said nothing. She only stood there, waiting.

"I . . . regret any . . . misunderstanding which may have arisen between us, Your Grace," Draskovic got out at last, and each word was like pulling a barbed splinter out of her flesh. "It's apparent that tempers have gotten . . . out of control here. I regret that, also. The fact that you and I do not agree politically and have had our public policy disagreements shouldn't be allowed to impair our professionalism as Queen's officers."

"I couldn't agree more," Honor replied with lethal affability, savoring the other woman's internal apoplexy, and Draskovic managed a rictus-like almost-smile.

"Good. It's possible that I was just a bit hasty in my judgment of the availability of some of the officers you've requested, Your Grace," she said. "I believe that it might not be inappropriate for me to reexamine my decision in those cases."

"I would be most grateful," Honor said. "However, I would have to insist—respectfully, of course—that the availability of *all* of the officers in question be . . . reexamined. It would be most unfortunate if the nonavailability of any of them made it impossible for me to accept the honor of the Sidemore command."

Her voice was calm, almost tranquil, but her eyes were like brown flint, backed by battle steel, and she felt something wilt inside Draskovic.

"It's Admiralty policy to be as forthcoming as possible in meeting the personnel requests of station commanders, Your Grace," she said after only the briefest pause. "I assure you that I will give your requests my complete and serious attention."

"Thank you. I appreciate that very much, Admiral," Lady Dame Honor Harrington said softly.

CHAPTER SIXTEEN

"**I** don't know what you did, Ma'am, but it certainly had some horsepower."

Captain (senior grade) Rafael Cardones smiled cheerfully and tipped back his chair while he nursed the stein of beer James MacGuiness had bestowed upon him. They sat in Honor's home office, and the sliding crystoplast wall of the bay window was open, turning it into a balcony onto the cool spring night. Night birds, both Manticoran and Old Earth imports, sang in the darkness, brilliant stars glittered above Jason Bay, and one of Manticore's moons poured silver light like syrup over the mansion's manicured grounds while the red, white, and green jewels of air car running lights drifted above the glassy smooth water.

"The last I'd heard," Cardones went on, "*Werewolf* was slated for a routine—and very boring—deployment to Trevor's Star. And then—"

He shrugged and waved his Old Tillman enthusiastically, and Honor used her stein to hide a smile as she sipped her own beer. She remembered rather clearly an inexperienced, overly anxious, bumbling, but extremely talented junior-grade lieutenant who'd suddenly found himself acting tactical officer aboard the elderly light cruiser *Fearless*. There was very little of that young man's anxiety or lack of confidence in the relaxed, handsome, competent-looking captain sitting across her coffee table from her, but the bright-eyed eagerness she also remembered was still very much in evidence.

"BuPers works in mysterious ways, Rafe," she said, after a moment, her expression serene. "I simply explained to Admiral Draskovic how badly I needed you, and she took it from there."

He cocked his head at her, his expression quizzical, and she tasted his amused disbelief. Apparently, he'd had the misfortune to meet Josette Draskovic, and he obviously suspected just how . . . congenial the Fifth Space Lord and Honor must have found one another's personalities. He started to say something, then visibly changed his mind and said something else entirely.

"Well, I can't say I'm going to miss Trevor's Star, Ma'am. It's a perfectly nice star system, and the San Martinos are perfectly nice people, but there's not a whole lot to do there except drill. And I hope you know without my saying it how pleased and flattered I am by the assignment. It's really good to see you again, and having you fly your lights aboard *Werewolf*— Well, that's something the entire ship's company was delighted to hear about."

"I'm glad . . . assuming you're not just buttering the Admiral up, of course," Honor told him with a grin, and he chuckled as he shook his head in denial of the charge. "Seriously," she went on, allowing her grin to fade, "I was really impressed by how well you and your ship performed in Operation Buttercup, Rafe. You did darned well, and your experience will stand us in good stead if it falls into the toilet in Silesia."

"How likely is that to happen?" her new flag captain asked. His expression was much more sober, and he sat forward in his chair, elbows on thighs and clasping his stein in both hands while he watched her face with sharp, dark eyes.

"I wish I could tell you for certain," Honor sighed. "ONI is supposed to be sending us complete copies of its analysis of Andy ship movements in and around Marsh. Our information on those should be pretty good for the immediate neighborhood, but from what I've seen so far, its reliability is going to fall off pretty steeply outside that area."

She paused and gazed at Cardones thoughtfully. She'd already decided not to discuss her confrontation with Draskovic with him, for several reasons. First, of course, it was her fight, and not his. Second, while she rather doubted even Draskovic would attempt to retaliate by wrecking the careers of the junior officers whose services Honor had requested, she couldn't be certain of that. And she *could* be certain that if Rafe upped the ante by choosing sides in his seniors' quarrel the consequences for his career would be catastrophic, at least in the short term. In the longer term, he would probably survive whatever happened, because eventually, Janacek was bound to lose his position at the Admiralty. When that happened, his successor's first priority was probably going to be the rehabilitation of the officers Janacek's administration had purged. But rehabilitation after the fact wouldn't make the sort of vengefulness in which someone like Draskovic would indulge any more enjoyable at the time, and she knew her Rafe Cardones. He gave his loyalty the same way he did everything else—with conviction, enthusiasm, and a hundred-and-ten-percent effort. Worse, he had a passion (carefully hidden, he fondly imagined) for dragon-slaying, which only reinforced her decision not to tell him everything. She didn't need anyone else to fight her battles for her, but if she wanted Rafe safely out of the line of fire, the only way to keep him there was never to tell him a battle was being fought.

Yet there were other unpleasant truths about the current Admiralty administration, and although she hadn't planned on going into them—not yet, at least—Rafe was going to be her flag captain. Her tactical deputy and right hand. Which meant she had no choice but to share her concerns with him. Not only was it absolutely essential for him to understand at all times what she was thinking and why she was thinking it, but she owed him that openness and honesty.

"This stays in this room unless I tell you differently, Rafe," she said after a moment, and watched him settle deeper into his chair. It was a subtle thing, more sensed through her empathic link than seen, but his shoulders squared ever so slightly and his eyes narrowed intently.

"I don't trust our intelligence assessments," she said quietly, meeting his gaze levelly. "Just between the two of us, Admiral Jurgensen isn't the right man for ONI. He's always been an administrator, a bureaucrat and not an actual 'spook.' And my impression is that he has a tendency to . . . shade, let's say, his analyses to suit his superiors' needs. Or desires."

She raised her artificial left hand, palm uppermost and slightly cupped in a questioning gesture, and Cardones nodded slowly.

"I'm not comfortable about the sources our assessments are

apparently based on, either," she went on. "ONI is always reticent about naming sources, and rightly so. But from reading between the lines, and especially from looking at what isn't there to be read at all, it looks to me like our human resources are thin on the ground in both Silesia and the Empire right now. Admiral Jurgensen has assured me that my concerns in that area were unnecessary, and I certainly don't have any hard evidence that he was wrong. But I've deployed to Silesia several times, Rafe, and there's a distinctly different feel between these assessments and the ones my captains or I were given then. I can't explain the difference exactly, but they feel . . . unfinished. Incomplete.

"The Foreign Office assessments aren't a lot better, either. In their case, however, it's not because of any lack of sources. Actually, it's almost a case of information overflow. There's too much detail, too much minutiae and not enough hard indicators of what it is the Andermani are up to. The official Foreign Office position at this moment is that the Andies themselves aren't certain just what they have in mind. That they're testing the waters, as it were, with these shows of force around Sidemore Station. The official opinion is that the Empire's position hasn't yet hardened, and that there's an opportunity for us to shape the ultimate Andermani intentions by demonstrating 'firmness and consistency.' "

"Excuse me, Ma'am," Cardones said, "but have any of these Foreign Office types ever actually *been* to Silesia? Or the Empire?"

Honor's lips twitched at his plaintive tone, and even more at the emotions behind it. But she ordered herself sternly not to smile and shook her head at him.

"I'm sure some of them have," she told him with admirable restraint. "At some point in their lives, at least."

"It certainly doesn't sound like it," Cardones said frankly. "You and I have both been there before, Ma'am, and somehow I don't think either of us believes that anyone this side of the Devil himself is going to do much 'shaping' of Gustav XI's foreign policy."

"I'll concede that the Emperor tends to exercise very direct control of the Empire's policy. For that matter, my own opinion is that he probably knows exactly what it is he has in mind. Unfortunately, he's always been a bit on the unpredictable side."

Cardones looked as if he wanted to interrupt, and she shook her head quickly.

"All right, not just unpredictable. Stubborn and obstinate to the point of bloody-mindedness, too. But those other qualities just make him even more unpredictable. I think he tends towards pragmatism, and it's obvious that there's nothing wrong with his IQ, but once he convinces himself to do something, no one's going to be able to talk him out of it, however hard they try. So figuring out what he ought to be doing is frequently worse than useless, because it can leave you making perfectly logical assumptions that bear absolutely no relationship to what he's actually *going* to do. All of which means that Imperial policies have also been unpredictable from time to time, given his control of them. And, no, Rafe, I don't think the Foreign Office analysts have it right this time. They're not particularly interested in hearing my opinion of their opinions, however. You might say that the current Government and I aren't exactly on the same page of the playbook."

Cardones turned a snort of laughter into a particularly unconvincing coughing fit, and this time Honor went ahead and smiled, although she personally didn't find the situation especially amusing.

"The point is, Rafe," she went on more briskly, "you have a right to know that we're sailing straight into a minefield here. Our intelligence is less than complete and, frankly, the motives of the people analyzing it are suspect, in my opinion. The Government has a very strong vested interest in keeping the lid on in Silesia, and I'm very much afraid that that means Foreign Secretary Descroix is pushing her people, if only by example, into making what I consider to be grossly overoptimistic assumptions. I hope I'm wrong, but I think the Andies are about ready at last to push outright territorial demands on Silesia. That's what I think their shows of force and beefed-up presence throughout the Confederacy are all about, and the fact that ONI is beginning to suggest that there may have been a few 'unspecified upgrades' in the IAN's weapons technology doesn't make me feel any better."

"This doesn't sound like fun, Ma'am." Cardones' earlier amusement had vanished. He didn't seem frightened—just focused and very thoughtful, his eyes dark with professional concern. "Have we been given any new policy directives?"

"No," Honor admitted with a grimace. "According to my briefings from both the Admiralty and the Foreign Office, it would be 'premature' to formulate new policy at this time. Which means that our traditional policy—that we aren't prepared to countenance any violations of Silesian territorial integrity by outside powers—

remains in force. We're supposed to make that stand up . . . without, of course, provoking any confrontations with the Empire."

"And if they want a confrontation with *us*?"

"In that case, we do the best we can." Honor sighed and pinched the bridge of her nose. "To be completely honest, Rafe, what I'm afraid of is that the Government will continue to refuse to enunciate clearly and concisely what its intentions are for the benefit of Gustav XI. In the absence of clear, unambiguous signals from the Star Kingdom, he may just find himself encouraged to push even harder and further than he originally had in mind. And if that happens, we're going to find ourselves squarely in the path of a situation which can all too easily slide right out of control."

"With all due respect, Ma'am, what in the world possessed you to accept this command? You know Silesia, probably better than ninety percent of the Navy's officer corps, much less the bureaucrats over at the Foreign Office. And you know the Andies, too. Unless they're ready to give you a lot bigger stick than anything I've seen yet suggests, we're going to come up mighty short if the Empire gets aggressive. And as you say, you and the Government aren't exactly on the same frequency."

He started to say something more, then stopped himself, but Honor knew what he hadn't said.

"It's entirely possible that you're right," she said quietly. "I won't go so far as to say that anyone in the Government actively wants a major deterioration in our relations with the Empire. If that happens, though, I don't doubt that at least some members of the current Government would be less than displeased to find themselves in a position to hang me out to dry. But I can't just sit by and watch the wheels fall off. There are too many innocent bystanders, and we have a responsibility to the Sidemorians. For that matter, we have a responsibility to the Silesians, as well."

"It's not your job to make the Star Kingdom's foreign policy make sense, Ma'am."

From anyone Honor hadn't known so long and so well, that statement might have carried overtones of disapproval. From Cardones, she didn't even need her sensitivity to emotions to know he meant exactly the opposite. It wasn't disapproval of her egotistical assumption that she might somehow make a difference; it was concern that if she tried and failed, she would find herself caught in the gears.

"No, it's not," she agreed. "But it is my job to do what I believe is right, and what I think the Queen would expect one of her officers to do. Sometimes that isn't the easiest thing in the universe, and sometimes it carries consequences we shouldn't have to face. But no one said it would be easy, and if we can't take a joke, we shouldn't have joined."

Cardones' mouth quirked in a smile at the hoary lower-deck proverb, and she smiled back crookedly.

"At the same time," she said seriously, "I'll understand if you have some reservations about accepting the flag captain's slot." He started to reply quickly, but she raised her hand. "I'm serious, Rafe. This could turn very ugly for everyone concerned. I believe you're still junior enough that no one's likely to be interested in making an example of you if things come completely apart. I can't guarantee that, though, and I want you to think very seriously about whether or not you're prepared to run that risk just because I think I'm a female reincarnation of Don Quixote."

"I don't need to think about it at all, Ma'am," he told her. "You're probably right that no one's going to be looking to pin the blame on a lowly captain if it all falls into the crapper. But even if they were, I can think of lots worse company to be in. And you're also right that I don't remember anyone at Saganami Island telling me they paid us our lordly salaries for doing the easy jobs. If you're crazy enough to take this one on, I'd be honored to take it on along with you."

"I knew you were going to say that," she said. "And I suppose I ought to be a little ashamed for having counted on it. But I'm not."

"I should hope not. For that matter, it's probably your fault, now that I think about it," he replied. "There I was, a young and impressionable lieutenant, and you went and set a completely unrealistic example for me." He shook his head mournfully. "When I think of how much simpler my life might've been if I'd never gone to Basilisk Station with you it just completely exhausts me."

"I don't know about simpler, but it probably would have been safer," she said wryly. "I don't think it's all my fault, though. You never were very smart about keeping your head down."

"Now that's not fair, Ma'am," he said severely. "It's not that I'm not very smart about keeping my head down—it's just that I'm not very smart. Period."

Honor chuckled, then lifted her stein in a brief salute. He responded in kind, and leaned back once more.

"Now that that's more or less settled, Ma'am, where do we go next?"

"I understand that *Werewolf* is just completing a refit cycle." Honor made the statement a question, and he nodded.

"Yes, Ma'am. The yard dogs are supposed to turn us loose in about two weeks. I think we're going to run a little longer than that, though. All of the yard work dropped back to a slower tempo once the peace talks began, and it's dropped even further now that we've formally begun to build down our force levels."

"I know. And to be honest, I'm not going to be upset if your refit does run a little over. My impression is that things are coming to a head in Silesia, but there's still some time in hand. I don't want to lose any time getting on station, but it's going to take the Admiralty the better part of a month to assemble the other reinforcements we're supposed to take out to Sidemore with us, anyway."

"I'm glad to hear it," he said frankly, "because I was sweating it just a little, actually."

"No flag captain wants her admiral to think she's slack, Rafe. But I've been a flag captain, too, you know. There's not a lot you can do to make the yard dogs turn your ship loose any sooner than they're good and ready to."

"Actually," he admitted, "that's not the only problem I have. Captain Thurmond, my COLAC, was just detached for compassionate leave. His wife was killed in a boating accident on Gryphon, and they have—had—three children. My understanding is that he won't be returning. Certainly not before we complete the refit and begin working up again."

"I know," Honor repeated. "I wouldn't worry about it, though. While Admiral Draskovic and I were discussing other personnel assignments, I requested a new COLAC for you. I believe you know him. A Captain Jay-Gee . . . Tremaine, I think it was."

"Scotty? You got *Scotty* for me?" Cardones' white teeth flashed in an immense grin. "Dare I hope that you got me Harkness, as well?"

"Where one of them goes, the other is certain to turn up," Honor said dryly.

"Outstanding!" Cardones grinned at her for another second or two, then shook his head. "I'm beginning to think you must have been exceptionally persuasive with Admiral Draskovic, Ma'am."

"You might say that," Honor allowed.

"And who else did you get for us, if I may ask?"

"Well, let's see. I got a task group commander named Truman, and another one named McKeon." Honor looked up at the ceiling and rubbed her chin thoughtfully. "And at my urgent request, High Admiral Matthews has agreed to release a Commodore Brigham to serve as my chief of staff. And for an ops officer, I got Captain Andrea Jaruwalski. I don't know if you know her, but she's good, Rafe. Very good. Oh, and I got Fritz Montoya as our senior medical officer, too." She shrugged. "There may be—oh, one or two other officers I specifically requested, but those are the high spots."

"It's going to be like old times, isn't it?" Cardones observed.

"Not too much like 'old times,' I hope." Honor frowned ever so slightly. "I think it's a good, solid team, but when I sat down to put it together, I couldn't help remembering the old *Fearless*."

"I'm not surprised, Ma'am. And we did lose some people in Basilisk. And at Yeltsin's Star, too, for that matter. But we also did what we set out to do both times, didn't we?" He held her eyes until she nodded, almost against her will. Then he shrugged. "Well, we'll just have to do it again, then. And at least we're all practiced up at it!"

"More practiced than I'd like," Honor agreed ruefully.

"That's the name of the game, Ma'am."

"I suppose it is."

Honor took a long pull at her beer, then made a face as her wrist chrono beeped.

"Rafe, I'm sorry, but I've got an appointment with Richard Maxwell and Merlin Odom. I've simply got to get some management details nailed down here in the Star Kingdom before I go haring off to Silesia!"

"Not a problem, Ma'am. I imagine you've got a whole bunch of 'details' to deal with, given the number of hats they've got you wearing these days."

"You're not wrong there," she agreed feelingly. "In fact, I'm going to have to make a quick run to Grayson to settle the same sorts of details there. I'm planning on taking the *Tankersley*, and I hope I'll be back by the time *Werewolf* gets out of the slip, but I can't guarantee it."

"We'll survive until you do get back," he assured her.

"I know. I'll be bringing Mercedes back from Grayson with me when I come. According to the last update I got from BuPers, Alistair should be arriving at *Hephaestus* day after tomorrow, before I leave, though. And Captain Jaruwalski is already here in the Star Kingdom. You should meet her tomorrow. I'm hosting a small dinner here at the house, and you're both invited." Cardones nodded, and she shrugged. "Alice may be here in time for dinner as well; if not, she'll be on hand within another day or two, and hopefully, between the four of you, you can handle almost anything that comes up before Mercedes and I get home. If not, just put it on hold. I explained to the Admiralty that my responsibilities as Steadholder Harrington were going to cause some delays in how quickly I could get up and running, so no one should be breathing too hard on the backs of your necks while I'm gone."

"I'm sure Admiral McKeon and Admiral Truman will be able to deal with any bureaucratic types in your absence, Ma'am," Cardones agreed.

"And if they can't, I know who can," Honor assured him with a chuckle. "Scotty and Sir Horace should be at dinner tonight, as well. So if things get too out of hand, just remember that Harkness has a certain way with computers and sic him on the Admiralty database."

CHAPTER SEVENTEEN

"Tell him one more time, Mecia," Captain Erica Ferrero, commanding officer, HMS *Jessica Epps*, said. Her voice was cold and flat. "And tell him we won't ask again."

"Aye, aye, Ma'am!" Lieutenant Mecia McKee, *Jessica Epps*' communications officer replied crisply. She turned back to her panel, pushed an errant strand of long red hair behind her left ear and keyed her microphone.

"Unidentified starship, you are instructed to cut your wedge and stand by to be boarded. I repeat, you are instructed to cut your wedge and stand by to be boarded. If you do not comply, we will employ deadly force. This is your final warning. *Jessica Epps*, clear."

The crimson icon on Ferrero's plot made absolutely no response to her youthful com officer's warning. It simply continued to flee at its maximum acceleration, which was fairly stupid, the captain reflected. Admittedly, it represented a much smaller starship, which, with equally efficient inertial compensators, ought to have enjoyed an acceleration advantage of at least thirty or forty gravities over a ship of *Jessica Epps*' tonnage. Unhappily for whoever commanded that icon, however, it didn't enjoy equal efficiency, because *Jessica Epps* mounted the very latest version of the Royal Manticoran Navy's improved compensator. The suspect vessel's actual advantage, even at the eighty-percent settings which represented the RMN's normal maximum power load, was barely twenty-one gravities, less than a quarter of a KPS². If Ferrero had chosen to go to maximum military power and run the risk of compensator failure, the advantage would have lain firmly in *Jessica Epps'* favor.

Not that it mattered either way, because Ferrero's cruiser had surprised the other ship skulking along at a low base velocity. That was what had attracted her tac officer's attention in the first place. Given its small size, its low velocity and position just inside the hyper limit of the Adelaide System, especially headed towards the primary, were a dead giveaway. The only logical reason for a vessel the size of a very small frigate to be moving in-system at such a low speed (especially in Silesia) was that it was a pirate or privateer trolling for prizes. The low velocity at which merchantmen normally made the final translation into normal-space from hyper made them extremely vulnerable to interception immediately upon arrival, particularly since it always took at least a short interval for their sensors to settle down enough for them to be able to detect anything in their vicinities. Until they could at least see what lay in proximity to them, they couldn't even know a threat was there to begin trying to evade it. Even when they realized they were in danger, merchantmen were slow and clumsy ships. When a potential enemy also had the advantage of surprise, the chance that a merchant skipper could evade him was remote, at best.

If evasion failed and an armed vessel, however small, managed to bring its weapons into range of an *un*armed freighter, the merchant ship would find itself completely helpless. And the best way for an armed vessel to do that was to be moving at a relatively low velocity on the same approximate heading a merchie might be expected to arrive upon. Too much relative speed, and it would overrun its intended victim, unable to decelerate to rendezvous before the merchantman could reverse her own acceleration, break back across the hyper limit, and escape into hyper-space. Too little, and even a whalelike merchantman might be able to somehow twist aside and make it back into hyper before she could be overhauled.

That was obviously what the ship on Ferrero's plot had had in mind. The fact that it had gone to maximum acceleration directly away from her own command the moment she identified herself and instructed it to heave to for examination was ample confirmation in her own mind that it was a pirate. Unfortunately for it, the same tactical considerations which applied to merchantmen at low velocity evading pirates applied to pirates at low velocity evading heavy cruisers . . . with one notable exception. A pirate needed to rendezvous with its prize if it wanted to loot it; a heavy cruiser was under no obligation to rendezvous with a pirate, because said pirate could be blown out of space in passing just fine. And that was the situation which obtained in this instance.

Ferrero and her crew hadn't really planned on doing any pirate-hunting this afternoon, but sometimes God rewarded the virtuous when they expected it least. This was clearly one of those times, and *Jessica Epps* had found herself heading in-system at just over sixty-three thousand KPS. Given the geometry of the cruiser's pursuit curve, that had worked out to an overtake advantage of forty-two thousand kilometers per second—well, 40,007.162 KPS, if Ferrero wanted to be fussy about it—over an initial range of three and a half light-minutes. Which meant that even with its slight acceleration advantage, the ship she was pursuing couldn't possibly evade her. In fact, assuming constant acceleration for both ships, *Jessica Epps* would overtake her prey completely in just under twenty-five minutes, and bring it into missile range well before that.

So it had to be obvious to the other ship's commander that Ferrero's only problem was when to begin reducing her own acceleration still further in order to give her sufficient time in passing to do a proper job of reducing her target to dispersing wreckage. Under the circumstances, his only real option was to heave to and allow her Marines to board him, and common prudence should have suggested that it would be wise of him to do that promptly, before *Jessica Epps'* obviously short-tempered captain decided it was too much bother to take prisoners and worry about trials.

It appeared, however, that prudence was in somewhat short supply aboard the fleeing vessel. Either that, or its crew was on the list of convicted pirates for whom no trials—beyond the necessary establishment of their identities—would be in order, anyway. This was Silesia, after all, and Silesian governors had a bad habit of "losing" condemned pirates whom the Star Kingdom had turned over to them rather than keeping said pirates safely locked up or executing them. That was the reason the RMN had authorized its skippers to summarily execute such "escapees" if they were captured by Manticoran ships a second time. Given that interstellar law mandated the death sentence for piracy, that authorization was completely legal, and Ferrero strongly suspected that the crew in front of her knew its names were on her list somewhere. In that case, being boarded and captured would leave them just as dead as being blown apart in combat, and there was always a possibility, however remote, that they might somehow manage to roll ship and squirm away from *Jessica Epps.*

They'll be ice skating in Hell before that *happens, Mr. Pirate!* she thought coldly. *But at least my conscience will be clear, because you'll have had your warning . . . and your chance.*

Which was just fine with Erica Ferrero, who liked pirates even less than most Manticoran officers.

"No response, Ma'am," Lieutenant McKee reported unnecessarily, and Ferrero nodded.

"Understood, Mecia," she said, and turned her attention towards the tactical section of the command deck. "I don't see any reason to muck around with this idiot, Shawn."

Lieutenant Commander Shawn Harris, *Jessica Epps'* tactical officer looked up from his own plot, and she smiled at him thinly.

"We'll give him a single warning shot," she said flatly. "Just like the rules of engagement require. After all, I suppose it's remotely possible that his com is down and no one in his entire crew knows how to fix it. But if he decides not to stop even after that hint, I want a full missile broadside right up the kilt of his wedge. No demonstration nukes, either; we'll go with laser heads."

"Yes, Ma'am," Harris acknowledged without surprise. At a hundred and ninety-one centimeters, the brown haired, mustachioed tac officer towered over his petite captain, but Erica Ferrero's record was ample proof that nasty things could come in small packages. She had a short way with pirates, did Captain Ferrero, and it had quickly become apparent to Harris that she regarded trials as an inefficient technique for dealing with them. She made it a point not to automatically assume guilt, and she was always scrupulous about giving any suspected pirate the chance to surrender—at least once. But if they declined the invitation to allow her to board and examine them in accordance with interstellar law, that was more than sufficient indication of a guilty conscience to satisfy her. In which case, she was perfectly prepared to pursue the options available to her under that same established interstellar law and give them a demonstration of peace through superior firepower.

Which, upon mature reflection, was perfectly all right with Lieutenant Commander Harris. It only took cleaning up the aftermath of one or two pirate attacks to make any naval officer . . . impatient with the entire breed.

He turned back to his own panel and began setting up his attack profile. It didn't look like it was going to be very difficult. The ship they were pursuing massed no more than fifty thousand tons, little more than twelve percent of an *Edward Saganami*-class cruiser like *Jessica Epps*, and no hyper-capable warship could mount very much offense or defense on that limited a displacement. Of course, she wouldn't have needed a lot of armament to deal with the completely unarmed and defenseless merchies upon which she preyed, and he felt a grim satisfaction at the way the tables had been turned in this instance.

He'd just locked his launch sequence into the loading queue for his broadside launchers when his earbug buzzed. He listened for a moment, eyebrows rising in surprise, and then turned towards his captain.

"CIC's just picked up another impeller signature, Ma'am," he reported.

"What?" Ferrero turned her chair to face him. "Where?"

"Approximately seventy million klicks at one-zero-seven by zero-two-niner," he replied. "She's headed straight for our bogey, too, Ma'am," he added, and the captain frowned.

"Why the hell didn't we see her sooner?" she asked. It was probably a rhetorical question, but it carried a lot of irritation, and Harris understood perfectly.

"I don't know for certain, Ma'am," he told her, "but from the accel she appears to be pulling, she's got to be military. Either that, or another pirate, and CIC estimates her tonnage is around three-fifty k-tons."

"What *is* her accel?" Ferrero asked, eyes narrowing. Assuming that displacement figure was even remotely accurate, the heavy cruiser-sized newcomer was much too large for a typical pirate. It might be a privateer licensed by one of the Confederacy's innumerable "revolutionary governments," but that seemed unlikely.

"CIC makes it right on five hundred and ten gravities from a base velocity of right on six-point-five thousand KPS," Harris replied. The captain's surprise showed, and he nodded. "Like I say, Skipper—she's got to be military, and she's running her wedge with just about zero safety margin on her compensator. Our closing velocity is approximately seventy thousand KPS on her current heading, and the only reason we wouldn't have seen a wedge pulling that kind of power and coming almost straight towards us a lot sooner than this is because she was hiding it under stealth."

"Any com traffic from her, Mecia?" Ferrero demanded.

"None, Ma'am," the lieutenant replied.

"Well, see if you can raise her," the captain directed. "At that much tonnage, she's almost got to be a warship, not another pirate coming to our idiots' assistance. Still, I don't want any misunderstandings here. Be polite and extend my compliments, but this is our bird, not anyone else's."

"Aye, aye, Ma'am," McKee agreed, and began speaking into her hush mike. "Unknown vessel bearing zero-three-seven, zero-two-niner, this is Her Majesty's Ship *Jessica Epps*, Captain Erica Ferrero, commanding, in pursuit of suspected pirate bearing zero-zero-six, zero-one-five from our position. Captain Ferrero extends her compliments and requests that you identify yourself and advise us of your intentions. *Jessica Epps*, clear."

Given the distance, it took three minutes and fifty-three seconds for McKee's hail to cross the vacuum between *Jessica Epps* and the unknown warship. Their closing velocity reduced the range by almost sixteen and a half million kilometers during that time, which meant that it required only a shade over two minutes and a half for the other captain's reply to arrive.

McKee twitched visibly in her chair when it did. Then she turned to her captain.

"I think you'd better listen to the direct feed, Ma'am," she said.

Ferrero started to ask her why, but then she shrugged and nodded, and a harsh, strongly accented Andermani voice sounded from the bridge speaker.

"*Jessica Epps*, this is His Imperial Majesty's Ship *Hellbarde*, *Kapitän der Sterne* Gortz, commanding." The male voice's tone carried a powerful dose of something. Ferrero couldn't precisely identify what that "something" was, but she didn't much care for it. "We are in a superior position to intercept the vessel you are pursuing. We will deal with it. Break off. *Hellbarde*, clear."

Ferrero understood McKee's reaction to that brusque message

perfectly. Captains of warships of sovereign star nations didn't necessarily have to waste fulsome military punctilio on one another, but there were certain standards of courtesy. This message was little more than a curt dismissal, an instruction to get out of *Hellbarde*'s way which did not even respond to Ferrero by name. Addressed to a warship of a navy which had so recently ratified its claim as the most powerful one within several hundred light-years, it amounted to a studied insult. Moreover, under established interstellar naval protocols, the fact that *Jessica Epps* was already clearly in pursuit and overhauling before *Hellbarde* entered the chase gave her priority in claiming the prize. As Ferrero had just observed, this was her bird, not *Hellbarde*'s.

"Put me on-mike, Mecia," she said flatly.

"Aye, aye, Ma'am." McKee tapped a command into her panel, then nodded to her commander. "Live mike, Ma'am."

"*Hellbarde*, this is Captain Ferrero." The CO forced her tone to remain pleasant but allowed an edge of crispness to intrude. "We appreciate the offer of assistance, but we have the situation in hand. Be advised that we will be firing our initial warning shot in approximately—" she checked the sidebar on her tactical plot "—eighteen standard minutes. Captain Ferrero, clear."

She waved one hand, gesturing for McKee to go ahead and transmit, then leaned back in her chair, wondering what in the hell this *Kapitän der Sterne* Gortz thought she was playing at. It wasn't as if a ship the size of the pirate they were chasing was going to be worth an enormous amount of prize money. No navy would buy something as small and lightly armed as a typical pirate vessel into service, so the only real possibility for prize money would be the thousand dollars of "head money" the Star Kingdom paid for each pirate captured—or killed resisting capture—in the course of a warship's cruise. Given the small size of the current candidate, that probably wouldn't amount to much more than forty or fifty thousand to be divided amongst *Jessica Epps*' entire crew. Neither Ferrero nor her personnel were out here expecting to get wealthy capturing pirates, but there was still a principle involved. Not to mention the fact that routine relations between interstellar navies required a certain minimum level of courtesy to be maintained. After all—

"Missile launch!" Harris snapped suddenly. "Confirmed multiple missile launches!"

Ferrero jerked upright in her chair, spinning towards Tactical in astonishment. Harris took another fraction of a second to confirm the preposterous readings, then looked up.

"The Andy just launched on the pirate, Skipper! I have three birds in acquisition!"

Ferrero's eyes dropped to her own repeater plot, and she swallowed a curse of disbelief as it updated. Harris was right. Preposterous as it sounded, *Hellbarde* had just launched missiles at *Jessica Epps'* prize in complete violation of all interstellar naval practice. Not to mention at least half a dozen solemn protocols Ferrero could think of right off hand.

There was nothing she—or anyone in the universe—could have done to change what happened next. *Hellbarde* was much closer to the target than *Jessica Epps* was, and the flight time on her missiles was little more than seventy seconds. None of them were warning shots, either.

The hapless suspected pirate altered course, rolling ship frantically in an effort to interpose the roof of its impeller wedge between it and the incoming warheads. It was wasted effort, and its pathetically outclassed counter missiles and point defense were equally useless. Seventy-four seconds after *Hellbarde*'s launch, what had been a forty-seven-thousand-ton starship had become a spreading pattern of very small pieces of wreckage.

"*Jessica Epps*, this is *Hellbarde*," the same harsh, hard voice said from the bridge speakers. "As we said, we will deal with it. *Hellbarde*, clear."

Every eye on *Jessica Epps'* command deck turned to Erica Ferrero. Most of them turned away, almost as quickly, for not one of her officers could ever recall having seen so much raw fury on their captain's face. She glared at her plot, lips tight in a snarl of anger, and every fiber of her being wanted to lash out at that smug, disdainful voice.

But a small, clear voice of warning sounded in the back of her brain, despite her rage. She had no doubt that *Kapitän der Sterne* Gortz—whoever the hell she was—had enjoyed what she'd just done, but the fact that she'd done it at all, coupled with the increased Andermani presence throughout this entire region, suggested a great many unpleasant possibilities. No warship captain in her right mind would gratuitously violate all accepted interstellar law and standards of behavior and simultaneously insult another navy the way Gortz just had . . . unless there was a very good reason for it.

It was always possible that Gortz wasn't *in* her right mind, but that seemed unlikely, to say the least. Another possibility was that she was one of the Andies who particularly resented the RMN's presence in Silesia—or, at least, the Star Kingdom's refusal to give her own star nation a free hand in the Confederacy—and who believed she was sufficiently well born (or had sufficiently powerful personal patrons within the IAN) to escape the consequences of her actions.

Or, Fererro thought, *it's also possible that she was under orders to do precisely what she just did. Or something else like it.*

The Andies had been confronting Manticoran warships more and more openly and aggressively for months now. There'd never been anything else quite this blatant, but if Gortz's actions did represent a deliberate, pre-sanctioned act, it was arguably a direct, straight-line evolution of what they'd already been doing. Yet if that were the case, it was also a substantial escalation, a deliberate provocation.

And whatever it was, it was Erica Ferrero's job to respond to it.

"Skipper?"

Lieutenant Commander Harris's voice drew her attention, and she looked up from the plot at which she'd been glaring.

"Yes, Shawn?" She was just a bit surprised by how calm her own voice sounded.

"CIC's just completed an analysis of the Andy missiles, Ma'am," Harris told her. "They were pulling ninety-one thousand gees. And they detonated over fifty thousand klicks from the target." Her eyes widened in surprise, and he nodded. "Not only that, but CIC estimates that they scored at least eighty-five percent of possible hits."

Ferrero understood immediately why CIC had passed its analysis on to Harris . . . and why Shawn had passed it on to her so quickly in turn. Those figures represented an increase of over seven percent in what ONI listed as the maximum acceleration for an Andermani shipkiller missile, and fifty thousand kilometers represented an increase of well over sixty percent in any standoff attack range the RMN had ever previously observed out of an Andy laser head, as well.

And eighty-five percent of possible is damned impressive target-ing for a laser head at any *range*, she thought.

The question was why Gortz should choose to deliberately reveal that improvement in capabilities to *Jessica Epps*. And it had to have been deliberate. She certainly hadn't needed to launch her birds at maximum accel—assuming, of course, that that was what she'd done, and that she hadn't had still more drive power in reserve—just as there'd been no compelling tactical need to show off her laser heads' reach and accuracy. It was entirely possible that the Andy *had* had still more performance in reserve, she reflected. Even if Gortz was deliberately making a statement, it would make sense to keep at least a little bit back to use as a surprise in an emergency. But whether or not what they'd just seen was the maximum possible performance envelope for the IAN's current generation of missiles, it was a substantial improvement in what everyone had thought were the limits of the Andies' hardware.

Which suggested that this entire episode did indeed reflect a new and even more dangerous level in the Empire's aggressive foreign and naval policy.

"Record for transmission, Mecia," Ferrero said after a moment.

"Recording, Ma'am," Lieutenant McKee acknowledged.

"Captain Gortz," Erica Ferrero said in icy tones, "this is Captain Ferrero. Your high-handed intervention in my pursuit of a *suspected* pirate represents a violation of the established protocols in existence between the Andermani Empire and the Star Kingdom of Manticore. Your destruction of the vessel in question, leading to the death of all aboard, whose guilt or innocence had not been confirmed and who had not received the warning shot specified by numerous interstellar accords, also represents an unacceptable violation of customary naval usage and interstellar law and arguably constitutes an act of cold-blooded murder. I protest your actions in the strongest terms, and I will be filing a record of this incident with my own command authorities and the Star Kingdom's Foreign Office. My recommendation will be that interstellar legal proceedings against you and your bridge officers be initiated immediately, and I look forward with anticipation to the time at which you may be invited before a court of admiralty to explain and justify your performance here this afternoon. Ferrero, clear."

"On the chip, Ma'am." McKee's confirmation was soft, and

Ferrero smiled humorlessly at the com officer's tone. Yet she had no choice but to respond to Gortz's actions in uncompromising terms . . . especially if they did represent a deliberate shift in the IAN's policy towards the Royal Navy. Higher authority could always back off from her initial hard-line position, but until those same higher authorities could be advised of what had just happened, it was up to her to do anything she could to make the Andermani rethink any inclination towards confrontation.

"Send it," she told McKee, then turned to Lieutenant McClelland, her astrogator.

"Turn us around, James," she told him. "Take us back out across the limit. And calculate a least-time transit to Marsh."

"Aye, aye, Ma'am." The short, brown-haired, brown-eyed officer— one of the few native Sidemorians in *Jessica Epps'* company— studied his plot, then looked at the cruiser's helmsman.

"Helm, reverse heading and go to five-zero-five gravities," he said.

"Reversing heading and going to five-zero-five gravities, aye, Sir," the helmsman replied, and *Jessica Epps* turned end-for-end and began decelerating towards the hyper limit.

"Captain," McKee said in a very formal voice, "*Hellbarde* is hailing us. They sound . . . pretty insistent about speaking to you."

"Ignore them," Ferrero told her in a voice of liquid helium.

"Aye, aye, Ma'am," McKee acknowledged, and Ferrero returned her attention to her plot.

CHAPTER EIGHTEEN

The woman waiting for Honor under the landing pad's crystoplast canopy when the shuttle landed in the misting Grayson rain was dark-haired and eyed. The hair might have been a little more thickly threaded with silver than the first time they'd met, but the comfortable, lived-in face was the same.

The uniform wasn't. Mercedes Brigham was a rear admiral in the Grayson Space Navy, but she was also one of the GSN's many "loaners" from the RMN, and she wore the Royal Navy's uniform this afternoon. In Manticoran service, her rank was that of a commodore, and Honor had been a little concerned over how she might feel at the notion of accepting a demotion to serve on someone else's staff. She'd known Mercedes well enough for long enough to feel fairly confident the older woman would genuinely wish for the assignment. But she'd also known her well enough to be afraid she would accept the job out of a sense of obligation and friendship whether it was really one she wanted or not.

The taste of Brigham's emotions, coupled with the commodore's enormous smile, put that concern, at least, instantly to rest.

"Mercedes!" Honor said, as she stepped off the foot of the shuttle ramp. The fresh, life-rich smell of the spring rain embraced her, and she felt a familiar twinge of irony. That scent was like the very breath of a living planet after a week on shipboard air, yet it was a world whose atmosphere was potentially lethal in the long term to any human, especially an off-worlder like herself. It was a point her intellect was only too well aware of, but her instincts were another matter, and she drew the smell deep into her lungs despite all her forebrain could do.

"It's good to see you again," she went on, gripping Brigham's proffered hand and squeezing it firmly but carefully, mindful of her heavy-worlder strength.

"Likewise, Your Grace," Brigham said, gripping back. She nodded to LaFollet, Hawke, and Mattingly, and the three armsmen came very briefly to attention in response before they reverted to their normal watchful stances. Two more HSG armsmen brought up the rear, shepherding Honor's personal baggage, and Brigham waved her free hand at a waiting air car in Harrington Steading colors.

"If you and your friends will step this way, Your Grace," she invited, still smiling, "your chauffeur is waiting to whisk you away to Harrington."

"Not to Austin City?" Honor asked in some surprise.

"No, Your Grace. High Admiral Matthews was called away to Blackbird this afternoon, and he won't be able to return until sometime late tomorrow morning. He and the Protector decided that it would make more sense for you to get yourself settled at home before any formal meetings. Your parents and the kids are waiting to have supper with you there, and I understand Lord Clinkscales and his wives will be joining you. Your mother said she . . . ah, had a few things to discuss with you."

Honor's lips twitched in a mixture of humor and affectionate dread. It had gotten progressively more difficult to keep her mother here on Grayson and out of the fray on Manticore, yet the effort had become even more urgent once Lady Emily had knocked the scandal on its head. Allison Harrington was not noted for moderation where her family was concerned, and Honor could just imagine the smiling, merciless "I told you so" daggers she would have planted—as publicly as possible—in at least a dozen prominent Manticoran political figures.

"I think the Regent also has a little Steading business he needs to discuss with you while he has the opportunity," Brigham continued. *And he probably wants to rip a few strips off various Manticoran politicos, too . . . at least vicariously, since he can't get at them physically*, Honor thought resignedly. "That's more than enough to keep you busy for your first evening on-planet, and you're scheduled for an informal private audience over lunch with the Protector tomorrow afternoon at the Palace. If it's convenient, we'll meet with the High Admiral afterwards."

"Of course it will be," Honor agreed, and glanced at LaFollet.

"I'm sure you want to check the car for possible assassins, Andrew," she told him with one of her slightly lopsided smiles.

"If Commodore Brigham is prepared to testify under oath that the car has never been out of her sight, then I'm prepared to forego my normal thoroughness, My Lady," LaFollet assured her with only the smallest gleam of humor, and she chuckled.

"In that case, we'd better go quickly, Mercedes—before he changes his mind!" she said, and Brigham laughed and fell into place a respectful half-step behind Honor as the armsmen spread out in their customary triangular formation about their lady and headed for the vehicle.

Honor climbed into the back seat of the luxurious, armored air limo and settled Nimitz in her lap, and Brigham followed her. LaFollet parked himself in the facing jump seat while Mattingly politely but firmly displaced the original driver and Hawke took the front passenger/EW operator's seat. Mattingly spent a moment or two familiarizing himself with the pre-filed flight plan, then lifted the vehicle smoothly into the air and headed for Harrington City. The inevitable stingships settled into their escort positions, even for this relatively short flight, and Honor turned towards Brigham.

"I almost didn't ask the High Admiral for your services, you know," she said. "Both because I know how much Alfredo depends on you in the Protector's Own, and because I hesitated to ask you to step down a grade, even temporarily."

"Much as I hate to say anything which might undermine your perception of my indispensability, Your Grace, the Admiral can get along without me if he really needs to," Brigham replied. "And given the fact that I never really expected to advance beyond lieutenant back when we first went out to Basilisk, commodore isn't too shabby. Besides, I seem to recall a few times you've stepped back and forth between navies yourself."

"I suppose you do," Honor acknowledged. "But I really do want you to know how much I appreciate your willingness to do it this time."

"Your Grace," Brigham said frankly, "I was honored you chose to ask for me again. And it's not as if I'm the only person who's going to be looking at a drop in grade," she added in a darker tone.

"I know." Honor nodded, and Nimitz's ears flattened ever so slightly as he tasted her emotional response to Brigham's obvious reference to Dame Alice Truman.

Like Hamish Alexander, but with even less excuse, Truman had found herself a victim of the Janacek purges. Honor's contacts within the current Admiralty were much less extensive than they'd been when Baroness Mourncreek was First Lord, but there were rumors that Alice had stepped on someone's rather senior toes when she'd been captain of HMS *Minotaur*. That, coupled with the fact that the Trumans had served in the Royal Navy for almost as many generations as the Alexanders had, and that they were equally fervent members of the anti-Janacek faction, had consigned Alice to half-pay and cost her confirmation of her promotion to vice admiral.

Even Sir Edward Janacek and Jeanette Draskovic had found that one just a bit difficult to rationalize away, given the fact that Rear Admiral Truman, temporarily "frocked" to the acting rank of vice admiral, had commanded Eighth Fleet's CLACs throughout the campaign which had driven the People's Republic to its knees. Not that they'd allowed that to stand in their way, and Alice's obvious and none too private disagreement with current Admiralty policies had made it easier for them to justify it—or her lack of employment, at least—on the basis of irreconcilable policy differences. Which, as Honor had fully recognized, was yet another reason for Draskovic's pettiness over the slate of officers she'd requested.

"At any rate," Honor went on after a moment in a deliberately more cheerful tone, "your misfortune—and Alice's—is my good fortune. Janacek and Chakrabarti may not be able—or willing—to cough up the ship strength I think we're going to need, but at least we're going to have an excellent command team. So if I can't get the job done, we'll know whose fault it is, won't we?"

"I wouldn't put it quite that way myself, Your Grace. But I do agree that you seem to have pulled together a pretty good bunch. And I'm looking forward to seeing Rafe and Alistair again. And," she grinned suddenly, "especially to seeing Scotty and 'Sir Horace!' "

✧　　✧　　✧

"That was delicious." Honor sighed and leaned back in her chair with a pleasant sense of repletion.

The picked-over rubble of lunch lay strewn across the table between her and Benjamin IX, Protector of Grayson. They sat on one of Protector's Palace's private, domed terraces, a continent away from Harrington Steading, but it was raining here, as well. Not the gentle, misty rain which had welcomed Honor, but a hard, driving fall downpour that pounded the overhead dome hard. The occasional rumble of thunder was clearly audible, and Honor glanced up as a fork of lightning split the charcoal overcast. The gray, water-soaked afternoon was dark, almost ominous, yet that only made the terrace's warm comfort even more welcoming.

They were alone, aside from Nimitz, LaFollet, and Benjamin's personal armsman and constant shadow, Major "Sparky" Rice, and the Protector chuckled at her comment as he reached for his wineglass.

"I'm glad you enjoyed it," he assured her. "My chef stole the stroganoff recipe from your father, and the fudge cake—of which, if memory serves, you had three slices—came directly from Mistress Thorne's recipe book."

"I thought they both tasted familiar. But Master Batson's added a little something to the stroganoff, hasn't he?"

"I'd be surprised if he hasn't," Benjamin agreed. "As to what it might have been, though—" He shrugged.

"Dill weed, I think," Honor said thoughtfully. "But there's something else, too . . ." She gazed thoughtfully up into the rainstorm, pondering, then shrugged. "Whatever it is, warn him that Daddy's going to be trying to steal it back from him."

"From something your mother said a couple of weeks ago, I think he already has," Benjamin said with a grin. "And I think Master Batson can't quite make up his mind whether to be outraged by the fact that a steadholder's father is raiding his recipe files, even in retaliation, or flattered by the competition!"

"Oh, flattered. He should definitely feel flattered!" Honor assured the Protector.

"I'll tell him that," Benjamin replied, then sipped his wine and cocked his head to one side. "And how are your parents? And my godchildren?" he asked.

"Fine, thank God," Honor said, then shook her head with a wry chuckle. "Mother and Daddy both wanted to strangle about a third of the population of the planet of Manticore—starting with the Prime Minister. And Howard—!" She shook her head again. "Your godchildren were just fine, too. And noisy." Her twin siblings had just celebrated their sixth birthdays, and she'd been appalled by the sheer energy level they'd demonstrated. Especially Faith, although James hadn't been far behind her. And neither of them had been able to compete with Samantha and Nimitz's kittens, now rapidly approaching adolescence and even more rambunctious than the twins. And, she thought with a mental shudder, far better, at their size, in getting into places they had no business being. Explaining to them why their mother hadn't returned with Honor this time had been difficult, but less traumatic than she'd feared. Probably because all of their foster mothers had been there to help them cope with it.

Of course, she reflected, it might also be because they were the first treecats ever to be raised from birth among humans. She couldn't be absolutely certain, since Nimitz had been fully mature when they first met, but it seemed to her that she already tasted a subtle difference in their "mind-glows." A sense of horizons that were . . . broader. Or more diverse. Something.

"In fact, the whole household was delighted to see me," she told Benjamin, shaking herself free of her thoughts. "I've got the hug bruises to prove it, too."

"Good." Benjamin took another sip of wine, then returned the glass to the table. Honor would have recognized the "time to get down to business" gesture even without her ability to taste the emotions behind it, and she cocked her head.

"There was a reason I asked you to dine privately with me," he said. "In fact, there was more than one. If Katherine or Elaine had been available, I would have invited them, as well. But Cat was already scheduled for that address to the Navy Wives Association, and then Alexandra came down with the flu." He shook his head quickly at the flicker of concern the news of his youngest daughter's illness sent through Honor's eyes. "It's not serious, but Alex is almost as stubborn about admitting she's not feeling well as Honor is, and she managed to get herself dehydrated before she told her mothers she was sick. So Elaine is playing the tyrannical mommy this afternoon."

"I see, and I'm glad to hear it's nothing more serious than that.

But I have to admit that you've made me just a little nervous with your ominous foreshadowing."

"I didn't mean to do that, but by the same token, I do have some serious concerns, and I've been looking forward to the opportunity to discuss them with you face-to-face."

His voice was calm, but his eyes were intent, and as Honor gazed at him, she was struck by the weariness and worry hiding behind his composed exterior. And by his age, she realized abruptly. He was forty-seven T-years old, thirteen years younger than she, yet he looked older than Hamish, and she felt a sudden pang, almost a premonition of loss.

She'd felt the same thing last night, sitting at the supper table with her parents, Faith and James, and the Clinkscales when she'd realized how much frailer Lord Howard Clinkscales had become over the past few years. Now she saw the same process, if on a lesser scale, as she gazed at the Protector. Like so many of her pre-prolong Grayson friends, age was inexorably creeping up on him, and it shocked and dismayed her to realize he was already into middle age. It was a vigorous, energetic middle age, yet his dark hair was going silver and there were too many lines on his face.

And, she thought with a sudden chill, sensing her armsman at her shoulder as thunder rattled the overhead dome once more, *he's five years* younger *than Andrew is.*

That was not a thought she wanted to consider at the moment, and she put it resolutely away.

"I wish I could say I were surprised to hear you're concerned," she told him soberly instead.

"But you're not, of course." Benjamin cocked his head, and his eyes were both measuring and compassionate as he regarded her. Then he shrugged ever so slightly.

"Honor, I haven't asked you if there was any truth to the rumors about you and Earl White Haven for two reasons. The first, and by far the most important, is that both of you have denied there is, and I've never known either of you to tell even the slightest untruth. Which is most certainly not the case where the people who keep asserting that you've lied are concerned. The second reason, quite frankly, is that even if there had been any truth to them, it would have been your business, not mine. And certainly not that of High Ridge and his toadies.

"I'm quite certain you didn't need me to tell you that," he

continued calmly. "I, on the other hand, needed to say it to you, personally and directly, because you deserve my assurances in that regard as your friend as well as in my official capacity as your liege. But also, I'm afraid, because you and I need to discuss how that entire sordid attack has affected Grayson's relations with the Star Kingdom."

"I know the effect hasn't been good," she said somberly. "You and I have corresponded enough on that topic."

"We have," he agreed. "But the fact that you're about to head off to Silesia isn't helping a great deal." He raised a hand as she started to protest. "I'm fully aware that you decided to accept this assignment because you feel a responsibility to the Sidemorians, and because you feel a duty to Elizabeth and the Star Kingdom which transcends the way the current Government's treated you. I admire your ability to reach that decision, and I don't disagree with it. But there's an element here on Grayson, particularly among the Keys who've been pressuring me to reconsider our status under the Alliance, which is openly viewing this assignment as a way for the High Ridge Government to 'run you out of town' without ever admitting that that's what it's doing."

"I was afraid there would be," she sighed. "Unfortunately, I don't really see a way around that."

"Neither do I. And I'm certainly not second-guessing your decision. As I say, I think that in many ways it was the right one, although I deeply regret the potential personal consequences for you if the situation in Silesia goes as badly as I'm afraid it's going to."

"Do you have some particular reason for those fears?" she asked intently.

"Not concrete ones." Benjamin shook his head. "But Gregory and I have been mulling over the reports from ONI and our own intelligence people, and we don't like the picture that seems to us to be emerging."

"I wasn't particularly happy over what Admiral Jurgensen's briefers had to say to me, either," Honor told him. "But you sound as if you and Greg are seeing something even worse than I saw from them."

"I don't know about 'worse,' but I've got a hunch that we're seeing more."

"What do you mean, 'more'?" Honor's frown was more than merely intense now. Gregory Paxton had been her staff intelligence

officer when she'd commanded her first battle squadron here at
Yeltsin's Star. He held multiple doctorates, and was one of the more
brilliant analysts she'd ever worked with. More to the point, Benjamin and his murdered chancellor, Lord Prestwick, had nabbed
Paxton from the Navy when they required a new director for Sword
Intelligence, and from everything she'd heard since, he'd done an
even more impressive job there than he had for her.

"I haven't wanted to say anything about it in my letters to you,"
Benjamin admitted, "because, frankly, you've had enough to worry
about in the Star Kingdom without my adding still more, possibly groundless, concerns to it. But before Admiral Givens . . . went
on vacation, she and Greg had arranged for us to see the raw take
from her sources, as well as her analysis of the data. Since she left
the Admiralty, what we're getting is much more restricted."

"How?"

"We're not seeing any of the raw data anymore. Officially, ONI
is concerned about maintaining security, and to be perfectly honest,
that concern—which started the day Admiral Jurgensen arrived on
the scene—has struck a lot of our intel people as fairly insulting."

Benjamin's tone was light, but Honor could taste the anger
behind it and knew his intelligence people weren't the only ones
who'd found the shutdown of information flow insulting.

"To the best of our knowledge," he continued, "and Admiral
Jurgensen hasn't provided any evidence that our knowledge is
incomplete, we've *never* had a breach of security where shared intelligence material was concerned. The same can't be said for ONI,
where the evidence is very strong that in at least two cases information we provided *them* somehow ended up in Peep hands. And
while Jurgensen hasn't quite come out and said so, he's made it clear
enough that his real concern is the 'Peep turncoats' in our service."

Honor's nostrils flared, and sudden anger sparkled in her eyes.

"Alfredo and Warner are two of the most honorable, reliable men
I've ever met!" she said roundly. "And for someone like Jurgensen
to—!"

"Calmly, Honor. Calmly!" Benjamin shook his head wryly. "I
knew you were going to explode when I got to that part. And,
frankly, I don't disagree with you. But please believe me when I
say that Jurgensen's paranoia doesn't mean a thing to anyone in
this star system. We have absolutely no qualms at all about trusting
our 'turncoats.' "

"I should hope not!" Honor snorted. Then she made herself sit back in her chair. Nimitz flowed from his high chair into her lap and stood up on his true-feet like an Old Terran prairie dog, leaning his back against her, and she wrapped her flesh-and-blood arm around him.

She knew Alfredo Yu and Warner Caslet far too well to doubt for a moment that both of them had been overjoyed by the changes taking place in the Republic of Haven under Eloise Pritchart and Thomas Theisman. Both of them had known Theisman well. Indeed, in many ways, Yu had been as much Theisman's mentor and exemplar as Raoul Courvosier had been for Honor, and both he and Caslet had felt the heart-yearning to return to their homeland to share in its rebirth.

But she also knew they were the honorable men she'd just called them. They'd given their allegiance to Grayson and to the Manticoran Alliance. Indeed, Yu had been a Grayson citizen for over three T-years. The decision of whether or not to remain loyal to Grayson, even if that risked pitting them someday against the Republic once more, had not come easy for either of them, yet there'd never really been any question of how they would choose.

And the fact that High Ridge's refusal to negotiate a genuine peace treaty means they're still technically traitors during time of war didn't make things any easier for them, she thought grimly, still quivering inwardly with fury that a political cretin masquerading as a naval officer like Jurgensen should dare to impugn their honor.

"At any rate," Benjamin went on once he was certain she had her temper back under control, "he's openly disparaged—politely, of course!—our security systems while studiously ignoring or denying the failures in his own. In light of the difference in our track records, and the sheer arrogance of the man, a lot of Greg's senior people, and especially the ones who've worked most closely with Alfredo since we organized the Protector's Own, are deeply affronted by his insinuation that somehow we're less security conscious than the Star Kingdom is.

"The problem though, in practical terms, is less about our hurt feelings than it is about the reliability of what they are sharing with us. Speaking purely as head of state of Grayson, I don't need the additional friction this is generating—not at this particular moment. It's bad enough to have the lunatic element in the Keys pressing for us to go it alone in the wake of the Star Kingdom's 'insults' to Grayson and to one of our steadholders in particular. I don't need to have senior officers of my own Navy pissed off, if you'll pardon the language, with their RMN counterparts, as well. But I can live with that, within limits, at least, because my officer corps knows how to take orders, including orders to get along with idiots like Sir Edward Janacek and his flunkies."

The Protector's tone remained almost whimsical, but there was a savage, cutting edge buried in the whimsy, and Honor once more realized how rare it was for him to be able to show his true feelings at moments like this to anyone outside his own family and the innermost circles of his Council.

"As I say," he continued, "our primary concern is that what we're getting from the ONI reports doesn't match what we're getting from our own sources. We realize Manticore has spent decades, or even longer, setting up its intelligence-gathering nets, whereas we're still very new to the game, but we also know exactly where our information is coming from. We don't have any way to know that where Jurgensen's synopses are concerned, and he won't tell us. The end result is that knowing our data's pedigree automatically makes it seem more reliable to us. And, frankly, the fact that so much of what we seem to be getting from ONI these days is pure fluff only aggravates that."

"I don't think I like what I'm hearing, Benjamin," Honor said quietly. "And not just because it's insulting to every officer in a Grayson uniform. Tell me if I'm wrong, but it sounds to me as if what you're saying is that the reports Jurgensen is sharing with you are not only incomplete but . . . slanted."

"I think that's exactly what they are," Benjamin told her flatly. "I don't know if his people are going as far as deliberately falsifying information, but it seems very evident to me and to Greg that at the very least they're disregarding evidence which doesn't support the conclusion they wanted to reach from the beginning."

"Do you have specific examples of that?" she asked very seriously.

"Obviously, we can't show you a smoking gun when we've never seen the original data in the first place. But I'll give you two possible examples, both of which I find particularly disturbing.

"First, Silesia. Everything in the official ONI reports suggests that Emperor Gustav is still in the process of deciding what policy to pursue towards the Confederacy. At the same time, until the last month or so, ONI showed absolutely no concern about possible increases in the Andermani's naval tech base. But according to our sources in the diplomatic community, both in the Confederacy and on New Potsdam, the Emperor made his mind up months ago. Possibly as long as a full T-year ago. We can't positively confirm that, of course, but the aggressive moves they've been making and the generally more confrontational attitude of their naval forces in and around Marsh all seem to us to confirm that thesis.

"Greg's conclusion, and mine, is that the Empire has decided this is the time to push in Silesia. The Andermani haven't issued any formal demands or ultimatums to the Silesians, and they certainly haven't sent any formal communiques on the subject to Lady Descroix, but we think that's because they're still testing the waters and getting themselves positioned. Once they're satisfied the Star Kingdom won't push back—or isn't in a position to do any pushing—they'll make their demands clear enough. And they'll be prepared to use military force to support them.

"Which brings us to our second concern about Silesia, which is the fact that we believe ONI is seriously underestimating the extent to which the Andermani have improved their naval capabilities. Our hard-and-fast observational data is pretty thin, but there's enough to convince us that we're looking at a major increase in their compensator efficiency, that they've made substantial improvements in the range and targeting capability of their missiles, *and* that they've been experimenting with their own LACs. We don't think their LAC technology, in particular, is anywhere near our own—not yet—but we can't rule out the possibility that they've been putting the LACs they do have onto carriers. The thing that makes this particularly disturbing is that we know they're fully aware of what Eighth Fleet did to the Peeps, and one thing the IAN isn't is stupid. They wouldn't be picking a fight with someone they know just kicked the Peeps' butts if they didn't think their own hardware was good enough to even the balance. And unlike us, they have a pretty good idea of exactly what kind of hardware they'd have to go up against, because their observers have seen ours in action."

He paused and cocked an eyebrow at Honor. She gazed back at him, her expression a mask while she considered what he'd just said. The implications were frightening. She'd suspected that the briefings Jurgensen and his staffers had laid on for her had been overly optimistic, but she hadn't suspected that they might actually be ignoring or even actively suppressing the sort of evidence Benjamin was implying existed. She wished she could feel confident that the Graysons were wrong, but she'd worked too closely with them to underestimate their abilities.

Which, she reminded herself, was definitely not the case where Sir Edward Janacek and Francis Jurgensen were concerned.

"Now I know I don't like what I'm hearing," she told him after a moment. "I hope you and Greg will share your own information and analyses with me."

"Of course we will!" Benjamin sounded testy, and she tasted his sudden flash of anger, almost as if he felt insulted that she should even wonder about such a thing for a moment. She waved her right hand in a small gesture of apology, and he continued to eye her sternly for a handful of heartbeats, then made a face and snorted.

"Sorry. I know you didn't mean it like that, but the fact that I even considered taking it that way is probably a sign of how hard High Ridge and Janacek and their cronies are making it for us to work with them. Trust me, the last thing I want is to let my frustration with them spill over onto you, Honor!"

"I know. And I know it's hard, too. Especially when I'm sort of caught between two stools the way I am. You'd have to be superhuman to forget that I was a Manticoran first, Benjamin, and right now you've got every reason in the universe to be irritated with all Manticorans."

"But not with one of them who happens to be not only a Grayson but the person who's catching the most grief from both sides," he pointed out.

"Trust me, compared to what I've been putting up with on the other side of the line, any 'grief' any Graysons have been giving me is a pillow fight!"

"Maybe," he conceded, then brushed that aside and returned to his original topic.

"I said there were two areas we were concerned about, and Silesia is only one of them. And, if we're going to be honest about it, Silesia is the lesser of the two."

"The lesser?" Honor tilted her head to one side and frowned. "It sounds more than bad enough to be going on with to me!"

"I didn't mean to imply that it wasn't, but compared to what we're hearing out of the Republic of Haven, it's definitely secondary."

"Out of Haven?" Honor sat bolt upright in her chair, and Nimitz stiffened in her lap as her sudden stab of anxiety went through him.

"Out of Haven," Benjamin confirmed grimly. "Again, we don't have a great deal of hard evidence and Jurgensen's refusal to share sources with us contributes to a major uncertainty factor, but there are three things we think his reports have significantly understated or overlooked completely.

"First, is his analysis of what the fighting against the StateSec holdouts and the regular Navy officers has meant for Theisman's officer corps."

"I think I know where you're going with this one," Honor interrupted, "and if I'm right, I agree with you completely. You're about to say that Jurgensen's view is that the fighting has constituted a steady drain on their experienced personnel. That it's left them weaker."

"That's exactly what I was going to say," he agreed.

"Well, only an idiot—or a political admiral, if there's a difference—could think anything of the sort," Honor said roundly. "Of course they've lost some people and some ships along the way. But a lot more of their officers and crews have survived, and they've spent the last few T-years picking up experience. During the war, we managed to keep their officer corps trimmed back, for the most part, although Giscard and Tourville were turning that around before Operation Buttercup. Now, though..." She shrugged. "I don't know any way to quantify what it's done for them, but I'm absolutely convinced that it's improved their combat worthiness by an uncomfortably large factor, not reduced it the way Jurgensen argues that it has."

"So are we." Benjamin nodded. "Which is one reason we're concerned about the second point I was going to raise. You know that Pierre's financial reforms actually brought about a significant improvement in the Havenite economy."

He made the statement almost a question, and Honor nodded back.

"Well, we've been doing our best to evaluate just how much their economy has improved. Obviously, it's a matter of guess piled on top of conjecture, particularly given the fact that any officially published figures on the Peep economy were completely fabricated to hide the rot for at least four or five decades before the war. But we've run our models backward and forward, and they all agree that there ought to be more cash in the Republic's budgets than is being publicly reported."

Honor looked a question at him, and he shrugged.

"We know what their tax structure is, and we've managed to come up with a ballpark figure for their total economy which we feel is probably within ten or fifteen percent of accurate. And even taking the lower limit we've been able to postulate, the revenues they say they're collecting and spending are low to the tune of several hundred billion Manticoran dollars per year. And if our higher limit is closer to correct, the discrepancy gets much, much worse."

"*Several* hundred billion?" Honor repeated very carefully. She tried to remember if any of the High Ridge Government's intelligence types had ever expressed any qualms about the announced budgetary figures of the new Republic to any member of Parliament. Right off the top of her head, she couldn't think of a single time they had. For that matter, she admitted, it had never occurred to her to ask them about it or to suggest that anyone run the sort of analysis Benjamin was suggesting Grayson had made.

Which, she reflected, *was uncommonly stupid of me.*

"At an absolute minimum," Benjamin told her. "We haven't been able to find out where the money's actually going—not with any degree of certainty, at any rate. Part of the problem is that the Republic's so large and constitutes such a huge internal market that virtually all of it could be being plowed back into the domestic economy. More to the point, so much of their economy's been so distressed for so long that it's literally impossible to single out all of the perfectly legitimate places they could be pumping funds back into it. Unfortunately, we don't think that's the case. Or, rather, we're afraid it is the case, but that we wouldn't like the place they're spending all of that money if we could confirm it."

"And that place is?" Honor prompted as he paused.

"We don't know," Benjamin admitted, "but we have two straws in the wind, as it were. One is the existence of some top-secret project, one that was apparently launched under the Committee as much as several years before the McQueen Coup but which has been continued under Pritchart and Theisman. All we know about it for certain is its codename: 'Bolthole.' That, and the fact that Pierre and Saint-Just funneled huge amounts of money into whatever it is even at the height of the war and despite their worst financial problems. We don't have confirmation that Pritchart and Theisman have continued the same level of funding, but the discrepancy between what their revenues ought to be and what they're reporting certainly seems to suggest that some 'black project' is continuing to siphon off an awful lot of cash.

"That's straw number one. Straw number two is the name of the one officer our sources have been able to identify as being closely associated with whatever 'Bolthole' is since Theisman's little revolution. I believe you know her."

"I do?" Honor was startled and it showed.

"Oh, indeed you do," Benjamin said with something almost like grim amusement. "Her name is Vice Admiral Shannon Foraker."

"Oh, my God." Honor abruptly sat all the way back in her chair. "Foraker? You're sure?"

"We can't be one hundred percent positive. All we can say for certain is that her name appeared on the promotion lists, that we haven't been able to find her anywhere else, and that at least two separate sources within the Republic have suggested that where she disappeared to is wherever 'Bolthole' hangs out." The Protector shrugged. "There's no possible way to confirm it, but if I were a secretary of war who had some sort of high-cost project in applied research and development going on somewhere and I had someone of Foraker's demonstrated abilities to put in charge of it, I know what I'd be doing with her."

"You and I both," Honor agreed feelingly. She shook her head. "You're right. That's a much scarier possibility than some sort of tussle with the Andies over Silesia. But I can't believe Thomas Theisman would be a party to renewing hostilities! He's too smart for that."

"I'd tend to agree with you. But President Pritchart is more of an unknown quantity, and even if she weren't, it's possible you and I would both be wrong about Theisman. Even if we're not, neither he nor Pritchart is operating in a vacuum."

"No. And even if they were, it would make perfect sense for them to be looking for ways to offset our tactical advantages. In fact, they'd be derelict in their duty if they weren't looking for them."

"Absolutely. That's what has me and Greg so worried. Well, that and the fact that so far no one—including our sources—has seen a single improvement in their pre-truce hardware. It's been the better part of four T-years, Honor. Do you really think that much time could have passed without a navy which knows exactly how badly outclassed it was by Eighth Fleet introducing even one new weapon improvement?"

"No," Honor said quietly, and kicked herself for not having wondered the same thing already as she read Jurgensen's confident reports about the technological gap between the Star Kingdom and the Republic.

"That's the real reason Wesley and I have been continuing to push the naval budget so hard," Benjamin told her. "We're beginning to catch some fairly powerful opposition, especially in the Keys, but we're determined to go right on building up the Fleet as long as we can. The problem is that we estimate we can only keep it up for another two T-years, three at the outside. After that, we'll simply have to cut back on our building programs. We may even have to suspend them entirely."

Honor nodded. Altogether too many of the Star Kingdom's politicians shared the Government's ill-concealed opinion that Benjamin's obsession with continuing to build up the Grayson Navy now that the war was 'over' was a reflection of megalomania on his part. After all, no single-planet system like Yeltsin's Star could possibly match the sort of fleet a star nation like the Star Kingdom or the Republic of Haven could build. But Benjamin hadn't seemed to realize that, and the GSN was up to a strength of very nearly a hundred ships of the wall. Not only that, virtually all of them were SD(P)s. And that didn't include the CLACs which had been built or ordered from Manticoran yards to support them. Only the vast increases in onboard automation which had been accepted in the newer designs made it possible for Grayson to man its new construction, even with all of the demobilized Manticoran naval personnel it had managed to attract and even with the scandalous, steadily increasing number of women entering the planetary work force. But she hadn't needed Benjamin to tell her that the financial strain of that continued buildup was ruinous.

"Have you shared this information with Jurgensen?" she asked after a moment.

"We've tried to," Benjamin said bitterly. "Unfortunately, he seems to suffer from a bad case of 'not made here' where anything he doesn't want to hear about is concerned."

"And he's not going to want to listen to me, either," Honor observed.

"I wouldn't imagine so," Benjamin agreed with mordant humor.

"Of course," she went on, thinking aloud, "the most likely explanation for why wc haven't seen any new hardware in the Peep fleet is that they haven't managed to produce it in useful quantities yet. One thing I do feel certain about where Thomas Theisman is concerned is that he's not likely to make the mistake of introducing it in dribs and drabs."

"Which only means that when he does get around to introducing it, he's going to do it in style," Benjamin pointed out.

"You do have a way of coming up with pleasant prospects, don't you, Benjamin?"

"I try. And while I hesitate to mention it, there's another one I suppose I ought to bring up." To Honor's surprise, he sounded almost hesitant, and Nimitz pricked his ears as both of them tasted a certain unhappiness—almost a sense of betraying a confidence—in his mind-glow.

"Which is?" she prompted gently when he continued to hesitate, and he sighed.

"None of this is official," he warned her, and waited for her to nod in understanding. "With that understood, I probably ought to tell you that we've been picking up a few worrisome diplomatic indicators. More like hints, really."

"Hints about what?" she said when he paused once more.

"About Erewhon," he said finally. "You know they were almost as angry as we were about High Ridge's unilateral acceptance of Saint-Just's truce offer, of course."

Honor nodded again. In fact, Benjamin was probably understating the Erewhonese reaction—not least because Erewhon had been forced to live under the shadow of Peep conquest for far longer than Grayson had. The fact that the Erewhonese government had elected to cut its treaty relationship with the Solarian League in order to sign on with the Manticoran Alliance had only exacerbated that anger, too. The perception had been that it had sacrificed a longstanding security arrangement with the most powerful political and economic entity in the history of the human race in order to stand shoulder-to-shoulder with Manticore only to be stabbed in the back by its own treaty partners.

"Well, neither Greg nor I have any proof of it, but in the last few weeks, we've started picking up hints that Erewhon is . . . rethinking its relationship with Haven."

"Rethinking?" Despite herself, Honor's voice sharpened, and her eyes narrowed. "Rethinking it how?"

"Remember that this is at least ninety percent conjecture from very limited evidence," Benjamin cautioned her, and she nodded again, with just a hint of impatience.

"Bearing that in mind," the Protector went on then, "what seems to me and Greg to be happening is that the current Erewhonese president and his cabinet believe Pritchart and Theisman are genuine about their intention to resurrect the Old Republic. And that they've genuinely renounced the Legislaturalists' and the Committee's expansionist foreign policy. Erewhon's a lot closer to the Republic than it is to Manticore, as well. And unlike us, it controls a wormhole junction of its own which connects it—and anyone it allies itself with—directly to the Solarian League."

"You're suggesting that Erewhon might be considering a . . . closer relationship with Haven?" Honor said sharply, and he nodded.

"As I say, we have no proof of it, but we've been conducting quiet, one-on-one negotiations with several of the Alliance's smaller members." She regarded him intently, and he shrugged with a curious mixture of apology and irritation. "No one's interested in sneaking around behind the Star Kingdom's back, Honor. Not really. But let's face it. Thanks to High Ridge's idiotic foreign policy, the Alliance is in serious disarray at the moment, and we've been doing our best to try to put out the various fires before they get entirely out of hand and bring the entire structure down."

"I see." Honor understood exactly what he meant, and she felt a dull throb of shame at the thought of how hard Benjamin had obviously been working to preserve the vital alliances High Ridge equally obviously never wasted a single night's sleep worrying about.

"At any rate," Benjamin went on after a moment, "some of the things the Erewhonese ambassador's said in those discussions sound a lot more like the sort of temporizing and qualifying that usually go on between states that don't entirely trust one another— or who have something to hide—than the way allies are supposed to speak to each other. I don't think it's his idea, either. I think he's acting on formal instructions from his government, and that makes me wonder just why they're holding not just the Star Kingdom but *all* of us at arm's length. And one possibility which suggests itself to me is that they might be considering jumping the other way."

"My God, but I hope you're wrong!" Honor said fervently after two or three heartbeats. "After Grayson, Erewhon has the largest navy in the Alliance."

"And access to all of our new hardware," Benjamin pointed out grimly. Honor inhaled sharply, and he shrugged. "Their industrial base isn't as good as ours is because it was never as completely modernized and overhauled as ours was. But at the very least, they have examples of everything short of Ghost Rider—and some of that technology, too, I think. And if the Peeps get a chance to reverse engineer that . . ."

Honor shivered as the possibility Benjamin had just evoked blew through her bones like the breath of space itself.

"I was going to try pressing the Admiralty to increase the force levels they're projecting for Sidemore Station on the basis of your first little bombshell," she told him after a long, thoughtful moment. "Now I'm not at all sure that would be a good idea. Not if the Peeps—I mean, not if the *Republic*—is likely to be taking the wraps off something Shannon Foraker came up with after they gave her a big budget to play with! And if there's even the possibility that you're right about what the Erewhonese might be considering, that only makes the situation even worse."

"I'd have to agree that thinning out the RMN even further probably wouldn't be a very good idea," Benjamin conceded. "I hate to admit it, but even though our navy is almost half the size of the Star Kingdom's active fleet, we're not the ones that exercise a deterrent effect. Everybody keeps their eye on Manticore; we're just the 'plucky little scrapper' that plays backup to the Royal Navy." Honor looked at him in quick alarm, but he shook his head. "That wasn't resentment talking, Honor. It's just the way things are, and it would be unreasonable to expect that perception to change this quickly, no matter what's happening to the relative size of our fleets. The important thing is that when it comes to the perception game, the size of the RMN's deployable assets matters a lot more than the size of the GSN."

"I'm afraid you're right," she said. "Mind you, I doubt that anyone who's had the personal pleasure of tackling a bunch of Graysons would make that particular mistake, but that's not really the point."

"No, it isn't. But it may be that there's a corollary to it that we ought to be considering."

"What sort of corollary?" she asked.

"Well, if no one's going to worry a lot about the size of *our* fleet, then maybe the solution to your problem in Silesia is to find you some reinforcements from here. Sending off Grayson ships isn't likely to encourage any sense of adventurism among the Peeps, but their arrival in Silesia might be enough to make Gustav think twice."

"Wait a minute, Benjamin! Given how shaky things are between Grayson and the Star Kingdom right this minute, just how do you think the Alliance's domestic opponents are going to react if you start sending your navy off to pull Manticore's chestnuts out of the fire?"

"Who said anything about the Navy?" Benjamin asked her with a lurking smile.

"You did!"

"No, I mentioned 'Grayson ships.' I don't recall having said a single word about regular naval vessels."

Honor's eyes narrowed, then widened in sudden surmise, and he nodded with a chuckle.

"I'm not going to send a naval detachment to serve under a Manticoran admiral on an RMN naval station, Honor. I'm going to send the Protector's Own on its first major interstellar deployment and training cruise under the direct supervision of its permanent commander, Steadholder Harrington."

"You're out of your mind! Even if that sort of legal fiction was going to do you a bit of good when the Opposition gets hold of this in the Keys, think about the possible consequences. If it does come to a shooting situation with the Andies, then you're going to get Grayson involved in it right alongside the Star Kingdom. And I can tell you that the IAN's always been a much tougher proposition than the Peep Navy ever was!"

"Do you really think that matters?" The brief flash of amusement had faded from Benjamin's eyes, and he shook his head wearily. "Baron High Ridge is an idiot, Honor. You and I both know it, just as we both know he's so obsessed with domestic political maneuvering that he's almost completely oblivious to the potential interstellar disaster we both think he's courting. But the Star Kingdom is still our natural ally, and if the worst happens, Manticore's going to find itself under different management very quickly. If the Star Kingdom goes to war, whether it's with the Andies or the Havenites, we have no realistic choice but to support it, because without the Star Kingdom, Grayson and every other member of the Manticoran Alliance become the natural targets of any aggressor. Which means that I find myself in the unenviable position of being forced to watch High Ridge's and Janacek's backs when they're too stupid to even realize they need watching!"

"I hadn't thought of it from just that perspective," Honor admitted. "But even if you're right, there's going to be heavy domestic political fallout from this, and you know it."

"I'll deal with that as it arises," he told her flatly. "And if the Opposition wants a fight, I'll give it one it won't enjoy. Besides, I may have to watch High Ridge's back, but at least I can do it by watching the back of someone I actually like, as well. So don't argue. It won't do you any good, anyway. If you're stubborn, I'll just send Alfredo along with orders to make an extended 'courtesy visit' to Marsh."

"You would, wouldn't you?"

"Damn straight I would." He laughed suddenly. "And compared to some of the other problems I've got, fixing this one is pretty straightforward!"

"If you think this is straightforward, I'd hate to see what you think is complicated!"

"Don't worry, you'll get to see exactly what I'm talking about after supper tonight."

"What devious thing are you up to now, Benjamin Mayhew?" Honor demanded.

"Not a thing," he assured her. "But it seems that Abigail Hearns graduated from Saganami Island this past Fall, and while it may have escaped your notice, Rachel just had her sixteenth birthday. And guess who wants to follow in Steadholder Denby's daughter's footsteps?"

"Oh, dear." Honor felt her mouth quiver, but managed somehow not to laugh. Nimitz, on the other hand, couldn't quite suppress a bleek of amusement, and Benjamin gave him a disgusted look.

"All very well for you and your six-footed friends," he told the treecat severely. "As a matter of fact, Hipper's been less than helpful about the whole thing."

"I can see where the timing might be less than ideal," Honor said carefully. "But she does have a point, Benjamin. Abigail did very well at Saganami, and I think Rachel would do even better. And it's not as if she were your heir. There's Bernard Raoul and Michael still between her and the succession, even if the Keys were prepared to accept a female Protector. Which you and I know very well they're not."

"I know. I know! And Cat and Elaine are busy telling me exactly the same thing, although at least they don't do it in front of Rachel, thank God! For that matter, I have to admit, speaking as the Protector of Grayson and not a nervous father, that under other circumstances it might be a wonderful idea. But at this particular moment, with relations as strained as they are and as much resistance as there is in the Keys to any closer accommodation with the Star Kingdom, sending the Protector's oldest daughter off to enroll in the RMN's naval academy could be a recipe for disaster."

"I can understand that. But even if you sent her off at the earliest age the Academy would admit her, she'd have to be at least seventeen T-years old, and that gives you a year to work with. A lot of things could change in that much time."

"But a lot of things might *not* change," Benjamin shot back. "And if they don't, if it's still politically unfeasible to send her to the Academy, I don't want to be in the position of having told her she could go and then breaking my word to her. I've never done that before, and I don't want to start now, even if it's because a reason of state gives me no choice."

"That's because of the good father in you," she told him gently, and smiled. "Tell you what. I'll have a talk with her tonight after supper, if you'd like. I know Rachel well enough to know she's been keeping an eye on what's happening politically in the Star Kingdom, whether she'll admit it to you and her mothers or not. She has to realize political factors are driving your decisions right now in a lot of ways . . . some of which are going to impact on her personally. Still, she may take it better from me than from you if I point out how unpleasant it is being used as a soccer ball by a bunch of cretins like High Ridge, Solomon Hayes, and Regina

Clausel and then explain as gently as possible why it simply may not be possible to send her to Saganami next year. After all, you're her father, and there have to be some authority issues tied up in that for any teenager. I, on the other hand, am simply Aunt Honor, and if any glamour attaches to 'Admiral Harrington,' maybe I can put it to good use with her."

CHAPTER NINETEEN

"**T**ake a look at this, Jordin."

Jordin Kare looked up from his own terminal and pivoted his work station chair in Dr. Richard Wix's direction. Wix was a strawberry blond, with a somewhat shaggy beard, a mustache several shades lighter than his hair, and quite a reputation as a hard-partying sort. Indeed, he rejoiced in the nickname "Tons of Joy Bear," although Kare wasn't quite sure where the "bear" part of it came in. On the other hand, when he wasn't establishing himself as the very soul of conviviality, Dr. Wix was also an extremely competent astrophysicist. Perhaps even more important, he possessed that unique intuitive sense which spotted data correlations almost more by feel than by analysis.

"What is it?" Kare asked.

"Well," Wix said with an air of calm, "I can't be certain of course, but unless I'm sadly mistaken, that last data run from Admiral Haynesworth's people just nailed down the entry vector."

"What?!" Kare was out of his chair and standing at Wix's shoulder, peering down at his display, without any conscious memory of having moved. "That's preposterous! There's no way! We don't even have a definitive locus yet—how the hell could we have an *entry vector*?"

"Because God works in mysterious ways?" Wix suggested.

"Oh, very funny, TJ," Kare half-snapped. He leaned closer to the

308

display, then reached over Wix's shoulder and punched a command of his own into the data terminal. The display considered his question for a moment, then obligingly reconfigured, and Kare muttered a half-audible oath his rabbi would not have approved of.

"See?" Wix asked with an ever so slight air of complacency.

"I do, indeed," Kare said slowly, his eyes fixed on the display's vector arrows and the sidebar of tabular numerical data. He shook his head, unable to look away from the ridiculous figures. "You do realize how astronomical—you should pardon the expression—the odds against this are, don't you, TJ?"

"The thought did pass through my admittedly shallow mind," Wix agreed. "By my most conservative estimate, it should've taken us at least another six or seven months just to nail the locus, much less this." It was his turn to shake his head. "But there it is, Jordin." He waved at the display. "The grav eddies don't leave very much room for doubt, do they?"

"No. No, they don't," Kare replied. He straightened up and folded his arms, frowning as he contemplated the staggering implications of Wix's discovery. So far as he and Michel Reynaud knew, they'd kept any of their political overlords from realizing they were in hot pursuit of the Manticore Wormhole Junction's long-sought seventh terminus. But they weren't going to be able to sit on this news. As Wix said, they'd just cut a minimum of half a T-year off the search time—more like a full year, really. Which suggested that there might be a slight amount of hell to pay when the politicos discovered the hired help had been trying to keep them in the dark about the state of their progress.

On the other hand . . .

"This is tremendous news!" Countess New Kiev said exultantly, with what Baron High Ridge privately considered an unsurpassed talent for stating the obvious. Not that the Prime Minister supposed he should really hold that against the Chancellor of the Exchequer under the circumstances.

He had assembled a working group from the Cabinet in the secure conference room underneath the Prime Minister's residence. That room was buried under almost fifty meters of solid earth and ceramacrete, although every effort had been made to avoid any "bunker atmosphere." The furnishings were both expensive and elegant, from the deep pile carpet in the blue and silver of the House of Winton to the powered chairs around the huge conference table of hand-rubbed dark wood. One entire side of the large room was a programmable smart wall, whose holographic technology and nanotech had currently combined to create a breathtakingly realistic illusion that it was actually a window overlooking Jason Bay.

Yet despite all attempts to convince them otherwise, everyone in that conference room was well aware of how far beneath the surface they were . . . and of how impossible that made it for anyone to eavesdrop upon their conversation.

"I agree that this is fantastic news, of course, Marisa," Stefan Young said. "Obviously, the entire business community is going to be electrified by the possibility of still another Junction trade route, and as Trade Secretary, I'm delighted at the prospect. At the same time, the announcement could pose a few . . . difficulties."

"Not any insurmountable ones," High Ridge told him with a slight, quelling frown he was careful not to let New Kiev see. This wasn't the time to be reminding the countess of any trifling accounting irregularities where RMAIA was concerned. In fact, that was one reason he'd wanted Melina Makris assigned to Reynaud's staff. Makris knew exactly where her true loyalties lay, and as New Kiev's representative at the agency, she provided the perfect cutout between New Kiev and the actual bookkeeping. Which was a very good thing, given the way the countess' political conscience had of pricking her at the most unpredictable of times. It seemed to do it more over lesser matters than over greater ones, too. Personally, High Ridge suspected it was some sort of defensive mechanism. Perhaps her subconscious fixated on such minor matters because her pragmatism prevented it from reacting to any major sins of commission.

"Certainly not!" Elaine Descroix seconded enthusiastically. "This is the greatest discovery in decades—no, centuries! The Junction's been the biggest single factor in the Star Kingdom's prosperity; if its capacity increases, it will be the biggest boost our economy's had in almost a hundred T-years. And it's an agency *we* created which found a new terminus to make that possible."

"Of course," New Kiev said in a somewhat more down-to-earth tone, as if she found Descroix's complacent contemplation of political advantage distasteful, "we don't know where this terminus leads. The odds are against its connecting to any settled regions."

"The 'odds' were against the original Junction termini connecting to places like Beowulf or Trevor's Star," Descroix replied crisply.

"And even if it connects to completely unexplored space," North Hollow pointed out, "that's exactly what Basilisk was when we first discovered it. The opportunity for additional exploration and survey work alone would constitute a significant economic impetus."

"I'm certainly not trying to suggest that this isn't an enormously important discovery." New Kiev sounded just a bit defensive, High Ridge thought. "I'm only saying that until we know more—until we've actually sent a ship through and brought it home again after taking a look at the other end—no one can know just how important it will be. Especially in the short term."

"Agreed," High Ridge said, nodding sagely. "At the same time, Marisa, I'm sure you'll agree that news of this magnitude must be announced as promptly as possible?"

"Oh, of course. I didn't mean to suggest that it shouldn't. I'm only cautioning against making the news public in a way which feeds expectations we may be unable to satisfy in the long term."

"Of course not," High Ridge soothed. After all, there'd be no need to feed any expectations with official pronouncements. Private sector speculation would do the job just fine, and if it didn't do it on its own, there were enough think tanks which owed his Government favors. He was confident he could prime the pump without leaving any fingerprints if he had to.

"How soon *will* we be able to send a ship through?" Descroix asked.

"We're not positive," High Ridge admitted. "The reports from Admiral Reynaud and Dr. Kare are filled with a lot of qualifications. It's obvious to me that there's an element of covering their backsides to it, but I suppose that's to be expected, and it would be unwise to try to override them. They've both stressed that no one could have predicted—or, at least, that no one did predict—a fundamental discovery of such magnitude. According to their reports, they more or less stumbled onto the critical observational data, and they both insist that it's going to take some time to refine their current rough figures. Apparently, they have the approach vector for this end of the new terminus fairly well defined, but they say they're going to have to send quite a few probes in to test their data to be sure there are no glitches in their numbers. And they also want to study telemetry from the probes on the transit itself. According to Reynaud, without that, and especially without the transit readings, they can't project a survey ship's required helm data with sufficient accuracy to assure a safe transit. Until they can do that, they're both on record as opposing the dispatch of any manned vessel."

"It sounds to me like they're scared of their own shadows," Descroix said roundly, with a scathing edge of contempt.

"And it sounds to me," New Kiev said sharply, "as if they're concerned about the possible loss of life unnecessary haste could cause! We've gotten along just fine with only six Junction termini for centuries, Elaine—we can wait another few months to explore a seventh one."

Descroix bristled angrily at the countess's tone, and High Ridge intervened hastily.

"I'm sure no one in this room wants to run any unnecessary risks with the lives of our survey people, Marisa. On the other hand, I can certainly understand Elaine's sense of impatience. The sooner we can survey this new Junction route, the sooner the Star Kingdom's economy can begin to profit from it. And although it may seem just a trifle on the calculating side, I don't think any fair-minded person could fault us for taking a degree of credit for the discovery." He held New Kiev's eyes steadily. "After all, the discovery was made by an agency which this Government created and funded—against, I might add, quite strong opposition from Alexander and his crowd. And just as a government takes the blame for things which go wrong on its watch, whether those problems stem from its decisions or policies or not, it's fair for a government to take credit for things which go right."

"Of course it is," the countess conceded. "I think it's important we not be overly strident in telling everyone that the credit for this discovery belongs entirely to us, but someone is going to get the political capital that comes out of it, and that someone clearly ought to be us. I'm simply saying that even from a purely political perspective, it would be most unwise of us to push Admiral Reynaud into any exploratory activity he thinks would be premature. If we do, and if lives are lost, we'll get the 'credit' for that, too."

"You certainly have a point there," High Ridge agreed, and cocked an eyebrow at Descroix. "Elaine?"

"Oh, certainly we don't need to be losing any lives unnecessarily," the Foreign Secretary said peevishly. "But by the same token, I don't see anything wrong with turning the pressure up a little bit on Reynaud and Kare. I'm not proposing that we override them, but knowing the Government is strongly committed to moving forward as quickly as possible could help to . . . focus their attention a bit more firmly on ways to expedite matters safely."

New Kiev seemed to hover on the brink of yet another sharp reply, but she subsided after another glance from High Ridge.

"Excellent," the Prime Minister said briskly. "In that case, I think we're in agreement on how to proceed with exploration. For right now, however, we also need to consider precisely how—and when—we'll make the announcement. My own thought is that we need to announce it as quickly as possible. The question in my mind is whether we should do it through Clarence or through an RMAIA news conference. Opinions?"

"Clarence" was Sir Clarence Oglesby, High Ridge's long-time public relations director and currently the official press secretary for the High Ridge Government.

"We should release the news through Clarence," Descroix said instantly.

"I don't know about that," New Kiev said almost as promptly. "The RMAIA would be the logical avenue for the initial announcement. Wouldn't it seem like we were making a blatant grab for publicity if the Government's press secretary 'stole their thunder'?"

"I do trust, Marisa," Descroix said with a thin smile, "that you don't object to our taking at least some small official notice of this insignificant little event?"

New Kiev opened her mouth angrily, but High Ridge intervened once more.

"Marisa never said that, Elaine," he said firmly, and stared her down when she seemed disposed to reply sharply. He could do that with Descroix. Unlike New Kiev, she was unlikely ever to allow principle to conflict with ambition, and she understood the finer points of manipulation, whether of the electorate or her cabinet colleagues, in a way New Kiev never would.

"Personally," he continued once he was certain his Foreign

Secretary wasn't going to pour more hydrogen on his Chancellor of the Exchequer's anger, "I think there's some merit to both suggestions. The fact that this is a scientific discovery certainly suggests that the scientific agency which made it ought to announce it. But it's also a major political event, with implications for the entire Star Kingdom, beginning with the financial sector, no doubt, but certainly not limited to it. So I think the proper way to proceed would be for Admiral Reynaud to announce a press conference, at which the news of his discovery would be made public, and which Clarence would also attend in the role of moderator. That would put him in position to address the political and economic implications of the discovery as well as being sure that the scientists who actually made it get full credit for their work."

He smiled brightly around the conference table, pleased with his compromise, and New Kiev nodded. Descroix's agreement was a bit more grudging, but it came anyway, and his smile grew broader.

"Excellent!" he said once more. "In that case, I'll have Clarence contact Admiral Reynaud immediately to arrange it. Now, about those new shipbuilding subsidies you wanted to recommend, Marisa. It seems to me..."

"It's good to see you home again, Honor!" Rear Admiral Alistair McKeon said feelingly as Honor walked into the flag briefing room aboard HMS *Werewolf*. He and Alice Truman had reached Honor's new flagship before the *Paul Tankersley*'s shuttle made rendezvous with her. Mercedes Brigham had arrived with Honor, and Rafael Cardones and Captain Andrea Jaruwalski had met them in the boat bay and accompanied them to the briefing room.

"Rafe and Alice and I have managed to keep things moving, more or less," McKeon went on as he reached out to grip her hand firmly. "But no one at the Admiralty seems to have the least sense of urgency about all of this, and I think we need someone a little more senior to kick ass over there!"

"If it's all the same to you, Alistair," she said mildly, squeezing his hand back, "I'd prefer to spend at least—oh, an hour or two, perhaps—getting my bags unpacked before I go over to do battle with Admiral Draskovic and the First Space Lord."

"Sorry." He grimaced, then grinned lopsidedly. "It's just that I've never been at my best dealing with bureaucrats. And to be completely honest, it seems to me that some of them are deliberately dragging their feet this time around."

"I wouldn't be at all surprised if Alistair's suspicions are justified," Dame Alice Truman put in, reaching out to shake Honor's hand in turn. Her own smile was genuine but carried a decidedly sour edge. "I don't know exactly what you did to Draskovic to make her sign off on your staff and command selections, but I suspect we'd be getting considerably more—and prompter— cooperation out of the Admiralty if you'd picked a slate that was in somewhat better odor with the Powers That Be. Starting with your choice for your second-in-command."

"Starting with the station commander herself, you mean, Ma'am," Jaruwalski put in. The dark, hawk-faced captain had come a long way from the defensive, half-defeated woman who'd once been branded with responsibility for the Seaford Nine disaster, and she met Honor's sharp look with a sardonic smile.

"That might not be exactly the most diplomatic possible thing to say, Andrea," Honor observed, and her new ops officer shrugged.

"One thing I've already learned about trying to work with the new management at the Admiralty, Your Grace—we're never going to get anything done if we count on Admiralty House to do it for us. And with all due respect, Ma'am, you know that as well as we do. So we might as well be open about it here 'in the family,' don't you think?"

"You're probably right," Honor conceded after a moment, then shrugged and turned back to McKeon. "We'll have to sit down and discuss exactly where we are now that Mercedes and I are back from Grayson," she told him. "And if it looks like there's something we need that I can get the Admiralty to move on, then I'll certainly use whatever size stick it requires. But if it's something we can take care of ourselves, even if we have to go through back channels to do it, then I'd prefer to avoid any more . . . Admiralty interviews that I can."

"I can understand that," he agreed. "And I suppose it wouldn't hurt any for the rest of us to carry as much of the weight as we can instead of consigning you to Admiralty House's tender mercies."

"I wouldn't put it quite that way myself—even 'here in the family,'" Honor replied. "But in general, it probably wouldn't be a bad idea to keep me in reserve whenever we can rather than squandering whatever clout I have. Speaking of which," she continued her interrupted trip to the chair at the head of the briefing room table and sat down, moving Nimitz from her shoulder to her lap, "where, exactly, are we?"

"About two weeks behind your projected timetable," Truman responded. Honor looked at her with one raised eyebrow, and the golden-haired rear admiral shrugged. "*Hephaestus* turned *Werewolf* loose ahead of schedule, and Rafe and Scotty have done really well at working up her LAC group. We're at least a week behind on assembling the rest of the carrier force, though, and until we get all of the CLACs and all of the LACs gathered in one place, it's going to be impossible to form any judgments on the LAC groups as a whole. I doubt they'll be fully up to *Werewolf*'s standards, but that would be true of just about anyone they could send us. Scotty's LAC jocks could use as much additional exercise time as we can steal for them, but at least two-thirds of them are veterans, and in my opinion, they're shaping up very nicely. Would you agree, Alistair?"

"It's certainly looks that way to me," McKeon confirmed.

"I see." Honor nodded and glanced at Jaruwalski. "And that other project we discussed, Andrea?"

"That much is on schedule, Your Grace," Jaruwalski assured her. "The data is tucked away as per instructions, and Commander Reynolds and I have already had a few thoughts about it. We're not quite ready to share them yet, but I don't think you'll be disappointed."

"Good." Honor smiled thinly. It was a strangely hungry smile, but it became broader and warmer as she tasted the puzzlement of her senior subordinates. Well, there would be time enough to enlighten them later. She didn't expect any of them to have any objections at all to the little side project she'd codenamed Operation Wilberforce. But given the . . . sensitive nature of the intelligence data which would make Wilberforce possible, she preferred to restrict the details to the smallest possible circle until they were safely in Silesia.

"So you think the LAC crews are going to be up to snuff by the time we reach Sidemore?" she asked, turning her attention back to Truman, and her second-in-command raised one hand and waggled it back and forth in a maybe-maybe not gesture.

"I think they ought to be," she said. "I'm confident that they'll be up to Scotty's standards eventually, but I won't absolutely guarantee that 'eventually' will happen before we reach our station."

"You're the LAC expert here, Alice," McKeon said, "but I think you may be being a bit overly pessimistic. To me, they look like they're already starting to shape up nicely from what I've seen in the sims. But what do I know? As I understand it, Her Grace," he grinned at Honor, "asked me along to ride herd on the old-fashioned side of things."

"Not all that old-fashioned," Honor demurred.

"More old-fashioned than you may have thought, Ma'am," Jaruwalski said sourly. She grimaced when Honor glanced at her. "The latest from Admiral Chakrabarti's office is that we're going to have to leave one of our squadrons of *Medusas* here with Home Fleet. They're going to give us two squadrons of the pre-pod types, instead. And according to my sources, at least two of the non-pod ships are going to be dreadnoughts, not super-dreadnoughts."

"Only two squadrons?" Mercedes Brigham demanded, and turned to face Honor. "I know you warned me they were being tight about turning tonnage loose, Your Grace, but that's ridiculous! There's no way two squadrons of pre-pod ships equate to a single squadron of SD(P)s!"

"No, there isn't," Honor agreed with massive restraint. Privately, she wondered if it was possible that some of Benjamin's apprehensions about the Republic of Haven might finally have begun to percolate through what passed for the brain of ONI. She reminded herself that she still had to bring William Alexander and Elizabeth up to speed on all of Benjamin's concerns . . . including Erewhon's possible intentions. But at the moment, that was secondary to her own immediate concerns, and she certainly couldn't think of any other reason to reduce the ships being sent off to deter the Andermani so severely. If the new force levels held up, the Admiralty would be giving her task force only one squadron of SD(P)s. Admittedly, there would be eighteen older-style superdreadnoughts—*or dreadnoughts, if Andrea is right,* she corrected herself—to back them, plus the two weak battle squadrons already on station under Admiral Hewitt. And it was also true that six of the new ships ought to be capable of destroying an entire fleet of the older types all by themselves, but it still seemed like a foolhardy move.

Should I tell them about the Protector's Own? she wondered. There was no real reason she shouldn't . . . except that she and Benjamin had agreed that no one would be told—except Alfredo Yu himself— until the Grayson ships actually reached Silesia. The Protector had decided upon more mature consideration that the simplest way to avoid potential domestic arguments over his decision was simply not to tell anyone about it. As far as the rest of the Navy and the Grayson population at large were concerned, the Protector's Own was merely being dispatched on an extended deep-space training cruise, accompanied by its organic support ships. The primary purpose was to demonstrate its ability to sustain itself out of its own logistic resources in long-distance, independent operations. The fact that its training cruise would just happen to take the entire Protector's Own to the star system where its official commander just happened to have been stationed by the RMN would just happen to be one of those happy coincidences which just happened to happen from time to time.

Besides, as Wesley Matthews had pointed out when his opinion was sought, if someone like Sir Edward Janacek or Simon Chakrabarti knew Grayson was planning to make up the difference in the force levels Honor would require, their response almost certainly would be to see it as an opportunity to reduce the purely Manticoran forces available to her even further. Which analysis took on an additional point in the wake of Jaruwalski's news.

No, she decided. *It's not really fair for me to tell them when Benjamin won't even be telling his own people about it. And even though it may not be very nice of me, if I don't tell them about it, it'll probably encourage them to try even harder to make what we do officially have adequate. Besides,* she hid a sudden mental grin, *think what a pleasant surprise it will be for them when Alfredo turns up in Marsh. Assuming, of course, that they don't decide to lynch the admiral who didn't warn them he was coming!*

"Well," she said aloud, "we'll just have to find a way to get along without them, I suppose, won't we?"

CHAPTER TWENTY

The brilliant white icon representing Trevor's Star glared at the center of the enormous holographic plot in *Sovereign of Space*'s CIC, but Shannon Foraker had no attention to spare for unimportant distractions like suns and planets. Her eyes were riveted to the dense rash of crimson dots sweeping outward from the larger bloody icons of the defending fleet.

"Looks like they've got us on their sensors, Ma'am," Captain Anders observed quietly beside her, and she nodded. Despite all the Republican Navy's improvements in its stealth technology, its systems remained far inferior to those available to the Manticorans. It had been a given that they would be detected on their inbound vector; what remained uncertain was how much of an edge that would give the other side.

"We're getting initial contact reports back from the lead LACs," Commander Clapp announced, and Foraker turned to look at him. "Composition is about what we'd projected, Admiral," the commander told her, cupping one hand over the earbug screwed into his right ear and listening intently. "It looks as if their missile LACs are taking the lead." He listened a moment longer, then grimaced. "We can't absolutely confirm that, Ma'am. Their EW is still too good to penetrate at this range, and CIC's interpretation of the contact reports suggests that they may already be seeding their formation with decoys."

"Understood," Foraker acknowledged, and returned her attention to the plot. Like Clapp, she would have preferred for CIC to have been able to download the raw sensor data directly, rather than relying on the interpretive reports of the LACs' tactical officers. Unfortunately, that wasn't possible . . . yet. On the other hand, no one on the other side (*we hope*, she amended dutifully) had any reason to suspect that the Republican Navy had finally managed to crack the secret of the Royal Manticoran Navy's faster-than-light communications capability. Actually, the RHN had known roughly what the Manties were doing for years; they just hadn't known how to do it themselves. Until now.

To be honest, Foraker's techs had needed a bit of a leg up from the Solarian League firms which had been trading military technology to Rob Pierre's People's Republic in return for combat reports and the largest payments the cash-starved Committee had been able to scrape up. But it had been a very small leg up, and Foraker felt a deep, uncomplicated sense of pride in the way her own R&D people had picked it up and run with it. She was far too self-honest to believe Haven's researchers were in the same league as Manticore's, yet they were much better than they had been. They were still playing catch-up, but they'd managed to considerably narrow the gap between themselves and their potential enemies.

And that's another of the things we can "thank" Pierre and his butchers for, she thought. *At least they blasted loose the old R&D hierarchies and actually found a few people who could think to take over instead!*

"I wish we could deploy drones like the Manties," Anders murmured beside her, and her mouth twitched in a small, wry grin at the confirmation that he'd been thinking exactly what she had. The power requirements and mass costs of the RHN's current grav-pulse transmitters were far too high to permit it to employ the remote drones the RMN and its allies could deploy. The Manties were considerably ahead in super-dense fusion bottle technology and several other areas—including the newest generation of superconductor capacitor systems—and Haven was unable to match the onboard power levels of their remote platforms. But even without that, the sheer size of the early-generation RHN hardware would have made it impossible to squeeze it into such tight quarters. Indeed, it could be fitted into nothing smaller than a LAC. And, as Foraker strongly suspected had been the case for the Manties when they first developed the system themselves, any LAC or starship had to temporarily cut its acceleration to zero in order to transmit a message. Coupled with the slow pulse repetition frequency rate they'd so far managed to achieve, that limited them to very short and simple messages or to the use of preplanned ones which could be transmitted in short-hand code groups. Which was the reason *Sovereign of Space*'s CIC couldn't receive the raw sensor data directly; there simply wasn't enough bandwidth available.

Yet, she reminded herself once again.

"They're coming in for a head-on engagement," Commander Clapp reported. "Our lead LACs are reporting radar and lidar hits consistent with known Manty fire control systems."

"Now that's a surprise," Commander Doug Lampert observed ironically. As Captain Reumann's tactical officer, he really ought to have been on *Sovereign*'s command deck, but this battle was going to be fought beyond the reach of even her broadsides. Since that was the case, Lampert had opted for a ringside seat here in CIC, with its superb instrumentation and far more detailed master plot.

"Maybe not," Anders replied. "But I'm still not sure this is their most logical response. They've got to realize we're sending in a wave of LACs, and they must know we wouldn't be doing it unless we figured our LACs can stand up to theirs."

"I think it was reasonable to assume this was how they'd respond," Foraker disagreed quietly, her eyes never leaving the plot as the crimson hostile icons swept closer and closer to the incoming green light codes of her own light attack craft. "Of course they realize we're sending in LACs. But they've never seen the new birds in action. As far as we know, they're not even aware the *Cimeterre* class exists. So the only way for them to find out what they're up against is to come out and see. And when you couple that with the edge their hardware's always enjoyed, this is a perfectly reasonable thing for them to do."

"I understand the logic, Ma'am," her chief of staff replied in a tone of quiet stubbornness. "I'm just uncomfortable planning our entire doctrine around that assumption."

"With all due respect, Captain," Clapp put in diffidently, "we're not actually planning doctrine around this specific response. We simply anticipated it for the first few engagements."

"Granted," Anders acknowledged. "But I can't help feeling that 'the first few engagements' are going to set the pattern for our doctrine. All I'm saying, Mitchell, is that we need to be aware that they're going to adjust their operational patterns as soon as they realize what we've got. Which means what we really ought to be modeling at this point is not only how we expect them to react the first time they see the *Cimeterres*, but also what we expect them to do to adapt to the new threat."

"No one's disagreeing with you, Five," Foraker intervened mildly. "Obviously they're going to adapt, just like we've done in introducing the *Cimeterres* in reaction to *their* LACs. But the only thing worse than not allowing for adaptation on their part at all would be to project too far ahead with too little data. We believe we know more about their hardware and capabilities at the moment than they know about ours, but there are still a lot of things we're only guessing about. Without a more definite idea of what their options are, we could easily doublethink our way into a complete misestimate of the ones they'll choose."

"I know." Anders glowered at the plot for a moment, then puffed his cheeks, exhaled, and gave his admiral a slightly sheepish smile. "Sorry about that," he said. "I guess it's the engineer in me. I know we live in the real universe, where we can't nail things down the way we would in an R&D program. Especially not when the one thing we can count on a potential enemy doing is whatever it is we didn't want him to do in the first place." He grimaced and nodded to Clapp. "I didn't mean to sound like I was carping, Commander. It's just—"

"Just that one of a chief of staff's jobs is to play Cassandra, especially when everyone else seems to be feeling overly optimistic," Foraker completed for him with a smile. "Not that you'd make a very good Greek princess, Five," she added, and her smile turned into a grin as she contemplated the shininess of his hairless pate.

"Thanks . . . I think," Anders replied.

"They're about to enter missile range," Lampert put in. *Sovereign of Space*'s tactical officer was not a student of Old Earth mythology at the best of times, and, unlike the other three, he'd never taken his eyes from the onrushing wavefronts of icons in the plot. Now his announcement pulled their attention back to it, as well.

He was right, and as Foraker's eyes sought out the tactical

sidebars, she saw the icons of the Manticoran LACs double, then redouble, then redouble yet again as the combination of their hellishly effective onboard EW and even more frustrating drones and remote platforms came online.

"Right on schedule," Clapp murmured to himself at her elbow, and she glanced at him. The commander was clearly unaware he'd spoken aloud, and Foraker hid a smile as she recognized an echo of her old self in him.

Mitchell Clapp had come to his present duties via a less than orthodox route. Unlike the majority of naval officers who aspired to senior command, he'd never even considered the shipboard engineering or tactical career tracks. His first love and lasting allegiance had been given to the Navy's small craft, and he'd made quite a name for himself as one of the relatively few homegrown officers to distinguish himself almost equally on the engineering and test pilot sides of the People's Navy's pinnace and shuttle development and upgrade programs. The job he'd done was a vital one, but it was also one which partook of very little martial glory, at least in the estimation of his fellow officers. Which was one reason a man who had accomplished so much had been a mere lieutenant when Oscar Saint-Just suffered a mischief.

"Just about . . . now," the commander breathed, and the plot altered suddenly as a vast wave of still tinier icons separated from the green dots of the Republican LACs and sped to meet the oncoming sea of red.

Foraker felt herself holding her breath as she watched his tiny, fiery green darts slashing into the Manties' faces. No doubt any Manticoran who saw that launch would have put it down to panic. Manifestly, no Republican LAC missile seeker was going to be able to penetrate the solid wall of decoys and jammers the Manties had thrown up, much less defeat the onboard electronic warfare systems of the Manticoran LACs themselves. Counter missiles raced to meet them anyway, of course, but not in the numbers one might have expected against more capable missiles from larger combatants. Scores of the incoming birds were wiped away, but clearly the Manty missile defense officers were holding onto their limited stores of counter missiles for use against a more credible threat than Havenite LAC missiles.

After all, they knew that the hundreds of Havenite missiles racing toward them couldn't possibly hurt them.

As it happened, they were even correct about that . . . up to a point. The point which was reached as the Republican missiles reached the ends of their runs while still almost forty thousand kilometers short of the Manticoran vessels and the first echelon detonated.

They had no standoff attack range against spacecraft, because they weren't laser heads. Nor were they standard nuclear warheads in any usual sense of the word. And they didn't carry any of the sophisticated and devilishly capable electronic warfare systems the Manticorans had produced, either, because much though it galled Shannon Foraker to admit it, it would be years—probably decades—before the Republic of Haven was able to match the technical competence of the Star Kingdom of Manticore. So as Commander Clapp had suggested to her over two T-years ago, the only practical solution was to find a way *around* the Manties' technological advantage.

Which was precisely what the *Cimeterre*-class LAC and its armament were designed to do. Clapp's solution undoubtedly owed a great deal to how much time he'd spent thinking about and modeling the short-range, cluttered, high-threat environment in which pinnaces and assault shuttles routinely operated. Very few tactical officers thought in terms of that sort of combat where "proper" spacecraft were concerned, even when the spacecraft in question were mere LACs. Pinnaces and assault shuttles, after all, were expendable. Everyone knew a certain percentage of them were going to be lost, whatever tactical doctrine they followed. Fortunately, they were cheap enough and had small enough crews compared to starships that even a relatively high degree of attrition was acceptable as long as it allowed them to accomplish their missions.

But that, Clapp had pointed out, was also the primary tactical advantage of the LAC. It was just that because it weighed in at thirty or forty thousand tons, people didn't really think of it that way. Even those who'd grasped the tactical reality intellectually hadn't done the same thing on a deep, emotional level. And so they'd continued to think in terms of standoff engagement ranges, sophisticated shipboard systems, and all the other elements which made a LAC a miniaturized version of larger, vastly more capable hyper-capable ships.

Mitchell Clapp had begun his own design process by going back to a blank piece of paper. Rather than designing a starship in miniature, he'd seen it as an opportunity to design a pinnace on the macro scale. He'd ruthlessly stripped out everything that wasn't absolutely essential to the combat role as he visualized it, and along the way he'd discovered it was possible to save a truly amazing amount of tonnage.

He'd started out by accepting a life-support endurance of only ninety-six hours rather than the weeks and months which most LAC designers insisted upon. Next, he'd eliminated all energy armament, aside from an extremely austere outfit of point defense laser clusters. It was pretty clear to NavInt that the Manties had adopted radical innovations to provide the energy supply their new LACs required. Those EW systems had to be energy hogs, and the humongous graser they'd wrapped at least one of their LAC classes around was even worse. NavInt's best current guess was that they'd gone to some sort of advanced fission plant with enormously improved and/or enlarged superconductor capacitor rings to manage their energy budget. They'd also done something distinctly unnatural with their beta nodes to produce impeller wedges of such power without completely unacceptable tonnage demands. Again, all of those were things Haven would be unable to match for years to come, but by ruthlessly suppressing the energy armament and accepting such a vast decrease in life support—and by eliminating over half of the triple-redundancy damage control and repair systems routinely designed into "real" warships—Clapp had managed to produce a LAC hull which came amazingly close to matching the performance of the Manties' designs. Its less efficient inertial compensator meant its maximum acceleration rate was more sluggish, but it was actually a bit more nimble and maneuverable than the observational data suggested the Manty LACs were.

Of course, it had also been effectively unarmed compared to the Manticoran designs, but that was the point at which Clapp had recruited others to his project. In the absence of energy weapons, the *Cimeterre* carried a pure missile armament, and the R&D teams had made enormous advances in marrying reverse-engineered Solarian technology with their own indigenous design concepts. The missiles they'd come up with, like the LACs which would carry them, weren't up to Manticoran standards, but they were much, much better than anything any previous Havenite LAC had ever boasted. Unless NavInt was entirely wrong about the performance parameters of the Manticoran weapons, the *Cimeterre*'s birds could approximately match their range and acceleration in a package which was only a very little larger. Once again, sacrifices had had to be made to cram that performance into something the Republic could produce, and in this instance that something had been the sophisticated seeking systems and penetration aids built into the Manticoran missiles. But when Clapp and his colleagues were done, they'd produced a ship which was faster on the helm, had almost as good an acceleration rate, and was armed with weapons which were almost as long-ranged as anything the Manticorans had yet demonstrated.

And because Clapp had been so ruthless in suppressing every single system which wasn't absolutely essential to the *Cimeterre*'s mission as he visualized it, each LAC could cram a truly amazing number of missiles into its sophisticated rotary-magazine launchers.

Like the missiles which suddenly detonated long before any Manticoran would have expected them to. Missiles which contained absolutely no seeking systems, no penetration aids, no standoff laser heads—only the biggest, nastiest, *dirtiest* nuclear warheads Mitchell Clapp or anyone he could recruit had been able to design. Those warheads weren't designed to destroy enemy LACs; they were designed to strip away the enemy's EW advantages, and it was evident from the plot that they'd done just that.

The brutal wavefronts of plasma and radiation lashed out from the tsunami of missiles. No one had adopted such a brute force application to clearing away decoys and jammers in centuries. Even after the missile pod had reemerged, with its vulnerability to proximity "soft kills," no one had ever attempted to apply the same technique to electronic warfare drones and remote platforms. But that was because of the ranges at which deep space engagements were fought, and the dispersal which warships with impeller wedges hundreds of kilometers across were forced to maintain. Neither of those factors applied to the overgrown pinnaces Clapp had designed. The *Cimeterre*, even more than its Manticoran counterparts, was designed to get in close. It was a knife-fighter, not a sniper, and it eschewed sophistication and finesse for up-close-and-personal, bare-knuckle, eye-gouging combat.

The initial detonations ripped a thermonuclear hole straight through the electronic shield which had sheltered the Manticoran LACs, and a second echelon of the same massive salvo raced

Southwest Airlines
Open Seating
26

MUSORRAFITI / JOSE
PNR. HS5AAC
SEP 26
17 MACARTHUR NY
   to CHICAGO MIDWAY

RETAIN RECEIPT FOR FLIGHT

A

through the opening. Its birds detonated ten thousand kilometers closer to the Manties, ripping the hole even deeper and wider, and the next echelon exploited the opening the second had created. The third echelon closed to within as little as two or three thousand kilometers of the Manticoran LACs before it detonated in a final wavefront of blast, heat, and hard radiation.

The cumulative effect was devastating. The "triple ripple," as Clapp had dubbed it, not only irradiated and seriously degraded the remote platforms (those it didn't destroy outright), but also wreaked grievous carnage, however briefly, on the Manticorans' onboard fire control systems and sensors. Like all warship sensors, they were hardened against EMP, but nothing had prepared them for the precisely synchronized and timed detonations of that many multi-megaton warheads in so small a volume of space and time. Indeed, it was unlikely that anything *could* have prepared them. It was as if they'd suddenly found themselves staring directly into the belly of a star, and for precious seconds they were dazzled and confused by the sheer, unimaginable ferocity of the event.

And while they were still dazzled, the *Cimeterres'* second salvo came slashing in. Inferior as the seekers and penetration aids of that salvo's missiles undoubtedly were, they were more than sufficiently effective against defensive systems which could barely even see them coming. They roared down on their targets, homing ruthlessly, following their intended victims through the last-minute, desperate evasion attempts which were all their half-blinded state allowed, and then they detonated at ranges as low as five thousand kilometers.

This time, they *were* standoff weapons, and the crimson icons of the Manticoran "super-LACs" which had mangled one Havenite fleet after another during Eighth Fleet's offensive, began to vanish with dreadful speed.

"Eighty-two-percent kills, by God!" Commander Lampert announced exultantly as the numbers came in. "*Eighty-two* percent!"

"Eighty-two percent so far," Foraker corrected quietly, and Lampert nodded in acknowledgment as the *Cimeterres* continued to charge down upon the broken and harrowed ranks of their Manticoran opponents.

The massive energy mounts of the Manticoran *Shrike*-class LACs came into their own, even with targeting systems that remained partially degraded, and Republican LACs disappeared from the plot as the powerful grasers harvested them. But there weren't very many of the *Shrikes* left, and those which remained found themselves targeted by storms of individually less capable but numerically overwhelming short-range missiles. The first four, or five, or six missiles might be evaded or picked off by active defenses, but the seventh, or eighth, or ninth got through. The *Cimeterres* lost perhaps ten percent of their total number, but in return, they destroyed every single one of the Manticoran LACs. The absolute tonnage loss was less one-sided, but even that was hugely in the Republic's favor, and Commander Clapp staggered as Captain Anders pounded him on the back in jubilation.

"Simulation concluded," a voice announced, but it was almost drowned out by the babble of excited exultation surging through *Sovereign of Space*'s CIC.

"It's only a simulation!" Clapp pointed out as coherently as he could through the background racket and Anders' pounding.

"But it's the best simulation we've been able to build," Foraker responded. "And we used the most pessimistic assumptions we could about our relative capabilities when we modeled it in the first place." She shook her head, grinning almost as broadly as Anders. "If anything, this understates the probable outcome, Mitchell!"

"But only for the initial engagements," Clapp countered, and gestured at her chief of staff. "As Captain Anders pointed out, once we've done this to them a time or two, they're going to begin adapting their tactics. If nothing else, they'll accept a greater degree of dispersal and use sequenced waves of EW drones to make it harder for us to kill them before we close."

"Of course they will," she agreed. "And," she went on more somberly, "you're quite right—our relative losses will go up steeply when that happens. But the entire point of your operational concept is that since we can't match their ability to kill starships with LACs, the best we can hope to do is to impose attritional losses on them. To neutralize their anti-shipping strike capability because we don't have the tech base to create a matching capability of our own. And that, Mitchell, is precisely what you've accomplished here. It isn't pretty, and it isn't elegant, but it *is* something more important than either of those things—it works." She shook her head. "To be honest, I hope we never get the opportunity to validate your creation, but if we do, I think it's going to do exactly what you set out to do."

CHAPTER TWENTY-ONE

"**I** don't care what the intelligence 'experts' have to say," Arnold Giancola grunted. "I'm telling you that the damned Manties don't have any intention in Hell of giving us back our star systems."

He pushed back in his chair and glowered around the table in the palatial, expensively paneled private meeting room in what had once been the Hall of the People. That edifice had once more reverted to its even older title—the Senate Building—and technically, the Secretary of State was here to address the Foreign Affairs Committee. But that committee meeting wasn't due to begin for another hour and a half. Since he seemed to have arrived a bit early, however, he'd decided to spend a few minutes passing the time in idle conversation with a few personal friends.

Now one of those friends, Senator Samson McGwire (who just happened to be the Chairman of the Foreign Affairs Committee and an old Giancola crony), managed almost visibly not to sigh and shook his head, instead.

"You've said that before, Arnold," he said. "And I don't say you're wrong. But let's face it—there's no reason I can see for the Manties to want to keep most of those systems, either. Hell, all but half a dozen of them were economic liabilities to the Old Regime! Why should a bunch of money-grubbing plutocrats want to hang onto money-losing possessions?"

"Then why haven't they gone ahead and given them back?" Giancola demanded irately. "God knows we've been negotiating about it with them long enough! Besides, according to the latest estimate I've seen, some of those systems' economies are beginning to turn around already. Oh, sure—they'd do even better participating in our own economic turnaround. And don't think for a minute that the people who live in them wouldn't prefer that to being no more than wage-earners in what are essentially Manty-owned enterprises and investments. But their economies are beginning to generate a positive cash flow—for the Manties, at least, if not the people the Manties stole them from. And if the Manties turn the occupied systems into still more money-makers, then there goes your argument for why they'd want to give them back."

"And don't forget the military considerations," Senator Jason Giancola put in sharply. "They seized those systems in the first place to use as jumping off points for operations deeper in the Republic. So I can see at least one reason for them to want to hang onto them that has nothing at all to do with their economies."

"I know," McGwire agreed heavily. Unlike most of the Republic's senators, McGwire had been a member of a minor Legislaturalist family before the Pierre Coup. His family hadn't been important enough to draw the People's Court's attention during the purges, but he'd lost two cousins and a nephew in the war against Manticore, and his hostility towards—and suspicion of—the Star Kingdom were profound. "In fact, that's why I'm inclined to support you, Arnold, despite the fact that I'm not at all sure your ideas make economic good sense."

"This discussion is all well and good," Representative Gerald Younger pointed out. Like the Secretary of State, he was technically an interloper in this building, but many representatives were in and out of the Senate Building on a regular basis. Younger was one of them. He was also several decades younger than any of the discussion's other participants, and his tone was brisk, almost impatient. "The fact is, though, that whatever we may think, President Pritchart doesn't agree with us. And with all due respect, Arnold, it looks to me like she's holding the rest of the Cabinet in line with her own policy."

"Yes, she is . . . so far," the older Giancola admitted. "But it's not as cut and dried as it may look from the outside. Theisman is completely in her corner, of course. So are Hanriot, LePic, Gregory, and Sanderson, to one degree or another." Rachel Hanriot was the Secretary of the Treasury, Denis LePic was the Attorney General, Stan Gregory was the Secretary of Urban Affairs, and Walter Sanderson was the Interior Secretary. "But Sanderson is more than half way to seeing things my way, and Nesbitt, Staunton, and Barloi have both told me privately that they agree with me." Toby Nesbitt was the Secretary of Commerce, Sandra Staunton was the Secretary of Biosciences, and Henrietta Barloi was the Secretary of Technology. "So if Sanderson decides to come out openly on our side, the Cabinet will actually be split almost straight down the middle."

"It will?" Younger sounded surprised, and his expression was thoughtful.

"Damn right it will," the Secretary of State replied.

"What about Trajan and Usher?" Younger asked. Wilhelm Trajan's Foreign Intelligence Service and Kevin Usher's Federal Investigation Agency both came under the Justice Department and reported to LePic, much to Giancola's resentful chagrin. In his opinion, Justice should have the FIA, but State should have jurisdiction over ForInt. Pritchart hadn't seen things that way, and her decision to place both under LePic was one more point of contention, as far as he was concerned.

"Both of them are lined up behind the President, of course," he said testily. "What else did you expect? But neither of them holds a cabinet-level appointment, either. They're just very senior bureaucrats, and what they think or don't think doesn't affect the balance of power, if you will, in the Cabinet."

"Which won't matter a great deal," McGwire pointed out calmly. "Eloise Pritchart is the President, after all. Under the Constitution, that means her one vote outnumbers all the rest of the Cabinet combined. And even if it didn't, do you really want to risk pissing off Thomas Theisman?"

"If he were a Pierre or a Saint-Just, I wouldn't," Giancola said frankly. "But he's not. He really is obsessed with restoring 'the rule of law.' If he weren't, he never would have brought in Pritchart in the first place."

"And if he thinks you're challenging the 'rule of law,' you're likely to get a chance to exchange personal notes with Oscar Saint-Just," McGwire said dryly.

"Not as long as I do whatever I do from within the framework of the Constitution," Giancola disagreed. "As long as I do that, he can't take direct action against me without violating due process himself, and he won't do that. It would be like strangling his own child."

"You may be right," McGwire conceded after a moment. "But if Pritchart decides to demand your resignation, he'll certainly back her up. Especially if LePic and Justice also support her."

"Well, yes . . . and no," Giancola said with a slow, nasty smile.

"What do you mean, 'no'?"

"Well, it just happens that there might be a slight difference of opinion as to whether or not a President can dismiss a Cabinet-level minister on a whim."

"That's ridiculous," McGwire said flatly. "Oh, I agree it might be convenient if she couldn't," he continued in a slightly placating tone as Giancola frowned at him. "But the precedents under the old Constitution were clear enough, Arnold. Cabinet ministers serve at the pleasure of the President, and she has the right to dismiss any of them whenever she chooses."

"That may not be entirely true," Jason Giancola put in. "Or, rather, it may have been true under the old Constitution without being true under the new one."

"But the new Constitution *is* the old one," McGwire said.

"Mostly," the older Giancola said, taking over control of the conversation once more. "But if you go back and read the minutes of the Constitutional Convention, and then take a close look at the exact language of the resolution readopting the pre-Legislaturalist Constitution, you'll find that the second clause of subsection three specifies that 'all acts, laws, resolutions, and executive decisions and/or decrees made to reimplement this Constitution shall be subject to the consideration and approval of this Convention and of the Congress which shall succeed it.' "

"So what?" McGwire's puzzlement was apparent.

"So arguably, Pritchart's selection of the members of her first Cabinet—the Cabinet under whose direction the Constitution's been officially put back online—would come under the heading of 'executive decisions and/or decrees made to reimplement this Constitution.' In which case, of course, the entire Congress would have the legal right and responsibility to approve any changes she might unilaterally decide to make. Especially a change which would replace the individual charged with heading the interim administration of the state if something happened to her."

"That's really stretching, Arnold," the senator said skeptically.

"I suppose some might think it was," Giancola conceded equably. "But others might not. And given the grave constitutional implications of the question at this crucial formative stage in the Republic's evolution, it would obviously behoove those in disagreement with the President to submit it to the judgment of the judiciary for definitive clarification. And, of course, to seek an injunction to stay the President's actions until the High Court can consider it."

"And," his brother Jason said with an edge of very poorly disguised jubilation, "I have it on fairly reliable authority that Chief Justice Tullingham would be prepared to give the question very careful consideration if that should happen."

"He would?" McGwire sat suddenly straighter and looked intently at Arnold, who appeared less than completely pleased with his brother's revelation. The Secretary glared at Jason for a heartbeat or two, then shrugged and turned back to McGwire.

"Jeff Tullingham is a very responsible jurist, and one who was present as a voting member of the Convention. He takes his duty to oversee both the Convention's final resolution and the Constitution very seriously. Which, of course, was the reason I so strongly sponsored him when he was nominated to the bench."

Something clicked visibly behind McGwire's eyes, and his gaze was much more overtly speculative as he considered Giancola's completely bland expression.

"This is all very interesting," he said slowly, "but it's also premature at this point. After all, there's been no open policy disagreement in the Cabinet, and so far as I know, the President hasn't asked for anyone's resignation."

"Of course not," Giancola agreed.

"If there were to be an open disagreement, however," McGwire went on, "what, precisely, would it be about? And why would it arise in the first place?"

"I would imagine that the most probable cause for disagreement would be a dispute over whether or not—and how hard—to press the Manties to restore our occupied star systems and sign a formal peace treaty whose terms would be acceptable to the Republic,"

Giancola replied. "Of course, we're speaking purely hypothetically at this point, you understand."

"Oh, of course. But, continuing in that hypothetical vein, why should any member of the Cabinet feel so strongly on this topic as to risk a potential public breach with the President?"

"Out of a sense of responsibility to the Republic's citizens and its territorial integrity," Giancola said. "Obviously, if the present Administration is unable or unwilling to move expeditiously towards an equitable and honorable peace settlement, then it's the duty of those who might advocate a more active policy to provide Congress and the electorate with . . . an alternative leadership choice."

"I see," McGwire said very softly. Silence hovered in the conference room, and then McGwire tipped his chair back, steepled his fingers across his chest, crossed his legs, and cocked his head sideways at Arnold Giancola.

"Is there some particular reason why the need to present the possibility of such an energetic policy should arise at this time?" he asked pleasantly.

"There may be." Giancola tipped his own chair forward, and his expression was no longer bland as the keen, ambitious brain behind his eyes dropped its mask. "The situation in Silesia is unraveling on the Manties. I don't think they even begin to realize just how true that is, either. Of course, they don't know that the Imperial Foreign Service has formally inquired as to exactly what the Republic's position would be should the Empire seek certain border adjustments in the Confederacy."

"Why haven't we heard anything about that on the Foreign Affairs Committee?" McGwire demanded.

"Because the inquiry was only made day before yesterday. It was also made confidentially, and it doesn't directly affect our own foreign policy, anyway. The Republic has no interests in Silesia," the Secretary of State said with a very slight smile, "and as a result, we feel no desire to become embroiled in someone else's dispute there. Which I explained to the Imperial ambassador when he and I spoke over a private dinner."

McGwire's eyes narrowed, and Jason Giancola was obviously hard put to suppress a chuckle.

"Are you planning on handing out any more green flags, Arnold?" McGwire asked after a moment. "As Chairman of the Foreign Affairs

Committee, I'd really appreciate it if you could give us at least a little warning before you effectively commit the Republic to turning a blind eye to someone else's territorial expansion."

"Why? I mean, we *don't* have any interests in Silesia, do we?" Giancola shot back. "And even if we did, and even if we objected to whatever the Andermani have in mind, what, precisely, do you think we could do about it? The Confederacy is *three hundred* light-years from Nouveau Paris, Samson. Until we manage to finally resolve the mess in our own front yard—the one the Manties have stuck us with—we certainly don't have any business becoming involved in confrontations over Silesia!"

"And was that President Pritchart's view, as well?" McGwire inquired in a carefully neutral tone.

"On the basis of our many past discussions on similar topics, I feel certain it would be," Giancola told him in an even more neutral voice. "And because I felt confident I already knew her views, I saw no reason to waste any of her valuable time discussing it with her yet again."

"I see." The tension in the conference room ratcheted upward. Then McGwire gave a desert-dry chuckle. "I don't suppose that it really is any of our business to attempt to dissuade the Empire from pursuing its long-term and arguably legitimate ambitions in Silesia. Particularly not when doing that would ease the Manties' problems."

"Not until they get the hell out of our star systems, at any rate," Younger agreed emphatically.

"That thought had crossed my own mind," Giancola admitted. "And I notice that the Manty navy has just announced that it's dispatching a substantial task force to reinforce their Sidemore Station. Jason?"

"According to the Naval Affairs Committee's last briefing, they're dispatching at least five squadrons of ships of the wall, plus at least one carrier squadron. Of course, that information is bound to be out of date, since the dispatch boat took the better part of two weeks to get here from Trevor's Star. Actually, if they stuck to their original schedule, they should have already sent them on their way, although NavInt says they seem to be running a bit behind on their timetable. But even if it's taking them a while to get organized, that's still a fairly substantial force. And they've put Harrington in command of it."

"Harrington, eh?" McGwire looked thoughtful.

"Exactly. Everyone knows she and High Ridge aren't exactly bosom buddies," the Secretary of State said. "But even he has to know she's one of the best naval officers they've got. The fact that they're prepared to send over thirty additional ships of the wall all the way to Silesia and put them under the command of someone like her suggests that they're prepared to take a rather firm line with the Andermani."

"And from the point Ambassador von Kaiserfest raised with you over dinner, it sounds as if the Andermani are prepared to be equally . . . firm with them, doesn't it?" McGwire mused.

"That thought had also crossed my own mind," Giancola replied. "As had the fact that if worse came to worst, the Manties would have to transfer even more of their available naval forces to Silesia to deal with it. Which, just coincidentally, would mean they had to transfer those forces directly away from us."

"I'm not sure I like the sound of that, Arnold." McGwire sounded suddenly more cautious, almost alarmed. "It's one thing to contemplate the possibility of a foreign distraction for High Ridge and Descroix, but it's quite another to deliberately court a fresh military confrontation with the Manties! I trust you haven't forgotten what their Eighth Fleet did to us. I certainly haven't, I assure you, and however much I might differ with the President's negotiating stance, I'm not about to support anything which might put us back in *that* position."

"Nor would I," Giancola assured him. "But that particular situation isn't really likely to arise again."

"You've been dropping smartass hints about that for months now, but all I've seen is a lot of smoke and no substance," McGwire told him in frosty tones, "And, frankly, it would take one hell of a lot of substance to convince me that we wouldn't be reaching right back into a meat grinder if we started screwing around with the Manties again. You may think we can avoid that situation, or at least survive if it hits us in the teeth. I don't happen to agree, and with all due respect, I'm not prepared to risk the survival of the Republic on the possibility that you know what you're talking about."

"It isn't a 'possibility,'" Giancola said calmly. "It's a virtual certainty. Whatever I may think of Theisman when it comes to foreign policy or his apparent inability to subordinate theory to reality when it comes to the 'rule of law,' I don't think there's much question about his ability as a naval officer. Would you agree with that?"

"Anyone but an idiot would," McGwire half-snapped.

"I'm glad to hear you say that," Giancola told him. "Because it just happens that that's what my 'smartass hints' have been about. It would appear that without his having bothered to tell anyone about it, the Secretary of War has been quietly but rather effectively doing something about our military inferiority."

"Doing what?" McGwire asked intently.

"By a fortunate turn of circumstances, we're actually in a position to answer that question for you, Samson," Arnold Giancola said calmly, and looked at his brother. "Jason, why don't you tell Samson and Gerald about the good Admiral's little Bolthole."

CHAPTER TWENTY-TWO

It wasn't the usual route for deploying to Silesia.

Under normal circumstances, a Manticoran task force making transit to the Confederacy would have gone out by way of the Manticoran Wormhole Junction's Gregor terminus. But Gregor was an Andermani star system located in the very heart of the Empire. The Star Kingdom might hold title to the terminus itself, along with the legally recognized right to fortify the area around it and to maintain a fleet base orbiting the system's secondary component, but it was the Empire who held sovereignty over the rest of it.

Which was why Honor had opted to travel the Triangle Route in reverse. Rather than making transit to Gregor, and from there to Silesia and home again by way of Basilisk, as most merchant skippers would have, she and the reinforcing units of Task Force Thirty-Four had moved "north" to Basilisk, and then "west" to Silesia. It wasn't the fastest possible way to get there, since it required her to effectively cross the entire breadth of the Confederacy to reach Marsh, but it was one way to avoid any possible . . . unpleasantness with the Andies before she even reached her new command area. She didn't really like tacking on the additional thirty-four light-years, but even in the zeta hyper-space band, that amounted to less than five days of travel time, and the additional delay was acceptable under the circumstances which actually applied.

Not that every one of her officers agreed with her about that.

"I still say that all of this pussyfooting around is ridiculous," Alistair McKeon grumbled.

He, Alice Truman, and their chiefs of staff had come aboard *Werewolf* by pinnace in response to one of Honor's dinner invitations. Her dinners were something of a legend in the Fleet, and everyone knew her guests were expected to bring their opinions and any problems they might be wrestling with along with them when they came. McKeon knew that even better than most, and she'd more than half-expected to hear from him—again—on this topic once the wine had been poured.

"It's not 'pussyfooting,' Alistair," she replied mildly, sipping her own cocoa while her guests nursed a particularly good Sphinxian burgundy. She knew it was a good one, although she personally didn't care for it particularly, because her father had selected it for her.

"I calls it as I sees it," he told her with a lopsided grin. "And pussyfooting is exactly what it feels like to me. No offense, Nimitz," he added with a nod to the treecat in the highchair beside Honor, who showed him bone-white fangs in a yawn of amusement.

"In a lot of ways, I have to agree with Alistair," Truman put in. "Not that Wraith and I can't find a lot of useful things to do with the additional time, of course."

She cocked her head at Captain (senior-grade) Craig Goodrick, her chief of staff. Goodrick, who'd earned the nickname "Wraith" for his work with the electronic warfare capabilities of the first *Shrike*-class LACs, was an unremarkable-looking officer. The brain hiding behind his unassuming façade, however, was one of the better ones in the RMN, at least when it could be pried away from contemplating a hand of spades. Now he shrugged.

"Actually, Ma'am, I don't mind the longer transit time at all. I'm not especially crazy about anything that looks like tiptoeing around the Andies' sensibilities when they're being such pains in the posterior, but given the realities where our LAC groups are concerned, I'll take all the exercise time I can get and be glad of it."

"Heresy!" McKeon proclaimed, but there was a twinkle in his eye, and Commander Roslee Orndorff, his own chief of staff, chuckled out loud. It was a very substantial chuckle from a very substantial woman, and the 'cat in the chair beside her bleeked a laugh of his own. Honor didn't know Orndorff very well, but the ash-blond commander was another of the handful of naval officers who had been adopted. Her Banshee didn't seem to mind that his human-style name was derived from a mythological female harbinger of death. He was a good bit younger than Nimitz, around Samantha's age, in fact, but it was obvious to Honor that he shared Nimitz's low sense of humor.

"You're outnumbered, Sir," Orndorff told McKeon now. "And it's not just the LAC jocks who need time to work up to full efficiency, is it?"

"We could take any batch of Andies I ever saw exactly like we are this minute," McKeon proclaimed.

"In your dreams, Alistair," Truman said dryly. McKeon looked at her, and she shook her head at him. "I make all due allowance for patriotism and *esprit de corps*, even parochialism, but you know better than that."

"Well, maybe," he conceded. "But the Andies aren't exactly four meters tall and covered with long, curly hair, either. And while I'm prepared to admit we have more than our fair share of rough edges, we also have a bunch of combat-experienced veterans, which is more than the Andies can say."

"That's fair enough," Honor acknowledged. "But you might want to think about the fact that before we and the Peeps started shooting at one another, they were the ones with all of the in-depth backlog of combat experience. We'd done our share of chasing down pirates and dealing with the occasional squadron of 'privateers,' but we didn't have any real, recent war-fighting experience to go with it. Which, if you think about it, is a pretty decent description of where the Andermani probably are right now."

"Maybe it is," McKeon agreed with a more serious expression, "but we're not exactly the Peeps. They might have had a lot of experience at knocking off single-star system opponents, but most of their 'wars' hadn't really amounted to all that much more than polishing off privateer squadrons of their own."

"Somehow I rather doubt President Ramirez would agree with your analysis where the San Martin navy was concerned," Truman pointed out in an even drier tone.

"You're ganging up on me," he complained plaintively.

"That's what happens when someone rushes in where angels fear to tread," Honor told him. "Besides, it's dangerous to draw too close an analogy between the prewar Peep navy and the one we actually wound up fighting. The officers who'd amassed all the experience tended to be Legislaturalists, and they disappeared in Pierre's purges without our having to face most of them in combat. The ones we did go up against, like Parnell—or Alfredo Yu, when he was still in Havenite service—certainly gave us a run for our money, even with our hardware edge."

"You're undermining your own argument," McKeon objected. "If we're supposed to be the overconfident Peeps and the Andies are supposed to be the underestimated but plucky underdogs, then pointing out how competent people like Parnell and Yu were sort of defeats your purpose, doesn't it?"

"Not really. Even Parnell clearly underestimated what we could do to him, and the fact that he was so good in so many ways only underscores how easy it is for it even a competent officer to get overconfident on the basis of his people's superior levels of experience. Which is what the lot of us are ever so gently suggesting to you that you might be doing, Alistair."

She smiled seraphically, and Truman snorted at his expression.

"Gotcha!" she announced.

"All right. All right!" McKeon surrendered. "I admit we can use the additional training time. But all joking aside, I really am more than a little . . . irked to see a Manticoran task force sneaking around through the backdoor route this way."

"I know," Honor acknowledged. "And I know you're not alone in feeling that way, either. But remember that our most recent reports on what's going on in Marsh were three weeks old before we even left Manticore. I don't want to appear any more provocative than we can help. If Emperor Gustav really is planning an aggressive move in Silesia, we don't need to go around providing any military pretexts he can capitalize on. And, by the same token, if there's a genuine probability of hostilities with the Empire, I don't want our task force to be caught deep in Imperial territory when the shuttle goes up."

"I understand entirely," McKeon said, and this time there was no humor at all in his expression or tone. "And I don't really disagree with you. That's the main reason I'm so irritated. We shouldn't have to be so worried about provocations that we go thirty-five light-years out of our way just to avoid the possibility. Much as I may complain about it, I understand exactly why no responsible station commander would be in a position to make any other routing decision. But understanding it doesn't mean I have to like the circumstances which make it the responsible thing to do."

"No," Honor agreed. "And on that level, I have to agree with you. But Alice and Wraith are right about how much we can use the additional time for training."

McKeon nodded, and she tasted the agreement behind the gesture. It was a bit grudging, but that wasn't because Alistair rejected her position. It was because he didn't like the reasons her ships' companies needed the additional drill time any more than he liked the reasons she felt no choice but to avoid actions which might be—or might be construed as—provocative.

And he's right, she reflected. *It's absolutely ridiculous for the Queen's Navy to have gotten so . . . out of shape in barely four T-years. I suppose this is what Hamish meant when he started talking about "victory disease." But I know darned well that it never would have happened if Baroness Mourncreek were still First Lord and Sir Thomas were still First Space Lord.*

But that was the real crux of the matter, when she came right down to it. Any military organization had a pronounced tendency to take its direction from the attitudes of its senior commanders, and the complacency and arrogance of the political admirals currently running the Admiralty were reflected among an unfortunately large and growing proportion of the Navy's officers. The manpower reductions mandated as part of the build down had been disproportionately concentrated among experienced personnel, particularly in the senior noncom and enlisted grades, which helped explain some of the problem, but it certainly didn't excuse it. Total numerical reductions in the regular officer corps had been lower than anywhere else, since the first priority had been to release reservist officers back to the merchant marine and civilian economy. That had actually increased the proportion of active-duty officers who were Academy graduates, but all too many of the better regulars had become so disgusted with the Janacek Admiralty that they had voluntarily gone on half-pay status and followed their reserve fellows into merchant service. The ones who remained were all too often the ones who found the current Admiralty attitude a comfortable fit. Which didn't say anything good about their own training and readiness attitudes.

It wasn't anything overt enough for the officers who hadn't been affected to effectively combat. It was just . . . sloppiness. It was the Navy's smugly comfortable belief in its own God-given superiority to anyone who might be foolish enough to cross swords with it. The belief that the inherent supremacy of the RMN would suffice to crush any opponent . . . which made the unrelenting drills and training exercises which had always been so much a part of the Royal Navy seem superfluous.

The inexperience of the LAC crews which had been assigned to Alice Truman's CLACs was one thing. The huge expansion in LACs which the Janacek Admiralty had undertaken as its low-cost answer to rear area security had spread the surviving combat-experienced LAC crews all too thin, and the LAC groups had taken their own losses of experienced personnel. The vast majority of her own LAC crews had been assigned to their present duties only after the truce had brought active operations to a close, which certainly explained their rough edges. Whether or not it *justified* them was another matter entirely. The people who'd trained them had had access to all of the after-action reports of the COLACs who'd actually led the *Shrikes* and *Ferrets* in combat. They'd also had Truman's original training syllabus and notes to draw upon. But no one would have guessed that from the initial performance of the LAC groups of green, inexperienced crews Honor had been assigned for Sidemore Station.

Yet however understandable her LACs deficiencies might be, her battle squadrons weren't a lot better, and with far less excuse. The same complacency and lack of attention to routine training had spread its subtle malaise through the ships of the wall, as well. Especially the older, pre-pod classes. Those ships were almost universally regarded as obsolescent, at best, and even the personnel assigned to them seemed to have come to regard them as secondary units. As little more than backup for the SD(P)s.

"To be completely honest," she told her guests, "I probably would have taken the long way around even if I hadn't been concerned about the Andies' sensibilities. God knows we needed the time to get the rust blown off." She shook her head. "I hate to admit it, but the whole time Earl White Haven and I have been fighting with Janacek and High Ridge over procurement policies, we managed to take our eyes off an even more important ball. We were so worried about the hardware that we forgot to worry about how well our people were trained to use the hardware they actually had."

"Even if you hadn't, how much could you realistically have expected to accomplish, Ma'am?" Mercedes Brigham's tone was respectful, but it was also firm, almost brisk. "There were only so many battles you could fight," she pointed out. "And if you'll forgive me for pointing it out again, there's no point for blaming yourself for the consequences of policies you opposed. And you did oppose the entire mindset that made this sort of mistake possible."

"Well, yes. But not because I saw this one coming. I think that's what actually bothers me most about it, to be honest. I like to think I'm smart enough to notice things like this sneaking up on me, and I *hate* finding out I wasn't."

"Everyone gets an egg in the face every so often," McKeon observed philosophically, then grinned. "Some of us get to savor the sensation more often than others, of course. Like your humble wall of battle commander."

"Or," Goodrick said in a darker voice, "the people who get into bed with people like Manpower."

The captain smiled thinly and very, very coldly. Of all the people in the dining compartment, Wraith Goodrick had the most intensely personal bone to pick with the Mesan slavers, because his mother had been genetically designed and sold like so much animate property. She'd been consigned to one of the notorious "pleasure resorts" whose whispered existence was an open secret, however well hidden they might be, and she'd escaped that fate only because she'd been loaded as cargo aboard a freighter which had enjoyed the unhappy experience of straying into the arms of an RMN light cruiser. Which was how she'd come to be emancipated in the Star Kingdom and why Goodrick had imbibed his searing hatred of all things Mesan literally at his mother's breast.

Which, in turn, explained his almost religious experience when Honor and Andrea Jaruwalski explained Operation Wilberforce to Task Force Thirty-Four's senior officers once they were *en route* to Marsh.

"We can certainly hope that will prove the case for some of them, at least," Honor told him, with no more doubt than anyone else in the compartment what he was referring to. "Not that we can absolutely count on it, of course," she added on a note of caution. "We are going to be operating in Silesia, not Manticoran space."

"Judging from the way the Manpower scandal worked out in the Star Kingdom, that may actually be an advantage where bigger fish are concerned, Your Grace," Orndorff pointed out.

"Maybe," Honor acknowledged. "On the other hand, I'm not entirely certain that whole affair has been as completely put to bed as it might appear just now. The circumstances which led to the . . . circumscribed nature of the investigation aren't going to obtain forever. And the information that was handed over to the Crown may not be all the information there is. Or that can still be turned up if someone looks in the right place."

"Well, someone certainly looked 'in the right place' for the Wilberforce information."

Alice Truman's observation came out in ever so slightly questioning a tone. Everyone in that dining compartment was consumed with curiosity about the source of Honor's private information on the network of Silesian system governors and Navy officers who'd reached highly profitable accommodations with Mesa. It was far too detailed and internally consistent for them to doubt its accuracy, but none of them could begin to imagine how she'd gotten her hands on it.

And she intended to keep it that way. She owed Anton Zilwicki that much for his trust in handing it over to her.

"That particular information does provide an example of what I'm talking about," she agreed with a slight smile which told Truman her fishing expedition was going to come up dry. "Not that any of it has any domestic Manticoran connections—or not direct ones, anyway. But I'll settle for progress anywhere, where genetic slavery is concerned. And given that we know which systems and which Silesian freight lines to watch, we may just make a little bit of a difference with Wilberforce, after all.

"None of which," she added, pulling the conversation back to its earlier thread, "has any particular bearing on whether or not the Opposition—and especially the Opposition's Navy types, like yours truly—should have realized how . . . flabby the Queen's Navy was getting. Or keeps me from wishing I'd paid enough attention to at least realize this particular mistake was being made in the first place!"

"Well," Goodrick said, accepting the change of subject for all of them, "we all realize it now, Your Grace. And since it's already been made, all we can do is dig in and undo as much of the damage as possible before we ever get to Sidemore."

"Agreed." McKeon nodded sharply, and leaned forward, his manner suddenly businesslike. "And all joking aside, Roslee and I have been thinking about a new series of joint exercises we can carry out in the simulators."

"I take it that the fact that you're bringing it up now means that you're not talking about exercises restricted solely to the wall?" Truman made the statement a question, and McKeon nodded again.

"We're already working on that side of it, Alice. What Roslee and I wanted to discuss is how we could best go about structuring our training schedule to exercise the wall and the LACs jointly, both in cooperation and against one another."

"That sounds like an excellent idea to me," Honor said firmly. In fact, that sort of discussion was precisely why she believed in inviting her officers to dine with her on a regular basis, and she looked over her shoulder at Andrew LaFollet.

"Andrew, would you please pass the word for Andrea to join us as soon as she finds it convenient?" she requested. Her personal armsman nodded in acknowledgment and reached for his com, and Honor turned back to her other guests and leaned forward in her own chair.

"I'm sure Andrea will be able to offer some extremely useful suggestions once we get her in on this," she said. "But in the meantime, we should be about it, so why don't all of you tell Mercedes and me exactly what it is you have in mind?"

"All units, this is *Cockatrice One*-Alpha. We'll go with Alpha Delta Niner-Six." Captain Scotty Tremaine listened to the voice in his earbug. "*Werewolf Four*, take the lead battlecruiser. *Werewolf Five* and *Six*, you're on Bandit Two. All *Chimera* squadrons, take your targets from Bandit Two along the targeting queue. *Centaur* and *Cockatrice* groups, decel to establish interval Baker Eight—you're on cleanup. Execute now!"

Tremaine watched his plot in *Werewolf*'s Primary Flight Control carefully as the massed squadrons of TF 34's four CLACs began to flow outward in response to Commander Arthur Baker's orders. This was the third attack exercise of the day, and the first two had not been outstanding successes.

At least they were better than yesterday's, he reminded himself wryly. *And, after all, that's what exercises are intended to do—find the problems so you can make things better.*

He would have preferred to be leading the attack in person, for several reasons. One of the things he most treasured about his assignment as the task force's senior COLAC was that despite his lofty position in its command hierarchy, he still got to go out in space with his personnel rather than staying back aboard a flagship somewhere. It gave him a better chance of getting himself killed than a battle squadron or task group commander might have enjoyed, but it also meant he didn't have to send people out to do something he wasn't doing himself.

Besides, there wasn't much of an option about it. Even with grav-pulse FTL communications, LACs operated much too far away from their motherships to be controlled from there. As Jackie Harmon had established with the very first LAC group, any COLAC's proper place was out with his attack birds and their crews.

But at the moment, Commander Baker, HMS *Cockatrice*'s COLAC, was subbing for him. After *Werewolf* herself, *Cockatrice*, Admiral Truman's flagship, was the next senior of the task force's CLACs, which meant that if anything happened to Tremaine, it would be up to Baker to take over. From what Tremaine had seen of him so far, the tall, black-haired commander had all the required skills and ability, but he was short on experience. He also still tended to think a bit too much like the destroyer skipper he'd been slated to become before he found himself transferred into the expanding LAC community. He was developing the proper "LAC jock" attitude, but he still had a few rough edges and he needed a bit more confidence.

Which was the reason he was the one running the squadrons through their paces while Tremaine and Chief Warrant Officer Sir Horace Harkness managed the training scenario.

Unlike the morning's two previous sessions, this was an all up exercise, with live hardware, not simply a simulation. The task force was currently transiting between two grav waves under impeller drive, which meant that ships without Warshawski sails—like LACs—could maneuver without being destroyed the instant they left their hangar bays. It also put a maximum limit on the time window for the exercise, since the hyper-capable ships would be entering the next grav wave in a tiny bit over three hours from now.

Now, as Tremaine watched, the battlecruiser squadron Admiral McKeon had detached from his screen to play the aggressor's role altered course to head directly towards the LACs which were obviously deploying to attack them. At the same time, the clear, clean icons which had represented them on PriFly's master plot disappeared into a mushy haze of jamming and decoys.

"Bet Commander Baker didn't much like that, Skipper," Harkness observed with a nasty grin, and Tremaine chuckled.

"I did warn him we'd arranged a few surprises," he pointed out.

"Yeah, but I bet he never figured you'd let Admiral Atwater's squadron turn Ghost Rider loose on him!"

"It's not my fault he wasn't around when Dame Alice did the same thing to us," Tremaine shot back. "And just because the Peeps don't have anything to match Ghost Rider doesn't mean the Andies haven't come up with something a lot closer to it than we'd like."

"No argument there, Skip," Harkness agreed in a much more serious tone. Although he was only a chief warrant officer, he was holding down a lieutenant commander's duty slot himself, as *Werewolf*'s senior LAC flight engineer. That made him effectively the chief electronics technician and ordnance officer for the entire task force's carrier force. As such he had clearance for access to all of the official ONI briefings on the situation in Silesia, and to say he'd been less than impressed by their thoroughness would have been a masterpiece of understatement.

"Matter of fact," he went on after a moment, watching Baker's carefully orchestrated maneuver disintegrate into apparent mass confusion as he and his tac officers tried to compensate for the sudden loss of at least eighty-five percent of their sensor capabilities, "I picked up on something yesterday that I meant to mention to you, Sir."

"Like what?" Tremaine asked, never taking his eyes from the display's icons. The seeming confusion was settling down into a revised attack pattern with a speed and precision which surprised him pleasantly. It was obvious that the sudden increase in his targets' electronic warfare capabilities had come as a complete surprise to Baker, exactly as Tremaine had intended, but the commander hadn't panicked. He'd realized he still had time before he entered the battlecruisers' engagement envelope, and he was adopting a rather more defensive formation, with the missile-armed *Ferrets* moving up to screen the energy-heavy *Shrikes* with their own decoys and jammers. Obviously he'd reached the same conclusion Tremaine would have in his place; against such capable EW, he was going to have to get in close with the *Shrikes*' grasers rather than relying on a missile engagement, and the *Ferrets*' electronic warfare birds were his best chance to do that.

"I was reading through those reports Grayson Naval Intelligence copied to us," Harkness said, his own eyes watching approvingly as Baker adapted to the new parameters of his problem. "I know everyone knows the Graysons don't know squat compared to our own all-knowing intelligence pukes. But I gotta tell you, Skip, I didn't like what the GSN had to say about Andy 'tronics systems."

"What?" Tremaine turned to look at the CWO in surprise . . . and chagrin. "I must have missed that one, Chief."

"Well, there's a lot to wade through," Harkness told him. "And I have to admit the indexing system they used seems kinda skewed. This one was tucked away under an engineering head, not tactics, which is probably why I noticed it and you didn't."

"Thanks, but stop making excuses for me and tell me what it said," Tremaine commanded with a lopsided grin, and Harkness shrugged.

"Like everything else, it's all a matter of interpreting a mighty slim data sample, Skip. But the Graysons managed to 'acquire' access to a confidential report from the Confed Navy. Looks to me like they probably crossed a couple of palms with good old-fashioned dollars.

"Anyway, however they got it, it's a report from one of the Sillies' cruiser captains. Seems he happened along just as a 'privateer' the entire Confed Navy had been trying to catch up with for over six months sailed straight into an Andy ambush. This particular Confed skipper seems to me to've been a couple of cuts above the average for a Silly officer. He'd already IDed the pirate, and he was busy sneaking up on it, using his own stealth systems, when a pair of Andy destroyers and a heavy cruiser just 'suddenly appeared' and blew the raider into dust bunnies."

"'Suddenly appeared'?" Tremaine repeated, and Harkness nodded.

"His exact words, Skip. Now, I know the Sillies' sensors aren't worth a hell of a lot, and I know their sensor techs aren't usually up to our standards, or even the Peeps'. But from his report, this bird runs a mighty taut ship for a Silesian, and he was real careful to emphasize that none of his people got so much as a sniff of the Andies until all three dropped their stealth and opened fire."

"What was the range?" Tremaine asked intently.

"That's what bothered me the most," Harkness admitted. "It looked to the guy writing the report like the pirates never saw the Andies at all, but those bastards tend to be even slacker than most Confed navy crews, so that don't necessarily prove a thing. But the Silly cruiser was only about four light-minutes from the nearest Andy ship when she opened fire, and *she* hadn't seen a damned thing, either."

"Four light-minutes, huh?" Tremaine chewed his lower lip unhappily for a moment. "I can see why you didn't much care for that one, Chief," he said after a moment. "Go ahead and copy the same reports to my mail queue, would you?"

"No problem, Skip."

"I'll probably need to flag it to be sure the Old Lady and Admiral McKeon and Admiral Truman get a copy of it, too. If they've improved their EW as much as your cruiser captain seems to be suggesting . . ."

"Absolutely, Skip," Harkness agreed, and nodded at the display, where Commander Baker had gotten his revamped attack formation organized and was closing in on his prey. "Might just turn out that having our boys and girls working out against first-string EW is an even better damned idea then you thought," he said quietly.

CHAPTER TWENTY-THREE

"You know," Erica Ferrero remarked to her bridge crew, "I'm getting really tired of these jokers."

No one replied to her observation. In part that was because her tone suggested that anyone unwise enough to draw her ire at this particular moment might live to regret it. But that was only a relatively minor consideration, compared to the fact that every one of *Jessica Epps'* bridge officers agreed with her.

"Do we have any particular idea just what they think they're doing this time around, Shawn?" the captain continued.

"Actually, Skipper," Lieutenant Commander Harris replied in a slightly hesitant voice, "I think I know exactly what they're doing."

Ferrero turned her command chair to face the tactical section and tilted her head in a "tell me more" gesture, and Harris shrugged.

"Unless I'm badly mistaken, Captain," he said more formally, "they're conducting a tracking exercise . . . on us."

"Oh, they are, are they?" Ferrero's conversational tone set alarm bells ringing inside most of her officers.

"Yes, Ma'am."

"And you think this because—?" the captain invited.

"Because they're altering course and acceleration every time we make a helm change, Skipper," Harris told her. "Whenever our vector changes, so does theirs. They're running a constantly updated mirror course on us."

"I don't suppose they happened to inform us of their intentions and you simply neglected to tell me about it, Mecia?" Ferrero said dryly with a glance at her com officer.

"No, Ma'am," Lieutenant McKee assured her.

"Somehow, I didn't think so," the captain replied.

It wasn't uncommon for a warship to run sensor and tracking drills on merchantmen and even the warships of other navies. But common courtesy—and common sense, as well—mandated that one inform another warship when one intended to track and shadow her. Unless, of course, one's intentions were less than friendly . . . which was the reason that practical-sense caution suggested that one request permission ahead of time. It was the only way to be certain of avoiding misunderstandings which could lead to unpleasant consequences, particularly at times when inter-stellar tensions were already running high.

"Any sign of active sensors?" she asked the tac officer after a moment.

"No, Ma'am." It wasn't as foolish a question as it might have sounded. Ferrero knew as well as Harris that they couldn't pos-sibly have been taking hits from any shipboard sensors at this range, but that wasn't what she was asking about. "I'm not picking up *any* sign of remote platforms," Harris continued, answering the question she'd really asked.

"I see," Ferrero said sourly. Given the current range between the two ships, Harris was only able to keep tabs on the other by using the remote scansats *Jessica Epps* had set up to cover the system periphery when Ferrero moved her anti-pirate operations into the Harston System. The remote platforms' grav-pulse transmitters allowed him to effectively real-time sensor data from most of the outer system without using all-up Ghost Rider recon drones. Those drones were not only expensive, but also something which the Royal Manticoran Navy didn't go out of its way to flaunt, on the theory that what other navies didn't see, they couldn't acquire sensor data on.

The scansats also had much greater endurance than the more costly drones, since they simply sat in place rather than being compelled to maintain impeller wedges. Because of all those fac-tors, the fact that patrolling RMN cruisers now routinely seeded the outer volumes of their star systems of responsibility with FTL scansats was well understood, however, and their stealth systems were fairly rudimentary. That meant people knew to look for them and that they were relatively easy for shipboard sensors to spot, so there wasn't too much question that the other cruiser had known for some time that *Jessica Epps* was aware of her presence, in general terms, at least. But it was equally obvious that at this distance extended-range remote drones were the only way the other ship could be tracking *Jessica Epps* in return, and Ferrero didn't like the fact that they were clearly so stealthy that even Manticoran shipboard sensors couldn't find them. But Harris wasn't quite finished with his report.

"Uh, excuse me, Ma'am, but I'm not certain you do see. Not entirely, that is," he amended hastily as she shot him a sharp glance.

"Then suppose you enlighten me, Mr. Harris," she suggested coolly.

"Ma'am, they're almost seventeen light-minutes away from us," he reminded her respectfully. "But they're making their course corrections on average within three minutes of each of our helm changes."

Ferrero stiffened, and the tac officer nodded and tapped his display.

"I've been running a passive track on their impeller wedge for the last eighty minutes, Ma'am. The longest interval so far has been six-point-seven minutes. The shortest was less than two. The data's on the chip if you want to review it."

"I'm not questioning your observation, Shawn," the captain told him in a deceptively mild voice. "I'm just not very happy to hear what you're telling me."

"I'm not very happy to be telling it to you, Skipper," Harris admitted, smiling ever so faintly as her warmer tone suggested that he wasn't about to be blasted to cinders after all.

Ferrero allowed herself a small smile in return, but her brain was busy as she gazed at the bland light icon representing *Hellbarde*. The Andermani cruiser had become something of a constant companion of *Jessica Epps'* over the past few weeks, and she didn't like it. This Captain Gortz—and she still didn't know even whether Gortz was a man or a woman—couldn't possibly be getting in *Jessica Epps'* way so often and so thoroughly by accident. She (or he) was deliberately following Ferrero's ship from system to system for the express purpose of harassing her. That was the only possible explanation, and the other ship's increasingly offensive behavior was not only doing bad things to Ferrero's blood pressure but also suggested her captain was working to an orchestrated plan. The question, of course, was whether the plan was the personal property of Captain Gortz or if it had been handed to her (or him) by higher authority.

But what Harris was telling Ferrero now added yet another dimension to whatever it was the other ship thought she was accomplishing.

Impeller signatures were the only normal-space phenomenon which propagated at what was effectively faster-than-light speed. That wasn't exactly what really happened, of course. What *really* happened was that the intense gravity distortion associated with an impeller wedge created a "ripple" along the interface between the lowest alpha band of hyper-space and normal-space. It was that ripple, which was actually little more than a resonance from a hyper-space signature, which a starship's Warshawskis picked up.

But the mechanics of what happened weren't really important at the moment. What was important was the fact that impeller signatures could be detected and tracked in real-time across the effective range of shipboard sensors. Which was all well and good, except that as Harris had just reminded her, they were well beyond shipboard detection range from the Andy cruiser. Which meant that it didn't matter that gravitic sensors were effectively FTL. For *Hellbarde* to be reacting that quickly to *Jessica Epps'* heading changes, the communications links between her and her remote *sensor platforms* had to be FTL, as well.

Which meant the Andermani Navy had not only managed to produce its own grav-pulse communicator, but also engineered it down to a size it could fit into something as small as a recon drone.

And a drone which is so stealthy, and has such a good shield against backscatter from its transmitter, that Shawn can't find it even when he knows it has to be out there, she thought unhappily.

And Gortz is showing us that, *too.*

"You've been looking for drones only on passives, right?" she asked after a moment.

"Yes, Ma'am. Until I realized what was happening, I didn't see any reason to go active. Do you want me to do it now?"

"No. Let's not advertise the fact that we didn't even realize she had drones on us. But I want to know where they are. So if we're not spotting them with our shipboard passives, let's put a few more drones of our own out there to hunt for them."

"When they spot the drone launches they'll have a pretty good idea of what we're up to, Skipper," Harris pointed out.

"Understood. But I think it's time to put Ghost Rider to work."

Harris looked up sharply, as if he were about to ask her if she was certain about that decision. But he wasn't quite foolhardy enough to do that, despite his surprise, and she hid a lopsided mental grin at his expression.

"Don't worry, Shawn," she reassured him. "I haven't lost my mind. But Ghost Rider's mere existence isn't on the Official Secrets List anymore. Everybody knows at least a little about its capabilities, and I'm sure Andy intelligence knows more than 'a little.' I don't intend to flash the system's full capabilities, but I want to know where those remotes are, and I want to find them without letting the Andies know how long it took us to realize they were out there."

"Understood, Skipper," he acknowledged, although she rather doubted that he did understand fully what she had in mind. On the other hand, he obviously understood enough of it, as his next remark made clear.

"I'll 'swim' them out of the tubes and program them for a strength-one wedge after, say, ten minutes. If we could cut our accel to a couple of hundred gravities about four or five minutes after launch and leave it there for a while, that should be enough to let them make up on us gradually without generating a signature powerful enough to burn through their stealth systems."

"That's excellent thinking, Shawn," she approved warmly, and looked at her astrogator. "You heard, James?"

"Aye, aye, Ma'am," the Sidemore lieutenant acknowledged. "Five minutes after Mr. Harris confirms launch, I'll cut our acceleration to two hundred gravities. Should I maintain the same heading?"

"No," Ferrero said thoughtfully. "I don't want him wondering why we should suddenly reduce power if we're just going to go right on bumbling along on the same course." She drummed on her chair arm for a moment, then smiled. "Page the Exec for me, Mecia," she said.

"Aye, aye, Ma'am," Lieutenant McKee said, and a moment later the slightly sweaty face of Commander Robert Llewellyn, *Jessica Epps'* sandy-haired executive officer, appeared on Ferrero's small com screen.

"You rang, Skipper?" he inquired.

"Yes, I did. Where are you?"

"I'm up in Number Four Magazine with a work party," Llewellyn replied, and gestured at something beyond the limited range of the bulkhead com pickup. "Chief Malinski and I think we've finally isolated the fault in the feed tube auxiliary cable harness, and we've been pulling up deck plates to get at it."

"I'm glad to hear you've found it, but something else has come up, Bob. I'm afraid you're going to have to leave the Chief to deal with the feed tube, because I need you in the boat bay."

"The boat bay?" Llewellyn repeated.

"Yes. I need to keep an overly inquisitive Andie heavy cruiser from figuring out the real reason I'm about to reduce accel. So I've decided that what we need to do is to set up a series of exercises against one or two of our own small craft, and I want you to coordinate them. I know it's short notice, but I figure you can start by running a simulated Dutchman search. By the time we complete that, you can probably have at least another couple of problems worked out for the pinnace crews. And while you're at it, come up with some sort of interception exercise that will give us an excuse to deploy a couple of tractor-tether EW drones. Think you can manage that?"

"I don't see why not," the exec agreed, although he clearly felt more than a bit mystified by whatever she was up to. Well, there'd be plenty of time to bring him up to speed.

"Good. Com me again when you get to the boat bay. I'll have Mecia warn them you're on your way."

"Aye, aye, Ma'am."

Llewellyn's face disappeared from her screen as the exec cut the circuit, and Ferrero gestured to McKee to send word of his impending arrival to the boat bay personnel. Then she looked at Harris and McClelland.

"All right. When the Exec tells us he's ready, I want the acceleration reduction we discussed, and a thirty- or forty-degree change of heading for the 'pinnace exercises.' And I want the drones dropped five minutes before that. Understood?"

Both of her subordinates nodded their understanding, and she leaned back in her command chair to smile at *Hellbarde*'s dot of light on her plot.

"That's it, Ma'am," Lieutenant Commander Harris said finally. "Four of them."

"Good work, Shawn," Ferrero said sincerely as she stood looking over his shoulder at his detailed plot. There were, indeed, four of the Andy drones, placed so as to bracket *Jessica Epps* regardless of any course changes the Manticoran cruiser might make. They were within a few thousand kilometers of where Ferrero would have placed them herself, which only underscored how difficult it had been for Harris to nail them down. They'd started looking for them where they'd expected to find them, and despite that it had taken almost four and a half hours for the tac officer to positively confirm locations on all of them. Even then, he might not have managed it if the Andies hadn't been forced to cycle in fresh drones to replace them as they exhausted their onboard power. He'd caught one of the replacement drones on its way in, and once he had its locus precisely defined, he'd managed to find the others by working his way out from there.

Which said some remarkably ominous things about the hellacious stealth technology the Andies had built into the damned things. At least their platforms' endurance time seemed to be lower than the RMN's, but that was rather cold comfort just at the moment.

Ferrero stood gazing at the icons of the elusive drones for several more moments. She was reasonably confident that they hadn't noticed the even stealthier Ghost Rider drones creeping up behind them, but she wasn't prepared to place any expensive bets on the proposition. Not after the way the Andies had managed to sneak their own platforms in on her. From everything Harris and Bob Llewellyn could detect or extrapolate, Ghost Rider's technology was still superior to what they were seeing. But that assumed the Andy systems were working at full power without holding anything in reserve. Which seemed likely, but couldn't really be confirmed.

On the other hand, whatever else they might be, those drones had to be equipped with extremely sensitive passive sensors. Which suggested the perfect way to deal with them to Erica Ferrero.

She glanced at the bulkhead time-date display, then rested one hand on Harris' shoulder and smiled evilly.

"I'm afraid your day isn't quite done yet, Shawn," she told him. "We're going to terminate our pinnace exercises at the end of the current evolution. When we do, I want you to track those things for another . . . seventy-nine minutes. I know it won't be easy to hold them without the Andies catching on, but I want to put a little more time between our course changes for the exercises and the moment of truth."

"Moment of truth, Ma'am?" Harris repeated.

"Exactly," she told him. "I don't know whether it's her idea or her superiors', but this 'Captain Gortz' is obviously trying to make a statement about the Andies' technical capabilities. That being the case, I think it's time we made a statement about our capabilities, too. So at the end of your seventy-nine-minute tracking period, I want you to bring both of our tethered platforms around so that their active sensors bear on the Andie drones. And then I want you to go to maximum power. I don't just want a radar hull map of those drones, Shawn. I want to be able to read the mag combinations on their service access ports. I want their frigging *serial* numbers and the fingerprints of the last tech to service them. And I especially want to reduce those things' passive sensors to slag. Got it?"

"Oh, yes, Skip!" Harris agreed with a smile every bit as evil as her own had been. "Fried recon drones in hollandaise sauce coming right up!" he promised.

"Good." She patted him on the shoulder again. "Very good," she repeated, then turned and walked across to her own command chair.

She sat back down, and her smile faded slightly as she gazed once again at her own plot, and the steady crimson dots of *Hellbarde*'s shadowing drones. However satisfying it might be to repay the Andy cruiser's rudeness with interest—and she was honest enough with herself to admit that it would be *extremely* satisfying—it wouldn't change the fact that *Hellbarde* had managed to get them into position undetected in the first place.

Exactly why Gortz had chosen to reveal the ability to do that remained as much a mystery as ever, but there was clearly a pattern to the other captain's actions. She (or he) was escalating slowly but steadily, revealing ever more capable layers of technology and, probably, using that same opportunity to probe at *Jessica Epps'* capabilities. That was one reason Ferrero had gone to such lengths to conceal the fact that she was using Ghost Rider. The tractor-tethered electronic warfare remotes she'd had Llewellyn deploy as part of his "exercises," were scarcely new. They'd been around for generations, and they'd undoubtedly be around for generations more, because unlike even the most capable drones, they could be powered directly from the ship which had deployed them, which gave them effectively unlimited endurance. It also allowed them to mount extremely powerful decoy, jammer, and sensor systems, since they could draw directly on their mother ships for the energy to power them. So when she used them to take out *Hellbarde*'s platforms, she would be using "old" technology.

But by the same token she would be showing Gortz that *Jessica Epps* had spotted *Hellbarde*'s spies, hopefully without revealing precisely when or how that had been accomplished. That should remind Gortz that however good Andie technology might have become, the RMN continued to have the best hardware in space. Which, Ferrero devoutly hoped, was still true.

Yet it was the other half of the message she most looked forward to delivering, she admitted to herself. Because when Lieutenant Commander Harris reduced the exquisitely sensitive passive systems aboard their drones to so much useless junk, the personal message from Captain Erica Ferrero to *Kapitän der Sterne* Gortz would be excruciatingly clear.

Don't fuck around with me, *smart ass!*

CHAPTER TWENTY-FOUR

"**I** don't like it." Thomas Theisman's voice was mild as he leaned back in his comfortable chair in President Pritchart's office. His expression was another matter, and he frowned fiercely as he considered what he'd just said. "In fact, I don't like it one bit," he amended.

"And you think I do?" Eloise Pritchart demanded. Her voice was harsh, although Theisman knew her anger wasn't directed against him. "On the other hand, Kevin's report doesn't seem to leave us a whole lot of options, does it?"

"You can always fire the son-of-a-bitch," Theisman suggested.

"I thought about that. Hard," Pritchart admitted. "Unfortunately, according to certain other sources, he's prepared to challenge any demand for his resignation as unconstitutional."

"*Unconstitutional?*" Theisman stared at her in disbelief, and she smiled bitterly.

"Well, illegal, at least. It seems that according to arguably competent legal opinion, the resolution readopting the Constitution gave Congress the right to approve or disapprove my Cabinet appointments . . . and any changes to them."

"That's ridiculous!"

"My own opinion exactly. Which doesn't mean Arnold won't take the matter to the courts anyway if I try to fire him."

"Have you asked Denis about this?"

"I have," the President confirmed. "He's of the same opinion you are. Unfortunately, the same source which told me Arnold might try something like this pointed out his longstanding friendship with Chief Justice Tullingham."

"Oh *shit*," Theisman muttered with intense disgust.

"Precisely," Pritchart agreed. "I doubt very much that he could win in the long run, but he could certainly tie things up in legal arguments for weeks—probably months. And that would be just as bad, in the long run. Which means there really isn't anything I can do to punish him."

"It leaves us at least one other possibility," Theisman growled. Pritchart cocked her head at him, and he smiled thinly. "If you can't fire him, then have Denis *indict* the scheming bastard, instead."

"Indict the Secretary of State?" Pritchart stared at him.

"Damned straight," Theisman shot back. "At the very least, he's already spilled classified information, and there's no way he did it 'accidentally'! Not to the bunch Kevin tells us he's been talking to about it."

"He's also a cabinet secretary," Pritchart pointed out. "And while I personally agree a hundred percent with you, the people to whom he's 'spilled' the information all hold Top Secret clearances of their own."

"And not one of them, aside from his lying brother, was cleared for this information, or has any demonstrated need to know it," Theisman shot back. "And you know perfectly well that if he's told them, it's only a matter of time before the information gets made public. Which brings us back to exactly the national security concerns I've been raising from the day we decided to proceed with Bolthole."

"I agree." Pritchart pushed back in her own chair and pinched the bridge of her nose wearily. "The problem is, Tom, that he's got us between a rock and a hard place on the information side. The same logic that puts too high a political price on firing him holds just as true for what you're suggesting, and you know it. If we have him indicted and tried, then the very information we're trying to keep secret will come out in open court. Unless you're prepared to suggest holding a secret trial of a cabinet-level minister of the government whose legitimacy we're still trying to sell to its own legislators?"

"I—" Theisman started to reply angrily, then stopped and drew a very deep breath. He sat completely still for several heartbeats, then shook himself.

"You're right." He shook his head. "And the worst of it is that I don't doubt for a moment that he planned it that way from the beginning to protect himself if we found out what he was up to."

"That's just the problem, Tom. We still don't know what he's up to. The information he's sharing with his political allies is a means to an end, not an end in itself. Oh, I've got some pretty firm suspicions of what his ultimate goals are in a general sense, but right this minute, we don't know exactly what immediate goal he's headed for."

"Kevin doesn't have any idea at all?" Theisman sounded the next best thing to incredulous, and Pritchart's lips quirked in a wry smile.

"Kevin Usher has the instincts of a paranoid cat and the heart of a lion. He also has an incredibly soft and gooey center, which he takes great pains to hide. But one thing he doesn't have is telepathy or clairvoyance. We're lucky he's picked up this much. And," she admitted, "we're also lucky that he decided to report it directly to me."

"And who else should he have reported it to?"

"The point," Pritchart explained patiently, "is that we chose Kevin for the FIA specifically because he's seen entirely too much of the downside of using domestic security information for political advantage. Arguably, anything Arnold's done so far could be put down to a case of bad judgment and loose lips. Even though what he's done is illegal, it could be nothing more than inadvertent garrulousness on his part, and Kevin is probably better aware than anyone else in this city of just how much tension there is between Arnold and me. So I will guarantee you that he thought twice, or even three times, before he handed me information I could use to hammer Arnold if that was what I decided to do with it. The fact that he knows me as well as he does is probably the only reason he passed his findings along to me."

"Are you saying that with another president he might have suppressed the information?" Theisman frowned. "Somehow, that doesn't jibe with my impression of him. Or, I guess what I mean is that if it had ever occurred to me that he might do something like that, I'd've been very, very unhappy when you chose him for his job."

"I'm not saying he would have suppressed anything. What I'm telling you is that this information didn't come to him through any of his official pipelines, and it wasn't part of any ongoing investigation. He wouldn't have had to actually 'suppress' it, because passing what started out as little more than unsubstantiated rumors along to me was a pure judgment call on his part. He was very careful to make sure that there was substance to those rumors first—which he did without opening any official investigation— but there was absolutely no reason why he had to go out of his way to pursue those rumors on his own discretion in order to be able to tell me about something I hadn't even asked about. He made that decision entirely on his own, and he did it because he judged that I wouldn't abuse the information, the system, or his trust in me. And, I think, because he agrees with me that Arnold Giancola and the people who agree with him are the single greatest danger we face at this moment."

"Internally," Theisman agreed. "Externally?" He shook his head once more. "I still think the Manties, and particularly that jackass Janacek, are more immediate and much more dangerous threats."

"Tom, Tom." Pritchart sighed and rubbed both eyes with the palms of her hands, then grimaced at him. "I don't question your estimate of the degree of stupidity Janacek, High Ridge, or any of the rest of them are capable of. The problem is that we can't control what they do, however hard we try. The only situation we can even hope to control is our domestic one. The interstellar one is just going to have to take care of itself this time. And if Janacek and his boss do decide to do something stupid, then it's going to be up to you and the Navy to protect us from its consequences."

Theisman gazed at her for several unspeaking seconds, and she could almost feel the intensity of the thoughts flickering through the brain behind his eyes.

"You're absolutely certain this is the way you want to handle it?" he asked finally.

"It's not the way I 'want' to do anything," she half-snapped. "It's only the least bad of the half-dozen or so miserable options I see. Kevin may not know specifically what immediate objective Arnold thinks he's going to accomplish, but I'll guarantee you that I know at least two of the directions he's headed in. One is to force my hand—and yours, I suppose—where our negotiating stance with the Manties is concerned. And the second is to position himself to make his own run for President at the next election. If he waits that long."

"What do you mean, 'if he waits that long'?" Theisman sat up very straight. "Do you actually think he's contemplating something along those lines?"

"No. No, I don't." He regarded her out of narrowed eyes, and she sighed again. "All right, maybe I do," she conceded, manifestly unwillingly. "And I wish to Hell that I hadn't let the possibility slip in front of you, Tom Theisman! Because all I have for certain at this particular moment is the fact that I don't trust him, I don't like him, and I know he's ambitious, opinionated, and pigheaded. None of which is grounds for any sort of 'direct action.' "

"Appearances notwithstanding, Eloise," he said in a deceptively mild tone, "I'm not really in the habit of staging coups. Not without a lot more provocation than this, at least."

"I know," she said contritely. "I guess I just get a little crazy where Arnold is concerned. Mind you, I don't think for a moment that he'd hesitate if the opportunity for some old-style maneuvers came his way. At the moment, though, Denis and Kevin between them have pretty much taken that possibility off the board for anyone. Which is why he's coming at it from another direction. And it's also why we can't afford to let him control the information flow. He's using the existence of Bolthole as a wedge, Tom. Dribbling the facts out helps to establish his credentials as an insider, someone with access to the levers of power and the information that goes with it. And when he sits down to recruit someone who's already unhappy or concerned by the way the Manties have been stalling any meaningful negotiations, he can use the new ships to make my policy look even weaker. After all, if we've managed to make progress in equalizing our military capabilities, and we're still not prepared to press the Manties, then obviously we're too timid to *ever* press the issue."

"And if we'd pressed the issue when he wanted us to begin pressing it, then we'd never have had time to do any equalizing!" Theisman shot back.

"Of course not, but do you think he's going to mention that

minor point?" Pritchart chuckled with very little humor. "And even if we were in a position to somehow bring it up without going public ourselves, it wouldn't do much good. Nobody's going to be interested in what the situation was three or four years ago. They're going to be looking at what the situation is now. And what the situation is now, according to Arnold, is that we have the military muscle to stand up to the Manties if we only had the strength of will to use it."

"So you're going to do what he wants you to do." Theisman's sentence could have come out as an accusation, but it didn't. It was clear that he still disagreed with her proposed policy, but it was also clear that he understood what was driving her hand. And that he realized she was right. There wasn't a "good" policy; only a choice between bad ones.

"I don't see any option but it to try to co-opt his own maneuvers," Pritchart replied. "If we announce the existence of the new ships ourselves and simultaneously began pushing the Manties at the negotiating table, we'll blunt a lot of his efforts. I hope."

"Just so long as we don't push the Manties too hard, too quickly," Theisman cautioned. "Even if they take this a lot more calmly than I expect them to, there's going to be a lag between the moment we admit Bolthole exists and the time they actually readjust their perceptions and strategic thinking. There's no telling how they'll react if we ratchet the pressure up too high before they make that readjustment."

"I realize that. But I think that situation is more controllable than letting Arnold ricochet around Nouveau Paris like an out-of-control null-grav bowling ball. At the very least, it's going to take the better part of a month for word of the press releases on Bolthole to reach Manticore. We'll time the diplomatic note announcing our new, firmer position to arrive a few days after it gets there, and we'll be careful to couch it in nonconfrontational terms."

"You're going to demand that they stop wasting our time in a 'nonconfrontational' way?" Theisman cocked a quizzical eyebrow, and she snorted.

"I didn't say they were going to like hearing about it. But we can be firm and make our point without sounding like some bunch of reckless lunatics who're just itching to try out their new military toys!"

"As the person whose toybox those toys are in, I can certainly approve of that," Theisman agreed fervently. Then he scratched his chin and frowned thoughtfully. "Still, I'd feel happier if Giancola weren't the Secretary of State. There's too much opportunity for him to put his own twist on anything we say to the Manties to make me happy."

"The same thought had occurred to me," Pritchart confessed. "Unfortunately, if we can't fire him and we can't indict him, then we're stuck with him. There are times I wish our system was a bit more like the Manties. Mind you, I think the stability of ours has its own major advantages—such as avoiding sudden, unanticipated shifts in government policy like what happened to them when Cromarty died. But since our cabinet officers require Congressional confirmation for specific posts, we can't just shuffle portfolios whenever it's convenient like they can. And as long as he's Secretary of State, we can't cut him out of the diplomatic channel.

"But by the same token, he already knows he's scarcely on my Christmas card list, however cordial our relationships have to appear in public. So I'm not going to lose any sleep over the possibility of hurting his tender feelings when I insist on reviewing any notes we send the Manties before they're dispatched." She snorted again, and this time there was an edge of true humor in her fleeting smile. "Who knows? Maybe he'll get offended enough to do us all a favor and resign!"

"Don't hold your breath waiting for that," Theisman advised. "Anoxia is a fairly miserable way to go."

"A woman can always hope," she shot back.

"I suppose." He thought for a few more moments. "So how exactly do you want to handle the initial disclosure about Bolthole? Should it come out of your office, or out of mine?"

"Yours," Pritchart said promptly. "I'm sure I'll be asked all sorts of questions about it at my next press conference, but the initial announcement should be a Navy affair."

"And if someone asks me how it happens that Bolthole never appeared in any of our official budgets?"

"As a matter of fact, I'm sort of hoping someone will ask you exactly that," Pritchart admitted. "If they do, I want you to point out to whoever asks that in the absence of a formal treaty with the Star Kingdom of Manticore, the Republic is still in a state of war. And that publicizing the naval budget would clearly be of enormous help to any potential adversary. Don't go out of your way to link Manticore and 'any potential adversary,' but don't back away from it if someone else suggests the linkage. It won't hurt to jar the Manties' thinking a little before we start sending them any formal diplomatic notes. And getting that argument out early should help to undercut anyone—like our own esteemed Secretary of State and his political allies—if they try to argue that we've been overly timid. I doubt that anyone's completely forgotten what the Manty Navy was in the process of doing to us a few years back, but it won't hurt to remind them of it."

"I see what you've got in mind. And if we have to walk up to a sleeping attack dog and kick it on the nose, we might as well do it in the most effective way we can." He shook his head. "You know, when Dennis and I decided Saint-Just had to go, I never expected that a republican government, freely and openly elected by its citizens, would have to go to such lengths to protect itself against one of its own cabinet secretaries."

"And that's why you prefer the military to politics," Pritchart told him half-sadly. "Not that I blame you, sometimes. But a lot of it's timing, Tom. Give us another fifteen or twenty T-years for the Republic to get its feet back under it and the electorate to get truly accustomed to the idea of the rule of law, and we wouldn't have to spend so much time worrying about one overly ambitious, unscrupulous politico. I could just insist on his resignation and feel confident that the Constitution could weather any repercussions. Unfortunately, we're not that far along yet."

"I know. And I'm looking forward to the time when we will be . . . assuming that Giancola's lunacy doesn't get us back into a shooting war with the Manties again first."

"I think that's a worst-case scenario," Pritchart said seriously. "High Ridge is even more unscrupulous and ambitious than Arnold, if Wilhelm and his analysts are reading him correctly. But he's also basically a coward. I don't discount the possibility that backing him into a corner might provoke him into doing something rash, but there's no way that he wants to go back to war with us, either. Especially not if it looks to him like Bolthole might genuinely have evened the odds. So as long as we're very, very careful not to crowd him too hard, he's not going to pull the trigger on a war with us. And I certainly don't have any intention of starting one!"

"I'd feel a lot better if I didn't know how many wars had started when neither side really wanted them to," Theisman said dryly.

"Granted. But I can't allow worrying about the possibility to paralyze us, either. It's an imperfect universe, Tom, and all we can do is the best we can."

"I wish I could disagree. But I can't. So I suppose I should get back over to my own office. If we're going to announce the existence of Shannon's little project, then I'd better sit down with Arnaud Marquette and light a fire under my planning staff. Whatever we may want or expect, it's my job to have a war plan ready if the wheels come off anyway."

CHAPTER TWENTY-FIVE

"⬥ ⬥ ⬥ So as soon as the necessary probe data are in hand, we'll be sending a fully equipped survey ship through," Michel Reynaud told the reporter.

"And how long will it take you to amass the information you need, Admiral?" the woman followed up quickly, before anyone else in the crowded auditorium could take the floor away from her.

"That's an imponderable, of course," Reynaud told her patiently. "As all of you are no doubt aware, there simply aren't that many junctions, even today, which means our comparative information base is limited. We can describe the observed properties of the phenomenon mathematically, but our grasp of the underlying theory lags behind our ability to model. All I can tell you for certain is that we know what data it is that we need, but until we actually insert the first probes, we don't have any idea how long it's going to take us to acquire it."

"But—" the reporter began stubbornly, and Reynaud gritted his teeth behind a pleasant smile. He could feel Sir Clarence Oglesby standing beside him, and that didn't help his mood at all. He didn't much like Oglesby at the best of times, and the Government spokesman's blandly optimistic comments about the vast possibilities the new terminus created were largely to blame for the press pool's demands that Reynaud somehow provide them with an exact timetable for the cornucopia's arrival.

I've never been at my best dealing with situations like this, he thought. *And if I told this airhead what I really think of her obvious inability to understand simple English* ...

"If I may, Admiral?" Jordin Kare, on his very best behavior here in the public eye, asked diffidently, and Reynaud managed to conceal his relief somehow and nodded.

"As Admiral Reynaud just suggested," the astrophysicist told the reporter in his best, authoritative professorial mode, "each wormhole junction with which we're familiar has been a distinct and unique case. Our own Junction isn't quite like any of the others which have been explored, and none of the others are identical to one another, either. I've spent the better part of my adult life studying this particular field, and while I can speak with authority about the known junctions, that doesn't apply to new ones. Or even to previously unexplored termini of known ones. We're largely in the position of, say, the last century or so Ante Diaspora where gravity was concerned. They could describe, model, and predict it in considerable detail, but no one had a clue how to generate and manipulate it the way we can today. All of which means that while we've made certain working assumptions about this terminus based on the Junction's other termini and what we know about other junctions, they remain just that: assumptions. Until we can positively confirm their accuracy, the notion of sending a manned vessel through is out of the question."

He smiled with easy authority, wrapped in the mantle of his academic credentials, and the reporter nodded with profound respect, as if he hadn't just told her exactly what Reynaud had already said. The RMAIA director was grateful for Kare's intervention, but that didn't prevent him from thinking slightly homicidal thoughts about the reporter as she finally sat down.

The rest of the newsies instantly stabbed at their attention buttons, and Reynaud nodded to a slightly built, dark-haired man as a holographically projected green light appeared above him to indicate he'd won the competition.

"Ambrose Howell, Admiral," the reporter identified himself. "*Yawata Crossing Dispatch.*"

"Yes, Mr. Howell?"

"We've heard a great deal about the potential value of this discovery, and you and Dr. Kare have both cogently explained the difficulties and scale of the discovery and exploration process. I have two questions, if I may. First, since we've known for centuries that the math models of the Junction suggested there were additional termini, why has it taken us this long to look in the right place for this one? And, second, why did we go looking for it at this particular moment?"

"Both of those are excellent questions," Oglesby replied, cutting in in his deep, resonant baritone before Reynaud could respond, "and, if I may, I'll answer the second one first."

He bestowed a self-deprecating smile on the RMAIA director, apparently totally oblivious to Reynaud's blistering anger at his uninvited intervention.

"Obviously," he went on, transferring his modest smile to Howell, "as a layman and a total ignoramus where hyper-physics are concerned, I'm not in any position to reply to your first question. The timing, however, was the result of equal parts serendipitous circumstance and foresight. Although the thorny issues which have prevented the negotiation of a final peace treaty remain, the determination by both parties to the recent war that even an uneasy truce is superior to active bloodshed provided a window of opportunity in which it was possible for the Government to consider other substantive issues. No one could reasonably blame previous governments for their preoccupation with matters of interstellar security and naval budgets. And, of course, until we do have a formal peace treaty, the present Government is also under a powerful obligation to secure the Star Kingdom's security as its first priority. But the present political realities mean we've been able to step back from the abyss of active warfare and turn our thoughts to something besides better ways to kill our fellow human beings.

"The present Government, aware of the absolute necessity of maintaining the momentum towards peace domestically, as well as internationally, sought an entire array of initiatives to, as the Prime Minister and Chancellor of the Exchequer put it, 'build the peace.' Some were designed to ease the transition of military personnel back into the civilian economy, while others were intended to repair the ravages individuals and certain sectors of the economy—as in Basilisk, for example—had suffered during the fighting. And the creation of the Royal Manticoran Astrophysics Investigation Agency, with Admiral Reynaud as its head, was another. The Government saw this as an ideal opportunity to make a fundamental investment in the Star Kingdom's future. And, to be perfectly honest, the Government also saw the RMAIA and its audacious search as precisely the sort of peaceful challenge which would bring out the very best in a citizenry weary of the sacrifice and violence of a decade-long war. I'm very pleased, as, I'm sure, is every other individual associated with the Government in general, and the RMAIA in particular, that success has attended the effort with such unanticipated promptness."

Oglesby beamed at Howell and the HD cameras, and Reynaud reminded himself that it would never do to strangle the pompous, fatuous opportunist in front of so many witnesses. And at least he wasn't as poisonous a personality as Makris. For a moment, the admiral considered the alternative of asking Oglesby to brief the newsies about the . . . ambiguities Reynaud's own staffers had discovered in the Agency budget statements Makris had approved. But, no, that would never do, either. And so he simply waited until Oglesby had stepped back from the podium, and then looked directly at Howell, ignoring the Prime Minister's press secretary entirely.

"Since Sir Clarence has done such an . . . admirable job of answering your second question, Mr. Howell," he said, "I'll confine my own response to the first one. The simplest answer is that there was a flaw in the most widely accepted models of our Junction—one which Dr. Kare and his team at Valasakis University first identified only about six T-years ago. To be perfectly honest, it was his work there which led to his selection to head this project.

"The discrepancy they identified wasn't really a fundamental error, but it was sufficient to throw all of our predictions as to the probable loci of additional termini off to a significant degree. The Manticoran Wormhole Junction is a spherical region of space approximately one light-second in diameter. That gives it a volume of approximately fourteen quadrillion cubic kilometers, and any given terminus within the Junction is vastly smaller than that, a sphere no more than three thousand kilometers across. Which means that a terminus represents less than seven hundred millionths of a percent of the total volume of the Junction. So even a very small error in our initial models' predictions had an enormous impact. In addition, this terminus's 'signature' was extremely faint, compared to those of the termini we already knew about.

Our theoretical studies had always suggested that would be the case, but that faintness meant we required further advances in the sensitivity of our instruments and their computer support before we could realistically hope to detect it."

The admiral shrugged.

"Compared to the difficulties associated with the hunt for this terminus, the proverbial needle in a haystack would have been no challenge at all. Indeed, honesty compels me to admit that even with the strong support RMAIA has received, it was as much old-fashioned luck as anything else which allowed us to detect the terminus this quickly.

"I trust that answers your questions, Mr. Howell?"

The reporter nodded and sat down, and Reynaud moved on to the next holographic halo.

"Well, I thought Clarence did rather well," Baron High Ridge remarked as he held up his cup. He'd brought his own butler to the Prime Minister's official residence with him, and now that well-trained servant responded instantly with his coffeepot to the silent, peremptory command. High Ridge sipped the fragrant brew appreciatively. He did not, of course, thank the man or even acknowledge his existence.

"I suppose," Elaine Descroix conceded across the remnants of her own breakfast. She drank a little coffee, patted her lips with an old-fashioned linen napkin, and then grimaced ever so slightly.

"Clarence certainly did his best to see to it that credit went where credit was due," she told High Ridge." And I particularly liked the way he kept managing to slip our 'building the peace' slogan into his replies. But that Kare, and especially Reynaud—!" She shook her head. "What a deadly dull pair!"

"One can hardly expect acute political awareness out of career bureaucrats and scientists, Elaine," High Ridge chided gently.

"No," she agreed. "But I was watching Reynaud, in particular. He didn't care one bit for the way Clarence kept 'stealing his thunder,' and it showed. Are we going to have problems with him down the road?"

"What sort of problems?" High Ridge frowned.

"Oh, come now, Michael! He's the RMAIA's director, and however much I may dislike him, he obviously has a brain. I'm quite certain he can do simple math, and not even Melina can change the fact that he has access to his own books."

High Ridge set down his cup, and glanced over his shoulder at the butler. Descroix had a disturbing tendency to ignore the ears of servants. The Prime Minister was particularly aware of it because it was something he had to constantly watch in himself, but he'd seen too many examples of what ungrateful and resentful servants could do to their employers when those employers were careless about what they said in front of them. It wasn't a lesson he intended to forget, and although his butler had been in his employ for almost thirty T-years, there was no point in taking chances.

"That will be all, Howard," he told the man. "Just leave us the coffeepot. I'll buzz when we're done."

"Of course, My Lord," Howard murmured, and disappeared with discreet promptness.

"Now then, Elaine," High Ridge said, gazing at her intently, "what, specifically, are you suggesting?"

"I'm suggesting that he has access to his own books. I admit that Melina has done a better job than I'd expected in managing the fiscal details, but in the end, she can't simply refuse to let the man who's technically her superior look at his own agency's accounts. And Reynaud may be an admiral, but he came up through Astro Control, Michael. He's had plenty of bureaucratic experience of his own. He may not be an accountant, but I'm not at all sure that he wouldn't be able to see through Melina's little . . . subterfuges. And given that he so obviously disapproves of Clarence, and so, by extension, of us, he also has the potential to see himself as a knight on a white horse. It's just possible that his delicate conscience could turn him into a whistleblower."

"I think that's unlikely," High Ridge said after a moment. "If he were likely to do something like that, why hasn't he already done it? So far as I'm aware, he hasn't even asked any difficult questions, much less shown any inclination to take his suspicions—if any—public. And even if it turned out that he were so inclined after all, it would effectively be his word against the full weight of Her Majesty's Government." He shook his head. "No. I don't see any way he could hurt us. under the circumstances."

"You're probably right . . . for now," Descroix replied. "On the other hand, I wasn't thinking about right this minute, or even any time in the next several months or even the next few years. But let's face it, Michael. You and I both know that eventually there's going to be a change of governments."

"Cromarty hung on to the premiership for the better part of sixty T-years with only three interruptions," High Ridge pointed out just a bit stiffly.

"And he had the enthusiastic support of the Crown the entire time. A happy state of affairs which," Descroix observed dryly, "scarcely obtains in our own case."

"If the approval of the Crown were critical to the survival of a government, we'd never have been permitted to form one in the first place!" High Ridge shot back.

"Of course we wouldn't have. But that's not really the point, is it? However temperamental the Queen may be, she's also an astute political observer, and she was right. Our differences in priorities and ideology—especially between you and me, on the one hand, and Marisa, on the other—are too fundamental for us to maintain our cohesion indefinitely. And that completely over-looks potential outside forces. Like that idiot Montaigne." Descroix grimaced. "I don't think she has a hope in Hell of pulling it off, but it's perfectly clear what she's up to with that dramatic renun-ciation of her title. And while I think the odds against her are high, I didn't expect her to win her precious little special election, either. So I don't have any desire to stake my own political survival on my faith that she can't do it after all."

"You think she could effectively challenge Marisa's control of her party leadership, then?" High Ridge asked.

"Probably not as things stand," Descroix replied. "But that's my point. You and I both know politics are a dynamic process, not a static one. Things change, and Montaigne's challenge could weaken Marisa enough for someone else higher up in the party hierarchy to challenge her successfully. Or, for that matter, to pull Marisa back towards the Liberals' 'true faith' and away from her coalition with us. Frankly, I think that's what's most likely to bring this Government down in the end, because let's face it, she's never really been comfortable working with us in the first place."

"It doesn't help any when you snipe at her in Cabinet meet-ings," High Ridge said in a painfully neutral tone.

"I know that. It's just that she's so damned sanctimonious and pious that I can't help myself. Come on, Michael! You know that when it comes right down to it, she's at least as willing as you or I—probably *more* willing—to do whatever it takes to hang on to power. But, of course, she's only doing it because of the absolute sanctity of her holier-than-thou, save-the-universe, rescue-mankind-from-original-sin ideology."

"I suppose so." High Ridge drank a little more coffee, using the cup to obscure his expression until he was certain he had it back under control. He'd known Descroix's impatience with New Kiev had been growing steadily, but the sheer venom in the Foreign Secretary's biting tone still came as something of a shock. Particularly if it proved to be the first rumbling of the very discord Descroix was warning him against.

"Oh, don't worry," she told him, almost as if she could read his mind. "I detest the woman, and I'm quite sure she detests me, right back. But we're both fully aware of how much we need one another right now, and neither of us is likely to do anything stupid.

"In the end, however," she went on, promptly undermining his momentary sense of relief, "we're either going to accomplish what made us political bedfellows in the first place, or else Alexander and the Queen are going to manage to take us out of office before we do. In the first case, I think we can take it for granted that there's going to be a certain . . . acrimoniousness to the ultimate dissolution of our partnership. And in the latter case—which, I hasten to add, I consider an unlikely, worst-case scenario—you can bet anything you like that Her Majesty's going to be out for blood. Our blood. Either way, there are going to be plenty of sharp knives waiting to be parked in someone's back, and Reynaud could be one of them."

"I think you're worrying unduly," the Prime Minister said after a moment. "There are always . . . irregularities of one sort or another, but neither side has any interest in making them public when the government changes hands. After all, as you've just pointed out, it will always change hands again at some point. If the incoming government smears its predecessors over every potential little discrepancy, then it invites the same treatment when it's time for it to leave office, in turn, and no one wants that."

"With all due respect, Michael, we're not talking about 'little discrepancies' in this instance," Descroix said coolly. "While I would be the first to argue that our decisions were completely justifiable, they hardly represent unintentional errors or sloppy paperwork.

There's not much point in pretending that someone like Alexander couldn't exaggerate them all out of proportion and start some sort of witch hunt. And whatever he might want to do as a realistic and pragmatic politician, the Queen is going to want the biggest, noisiest witch hunt she can possibly arrange in our case. In fact," Descroix smiled thinly, "I'm pretty sure she's already stockpiling wood for the barbecue at Mount Royal Palace."

"It's just a bit late to be developing a case of cold feet, Elaine," High Ridge told her. "If you thought we were taking unjustifiable risks, you should have said so at the time."

"I just finished saying that I felt they were justified," she said with calm deliberateness. "I'm simply pointing out that that doesn't mean I'm blind to the potential consequences if they come home to roost later."

"And just why are you so assiduously pointing it out?" he asked in a tone he realized was beginning to verge rather too closely on querulous for the Prime Minister of Manticore.

"Because Reynaud's attitude towards Clarence crystallized my concerns about them. I've been aware of them from the beginning, but the need to concentrate on day-to-day tactics has tended to push them further down my list of things to worry about. Unfortunately, if we don't start worrying about them now, then we're going to spend a lot more time worrying about them later."

"Meaning what?"

"Meaning that it's time you and I started making sure our lifeboats don't spring any leaks when the ship finally sinks." She allowed herself a small, amused smile at his exasperated expression, but she also decided it was time to show some mercy and come to the point at last.

"Eventually, someone's going to ask some very pointed questions, Michael. Elizabeth will see to that, even if no one else wants to. So it's occurred to me that this would be a very good time to begin establishing the documentary evidence to support the answers we're going to want to give."

"I see," the Prime Minister said slowly, leaning back in his chair and regarding her speculatively. And, he admitted, respectfully.

"And just how do you suggest we do that?" he asked finally.

"Obviously, we begin by seeing to it that any little . . . financial irregularities lead back to our esteemed Chancellor of the Exchequer and Home Secretary MacIntosh." She sighed. "How tragic! To think that such high-minded and selfless servants of the public weal should turn out to have actually been so venal and corrupt as to divert government monies into slush funds and vote-buying schemes. And how truly unfortunate that your own trust in the Liberal Party's well-known probity prevented you from realizing in time what they were doing."

"I see," he repeated, even more slowly. He'd always known Elaine Descroix was about as safe as an Old Earth cobra, yet even now, a part of him was appalled by her ruthlessness.

"Of course," she admitted cheerfully, "it needs to be done carefully, and to be completely honest, I'm not at all sure how to go about doing it properly. A clumsy job, with fingerprints pointing in our direction, would be worse than useless."

"I can certainly agree with that!"

"Good. Because in that case, I think we should put Georgia to work on it."

"Are you sure you want to bring her that fully into this?" High Ridge knew his doubtfulness showed, but Descroix only smiled.

"Michael," she said patiently, "Georgia already has access to the North Hollow Files. I'm sure there are more than enough smoking guns tucked away in there to destroy anyone she really wants to destroy. She doesn't need any more information to be a threat to us, if that's what she decides to become. Besides, you've already used her for half a dozen things I can think of whose legality might be . . . questioned by a real stickler. The surveillance of Harrington and White Haven springs to mind.

"My point is that she already knows enough to blow us out of the water. But she can't do that without doing herself in right along with us. The same is true of Melina. After Reynaud, she's the most dangerous potential leak where RMAIA is concerned. but she's also the one who's done such a good job of insulating Marisa from harsh reality, which means that if the Agency goes down, she goes right with it."

Descroix shrugged.

"Georgia and Melina both have very, very good reasons to see to it that any nasty suspicion is directed away from themselves to someone else. In fact, if I thought Melina were up to it, I'd advise leaving the entire affair in her hands. Unfortunately, I don't think she is . . . whereas Georgia has clearly demonstrated her own capability in such matters. So, given how very good she is at this sort of thing anyway, it strikes me that it wouldn't make any sense to bring anyone else in. The more people we involve, the more likely something is to leak entirely by accident, much less what someone like Reynaud could do to us if our efforts came to his attention. So let's put the project in the hands of a single individual with a powerful interest in seeing to it that her tracks are buried right along with ours."

"I see," he said for a third time. And then, slowly, he smiled.

CHAPTER TWENTY-SIX

The G6 star at the heart of the Marsh System was a thoroughly average system primary. Nothing much to write home about, Honor thought, leaning against the bulkhead beside the armorplast viewport as she gazed out into the dark, diamond-dusted clarity. Just one more insignificant furnace in which the fires of creation blazed with inconceivable fury, shedding their stupendous glory down the halls of God's endless night.

Certainly not anything important enough for the Star Kingdom of Manticore to risk a war over.

She snorted, and tasted Nimitz's echo of her own dark moodiness from where he reclined on the perch beside his bulkhead-mounted life-support module. Of course, she also knew that the somberness they shared sprang from more than her awareness of the all but impossible task she faced here. For the 'cat, it was the loneliness, the separation from his mate. But that was a separation Nimitz and Samantha had endured before, and would again, and at least he and Honor had one another, while Samantha had Hamish. Both 'cats knew this was one of the inevitable prices of their bonds with their humans, and in its own way, that knowledge was a form of armor. It didn't lessen the pangs of their separation—a separation which was far worse for empaths than for the "mind-blind"—but at least both of them knew exactly how vital they were to one another . . . and that they would be together once again at deployment's end.

Which was far more than Honor knew. She deeply regretted separating Nimitz and Samantha, and her regret carried a strong overtone of guilt, yet deep inside, she couldn't quite stifle an ignoble envy, almost jealousy. However much the two 'cats might miss one another now, their separation would come to an end. Honor's wouldn't. She knew that, but at least this empty, lonely ache at the heart of her was better than the pain and hopeless longing she'd felt before she put distance between her and Hamish. She told herself that at least a dozen times a day, and for the most part, she believed herself.

For the most part.

She turned her head, letting her gaze sweep over the nearest ships of her gathered task force. They floated in orbit about the planet Sidemore, the space-going equivalent of a fleet anchored in a safe harbor, but she'd been pleased when she arrived to find that Rear Admiral Hewitt had insisted upon maintaining a heightened state of readiness. All of his vessels' parking orbits had been carefully arranged to avoid any problems with wedge interference if it was necessary to bring up their impellers quickly. And he'd also seen to it that at least one of his battle squadrons' impeller nodes had been hot at all times. The ready duty rotated among his squadrons on a regular basis, but his precaution meant that its units could bring up their wedges in as little as thirty to forty-five minutes.

Honor had not only told him how much she approved of his wariness but also maintained and extended his standing orders, including the dispersal of their orbits, to the units of Task Force Thirty-Four, as well. Which meant, of course, that even ships as stupendous as *Werewolf* or Alister McKeon's superdreadnought flagship *Troubadour* were the tiniest of models when she gazed at them with the naked eye.

Of course, not all naked eyes had been created equal, and Honor smiled despite her moodiness as she brought up the telescopic function of her artificial left eye and the distant, floating mountains of battle steel grew and blossomed magically.

They hung there in the void, like killer whales in an endless sea of dark kelp, spangled with the green and white lights of starships in orbit, their flanks dotted with the precise geometry of weapon bays or LAC launch tubes. There were dozens of them, huge capital ships, pregnant with firepower and destruction and awaiting her orders. With the reinforcements she'd brought out from Manticore, she had eight full battle squadrons, plus Alice's understrength CLAC squadron, screened by five battlecruiser squadrons, three light cruiser squadrons, and two destroyer flotillas . . . which didn't even count the dozens of cruisers and destroyers scattered through the nearer sections of the Confederacy on anti-pirate duties. She had no less than forty-two ships of the wall under her command, which made her "task force" a fleet in all but name. It was also far and away the most powerful force which had ever been placed under her orders, and as she gazed out the viewport at the might and power ready to her fingertips, she supposed she ought to feel confident in the strength of her weapon if she should be called upon to use it.

Yet what she really was was aware of its flaws.

She couldn't fault the readiness state which Hewitt had maintained during his time on the station any more than she could fault the cheerfulness with which he'd surrendered his authority to her upon her arrival. Alister and Alice had managed to sharpen Task Force Thirty-Four to a far keener edge than she'd allowed herself to hope for during the voyage here, and Hewitt's squadrons had managed to maintain a far higher degree of readiness than Home Fleet. No doubt because his captains, like he himself, had been altogether too well aware of how far from any other help they'd be if it hit the fan out here in Silesia.

But all the readiness in the galaxy couldn't change the fact that only six of her forty-two ships of the wall were *Medusa*-class SD(P)s and none of them were the even newer *Invictus*-class ships. Or that eleven of the others were mere dreadnoughts, scarcely two-thirds the size and fighting power of even her older, pre-SD(P) ships. She had no doubt Janacek and High Ridge would roll the number forty-two out in suitably weighty tones for the benefit of any newsy or member of Parliament who asked pointed questions about the state of Sidemore Station. And she had just as little doubt that neither of them would mention just how obsolescent and undersized some of those forty-two ships were. Or that she had been allowed only four of the eight CLACs she'd requested. Or that ONI's most recent estimate gave the Imperial Andermani Navy something in excess of two hundred ships of the wall.

She inhaled deeply, then straightened up, squared her shoulders, and scolded herself for allowing herself to fall into a slough of despond. She'd known when she accepted the posting that this was exactly what was going to happen, although, to be honest, she hadn't anticipated that even Janacek would be quite so blatant as to assign every single Manticoran dreadnought still in commission to her. But even if he'd replaced every one of them with pre-pod superdreadnoughts, her strength would still have been totally inadequate if the Andies truly were willing to push things to the brink of outright hostilities. So it probably made sense, from Janacek's viewpoint, to pile as many as possible of his obsolescent assets into the same heap. After all, if he lost them, it wouldn't be as if anything vital had gone with them. Except, of course, for the people aboard them.

She scolded herself again, although a bit less forcefully. She really should be careful about imputing sordid motives to the First Lord. Not because she doubted that he had them, but because not even Sir Edward Janacek could have *only* sordid motivations. That would have completely devalued his ability to do such things out of simple stupidity, instead of calculation.

Her lips quirked in a smile, and she surprised herself by producing a chuckle. It was a small one, true, but it was also born of genuine amusement, and she felt Nimitz's flicker of shared amusement. And his gladness that she could at least still laugh.

She let her eyes sweep over the panorama beyond the viewport once again, ordering herself to let the infinite beauty of God's jewel box sweep through her like a cleansing breeze. The silent, pinprick glory of the endless stars blazed before her, and the blue-and-white, cloud-swirled beauty of Sidemore filled the lower quarter of the port. With her cybernetic eye, she could make out the floating gems of the planet's orbital solar power collectors, and the smaller reflections of communications relays, orbital sensor arrays, and all of the other clutter of an industrialized presence in space.

None of those things had been here when she'd first visited Marsh almost ten T-years ago. Then, Sidemore had been a backwater, a place merchant ships visited only by mistake, and thus the perfect hideout base for the brutal "privateers" who had taken it over. Thirty-one thousand of Sidemore's citizens had died during that occupation, over a third of them in a single, horrific instant when Andre Warnecke detonated his demonstration nuke as a mere bargaining ploy. But that wasn't going to happen again, she thought with deep satisfaction. Even if the RMN pulled out tomorrow, the Sidemore Navy would make mincemeat out of any privateer or pirate stupid enough to poke his nose into this system again.

Sidemore wasn't in the same league as Grayson, but Honor was honest enough to admit that that was at least partly because Sidemore had never been as important to Manticore as Grayson was. The Star Kingdom had pulled out all the stops to build Grayson into the industrial powerhouse it had become, and for all the crudity of its pre-Alliance tech base, Grayson had been aggressively dragging itself up by its own bootstraps for well over sixty years before Manticore ever arrived in its neighborhood. And much as Honor loved her adopted planet and respected the industry and determination of its people, she was also honest enough to admit that it had been only Grayson's astrographic position which had attracted the Star Kingdom's notice in the first place.

Which was also true for Sidemore. But Grayson had been seen as essential to Manticoran security; Sidemore had simply been a convenience. And so Sidemore hadn't received the same loan guarantees, or been the subject of the same investment incentives and tax breaks, or been the site of major shipyards, as Grayson had been. Which, in its way, made what the Sidemorians had achieved even more impressive, despite how modest it appeared in the shadow of Grayson's accomplishments.

Honor was delighted to see the unmistakable signs of a planet whose industrialization process had taken on a self-sustaining life of its own. There were freighters building in Sidemore orbit these days, not just the light warships of the Sidemore Navy, and the planetary president had already conducted Honor on a proud tour of the planet's new orbital resource extraction facilities and smelters. Those facilities had grown almost entirely out of the RMN's need for them to support the orbital repair yard it had built here to service its ships on Sidemore Station, but they'd become self-perpetuating since then. The Marsh System wasn't going to be posing any threats to the Manticoran balance of payments with Silesia any time soon, but Honor was delighted to see how shrewdly and successfully the planet was exploiting its new industrial power by expanding into the Silesian trade. Unless something very unfortunate happened—like a war which brought the Andermani navy rampaging through the system—Sidemore would be able to sustain its new prosperity and expand upon it even if Manticore withdrew from the region.

And that's the only way we are ever going to turn the Confederacy into something besides an ongoing, low-level bloodbath, Honor thought with a touch of grimness. *God knows we've tried to exterminate the pirates long enough! The only way to get rid of them in the end, though, is going to be by giving the people who live here the prosperity that'll create the capacity to squash the vermin themselves.*

It's a pity the Confederacy's government is too corrupt to let that happen.

And that, she knew, as much as Manticore's interest in the system and the industriousness of its people, was why Marsh was succeeding in turning itself into a modern, prosperous star system. There were no Silesian governors to batten on the opportunities for graft and corruption and strangle any sustained industrial expansion at birth.

None of which, she reminded herself briskly, had any particular bearing on the task which had brought her back to Marsh after all these years.

She turned her back on the viewport and headed for her desk. She had entirely too many reports waiting for her. Mercedes had flagged the most important dozen or so for her attention, but Honor was still behind in her reading, and Mercedes was altogether too capable of making her feel intolerably guilty just by looking reproachfully at her. Honor suspected she'd been taking Reproachful 101 lessons from James MacGuiness. And since she'd scheduled a meeting of the entire task force's staffs for this afternoon, it would probably be a good idea to give her chief of staff one less reason to employ The Look.

She chuckled again and punched up the first report in the queue.

"Excuse me, Ma'am."

Honor looked up from the letter to Howard Clinkscales she'd been recording as James MacGuiness appeared in the open hatch of her day cabin.

"Yes, Mac? What can I do for you?"

"Lieutenant Meares asked me to inform you that a merchant captain just screened the com center with a request to make a courtesy call on you."

"Really?" Honor frowned thoughtfully. Timothy Meares, her flag lieutenant, was a bit on the youthful side, but he'd very early shown the good sense of accepting MacGuiness' assistance in managing his Admiral. Among other things, Meares had quickly grasped that MacGuiness usually had a better idea than anyone else aboard *Werewolf* of how busy Honor actually was at any given moment, and the flag lieutenant had come to trust the steward's judgment about when and whether or not to interrupt her with some routine matter.

He'd also recognized the fact that Honor expected him to use his own discretion about those same routine matters, and he had a somewhat more exalted opinion of her importance than she herself did. Which made the fact that he'd passed the request along to MacGuiness at all informative. Obviously, there was some reason he hadn't seen fit to reject this particular captain's attempt to invite himself to dinner—figuratively speaking, of course—out of hand. At the same time, he'd passed it along through the filter of MacGuiness, which suggested that perhaps he'd wondered if an older and wiser head who'd been with Honor much longer than he had might decide to quash it.

If that had been his intention, MacGuiness clearly hadn't opted to do any quashing, and she felt her initial prick of curiosity grow into something stronger as she reached out to taste the steward's emotions. He radiated a combination of anticipation, curiosity of his own, minor trepidation, and an echo of something which wasn't quite amusement.

"May I ask if this merchant captain said who he is and why he wants to see me?" she asked after a moment.

"I understand, Ma'am, that he's a Manticoran national, although he's been here in the Confederacy for many years now. According to my information, he's managed to acquire ownership of a small but extremely successful shipping line. In fact, he holds a special warrant from the Confederacy to permit his vessels to be armed, and Lieutenant Meares tells me that our records indicate that he's destroyed at least a dozen pirate vessels we know about over the past ten T-years. As to precisely why he wants to see you, all he's actually told the Lieutenant is that he'd like to pay a courtesy call on you. I believe, however, that the Lieutenant suspects that the good captain has come across some sort of local information which he believes it would be beneficial to share with you."

Nothing could have been blander than MacGuiness' expression or tone, but that edge of not-quite-amusement was stronger than ever as he regarded her gravely. And, she noted, his sense of trepidation had grown in direct parallel.

"That's all enormously interesting, Mac," she told him with a twinkle of moderate severity. "It didn't exactly answer my first question, though. I would imagine this mystery skipper has a name?"

"Oh, of course, Ma'am. Did I forget to mention it?"

"No," she told him. "You didn't 'forget' anything. You chose not to tell me because that curiously twisted faculty which serves you as a sense of humor told you not to."

He grinned as her shot went home, then shrugged just a bit too casually.

"You have a naturally suspicious personality, Ma'am," he told her in virtuous tones. "As it happens, however, the gentleman *does* have a name. I believe it's . . . Bachfisch. *Thomas* Bachfisch."

"*Captain Bachfisch?*" Honor jerked bolt upright in her chair, and Nimitz's head snapped up where he reclined on his bulkhead perch. "Here?"

"Yes, Ma'am." MacGuiness' grin had vanished, and he nodded seriously. "Lieutenant Meares didn't recognize the name. I did."

"Captain Bachfisch," she repeated softly, and shook her head. "I can't believe it. Not after all this time."

"I've heard you speak of him," MacGuiness told her quietly. "According to Lieutenant Meares, he sounded a bit hesitant about asking to see you, but I felt certain you wouldn't want this opportunity to slip away."

"You're certainly right about that!" she said firmly, then cocked her head. "But you said he sounded 'hesitant' about asking to call on me?"

"That was the way Lieutenant Meares put it, Ma'am," MacGuiness replied. "I'm sure the com section has the actual request on record, if you'd care to view it, but I haven't seen it myself."

"Hesitant," Honor repeated and felt an obscure sort of pain somewhere deep down inside. Then she shook herself. "Well, he may be hesitant, but I'm not! Tell Tim that his request is approved, and that I'll see the Captain at his earliest convenience."

"Yes, Ma'am," MacGuiness acknowledged, and disappeared as quietly as he had come, leaving Honor to her thoughts.

He's aged, Honor thought, hiding a pang of dismay as the stoop-shouldered man in the blue uniform swung himself across the interface from the boarding tube's zero-gee into the boat bay gallery's standard single gravity. She'd checked *Werewolf*'s copy of the officers' list and found Bachfisch's name on it. Her old captain was a full admiral now, but solely because seniority continued to accrue even on half-pay, because that was precisely where he'd been for almost forty years. Forty hard years, she thought as she gazed at him. The dark hair she remembered was liberally laced with silver, despite his first-generation prolong, and Nimitz shifted ever so slightly on her shoulder, uneasy as both of them tasted the sense of pain and loss which flowed through him as he found himself once again upon a Queen's ship.

"*Pirate's Bane*, arriving!" the boat bay intercom system announced crisply, and the side party came to attention as the bosun's pipes shrilled in formal salute.

The dark eyes widened in surprise, and the shoulders squared themselves. That pain and loss intensified almost unbearably for just a moment, then turned into something far warmer. Not gratitude, although that was part of it, so much as understanding. An awareness of exactly why Honor had chosen to extend full formal military courtesies to a mere merchant skipper, whatever his half-pay rank might be. He came to full attention and saluted the junior-grade lieutenant boat bay officer at the head of the side party.

"Permission to come aboard, Ma'am?" he requested formally.

"Permission granted, Sir," she replied, snapping him a parade ground-sharp salute of her own, and Rafe Cardones stepped forward to greet him.

"Welcome aboard *Werewolf*, Admiral Bachfisch," Honor's flag captain said, extending his hand.

"That's 'Captain Bachfisch,' Captain," Bachfisch corrected him quietly. "But thank you." He shook Cardones' hand firmly. "She's a beautiful ship," he went on sincerely, but his eyes looked over Cardones' shoulder at Honor, and the emotions swirling through him were too intense and complicated for her to sort out.

"Thank you," Cardones told him. "I'm rather proud of her myself, and if you can spare the time, I'd be delighted to take you on the five-dollar tour before you return to your own ship."

"That's very kind of you. And if it's at all possible, I'll certainly take you up on it. I've heard a lot about this class, but this is the first opportunity I've had to actually see one."

"Then I'll see if our COLAC, Captain Tremaine, can accompany us," Cardones promised. "He'll be able to give you the LAC jock's viewpoint, as well."

"I'll look forward to it," Bachfisch assured him, still looking at Honor, and Cardones smiled just a bit crookedly and stepped back to make room for his Admiral.

"Captain Bachfisch," she said softly, reaching out her own hand. "It's *good* to see you again, Sir."

"And you . . . Your Grace." He smiled, and there was an entire universe of satisfaction and regret behind that expression. "You've done well. Or so I hear." His smile grew broader, losing some of its hurt.

"I had a good teacher," she told him, squeezing his hand firmly, and he shrugged.

"A teacher is only as good as his students, Your Grace."

"Let's just say it was a joint effort, Sir," she said, relinquishing his hand at last, and nodded her head at Cardones. "And let me repeat Captain Cardones' welcome. I hope you'll be good enough to join us for supper and allow me to introduce you to the rest of my senior officers?"

"Your Grace, you're very kind, but I wouldn't want to impose, and—"

"The only imposition would be for you to decline the invitation, Sir," Honor interrupted firmly. "I haven't seen you in almost forty T-years. You're not getting off the ship without dining with me and my officers."

"Is that an order, Your Grace?" he asked wryly, and she nodded.

"It most certainly is," she told him, and he shrugged.

"In that case, of course, I accept."

"Good. I see you still have a firm grasp of the tactical realities, Sir."

"I try," he said with another small smile.

"In that case, why don't you accompany me to my day cabin?" she invited. "We have a lot of catching up to do before supper."

"Indeed we do, Your Grace," he agreed softly, and followed her into the lift car, while Andrew LaFollet trailed along behind.

Chapter Twenty-Seven

"It really is wonderful to see you again, Sir," Honor said quietly as she ushered him into her day cabin and waved for him to seat himself in one of the comfortable chairs around the beaten copper coffee table. She saw him glance down at the table and watched the corners of his eyes crinkle in amused pleasure as he saw the bas relief Harrington Steading coat of arms which adorned it.

"It was a gift from Protector Benjamin," she half-apologized, but he only shook his head.

"I was only admiring it, Your Grace. And reflecting on just how well you truly have done . . . not on the vainglory of putting your monogram on a simple piece of furniture."

"I'm relieved to hear it," she said dryly, and she was immensely relieved by the sparkle of mischievous humor which accompanied his words.

"To be perfectly honest," he said more seriously, "the galaxy would probably cut you at least a little slack if your head had gotten a bit too big for your beret. On the other hand, I'd have been surprised if the midshipwoman I remembered had let that happen."

"I try to remember I'm merely mortal." Her attempt to make it come out humorously wasn't entirely successful, and she felt her cheekbones heat slightly. He glanced at her sidelong, then shrugged.

"And I'll try not to embarrass you any more, Your Grace. Except to say that one of my greatest regrets is that Raoul Courvoisier didn't live to see you now. He wrote to me after Basilisk Station to make sure I had the entire story straight, so I know he'd had proof his faith in you had been amply rewarded. But I also know how delighted he'd have been to see that others had seen fit to reward it, as well."

"I miss him," Honor said softly. "I miss him a lot. And it means a lot to me to know that you and he stayed in touch."

"Raoul was always a loyal friend, Your Grace."

"Captain," Honor said, meeting his eyes, "it's been thirty-nine T-years, but the last time we saw each other, I was only a midshipwoman. And half-pay or not, you are an admiral yourself. If it's all the same to you, I'd be grateful if you could remember that I was once one of your snotties and forget about the 'Your Graces.' "

"That's easier said than done, Yo—" Bachfisch paused, then chuckled. "Put it down to automatic social reflexes," he requested. "On the other hand, if I'm not supposed to call you 'Your Grace,' what would you prefer? Somehow, I don't think 'Ms. Midshipwoman Harrington' is really appropriate anymore, do you?"

"Probably not," she conceded with a chuckle of her own. "And I don't think I'd prefer 'Admiral Harrington,' either. So suppose we try just 'Honor.' "

"I—" the captain started, then paused again and cleared his throat. "If that's what you'd really prefer . . . Honor," he said after a moment.

"It is," she told him, and he nodded, then sat in the indicated chair and created a small space in the conversation by leaning back and crossing his legs before he let his attention sweep around the rest of the day cabin.

His eyes rested for just a moment on the crystal case protecting the sword rack, the glittering key of a steadholder, and a multi-spired golden star whose crimson ribbon was stained with darker, browner spots. A bronze plaque hung above it, one corner twisted and broken as if by a great heat, bearing the image of an old-fashioned sailplane. And another case held Honor's anachronistic .45 . . . and a more modern ten-millimeter dueling pistol.

He gazed at all of them for several seconds, as if absorbing the evidence of how much time—and life—had truly passed since last he'd seen her. Then he drew a deep breath and returned his attention to her.

"Quite a change since the last time you and I were in Silesia together," he observed wryly.

"I suppose so," she agreed. "But it brings back a lot of memories, doesn't it?"

"That it does. That it does." He shook his head. "Some of them good . . . some of them not so good."

"Sir," she said just a bit hesitantly, "at the court of inquiry after we got home. I asked to testify, but—"

"I know you did, Honor. But I told the court I felt you had nothing to add."

"*You* told the court?" she looked at him in disbelief. "But I was right there on the bridge. I knew exactly what happened!"

"Of course you did," he agreed, almost gently. "But I knew you too well to let them put you on the stand." She continued to stare at him, her eyes shadowed with sudden hurt, and he shook his head quickly. "Don't misunderstand me. I wasn't worried about anything you might say hurting me or my chances. But the official record already contained everything you could have testified to, including your own after-action report, and you've never been noted for your overly powerful self-preserving instincts. If they'd gotten you on the stand, you were almost certain to say something fierce in my defense, and I didn't want anything splashing on you."

"I'd have been honored to be 'splashed on' if it could have helped you, Sir," she said quietly.

"I know that. I knew it when I refused to let my advocate call you as a witness. But you had enough enemies of your own already for any midshipwoman, and I wasn't about to see you throw away the credit you so richly deserved for saving my ship. Not when anything you said wasn't going to matter, anyway."

"You couldn't know that it wouldn't matter," she protested.

"Oh, yes, I could, Honor," he said with a half-bitter, half-amused smile. "Because the fact of the matter was that I deserved to be dismissed from my ship."

"You did not!" she disagreed instantly.

"I think I'm hearing the midshipwoman who served under me, not the admiral sitting across her coffee table from me," he observed almost lightly. She opened her mouth, but he raised one hand and shook his head at her. "Think about it—as a flag officer, not a midshipwoman. I don't say there weren't extenuating circumstances, but let's be honest. For whatever combination of reasons, I allowed Dunecki and his ship into point-blank range, and I damned near got my own ship blown out of space, as a consequence. I did get too many of my people killed," he added in a much darker tone.

"But you couldn't have known," she protested.

"You were one of Raoul's proteges," he replied. "What did he always tell you about surprises?"

"That they were usually what happened when one captain made a mistake about something she'd actually seen all along," she admitted slowly.

"Which is precisely what I did." He shrugged. "Don't think it wasn't important to me to know you wanted to speak up in my defense, because it was. And don't think that because of that one incident I regard myself as some sort of total failure. But neither of those things changes the fact that I hazarded the ship the King had entrusted to me and that I would have lost her, with all hands, if not for the actions of a midshipwoman on her snotty cruise and a quite disproportionate amount of good luck. To be perfectly honest, I was surprised when they only placed me on half-pay rather than dismissing me from the Service entirely."

"I still say they were wrong," Honor said stubbornly. He looked at her quizzically, and it was her turn to shrug uncomfortably. "All right. I suppose that if I were sitting on a court of inquiry on a similar incident and all I had was the official record, I *might* have agreed some penalty was appropriate. I might have. But I like to think that by now I've seen enough of the ways in which good, competent officers can do everything right and still crap out to give anyone the benefit of the doubt."

"Perhaps you have," he agreed. "And perhaps, if it hadn't been an incident in peacetime, if the officers of the court had had the sort of experience you have now, their decision might have been different. But it was a different set of rules in a different time, Honor." He shook his head. "I won't pretend it didn't hurt. But I've never felt it was a gross miscarriage of justice, either. And," he gestured at the blue uniform tunic he wore, "it wasn't exactly the end of my life."

"No, I suppose it wasn't. But you'd still look better in black and gold than in blue, if you'll pardon my saying so. And the Navy could darned well have used your experience when the war finally began."

"I suppose if I'm honest, that was what hurt the most," he admitted in a slightly distant tone, gazing at something only he could see. "I'd spent so many years training for exactly what happened, and I wasn't allowed to use all I'd learned in the Star Kingdom's defense when the storm finally broke." He gazed at that invisible something for several more seconds, then shook himself. "But," he said briskly, focusing on her face once more, "there was absolutely no point in sitting around and brooding over what had happened, and I've found the odd project here and there since to keep myself busy."

"I understand you own your own shipping line," Honor said.

"That might be putting it just a bit grandly," he replied wryly. "I do own two ships outright, with majority shares in three others. Not quite on the scale of the Hauptman Cartel—or Skydomes of Grayson—but not too shabby an accomplishment here in Silesia, I suppose."

"From all I've heard that's a pretty severe case of understatement. And they tell me you have at least two armed merchant-men?"

"True," he said. "You're wondering how I managed it?" She nodded, and he shrugged. "Like everything else here in the Confederacy, it all depends on how deep your pockets are, what contacts you have, and who you know. Silesia may be a dangerous place to be a merchant skipper, but for that very reason, there's a lot of money in it if you manage to survive. And I've been out here long enough to've amassed quite a few debts and favors . . . and to learn where a few useful skeletons were buried." He shrugged again. "So, technically, *Pirate's Bane* and *Ambuscade* are auxiliary units of the Confederate Navy. Technically."

"Technically," Honor repeated, and he smiled. "And practically speaking?" she inquired.

"Practically speaking, the Confed Navy's official warrants are nothing but ways around the prohibition against armed merchant-men which are available to those with sufficiently well-placed government patrons. Everyone knows the auxiliaries will never be called upon in their naval capacity. For that matter, at least some of them are pirates themselves!" He seemed, she noted, to actually find that amusing, in a grim sort of way.

"May I ask who your patron is?" she asked in a carefully neutral voice, and he chuckled.

"I believe you've probably met her, at some point," he told her. "Her name is Patricia Givens."

"*Admiral* Givens?" Honor stared at him, startled by the name.

"Indirectly speaking," Bachfisch qualified. "Mind you, I probably would have reached the same point eventually on my own— or I like to think so, anyway. I'd already acquired a half-ownership in *Ambuscade*, and to be completely honest, I'd already armed her on a minor sort of scale. My partner wasn't entirely happy about that, but we both understood that if the Sillies ever complained about it, I'd take the fall by claiming full responsibility. At least a half dozen Confed skippers—and, for that matter, at least one flag officer—knew she was armed, of course, but by then I'd been out here long enough that I was considered a Silly myself, not one of those pushy Manticoran interlopers.

"Actually, there've always been more more-or-less-honest private armed vessels in Silesia than most people realize. I'm sure you've encountered quite a few of them yourself, during your deployments here?" He raised his eyebrows at her, and she nodded. "The problem, of course, has always been telling the good guys from the bad guys," he went on, "and for whatever reason, the Confed Navy had decided I was one of the good guys. It may have had something to do with the first couple of pirate vessels which suffered a mischief when *Ambuscade* was in the area."

"I hope you won't take this wrongly, Sir, but why did you stay out here in Silesia at all?" He looked at her, and she waved one hand in the air above her desk. "I mean, you've done well, but surely you had more and better contacts in the Star Kingdom than you did out here, and the Confederacy was scarcely the most law-abiding environment available."

"I suppose shame might have been a part of it," he admitted after a moment. "The language in which the court of inquiry couched its verdict was actually pretty moderate, but the subtext was clear enough, and there was a part of me which wanted sympathy about as little as it wanted condemnation. So there was certainly an element of starting over somewhere where I'd have a clean page.

"Then again, I was one of the Navy's old 'Silesian hands.' Like you, I'd been deployed out here several times in the course of my career, and there were people who knew me, either personally or by reputation. They don't get to see too many Manticoran officers of my seniority or experience in private service out here, so in some ways it was easier for me to write my own ticket in the Confederacy than it would have been in the Star Kingdom."

He paused for several seconds, and she tasted his emotions as he considered whether or not to leave it at that. Then he gave his head a little toss—a mannerism she remembered well as an indicator of decision.

"And if the truth be known, I think it was also a case of looking for the grand gesture. A way of proving to the galaxy at large that whatever the court of inquiry might have decided, I was—well, a force to be reckoned with, I suppose. I needed to go out and demonstrate that I could succeed out here and simultaneously cut a swathe through any pirates who got in my way."

"And perhaps just a bit of knight errantry?" Honor asked gently. He looked at her expressionlessly, and she tipped her chair back and smiled. "I don't doubt anything you just said, Sir. But I think there's also at least a trace of 'once a Queen's officer, always a Queen's officer.'"

"If by that you mean I thought the universe would be a better place with fewer pirates in it, you may have a point," Bachfisch conceded. "But don't make the mistake of assigning me too much purity of motive."

"I didn't say anything about purity of motive," Honor replied. "I just couldn't quite picture you quietly fading away under any circumstances. Finding you out here in command of what amounts to privately flagged Q-ships simply suggests to me that you're still in the business of suppressing piracy. And given that you just let drop the name of the previous Second Space Lord, my naturally suspicious mind suggests that there might be a more direct connection between you and Her Majesty's Navy than most people would suspect."

"There's something to that," he admitted. "Not that I started out with any such connection in mind. Even if one had occurred to me, the circumstances which had gotten me placed on half-pay in the first place would have discouraged me from approaching anyone in the Admiralty. But ONI has always done its best to keep

track of the Navy's officers, active-duty or not, and as my support base grew out here, ONI approached me. In fact, it was ONI
which quietly greased the way for me to acquire official approval
for *Ambuscade*'s guns. And unless I'm very much mistaken, it was
also ONI which even more quietly helped send the *Bane* in my
direction when she was listed for disposal by the Andies. No one
ever said so in as many words, but there were one or two coincidences too many in the way things came together when I put
in my bid on her.

"And whether I'm right about that or not, Admiral Givens—
or her minions, at least—were in fairly regular contact with me
right up to the truce with the Peeps. I suppose that technically I
was one of those 'HumInt' sources ONI keeps referring to when
they brief officers for Silesia."

"You said ONI *was* in regular contact with you?" Honor asked,
looking at him very thoughtfully, and he nodded.

"That's exactly what I said," he agreed. "And I meant precisely
what you think I meant. Since Jurgensen took over from Givens,
Intelligence seems to've cut back drastically on its use of human
resources here in Silesia. I can't say what the situation might be
elsewhere, but here in the Confederacy, no one seems to be pay-
ing much attention to old sources or networks. And, frankly, Honor,
I think that's an enormous mistake."

"I wish I could say I disagreed with you, Sir," Honor said slowly.
"Unfortunately, if you're right, it only confirms fears I already had.
The closer I look at the intelligence packets they sent out here with
me, the less in touch with reality the analysts who wrote them up
seem to be."

"I was afraid of that," he sighed. "Obviously, there was no way
for me to know what ONI was or wasn't telling the officers the
Navy was sending out, but the fact that no one was asking me
any questions anymore suggested that the information contained
in their briefings was probably . . . incomplete. And unless I'm very
mistaken about the Andies' intentions, that could be a very, very
serious oversight on someone's part."

"Do you think he's right, Your Grace?" Mercedes Brigham asked
quietly as she, Honor, Nimitz, Lieutenant Meares, and LaFollet rode
the lift towards the flag briefing room and an already scheduled
meeting with Honor's entire staff.

"I'm afraid I do," Honor replied equally quietly.

"I know you and he go way back, Your Grace," Brigham said after a moment, and Honor chuckled humorlessly.

"Yes, and he was my very first captain. And, yes, again, Mercedes, that gives him a certain aura of authority in my eyes. But I'm not blind to the ways people can change in thirty or forty T-years. Nor am I overlooking the possibility that however good his intentions, his information—or his interpretation of it—could still be badly flawed." She shook her head. "I'm considering what he's said as impartially and skeptically as I can. Unfortunately, too much of it fits entirely too well with all the other straws in the wind we've been identifying."

"I didn't mean to suggest that he might be trying to dump disinformation on you, Your Grace. And to be honest, I have to agree that his analysis of what the Andies probably have in mind jibes altogether too damned well for comfort with what we were already afraid they were thinking. I guess my greatest concern is that he's so much more emphatic about the Andies' new hardware than anything we had from ONI suggests. For that matter, he's more emphatic than anything we got from the *Graysons* would suggest."

"Agreed. But by the same token, he's had a much closer look at the Andies than either ONI or Benjamin's people. In ONI's case, that's purely because Jurgensen and his people have chosen not to avail themselves of the resource that was available to them. Unless I'm mistaken, the Captain wasn't the only human source Jurgensen decided he could dispense with, either. In the Graysons' case, it's simply a matter of time and distance. Well, that and the fact that they never even knew the Captain was here, so they can hardly be blamed for not getting his input.

"Even conceding all of that, though, what he's been able to piece together about the new Andermani systems tallies much too closely for comfort with what Greg Paxton did manage to put together. Not to mention what Captain Ferrero's had to say in her reports. Or that Sidemorian analyst, what's-his-name?" She frowned, then nodded. "Zahn."

"Lieutenant Commander Zahn's husband?" Brigham asked.

"That's the one," Honor agreed. "George just finished reading one of his position papers and briefed me on it last night."

Brigham nodded. Commander George Reynolds was Honor's

staff intelligence officer, and Honor had selected him for the post of "spook" at least partly on Brigham's recommendation. The chief of staff had worked with him before and been impressed by his ability to think outside the box.

"George wasn't prepared to unreservedly endorse Zahn's conclusions," Honor continued, "but he did say that the logic seemed tight, assuming the basic facts on which it was based were accurate. And now Captain Bachfisch seems to be confirming those facts from an entirely independent perspective."

"If both of them are right," Brigham said unhappily, "then we're holding an even shorter stick than we thought, Your Grace."

"I wish you were wrong," Honor told her. "Unfortunately, I don't think you are."

"So what do we do about it?"

"I don't know. Not yet. The first thing is this meeting, though. We need to get the rest of the staff brought up to speed, get them started thinking on possible threats and responses. And, of course, I'll want to get Alice and Alistair briefed in and thinking about it, too. Hopefully, at least one or two useful ideas will come out of it. And I'm enlarging the invitation list for dinner tonight, as well. I want you, George, Alistair, Alice, Roslee, Wraith, and probably Rafe and Scotty, at a minimum to join the Captain and me over supper."

"Will he be comfortable with that, Your Grace?" Brigham asked. Honor looked a question at her, and she shrugged. "It's pretty obvious he's spent a lot of time establishing himself out here. If word leaks that he's a Manticoran intelligence asset, it could do him a lot of damage. It might even get him killed. I just wondered if he really wanted that many people to know who your information source is. I don't expect any of them to let it get to the wrong ears, but he doesn't know them the way we do."

"I asked him that, more or less," Honor replied after a moment. "He'd already considered the same questions before he ever asked to come aboard *Werewolf*. I don't think he'd be here in the first place if he weren't prepared for the sorts of questions we're likely to ask him. And he may not know them, but he does know me, and I think he trusts my judgment about who might or might not be a threat to his own security."

"In that case, Your Grace," the chief of staff said as the lift car reached its destination and the doors hissed open, "we'll just have to make certain that none of us *is* a threat, won't we?"

CHAPTER TWENTY-EIGHT

"   So I did exactly what Mister Pirate told me to," Thomas Bachfisch said with an evil grin. "We hove to, opened our personnel locks, and stood by to be boarded. And then, when their boarding shuttles were about five hundred klicks out, we opened the weapons ports and put an eighty-centimeter graser straight through their ship."

More than one of his listeners winced at the thought of what it must have been like aboard that piratical cruiser in the fleeting instant its crew had to realize what had happened. There was, however, a marked absence of sympathy for the crew in question. These were all experienced naval officers; they'd seen too much of the wreckage pirates left behind.

"Your ships must have come as a nasty surprise to the pirate community out here, Sir," Roslee Orndorff observed as she handed another celery stick to Banshee.

"Not so much to the community as a whole, as to the individuals who ran into us," Bachfisch. "We haven't really tried to make our presence a secret—after all, half the effect of a Q-ship derives from the fact that potential raiders know she's out there somewhere. If they don't know she exists, then they're not going to be worried over the possibility that any given merchantman might be her. But by the same token, we haven't exactly broadcast a description of any of our ships, and we've been known to change the paint

401

scheme from time to time. The smart paint cost us a pretty penny, but it was worth it."

"I often think it's more useful to Q-ships than it's ever been to regular men-of-war," Alistair McKeon observed, and several heads nodded. The "paint" used by the RMN and most other navies was liberally laced with nanotech and reactive pigments which allowed it to be programmed and altered, essentially without limit, at will. Unfortunately, as McKeon had just suggested, that was of strictly limited utility for a warship. After all, the distinctive hammerhead hull form of a warship could scarcely be mistaken for anything else, whatever color it might be. Besides, no one was likely to rely on visual identification of any man-of-war, which was one reason most navies also had a distinct tendency to choose one paint scheme—like the RMN's basic white—and leave it that way.

But merchantmen were another matter entirely. Even there, cruisers and pirate vessels alike tended to rely primarily upon transponder codes, but anyone who wanted to steal a ship's cargo had to come close enough to do it. And at that point, visual identifications—or *mis*identifications, in some very special cases—became the norm.

"I'm guessing that if you're using smart paint, you're also using . . . inventive transponder codes, Admiral," Lieutenant Commander Reynolds put in. Bachfisch looked as if he were about to correct the rank title yet again, then visibly gave up and simply nodded once more.

"I'm confident my people could take just about any pirate out here in straight fight," he said. "But to be honest, our primary function is to carry cargo. Besides, we may be armed, and *Pirates' Bane* may have started life as an armed auxiliary, but that doesn't make her a dreadnought. She's got a military-grade compensator and the impellers and particle shields to go with it, and she and *Ambuscade* both have fairly respectable sidewall generators. But none of our ships have real military hulls or damage control capability.

"You were with Her Grace when her Q-ships deployed out here several years back, weren't you, Admiral Truman?" he asked, turning to Honor's second-in-command, and shrugged when Truman nodded in agreement. "Well, then you know what happens to a merchant hull that takes a hit from any heavy shipboard weapon. So under the circumstances, neither my crews nor I are particularly interested in 'fair fights' with pirates. Which is why we practically never sail under our own transponder codes until we're actually ready to make port."

"And the Confed Navy doesn't have a problem with that, Sir?" Rafe Cardones asked. It was a reasonable question, given that falsifying transponder codes was a moderately severe offense under the law of most star nations . . . including the Silesian Confederacy.

"Officially, they don't know anything about it," Bachfisch replied with a slight shrug, "and what they don't know about, they don't object to. In fact, most of their skippers know we're doing it, but they're not going to object to almost anything we do as long as we keep nailing the occasional pirate for them."

"Makes sense to me," Truman agreed, and reached for her wineglass. James MacGuiness materialized magically to refill the glass before she quite touched it, and she smiled her thanks at him, sipped the ruby wine, and turned her attention back to Bachfisch.

"I have to say that we're probably luckier than we deserve to have you run into us, Admiral Bachfisch," she said in a more formal tone.

"I didn't exactly 'run into' you, Admiral," Bachfisch replied with a crooked smile. "I came looking for you."

"I know." Truman considered him thoughtfully. "I'm grateful that you did. But at the same time, I'm sure you understand why we might be a little hesitant to accept one person's testimony, however credible that person might seem, when it flatly contradicts certain aspects of our ONI briefings."

"Well," Bachfisch said, letting his smile grow a bit broader, "I know why *I* might be a little hesitant, but then, when I was on active duty, the people running ONI could usually find their own asses . . . if they used both hands, at least."

Despite herself, Truman's lips twitched, and Cardones grinned openly.

"What I meant to say, Sir," the golden-haired admiral said after a moment, when she was confident she had her voice fully under control once more, "was that I'd feel more comfortable about relying on your information if you could describe firsthand how you came into possession of it."

"I understand what you're getting at, Dame Alice," Bachfisch said more seriously. "And I certainly don't blame you for wanting to be a bit cautious about relying on fortuitous windfalls of information. I've already promised Admiral Harrington to make my sensor log recordings available to support some of my observations—like the acceleration rates I've seen the new cruisers pulling, and the stealth capabilities that Andy heavy cruiser demonstrated in the Melbourne System. You can make your own analysis of those events from them, and, frankly, you have better facilities for doing that than I do.

"But I suspect that what probably concerns you most are the reports I don't have any log recordings to back up. Especially the ones about the new Andy battlecruisers."

"I will admit that that's one of the areas which causes me concerns," Truman agreed, clearly relieved that Bachfisch understood her worries and chose not to take them as aspersions upon his veracity.

"I've already given Commander Reynolds here as detailed a written description as I could put together," Bachfisch told her. "You'll probably do better to get the details from him, because it's based on notes I jotted down immediately after I saw the ship, not on what I can recall from unaided memory right this moment. But the way I came to be in a position to observe it has a lot to do with the Q-ship operations we were just discussing. I had a fresh crop of pirates to turn over to the Silly authorities in Crawford, but an Andy battlecruiser squadron was passing through the system and shortstopped my delivery. Not," he added wryly, "that the Confederate governor was at all happy about it. He seemed to feel the Andy admiral was being just a bit high-handed about the whole thing."

"Why am I not surprised?" McKeon murmured with a grimace. "Lord knows the only people the Sillies think are more arrogant and high-handed than the Andies are Manticorans, after all!"

"With all due respect, Admiral," Bachfisch told him, "and speaking as someone who's seen it from both sides, the Sillies have a point. From their perspective, both the RMN and the IAN *are* high-handed as hell. The fact that they know perfectly well, whatever they may choose to pretend, that they don't have the capability to police their own space lanes without outside interference only makes it worse, but how would you feel if foreign navies came sweeping into the Star Kingdom at will to police our commerce? Or if they took custody of criminals captured in our space because they distrusted the integrity of our legal system . . . or the honesty of our government officials?" He shook his head. "I know the situations are different, but the fact that our lack of confidence in them is justified so much of the time only makes them resent it even more. And too many Andy and Manty naval officers let their contempt for the locals show. For that matter, I probably did the same thing when I was on active duty!

"At any rate, I don't think the squadron CO realized I was a Manticoran myself when he ordered me to deliver my prisoners to him. He certainly didn't realize I was a half-pay Navy officer, anyway! I was just as happy to hand them over to the Andies, because I could be fairly confident they weren't going to simply be turned loose again that way, but I have to admit that I didn't much care for his attitude, myself. Interesting how it changed when he realized he wasn't talking to a Silesian after all.

"On the other hand, I don't think he was especially pleased to realize he'd allowed anyone who might be connected with the Star Kingdom close enough to get a good look at the after hammerhead of his flagship. Under the circumstances, I didn't think it would be especially wise of me to pull out a pocket camera and snap a few shots, and the Andies were pretty careful to keep their bow towards the *Bane* after I got back aboard her, so I couldn't get any good visuals from her, either. But there were definitely some major differences between her construction and a regular battlecruiser's. My personnel shuttle crossed her stern at less than half a klick on the run to deliver our 'guests,' and it was obvious that she didn't have much in the way of conventional stern chasers. But what she did have was a great big cargo hatch."

"I don't much like the sound of that," McKeon observed unhappily.

"Well, I can see where a battlecruiser built on the pod format would have a lot of short-term firepower," Wraith Goodrick replied. "But how sustainable would that firepower be? And how long could any battlecruiser's defenses stand up to a real ship of the wall, especially a pod design, if it came down to that?" He shook his head. "I don't know. It just doesn't sound like a really practical concept to me."

Honor and Brigham glanced at one another, and Honor gave her chief of staff a very small nod.

"Actually," Mercedes said then, turning to the rest of the table, "the Andies weren't the first ones to come up with the idea. Or, at least, if they've had it, the Graysons have, too, completely independently."

"Really?" McKeon looked at her sharply. "Why haven't I heard anything about it, then?"

"You'd have to take that up with High Admiral Matthews, Sir," Brigham told him calmly. "If I had to guess, though, I'd say it was probably a bit of tit for tat. First Lord Janacek and Admiral Chakrabarti decided to shut down the joint Grayson-Manticoran R&D teams shortly after they took over at the Admiralty. Officially, it was another economy measure, but I'm afraid there were persistent rumors in the GSN that the new management wanted to close down the information flow to Grayson."

"Why in the world would anyone think that?" Truman demanded in disbelief. "We're allies, for God's sake!"

"I'm only telling you what the rumors said, Ma'am," Brigham replied in a very carefully neutral voice. "No one ever said rumors have to make sense."

"But—"

Truman started to reply hotly, then closed her mouth with an almost audible click, and Honor hid a bitter little smile as she tasted her friend's sudden understanding of just how much damage Janacek and High Ridge truly had managed to do to the bonds Grayson and the Queen's Navy had forged out of so much shed blood.

"At any rate," Brigham went on, returning her attention to McKeon, "the new *Courvoisier II*-class battlecruisers are a pod design. The Office of Shipbuilding reduced their conventional missile broadsides by over eighty percent, which let them build in superdreadnought-sized energy weapons." McKeon's eyes widened and turned suddenly thoughtful, and the chief of staff shrugged. "I think there was some pressure to go to something more on the lines of the *Invictuses* and suppress the broadside tubes entirely, but Shipbuilding decided against it. Still, Wraith is right that they can't sustain their maximum rate of missile fire for anything like as long as a pod superdreadnought. But then, a conventional battlecruiser design couldn't sustain the missile fire of a pre-pod ship of the wall, either. And the exercises we've conducted in Grayson certainly seem to suggest that the new design has a much better chance of surviving against ships of the wall."

"Not on any sort of one-to-one basis, though," Goodrick argued.

"Depends on how old the ship of the wall's design is," Brigham said. "Against a pre-pod ship, a *Courvoisier* has a damned good chance, actually. She can roll enough pods to throw salvos that can saturate even an SD's missile defenses. Not a lot of them, maybe, but enough to do the job against one, maybe even two, of the older classes. And once she's beaten down the SD's offensive fire, she's actually got the energy weapons to get through its defenses, as well. And if two or three *Courvoisiers* concentrate on a single target, even an SD(P) will find herself in trouble. She'd have to get through to them and start killing them really quickly if she didn't want them to do exactly the same thing to her."

Goodrick looked shocked by the very notion, and Brigham grinned at him.

"Not only that, and not only are the *Courvoisiers* a hell of a lot more dangerous in energy-range, but the designers used the new automation systems even more heavily than they did in the design of the *Harrington* class, as well. The crews are really, really small. As a matter of fact, you can run one of the new ships with a few as three hundred people if you really have to."

"Three hundred?" Goodrick repeated in something very like disbelief, and Brigham nodded.

"Three hundred," she confirmed. "That kind of reduction in life-support requirements, coupled with the hollow core design, explains how they were able to pack an enormously powerful graser broadside into the new design. They only have about two-thirds as many mounts as their predecessors did, but the ones they have are just as powerful as those the *Harrington*-class mount."

"Which was the real point of the design, when you come right down to it, Wraith," Honor put in. "Oh, not the energy broadside, *per se*, and not the ability to go toe-to-toe with superdreadnoughts, either. What the Graysons have built is a battlecruiser to do to older battlecruiser designs what the SD(P) can do to older superdreadnoughts. So if the Andermani have been pursuing the same design philosophy, the ships Captain Bachfisch has just described to us are going to be even more dangerous than anything we've predicted this so far."

"That was my own thought," Bachfisch agreed.

"Have you seen—or heard anything about—proper pod-armed ships of the wall, Sir?" Lieutenant Commander Reynolds sounded more than a little anxious, and Bachfisch shook his head.

"No, I haven't, Commander. Unfortunately, that doesn't mean they don't have any; only that if they do, I haven't seen them. By the same token, though, it occurred to me the other day that you can build battlecruisers a hell of a lot faster than you can build ships of the wall. It may be that they have SD(P)s in the final design stage or even under construction but not yet in commission."

"Which could be why they're still ratcheting up the pressure but haven't actually made their move yet," Rafe Cardones thought aloud.

"I wouldn't rely too heavily on that possibility, Rafe," Honor cautioned. "Even if that's what's happening, we don't know how far along they are in their preparations. And if it isn't what's happening, and we assume that it is . . ."

"Understood, Your Grace," Cardones acknowledged. "Still, I think it's an interesting possibility."

"It is," Bachfisch agreed. "And to be honest, I wouldn't be too surprised if that consideration, or one very like it, didn't play a part in their calculations. But as Her Grace says, I wouldn't care to rely on it."

"No, I can see that," Truman agreed, and leaned back in her chair, her eyes intent as she considered what Bachfisch had told them. It was obvious from her expression, and even more from the taste of her emotions, that if she'd had reservations about their information source, those reservations were dissipating rapidly.

"Wraith and I are looking forward to examining those sensor recordings of yours, Captain," she said. "Especially the ones of the Andies' new LACs."

"I'm not surprised," Bachfisch told her with a small smile. "And, to be honest, I was very interested in the readings I got on your own LACs here in Marsh, Admiral. I haven't had the leisure to compare them exhaustively, but my initial impression is that your design is still faster and more powerful than anything of theirs I've seen."

"But you haven't seen any sign of Andy CLACs?" Truman asked.

"No, I haven't. But if I were the Andies, I'd probably be even more leery of showing off my CLACs than of letting out the fact that I had pod-battlecruisers. And it wouldn't be all that difficult to keep them a secret, either. You know how easy it would be to hide CLACs in some out-of-the-way star system while they worked up."

"As a matter of fact, Captain, I know *exactly* how easy it would be," Truman told him with a small chuckle. Then she sobered, and looked at Honor.

"I agree with Alistair, Honor. I don't much like the sound of any of this. Not when you combine it with things like Zahn's analysis and Ferrero's reports. *Especially* not combined with what Ferrero's had to say. If the Andies are deliberately showing us the sort of technology advances she's reported, but at the same time they're busy concealing the existence of these new pod-battlecruisers—or trying to conceal it, at any rate . . ."

She let her voice trail off, and Honor nodded. The same thought had already occurred to her. The actions of *Hellbarde*'s captain looked more and more like deliberate provocations. If they were, then Gortz's revelation of the new weapons and sensor capabilities of the Andermani Navy took on the appearance of a deliberate attempt to intimidate, or at least to make Honor, as Sidemore Station's CO, worry about what else they might have in store for her. For that matter, they were busy doing exactly the same thing to the Sillies, according to all reports. Which suggested that they were busy attempting to intimidate the Confederacy's navy, as well. But the fact that they hadn't also flaunted their new warship types was an ominous suggestion that whatever new technology they were prepared to reveal, they were keeping some major surprises tucked away up their sleeves.

She drew a deep breath and looked around the table at the assembled officers . . . and at Thomas Bachfisch. His merchant service uniform looked totally out of place amid the black and gold of the RMN, and yet for all that, she felt a curious sense of completion at seeing him there. It was right that her first commanding officer should be here when she assumed her first station command, and as she looked at him, she felt the same awareness—or something very like it—radiating from him, as well.

"Very well, Ladies and Gentlemen," she told them all. "Thanks to Captain Bachfisch, we have significantly more information about possible threat levels than we had when we arrived. What I'd like to do now is to move down to the flag deck simulator and play with some of the new possibilities. And if you have the time, Captain," she said, gazing directly into his eyes, "I would be both pleased and honored if you'd join us there. I would value your input greatly."

"The honor would be mine, Your Grace," Bachfisch replied after a moment.

"Good!" Honor said with a huge smile, then stood and scooped Nimitz onto her shoulder.

"In that case, People," she told her officers with another smile for Bachfisch, "let's be about it."

CHAPTER TWENTY-NINE

"**W**ayfarer, this is *LaFroye*. Our pinnace is closing from your six o'clock and low. ETA is now twelve minutes."

"Understood, *LaFroye*. Ah, may I ask just what it is you're concerned about?"

Jason Ackenheil sat back in his command chair, watching Lieutenant Gower, his com officer talking to one Captain Gabrijela Kanjcevic, mistress after God of the Solarian-flag merchant ship *Wayfarer*, and smiled thinly. It was safe enough, since he was far outside the range of Gower's visual pickup. *Wayfarer* wasn't that huge for a merchie—a fast freight hauler configured for relatively small cargos (by the standards of the leviathans which roamed the interstellar deeps) and limited passenger service—although she still dwarfed *LaFroye* to minnow-status. But the minnow had teeth and the whale didn't, so the whale had better be extremely polite to the minnow. On the other hand, some merchies were more equal than others, and *Wayfarer* undoubtedly felt reasonably secure in her League registry. After all, no Manticoran captain in his right mind wanted to provoke a career-ending incident with the League. Which explained why, so far at least, Kanjcevic sounded wary but not truly concerned.

But that was about to change . . . assuming, of course, that his information was accurate.

Which, all things being equal, it had damned well better be.

411

"It's only routine, Captain," Gower assured the face on his com screen. Then he glanced over his shoulder, as if checking to see if anyone were in proximity, and leaned back towards Kanjcevic's image.

"Just between you and me, Ma'am, it's pretty silly, actually. We've had reports of a rash of merchant losses in this sector over the last few months, and Intelligence has decided someone's using an armed merchant raider. So orders came down from Sidemore to make an eyeball check on every merchant ship we can." He shrugged. "So far, we've checked eleven without finding a thing." He did not quite, Ackenheil noticed, add "of course," but his tone made it superfluous, anyway. "Shouldn't take more than a few minutes for our pinnace to dock, come aboard, make sure you don't have any grasers hidden away, and let you go on about your business. But if we don't check it out, well . . ."

He shrugged again, and Kanjcevic smiled.

"Understood, Lieutenant," she said. "And I don't suppose I should complain about anything designed to make life harder on pirates. We'll give your people full cooperation."

"Thank you, Captain. We appreciate it. *LaFroye*, clear."

Gower cut the connection and turned to grin at his captain. "How was that, Skip?"

"Perfect, Lou. Just perfect," Ackenheil assured him. *Now let's just hope Reynolds knew what he was talking about in that intelligence brief,* he added very quietly to himself.

Captain Denise Hammond, RMMC, stood and moved to the center of the pinnace troop compartment. Quarters were more than a little cramped, given that she had two entire platoons of battle-armored troopers.

"All right, People," she told them. "We're docking in five mikes. You know the drill. No nonsense off anyone, but no bloodshed if we can help it either. Copy?"

A chorus of assents came back over her helmet com, and she nodded in satisfaction. Then she turned back to the hatch and waited with a hungry grin of anticipation. If the Skipper was right about what they were about to find, then this would be one of the best days she'd had in months, possibly years. And if he was wrong . . . Well, she was only a Marine. None of the crap was going to splash on her for following orders, and she'd never much liked Sollies, anyway.

The pinnace settled into the docking arms, the personnel tube mated with the lock, and the Solarian merchant marine lieutenant Kanjcevic had sent down to greet their visitors straightened into what might charitably have been called a posture of attention. He didn't much care for Manties—damned arrogant upstarts; that's what they were, crowding Solarian shipping lines all the time—but he'd been ordered to make nice this time. Given the circumstances, he thought that was an excellent idea, however much it might gripe him to do anything of the sort, and he pasted a smile on his face as the green light of a good seal showed above the tube hatch.

The smile disappeared into sickly shock as that same hatch slid open and he suddenly found himself looking down the business end of a stun rifle. One held in the powered gauntlets of a Royal Manticoran Marine in the menacing bulk of battle armor. A Marine, a corner of the lieutenant's stunned brain noted with something almost like detachment, who appeared to be followed by dozens of other Marines . . . most of whom appeared to be armed with things considerably more lethal than stunners.

"My name is Hammond, Lieutenant," the Marine behind the stun rifle said over her armor's external speakers in a soprano which would probably have been pleasantly melodious under other circumstances. "Captain Hammond, Royal Manticoran Marines. I suggest you take me to your captain."

"I—I—" The lieutenant swallowed hard. "Uh, what's the meaning of this?" he demanded. Or tried to demand, anyway; it came out sounding more like a bleat of terrified confusion.

"This vessel is suspected of violating the provisions of the Cherwell Convention," Hammond told him, and felt a profound sense of internal satisfaction at the way his face went suddenly bone-white. "So I suggest," she went on as the rest of her boarding party swiftly and competently secured the boat bay, "that you see about getting me to your captain. Now."

"It's confirmed, Skipper," Denise Hammond told Captain Ackenheil. There was no visual, because she was speaking to him over her helmet com, but he didn't need a visual from her. He'd already seen the imagery from the external cameras of the Marines who'd forced the hatches into *Wayfarer*'s "passenger cabins." Even in Silesia and even aboard freighters with strictly limited personnel space, passengers were seldom packed in twelve to the cabin.

Of course, *Wayfarer*'s crew had managed to save a little space for them in their quarters. After all, they didn't need much space to store their personal belongings when they didn't have any . . . including clothing of any sort.

The expressions of abject terror on the faces of those naked, hopeless "passengers" had been enough to turn a man's stomach. But the moment when they realized they were looking at Royal Marines, not the bully boy guards of the owners to whom they had been consigned, had been something else again. Indeed, seeing it had given him almost as much pleasure as the sick, stunned expression on Kanjcevic's face when she realized what had happened. And when she remembered that under the terms of solemn interstellar treaties, the Star Kingdom of Manticore equated violation of the Cherwell Convention's prohibitions on trafficking in human beings with piracy.

Which was punishable by death.

"Good work, Denise," he said sincerely. "Very good work. Keep an eye on things over there for another twenty minutes, and I'll have the prize crew across to you."

"Aye, aye, Sir. We'll be here."

"Do you know what I hate most about our political lords and masters?" Dr. Wix demanded.

Jordin Kare tipped back his chair and cocked his head with a quizzical expression as he regarded the astrophysicist who'd just burst unceremoniously through his office door. It was very early in the day—which was the only reason Wix had gotten past the secretary who would have intercepted him during regular working hours—and Kare's coffee cup sat steaming on the corner of his blotter beside a half-eaten croissant.

"No," he said mildly, picking up his napkin and brushing crumbs from his lips. "I don't know what you hate most about our political lords and masters, TJ. But I feel somehow certain that you can scarcely wait to enlighten me."

"Um?" Wix stopped just inside the door, alerted by his superior's tone of voice that he'd just committed a social *faux pas*. Then he had the grace to blush. "Oops. Sorry, Boss. I forgot it was breakfast time for you."

"For me? Most people eat breakfast even earlier than I do, TJ— between the time they get up and the time they begin work," Kare pointed out. Then he noticed Wix's somewhat scruffy appearance and sighed. "TJ, you did go home last night at some point, didn't you?"

"Well, actually . . . no," Wix admitted. Kare drew a deep breath, but before he could deliver yet another homily on the desirability of something resembling a normal sleep schedule, the younger scientist hurried on.

"I was going to, honest. But one thing led to another, and, well—" He twitched one shoulder in impatient dismissal. "Anyway," he went on more enthusiastically, "I was looking at that latest data run—you know, the one *Argonaut* pulled in last week?"

Kare recognized the futility of trying to introduce any other topic until Wix had run down about this one and resigned himself.

"Yes," he said. "I know the data you're talking about."

"Well," Wix went on, starting to bounce around the office in his excitement, "I went back and reran them, and damned if I don't think we've actually hit the proper approach vector. Oh," he waved one hand as Kare let his chair come suddenly back upright, "we still have a lot of refining to do, and I want to make at least two or three more runs to get a broader observational base to double-check my rough calculations. But unless I'm mistaken, the analysis is going to confirm that we've hit the target pretty much on the nose."

"I wish," Kare said after a moment, "that you'd stop doing this, TJ."

"Doing what?" Wix asked, obviously confused by his superior's tone of voice.

"Finding things ahead of schedule," Kare told him. "After the Director and I spent days hammering home the need for us to do all of the time-consuming detail work, you turn around and find the damned approach vector a good four months early! Do you have any idea how hard this is going to make it to convince the politicos that they should listen to us the next time we tell them we need more time to complete our research?"

"Of course I do," Wix told him in a moderately affronted tone.

"That's what I hate most about our political lords and masters, if you'll remember the way I began this conversation. Besides, it really sours my day to start it off by literally stumbling across something which I ought to feel only pleased about finding and then realize how much it pisses me off to realize I'm going to do exactly what the idiots I work for wanted done all along. Well, that and the way the assholes are going to steal the credit for it."

"You do realize how paranoid—if not petty—this entire conversation makes two reasonably intelligent adults sound, don't you?" Kare asked with a wry grin, and Wix shrugged.

"I don't feel particularly paranoid, and I don't think we're the petty ones. In fact, that's why it pisses me off—I don't like working for a *prime minister* who's so damned petty. Besides, as soon as we tell them about it, that asshole Oglesby is going to be back over here for another news conference. At which you and Admiral Reynaud will be doing well to get a single word in edgewise."

"Oh, no, TJ! Not this time," Kare said with a seraphic smile. "You found it, so this time *you're* the one who's going to be doing well to get a single word in edgewise."

"That was delicious, Your Grace," Mercedes Brigham sighed, sitting back from the breakfast table with a comfortable sense of repletion. The plate before her bore the sticky remains of her eggs Benedict's hollandaise sauce and a few bacon crumbs, while the rind of a musk melon stood up like the keel of a stripped ark on a smaller plate, accompanied by two purple grapes which had somehow escaped the massacre of their fellows.

Honor's breakfast, as always, had been considerably more substantial, as a concession to her enhanced metabolism, and she smiled at Brigham's comment as she reached for the cocoa carafe and poured herself another mug.

"I'm glad you enjoyed it," she said, her smile broadening as James MacGuiness stepped in from his pantry with a fresh cup of the hot tea her chief of staff preferred. "Of course, I'm not the person you ought to be complimenting about it."

"No, and I wasn't complimenting you," Brigham told her. "I was simply commenting. The person I intended to compliment about it wasn't here at the moment. Now he is." She sniffed and looked up at MacGuiness. "That was delicious, Mac," she said with dignity.

"Thank you, Commodore," MacGuiness said gravely. "Would you like another egg?"

"Some of us, unfortunately, have to be a bit more careful than others about what we eat," Brigham said in regretful tones.

"Cheer up, Mercedes," Honor told her while Nimitz bleeked a laugh of his own around a stalk of celery. "There's always lunch."

"And I'll look forward to it," Brigham assured her with a chuckle while she smiled at the steward.

"I'll do my best not to disappoint," MacGuiness assured her. He was just about to say something more when the com attention signal chimed softly. He made a small face—the grimace of irritation he saved for moments when the outside universe intruded itself into his admiral's mealtimes—and then stepped over to the bulkhead-mounted terminal and pressed the accept key.

"Admiral's day cabin, MacGuiness speaking," he told the pickup in decidedly repressive accents.

"Bridge, Officer of the Watch, speaking," Lieutenant Ernest Talbot, *Werewolf*'s communications officer, replied in a respectful voice. "Sorry to interrupt Her Grace's breakfast, Mr. MacGuiness. But the Captain asked me to inform her that Perimeter Security has just picked up an unidentified incoming hyper footprint. A big one, twenty-two light-minutes from the primary. According to CIC, there are over twenty major drive sources."

MacGuiness' eyebrows rose, and he started to turn towards Honor, but she was by his side before the movement was more than half completed. She laid one hand on his shoulder and leaned a bit closer to the pickup herself.

"This is the Admiral, Lieutenant Talbot," she said. "I assume that the grav-pulse challenge has already been sent?"

"Of course, Your Grace." Talbot sounded suddenly crisper. "It was transmitted as soon as they were picked up, exactly—" he paused, obviously checking the time "—seven minutes and forty-five seconds ago. There's been no response."

"I see." Honor refrained from pointing out that if there *had* been a response, the hyper footprint would scarcely have still been unidentified. Then she felt a tiny pang of guilt at the thought. Good officers learned never to assume that someone else was aware of all they were aware of, and subordinates who were willing to risk sounding foolish to be certain their superiors had all relevant information were to be cherished, not scorned.

•

"Well," she went on, "they could still be friendlies who're just a little slow responding, I suppose." Her tone was that of someone thinking out loud, and Talbot made no response. Nor was any required. Both of them knew that by now every Manticoran or Allied man-of-war was equipped with FTL grav-pulse transmitters . . . and that no Allied com officer was "slow" enough to not have responded by now.

"Still," Honor continued, "this isn't a good time to take chances. My compliments to Captain Cardones, Lieutenant, and ask him to bring the task force to Action Stations."

"Aye, aye, Ma'am!" Talbot said crisply, and the General Quarters alarm woke to clamorous, ear-hurting life less than four seconds later.

Admiral of the Green Francis Jurgensen felt his belly congeal into a single, massive lump of ice as he stared at the report on the display in front of him. For several seconds, his brain simply refused to work at all.

Then the real panic set in.

Sheer, shocked disbelief had held him paralyzed as he read through the brief, terse communique and the attached copy of the official news release. None of it could possibly have been true! Except that even as he'd told himself that, he'd known that it was. Now the shock had worn off enough to lose its anesthetic edge, and he jerked up out of his comfortable chair with an abruptness which would have startled anyone familiar with the eternally self-possessed exterior he was always so careful to present to the rest of the universe. For a moment, he stood poised, looking almost as if he wanted to physically flee the damning information contained in the report. But, of course, there was nowhere to run, and he licked his lips nervously.

He walked over to the window of his office, his strides jerky, and leaned against the towering panel of crystoplast as he gazed out over the early evening skyline of the City of Landing. The Star Kingdom's capital's air traffic moved steadily against the darkening cobalt vault of the planet Manticore's star-pricked heavens, and he closed his eyes as the serene, jewel-bright chips of light floated steadily about their business. Somehow, the tranquility of the everyday scene only made the report's contents and conclusions even worse.

His brain began to function again, after a fashion. It darted about, like a frightened fish in too small an aquarium, bumping its snout again and again against the unyielding crystal wall which kept it pent. But, like the fish, it found no escape.

There was no point even trying to suppress this information, he realized. It wasn't an agent report, or an analyst's respectfully-phrased disagreement with his own position which could be ignored or conveniently misfiled. In fact, it was little more than a verbatim transcript of Thomas Theisman's own news release. The high-speed courier the agent-in-charge in Nouveau Paris had chartered to get it to him as quickly as possible couldn't have beaten the normal news service dispatch boat by more than a few hours. Perhaps a standard day, at most. Which meant that if he didn't report it to Sir Edward Janacek—and thus to the rest of the High Ridge Government—they would read about it in their morning newsfaxes.

He shuddered at the thought. That prospect was enough to quash any temptation, even one as powerful as the auto-response defensive reaction which urged him to "lose" this particular report the way he'd lost others from time to time. But this one was different. It wasn't merely inconvenient; it was catastrophic.

No. He couldn't suppress it, or pretend it hadn't happened. But he did have a few hours before he would be forced to share it with his fellow space lords and their political masters. There was time for at least the start of a damage control effort, although it was unlikely to be anywhere near as effective as he needed it to be.

The worst part of it, he reflected, as his brain settled into more accustomed thought patterns and began considering alternative approaches to minimizing the consequences, was the fact that he'd assured Janacek so confidently that the Peeps had no modern warships. That was what was going to stick sideways in the First Lord's craw. Yet even though Jurgensen could confidently expect Janacek to fixate on that aspect of the intelligence debacle, he knew it was only the very tip of the iceberg of ONI's massive failure. Bad enough that the Peeps had managed to build so many ships of the wall without his even suspecting they were doing it, but he also had no hard information at all on what sort of hardware they'd come up with to put aboard them.

He thought still harder, pushing the unpalatable bits of

information about, studying them from all angles as he sought the best way to present them.

However he did it, it was going to be . . . unpleasant.

The rest of Honor's staff was waiting on *Werewolf's* flag bridge when she and Mercedes, both now wearing their skinsuits, stepped out of the lift. She nodded to them all, but her attention was on Andrea Jaruwalski.

"Still no reply to the challenge?" she asked. She reached up to rub Nimitz's ears where he sat on her shoulder in his custom-built skinsuit, and he pressed back against her hand. He held his miniature helmet tucked under one mid-limb, and she smiled as the taste of his emotions flowed through her.

"No, Ma'am," Jaruwalski replied. "They're accelerating in-system at a steady four hundred gravities, and they haven't said a word. CIC has managed to refine its data a little further, though. They make it twenty-two superdreadnoughts or dreadnoughts, eight battlecruisers or large heavy cruisers, fifteen or twenty large destroyers or light cruisers, and what looks like four transports."

"Transports?" Honor raised an eyebrow at her operations officer, and Jaruwalski shrugged.

"That's CIC's best guess so far, Ma'am. Whatever they are, they're big, but their wedge strength looks low for warships of their apparent tonnage. So it looks like they're military auxiliaries of some sort, whether they're actually transports or not."

"I see." Honor continued across the flag deck to her command chair and racked her own helmet on its side. Her command station was no more than three long strides from the flag plot, and her small com screen blinked to life as she eased Nimitz down from her shoulder and set him on the back of her chair. Rafe Cardones' face looked out of it at her, and she smiled in welcome.

"Good morning, Rafe," she said.

"Good morning, Ma'am," he responded more formally, and his smile was a bit tighter than hers had been. "It looks like we've got visitors," he added.

"So I've heard," she agreed. "Give me a few minutes to get myself brought up to speed, and we'll decide what sort of welcome mat we want to put out."

"Yes, Ma'am," he said, and she turned her attention to the plot. *Werewolf* was a new ship, and she and her sisters had been designed from the keel out to serve as task force or fleet flagships, so her flag plot's holo sphere was at least two-thirds the size of CIC's master plot. It was less cluttered than the master plot because the automatic filters removed distracting items—like the Marsh System's civilian spacegoing infrastructure—which were both unnecessary and possibly confusing. They could be put back if Honor really wanted to see them, but at the moment she had eyes only for the red icons of unknown starships sweeping steadily inward from the system hyper limit.

"What's their time to Sidemore orbit?" she asked.

"They came out on our side of the primary, Your Grace," Lieutenant Theophile Kgari, her staff astrogator, replied crisply. Kgari's grandparents had migrated to the Star Kingdom directly from Old Earth, and his skin was almost as dark as Michelle Henke's. "They made transit at a very low velocity—no more than a hundred KPS or so, almost directly in-system. But they've been piling on the accel ever since. They translated out of hyper just under—" it was his turn to consult a time readout "—nineteen minutes ago, so they're up to four-point-three-four thousand KPS. Assuming a zero/zero intercept with Sidemore, they'll hit turnover in almost exactly two hours, at which time they'll be up to approximately three-two-point-niner thousand KPS at seven-point-six-five light-minutes from the planet."

"Thank you, Theo," Honor said, turning to smile briefly at him before she returned her attention to the plot. She reached down to caress Nimitz's ears once more as he sat upright on the back of her command chair. She stood that way for several thoughtful seconds, gazing at the light dots in the plot silently, then drew a deep breath, shrugged, and turned to face her staff.

"Until they tell us differently, we'll consider them hostiles," she told them. "It would take a lot of chutzpah for anyone to come in on us with only twenty-two of the wall, but that's not to say someone might not be crazy enough to try it. So we won't take any chances. Andrea," she looked at the ops officer, "this looks like an excellent opportunity to dust off Buckler Bravo-Three, wouldn't you say?"

"Yes, Ma'am, I would," Jaruwalski agreed.

"Mercedes?" Honor asked, cocking her head at her chief of staff, and Brigham frowned ever so slightly.

"As you say, Your Grace, it would take someone with more guts than good sense to take us on with what we've seen so far. The only thing that bothers me about that supposition is that presumably whoever they are, they realize that too. Which leads me to reflect upon that axiom of Admiral Courvoisier's you're so fond of quoting."

"The same thought had occurred to me," Honor told her. "That's why I figure this is a good time to run Buckler Bravo-Three. If it turns out it's only an exercise, well and good. But if it should turn out we need it, I want those pods and those LACs in space and in position when it hits the fan."

"That's more or less what I was thinking, Ma'am," Brigham said. "My only problem is that Bravo-Three takes us out of Sidemore orbit towards them. If it's all the same to you, I'd really prefer Bravo-Two." She shrugged. "I may be being paranoid, but if these really are hostiles and not just terminally stupid friendlies who think it's humorous not to respond to our challenges, then I'd just as soon not be drawn any further from the planet than we have to be."

"Um." Honor rubbed the tip of her nose thoughtfully, considering what the chief of staff had said.

Buckler Bravo-Three called for the task force to advance to meet any potential enemy, closing into extreme Ghost Rider missile range with the ships of the wall behind an advanced screen of LACs. Bravo-Two, on the other hand, kept the ships of the wall in close proximity to Sidemore while LAC scouting forces fanned out to make a more precise ID and, if appropriate, launch the initial attacks independently of the wall. It was the more cautious approach, and the LACs, unlike the capital ships, would have to enter any adversaries' range to engage them. That meant exposing them to potential losses the ships of the wall could avoid, thanks to the range advantage Ghost Rider gave their missile pods. On the other hand, the LACs could go out, make positive identification, and then report back rather than sweeping in to attack automatically, and there ought to be time to bring the wall into range instead if that seemed appropriate.

She considered a moment longer, then nodded.

"I can't think of any good reason for them to be trying to suck us away from the planet—not on the basis of anything we've seen up to this point, anyway. But that doesn't mean there isn't one, and you're right. Bravo-Two will do the job just as well as Three."

She turned her attention to the com screen and her flag captain. "You heard, Rafe?"

"Yes, Ma'am. Bravo-Two, it is. Shall I pass the word to Admiral McKeon and Admiral Truman?"

"Yes, please. And tell them we'll be setting up a four-way com conference in fifteen minutes, as well."

"Aye, aye, Ma'am. I'll see to it."

"Thank you," she said, and slid into her command chair, then rotated it to face her staff once more.

"And now, ladies and gentlemen," she said calmly, "the Chair will entertain theories as to just what these people think they're doing."

Ninety minutes trickled past without a single transmission from the incoming strangers. The transports—or whatever they were— had fallen back, trailing along behind the probable ships of the wall with what looked like three light cruisers or large destroyers riding herd on them. The rest of the unidentified formation simply continued to bore straight in, and tension had ratcheted steadily higher on *Werewolf's* flag deck as the range continued to drop just as steadily.

"Scotty is about fifteen minutes from contact, Ma'am," Jaruwalski reported.

"Has he gotten a visual yet?" Honor asked.

"No, Ma'am," the ops officer admitted with an unmistakable edge of chagrin. "Whoever this is, they're clearly familiar with our remote sensor platform doctrines. They haven't tried to take any of them out, but the formation they've adopted makes that unnecessary . . . so far, at least."

Honor nodded in understanding. The strangers' formation was unorthodox, to say the least. Rather than a conventional wall formation, the capital ships had settled into a roughly spherical alignment, then rotated ever so slightly on their axes. The result was to turn the roofs and floors of their impeller wedges, which had just as powerful a warping effect on visible light as on anything else, outward in all directions. In effect, they had created a series of blind spots directed towards their flanks, which just happened to be where doctrine called for sensor drones to be deployed.

"Has Scotty considered vectoring his drones around behind them for a look up their kilts?" she asked.

There wasn't that much to choose between looking down the throat or up the kilt of an impeller wedge, except that the throat was deeper than the kilt, which gave a sensor drone a better angle on its target. Unfortunately, the forward sensors and point defense armament of a warship were better than those guarding its stern precisely because the throat was more vulnerable than the kilt. Given these people's apparent awareness of the defenders' probable doctrine, it was a fairly safe bet that any drone, however stealthy, which wandered in front of them would be dead meat unless they chose not to kill it.

"Yes, Ma'am, he has," Jaruwalski acknowledged. "But they should be going for turnover in another ten minutes or so."

"Understood," Honor said. When the bogeys flipped to begin decelerating towards Sidemore, they'd turn their own kilts directly towards Scotty's shipboard sensors.

She leaned back in her command chair, with Nimitz curled comfortably in her lap, and let her gaze wander around her flag bridge. The tension was palpable, but her people were functioning smoothly and efficiently under it. None of them had been able to come up with an explanation for the intruders' actions, but from the taste of their emotions, most of them had come to the conclusion that the bogeys were most probably Andermani.

Mercedes and George Reynolds, Honor knew, both suspected that this was one more provocation, this time on a grand scale. A sort of interstellar game of chicken between task forces. Jaruwalski disagreed. She didn't know who these people were, but she was firmly convinced they *weren't* Andies. There was entirely too much potential for someone to panic and start shooting if those were Andermani warships out there, and nothing anyone had reported, including Thomas Bachfisch, suggested that the Andermani could possibly be able to overcome such unfavorable numerical odds. If Honor's staff was aware of that, then surely the Andermani were, as well, and risking that much tonnage and the personnel required to crew those ships just to "send a message" was a far cry from risking a single cruiser here or there. And whatever else the Andies might be, it struck her as extremely unlikely that any senior Andermani officer could be crazy enough to take such a chance. She'd been polite about it, but she'd also made her disagreement with both the chief of staff and the staff spook clear, and Honor smiled ever so slightly at the thought. Then she glanced at the time and date display on the bulkhead, and beckoned to Timothy Meares.

"Yes, Your Grace?" the youthful flag lieutenant said quietly as he stopped beside her command chair.

"I think it's about time, Tim," she told him, equally quietly.

"Yes, Ma'am," he said, and walked casually across the bridge towards Lieutenant Harper Brantley, Honor's staff communications officer.

She watched him go, then turned her head as she tasted a sudden spike in Mercedes Brigham's emotions. Her chief of staff was gazing at her in intent speculation. Speculation that became something else when Honor grinned cheerfully at her. Brigham's eyes narrowed, then snapped from Honor to Meares and Brantley, and Honor felt Nimitz's delighted amusement. Which was only to be expected from someone whose treecat name was "Laughs Brightly," she reflected.

Brigham looked back at Honor and opened her mouth as if to say something, then closed it again and shook her head severely at her admiral, instead.

None of the other staffers had noticed the silent exchange. They were all far too intent on their own duties to pay any attention to Meares' movements or the chief of staff's expression. Nor did they notice when the flag lieutenant bent over Brantley's shoulder to whisper quietly in his ear.

The com officer's head popped up, and he looked incredulously at Meares for just a moment, then darted a half-accusing, half-amused looked at his admiral before he bent back over his console. He murmured something into his hush mike, then leaned back in his chair and crossed his arms.

Nothing at all happened for perhaps ninety seconds, and then quite a lot of things happened in rapid succession.

The incoming bogeys suddenly and simultaneously made turnover over ten minutes early, and as they did their icons began to multiply in the plot. Dozens—scores—of additional light codes appeared, spreading outward like captive constellations, and Honor tasted her staffers' consternation as they recognized what they were seeing. It was a sight they'd seen scores of times over the past three or four T-years; it was just that they'd never seen anyone *else* lunching full deckloads of LACs.

For a few, brief moments consternation (and something just a bit more akin to panic than any of them would ever have admitted) was all they felt as they grappled with the sudden awareness of how far the bogeys' unexpected possession of LACs would go towards evening the tactical imbalance they had assumed favored Task Force Thirty-Four so heavily. But before they could react, the flood of LAC icons began to blink from the crimson of unknown, assumed hostiles to the steady green of friendly units. The color change flowed through the formation in a cascade, one LAC squadron at a time as each of them brought its transponders online. And as each LAC group completed its transition, its mothership's icon blinked to green, in turn.

"Your Grace," Jaruwalski began, "we know those ships! They're—"

She chopped herself off abruptly and turned to favor Honor with a much more old-fashioned glance than the one Brigham and turned upon her as she realized how superfluous her report actually was. Honor returned her look—it would never have done to call it a glare, of course—with her best innocent smile.

"Yes, Andrea?" she said.

"Never mind, Your Grace." For a moment, the ops officer sounded remarkably like a Grayson nanny who had surprised her charges in the act of painting the nursery purple. But then, almost against her will, she began to grin and shook her head at her Admiral.

"Never mind, Your Grace," she repeated, in quite a different tone. "I suppose by now we should all be accustomed to what passes for your sense of humor."

CHAPTER THIRTY

"**I** expected better than this from you, Edward."

Michael Janvier, Baron High Ridge and Prime Minister of Manticore, looked down his aristocratic nose at his First Lord of the Admiralty, and his tone was rich with disapproval. The conference room's smart wall had been reprogrammed to create a moonlit forest glade behind him, but he appeared totally oblivious to the bizarre contrast between its calm tranquility and his own almost petulant expression.

"Not seven months ago," he went on in precisely metered words, "you assured us that the Republic of Haven had no pod-superdreadnoughts. Now you're reporting that they have a minimum of at least sixty in commission . . . which is only four less than *we* have. And, I might add, that they've managed to assemble this force without our so much as suspecting they might be doing so."

He paused, gazing at his First Lord with his best, patented look of disappointment, and Sir Edward Janacek resisted a powerful urge to glare back at him. It was just like High Ridge to try to make this all his fault, he reflected. But of course he couldn't say that. And however typical of the Prime Minister the automatic search for a scapegoat might be, his own position at the Admiralty made him the natural choice for the role in this case, which meant this conference had to be handled very carefully, indeed.

"What I'd like to know," Lady Elaine Descroix put in as the Prime Minister's pause lingered, "is exactly how bad the situation really is."

"Yes," Countess New Kiev agreed. "And not just the military situation, either." She gave the Foreign Secretary a sharp glance, to which Descroix did her best to appear completely oblivious.

"I believe Elaine speaks for all of us, Edward," High Ridge pronounced in those same, measured tones, and Janacek gritted his teeth for a heartbeat or two.

"Obviously," he began once he was confident he could keep his own tone level, "the fact that we've suffered an Intelligence failure on this scale makes any precise estimate of the situation difficult, if not impossible. I have, of course, discussed the nature and extent of that Intelligence failure with Admiral Jurgensen, and I assure you that we will be using every resource available to us in our efforts to repair it."

"Is Jurgensen the right man to be repairing anything?" Descroix asked, and twitched one shoulder when Janacek looked at her. "Whatever else may have happened, Edward, one thing is certain. As you just said, we've suffered an enormous intelligence failure, and Admiral Jurgensen *is* Second Space Lord. Ultimately, the performance of ONI is his responsibility, and it would appear to me that he's failed in it."

"Francis Jurgensen is a dedicated and conscientious officer," Janacek replied. He spoke with careful, deliberate emphasis, every centimeter the First Lord of the Admiralty defending a subordinate, even as he heaved a huge internal sigh of relief that Descroix had pointed her accusing finger at someone besides himself. "Obviously, we're currently engaged in a major reassessment of ONI's performance, and we believe we've already identified several weak links. The majority of them are holdovers from the Mourncreek Admiralty, but I must admit that a substantial percentage of them are people we put into place after assuming office. The problem is that someone can look very good on paper or even on the basis of his past record and still conceal serious weaknesses. Unfortunately, those sorts of weaknesses only become apparent after a failure calls attention to them. That happens fairly frequently in intelligence work, I'm afraid, but this time the failure was rather more . . . spectacular than most.

"I feel it would be inappropriate to relieve Admiral Jurgensen at this time. In part, that's because I believe he deserves an opportunity to correct the problems he's only recently discovered rather than being scapegoated individually for the failures of a great many people. But I also feel that 'changing horses in midstream' is often a serious mistake. Any newcomer as Second Space Lord would start from scratch in his new position. He'd have to learn everything about his job, and there would be an inevitable period of disruption and distraction while he did so. Admiral Jurgensen, on the other hand, already has ample evidence of things which have gone wrong. With that evidence in hand and the intimate familiarity with the mechanics and internal dynamics of his command which he's gained over the last several T-years, I feel he's in a position to offer a continuity and effectiveness any new appointee would find very difficult to match."

"Um." High Ridge frowned, and Janacek waited, his expression calm, while he pondered. Then the Prime Minister nodded slowly.

"I'm not certain I entirely agree with you, Edward," he said pontifically, "but the Admiralty is your shop. And certainly your loyalty to your subordinates is commendable. I would advise you not to allow that loyalty to blind you to realities. Or to create a situation in which someone else's incompetence destroys your own career. But I'm not prepared to overrule you where Jurgensen is concerned at this time."

"Thank you, Michael. I appreciate that," Janacek said gravely, and it was true. He especially appreciated the fact that keeping Jurgensen around offered him a ready-made scapegoat he could blame and—regretfully, of course—sack after all if any other disasters came home to roost.

"In the meantime," the First Lord continued, "and having admitted that, for whatever reason, we've suffered an Intelligence failure of the first magnitude, I would like to point out two things. First, the only source we have for the number and capabilities of the Peeps'—I mean, the Republic's—new ships is Theisman's own news conference. There is absolutely no independent confirmation of any of his claims at this time. Second, the mere fact that they may possess pod-superdreadnoughts doesn't necessarily equate to anything like equal capabilities in combat."

"Are you suggesting that the Republic doesn't, in fact, have the ships it claims it does?" New Kiev managed not to sound overtly incredulous, but her automatic distaste for and distrust of all things military still colored her voice.

"I'm not suggesting anything where numbers of hulls are concerned," he replied, his eyes hard. "I'm simply pointing out that the only numbers we have are the ones Theisman supplied. It's certainly possible he exaggerated those numbers. By the same token, it's equally possible that he underrepresented them, instead."

"Why would he do either of those?" Descroix asked.

"I haven't said he did do either of them." Janacek heard an edge of exasperation creeping into his voice and made himself stop and draw a deep breath. Then he continued. "What I said was that he might have done either of them, and that we wouldn't have any way of knowing which—if either—it was. As to why he might have announced inaccurate numbers, I can think of at least a handful of reasons to go either way. If this is the first step towards a more aggressive and assertive foreign policy, then obviously it would be to the Republic's advantage for its opponents to overestimate its military potential. In that case, telling us that they have more ships than they actually do would be a reasonable piece of disinformation for them to throw out. That might also be true if they're concerned about the possibility of preemptive action on our part. On the other hand, if their objective is to lull us into a sense of false security, then it would make sense for them to understate their actual strength in order to avoid alarming us. For that matter, they might also believe that understating their true strength would cause us to feel less alarmed and so be less likely to act preemptively. The problem, of course, is that we have absolutely no way to know which, if any, of those possibilities might actually be true. That's why I raised the point in the first place. We need to be aware— *all* of us need to be aware—of exactly how limited our current information really is. Not only about these new ships of theirs, but about their possible intentions, as well."

He paused again, this time without grinding his teeth together, and glanced around the conference room. The expressions on the faces looking back at him had become at least a little more thoughtful as he spoke, and he allowed himself to feel a very slight flicker of satisfaction at the evidence that his own reasoned manner was having an effect.

"Whatever their intentions, though," he continued, "the second point I raised is probably the more important one. In the final analysis, ships of the wall are only platforms for weapons. What really matters is the weapons those platforms carry, and at the moment nothing we know suggests that the Republic has somehow managed to overcome the technological gap between our capabilities. While Theisman and Pritchart may have managed to build a shipyard complex somewhere that we didn't know about, the mere fact that a yard exists says nothing about the sophistication of its technical capabilities. It's going to take longer for us to develop that sort of information, but Admiral Jurgensen's technical people have been running continual threat update assessments of the Republic's technology."

He made certain that neither his tone nor his expression revealed his awareness that he was heading out onto thin ice.

"By their most pessimistic estimates, the Republic's R&D is still years from matching our capabilities. In that regard, it's significant that Theisman hasn't claimed that they've managed to put any CLACs into commission. Building the carriers themselves isn't any more difficult than building SD(P)s. In fact, it's a simpler problem in naval design. So the fact that they apparently don't have any of them may well be an indicator that their tech base still isn't up to the task of producing a LAC design good enough to justify building carriers to put it on.

"Obviously, that's nothing more than a hypothesis at this point. We certainly can't prove or *dis*prove it on the basis of the evidence available to us. But if it's true, then it's just one more indication of the wide gap between our basic military technology and theirs, and that's the significant point. Until they can deploy weapons systems which match the range and accuracy of ours—or, perhaps even more important, the defensive capabilities of our electronic warfare systems—the actual tonnage ratios are relatively unimportant."

"Unimportant?" New Kiev repeated. The single word came out with an utter lack of emphasis which, in its own way, was as emphatic as a snort of disbelief.

"*Relatively* unimportant," he corrected in a voice just barely on the warm side of frosty. "Obviously that's not the same thing as 'insignificant,' Marisa. But as Eighth Fleet demonstrated in Operation Buttercup, capability trumps simple numbers. To put it in its simplest possible terms, if our ships can kill their ships at twice their effective range, then it really doesn't matter if they have more hulls than we do. All it does is give our fire control crews more targets."

"I see what you're saying," High Ridge said, and his voice was noticeably warmer than it had been at the beginning of the meeting. Which, Janacek knew, was because he wanted to find his First Lord's reassurances reassuring.

"So do I," Descroix seconded with a vigorous nod.

"I follow your logic," New Kiev agreed, although her voice and manner were considerably cooler than those of her two colleagues. Then she paused for a moment, and Janacek held his mental breath, wondering if she were about to point out the gaping hole in what he'd just said.

"I follow your logic," she repeated, "but even granting all you've just said, I have to admit that the mere fact that they've announced the existence of these ships worries me badly. They've obviously spent years successfully concealing it, given how long it takes to build a ship of the wall, so what inspired them to voluntarily stop concealing it? And why do it at this particular moment?"

Janacek exhaled internally, his attentive expression hiding his enormous relief that she hadn't pointed out that the ONI which was confident of the RMN's technological superiority was the same ONI which had been equally confident of its *numerical* superiority up until approximately thirty-six hours before this meeting.

"I have to admit to concerns of my own in that regard," he told her, and turned to the Foreign Secretary. "I'm not aware of any compelling military reason for Theisman to have made this information public," he said. "Which leads me to suspect that there must be some other consideration which justifies him and Pritchart, at least in their own minds, in making this announcement. Have your people been able to come up with anything in that regard, Elaine?"

Descroix returned his bland gaze with a composure he suspected was equally false. It was obvious that she fully understood his relief at finding another target against which he might direct the attention of their ministerial colleagues. Fortunately, he thought, there wasn't very much she could do about it.

"We haven't had a great deal of time to think about it, Edward," she said with an air of reason. "Given how completely . . . unexpected Theisman's announcement was, none of my diplomatic analysts had seen any reason to allow for anything like it in their evaluations of the Republic's negotiating posture. After all, since no one had even hinted to them that these ships existed, they could hardly have factored them into their analyses, now could they?"

Her sweet smile held more than a hint of malice, and Janacek hid a mental wince as her swift riposte drew blood.

"I've spent several hours conferring with my senior people since we received the news, however," she continued in a tone which added an unspoken "of course" to the sentence. "At the moment, we see two main possibilities where political and diplomatic considerations are concerned.

"First, and simplest, is a possibility you've already raised yourself. It's been apparent for some time that Pritchart has been less than delighted with our refusal to make the ridiculous concessions her negotiators have demanded from us." New Kiev shifted ever so slightly in her chair, but she didn't interrupt, and Descroix went on smoothly. "Our best analyses suggest that Secretary Giancola is even unhappier than she is. In fact, it would be completely unreasonable for us to expect either of them not to be displeased, under the circumstances. After all, one of the realities of interstellar diplomacy is that someone is in the weaker position in almost any negotiation, and since Saint-Just sued for a truce, that someone has been the Republic.

"Obviously, Pritchart and her administration would very much like to change that. They've failed to do so at the negotiating table, and so it's very possible—even probable—that this entire announcement is designed to do so in another venue. If they've been able to offset our military advantage, or even to create a false impression that they've done so, then the entire balance of power shifts. In which case," she transferred her attention from Janacek alone to everyone else around the table, "Edward's suggestion that this might be the first step towards a new, more aggressive foreign policy stance would make perfectly good sense."

"I see." High Ridge nodded thoughtfully, then pursed his lips. "But you said that was the first possibility. What's the second one?"

"The second one," Descroix said, "is that this announcement represents an escalation of a purely internal political agenda."

"How?" New Kiev asked. Descroix glanced at her sharply, and the Chancellor of the Exchequer shrugged. "I'm not discounting the possibility, Elaine. I'm just curious about how an announcement of enhanced military capabilities could affect any sort of domestic agenda."

Her tone was conciliatory, despite the growing antipathy between her and Descroix, and the Foreign Secretary relaxed visibly.

"The internal dynamics of the Republic aren't as clear as we could wish," she said. "In large part, that's because their entire system is so new. In a lot of ways, they're still working out precedents and spheres of authority as they go along, and if *they* don't know exactly where the lines lie, it's even more difficult for us to know. Even so, though, it's pretty clear that Pritchart and Giancola are rivals, despite his membership in her Cabinet. As you know, he ran a fairly respectable campaign against her in the presidential election, and there are several indications that he sees foreign policy as an issue on which he might base an even more effective campaign when she runs for reelection.

"We don't have a formal ambassador to Haven, of course, but we do have extensive third-party contact with their government through several other nations' embassies and consulates. On the basis of that contact, it seems evident to us that Giancola's been pressing Pritchart to assume a more assertive stance in their treaty negotiations. Not only that, but he also appears to be in the process of establishing his own clique within their Congress and the upper tiers of the Administration, and he's using discontent with Pritchart's stance to do it."

"I assume that if we're aware of this, President Pritchart also has to be aware of it." New Kiev's observation came out as a question, and she cocked an eyebrow at Descroix.

"I'm sure she is," the Foreign Secretary agreed.

"In that case," New Kiev asked, "why doesn't she simply fire him as Secretary of State?"

"Probably because she can't," Descroix replied. "She has to consider the balance of power between domestic political factions just as carefully as we do, Marisa. Probably even more carefully, given how . . . unsettled the Republic's internal affairs have been. It's obvious that Giancola has a substantial power base of his own, and she probably figures that she can't afford to openly alienate it. Especially if he has been succeeding in strengthening it."

"All right." New Kiev nodded. "I can see that. But if Giancola's been advocating a more confrontational foreign policy, wouldn't she appear to be giving in to his demands if she adopted one?"

"That would certainly be one way to look at it," Descroix conceded. "On the other hand, she may see it as her best opportunity to undercut his power base by co-opting his position and effectively taking it away from him. Which is why I said that announcing the existence of these new ships could reflect domestic tensions even more than interstellar ones. It's entirely possible that Pritchart does intend to become more aggressive—on the surface, at least—in her negotiating stance, and that she sees Theisman's announcement as a stick she can use against us. But if that's the case, I would be extremely surprised if she were really willing to push us hard."

"Why?" High Ridge asked. "I don't necessarily disagree," he said when she glanced at him. "I'm just curious as to your reasoning."

"As Edward's just pointed out," the Foreign Secretary said after a moment, "the mere fact that they have more ships than we thought they did doesn't necessarily indicate that they've actually managed to equalize the military balance. In fact, now that I've had time to think about it, the fact that Pritchart hasn't already become more assertive in the treaty negotiations is probably an indication that it doesn't. After all, whatever we may or may not have known about their naval building policies, she obviously had full information on them all along. So if she believed these new ships of the wall Theisman's just told the galaxy about really would significantly change the military equation, I doubt that she would have waited this long to stiffen her negotiating stance. Especially not if delaying such a change has permitted Giancola to do any successful empire-building inside her administration.

"Given all of that, I'm very much inclined to think that we're probably going to see a few strongly worded notes and probably some fairly emphatic news releases and press briefings from their State Department over the next few months. But all of that will probably be posturing, intended at least as much for domestic consumption as for us. Certainly, if Pritchart really intended to take a hard line in our negotiations, we'd have seen some sign of it before this."

"I have to say that that makes sense to me," Janacek put in. "And if she were truly insane enough to contemplate some resumption of active operations against us, they would have been much less likely to tell us these ships existed. The mere fact that we know about them enormously reduces the military impact they could have asserted if they'd taken us completely by surprise with them."

High Ridge nodded exactly as if he hadn't expected the First Lord to agree with anything which might make the Admiralty's Intelligence failure look even a little less ominous.

"So what you're basically saying, Elaine," he said instead, "is that you believe we can expect a certain degree of surface agitation but that the fundamental diplomatic equation remains effectively unchanged?"

"I don't know that I'd put it quite that strongly," she temporized cautiously. "That's certainly what I think right now, but at the moment our information about these additions to their navy seems to be extremely incomplete. If it turns out they really have narrowed the military gap—or even if they only think they have, whether or not they're correct—I'd have to reconsider my position."

"That's reasonable," he agreed, and turned back to Janacek.

"Assuming the ship numbers Theisman announced are accurate, and further assuming that the Republic does become more confrontational in the wake of his announcement, then I think it will be incumbent upon us to reconsider our own naval stance," he said. "How soon will you be able to recommend any appropriate changes, Edward?"

"I can't say at this point," Janacek admitted. "It's going to take time for us to verify Theisman's claims, and even longer for us to get any realistic appreciation for possible changes in their hardware. I wish that weren't the case, but it is."

"Couldn't we begin considering possibilities while we go about getting that verification?" For a change, New Kiev's question was untainted by her habitual dislike of the military. She was simply considering their options, and Janacek made himself smile at her.

"Certainly I can—and will—put my people to work considering best-case and worst-case scenarios, Marisa. And I'm sure they'll be able to give me detailed proposals for dealing with either of them. The problem is that once a set of proposals has been presented and adopted, it tends to become self-fulfilling. I think that as important as it is for us to formulate the proper response to the new situation, it's equally important that we not go off half-cocked and adopt radically new policies of our own before we're certain we're justified to do so."

"I fully agree that we need to avoid panicking," High Ridge responded. "But at the same time, we can't afford to do nothing, Edward. For one thing, I think we can be confident that Alexander and White Haven and their cronies are going to insist—loudly—that this news validates their continual criticism of our naval policies."

"I know," Janacek growled in what was very nearly a snarl as the Prime Minister put an unerring finger on a consideration which had occurred to him the instant Jurgensen screened him with the information.

"Well," High Ridge continued, "when they do, we have to be ready to respond. I think it's equally important that we demonstrate not only that we're prepared to realistically modify our policies in the light of new information, but also that our existing policies have been basically sound. Which, of course, they have."

He looked around the conference room, and no one chose to dispute his last sentence.

"I understand." Janacek sighed, and sat back in his chair.

"I'm afraid that the first thing were going to have to do," he said, manifestly unhappily, "is reconsider the present naval budget. I don't want to do it, especially after the amount of grief the Opposition gave us over adopting it in the first place. Worse, I'm not at all convinced at this point that a decision to reconsider it is justified by the actual situation. Unfortunately, we can absolutely count on White Haven, if no one else, to seize upon any excuse to demand that we do so. In light of that, it seems to me that our only real option is to make it clear that we've already done it. If we take the lead ourselves, we can exert more control over the process. And if we present our own suggestions in a reasoned, calm sort of way, we may even be able to make him and his cronies look as hysterical as they actually are."

And, he added to himself, *thank* God *that maniac Harrington isn't here to add* her *voice to the chorus!*

"What sort of 'reconsideration' did you have in mind, Edward?" New Kiev asked, and despite her obvious intention to avoid confrontations with the First Lord, her tone bristled with automatic defensiveness of her cherished programs for "building the peace."

"There's going to be a lot of pressure from the hysterics to begin all sorts of emergency construction programs and major dislocations of existing policies," Janacek told her. "People like White Haven won't really care about the facts; they'll be too busy twisting them to their own advantage to justify the policies they wanted to put in place all along. If we want to prevent them from succeeding, then we're going to have to be willing to propose a more rational set of alternatives which will still soothe the inevitable public . . . disquiet. I have no more desire than you do to disrupt our existing budgetary priorities, Marisa, but we're going to have to propose at least some changes.

"Unless the actual situation is much worse than anything Admiral Jurgensen has so far been able to determine suggests, I think we can reasonably reject the most panicky demands. At the very least, however, we're going to have to announce that we're resuming construction on at least some of the incomplete SD(P)s and CLACs. After all, a large part of our current naval spending priorities was based on the fact that those ships are there, waiting to be finished and commissioned if circumstances warranted it. In fact, I think we'll want to reemphasize that point in order to quell any unjustified panic."

And demonstrate in the process that our policies were sound all along, he did not add aloud.

"Even assuming that Theisman's numbers are accurate, simply completing the ships already under construction will more than offset them," he continued, then snorted harshly. "For that matter, just completing the ships under construction at Grendelsbane would match every modern ship of the wall Theisman says they've built!"

His colleagues relaxed visibly at his assurance. He was relieved to see it, but he was also too experienced a politician not to cover his back.

"At the same time," he cautioned, "there's going to be a window between the time when we authorize resumption of construction and the time the ships are actually completed. I haven't got detailed projections at this point, but the rough estimate from BuShips is that it will take at least six T-months, more probably eight, to reactivate the building slips and assemble the workforce required. In addition, Mr. Houseman, Admiral Draskovic, and I are going to have to go over the manpower numbers very carefully, since it won't do us any good to build ships we don't have the personnel to crew."

"Just how wide is this 'window' of yours likely to be, Edward?" Descroix asked.

"It's not *my* window," Janacek replied. "It's a simple physical limitation we're going to have to live with." He held her eyes levelly for a second or two, then shrugged. "As I say, it will take around six T-months to get construction back underway. After that, we can assume between another six months and a year to complete each existing hull, depending on how advanced its construction was before we halted it. So the window will be from twelve to eighteen T-months wide."

There was a sudden, profound silence in the conference room as all of them were brought face-to-face with the unpalatable numbers. Janacek was hardly surprised, although nothing he'd said should have come as a shock to them. The time lag was an inevitable consequence of their decision to suspend construction in the first place, and he and Houseman had both warned the others about it. They hadn't exactly dwelt on it, of course, but they *had* mentioned it. It was right there, in black and white, in their initial budgetary analysis, which at least meant no one who felt surprised now could blame them for it.

"That's a wider period of vulnerability than I like," High Ridge said finally. He did not, Janacek noticed, ask what the Republic of Haven's shipyards might be producing during that same period. That was a point which had exercised a considerable influence on the First Lord's own thought processes over the last day or so, but if no one else was going to bring it up, he certainly had no intention of doing so.

"I don't much care for it myself, Michael," he said instead. "Unfortunately, there's not much we can do to narrow it. Not by simply increasing our own forces, that is."

"What are you suggesting?" Descroix asked.

"I'm not suggesting anything . . . at this point," Janacek replied. "But we have to be aware of *all* of our alternatives, Elaine."

"And which alternative haven't you already mentioned?" she inquired, gazing at him intensely.

"We could always opt for a preemptive strike on their new ships," he said flatly.

"That would be an act of war!" New Kiev protested instantly, and Janacek ordered himself not to let his contempt show.

"Yes, it would," he acknowledged with massive restraint. "I'd like to point out, however, that legally we're still *at* war with the Republic of Haven. If you've read the transcript of Theisman's news conference, then you know he made that point himself, when one of the newsies asked him why the Pritchart administration had been so secretive about its own naval budget. He was right, too. So to the best of my knowledge, there's absolutely no domestic or interstellar legal obstacle to our resuming military operations at any time we choose."

"But we happen to be in the middle of a truce . . . and negotiating to extend that truce into a permanent treaty!" New Kiev pointed out sharply.

She glowered at Janacek, her nonconfrontational attitude clearly in abeyance as her maternal pride in the truce agreement she had negotiated during her own tenure as Foreign Secretary roused.

"I'm fully aware of that, Marisa," he told her. "And I'm not proposing any sort of attack at this time. I'm simply enumerating all of our potential responses. Personally, I find the notion of resuming active operations the least appetizing of any of them, but I don't think we can afford to overlook it."

"Especially not when it's the Havenites, not us, who have seen fit to destabilize the existing military balance," Descroix put in virtuously. New Kiev turned her attention to the Foreign Secretary, who shrugged. "They can't reasonably expect us to negotiate in good faith under threat, Marisa!"

None of her colleagues saw any reason to point out that all of them had certainly expected the *Republic* to negotiate "under threat."

"But we still have a responsibility to observe the terms of the existing truce," New Kiev argued.

"I'm sure we all agree with that in principle, Marisa," High Ridge said soothingly. Her eyes flashed angrily, but he continued in those same, smooth tones. "As Edward says, however, we have a responsibility as Her Majesty's Government to consider all options and alternatives, don't we?"

New Kiev had opened her mouth, but now she shut it again. Her expression remained thunderous, but she drew a deep breath and nodded, despite her obvious unhappiness with the thought.

"Actually," Janacek said after a moment, "there probably isn't any conflict between the truce terms and the operational requirements of a preemptive strike."

All of them looked at him in varying degrees of surprise, and it was his turn to shrug.

"For obvious reasons, we've paid particularly close attention over at Admiralty House to the terms which bear specifically on military operations," he said. "Those terms require both sides to refrain from hostile actions as long as the negotiations are proceeding. If they *stop* proceeding, then that requirement no longer applies."

"You mean—?" Descroix's eyes widened in speculation as she looked at him, and he smiled thinly.

"Technically, we could decide at any time we wished to break off talks and terminate the truce. Or we could determine that the Republic has already effectively done so."

"In what way?" Descroix asked.

"As you just pointed out, Elaine, they've destabilized the balance by secretly building this new fleet of theirs. Certainly we could argue that such a massive escalation of their war-fighting ability—particularly when we've been unilaterally building down our own naval strength in the interest of reducing tensions and promoting the peace—represents a 'hostile action.' Under those circumstances, we would have every right to act to neutralize that action."

He shrugged again, and New Kiev stared at him in a shock that verged on horror. Descroix and High Ridge, on the other hand, returned his thin smile with broader ones of their own. He was hardly surprised by any of the reactions he'd elicited, but his attention was focused on New Kiev.

"I'm not suggesting that we do anything of the sort, Marisa," he told her in his most reasonable voice. "I'm simply pointing out that if they drive us to it, we have options. To be perfectly and brutally honest, I would advocate launching an attack with no notice at all if I believed the situation were sufficiently desperate to justify it. As it happens, I don't believe that's the case at this point, and I would never suggest doing anything of the sort if the situation *isn't* desperate. But as Michael says, we have a responsibility as Ministers of the Crown to consider all possible avenues of action, however distasteful we may personally find some of them to be."

"Edward is right, Marisa." High Ridge was careful to project an equally calm and reasonable attitude. "No one disputes that we have a responsibility to set an example of proper behavior in our conduct of our diplomacy. Certainly, I would never wish to be the Prime Minister who violates any interstellar agreement to which the Star Kingdom is a party. Any such action must be repugnant to any of us, even when—as Edward has just pointed out—we wouldn't be technically violating anything. At the same time, however, I have to agree with him that under certain circumstances, military necessity clearly trumps any treaty clause or agreement."

New Kiev hovered on the brink of hot disagreement, but then she looked around at the others' expressions and hesitated. And in that moment of hesitation, her urge towards rebellion perished. It was obvious that she couldn't bring herself to agree, but neither was she willing to disagree. Not, at least, while the question remained hypothetical.

"Very well, then," the Prime Minister said briskly as the Chancellor of the Exchequer sank unhappily back in her chair. "Edward and Reginald will begin work immediately to project the necessary budgetary adjustments to respond to the Republic's new ships. Edward, I'll want to see both minimum and maximum projections. How quickly can you have them for us?"

"I can probably have rough numbers for you by tomorrow evening," Janacek replied. "Until we manage to confirm or disprove the accuracy of Theisman's claims, 'rough' is all they'll be, though," he cautioned.

"Understood." High Ridge rubbed his hands together, frowning in thought, then nodded. "All right. While Edward works on that, the rest of us need to concentrate on the spadework to prepare public opinion. We have at most another twelve to eighteen hours before this hits the 'faxes. Between now and then, we have to convene a meeting of the entire Cabinet and prepare an official response to the news. Something that combines the proper balance of gravity and confidence. Elaine, I think you should prepare a separate statement as Foreign Secretary. Marisa, I'd like you to work with Clarence on a more general statement for the Government as a whole."

He watched New Kiev with carefully concealed intensity as he made the request. She seemed to hesitate for just a moment, but then she nodded, and he relaxed internally. She would be far less likely to break ranks with the rest of the Government's position later if she bore formal responsibility for the statement which had announced it in the first place.

"In that case," he said calmly, "I would suggest that we adjourn and get started."

CHAPTER THIRTY-ONE

"How well did we time it, My Lady?" Admiral Alfredo Yu asked. He and Rafe Cardones had arrived in Honor's day cabin together, and now the slender, one-time Peep grinned broadly at his hostess while James MacGuiness began distributing potable refreshments. "I tried not to interrupt your breakfast."

"Mercedes and I were just finishing dessert, actually," Honor told him with an answering smile. She glanced at Brigham, almond eyes twinkling wickedly, and Nimitz groomed his whiskers cheerfully at the other woman from her shoulder.

"And did our arrival come as a pleasant surprise?" Yu asked as he also turned to the chief of staff . . . who'd commanded a division of SD(P)s in the Protector's Own before accepting her position on Honor's staff.

"After we got over the collective heart failure you and Her Grace managed to inflict on all of us," Brigham replied wryly, and shook her head. "I can't believe that neither of you even told *me* this was coming!"

"Well, it wouldn't exactly have been fair to tell you if I didn't tell anyone else on the staff, now would it?" Honor asked, and chuckled at the very old-fashioned look Brigham bestowed upon her.

"Was there a particular reason why you didn't tell the entire staff?" the older woman asked after a moment, and Honor shrugged.

"I suppose not, really," she conceded. "But since none of Alfredo's people knew they were headed out here when they first sailed, it just seemed that it would be . . . I don't know, inappropriate, perhaps, to tell you what they didn't know. Besides," her crooked smile turned impish, "Alfredo and I had already decided all of you could use a little unscheduled drill you didn't know was a drill. And it did get all of us up on our toes, didn't it?"

"I imagine someone given to understatement might put it that way, Your Grace," Cardones agreed in a dust-dry tone. "Not," he continued, turning to Yu, "that we're not all delighted to see you, Admiral."

"I believe Captain Cardones speaks for all of us in that, Sir," Andrea Jaruwalski put in, and shook her head. "You've just more than doubled our strength in both SD(P)s and CLACs, after all!"

"And no one knows you have. Not yet, at least," Brigham observed with profound satisfaction.

"But that cuts both ways," Jaruwalski pointed out. "If the Andies do decide to try something, then the fact that we have Admiral Yu's units to back us up is going to come as a profoundly unhappy surprise for them. But if they did know he was here, then his presence might well . . . dissuade them from any risky adventures."

"The word will get around soon enough," Honor reassured her, then paused to accept a stein of Old Tillman from MacGuiness. She smiled her thanks at the steward and turned back to the ops officer.

"The Silesian grapevine is the only genuinely faster than light means of interstellar communications I've ever encountered, Andrea," she continued. "And, frankly, I'm not at all unhappy at how quickly I expect the word to get out. The secrecy about Admiral Yu's destination wasn't aimed at the Andies in the first place."

"Worried about the Opposition in the Keys, Your Grace?" Brigham asked shrewdly, and Honor nodded.

"That doesn't get mentioned outside 'the family,'" she cautioned, and Jaruwalski, Brigham, and Cardones all nodded in understanding.

"May I ask how long the Protector's Own will be staying?" Jaruwalski inquired after a moment, glancing back and forth between Honor and Yu.

"Until Steadholder Harrington tells us to go home," Yu replied in an emphatic tone. Jaruwalski's expression showed her flicker of surprise at the strength of his response, and he shook his head. "Sorry, Captain. It's just that my instructions from High Admiral Matthews and the Protector were a bit on the . . . firm side."

"I appreciate that, Alfredo," Honor said. "At the same time, though, I don't see how I could justify hanging onto this much of the Protector's Own indefinitely."

"You don't have to justify a thing, My Lady," Yu told her. "Part of our mission profile is to demonstrate our ability to maintain ourselves out of our own resources. That's why we brought along our own supply and service ships. At the moment, we've got everything we need to meet our logistical needs for a minimum of five T-months, and the High Admiral told me that he doesn't expect to see me back until we reach the bottom of the barrel."

"That's very generous of him—" Honor began, only to have Yu interrupt, politely but firmly, before she could complete the sentence.

"He told me that was exactly what you'd say, My Lady. Not that I really needed telling. And he also told me to tell you that you are a vassal of Protector Benjamin, and that as a loyal and obedient vassal you'll take the forces that the Protector chooses to send you, and you'll use them to accomplish the mission which you and the Protector discussed before your departure from Grayson. That was just before he added the bit about 'suffering your liege's displeasure' if you were foolish enough to turn down the reinforcements which both of you know you need."

"He's right, you know, Your Grace," Brigham said quietly. Honor looked at her, and the chief of staff shrugged. "I know you haven't specifically discussed this aspect of our assignment with any of us, but I think I've spent enough time in Grayson service to know what the Protector is thinking. As a Manticoran, I find it humiliating that we need someone else's support. As a Grayson, I can see exactly why the Protector is willing to provide that support. The last thing any of us need is for the situation in Silesia to blow up in all of our faces."

"Whether the Government recognizes that or not," Cardones agreed in an uncharacteristically grim tone.

"Well," Honor said mildly after a moment, a bit taken back, despite her ability to taste their emotions, by her subordinates' emphatic, unanimous agreement with one another, "I don't plan on sending Alfredo home tomorrow morning. For that matter, I don't really plan on sending him home at all until I'm certain the situation out here is under control. And to be completely honest, I expect that situation to work itself out, one way or another, within no more than another three or four T-months. Either the Andies will discover Alfredo's presence here and take it as conclusive proof that the Alliance means business and shelve any plans which might lead to a shooting incident, or else they'll go ahead and shoot anyway."

"And which way to you expect them to jump, My Lady, if I may ask?" Yu asked quietly.

"I wish I could tell you that," Honor replied.

"Now what do we do?"

Arnold Giancola looked up from the display of his memo pad as his brother asked the plaintive question. He hadn't heard Jason come in, and he grimaced as he realized his brother had just stepped in from the outer office . . . and that the door was standing wide open behind him.

"I think it might be a good idea if you came in and closed the door, first," he suggested testily. "I realize it's after hours, but I, for one, would just as soon not share our discussions with whoever happens along down the hallway."

Jason flushed at the acid tone, but it was one with which he had an unfortunate degree of familiarity. Arnold had never been a particularly patient individual, and he'd become progressively less patient over the past two T-years or so. In this instance, however, Jason had to admit he had a point, and he hastily stepped forward to clear the powered door's sensors and allow it to close.

"Sorry," he half-muttered, and Arnold sighed.

"No, Jase," he said, shaking his head ruefully. "I shouldn't have bitten your head off. I guess I'm even more irritated than I thought I was."

"I wouldn't be surprised if you were," Jason said, and produced an off-center smile. "Seems like every time we turn around someone's giving one of us a fresh reason to be pissed off, doesn't it?"

"Sometimes," Arnold agreed. He tipped back his chair and squeezed the bridge of his nose. It would have been nice if he could have squeezed the overwhelming sense of fatigue out of himself, but that wasn't going to happen.

Jason watched him for several seconds. Arnold had always been the leader. Partly that was because he was over ten T-years older than Jason was, but Jason was honest enough to admit that even if their ages had been reversed, Arnold would still have been the leader. He was smarter than Jason, for one thing, and Jason knew it. But more importantly, he possessed something that had been left out of Jason's personality. Jason wasn't entirely certain what that "something" was, but he knew it gave Arnold a spark, a presence. Whatever it was, it lay at the heart of the almost frighteningly powerful magnetism Arnold could exert upon those around him when he chose.

Well, upon almost all of those around him. Eloise Pritchart and Thomas Theisman appeared remarkably resistant to what several of their congressional allies referred to as the "Giancola Effect." Which unhappy reflection brought Jason back to the purpose of his visit.

"What do we do now?" he repeated, and Arnold lowered his hand to look up at him.

"I'm not sure," the Secretary of State admitted after a moment. "I hate to admit it, but Pritchart and Theisman completely surprised me with that news conference. I guess they were more alert to where I was headed than I thought they were."

"Are you sure? I mean, it could have been a genuine coincidence."

"Sure it could," Arnold said acidly. "But if you think it was, I've got some bottomland I'd like to sell you. Just don't ask me what it's on the bottom of!"

"I didn't say I thought it *was* a coincidence," Jason said with some dignity. "I only said that it could have been, and it could have."

"In the theoretical sense that *anything* could be a coincidence, you probably have a point, Jase," Arnold replied a bit more patiently. Not a lot, but a bit. "In this particular case, though, it had to be deliberate. They knew we'd been talking to people, and they must have suspected that we were just about ready to announce the existence of the new ships ourselves. So Pritchart had Theisman make the announcement instead as a way to take the wind out of our sails."

"McGwire asked me about her speech," Jason told him, and

Arnold grunted. The mysterious speech all of the news services planned to carry live from Eloise Pritchart's presidential office the next evening was another source of his current unhappiness.

"He wanted to know what she intends to announce," the younger Giancola continued, then shrugged. "I had to tell him I don't really know. I don't think that was what he wanted to hear."

"No, I doubt it was," Arnold agreed. He swiveled his chair gently from side to side for two or three seconds, gazing at his brother contemplatively, then shrugged. "I haven't seen a draft of her speech, but based on a few things she's said to me over the last week or so, I have a pretty shrewd notion of what she plans to say, and I can't say I'm exactly thrilled by it."

"You think she's going to talk about the negotiations with the Manties, don't you?" Jason said.

"I think that's exactly what she's going to talk about," Arnold acknowledged. "And I think she's going to tell Congress—and the voters—that she intends to pursue an actual peace treaty with considerably more vigor. Which is why there's no way in Hell Theisman's news conference was a coincidence."

"I was afraid that was what she was going to say," Jason admitted. He sighed. "She's taking your position away from you."

"Tell me something I don't already know." Arnold snorted. "It has to be Pritchart, too. She's a much better political tactician than Theisman. Besides, Theisman was our best ally as far as timing the announcement of the new fleet elements was concerned. He was so obsessed with maintaining operational security that we could have counted on him to keep his mouth shut until we were completely ready to go public. No, it was Pritchart. She overruled him, and now, like you say, she plans to co-opt my position on the negotiations."

"Is there anything we can do about it?" Jason asked.

"Not that I can think of right off the top of my head." Arnold's voice was sour. "I'm beginning to wonder if maybe she didn't deliberately let me entirely commit myself on the issue. Maybe she was just giving me enough rope to be sure I hung myself with every insider in Nouveau Paris. Everyone we've talked to knows exactly where I stand, and now that she's going to very publicly give me what I wanted all along, it cuts the legs right out from under any opposition to her I could mount."

He tipped his chair even further back and gazed up at the ceiling, eyes slightly unfocused in thought, and Jason watched him silently. He knew better than to interrupt his brother when he was thinking that hard, so he found himself a chair and sat down to wait it out.

It took a while, but finally Arnold's eyes dropped back into focus, and he smiled at Jason. It was unkind, but true, that Jason wasn't exactly the sharpest stylus in the box. He was loyal, energetic, and enthusiastic, but on his best day, no one had ever accused him of having an excess of intellect. There were times when he let his enthusiasm get the better of him, and he was entirely capable of putting his foot squarely into his mouth. And, to be honest, he had a way of asking irritating questions—the sort which either had no answer at all, or whose answer was so blatantly obvious any moron ought to know what it was without asking. But at the same time, there was something about him, something about those selfsame irritating questions, which had a way of striking sparks in Arnold's own thinking. It was as if the need to figure out how to explain things to his brother caused his own thoughts to gel magically.

Jason sat up straighter as Arnold smiled at him. He knew that expression, and his flagging spirits perked up instantly.

"I think, Jase, that I've been coming at this the wrong way ever since Theisman opened his mouth," Arnold said thoughtfully. "I've been thinking about the way Pritchart is about to try to take over my own position and squeeze me out. But when you come right down to it, she can't. Not as long as I'm Secretary of State. She can try to take credit for any success our negotiations might achieve, and she can try to convince the public that she's the one who decided to take a firmer position with the Manties. But in the end, I'm the one who's going to be carrying out those negotiations."

"So she's going to have to share at least some of the credit for any successes with you," Jason said, nodding slowly.

"Well, yes, she is," Arnold agreed. "But that isn't really what I was thinking about." Jason looked confused, and Arnold grinned. "What I was thinking about," he explained, "was that any communication with the Manties is going to pass through my office. Which means that what I really need to be concentrating on is the opportunity that offers to put my own little imprint on things."

Jason still looked less than totally enlightened, and Arnold decided not to be any more specific. Not yet. In fact, he almost wished he hadn't said as much as he already had, given Jason's propensity for occasionally blurting out things at inconvenient moments.

Fortunately, Jason was accustomed to leaving the heavy intellectual lifting to him. It wasn't really necessary to explain things at this point. Indeed, it might be just as well not to explain them at all. Jason was very good at carrying out instructions, as long as those instructions were specific and uncomplicated, so perhaps it would be wisest not to burden him with more than he absolutely needed to know.

Jason was also accustomed to the way Arnold wandered off into his own thoughts, and he was perfectly content to sit and wait in companionable silence for however long it took for Arnold to complete the process and remember his presence. Which was just as well, since Arnold was very busy thinking indeed just now.

Yes, indeed. He'd been overlooking his greatest single advantage all along. Or, no, not "overlooking" it precisely. He just hadn't realized how big an advantage it truly was if he handled it properly. But now that it had occurred to him, he could see all sorts of possibilities. The public might be gulled into believing any new, assertive negotiating stance was Eloise Pritchart's idea, not Arnold Giancola's. But whatever the public might be prepared to think, Arnold knew that, in the end, and despite any confidence she might project through her much-anticipated speech, Pritchart lacked the intestinal fortitude to go to the mat with the Manties if that was what success required. If it came down to going eyeball-to-eyeball with the real possibility of a resumption of hostilities, Pritchart—and Theisman—would blink and let the damned Manties walk all over them all over again.

But Arnold had spent too much time dealing directly with the Manticoran negotiators and corresponding personally with Elaine Descroix. He knew that if the Republic only had the guts to really turn the screws on them, it was the Manties who would blink. Baron High Ridge, Lady Descroix, and Countess New Kiev between them had the moral fortitude of a flea and the spine of an amoeba. It might have been different when Cromarty was Prime Minister, but that had been then, and this was now, and the present Manticoran government was composed of pigmies.

So the trick was going to be stage-managing things properly.

He had to create the right atmosphere, the right confluence of events. A situation in which anyone who didn't know the Manties as well as he did would believe the resumption of hostilities *had* to be the next step in the process . . . unless the Republic conceded every single thing they demanded. If he could generate a situation which gave Pritchart her opportunity to cave in and reveal her lack of grit to the electorate while simultaneously allowing him to step into the breach her indecision created and push things to a successful conclusion despite her . . .

Oh, yes. He smiled deep inside at the alluring prospect. It would be tricky, of course. He'd have to find a way to lure her into provoking the proper response from the Manties, but that shouldn't be too difficult, given the arrogance which was so much a part of High Ridge and Descroix. Of course, he'd need to find someone reliable he could assign as his direct contact with the Manties, especially since he might have to do a little . . . creative editing here and there. Whoever passed on those communiques would have to be in the loop and prepared to support the process, but he rather thought he had the perfect candidate for that job.

Of course, if it did become necessary to do any editing he'd have to be careful to see to it that that busybody Usher didn't find out what he was up to. After all, if the President wanted to get picky about it, what he was thinking about might technically be illegal. He'd have to check on that. Maybe Jeff Tullingham could advise him if he was careful to keep his inquiry sufficiently hypothetical? But illegal or not, it would certainly be embarrassing—possibly terminally so—if anyone ever figured out just how he'd shaped the international situation. But in the end, he would emerge as the iron-willed, insightful statesman who'd seen what was needed and done it despite the interfering instructions of the nonentity who happened to hold the presidency.

Of course, part of the trick would be to copper his bets by making *certain* the Manties wouldn't actually be willing to go back to war when Pritchart thought they would. But there was a way to see to it they were suitably distracted.

Now then, he thought. *The* first *thing to do is to invite the Andermani ambassador to lunch. . . .*

CHAPTER THIRTY-TWO

" **. . .** The excitement we all feel at this historic moment. The honor of speaking for the entire Star Kingdom, of somehow finding the words to express the pride Her Majesty's subjects all feel in our incomparable scientific community on an occasion such as this, does not come often to any political leader, and I approach it with mingled pride and anxiety. Pride that it has fallen to me to attempt to speak aloud what all of us feel at this moment, and anxiety for how inadequate I know any words of mine must be. Yet I take courage from the reflection that, in the end, anything I may say will be only the first words spoken. They will be far from the last, and as the citizens of the Star Kingdom add their own, far more worthy thanks to my own, I know that . . ."

"My God," T.J. Wix muttered out of the corner of his mouth. "Is he *never* going to shut up?!"

Jordin Kare and Michel Reynaud, seated to either side of him, managed not to glare repressively at him. They also managed not to grin in appreciative agreement with his plaintive tone . . . which was considerably more difficult. They sat with him on the raised stage of the press room, behind the lectern and the tall, narrow, stoop-shouldered form of the Prime Minister of Manticore, listening to his apparently interminable speech, and not one of them would have accepted the invitation to this prestigious moment if he'd had any choice in the matter.

452

Unfortunately, none of them had. And equally unfortunate, Kare reflected, was the fact that the High Ridge Government had found itself in greater need than usual of a public relations windfall at precisely the wrong moment.

I don't suppose we ought to have expected anything else out of them, he reminded himself. *Not that knowing what was coming would have made it any better.*

The Prime Minister and his First Lord of the Admiralty had suffered a sharp downtick in their popularity and job approval ratings when the HD footage of Secretary of War Theisman's Nouveau Paris news conference reached the Manticoran public. The public's reaction hadn't been as severe as it might have been, but it had been undeniably sharp, and the Centrists and Crown Loyalists had done their best—with some initial success—to capitalize upon it.

Kare had entertained at least a faint hope that the shock of the news might weaken High Ridge's grip on power, and he supposed it could still have a cumulative effect in that direction. But damaging as the revelation of the Peeps' new naval capabilities might have been, it was obviously insufficient to do the job by itself.

It was difficult for the astrophysicist to keep his own highly disrespectful thoughts from shadowing his attentive expression as he sat watching the Prime Minister speak into the lenses of the newsies' HD cameras, but he managed. He didn't have much choice. Besides, disgusting as he might find High Ridge, he didn't have a great deal more respect for his fellow citizens, either. In any reasonably run universe, the Manticoran electorate and even—God help them all—the Manticoran peerage ought to have been smart enough to rise up in revolt now that the consequences of the High Ridge-Janacek naval policies had become manifest. In the universe they actually occupied, things hadn't quite worked out that way.

Although he knew his rabbi would disagree, Kare had often suspected that the Manticoran domestic political arena was the direct present-day heir of the same divine thinking which had led to the *Book of Job.* Certainly he couldn't think of anything besides a deliberate decision on God's part to turn the Devil loose on hapless humanity under carefully delimited conditions which could explain the current political process in the Star Kingdom.

He scolded himself, more dutifully than out of any sense of conviction, for being too hard on the Manticoran public. Up until the past few weeks, after all, there'd been plenty of evidence which could be adduced to support the thesis that the war was over. Not a shot had been fired in almost four T-years, and there was no immediate prospect of that changing. And even leaving aside the obvious assumption on the Government's part that the Peeps had been licked once and for all, there'd been the heady assurance that if the Peeps had been foolish enough to start something new, the technical and tactical supremacy of the Royal Manticoran Navy would crush them with ease. Not to mention the fact that the generally conciliatory tone the Republic's diplomatic teams had pursued in the peace negotiations had been another example which could be cited by proponents of the theory that peace had actually come, whether it had been sealed by a formal treaty yet or not. Kare hadn't happened to subscribe to that theory himself, but he could readily understand why it had been so attractive to the public at large. After the pain, losses, and fear of fighting the war, it would have been profoundly unnatural for people *not* to have wanted to believe that the killing and the dying were over. The inevitable (and proper) need of individuals to focus on their individual concerns, to worry about the day-to-day details of their own lives, jobs, and families, only made the electorate's willingness to turn its attention to domestic concerns even stronger.

On the other hand, there'd also been plenty of countervailing evidence for people with the will to see it. And there'd been plenty of people like Duchess Harrington, Earl White Haven, and William Alexander who'd pointed that out. Unfortunately, in some ways the very strength and determination with which they'd made their case undermined it with those who weren't already disposed to share their views. If a politician was unscrupulous enough, it wasn't all that difficult for him to make his opponents look obsessed and vaguely ridiculous, or at least terminally alarmist, when they kept hammering away with warnings that the sky was falling.

Until, that was, Kare thought grimly, the sky finally came crashing down.

In his book, that was exactly what had happened the moment Thomas Theisman admitted that the Republican Navy had virtually completely rebuilt its war-fighting capabilities, apparently without anyone in the High Ridge Government even suspecting they were doing it. A sizable chunk of the electorate appeared to be inclined to agree with him, but not a large enough one. Government spokesmen—and especially "nonpartisan" representatives from the so-called strategic think tank of the Palmer Institute—had instantly begun providing tranquilizing public statements to prove things weren't really as bad as they seemed to be, and those statements were already beginning to have their effect. Even if they hadn't been, any immediate alarm on the part of the voters was completely unable to affect the Government's control of the House of Lords.

And then, of course, there was Jordin Kare's personal contribution to sustaining the High Ridge Government in power.

It became momentarily more difficult not to scowl ferociously as that thought flowed remorselessly through his brain. It wasn't really his fault any more than it was Wix's, but the timing of this first manned transit of the newly discovered terminus could not have come at a more propitious moment for Michael Janvier and his henchmen. The Government's spin strategists had recognized that instantly, and their successful drive to capitalize upon it had survived even the Prime Minister's unpleasant, droning voice and interminable speeches.

Which was what had brought all of them to this particular news conference.

" . . . and so," High Ridge said finally, "it is my enormous pleasure and privilege to introduce to you the brilliant scientific team responsible for making this momentous breakthrough so much more rapidly than even they were prepared to predict might be possible."

It was really a pity, Kare thought, that even at a moment like this High Ridge was unable to project the image of anything but the supercilious aristocrat presenting the unusually clever lowborn servants who had somehow stumbled into doing something of actual value. The man was clearly trying. Worse, from the smile painted onto his vulpine face, he seemed to think he was succeeding. The man had all the personality and spontaneity of an overaged cake of warm *gefilte* fish.

The Prime Minister half turned to sweep his right hand in an arc at the three men seated behind him. It was somehow typical of him that he should refer to them collectively as the "scientific team," completely overlooking the fact that what Michel Reynaud actually was was the extraordinarily competent administrator who'd somehow kept the RMAIA functioning despite the technical illiterates with which his own staff had been lumbered.

Or perhaps he hadn't "overlooked" anything. Perhaps he was deliberately choosing to ignore Reynaud for some reason. His next words certainly suggested that he was, anyway.

"Ladies and gentlemen of the press, I present to you Dr. Jordin Kare and Dr. Richard Wix, the extraordinary intellects responsible for this historic moment."

Kare and Wix rose as the assembled dignitaries and newsies broke into applause. The fact that the applause was genuine, that the press corps of the Star Kingdom was as excited and eager as even the Prime Minister could have wished, only made it worse. Kare managed to smile, and he and Wix both inclined their heads in acknowledgment of the clapping hands. It was more of a semi-bob than a bow on Wix's part, but at least he'd tried.

The Prime Minister beckoned for the two of them to join him at the podium in what was clearly intended as a spontaneous gesture of invitation. Kare gritted his teeth and obeyed it, as did Wix . . . after a surreptitious elbow-jab in the ribs. Kare's smile became a trifle more fixed as the applause redoubled. It was extraordinarily perverse of him, he reflected, that he should feel equally irritated by the Prime Minister's invincible aura of aristocratic dismissal of anyone else's competence, on the one hand, and by the other man's hyperbolic praise of his own sheer brilliance, on the other. He was entirely too well aware of how huge a part good fortune, not to mention the hard work of all the other members of the RMAIA research staff, had played in the chain of discoveries and observations leading to this moment.

"Dr. Kare will now offer a brief summary of his team's progress and immediate plans," High Ridge announced as the applause finally faded. "After that, we will entertain questions from the ladies and gentlemen of the press. Dr. Kare?"

He beamed at the astrophysicist, and Kare smiled back dutifully. Then it was his turn to turn to face the audience.

"Thank you, Prime Minister," he said. "Ladies and gentlemen of the press, I'd like to welcome you here aboard *Hephaestus* on behalf of the Royal Manticoran Astrophysics Investigation Agency, its scientific team, and its Director, Admiral Reynaud." He turned his head to smile at Reynaud, then returned his attention to the spectators.

"As you know," he began, "over the past two and a half T-years, we've been engaged in the systematic search for additional termini of the Manticore Wormhole Junction. It's been a painstaking process, and a time-consuming one. But thanks in no small part to the observations and diligent work of my colleague, Dr. Wix, and to a quite disproportionate amount of pure good fortune, we are considerably ahead of any schedule we could have realistically projected as little as six, or even four, months ago. In fact, we are now in a position to dispatch a properly manned survey ship through the Junction's seventh terminus.

"That ship will depart from the Manticore System next Thursday." The entire audience seemed to inhale simultaneously, and he produced his most genuine smile of the entire news conference. "Precisely where it will depart to, and precisely when it will return, are questions I will not be able to answer today. No one will . . . until the ship and its crew have done both of those things. If you have any other questions, however, I'll do my best to answer them."

"Excuse me, Ma'am. I apologize for interrupting, but you wanted to know when the Secretary of War's pinnace was fifteen minutes out."

"Thank you, Paulette." Shannon Foraker looked up from her earnest conversation with Lester Tourville and smiled briefly at her flag lieutenant. "Please inform Captain Reumann that we'll be joining him in the boat bay momentarily."

"Of course, Ma'am," Lieutenant Baker murmured and withdrew from the day cabin almost as unobtrusively as she'd entered it.

Foraker turned back to her guests. Tourville half-reclined in the cabin's largest chair with all of his usual loose-limbed, casual ease. No one had seemed inclined to dispute his possession of it . . . particularly since it was positioned directly under an air return. Javier Giscard sat rather more neatly in his own chair, his mouth quirked in a fond half-smile as he watched the tendrils of smoke wreathing up from Tourville's cigar towards the ventilator grille. Their chiefs of staff formed the perimeter of the conversational group along with Captain Anders, but Commander Clapp, the most junior officer present, sat directly to Foraker's right. It probably wasn't evident to anyone who didn't know him as well as she did, but the commander was clearly more than a little uncomfortable at finding himself in such high-ranked company. Not that he'd allowed any trace of that to color the informal briefing he'd just given Tourville and Giscard.

"Obviously," Foraker told the two senior admirals as the hatch closed behind Baker, "we're going to have to head on down to the boat bay shortly. Before we do, though, did you have any more questions you wanted to ask Mitchell?"

"Not really. Not any specific ones, anyway," Tourville replied. "I'm sure some questions will occur to me eventually, but for now I think I need to spend some time digesting what he's already told us. Javier?"

"That sums up my own reaction pretty well, I think," Giscard agreed. "But I would like to say, Commander Clapp, that what you've already told us is impressive. To be perfectly honest, I'll be much happier if we never have to put your doctrine to the test, but the fact that we've got it if we need it is a vast relief."

"I'm flattered that you think that, Sir," Clapp said after a moment. "But as I keep pointing out, however well it may have performed in the sims, it hasn't been tested under real-world conditions."

"Understood." Giscard nodded. Then he shrugged. "Unfortunately, the only way to test it in the real world is to find ourselves back in a shooting war with the Manties. That may be going to happen whether we want it to or not, but just between you and me, I'd like to go on being short of real-world test results for as long as possible."

"I'm sure we all would, Sir," Foraker agreed, then glanced at her wrist chrono and made a small face. "And now, I'm afraid, we really do have to head for the lift."

Thomas Theisman didn't have to be a mind reader to recognize the disciplined anxiety behind the faces of the three admirals assembled in *Sovereign of Space*'s flag briefing room to meet with him and Admiral Arnaud Marquette, the chief of the Naval Staff which Theisman had painfully rebuilt after its predecessor's destruction in the McQueen coup attempt. The five admirals were alone, aside from the fleet commanders' chiefs of staff and his own senior military aide, Captain Alenka Borderwijk, and he knew Tourville and Giscard, at least, had been a little surprised by his decision to exclude everyone else. Foraker hadn't, but then, he'd spoken directly with her when *Sovereign of Space* first arrived in the Haven System. Tourville and Giscard might look a bit anxious at the departure from the norm; Foraker, despite her best effort to conceal it, looked a *lot* anxious because she already knew—or suspected—the reason for that departure.

"First," the Secretary of War said after everyone was seated, "let me apologize for the somewhat unusual circumstances of this conference. I assure you all that I'm not trying to be melodramatic, and that I don't think I'm allowing my megalomania or paranoia to get the better of me. On the other hand," his smile was thin, but it carried an edge of genuine humor, "I could be wrong about that."

"Well, Tom," Tourville said with the answering lazy grin permitted to the Republican Navy's third ranking flag officer, "I seem to remember an old saying. Something about sometimes even paranoiacs having real enemies. Of course, I can't speak to the megalomania question."

"How unwontedly tactful of you," Theisman murmured, and all his junior admirals chuckled. The amusement barely touched their eyes, however, and the Secretary of War leaned slightly forward in his chair.

"All joking aside," he said quietly, "one of the main reasons I wanted to come out here with Arnaud to talk to all three of you at once, face-to-face, instead of inviting you down to the New Octagon, was to keep any newsies from realizing we were talking at all. And another, frankly, is my confidence that we can control the information flow and guarantee security here. Not just against the Manties, either, I'm afraid."

Tourville and Giscard tightened almost visibly, and the temperature in the briefing room seemed to drop perceptibly. Theisman bared his teeth in a grimace which could never have been confused for an expression of amusement, because he knew exactly what sort of memories and resonances his last sentence had to have provoked in officers who had survived both State Security and his own coup.

"Don't worry, the President—" he bestowed a brief, genuine smile on Giscard "—knows exactly where I am, and exactly what I'm going to be talking to you about. In fact, she sent me. And, no, she's not planning a *coup d'état*, either. In some ways, it might be simpler if we were, but neither of us is that far along towards throwing out the baby with the bathwater."

"Well, that's a relief, anyway," Giscard murmured. "And it's not *much* more frustrating than the vague hints and dark mutterings in Eloise's last few letters to me, either," he added pointedly.

"Sorry," Theisman said sincerely, and waved his right hand at Marquette and Captain Borderwijk. "Alenka's brought along a full briefing packet for each of you, and before we head back to Nouveau Paris, Arnaud and I want to hold at least one general session with all of your senior staffers. But I wanted us to meet with just the six of you first, because it's particularly important that all of us be on the same page before we start bringing your staffs into it."

He tipped his chair back, propped his elbows on the chair arms, and folded his hands across his midsection. For just a moment, as his facial muscles relaxed, the admirals saw the fatigue and worry the animation of his expression normally cloaked. Then he inhaled sharply and began.

"All of you know that, left to my own devices, I still wouldn't have admitted the existence of Bolthole or any of the new ships. Shannon's done a miraculous job at the yards, and people like Captain Anders and Commander Clapp have performed more than a few minor miracles of their own along the way. Despite that, I think everyone in this briefing room has to be aware of the fact that our capabilities on a ship-for-ship basis continue to lag behind those of the RMN. I hope to God all of us are, at any rate!

"Unfortunately, what I wanted—or any of us wanted—doesn't really matter. Thanks to domestic political considerations, like the empire-building ambitions of a certain Secretary of State who shall remain nameless, the President and I found ourselves with no option but to go public with the new fleet. What we haven't yet told Congress, although I feel confident that some of them at least suspect the announcement is coming in the President's speech tonight, is that she also feels we have no option but to adopt a more aggressive stance in our negotiations with the Manties."

His gaze swept over all of them, but it settled on Giscard, and his eyes held the admiral's steadily as he continued.

"I'm not at all certain I agree with her reasoning. I can't really offer a better plan, however. And even if I could, the fact is that she's the *elected* President, and that means policy is hers to make, not mine. To be perfectly honest, that principle is important enough that even if I vehemently disagreed with her, I'd shut up and carry out my orders when she gave them.

"In this instance, those orders were to announce the improvements in our combat capabilities in a way which was certain to catch the Manties' attention as publicly as possible. And they were also to prepare—as unobtrusively as possible—to meet and defeat any preemptive strike Janacek and Chakrabarti might be inclined to launch. And as a third point, they were to prepare the best possible plan for a renewed general war with the Star Kingdom of Manticore."

If the temperature had seemed to drop earlier, now it was as if an icy wind had blown through the briefing room. The fleet commanders and their chiefs of staff sat very, very still, eyes fixed on the Secretary of War. Only Marquette, Borderwijk, Foraker, and Anders had known what he was about to say; the other four looked as if they wished they had never heard it.

"Let me emphasize," Theisman went on in a firm, quiet voice, "that neither the President nor I are actively contemplating operations against the Manties. Nor do we have any desire to contemplate them at any time. But it's our responsibility to be certain that if something goes wrong, the Navy is prepared to defend the Republic."

"I'm sure all of us are relieved to know we're not planning to attack the Manties," Tourville said. "However, I'm also sure that everyone in this compartment recognizes that however much the current tech balance may favor them, at the moment the overall military balance is probably as close to favoring us over them as it's ever going to get."

"I take your meaning, Lester. And I agree with you," Theisman said after a moment. "In fact, that's one of the main reasons I announced only the existence of the new ships of the wall, not the CLACs. And why I understated the number of SD(P)s we have in commission, as well. Obviously, I didn't want to panic Janacek into recommending that the Manties do something foolish and preemptive. But the longer we can keep them unaware of our true capabilities, the longer they'll be less likely to begin *any* vigorous countermeasures. Which, hopefully, translates into a longer period in which we can maintain whatever military edge we currently have."

"I don't know how 'vigorous' their countermeasures are likely to be, assuming they don't go for a military option," Giscard observed. "But all they really have to do to offset any edge we may have is to complete all of those damned SD(P)s and CLACs they laid down before the Cromarty Assassination."

"Exactly," Theisman agreed. "I'm hoping, probably with more optimism than rationality, that High Ridge will authorize as small an increase in naval spending as he thinks he can get away with. That would extend our window of relative naval security."

"I think you're right about optimism getting the better of reason, Tom," Giscard replied. "Not necessarily about how High Ridge's priorities would work out if he were left to his own devices, but about how likely we are to be able to keep Manty intelligence in the dark about our true capabilities indefinitely. I know we seem to've kept the wool pulled over their eyes for a lot longer than I would have thought we could have, but the cat's out of the bag now. They know we fooled them, and that's going to make them even more determined to get at the real numbers. Even someone like Jurgensen is going to be able to form a much more realistic estimate of our total ship strength than we'd like if he makes it the number one priority of their ONI."

"I know," Theisman admitted. "And all I'm really hoping to do is to delay that moment for as long as possible. Our own building programs are continuing to accelerate out at Bolthole. And Shannon—" he smiled at Foraker "—tells me that she's shaved another three months off the projected construction schedules for the new *Temeraire*-class units. So if we can just keep them from laying down new construction of their own for the next two or three T-years, I think we'll probably be in a position to stay ahead of them, or at least even with them, in effective naval power no matter what they may do.

"But there's no denying that we face both a window of opportunity and a window of vulnerability," he continued in a graver voice. "The window of opportunity is defined by however long we can keep the Manties from realizing our actual military potential and taking steps to neutralize it. The window of vulnerability is the period in which the Manties have time to neutralize it if they decide to do so. The most dangerous aspect of the entire situation, in many ways, is that the awareness of our opportunity makes it very tempting for us to take action in order to close the window of vulnerability. Frankly, that temptation becomes even stronger whenever I consider our responsibility to devise a general war-fighting plan with the Manties as our most probable opponent."

"That's a very dangerous temptation, if you'll allow me to say so, Tom," Tourville said in the quiet voice which always seemed so startling, even to his intimates, in contrast to his public "cowboy" persona. "Especially since I'm sure that somewhere deep inside, at least a part of a great many of our officers and enlisted personnel would not so secretly like to get a little of our own back against the Manties."

"Of course I'll allow you to say it," Theisman told him. "In fact, I'm delighted to *hear* you say it. I assure you that it's something I'm trying very hard to keep in mind at all times, and having other people remind me of it can't hurt.

"Nonetheless, I think it behooves us all to admit that if worse came to worst and we went back on active operations against the Manties, our best option at this point would be to adopt a basically offensive stance. Particularly now, while they're hopefully unaware of our true potential, a hard, carefully coordinated offensive offers us at least the potential of neutralizing their fleet and driving them back onto the defensive in a way which might convince them to negotiate seriously with us for the first time.

"No one in the administration, with the possible exception of the Secretary of State, would even consider suggesting that we run such military risks in an effort to unjam the diplomatic process. I'm certainly not proposing that we do any such thing, either. I'm simply pointing out that when it comes to devising war plans, I feel we need to look very closely at the advantages of a powerful offensive strategy rather than restricting ourselves to a purely defensive one."

"In the final analysis, an offensive strategy *is* a defensive one," Giscard said thoughtfully. "When it comes right down to it, for us to win, the Manty fleet and industrial infrastructure both have to be neutralized. If they aren't, and if we don't manage to do it early, then even with all Shannon's accomplished at Bolthole, it's likely that we'll end up looking at a situation very similar to the one Esther McQueen faced. Except that with the new ship types, any lengthy stalemate will be even bloodier than it was then."

"Exactly." Theisman nodded firmly. "Only an idiot would willingly go back to war with the Manties at all. If we have to, though, then I intend to fight to win, and to win as early as we possibly can. I don't plan to ignore the possibility of a more defense-oriented strategy, and Arnaud and the rest of the staff will be working on that as well at the New Octagon. But to be perfectly honest, any defensive plans are going to be primarily fallbacks in my thinking. That's one reason I wanted to talk to the three of you in person. If it comes down to it, you and Lester are going to be our primary field commanders, Javier. And your position at Bolthole is going to become even more critical, Shannon. So I want all of you to understand exactly what and how the President and I are thinking."

"I think we all do," Giscard told him. "Or, at least, I'm confident we all will before you head back to Nouveau Paris, at any rate. The thing I wonder is whether or not the Manties are smart enough to figure out the same thing."

"You and me both," Theisman told him with a sigh. "You and me both. In a way, I hope to Hell they are, because maybe then they'll also be smart enough to help avoid ever letting it come to that. Unfortunately, I don't think we can count on it."

Chapter Thirty-Three

"**S**o, Senator McGwire. What, in your opinion, does the President's speech really mean for our relations with the Manties?"

Thomas Theisman tipped back his chair at the head of the enormous table in the New Octagon conference room as Roland Henneman's deep-voiced question rolled from the HD mounted above the table.

Henneman had been an employee of the now defunct Office of Public Information for the better part of four standard decades. He'd begun in the usual way, working as a writer, and then as a reporter. Like all reporters in the People's Republic of Haven, he'd been very careful about what he reported, but he was a handsome man, with a resonant baritone voice and a reassuring manner. As such, he'd soon found his way to a larger and more visible role, and for the last five T-years of the People's Republic's existence, he'd hosted a daily talk show on HD here in the capital.

But PubIn had been thoroughly discredited in the eyes of the PRH's citizens. Universally recognized as no more than the Committee of Public Safety's propaganda mouthpiece, no one had trusted it. It had, in fact, been seen as one of the emblems of the discredited governments of the past, and its elimination had been one of Eloise Pritchart's first priorities as President. Which meant that, like all of his fellow employees, Henneman had found himself abruptly out of a job.

Fortunately for him, the new administration had disposed of PubIn's massive holdings in broadcast facilities and equipment at rock-bottom prices as a part of its media privatization drive. Although Henneman had been no more than modestly wealthy by the standards of the pre-Committee of Public Safety Legislaturalists, he'd managed to amass sufficient wealth under Rob Pierre to put him in position to organize a bidding cartel. He'd mortgaged himself to the hilt, even taking full advantage of the low-interest loan programs the Pritchart Administration had made available, but he and his colleagues had been able to acquire more than enough of PubIn's old infrastructure to emerge as a power in the fledgling private broadcast industry.

Henneman's own visibility during the heady days of PubIn's monopoly of the airwaves had paid another sort of dividend when it came to finding programming to fill his new network's broadcast schedule. He continued to host his daily talk show, although the blend of topics it examined had acquired a new, eclectic balance (and a harder edge) that PubIn would never have permitted. In addition, however, he produced, directed, and anchored *The Henneman Hour*, a political analysis and commentary program which aired every weekend.

In Theisman's opinion, Henneman remained more of a showman than a brilliant political analyst. But the Secretary of War had to admit that, whatever his shortcomings in that role, Henneman was probably the closest thing to it that the resurrected Republic had so far managed to produce. It never ceased to amuse Theisman when he reflected on the total disappearance of the "analysts" who had once served Public Information. One or two of them had actually found niches as producers on the programs which featured their replacements, but most of them had simply vanished into total obscurity. Not because of any deliberate purge on the part of the new government, but simply because they were supremely unsuited to the new political matrix. Most of them had excelled at delivering the "analysis" which PubIn had wanted delivered. Very few of them had possessed the skill, the tools, or the backbone to dig into questions of public policy and report things the government might not want reported.

Henneman, at least, didn't have that particular problem, and

Theisman had deliberately scheduled this meeting so that all of its participants could watch this interview with him.

"Well, Roland," Senator McGwire replied now, "that's a complicated question. I mean, while the President and Secretary Giancola have, of course, consulted with Congress all along, the entire situation where the Manticorans are concerned has been in something of a state of flux ever since the collapse of the Committee of Public Safety."

"Don't you mean, Senator, that the Manties have persistently refused to negotiate seriously with us? Or, for that matter, that they've systematically rejected, ridiculed, or ignored every proposal our negotiators have made?"

Theisman winced internally. Henneman hadn't raised his voice, and his expression remained courteously attentive, but that only lent his questions even more weight.

And that, the Secretary of War thought unhappily, *is because he isn't saying anything a surprisingly large percentage of the electorate hasn't already thought.*

"I don't think I'd put it in quite those terms myself, Roland," McGwire reproved mildly. "Certainly, the negotiations have dragged on far longer than anyone might have anticipated. And I would have to admit that it's often seemed to me, as to many of my colleagues in the Congress and, especially, on the Foreign Affairs Committee, that Prime Minister High Ridge and his government have preferred for them to do so. So I suppose I would have to agree with you that the Star Kingdom has declined to negotiate in what we might consider a serious or timely fashion. But I assure you that they have not 'ridiculed' our negotiators or the Republic."

"I think we're going to have to agree to disagree—respectfully, of course—about the exact verb we want to use for what they *have* done in that case, Senator," Henneman said after a moment. "But you would agree with me that the practical effect has been a complete deadlock?"

"I'm afraid I'd have to say yes," McGwire agreed, nodding regretfully. "In particular, I would have to acknowledge that it doesn't seem to me, both as an individual and as Chairman of the Foreign Affairs Committee, that the present Manticoran government has any interest whatsoever in restoring the occupied systems of the Republic to our control."

One of the other officers in the conference room inhaled sharply, and Theisman bestowed a wintery smile on the HD. He couldn't really say McGwire's pronouncement came as a surprise, but it was one the senator had been careful not to make publicly before Pritchart's speech.

"You believe that they intend to keep all of those systems permanently? Like Trevor's Star?" Henneman asked intently, and McGwire shrugged.

"In fairness to the Manticorans, Trevor's Star is something of a special case," he pointed out. "Given the brutality with which Internal Security and State Security operated on San Martin, I would have to say I don't find it surprising that the San Martinos should desire a complete break with the Republic, despite all of our reforms. At the same time, Trevor's Star is one terminus of the Manticorans' wormhole junction, and the Star Kingdom no doubt has a legitimate interest in maintaining its security. I don't say I'm happy by the precedent the star system's annexation represents. If it does turn out that they're inclined to keep other occupied systems, they might choose to argue they were doing nothing more than following the example set in Trevor's Star's case and for the same reasons. Should they choose to employ that pretext—which, I hasten to add, we've seen no indication they intend to do—it would be a lie. But despite any concerns I might have for the future, I believe we have no choice but to accept the Star Kingdom's decision to permanently retain control of this particular star."

"Even without a formal treaty under which the Republic agrees to resign sovereignty?" Henneman pressed.

"I would certainly prefer to see the situation regularized under a formal treaty," McGwire replied. "But in light of the San Martin electorate's clearly expressed desire to become subjects of the Star Kingdom, and bearing in mind the formal declaration of the Constitutional Convention that no star system of the old People's Republic would be compelled against its will to remain a part of the new Republic, I see no other practical outcome."

"I see."

It was obvious to Theisman that Henneman was dissatisfied with McGwire's position on Trevor's Star. That was disturbing. McGwire was entirely too close to Arnold Giancola for Theisman's peace of mind, but it had begun to seem evident, especially in the thirty-six hours or so since Pritchart's speech, that in some respects the man in the street had become even more of a hardliner than Giancola. Trevor's Star, in particular, had become a hot-button issue. So far as Theisman could see, what McGwire had just said should have been self-evident to anyone, but a sizable chunk of the newsfaxes and the public discussion groups appeared to disagree.

The disappearance of the People's Republic's onetime curbs on freedom of speech had created a chaotic, often vociferous ferment on the boards. The mere fact that people were now free to speak their minds seemed to provoke a large number of them into what often struck Theisman as public lunacy. Certainly, the old term "lunatic fringe" was the only one he could think of to describe a great deal of what found itself posted, and among the inhabitants of that fringe, there was a near hysterical demand that *all* of the occupied systems be restored to the Republic. Including Trevor's Star. In fact, especially Trevor's Star, which had become a rallying cry for the extremists despite the fact that anyone with half a brain had to know it wasn't going to happen.

What Theisman couldn't decide right now was whether Henneman belonged to that extreme fringe himself, or if he'd simply been looking for a sound bite which could have been used to play to it. He rather hoped it was the latter.

"But you do agree that, as the President seemed to be saying, all of the other occupied systems must be restored to us?" the commentator asked McGwire after a moment.

"That isn't precisely what President Pritchart said, Roland," McGwire replied.

"It certainly sounded like it to me, Senator."

"If you go back to the actual text of her speech," McGwire disagreed, "what she said—what she demanded, I should say—was that the status of the occupied systems be resolved in a fashion consistent with our domestic law."

"Which sounds an awful lot like requiring that they be returned to us."

"No. What it requires is that those planets and those star systems be restored to our jurisdiction long enough for us to ascertain what the expressed will of their citizens is under conditions which let us be positive they're not being intimidated or coerced by an occupying power. Demanding that they be 'restored to us' could be interpreted as a demand that they be returned to our permanent political control, regardless of the desires of their inhabitants."

"But the determination of exactly what their will is would have to be made under our oversight. Is that what you understand the President to have been saying, Sir?"

"In its essentials, yes."

"And do you believe the Manties will ever allow that to happen?" Henneman pounced, and Theisman suddenly realized he was holding his breath as McGwire hesitated. Then the senator shook his head.

"To be completely honest with you, Roland, I don't know," he said regretfully. "I'd have to say that on the basis of their past positions and performance they would be . . . disinclined to do so."

Theisman cursed silently. Up to that point, he hadn't had any particular problem with anything McGwire had said on today's program. That wasn't true about comments he'd made in other venues, perhaps, and he did rather wish the man hadn't brought up that bit about using Trevor's Star's annexation as a pretext for additional territorial expansion. But he supposed that if he was going to be fair about it, the senator had a right to express whatever opinion he chose. Unfortunately, however reasonable they might be on the surface, McGwire's remarks, and especially that last one, were only going to pour additional fuel on the public resentment the Manticorans' ongoing occupation of the disputed star systems had generated.

And the senator had to be at least as well aware of that as Thomas Theisman was.

"And do you think President Pritchart would be prepared to accept their 'disinclination' in this matter?" Henneman asked.

"In the past," McGwire said, choosing his words with obvious care, "the President's options, as those of the Republic as a whole, have been limited by the disastrous military position we inherited from the Pierre Regime. Whatever we may have believed or desired, we were not, unfortunately, in a position of sufficient strength to press demands."

"A situation which you believe has changed?"

"A situation which *may* have changed," McGwire corrected. "Certainly Secretary of War Theisman's announcement of our increased naval strength is something which must be weighed by all parties to the ongoing negotiations. And certainly, from the tone of President Pritchart's speech, she expects that to happen. As she so eloquently explained, we've tried for years now to resolve this fundamental issue through peaceful negotiation with absolutely no sign that the Star Kingdom was prepared to meet us halfway. No one in his or her right mind would willingly contemplate a return to open military confrontation with the Manticoran Alliance, and we've done our very best to avoid any situation in which that outcome might become likely.

"Nonetheless, there comes a time, as the President also reminded us, when avoidance of risk threatens to become the surrender of principle. I believe the demands which she's issued to the Star Kingdom—that they negotiate in good faith and that they accept the principle of self-determination, expressed in plebiscites under Republican oversight and jurisdiction, for all of the occupied planets and star systems—are completely appropriate and proper. I feel confident that I can accurately say she enjoys very strong support by all parties in the Congress, and that we stand united behind her and Secretary of State Giancola in this matter."

"So, if I understand you correctly, Senator," Henneman said intently, "you're saying you would support the President's demands even at the risk of resuming active military operations against the Manties."

"Some things, Roland," McGwire said solemnly, "are sufficiently important, both as matters of national self-interest and of principle, to justify even the most serious risks. In my opinion, the well-being and right to self-determination of citizens of the Republic living under the military occupation of a foreign power certainly fall into both those categories."

The senator's timing was excellent, Theisman thought sardonically, as the program dissolved to a commercial message, leaving the viewers with the impression of his somber, strong-jawed face and steady brown eyes.

"Turn it off," the Secretary of War said, and the HD unit went obediently dead and then withdrew silently into its ceiling nest.

Theisman brought his chair fully upright and allowed his eyes to circle the conference table. It was a very large table. It had to be to accommodate all of the officers seated around it. Counting himself and Arnaud Marquette, there were no fewer than eighteen flag officers, and each of those commodores and admirals was accompanied by at least two or three aides and staffers.

A lot of those officers looked unusually young for their seniority, because they were. Saint-Just's destruction of the original Octagon and every single military officer in it had torn an enormous hole in the Navy's senior ranks. The purges which followed had only turned that hole into a yawning chasm. Theisman had been given no choice but to promote to fill all of those vacancies when he resurrected the Naval Staff, and he (and most of those whom he'd promoted) recognized the relative inexperience of the replacements. That was one of the major reasons why Theisman had combined the offices of Secretary of War and Chief of Naval Operations in his own person. Preposterous as it still seemed to him, he was very probably the single most experienced officer in the entire Republican Navy.

And he'd been a mere commander fifteen T-years before.

But young for their positions or not, they were the General Staff he had to work with. And to be fair, they'd acquired quite a lot of experience and on-the-job training over the last four years or so.

"Well, Ladies and Gentlemen," he observed after a moment, "there you have it. I suppose if the Chairman of the Foreign Affairs Committee said it on *The Henneman Hour* it has to be official."

A dutiful chuckle ran around the conference room, and he smiled thinly. Not that he felt particularly amused. Actually, McGwire had been considerably less inflammatory than Theisman had feared he might be, particularly in light of his close working relationship with Giancola. Theisman wasn't certain that his restraint reflected his actual position, but he was inclined to think it did. McGwire had never made any secret of his intense wariness about anything which might have brought the Republic and the Star Kingdom back into open conflict, despîte his relationship with Giancola. In a way, though, that gave even more force to what he'd said at the very end, and Thomas Theisman didn't like what he sensed building about him.

He strongly suspected that even Eloise Pritchart had seriously underestimated the strength of the public reaction her speech was likely to provoke. But it seemed that the electorate's outrage and growing disgust and anger over the Manticorans' procrastination were beginning to outweigh its war weariness. For that matter, they even seemed to be starting to outweigh the public's deep-seated fear of the Manticoran Alliance. Perhaps even worse was the strength of the public's deep resentment of the humiliating and crushing defeat the Manticorans had inflicted upon them. Theisman had seen enough of human nature to realize that *revanchism* spawned by resentment was far more dangerous than any anger based on reason or logic, and the strength of this resentment had surprised him.

It shouldn't have, and he knew it. But it had. Perhaps that was because it had seemed to him that his own awareness of how catastrophic any fresh confrontation with the Star Kingdom could prove ought to have been agonizingly obvious to anyone who thought about it for a moment. Yet whatever the reason for his own blindness, the sheer strength of the public's emotional response to Pritchart's speech had been far, far stronger than he'd ever anticipated that it might.

He didn't like that. He didn't like that at all . . . and he especially didn't like the way his own announcement of Bolthole's existence seemed to have fanned that outrage and anger to even hotter flame. The situation wasn't out of control yet. In fact, it was a long way short of that. But the potential for a groundswell of support for Giancola's style of confrontational foreign policy, regardless of its possible consequences, was there.

"It isn't our job to make foreign policy here at the Octagon," he told his subordinates after a moment. "That was a point the Navy tended to forget under the Legislaturalists, and that helped produce the Committee of Public Safety. But it *is* our job to evaluate the potential military threats which may confront of the Republic or hinder the attainment of its foreign policy objectives.

"Obviously, from the moment we made the existence of our new units public, the parameters of the potential threats we face changed dramatically. All of you are aware of that."

Heads nodded. *And they'd damned well better!* he thought. *We've certainly spent long enough discussing those threats.*

"The President's speech, and our more assertive position in the peace talks, are going to change those parameters even further," he continued. "Frankly, I don't know how the Manticoran Alliance is going to respond to all this. So far," he emphasized the two words ever so slightly, "the President assures me she has no intention of resorting to the actual use of military force except in self-defense. Unfortunately, defending ourselves successfully, especially when so many of our star systems are already occupied by the potential enemy, creates a situation in which the best defense may indeed be a strong offense.

"The purpose of this meeting, Ladies and Gentlemen, is to bring all of you fully up to speed on the considerations which are currently shaping the way Admiral Marquette and I view our responsibilities. And our opportunities."

Some of the officers seated around the table stiffened visibly, almost like eager hounds scenting the prey, at his last three words, and he gave them an icy smile.

"Understand me," he said very softly. "I do not want a fresh war with the Star Kingdom of Manticore. Admiral Marquette doesn't want a war. More importantly, President Pritchart doesn't want one, either. If any one of you doesn't understand that very clearly, that situation had better change. Yes, I used the word 'opportunities,' and as military planners, we have to be just as aware of those as we must of threats. But those opportunities are *not* going to serve as excuses for launching a war when there is any way at all that we can avoid that. I trust I have made myself sufficiently clear."

He let his eyes sweep over them. No one said a word, but, then, no one needed to, and his nostrils flared briefly in satisfaction. Then he allowed the intensity of his gaze to ease just a bit and sat back in his chair once more.

"Having said that, however," he continued, "it's clearly necessary for us to revise our existing war plans to reflect the new realities stemming from Admiral Foraker's success at Bolthole. The new ships which have entered our order of battle give us many more options, and it's our responsibility to recognize them and plan accordingly.

"Admiral Marquette and I have discussed the implications of the changing diplomatic situation with President Pritchart and her Cabinet. We've also discussed our current military capabilities with Admirals Giscard, Tourville, and Foraker. On the basis of those considerations, I want a complete reevaluation of our current war plans. As you conduct that reevaluation, you will concentrate on and think in terms of three basic operational cases.

"Case Blue will concentrate on our defensive requirements in the face of an attack by the Manticoran Alliance upon the Republic. You will, of course, consider the possibility of an all-out attack on our territory, but, frankly, I think that's unlikely. Which is why your primary emphasis will be directed towards defeating any Manticoran preemptive counterforce attack intended to destroy our new ships.

"Case Amber will concentrate upon a limited offensive against the Star Kingdom of Manticore. The object of Case Amber will be the recovery by force of the star systems currently occupied by Manticoran forces. Again, let me emphasize that this will be a *limited* offensive. Our intentions under Case Amber will be to reoccupy our territory with a minimum of combat or loss of life on either side. I recognize, however, that minimizing combat may be difficult, particularly if the other side declines to cooperate."

He smiled again, this time with an edge of true humor.

"Accordingly, I want Case Amber split into two contingency plans. Case Amber Alpha will be predicated on the assumption that the Department of State and our diplomats have managed to prepare a situation in which a show of force will be sufficient to cause the Manticorans to withdraw their units. Assuming that that happy state of affairs can be created—which, frankly, I think is unlikely—Case Amber Alpha would require primarily logistical planning. Nonetheless, I want provision for the possibility that the Manticorans may decide not to withdraw after all. If they decide to fight, I don't want our commanders on the spot to be caught flatfooted by their response.

"Case Amber Beta, on the other hand, will assume from the beginning that occupying Manticoran forces will resist wherever possible. Amber Beta will distribute our forces in a fashion designed to provide sufficient strength to neutralize any hostile naval detachments occupying Republican territory while maintaining a powerful defensive force to fend off any counterattacks against the Republic as a whole.

"In either case, Case Amber will not envision an all-out offensive against the Star Kingdom or deep operations into the territory of the Manticoran Alliance. Its purpose will be solely to reoccupy our own territory."

He paused, considering their expressions and body language once more until he was satisfied that they all understood. Then he nodded.

"And then," he said quietly, "there's Case Red."

Something like a sigh ran through the conference room.

"Case Red will concentrate on an all-out offensive against the

Star Kingdom and the Manticoran Alliance. Its object will be the neutralization of the enemy's war fighting capability. Operations will be planned in such a way as to retake the occupied systems using the most economical possible mix of pre-pod capital ships and CLACs, but the primary focus will be upon the location of the enemy's SD(P)s and CLACs and their complete destruction. The purpose of Case Red will not be to annex any system which was never a part of the People's Republic. It may be necessary to temporarily occupy some additional systems, but any such occupation will be just that: temporary.

"Once the RMN has been neutralized, we will be in a position to dictate terms to the Manties for a change. But for there to be any chance of a lasting peace between the Star Kingdom and the Republic, we must demonstrate our willingness to return to the prewar *status quo* so long as our own territorial integrity is respected. President Pritchart and I have discussed this point at some length, and she feels very strongly about it. I mention this because I know some of the officers in this room would very much like to permanently retake Trevor's Star. Ladies and Gentlemen, that isn't going to happen. It will undoubtedly be necessary for us to temporarily reoccupy that star system, but its citizens have made their decision to become a part of the Star Kingdom abundantly clear, and the Star Kingdom has formally ratified that decision. This is the Republic of Haven, not the *People's* Republic of Haven, and we are not going to return to the days of repression by InSec or StateSec. Moreover, by making it clear to the Manticorans that we are prepared to return Trevor's Star to them, we will give the strongest possible evidence that our motives are essentially defensive and that our ultimate desire is to live in peace with our neighbors.

"Of course," he allowed himself a wintery chuckle, "before we can convince them of that, we'll probably have to beat the holy living hell out of them."

This time the mutter of laughter was louder, and he grinned.

"One point I'd like to make, if I may, Sir," Marquette put in after a moment, and Theisman nodded to him.

"As the Secretary already said, Ladies and Gentlemen," the Chief of Staff said, "he and I have discussed the bare bones of all three of these planning cases with Admirals Giscard, Tourville, and Foraker. We're in basic agreement that while none of us wants to go back to war, if we're forced to, we'll fight to *win*. If it comes to Case Red, that means that we'll go in hard, fast, and dirty.

"At the same time, as the Secretary also said, there are certain opportunities which our planning must not overlook. Specifically, at this time, it seems fairly evident that the Manties still don't realize just how much Admiral Foraker has actually accomplished. We've seen no evidence that they even suspect the existence of our CLACs, and so far as we're currently aware, they're also ignorant of the increases in our system efficiencies Admiral Foraker and her people have managed.

"Even if they become aware of all those factors, however, the building policies they've adopted over the past three years give us a substantial—I repeat, a *substantial*—advantage over them in modern ship types. Our best estimate at NavInt is that even if they realize tomorrow what they're actually up against, it will take them a minimum of two or even three T-years to regain parity in hulls."

"Sir," Vice Admiral Linda Trenis, the director of the Bureau of Plans, said very carefully, "are you suggesting that Case Red is actually likely to be put into effect?"

"No," Theisman replied for Marquette. Then he grimaced. "Let me rephrase. If, and I say *if*, it comes to open conflict with the Manties, I consider that Case Red is the war plan which we would be most likely to adopt. Under the circumstances, and especially in light of how close they already are to the Haven system with their advanced elements at Lovat, we simply don't have the depth to absorb a fresh, major offensive. Admiral Marquette is completely correct about the numerical advantage we currently enjoy over the RMN. Until and unless our hardware is tested against theirs in actual combat, no one can accurately estimate what the actual balance of military power is, although I genuinely believe it's presently in our favor. But it doesn't matter if our fleet is stronger than theirs if they manage to break through to Haven and occupy the high orbitals of the capital. And given the astrophysics of our starting positions, they're one hell of a lot closer to our capital system than we are to theirs.

"Because of that, if worse comes to worst and we're forced to resume operations, we must seize the initiative at the very outset and be certain that we retain it throughout. And to do that, Ladies and Gentlemen, is going to require that we go on the offensive and stay there. Which brings us directly to Case Red.

"That happens to be an inescapable consequence of the starting situation. But what you were really asking, Linda, was whether or not we should be planning a preemptive strike against them during the period in which we believe we enjoy military superiority. The answer to that question, is no. In fact, it's emphatically no. Does that clarify the situation for you?"

"Yes, Sir. It does," Trenis replied.

"Good."

"At the same time, Sir," the vice admiral went on, "what Admiral Marquette has just said is quite true. And for the immediate future, at least, the Manties' preoccupation with the Andermani only increases our probable advantage."

"That's true to a point, Linda," Vice Admiral Edward Rutledge, director of the Bureau of Logistics, said. "But they didn't actually commit very much of their modern fleet to Sidemore, you know."

"Agreed." Trenis nodded. "Every little bit helps, though, and they don't have all that many SD(P)s to begin with. And," she added, "they only have *one* Harrington, thank God! The longer they leave her at Sidemore, the better I'll like it."

Several people laughed, but there was more than a trace of genuine anxiety, not to say fear, in some of the laughter.

"'The Salamander' isn't three meters tall, Linda," Theisman said after a moment. "Mind you, I'm not saying she isn't a tough customer. She is. I know, because she's beaten me twice. But she's also been beaten, you know. I certainly won't object if the Manties are stupid enough to leave her in Silesia, but I'm almost more grateful that they were dumb enough to put White Haven on the beach."

"Not to mention firing Caparelli. And Givens," Marquette put in, and Theisman nodded in emphatic agreement.

"Janacek has done his best to drive all of their better commanders onto half-pay. Webster, D'Orville, White Haven, even Sarnow. In fact, Kuzak is about the only one of their first-rate admirals who's still on active duty. And it's also true that the size of the commitment they've had to make to Silesia has moved the tonnage balance on this side of the Star Kingdom even further in our favor."

"You're right about that, Sir," Trenis said, and frowned thoughtfully. "In fact, as long as they're going to place themselves in a false position, perhaps we should be thinking in terms of taking advantage of their deployments if it does come down to Case Red."

"Meaning what?" Theisman asked, cocking his head at her.

"They've divided their Navy into three major fleets and a host of small detachments," Trenis pointed out. "I'm assuming from everything you've said, both today and in the past, that we shouldn't be thinking of a direct, immediate attack on the Manticore System itself."

She made the statement a question, and Theisman shook his head.

"Not an immediate attack, no. If it comes down to it, we'll probably have to move to at least threaten their capital system, but we can't afford to attempt that deep a strike until we've removed the threat of their doing the same thing to us."

"That's what I thought," Trenis said. "So we can more or less disregard their Home Fleet for the moment. With the mothballing of so many of their wormhole junction forts, they're going to be in an even worse position to reduce Home Fleet's strength, anyway. So that leaves only two major concentrations: Kuzak's fleet at Trevor's Star, and Harrington's at Sidemore. I believe those are our natural targets and that we should focus on ways to destroy both of them."

"Both of them?" Marquette's eyebrows arched. "You are aware, Linda, that the Marsh System is the next best thing to four hundred light-years from where we sit right now?"

"Yes, Sir. I am."

"In that case, you're probably also aware that it would take two and a half T-months for our ships to get from here to there." Trenis nodded again, and the chief of staff shrugged. "While I appreciate the fact that you're thinking in large terms, if you're proposing that we attempt to coordinate two offensives over that great a distance, you may be thinking just a bit too large."

"With all due respect, Sir, I don't think that's the case," Trenis replied. "I'm not proposing any sort of fine coordination. Obviously, at that distance from the capital, whoever was in command of any forces we sent to Silesia would have to exercise independent judgment. On the other hand, it might be possible to coordinate things a bit more effectively than you're assuming."

"I'd like to know precisely how you propose to do that," Marquette said. "Especially since the Manties would be in a position to move forces back and forth to and from Silesia through either Basilisk or Gregor faster than we could possibly move them."

"Obviously, Sir, we'd have to preposition our forces in Silesia. Once we got them there, there are plenty of uninhabited star systems in the Confederacy where they could lie low until and unless they were required to attack. If we positioned them and then decided, for whatever reason, not to use them, they could simply turn around and come home with no one the wiser. As far as anyone else would be concerned, they were never there, and we never even contemplated an attack on Sidemore."

"Um." Theisman rubbed his upper lip. "That sounds just a bit cynical, you know, Linda," he pointed out. "Not necessarily wrong. Just . . . cynical."

"Sir," Trenis said, perhaps just a little bit more patiently than she really ought to have, "if we're seriously considering the possibility of going back to war against the Manticoran Alliance, then it seems to me that whether or not we're being cynical is probably the least of our worries."

"Oh, you're right about that," Theisman agreed. "But to make what you're proposing work, we'd need two things. First, we'd have to have sufficient advance warning to spend the two and a half months it would take to send them there from here without using the Manticoran Junction. And, second, we'd have to have some means of being certain our forces in Silesia didn't attack if tensions eased here. I won't countenance a situation in which we find ourselves forced to attack here, even if a peaceful resolution would otherwise be possible, because we know a remote commander we can't recall in time is going to attack the Manties somewhere else."

"I'd already considered both of those points, Sir," Trenis said respectfully. "May I respond?"

"Of course you may. Please do."

"First of all, Sir, we can substantially reduce the time it would take for our forces to reach Silesia by stationing them closer to the frontier. If we were to move them over to Seljuk, for example, they'd be over a hundred and fifty light-years closer to Silesia, which would reduce their transit time by almost three weeks if we decided to commit them. Or, we could go ahead and deploy them all the way to Silesia immediately, as long as your second major concern is addressed."

"I suppose so," Theisman conceded slowly. "Of course, I'd want to be confident we didn't need those same ships here to deal with Kuzak. And, for that matter, that whatever we sent to Silesia would be adequate to deal with Harrington's forces there. There isn't much point in splitting our forces if it simply weakens us enough to be beaten in detail."

"Understood, Sir. In fact, I took that as a given before I ever raised the possibility. Unless the Manties have considerably more in the way of SD(P)s squirreled away somewhere than we know about, I think we can make up the numbers on both fronts."

"You're probably right. But that still leaves the problem of communicating with someone we've sent off with orders to attack if the situation changes here."

"Not really, Sir," Trenis said in that same respectful tone. "What I would propose doing would be something like this. We'd go ahead and preposition an attack force in Silesia, preferably somewhere close to Marsh but sufficiently out of the way that no one would be likely to stumble across them, and somewhere between Marsh and either Basilisk or Gregor. But that force would be authorized to attack only after receiving a specific release order from here."

"Which would get there exactly how?" Marquette asked skeptically.

"Actually, Sir, that's the easiest part of all," Trenis told him. "The order to attack in Silesia wouldn't be issued until after the order to attack Trevor's Star and the other Manticoran detachments in our space had been given. What would happen is that when our primary attack force, presumably the one tasked with retaking Trevor's Star, received final orders to begin its sortie, its commander would send a dispatch boat to Trevor's Star. That dispatch boat wouldn't be Navy; it would be a civilian vessel, with impeccable documentation to prove that it was. The dispatch boat would arrive at Trevor's Star at least forty-eight hours before our attack force, and it would make transit through the Manties' wormhole junction to Basilisk or Gregor. From there, it would proceed as rapidly as possible to rendezvous with our Silesian attack force to deliver its orders to attack March. If it passed through Trevor's Star forty-eight hours before we attacked, then it would have a forty-eight-hour head start on any possible warning to Harrington—more than that, if our attack force was positioned between the courier's arrival terminus and Marsh. Which means that our Silesian units would receive their orders and move to attack her before she had any reason to expect it. Especially since she would never know they were in the area at all, and all of her attention would be directed towards keeping an eye on the Andermani, rather than worrying about anything we might do."

Theisman looked at her and rubbed his upper lip some more. Then he nodded slowly. "I'm not saying I think it would be a good idea to spread our forces so widely that it would be effectively impossible for either of them to support the other if it became necessary. That would have to be something we considered very carefully before we did it. But you're right. If we used a scenario similar to the one you're describing, we wouldn't have to worry about an attack in Silesia committing us here, but we could still get the order to attack there into the CO's hands well before Harrington—or whoever was in command there at the time—knew we were at war."

"It sounds like an excellent idea to me, too," Marquette agreed. "Except, of course, that if there was a period of escalating tension between us and the Manties before we attacked Trevor's Star, then Kuzak would probably do what she's done before and close the Trevor's Star terminus to all nonmilitary traffic. Which would freeze our messenger out."

"I can think of two ways to solve that problem, Sir," Trenis said confidently. "One would be to use a diplomatic courier. If nothing else, the Silesians do maintain an embassy right here in Nouveau Paris and, let's be honest, if we offer a sufficiently toothsome bribe to their Ambassador, he'd be perfectly willing to make one of his official dispatch boats available to us. That would still allow us to send the orders to our Silesian commander with a forty-eight-hour head start over any message that could reach Harrington, and Kuzak would never close the junction to a vessel with diplomatic immunity. Not, at least, when no shots had actually been fired.

"The second solution would lose some of our head start time, but it would be even simpler than that. All we really have to do is to plant our courier in the Manticore System ahead of time. I'm sure that if we put our intelligence types to work on it, they could come up with any number of covers for an ostensibly civilian ship—probably one that doesn't even have a Republican registry—to hang around in Manticore for several days, or even a few weeks. If we attack Trevor's Star, it's going to be pretty damned obvious very quickly to everyone in the Manticore System that we've done so. If nothing else, there are going to be enough ship movements in and out of the junction to give it away. So as soon as the skipper of our courier knows that the attack has actually commenced, she goes ahead and transits through the junction to either Basilisk or Gregor and proceeds to rendezvous. She'll probably still have a little bit of head start, since no one in the Star Kingdom, especially with Janacek and his crowd running their Admiralty, is going to spare as much as a single thought for the possibility that we might be contemplating hitting them simultaneously someplace that far away. That means they'll probably be slow off the mark getting word of the attack to their Sidemore Station commander. And even if they're not, the fact that no one is going to be anticipating an attack that far from any of our bases should still give us tactical surprise."

"Well," Marquette said with a crooked smile, "that's knocked that objection on the head, too. You do seem to be in fine form today, Linda."

"Yes, you do," Theisman agreed. "Mind you, I'm still far from convinced that splitting our forces in the first place would be a good idea. Especially when we don't know which way the Graysons are likely to jump. But if we did decide to do any such thing, I think the arrangements you've sketched out would probably work."

"I'm fairly certain they would, Sir," Marquette told him. "And as far as the Graysons are concerned, at the moment Janacek and High Ridge seem to be almost as intent on pissing them off as they were on firing all of their best admirals! According to all our sources in the Star Kingdom, it's pretty obvious Janacek doesn't trust Benjamin Mayhew as far as he could throw him in a two-grav field. Which is uncommonly stupid even for Janacek, but let's not look a gift horse in the mouth."

"Admiral Marquette is right about that, Sir," Trenis observed. "And for that matter, right this minute, Grayson has just sent a sizable chunk of its total navy off on some sort of long-term, long-range training deployment. According to NavInt's sources, they'll be gone for at least the next four to five standard months. If the balloon should happen to go up during that time period, well . . ."

She shrugged, and Thomas Theisman nodded slowly and thoughtfully.

CHAPTER THIRTY-FOUR

"**H**arvest Joy, you are cleared to proceed. Good luck!"

"Thank you, Junction Control," Captain Josepha Zachary, commanding officer of the improbably named survey ship HMS *Harvest Joy*, acknowledged the clearance and the good wishes simultaneously, then turned to Jordin Kare and quirked an eyebrow.

"Junction Control says we can go now, Doctor," she observed. "Do you and Dr. Wix agree?"

"Captain, Dr. Wix and I have been ready to go for days!" Kare replied with an amazingly youthful-looking grin. Then he nodded more seriously. "Our people are ready to proceed whenever you are, Captain."

"Well, in that case . . ." Captain Zachary murmured, and crossed the three paces of deck between her and her command chair. She settled into it, turned it to face her helmsman, and drew a deep breath.

"Ten gravities, Chief Tobias," she said formally.

"Ten gravities, aye, Ma'am," the helmsman confirmed, and *Harvest Joy* began to creep very slowly forward.

Zachary crossed her legs and made herself lean confidently back in her comfortable chair. It probably wasn't strictly necessary for her to project an aura of complete calm, but it couldn't hurt, either.

Her lips tried to twitch into a smile at the thought, but she suppressed it automatically as she watched the navigation plot repeater deployed from the left arm of the command chair. The com screen beside it showed the face of Arswendo Hooja, her chief engineer, and she nodded to the blond-haired, blue-eyed lieutenant commander. Arswendo and she had served together often over the years, and Zachary was grateful for his calm, competent presence at the far end of the com link.

She was just as happy to have avoided a few other presences, whether on the other end of com links or in the flesh. First and foremost among them was Dame Melina Makris, who had made herself a monumental pain in the posterior from the moment she came aboard. So far as Zachary had been able to determine, Makris had no redeeming characteristics, and the captain had taken carefully concealed but nonetheless profound satisfaction in banning all civilians—except Dr. Kare, of course—from *Harvest Joy*'s bridge for the moment of transit.

Now she nodded to Hooja in welcome. Neither of them felt any particular need for words of a time like this, and in Arswendo's case, she was reasonably certain that calm was completely genuine. Which was more than she could say for most of the people aboard her ship. She could feel the tension of her entire bridge crew. Like her, they were all far too professional to be obvious about showing it, yet it was almost painfully evident to someone who knew them as well as she did. And not surprisingly. In the entire two-thousand-T-year history of humankind's expansion through the galaxy, exploration ships had done what *Harvest Joy* was about to do less than two hundred times. It had been almost two T-centuries since the Basilisk terminus of the Manticoran Wormhole Junction had been mapped, and so far as Zachary knew, no living officer in the Star Kingdom, naval or civilian, had ever commanded the first transit through a newly discovered terminus . . . until her. And although she'd been a survey and exploration officer for the better part of fifty T-years, during which she'd made more Junction transits than she could have counted, *no one* had ever made this particular transit before. That would have been exciting enough, but, logical or not, the perversity of the human imagination persisted in projecting potential disaster scenarios to hone anticipation's edge still sharper.

The icon representing *Harvest Joy* on the astrogation plot slid slowly down the gleaming line of her projected transit vector. In some respects, it was exactly like a routine transit through one of the well-established Junction termini. And, as far as the navigation guidance from ACS and the pre-transit calculations from Dr. Kare's team were concerned, it might as well have been precisely that. But for all the similarities, there was one enormous difference, because in this case, the figures upon which those calculations were based had never been tested by another ship.

Stop that, she scolded herself. *They may never have been tested by another* ship, *but Kare and his crowd have put over sixty probes into this terminus to compile the readings your precious numbers are based on!* Which was true, as far as it went. *On the other hand*, she reflected with another almost-smile, *not a single one of those probes has ever come* back *again, has it now?*

Of course they hadn't. Nothing smaller than a starship could mount a hyper generator, and only something with a hyper generator could hope to pass through a wormhole junction terminus. The scientists' probes had reported faithfully right up to the moment they encountered the interface of the terminus itself, at which point they had simply ceased to exist.

Unlike them, Zachary's ship *did* have a hyper generator. Which mean *Harvest Joy* could pass safely through the hyper-space interface which had destroyed the probes . . . probably. Whether or not she would survive whatever lay on the other side of it was another matter, of course. After all, there were all of those deliciously terrifying, venerable legends about the rogue wormholes whose termini deposited doomed travelers directly into the heart of a black hole or some other suitably lethal destination. Not that anyone had ever actually found a wormhole where warships made transit in but never made transit out again.

As if anyone were about to let anything as boring as reality interfere with perfectly good legends, she told herself, and glanced sideways at Kare.

If the astrophysicist cherished any concerns of his own, they were admirably concealed. He stood at the astrogator's shoulder, blue-gray eyes intent as he watched *Harvest Joy*'s progress with total concentration, and the mere fact of his presence ought to be reassuring. Certainly, the RMAIA would scarcely have allowed its chief scientist, his three senior assistants, and over two hundred of its other scientific personnel to depart aboard *Harvest Joy* if it hadn't been completely confident of their safety, Zachary thought.

Then she snorted. From what she'd seen of Kare and Wix, it

would have taken armed Marines to keep them off *Harvest Joy*, danger or not. If a first transit was exciting for Zachary, it represented the culmination of Kare's entire academic and professional life, and the same was true for Wix.

"We're starting to pick up the eddy right on schedule, Ma'am," Lieutenant Thatcher reported from Astrogation. "The numbers look good."

"Thank you, Rochelle."

Zachary gazed intently at her display, and her nostrils flared as a bright crosshair icon ahead of *Harvest Joy*'s light code blinked the sudden, brilliant green of a transit threshold. The survey ship was precisely where she was supposed to be, tracking straight down the precalculated vector into the frozen funnel of hyper-space which was all a wormhole junction truly was.

"Dr. Kare?" Zachary said quietly. She was the captain, and hers was the ultimate authority to abort the transit if anything looked less than optimal to her. But Kare was the one in charge of the entire expedition; the official organization chart in Zachary's orders from Admiral Reynaud made that clear, whatever Makris thought. Which meant he was the only one who could finally authorize them to proceed.

"Go ahead, Captain," the scientist replied almost absently, without ever looking up from Thatcher's plot.

"Very well," Zachary acknowledged, and looked back down at the face on the small screen beside her left knee. "Prepare to rig foresail for transit, Mr. Hooja," she said formally, precisely as if Arswendo hadn't been prepared to do just that for the last twenty minutes.

"Aye, aye, Ma'am. Standing by," he replied with equally redundant formality.

"Threshold in three-zero seconds," Thatcher informed her captain.

"Stand ready, Chief Tobias," Zachary said.

"Aye, aye, Ma'am," Tobias responded, and Zachary consciously reminded herself not to hold her breath as *Harvest Joy*'s icon continued to creep ever so slowly forward.

"Threshold!" Thatcher announced.

"Rig foresail for transit," Zachary commanded.

"Rigging foresail, aye."

To a visual observer, nothing about *Harvest Joy* changed in any respect as Hooja threw the switch down in Main Engineering, but Zachary's instruments were another matter entirely. *Harvest Joy*'s impeller wedge dropped instantly to half strength as her forward beta nodes shut down and the matching alpha nodes reconfigured. They no longer generated their portion of the survey ship's normal-space stress bands; instead, they projected a Warshawski sail, a circular disk of focused gravitational energy, perpendicular to *Harvest Joy*'s long axis and extending for over three hundred kilometers in every direction.

"Standby to rig aftersail on my mark," Zachary murmured, and Hooja acknowledged once again as *Harvest Joy* continued to creep forward under the power of her after impellers alone and another readout flickered to life. Zachary watched its flashing numerals climb steadily as the foresail moved deeper and deeper into the Junction. The normal safety margin was considerably wider than usual because of the survey ship's relatively low acceleration and velocity, but that didn't make Zachary feel any less tense.

The numbers suddenly stopped flashing. They continued to climb, but their steady glow told her that the foresail was now drawing sufficient power from the grav waves twisting down the invisible pathway of the Junction to provide movement, and she nodded sharply.

"Rig aftersail now," she said crisply.

"Rigging aftersail, aye," Hooja replied, and *Harvest Joy* twitched as her impeller wedge disappeared entirely and a second Warshawski sail flicked into life at the far end of her hull from the first.

Zachary looked up from her displays to watch Chief Tobias take the ship through the transition from impeller to hyper sail. The maneuver was trickier than the experienced petty officer made it look, but there was a reason Tobias had been chosen for this mission. His hands moved smoothly, confidently, and *Harvest Joy* slid through the interface into the terminus without so much as a quiver. He held the survey ship rock-steady, and Zachary grimaced around a familiar wave of queasiness.

No one ever really adjusted to the indescribable sensation of crossing the wall between n-space and hyper-space. Precisely what physical sense reported that sensation was debated. Everyone seemed to have his or her own opinion as to which one it was, but however much they might disagree about that, everyone agreed about the ripple of nausea that accompanied the transition. It wasn't particularly severe in a normal transit, but the gradient was far steeper in a Junction transit, and Zachary swallowed hard.

But if the nausea was sharper, it would also be over sooner, she reminded herself. The familiar thought wound its way through the groove decades of naval experience had worn in her mental processes, and then the maneuvering display blinked again.

For an instant, a fleeting interval no chronometer had ever been able to measure, HMS *Harvest Joy* ceased to exist. One moment she was where she had been, seven light-hours from Manticore-A; the next she was . . . somewhere else, and Zachary swallowed again, this time in relief. Her nausea vanished along with the brilliant blue transit energy radiating from *Harvest Joy*'s sails, and she inhaled deeply.

"Transit complete," Chief Tobias reported.

"Thank you, Chief," Zachary told him, even as her eyes dropped back to the sail interface readout. She watched the numbers spiral downward even more rapidly than they'd risen, and nodded in profound satisfaction at their reassuring normality.

"Engineering, reconfigure to impeller now."

"Aye, aye, Ma'am," Hooja replied, and *Harvest Joy* folded her sails back into her impeller wedge and moved forward, once again at the same, steady ten gravities.

"Well, Dr. Kare," Zachary said, looking up from her displays to meet the scientist's eyes. "We're here. Wherever 'here' is, of course."

"Here" proved to be a spot in space approximately five and a half light-hours from an unremarkable-looking, planetless M8 red dwarf. That was disappointing, because the next nearest star, a G2, was just over four light-years away. That was a bit less than fourteen hours of travel for a warship, which wasn't really all that bad in a lot of ways. But the local star's lack of planets was going to deprive this terminus of any convenient anchor for the sort of infrastructure which routinely grew up to service wormhole traffic.

But if Zachary was disappointed by the absence of planets, the horde of scientists infesting her ship scarcely even seemed to notice it. They were too busy communing with their computers, *Harvest Joy*'s shipboard sensors, and the reports from the expanding shell of sensor drones they'd deployed even before Zachary reduced velocity to zero relative to the dim dwarf.

She was a bit amused by the fact that none of them seemed to have any interest whatsoever in the local star or even in determining where in the universe they might be. All of their attention was focused on their Warshawskis.

Actually, Zachary reflected, that was completely understandable—from their perspective, at least. And, upon more mature consideration, it was a focus she approved of heartily. After all, until they were able to nail down the precise location of this end of the terminus through which they'd come, it would be impossible for *Harvest Joy* to find her way home through it once more. Given how faint the readings which had guided them to the Junction end of the terminus had been, and how long and how hard the RMAIA had searched for it, Josepha Zachary was completely in favor of staying precisely where she was until Kare and his crew were totally confident that they'd pinned this one down.

But while they concentrated on that, the merely human hired help who had chauffeured them to their present location were busy with other observations. It was extremely rare—in fact, virtually unheard of—for any modern starship to be required to start completely from scratch in order to determine its location. Navigation through hyper-space depended heavily upon the hyper log, which located a ship in reference to its point of departure, since it was impossible to take observations across the hyper wall into n-space. In this case, however, even the hyper log was useless. There was no way to know how far *Harvest Joy* had come in Einsteinian terms, because a junction transit could theoretically be of literally any length. In fact, the longest transit "leg" for any known junction spanned just over nine hundred light-years, and the average was considerably shorter than that. Basilisk, for example, was barely two hundred light-years from the Manticore System, while Trevor's Star and Gregor were both even closer than that. Sigma Draconis and Matapan, on the other hand, were each the next best thing to five light-centuries from Manticore, while Phoenix was over seven hundred light-years away, although in terms of actual transit time all of them were equally close.

In this instance, however, with absolutely no way to judge how far from home they'd come, Lieutenant Thatcher and her assistants had to begin with a blank map. The first order of business was to isolate and determine the exact spectral classes of the most brilliant stars in the vicinity. Once that was done, the computers could compare them to the enormous amounts of data in their memory until they managed to positively identify enough of them to tell Thatcher just where the terminus had deposited them. In the immediate sense of this particular mission, Kare and Wix's work was considerably more important than Thatcher's, since they might never get home again if the scientists failed to nail down their target. In the grand scheme of things, though, Thatcher's quest held far greater significance for the Star Kingdom as a whole.

The only true utility of the terminus was to go from one place to another, after all, and there was no point in going if one didn't know where one was after one arrived. Besides, while it was theoretically possible that they were so far from Manticore that return would be possible only by retracing their course through the terminus, that was also extremely unlikely. *Harvest Joy* had a cruising endurance of just over four months before she would have to rebunker. That gave her a radius of over eight hundred light-years even assuming she had to make the entire hyper voyage under impellers, instead of Warshawski sail, which ought to be enough to get her back to civilization somewhere, assuming that Thatcher could figure out where they were.

As for Zachary herself, she had absolutely nothing to do until one batch of hunters or the other, or preferably both, succeeded in their quest.

"So," Zachary said nineteen hours later. "What do we know?"

She sat at the head of the table in *Harvest Joy*'s captain's briefing room and let her eyes run around the faces of the other people assembled around it. There were five of them: Lieutenant Commander Wilson Jefferson, her executive officer; Lieutenant Thatcher; Jordin Kare and Richard Wix; and Dame Melina Makris. Of that five, Zachary had discovered that she liked four, which was probably a bit above the average for any group of people. Unfortunately, the one member of the group she actively disliked—Makris—more than compensated for that happy state of affairs. To be honest, Zachary would have preferred to exclude Makris from this meeting (or anything else happening aboard *Harvest Joy*), but the immaculately coiffured blonde was the Government's personal representative. It was painfully obvious that in her own not so humble opinion, Makris also considered herself to be the true commander of this entire expedition, whatever the merely official table of organization said. She'd made that painfully evident from the moment she first came on board, and the situation had gotten no better since. The fact that she regarded the personnel who crewed *Harvest Joy* as the sort of menials who'd obviously joined the Navy because they were incapable of finding anything better to do with their lives was equally apparent.

Now Makris proceeded yet again to demonstrate her enormous natural talent for making any Queen's officer detest her. She cleared her throat loudly and gave the captain a pointedly reproving glare for daring to usurp her authority. With that out of the way, she officiously straightened the sheets of hardcopy in front of her, jogged them sharply (and noisily) on the table just in case anyone had missed the point of her glare, and turned her attention to Kare.

"Yes," she said in a hard-edged, slightly nasal voice which suited her sharp-featured face quite well. "What *do* we know, Doctor?"

It was remarkable, Zachary mused. Makris obviously had a detailed checklist of Things to Do to Piss Off Survey Ship Captains, and she was determined not to leave any of them undone. The captain couldn't decide which irritated her more: Makris' usurpation of her own authority . . . or the peremptory, almost dismissive, mistress-to-servant fashion in which she'd just addressed Kare.

"Excuse me, Dame Melina," Zachary said, and waited until the civilian turned to give her a look of pained inquiry.

"What?" Makris asked sharply.

"I believe that I was speaking."

Jefferson and Thatcher looked at one another, but Makris didn't know Zachary nearly as well as they did. She only tossed her head dismissively with a grimace of distaste.

"I hardly think—" she began.

"Regardless of what you may believe, Dame Melina," Zachary interrupted in calm, measured tones, "you are not in this vessel's chain of command."

"I *beg* your pardon?" Makris quite obviously couldn't believe she'd heard Zachary correctly.

"I said that you're not in this vessel's chain of command," Zachary repeated. Makris stared at her, and Zachary smiled thinly. "In point of fact, you're a guest aboard my ship."

"I don't believe I care for your tone, Captain," Makris said coldly.

"You may find this difficult to credit, Dame Melina, but I don't particularly care whether you do or not," Zachary informed her.

"Well you'd better!" Makris snapped. "I warn you, Captain— I'm not prepared to put up with insolence!"

"How odd. That's precisely what *I* was just thinking," Zachary replied, and something seemed to flicker in Makris' eyes. She opened her mouth again, but Zachary leaned forward in her chair before she could say anything more.

"I understand that you're aboard as the Government's representative, Dame Melina," the captain said flatly. "However, I am the captain of this ship; you are not. Neither are you the chairwoman of this meeting. That, too, is my role. In fact, you have no standing whatsoever in the chain of command aboard this ship, and I'm becoming rather tired of your manner. I think—"

"Now, see here, Captain! I'm not about to—"

"Be quiet." Zachary didn't raise her voice, but it cut through Makris' outraged splutter like a chill scalpel. The other woman closed her mouth with an almost-audible click, her eyes wide with astonishment that anyone should dare to address her in such tones.

"That's better." Zachary's hard eyes considered the bureaucrat as if she were inspecting some particularly loathsome bacterium. "As I was saying," the captain resumed, "I think you would do well to practice a certain minimal courtesy while you're aboard my ship. So long as you do, I assure you, the members of the ship's company will reciprocate. If, however, you find that to be beyond your capability, I feel sure we could all dispense with your presence. Do I make myself clear?"

Makris stared at her, looking as if someone had just punched her. But then the paralyzing moment of shock passed and a dark red tide of outrage suffused her face.

"I'm not in the habit of being dictated to by uniformed flunkies, *Captain*!" she spat. "Not even by ones who seem to think they—"

Zachary's open palm cracked like a pistol shot when it landed on the tabletop. The sharp, explosive sound made more than one person jump, and Makris recoiled as if the blow had landed on her cheek instead. A stab of pure, physical fear chopped her off in mid-sentence, and she swallowed as the cold fury burning behind Zachary's eyes seemed to truly register at last.

"That will be enough," the captain said, very softly, into the ringing silence. "Since you obviously cannot comport yourself with anything like adult self-control, Dame Melina, I believe we can dispense with your presence. Leave."

"I— You can't—" Makris spluttered, only to chop off again under the searing contempt of Zachary's gaze.

"Yes, I can," the other woman assured her. "And I have. Your presence is no longer required here . . . nor will it be required at any other staff meeting for the duration of this cruise." Her impaling gaze nailed the Prime Minister's personal representative into her chair, daring her to open her mouth once more as she was exiled from any further direction of the survey mission.

"And now," Zachary went on after a two-heartbeat pause, "you will leave this compartment and go directly to your berthing compartment. You will remain there until I send word you may leave it."

"I—" Makris shook herself. "The Prime Minister will be informed of this, Captain!" she declared, but her voice was much weaker than before.

"No doubt he will," Zachary agreed. "For now, however, you'll obey my orders or I will have you escorted to your quarters. The choice, Dame Melina, is yours."

Her eyes were unflinching, and Makris' attempt to glare defiantly back shattered on their flint. The civilian's gaze fell, and, after one more awkward second, she stood and walked wordlessly through the compartment hatch. Zachary watched her go, then turned back to those still seated around the table as the hatch closed behind her.

"Please excuse the interruption, Dr. Kare," she said pleasantly. "Now, you were about to say—?"

"Ah, you do realize she really will complain to the Prime Minister, don't you, Captain?" Kare asked after a moment, rather than answering her question, and she sighed.

"If she does, she does." The captain shrugged. "In either case, I meant every word I said to her."

"I can't disagree with any of them myself," the astrophysicist admitted with a wry grin. Then he sobered. "But she does have influence at the cabinet level. And a vindictive streak a kilometer wide."

"Somehow, I find that very easy to believe," Zachary observed with a wintery chuckle. "But while I also realize that she undoubt-edly has a certain amount of influence even with the Admiralty—" that was as close as she was prepared to come to mentioning Sir Edward Janacek by name, not that anyone failed to recognize her meaning "—I still meant it. And while there may be repercussions, they may also be less severe than you expect. After all, we're all heroes, Dr. Kare!" She grinned suddenly. "I expect our towering contribution to the expansion of humanity's frontiers to provide at least a little protection against any winds of official disfavor Dame Melina can stir up. If it doesn't—"

She shrugged and, after a moment, Kare nodded. He was still unhappy, not least because a part of him thought he should have been the one to slap Makris down. But there wasn't much he could do about that now, so he returned to the matter in hand, instead.

"In answer to your original question, Captain, TJ and the rest of our Agency people may not have the exact vector information we need yet, but our preliminary readings have managed to nail down the terminus locus. In fact, we've managed to derive a much tighter initial approximation than anyone anticipated." He chuckled. "It's almost as if all the things that made our end of the termi-nus so hard to spot for so long were reversed at this end."

"So you're confident that at least we'll be able to go home again?" Zachary asked with a smile.

"Oh, yes. Of course, TJ and I were always confident of that, or we'd never have volunteered to come along in the first place!"

"Of course you wouldn't have," Zachary agreed. "But confidence aside, do you have any sort of estimate on how long it will take you to derive the approach vector?"

"That's harder to say, but I shouldn't think it will take a great deal of time. As I say, our instruments are doing a much better job with this terminus. And we have a great deal more informa-tion about its strength and tidal stresses now that we've been through it once from the other side than we had when we began calculating for the trip here. If you want my best guess, bearing in mind that a guess is mostly what it would be, I'd say that we ought to have the numbers we need within the next two weeks— possibly three. I'll be surprised, frankly, if we can pull them together much more rapidly than that. On the other hand, we've rather persistently surprised ourselves with how quickly things came together ever since we finally found this terminus."

"So I understand." Zachary nodded pensively, then pursed her lips as she considered the time estimate. It was considerably better than she'd anticipated, she reflected. Which ought to make everyone—with the possible exception of Dame Melina—happy. She suppressed a sour smile at the thought and turned her attention to Jefferson and Thatcher.

"Well, Wilson. The boffins seem to be holding up their end. Are we holding up ours?"

"Actually," the exec replied with what she suddenly realized was studied calm, "I believe we might reasonably say that we are, Skipper."

"Ah?" Zachary arched both eyebrows, and Jefferson grinned. He was obviously pleased about something, but Zachary had known him for quite some time. It was equally apparent to her that his pleasure was less than complete. In fact, she seemed to sense an undertone of what could almost be anxiety.

"You're the one who put it together, Rochelle," he told Thatcher. "Suppose you break it to her?"

"Yes, Sir," Thatcher said with a smile of her own, then seemed to sober slightly as she turned to her captain.

"Our people have done just about as well as Dr. Wix and his people, Ma'am. So far we've already identified no less than six 'beacon' stars, which has let us place our current position with a high degree of confidence."

"And that position is—?" Zachary prompted when Thatcher paused.

"At this particular moment, Ma'am, we're approximately six hundred and twelve light-years from Manticore. And we've been able to identify that G2 star at four light-years as Lynx."

"Lynx?" Zachary's brow wrinkled, then she shrugged. "I can't say the name rings any bells, Rochelle. Should it?"

"Not really, Ma'am. After all, it's a long way from home. But the Lynx System was settled about two hundred T-years ago. It's part of the Talbott Cluster."

"Talbott?" This time Zachary recognized the name, and her eyes narrowed as she considered the implications of that recognition.

The Talbott Cluster was the thoroughly inaccurate name assigned to one of several regions, most of them rather sparsely settled, just beyond the frontiers of the Solarian League. Whatever else the "cluster's" stars were, they were nothing which remotely resembled anything an astrophysicist would have considered a cluster, but that didn't matter to the people who'd needed to come up with a convenient handle for them.

Most such regions were relatively hardscrabble propositions. Many of them contained colonies which had backslid technologically, severely in some cases, since their settlement, and only a few of them contained star systems which anyone from the Star Kingdom would have considered economically well established. And eventually, all of them would inevitably be incorporated into the glacially expanding frontiers of the League. Whether they wanted to be or not.

No one would resort to anything as crude as outright conquest. Sollies didn't do things that way . . . nor did they have to. The Solarian League was the largest, most powerful, wealthiest political entity in human history. On a per capita basis, the Star Kingdom's economy was actually somewhat stronger, but in absolute terms Manticore's entire gross domestic product would disappear with scarcely a ripple into the League's economy. When that sort of economic powerhouse expanded into the vicinity of star systems which could scarcely keep their heads above water, the train of events leading to eventual incorporation extended itself with the inevitability of entropy.

And if it didn't, the League could be counted upon to give the process a swift kick, Zachary reflected sourly.

Josepha Zachary was scarcely alone among the Star Kingdom of Manticore's naval officers in her dislike for the Solarian League. Actually, a lot of people who had been denied the honor and privilege of Solly citizenship disliked the League. It wasn't because the League went around conquering people. Not officially, anyway. It was just that the towering sense of moral superiority which the League seemed to bring to all of its interstellar endeavors could be absolutely relied upon to irritate every non-Solly who ever experienced it. The antipathy was exacerbated for the Royal Manticoran Navy, however, and Zachary was honest enough to admit it. The embargo which the Cromarty Government had managed to secure on weapons sales and technology transfers to the belligerents in the Star Kingdom's war against the Peeps had irritated the hell out of an awful lot of Sollies. Some of them had been none too shy about making their ire known, and some of those who hadn't been were officers in the Solarian League Navy or Customs Service who had expressed their personal irritation by harassing Manticoran merchant ships in Solarian space.

Even without that, however, Zachary knew, she wouldn't have cared for the Sollies. When the Solarian League was created, the local governments of Old Earth's older daughter worlds had already been over a thousand T-years old. Few of those planets had been prepared to surrender their sovereignty to a potentially tyrannical central government, so the League Constitution had been carefully designed to prevent that from happening. Like the founders of the Star Kingdom, the men and women who'd drafted that Constitution had limited the funding sources for the government they were creating as the best means of ensuring that it could never grow into the monster they feared. Unfortunately, they hadn't stopped there. Instead they'd gone on to give every member system of the League effective veto power in the League legislature.

That combination had created a situation in which the League effectively had no official foreign policy. Or, rather, what it had was a consensus so mushy that it was hopelessly amorphous. About the only clear and unambiguous foreign policy principle the League maintained was the Eridani Edict's prohibition against the unrestricted use of what were still called "weapons of mass destruction" against inhabited planets. And even that was only because the edict's proponents had used the Solarian Constitution's referendum provisions to do an end run around the Assembly and amend it to incorporate the edict into the League's fundamental law after the horrific casualties of the Eridani Incident.

But if the League had no official foreign policy, that didn't mean it lacked a *de facto* one. The problem was that the League Assembly as such had virtually nothing to do with that policy's formulation.

While the restrictions on the central government's ability to tax had indeed limited that government's power, the limitation was purely relative. Even a very tiny percentage of the total economic product of something the size of the Solarian League was an inconceivable amount of money. Despite that, however, the League was perpetually strapped for revenue, because the relative ineffectuality of the veto-riddled Assembly had resulted in the transfer of more and more of the practical day-to-day authority for managing the League from the legislature to bureaucratic regulatory agencies. Unlike laws and statutes, bureaucratic regulations didn't require the item-by-item approval of the entire Assembly, which, over the centuries, had led to the gradual evolution of deeply entrenched, monolithic, enormously powerful (and expensive) bureaucratic empires.

For the most part, the Sollies appeared to have no particular problems with that. Those regulatory and service agencies seldom intruded directly into the lives of the citizens as a whole. And however distasteful Zachary might have found their existence, they did perform many useful functions which the veto-hobbled Assembly would never have been able to discharge efficiently. But there was an undeniable downside to their existence, even for League citizens.

For one thing, the ever-growing sprawl of regulatory overreach required larger and larger bureaucracies, which, in turn, absorbed an ever-growing percentage of the central government's total income. That, Zachary suspected, was one reason the Solarian League Navy, for all of its numerical strength and its perception of itself as the most powerful and modern fleet in existence, was probably at least fifty T-years out of date compared to the RMN. The Navy's budgets were no more immune to the hemorrhaging effect of such uncontrolled bureaucratic growth than any other aspect of the League government, which left too little funding for aggressive research and development and meant that far too many of the SLN's ships of the wall were growing steadily more obsolete as they moldered away in mothballs.

Had Zachary been a Solly, that alone would have been enough to infuriate her. Unfortunately, the Navy was only one example of the pernicious effect of siphoning more and more of the available resources of government into the clutches of bureaucratic entities subject to only the weakest of legislative oversight. But what Zachary found even more objectionable as someone who was *not* a Solly was the way in which the League bureaucrats made foreign policy without ever bothering to consult with the League's elected representatives. And probably the worst of the lot in that regard was the Office of Frontier Security.

The OFS had originally been conceived as an agency intended to promote stability along the League's frontiers. It was supposed to do that by offering its services to mediate disputes between settled star systems which were not yet part of the League. In order to provide incentives for quarreling star systems to seek its arbitration, it had been authorized to offer security guarantees, backed by the SLN, and special trade concessions to those systems which sought the League's protection.

No doubt the OFS' creators had anticipated that the agency's operations would smooth the inevitable gravitation of such single-system polities into the benign arms of the League. But whatever they might have intended when the OFS was first authorized five hundred T-years ago, what it had become since was an arm of naked expansionism. These days, the OFS manufactured 'requests' for League protection. It didn't worry particularly about whether or not the people making those requests represented local governments, either. All it cared about was that *someone* had requested 'protection'—often *against* a local government, in fact—to offer the necessary pretext for its intervention. And there had been occasions when no one at all had requested OFS intervention. Instances in which the OFS had sent in the League Gendarmerie to enforce protectorate status . . . purely in the interests of safeguarding human rights, of course.

Over the centuries, the Office of Frontier Security had become the Solarian League's broom, sweeping the small, independent, poverty-stricken star systems along the League's periphery into its maw, whether they chose to be swept or not. To be completely fair, which Zachary admitted she found it difficult to be in this instance, most of the worlds which were dragged into the League eventually found themselves far better off materially.

Eventually. The rub was that in the short term their citizens were given no choice, no voice in their own future. And anyone who objected to becoming a Solly was ignored . . . or repressed. Worse, the OFS was no more immune to the temptations of graft and corruption than any other agency run by fallible human beings. The lack of any sort of close legislative oversight only made those temptations stronger, and by now the agency was in bed with powerful vested interests, using its power and authority to create "sweetheart deals" for favored interstellar corporations, shipping lines, or political cronies and contributors as it reorganized the "protected" worlds under its nurturing care. There were even persistent rumors that some of the OFS administrators had forged connections with the Mesan genetic slavers.

Which brought Zachary right back to the Talbott Cluster, because

Talbott had perhaps another twenty or thirty T-years to go until the League's creeping frontiers brought the OFS to it.

"The Talbott Cluster," she mused, half to herself, and Jefferson nodded.

"Yes, Ma'am. I did a little research when Rochelle identified Lynx, too. According to the most recent data in our files, which is probably at least ten or fifteen T-years out of date, the system population is around two-point-three billion. It looks to me as if economically they're about where the Graysons were before they joined the Alliance, or maybe not quite that far along, although their base tech level is probably a bit higher. From what I've found so far, Lynx seems to be one of the two or three more heavily populated systems in the cluster, but the average seems to work out to around one-point-five billion."

"And Lynx is only about fourteen hours from this terminus," Thatcher pointed out.

"That thought had also occurred to me," Zachary said mildly.

"Well, that certainly sounds good!" Kare said. The captain looked at him, and the scientist grinned. "We're going to need someone to help us anchor the terminus, Captain. It might be nice if they were a bit closer than that, but it should still make developing this terminus a lot easier!"

"Yes," Zachary agreed. "Yes, I suppose it will, Doctor."

She watched Kare and Wix smiling at one another in delight, and then her gaze met Wilson Jefferson's and she saw the reflection of her own worry in the exec's eyes.

Erica Ferrero reminded herself not to snarl. It wasn't easy.

She stood at Lieutenant Commander Harris' shoulder, gazing into his tactical display at a flashing crimson dot which had become entirely too familiar.

"Definitely *Hellbarde*, Skip," Harris reported. "It matches her emissions signature across the board."

"Still nothing from our friend Gortz, Mecia?" Ferrero asked without ever taking her eyes from the plot.

"Not a word, Ma'am," the com officer reported.

"Figures!" Ferrero snorted, continuing to stare hard-eyed at the icon. At least Sidemore's Intelligence files had been able to finally ID *Kapitän der Sterne* Gortz as one Guangfu Gortz. Intelligence didn't have as much information on him as Ferrero might have wished, but what they did have clearly indicated that he was one of the IAN's cadre of Manticore-haters. Which probably meant that he was enjoying himself immensely at the moment, she thought, baring mental teeth at the memory of the florid, jowly face from the ONI file's imagery. Then she patted Harris lightly on the shoulder, turned, and stalked across to her command chair. She settled herself into it and glared at the small repeater plot that duplicated Harris' in miniature.

Jessica Epps had been spared the company of IANS *Hellbarde* for almost four weeks—long enough for Ferrero to begin to hope *Kapitän zur Sternen* Gortz had found someone else to irritate. It had, she'd realized even at the time, been a triumph of optimism over experience, but she'd been properly grateful for the respite anyway.

Now, unfortunately, that respite had come to an end, and Ferrero felt a slow, intense boil of anger bubbling away deep down inside.

She drew a deep breath and forced herself to remember Duchess Harrington's orders. Like most of the ship commanders assigned to Sidemore Station, Ferrero had been delighted when she learned Harrington was being sent out to take command. It wasn't that she had a thing against Rear Admiral Hewitt. He was a good man and a competent flag officer, but Ferrero had hoped Harrington's assignment indicated that someone back home was finally taking the situation in Silesia seriously. Certainly they wouldn't have sent "the Salamander" all the way out here if they hadn't meant for her appointment to send a message to the Andermani!

Unfortunately, it was beginning to look like the people who'd hoped that were going to be disappointed.

It wasn't Harrington's fault. That much was obvious. But the nature and number of the reinforcements the Janacek Admiralty had decided to send out with the duchess made it painfully evident that—to use Bob Llewellyn's colorful phrase—Sidemore was still "sucking hind teat." The astonishing arrival of so many Grayson warships had only underscored the weakness of the reinforcements the Admiralty had seen fit to spare Harrington, and the duchess' instructions to the ships assigned to her new command had been another sign that no one back home gave much of a damn about what was happening out here.

Ferrero knew that no flag officer with Harrington's reputation could have been happy issuing those orders. And the fact that she'd done it had said volumes about just how out of touch with reality the Star Kingdom's government really was. Her Majesty's starships in Silesia were to maintain and protect the traditional interpretation of freedom of space, as well as the territorial integrity of the Silesian Confederacy, against anyone who threatened to violate either, while simultaneously avoiding "provocations" of the Imperial Andermani Navy . . . or responding in kind to Andermani provocations.

That mouthful of platitudes and qualifications must have stuck in Harrington's craw sideways, Ferrero thought. That much had been evident even through the officialese of her orders. And if it hadn't been, the revision of the controlling rules of engagement which had accompanied those orders would have made it clear enough. Although the modified ROE strongly reiterated that officers were to avoid counter provocations—which, Ferrero suspected, was at least partly aimed at her own destruction of *Hellbarde*'s remote sensor platforms, despite the fact that Harrington had officially approved her report of that patrol—they also emphasized that "These orders shall not be construed to in any way supersede or compromise a captain's responsibility to safeguard the vessel entrusted to her command. No officer can do very wrong by taking all such defensive actions as shall seem necessary and prudent in her judgment." Taken together, those seemingly contradictory provisions told Harrington's officers a lot. The most important message was that she really meant it when she ordered them to avoid responding in kind to Andermani provocations . . . and that she would back them to the hilt in any reasonable action they took in self-defense.

It was a dangerous set of instructions for any station commander to issue, and Ferrero knew it. If something did go wrong, Harrington could absolutely rely on someone to suggest that she'd actually encouraged her captains to respond with force if challenged. And to be fair to the sort of rear-area genius who would come up with that sort of suggestion, there were undoubtedly captains who would interpret Duchess Harrington's orders in precisely that fashion. Fortunately, few of them were currently assigned to Sidemore Station, but even one in the wrong place at the wrong time could be enough.

And, Ferrero told herself with bleak honesty, *I know who one of those officers could be . . . especially with Gortz pushing me this way.*

She drew a deep breath and made herself settle deeper into the command chair. *Hellbarde* had been matching *Jessica Epps'* every course change at close range for over sixteen hours . . . and refusing to identify herself when challenged. At the moment, the other cruiser was at least two hundred thousand kilometers inside normal missile range of Ferrero's ship, which put Gortz into a very gray area. *Hellbarde* hadn't quite violated interstellar law by shadowing *Jessica Epps* from within weapons range and ignoring all requests that she identify herself and state her intentions. Not quite. But she was pressing the limits. Indeed, Ferrero could have made a strong case before any interstellar court of admiralty for justifying herself in peremptorily ordering the Andermani to stand clear of her own vessel . . . and locking *Hellbarde* up with her fire control systems to emphasize her point.

Which, she admitted, was precisely what she wanted to do. And, for that matter, precisely what Gortz *deserved* for her to do.

But it wasn't what she'd done. Not given Lady Harrington's orders. Instead of slapping Gortz down, she'd gritted her teeth, brought *Jessica Epps* to level two readiness, and manned missile-defense stations. And she had Shawn Harris running constant targeting updates on *Hellbarde* using passive sensors only. But aside from that, she'd done nothing else. Indeed, after the first three challenges, she hadn't even hailed the other ship.

I wonder if Gortz is as pissed off by the way I'm ignoring his ship as I am by the way he's shadowing mine? Ferrero thought with a sort of mordant humor that did very little to mask the seething heat of her own anger from her.

But at this particular moment, what Gortz felt didn't really matter. Because however angry Erica Ferrero might be, she was going to follow her orders. She would *not* provide whatever pretext *Hellbarde* might be seeking to suck her into providing.

But if that bastard even blinks *in my direction,* she told herself harshly, *I'm going to blow him and his goddamned ship to dust bunnies.*

CHAPTER THIRTY-FIVE

Elaine Descroix had never really enjoyed her appearances in the House of Lords at the best of times. Which might have struck some observers as being just a little bit odd, since the upper chamber of the Star Kingdom's parliament was the logical spiritual home of the defenders of the *status quo* to which the current government was so devoted. But although the Descroix family was well ensconced among the wealthiest upper crust of Manticoran society, its connections with the true aristocracy were tenuous, at best. And Elaine, who had married into the family, was even more tenuously connected than that, especially since Sir John Descroix's death fourteen T-years before. She'd never seen any reason to replace the deceased husband who'd been her original passport to the stratified heights of Manticoran society, and most people had forgotten that she was a relative newcomer to it. Yet despite the outward assurance with which she rubbed elbows with the most nobly born, neither she—nor they—ever quite forgot that she was an interloper in their territory.

In many ways, that sense of inherent inferiority, by birth, at least, explained a great deal of the ambition which had driven her so far in her quest for political power. It was one of the more bitter ironies of her current position that the coalition to which she belonged was absolutely dedicated to preserving a political balance in which Elaine Descroix could never hold the one post she

505

most hungered to hold: the premiership. Unless, of course, she wound up ennobled in recognition of her selfless service to the Star Kingdom.

Not, she reflected, that Michael Janvier would nominate her for a title if he wanted to hang onto the Prime Minister's residence and had a single gram of sense.

None of which made her feel any happier about the prospect of today's session in the Lords. Unfortunately, there was no way to avoid it. That pain in the ass William Alexander and his even greater pain in the ass of a brother had put Eloise Pritchart's speech and the general state of the ongoing negotiations with the Republic of Haven on the Official Questions list for the upper house. Which meant someone from the Government had no option under the unwritten portion of the Constitution but to appear before the Lords to be suitably grilled.

And that someone, whether she herself was a member of the Lords or not, was the Foreign Secretary.

Now she listened to the boring, droning formalities of her introduction by the Speaker and drew a deep mental breath in preparation for the coming ordeal.

"And so," the Speaker wound up at last, "it is my pleasure to yield the floor to the Honorable Foreign Secretary. Madame Secretary?"

He turned to her with a smile she suspected must be at least as false as the one with which she responded, and she stood and crossed to the combination lectern and data console provided for those called to testify before the House.

"Thank you, Mr. Speaker," she said graciously, then turned to look out over the tiers of seats. "And may I also thank the noble members of this House for permitting me to appear before them."

She produced another of her patented, gentle smiles and then spent a few seconds arranging a dozen or so old-fashioned hardcopy note cards before her. They were purely nonfunctional props, but she'd long since learned to use them as a delaying tactic, something to shuffle through as if checking her facts while she actually considered exactly how to respond to a particularly sensitive question.

In the end, however, she had to stop playing with the pieces of paper and face up to the reason she was here.

"As the noble members are aware," she began, "this is Questions

Day. And because the first Question on the List is the state of the Star Kingdom's foreign policy, it seemed most appropriate to the Government for the Foreign Secretary to appear before you to respond. I await your pleasure."

There was silence for a few seconds, and then the blinking green light which indicated that someone sought recognition from the floor lit. Inevitably, it was above the White Haven cadet seat.

"I recognize Lord Alexander," she said in a voice whose pleasant tone fooled no one in the chamber.

"I thank the Honorable Secretary." Alexander's tone probably fooled even fewer people than her own had. He paused for a moment, then continued. "Madame Secretary. In a recent speech before both houses of the Congress of the Republic of Haven, President Eloise Pritchart announced that her administration intended to press the Star Kingdom's negotiators for concrete progress in the peace talks between the Star Kingdom and the Republic. She stated at that time that new proposals from the Republic would be forthcoming, and the implication of her speech appeared to be that she intended to demand a prompt response from us. Have those proposals, in fact, been received? And if so, of what do they consist and what response does the Government propose to make to them?"

Descroix suppressed an urge to shuffle through her note cards. It wasn't as if Alexander's questions came as any sort of a surprise.

"I am, of course, familiar with the text of President Pritchart's speech, My Lord," she began carefully. "While I would agree that the general tone of her remarks was more assertive and potentially confrontational than we might have wished, I'm not certain they indicated that she intended to 'demand' anything from us. There must, of course, be a certain degree of impatience on the part of anyone whose government has been engaged for so long, and with so little success, on the negotiation of a treaty to end such a bloody conflict. Her Majesty's Government is fully aware of the extent to which this must be true for the Republic of Haven, which, after all, stands in the weaker position in those negotiations. Nor are the members of Her Majesty's Government immune to such impatience in their own right. Unfortunately, there remain fundamental points of disagreement between the Star Kingdom and the Republic of Haven which continue to preclude the prompt and amicable settlement of our differences which I am certain both governments earnestly desire. President Pritchart's speech undoubtedly reflected the frustration all of us feel."

She smiled again. Alexander did not smile back, and her own expression stiffened ever so slightly.

"In response to your first question, My Lord, Her Majesty's Government is in receipt of a communique transmitted to us from President Pritchart through the offices of Secretary of State Giancola. I would not characterize its contents as a 'demand,' however. Certainly, they constitute a body of proposals to which President Pritchart obviously expects Her Majesty's Government to respond, but the term 'demand' implies a far greater degree of confrontationalism than is contained in President Pritchart's note.

"The exact nature of the proposals contained in her note is somewhat sensitive," she continued, edging very carefully into potentially murky waters. "The nature of such complex, ongoing negotiations, particularly those in which feelings have indeed, upon occasion, run high on both sides, demands a somewhat greater degree of confidentiality than might otherwise be the case. Her Majesty's Government craves the indulgence of this House and requests that that confidentiality be respected in this case."

"While I fully appreciate the need to maintain confidentiality under some circumstances, Madame Secretary," Alexander replied, "I find it somewhat difficult to believe these circumstances require it. These negotiations have been ongoing for more than four T-years. The newsfaxes have covered every aspect of them in minute detail. Unless President Pritchart's note contains some new and total departure from the Republic's previous positions, I cannot see any legitimate need to conceal her 'proposals' from the members of this House. After all," he allowed himself a wintery smile, "*she* already knows what they are."

Descroix found it even more difficult not to play with her note cards this time. Under the unwritten but ironbound constitutional precedents which governed the Official Questions List, she could refuse to answer Alexander's questions only if she were prepared to assert that the security of the Star Kingdom required that she do so. That option was always available to her, but while there might be one peer who would be stupid enough to believe her claim was anything other than a desperate political maneuver, there couldn't possibly be two of them. And if she invoked security concerns, then she effectively confirmed that Pritchart's "proposals" did, in fact, constitute a major escalation in the tension between the two star nations.

There was, however, an appeal which should remove her from the horns of this particular dilemma without resorting to that dangerous alternative.

"I regret that Her Majesty's Government must find itself in disagreement with you on this point, My Lord," she said firmly. "In the Government's opinion, and in my own, as Foreign Secretary, the best interests of the Star Kingdom and our hope for progress in our negotiations with the Republic of Haven would not be well served by a violation of the confidentiality of the negotiating process. I must, therefore, appeal to the judgment of the House at large, praying that its noble members will sustain my position and that of Her Majesty's Government."

"Ladies and Gentlemen of the House," the Speaker announced, "the Honorable Secretary craves your indulgence and asks you to sustain her in declining further specific response to the noble member's Question. Please indicate your pleasure on this matter."

Descroix stood calmly, her expression confident, as the members of the House entered their votes into their own consoles. It didn't take long, and then the Speaker looked up from the display which tallied them before him.

"Ladies and Gentlemen of the House," he said, "you have indicated your pleasure. The vote is three hundred and seventy-three in support of the Honorable Secretary's position and three hundred and ninety-one opposed, with twenty-three abstentions. The Honorable Secretary's position is not sustained."

Descroix stiffened. Several decades of political experience allowed her to maintain her calm expression, but she felt herself pale in dismay. In the entire four-plus T-years of the High Ridge Government, the House of Lords had never failed to sustain the Government when it declined to answer an Official Question. The same could not be said in the Commons, but the Lords had been a bastion of solid support, and she'd expected it to sustain the government today, as well.

The fact that it had chosen not to left her with no option but to answer or flatly refuse on the basis of national security. She could do that, but it would strip the Government of any cover of mature, considered support from the House of Lords at large. That was bad enough, but the vote totals were even worse. The number of abstentions was a sufficiently unpleasant shock, but the Opposition in the Lords could normally count on no more than three hundred and fifty votes. Which meant that at least sixty peers upon whose support the Government usually could have firmly relied had either abstained or actively supported the Opposition.

She stood there for a moment, making certain she remained firmly in command of her voice, then made herself smile at Alexander.

"If it is not the pleasure of the House to sustain the Government's position, then, of course, I am at your disposal, My Lord."

"I thank you for that gracious acknowledgment, Madame Secretary," Alexander replied, with a small bow. "In that case, may I renew my request that you share President Pritchart's 'proposals' with this House?"

"Certainly, My Lord. First, President Pritchart notes that, from the beginning of the negotiation process, the position of the Star Kingdom in relation to Trevor's Star has been that . . ."

Elaine Descroix stormed into the conference room. Her normal, benign expression was notably in abeyance, and Michael Janvier hid a mental wince at the ferocity of the scowl she turned upon the waiting members of the working Cabinet as she slammed through the door.

Despite his own membership in the House of Lords, the Prime Minister had decided that prudent tactics required him to be unavoidably detained on official business rather than attend the session Descroix had just endured. Had he been there, and had the session gone poorly—as, in fact, it had—then he might have found himself, as Prime Minister, drawn into responding to the Opposition, as well. Under the circumstances, that was not an acceptable situation. Descroix, as a mere Foreign Secretary, could get away with evasions a Prime Minister could not. And ultimately, a Foreign Secretary was expendable. He could always request her resignation from her current office if some minor prevarication came home to roost or if a sacrificial victim were required to propitiate the newsies. Her position in the Progressive Party would make it necessary to find her another Cabinet level post if he did, but such reorganizations were scarcely unheard of.

The fact that he hadn't attended the session, however, hadn't prevented him from monitoring it from his office. Which meant he understood exactly why Descroix looked ready to strangle Opposition peers with her bare hands.

And, he thought mordantly, *she'd probably just as soon throttle some of our peers, for that matter.*

"Hello, Elaine," he said as she stalked across to her chair at the conference table.

She snarled something which might have been interpreted as a greeting, jerked out her chair, and flung herself into it.

"I regret that you've had such an unpleasant morning," High Ridge continued, "and I deeply appreciate your efforts on the Government's behalf. I mean that sincerely."

"You'd damned well better appreciate them!" Descroix half-snapped. "Jesus! And you'd damned well better have a long heart-to-heart talk with Green Vale, too!"

Jessica Burke, Countess of Green Vale, was the Government Whip in the Lords. That post was far from a sinecure in a coalition of such diverse ideologies as that of the current government, and everyone in the conference room knew it. Nonetheless, High Ridge reflected, it was undoubtedly fortunate that Green Vale wasn't present at the moment.

"I assure you that I'll be speaking with her," he said mildly after a moment. "In all fairness, however, I feel confident she did all that could have been done under the circumstances."

"Oh?" Descroix glowered at him. "And what sort of Whip doesn't even warn us when we're likely to lose a vote like that?"

"The margin was only eighteen votes," High Ridge pointed out. "That's barely two percent of the members actually present."

"But the total shift was *sixty-three* votes, counting the abstentions," she pointed out in venomous response. "And by my math, that's over *eight* percent. Which doesn't even count the thirty-seven members of the House who managed to not even be there in the first place." Her eyes would have sent daggers through the heart of anyone less stoutly armored by his own sense of who he was than High Ridge.

"Admittedly, it was a most unfortunate occurrence," the Prime Minister conceded. "All I meant to indicate was that the margin of votes actually cast was close enough that I believe it would be unfair to fault Jessica for failing to realize ahead of time that the House wouldn't vote to sustain."

"Then why the hell do we have a Whip in the first place?" she demanded.

He didn't respond to the obviously rhetorical question, and, after a moment, she shrugged in petulant acknowledgment of its pettiness.

"At any rate," she went on after a moment, "I don't see any way we can regard today's fiasco as anything but a potentially serious setback, Michael."

"A setback, certainly," he agreed. "Precisely how serious it may prove is another question, however."

"Don't fool yourself," she said flatly. "Alexander and White Haven were both out for blood . . . and New Dijon wasn't any damned help, either. Goddamned Liberal hypocrite!"

High Ridge didn't manage to conceal his wince this time. Fortunately, the Chancellor of the Exchequer wasn't present. It had taken a little creative scheduling on his part to ensure that she would be otherwise occupied meeting with the Chairman of the Bank of Manticore and the Board of the Royal Interstellar Development Fund at the exact time he was "forced" to schedule this meeting. He strongly suspected that New Kiev knew exactly why he'd done it, and the fact that she hadn't protested even mildly suggested even more to him. On the other hand, she'd undoubtedly managed to assuage her own conscience by reflecting that her good friend and fellow Liberal Sir Harrison MacIntosh would be present to deputize for her and see to it that their party's interests were represented. Which he was. And at the moment, he looked almost as unhappy with Descroix's characterization of the Earl of New Dijon as New Kiev would have looked.

Not that High Ridge had any personal quibble with Descroix on that particular point. New Dijon had always been careful to distance himself from the current government. That hadn't meant he was unaware of which side of his bread was buttered, however, and while he'd been careful to maintain his public stance of independent thought, his actual voting record had been another matter.

But today had been different. The fact that William Alexander and his brother would lead the attack had been as inevitable as the next sunrise, and no one had been surprised when a dozen other Opposition peers piled on with their own pointed questions. But three of the Independent peers who had routinely supported the Government had joined the Opposition in indicating serious concern over the Republic's new, more aggressive negotiating stance . . . and so had New Dijon.

"Actually," the Prime Minister said after a moment, "New Dijon's position may work out in our favor."

"Excuse me?" Descroix looked at him incredulously, and he shrugged.

"I don't say that's what he had in mind, but the fact that he publicly 'took us to the woodshed,' as my grandfather used to put it, could actually help us out down the road. As far as the newsfaxes are concerned, he's indicated his independence of thought and willingness to speak his mind. And the questions he asked were actually on the mild side, you know. So he's positioned himself to act as a sort of buffer without doing us any real additional harm. Which means that if he later expresses himself as moderately concerned and yet confident in Her Majesty's Government's handling of the negotiations, his statement will carry even more weight because of his earlier doubts."

"Do you honestly believe that's what he had in mind?" Descroix demanded in obvious disbelief, and High Ridge shrugged again.

"Personally, I doubt it," he conceded. "His support, however indirect, has always been shakiest where our foreign policy was concerned, you know. I think, however, that he's clearly indicated his awareness of the consequences for the authority of the House of Lords if this Government should fall. So I wouldn't be surprised if his own party leadership was able to convince him of the necessity of supporting us against this particular attack. Wouldn't you agree, Harrison?"

He looked at MacIntosh, and the Home Secretary scowled. But then, obviously against his will, he nodded slowly.

"I'm sure," the Secretary of Trade put in, "that the Earl will be . . . open-minded if we approach him properly."

Everyone at the table glanced in the direction of the Earl of North Hollow with varying degrees of openness. Interesting, High Ridge thought. He hadn't realized the North Hollow Files might contain anything useful for influencing New Dijon.

"However that may work out in the end," Descroix went on after a moment, her voice slightly less acid, "we got hurt today. There's no point pretending otherwise."

"I wish you were wrong," High Ridge said. She wasn't, of course.

Alexander had hammered away at the exact nature of the Pritchart "proposals" with merciless energy. Descroix had managed to avoid simply handing over the note from Secretary of State Giancola, which had at least allowed her to paraphrase the taut, uncompromising way in which some of those proposals had been phrased. But nothing she'd been able to do had been sufficient to conceal the fact that the Republic of Haven had, indeed, taken a much harder line. It was painfully obvious that Eloise Pritchart was done responding to Manticoran proposals. She clearly intended to put her own demands on the table and insist that Manticore respond to *them*, instead.

That had been quite bad enough, but then Alexander's insufferable brother had dived into the fray. What, he had asked, was the Government's view of the effect the Republican Navy's newly revealed combat capabilities was likely to have on the future course of the negotiations?

Descroix had insisted that the consequences of the Republic's naval strength would be minimal, particularly in light of the steps the Government had already taken to offset the so far unproven increases in Haven's capabilities. It had been an unfortunate position for her to maintain, in some ways, given White Haven's earlier insistence that the Government's naval reductions were dangerously unsound. Yet it had also been the only one she could possibly take, and so she'd done her best to defend what was at best a weak position.

She had not come off well in the confrontation.

Yet for all that, High Ridge reminded himself, the Government's position in the Lords almost certainly remained sound. At least fifteen or twenty of the peers who'd managed to find reasons to be elsewhere during today's session could be counted upon in a pinch to vote to sustain the Government. They'd absented themselves to avoid potential embarrassment, perhaps, but like New Dijon, they knew where their own interests ultimately lay. And they'd actually lost even fewer of the Independent peers on the vote to sustain Descroix than he might have expected, under the circumstances.

"I think you handled Alexander about as well as anyone could have," he told her after a moment, and it was probably true. Under the circumstances, no one could have prevented the Opposition leader from making an unfortunate amount of political capital out of the situation, yet Descroix had managed to at least somewhat blunt his attacks.

"Do you?" she asked, her mouth twisting as if she'd bitten into something spoiled. "I wish I could say the same where his asshole of a brother was concerned!"

High Ridge grimaced, partly over her language, but far more because he agreed with her assessment. White Haven had hurt them on the military preparedness issue. Possibly hurt them badly, although that remained to be seen.

"Tell me, Edward," Descroix went on, turning her scowl upon Janacek. "How would you have responded to his little inquisition?"

"I've already had to do that, thank you," Janacek said sourly. "This is the first time you've had to deal with it, but we haven't been quite that fortunate over at Admiralty House."

"Well, perhaps if you'd seen it coming and managed to give any of us any warning," she said icily, "it wouldn't have been quite so embarrassing for you. Or for the rest of us, either."

"And perhaps if anyone at the Foreign Office had been awake enough to warn us that Pritchart was going to start issuing demands when you'd assured us you were completely in control of the negotiating process, *that* wouldn't have embarrassed us, either!" Janacek shot back.

"Which wouldn't have mattered if they hadn't managed to sneak their fleet increases past you," Descroix rejoined hotly. "Without having improved their military position, they wouldn't have had the gall to take this sort of high-handed tone with us!"

"I'm not as sure of that as you seem to be," Janacek growled. "And another thing, I'm getting tired—"

"That will be enough." High Ridge didn't quite raise his voice, but its hard edge cut through the burgeoning quarrel like a knife, and Janacek closed his mouth. That didn't keep him from bestowing a final glare on Descroix, who returned it with interest, but at least it shut them both up.

"I think," the Prime Minister continued, "that we're all in agreement that our position today is weaker than it was a few months ago." He shrugged. "That sort of thing happens in politics, and the same trends that are working against us right now may well turn around and work in our favor once the current furor's had an opportunity to quiet down. After all, the Opposition has been crying wolf for so long that a substantial portion of the public is tired of hearing it. At the moment, Alexander and his crowd may have managed to engender a certain degree of concern, possibly even panic. But if we can keep a lid on the situation, that concern will begin to fade into a 'business as usual' attitude. That's also the nature of politics.

"The point to which we ought to be turning our attention is just how we go about keeping that lid in place. And to be completely frank, Edward, I think the public is more exercised over the potential increases in the Havenites' naval power than over the exact language of diplomatic notes."

"I know it," Janacek conceded.

"And how do you suggest we go about addressing that concern?"

"Admiral Jurgensen and I have been focusing closely on that very question, I assure you," the First Lord replied. "As I told you when the existence of the new Havenite ships of the wall first came out, what really matters more than the ships themselves is the technology and sophistication of the weapons and defensive systems they mount. With that in mind, Admiral Jurgensen has ordered an exhaustive analysis of all the information in our possession. That includes direct reports from our own naval attaches, reports from agent networks in the Republic, technical intelligence, and even Havenite news accounts. The consensus of his analysts is that Theisman's 'new navy' is probably a lot less impressive than he wants us to believe."

"Really?" High Ridge leaned back and raised one eyebrow.

"Really. As I say, the key consideration is the capabilities of the hardware that goes inside the ships. Now, admittedly, there's no way short of actually physically examining those vessels to be positive about what those capabilities are, but there are certain significant indicators. Probably the strongest single one of those is the fact that they haven't shown anyone a single CLAC. It's extremely unlikely—indeed, according to BuWeaps it's virtually impossible—that the Havenite tech base is capable of matching the range performance of Ghost Rider, much less the fire control and electronic warfare capabilities of our new systems. Don't forget, we've had plenty of experience with examining captured Havenite equipment, so we know exactly what they had in their first-line units at the time of the cease-fire. Projecting from that basis, and bearing in mind that Havenite R&D has never been able to match our own, their SD(P)s are almost certainly shorter ranged and much easier to kill than our own are. Substantially more dangerous than any of the classes they had in service prior to the cease-fire, certainly, but not in a class with our own SD(P)s.

"The fact that they haven't put any CLACs into service is another indicator. We certainly showed them what the new LACs could accomplish, so, logically, they must have been working all out in an effort to duplicate those capabilities. Obviously, they've so far failed to do so. If they'd succeeded, Theisman would have announced that, as well. But many of the technologies required to produce Ghost Rider also have applications in the production of the new LACs. So if they don't have the one, it seems reasonable to assume they don't have the other."

He shrugged.

"I'm not certain how best to go about making the point to the man in the street, but it's becoming increasingly apparent to those of us at Admiralty House that to a large extent, this 'new navy' of theirs is a paper hexapuma."

"You're confident of that?" Descroix asked, and her voice was no longer acrimonious. Instead, she regarded Janacek narrowly, her eyes alight with interest.

"Obviously I can't make any promises, Elaine. As I said, without the opportunity to actually examine the physical hardware involved, all we can do is draw inferences and ask what we believe are significant questions. With that proviso, though, yes. I'm confident that Secretary Theisman has substantially overstated—or, rather, drawn certain so-called naval experts of our own into overstating—the actual combat power of the Republican Navy."

"I see." Descroix propped an elbow on the left arm of her chair and rested her chin on an upraised left hand. She sat like that for several seconds, thinking hard, then shrugged.

"I see," she repeated. "And I also see what you mean about the difficulty of getting that sophisticated analysis across to the average voter. Especially when someone like White Haven is busy beating the panic drum at the same time."

"Exactly," Janacek said sourly. "The public still thinks that sanctimonious son-of-a-bitch walks on water. No one's interested in listening to mere logic or something as unimportant as evidence when he shouts that the end is near every time he opens his overrated mouth!"

Sir Edward Janacek might not be the most disinterested observer where Hamish Alexander was concerned, High Ridge reflected. But that didn't mean he hadn't put his finger on exactly what White Haven had been doing to them ever since Theisman's announcement became public knowledge in the Star Kingdom.

"I'm afraid you're right," Descroix said, and this time her voice was almost completely back to normal and her expression was thoughtful, no longer angry. "But if we're not going to be able to get that across, anyway, perhaps we shouldn't waste the effort trying to."

"What do you mean?" High Ridge asked her.

"I mean we should certainly go on trying to calm public opinion by emphasizing the naval precautions we've taken," she replied. "By all means, let's keep reminding them of the ships we've authorized the yards to resume construction on. And while I'm not sure it would be a good idea to openly denigrate the Havenites' technological capabilities—that might sound too self-serving—I think it would be entirely appropriate for us to emphasize our own capabilities. Let's remind the voters that we've held the technological edge from the beginning. If we do that with sufficient confidence, at least some of them are going to draw the proper inference.

"But even more importantly, I think the way we conduct ourselves is going to be at least as important as anything we say. If we seem to be acting as if we're afraid, then any effort on our part to reassure the public is going to be futile. But if we make it obvious that we *aren't* afraid—that we remain confident of our ability to handle the Havenites diplomatically, or even militarily, if it comes down to it—then that message is going to soak into the public awareness, as well."

"So what exactly are you proposing?" High Ridge asked.

"I'm proposing that we make it clear, both here at home and in Nouveau Paris, that we don't intend to be bullied," Descroix said flatly. "If Pritchart wants to get confrontational, then we need to push back just as hard as she pushes us. From what Edward's just said, it sounds very much to me as if she's basically trying to run a bluff."

"I haven't said that they haven't made some substantial improvements in their war-fighting ability, Elaine," Janacek cautioned.

"No. But you have said you're confident that whatever improvements they've made, we still have the edge."

She made the statement an almost-question, and he nodded.

"Very well, then. If you can be confident of that without actually examining their hardware, then surely they have to be aware of it as well. After all, they know exactly what they have and also exactly what Eighth Fleet did to them before the cease-fire. That's what I meant when I said I think Pritchart is essentially bluffing. She certainly isn't going to be stupid enough to want to go back to war with us when she can't be confident of achieving a military victory. So we call her bluff.

"I'm not proposing that we issue any ultimatums," she went on quickly, reassuring the incipient alarm she saw on one or two faces. "I'm simply proposing that we stand firm. We won't demand any fresh concessions on their part; we'll simply refuse to be panicked into conceding the concessions they've demanded from *us*. Once the public realizes we feel sufficiently confident to hold our position and recognizes the patience with which we're prepared to wait out this diplomatic tantrum Pritchart is throwing, the sort of borderline panic Alexander and White Haven are working so hard to generate will die a natural death."

She raised her right hand, palm uppermost, and made a throwing-away gesture.

"You may be right," High Ridge said. "In fact, I think you probably are. But it's likely that things are going to be pretty unpleasant in the short term, whatever we do."

"Like you said earlier, Michael," she pointed out, "politics ebb and flow. As long as Green Vale and the party whips can hold our majority in the Lords, there isn't really anything Alexander and his crowd can do except view with alarm. And when the current 'crisis' passes without Armageddon actually descending upon us, their efforts to generate panic will turn around and bite them in the opinion polls.

"And that," she said with a thin, cold smile, "will make all of this worthwhile."

Chapter Thirty-Six

"**A**stro Control, this is *Harvest Joy*, requesting inbound clearance and vector. *Harvest Joy*, clear."

Josepha Zachary leaned back in her command chair and grinned hugely at Jordin Kare. The astrophysicist returned her grin with interest, then raised his right hand in the ancient thumbs-up gesture.

There was a moment of silence, and then the voice of the Astro Control approach officer sounded clearly over the survey ship's bridge speakers.

"Welcome home, *Harvest Joy*! We've been waiting for you. Clearance granted; stand by to copy vector."

"I, for one, think this is wonderful news," Abraham Spencer announced firmly.

The renowned financier looked around at his fellow guests. They were seated about a large conference table on an HD set, and among them they represented half a dozen of the best-known financial analysts of the entire Star Kingdom. Spencer himself was probably the most widely known and respected of them all, the long-time Chairman of the Crown Council of Financial Advisors and a confidant and advisor of many of the wealthiest individuals in the Star Kingdom, including Klaus Hauptman. He was also almost a hundred T-years old and one of those same wealthiest individuals in his own right . . . not to mention being handsome, silver-haired, and nearly as photogenic as he was rich.

"With all due respect, Abraham, I can't quite share your unbridled enthusiasm . . . again." Ellen DeMarco, CEO and chief analyst for the sprawling brokerage firm of DeMarco, Clancy, and Jordan, smiled. She was also a member of the CCFA and one of Spencer's closer friends, but they often found themselves on different sides of questions. "I think you may be allowing enthusiasm to get the better of levelheaded judgment this time. The Talbott Cluster is scarcely what I would call a high-return market area!"

"Of course it isn't," Spencer replied. "But then, neither is Silesia, when you come right down to it, Ellen. I mean, let's face it. Silesia is riddled with pirates, graft, political corruption, human rights abuses—all of the things which make commerce risky and certainly fail to provide the kind of stable investment climate any rational person would look for. Nonetheless, the Star Kingdom shows an enormous profit in our trade with Silesia. However chaotic conditions there may be, it's a huge market. The margin may be low, but the sheer volume of the trade compensates."

"Perhaps it does," DeMarco conceded. "Although," she added with a wry smile, "you chose that particular example with malice aforethought, Abraham! You know perfectly well that I've been advising for years now against further exposure in Silesia."

"I?" Spencer asked innocently. "You think that I would be guilty of choosing an example on such an ignoble basis?"

"Of course I do. But to return to the point you've just made, Silesia, as you so accurately say, is a huge market. It contains scores of inhabited systems, each with its own population and needs. And for all the chronic instability in the area, we have long-standing relationships with the powers that be. We have no such relationships in the case of Talbott; there are only seventeen inhabited star systems in the entire 'cluster'; none of them have a system population in excess of three billion; and the Solarian League has very strong, direct interests in the region. As I see it, the potential economic return on expanding into that region is offset by the danger it poses to our relations with the League."

"There's something to that," Spencer agreed more seriously. "By the same token, though, I'd argue that our current relations with the Andermani aren't all that good where Silesia is concerned, either. I know that having problems with one neighbor isn't exactly the best reason to go around borrowing problems with another, but in this instance, I really don't see that we have a lot of options."

"Excuse me, Abraham," another participant said, "but we always have options."

"Does that reflect your personal view, Ms. Houseman?" Spencer asked. "Or does it reflect the opinion of your brother?"

"I haven't specifically discussed it with Reginald." There was the faintest hint of an edge in Jacqueline Houseman's voice, but she made an obvious effort to smile pleasantly at the older man. The two of them detested one another cordially, and it was an open secret that Spencer had strongly supported Elizabeth III when the Crown declined Prime Minister High Ridge's nomination of Ms. Houseman for membership on the CCFA. "On the other hand, I don't really have to. Options are what are available to anyone who keeps an open mind and is willing to question the comfortable assumptions of established thinking."

"A point I can entirely agree with." Spencer nodded. "In fact, it's a proposition which I've debated many times with your brother. I only asked because I wondered if the Government is finally prepared to comment officially on this matter."

"As I say, Reginald and I haven't really spoken about it," Houseman said. "And if the Government were about to take any sort of official position, I scarcely think I would be the proper spokesperson for it. On the other hand, you might reflect that *Harvest Joy* has been home for less than a week. It's just a bit early, don't you think, for the Government to be announcing any official policy decisions?"

"Perhaps. But I don't think it's too early for the Government to at least acknowledge that those decisions are going to have to be made," Spencer replied with a thin smile, and Houseman bristled.

"I scarcely think—" She began in a hotter tone, but Stephen Stahler, the program host, interrupted her smoothly.

"I think we're straying just a bit afield," he said firmly but pleasantly. "We're scheduled to discuss the political aspects of the situation in our next segment. In fact, I believe you and Mr. Spencer are both on that panel, as well, Ms. Houseman. Our focus at the moment, however, is on the economic aspects."

"You're quite correct, Stephen," Houseman said, and smiled more naturally. "Of course, as I'm sure Mr. Spencer would agree, government policy is going to have a major impact on the economic possibilities."

"Oh, certainly. There's no question of that," Spencer agreed.

"Well, in that case, and without trying to lead the discussion off topic, I do think that it's legitimate to point out that whether or not we permit the location and . . . diplomatic considerations of this new terminus to dictate our attitude towards it is entirely up to us."

"I'm afraid I can't quite go along with that argument," Spencer said. "Leaving aside the political or diplomatic side of the equation, look at where Talbott lies. It's almost a third of the way around the periphery of the League from Manticore. When you add it to the connections we already have through Phoenix, Matapan, and—via Gregor—Asgerd, our shipping lanes will cover well over two-thirds of the League's *total* periphery, with huge reductions in transit times for cargos between points as distant from one another as, say, New Tasmania and Sondermann's Star. And that doesn't even consider the Beowulf terminus, which already gives our shippers direct, immediate access to be very heart of the League. That makes this terminus of literally incalculable value, completely regardless of the potential market in the Talbott Cluster itself. And that reality isn't going to go away simply because we decided not to allow it to 'dictate our attitude,' Ms. Houseman."

"I think I have to agree with that portion of your analysis," DeMarco put in. "But by the same token, the potential for further straining our relations with the League also needs to be carefully considered. After all, the extent to which we're able to exploit the astrographic possibilities you've brought up is going to be influenced to a major degree by the attitude of the League government."

"Why?" Spencer asked. "It's not as if the League government were a particularly coherent entity, Ellen. And whatever it might attempt to decree by government fiat, reality will be driven by the potential utility of the connection. Not simply for us, but for all the shippers who will be able to cut months off of their transit times and reach markets they otherwise never could have. So, in my opinion . . ."

"What do you think, Elaine?" Baron High Ridge asked.

He and the Foreign Secretary sat before the HD in the Prime

Minister's residence, watching the roundtable discussion. They'd been joined by Edward Janacek, and Stefan Young was also present in his capacity as Trade Secretary. Technically, High Ridge supposed, New Kiev ought to have been present, as well. Certainly, the Exchequer had a very strong natural interest in anything which promised to have this great an impact on the Star Kingdom's economy, and in this instance, the Prime Minister had made no particular effort to hold New Kiev at arm's length. In fact, he'd invited her to attend, and he wasn't entirely certain why she'd declined the invitation. Her official reason had been her daughter's wedding, and High Ridge was inclined to think the official reason was also the actual one. Of course, one could never be completely confident of that.

"What do I think about what?" Descroix asked. "About Spencer's argument? Or about whether or not Reginald's sister is an idiot?"

"I was thinking about Spencer's analysis of the situation," High Ridge said on a slightly reproving note. She hadn't exactly said "as big an idiot as Reginald," but the implication had been clear enough.

"Oh, that." Descroix's crooked smile told him exactly how much his reaction to her shot at the Housemans amused her. But then she sobered and twitched one shoulder in a half-shrug.

"I don't think there's any doubt at all about its fundamental soundness. One look at a star chart should make that evident enough! And I think the point he's trying to make is that this is one of those situations where the whole is greater than the sum of the parts. What this new terminus does is to fill in a whole arc of the League perimeter. But it doesn't really come into its own until you connect it with all of the other coverage available to us through the Junction." She shook her head. "I'm sure Stefan's people—or Marissa's people over at the Exchequer—could give us a much better sense of the dollar-and-cents value, but it doesn't take a financial genius to realize that this can only further enhance the value of our merchant marine."

"Edward?" High Ridge looked at Janacek.

"I have to agree with Elaine," Janacek replied. But where Descroix was obviously pleased over the potential she saw, his admission came grudgingly, and High Ridge knew why.

"I realize you were never very happy about the annexation of Basilisk," the Prime Minister said after a moment, having decided to grasp the dilemma's horns. "I wasn't particularly pleased with it either, you know. And I've had my own strong doubts about the wisdom of territorial expansion in general, as I'm sure you're quite aware. For that matter, the consequences we already face as the result of annexing someplace like Trevor's Star lend added point to the concerns we both share. Nonetheless, I think we would have to agree that this terminus is in a different class from Basilisk."

"Of course it is," Descroix said briskly. "There's no inhabited planet full of alien aborigines for certain political parties to agonize over, for one thing. And it's not going to help bring us into potential armed conflict with something like the People's Republic, either, however much the League might prefer for us to stay out of the region. Not to mention the fact, if we're going to be honest, that Basilisk was on the backside of nowhere when we first discovered it. Everything worthwhile beyond Basilisk has been surveyed and settled only since we opened up the terminus. *This* terminus gives us direct, immediate access to an already inhabited region and the shipping lanes which serve it. Not to mention the fact that the League's expansion in Talbott's direction means that the economic opportunities will grow by leaps and bounds over the next few decades."

"Elaine is right," the Earl of North Hollow said. "My senior analysts are still putting the final touches on their survey report, but I've seen the rough draft of their conclusions. Basilisk has been an enormous economic boon to the Star Kingdom, whatever the pros and cons of actually annexing the system. But by the most conservative estimate I've seen so far, the Talbott Cluster terminus offers us a minimum increase of over a thousand percent over what Basilisk did for us. *A thousand percent.*" It was his turn to shake his head. "What it boils down to is that this is the most significant single economic event in the history of the Star Kingdom since the original discovery of the Junction itself."

"I realize that," Janacek put in before the Prime Minister could respond. "And you're right, Michael. I don't like the logical consequence, but that doesn't mean I don't recognize what it is. In most ways, I'm still convinced that the last thing we need to be doing is embarking on some sort of interstellar imperialism. Unfortunately, I don't see that we have any real choice but to secure control of the Talbott terminus."

"Even if it brings our interests into potential conflict with those of the Sollies?" High Ridge pressed, and Janacek snorted.

"Spencer's right about that, too," the First Lord replied. "Unless we want to hand the terminus over to the League and unilaterally promise we'll never send our shipping through it, then we're automatically in 'potential conflict' with the Sollies! Their shipping lines are already about as pissed off with us as they can get over the advantages the existing Junction termini give us. I can't see them being any less pissed off when we add this one to the others!"

"In for a penny, in for a dollar, is it?" High Ridge asked with a smile.

"Something like that," Janacek said sourly. "Besides, it's always been established policy for us to at least secure effective extraterritorial control over the Junction's termini even when someone else held system sovereignty. Aside from Beowulf, we've managed to do just that, too. And at least in this instance, as Elaine points out, the terminus system is uninhabited. Not only that, it's never been claimed by anyone else, either. Legally, at least, the door is wide open for us to simply assert ownership."

"And the rest of the Talbott Cluster?" Descroix asked him.

"What about it?" Janacek looked at her warily.

"You know exactly what I mean, Edward," she chided. "Melina Makris may not have been all that happy with your Captain Zachary, but even she had to endorse Zachary's report on the Lynx System government's reaction to *Harvest Joy*'s arrival in their space."

Janacek made an irritated sound deep in his throat, and Descroix smiled sweetly at him. She knew how badly the First Lord wanted to argue that Zachary had exceeded her mission brief in taking her ship to Lynx. Unfortunately, she hadn't, and the Lynxians' reaction to the mere possibility of closer contact with the Star Kingdom had been . . . well, "ecstatic" was one word that came to mind.

"It's hard to blame them, really," the Foreign Secretary went on after a moment, her tone more serious than was its wont. "If they're left to the mercies of Frontier Security, they can look forward to at least fifty or sixty T-years of systematic economic exploitation, probably more like a century of it, before they achieve anything like equality with the League's other star systems. If they can reach some arrangement with us, instead . . ." She shrugged.

"What?" Janacek demanded. "You think they're going to turn out to be another bunch of Graysons? Or that we should even *want* another batch of neobarbs?"

"I fully appreciate your feelings where Grayson is concerned, Edward. And while I may not share them entirely, I don't reject them out of hand, either," Descroix replied. Which, High Ridge knew, was less than accurate. Descroix might not *like* Graysons any more than Janacek or he himself did, and she certainly didn't care for their uppity independence of attitude. But despite that, she was firmly of the opinion that bringing Yeltsin's Star into the military alliance against the Peeps had been one of the smarter moves the Cromarty Government had made.

"But whatever Grayson's actual value to us may have been," she continued, "the example of what Grayson has accomplished with our help, like the example of Sidemore, isn't lost on any under-developed star system which might find itself falling into our economic sphere. Which may not be such a bad thing, when you come down to it. Frankly, speaking as Foreign Secretary, I think that's a perception we ought to be encouraging, not just for the additional diplomatic pull it gives us with minor star systems, but in our own ultimate economic interest, as well."

Janacek's expression had turned sourer than ever at the mention of Sidemore, and he glowered at her. High Ridge could wish she'd chosen another moment and another way to make her point, but that didn't make what she'd just said untrue, and he shrugged.

"There's undoubtedly something to that," he conceded. "But what, exactly, are you suggesting, Elaine? That we extend the same sort of commercial relationship we have with Grayson to Lynx and the rest of the Talbott Cluster?"

"No," she said. "I'm suggesting that we go further than that."

"Further?" Janacek asked suspiciously.

"Precisely." She shrugged. "We've just agreed that our mere presence in the region is going to create problems for us where the Sollies are concerned. So I don't see any reason to be particu-larly careful of their exquisite sensibilities. But what I do see is an entire cluster of star systems, most of whom would much prefer to find themselves in our custody rather than ending up as Solly protectorates under the compassionate management of the OFS. And we're also looking at a domestic situation in which public opinion has found itself whipsawed between its negative reaction to the combination of the Havenites' new naval units and their new, more confrontational attitude, on the one hand, and the excitement and enthusiasm *Harvest Joy*'s voyage has whipped up, on the other. What I see here is an opportunity for us to take the lead in exploring the possibility of offering the Talbott Cluster's star systems some sort of protectorate status—or even actual membership in the Star Kingdom."

Janacek made a sound of protest, but she continued over it, speaking directly to High Ridge.

"I understand your party's fundamental opposition to expansionism, Michael. But this is a God-given chance to recapture any public support we may have lost in the wake of developments in Haven. For that matter, if we play it properly, we should be able to do one hell of a lot better than simply regain lost ground!"

Eloise Pritchart walked briskly to her chair at the head of the table, sat down in it, and turned to face the rest of her assembled Cabinet. No one who didn't know her well could have suspected her anxiety level for a moment from her expression or body language.

"Thank you all for coming, Ladies and Gentlemen," she said with her normal courtesy. "I apologize for convening this meeting on such relatively short notice, but given the nature of the latest reports out of Manticore, I felt it would be wise for all of us to discuss them before the press gets hold of them.

"May I assume all of you have reviewed Director Trajan's report?"

She let her gaze circle the table, and one by one, the Cabinet secretaries nodded.

"Good. In that case, I suppose, we should start with State. Arnold?"

It said volumes for her thespian skills that her tone was pleasant and her smile apparently genuine as she turned to the Secretary of State.

"At first glance," Giancola said after the briefest of pauses, "it's relatively straightforward. The Manty government hadn't taken an official stance before Wilhelm's people dispatched their reports through Trevor's Star, but it was pretty clear which way High Ridge was inclining. They're going to go ahead and annex Lynx as well

as the actual terminus system, however much they may be pussyfooting around announcing that fact."

"You're really confident that it's that cut and dried?" Secretary
of the Treasury Hanriot asked.

"In the end?" Giancola shrugged. "Yes, I am. They may go
through the motions of public debate, but I can't see High Ridge
or Descroix commenting so positively on the economic opportunities that decision would offer if annexation wasn't what they
ultimately intended. Or, especially in Descroix's case, carrying on
at such absurd length about how membership in the Star Kingdom would help to safeguard the human rights and self-
determination of the citizens of the Cluster. I might have put some
credence in an argument like that out of someone like New Kiev,
but Descroix—?"

He shook his head.

"Speaking of New Kiev," Secretary of Commerce Nesbitt put in,
"what's your read on her, Arnold?"

"I think she's unhappy about it," Giancola said promptly. "But
I also think she's been overruled by High Ridge, and that she's
not going to break ranks with him at this point."

"I see." Pritchart cocked her head, regarding him thoughtfully.
"I noticed, though, that you said their positions seemed relatively
straightforward 'at first glance.' Would you care to elaborate on
that?"

"Of course." Giancola tipped his chair back slightly, resting his
elbows on the arms and half-turning it in her direction.

"Basically, what I meant was that while all of the arguments
they've put forward are rational enough on the surface, particularly from their perspective, I don't believe that they're publicly
stating their complete rationale for pursuing this expansion into
Talbott."

"What they have publicly stated seems comprehensive enough
to me," Thomas Theisman observed mildly.

"On the surface," Giancola repeated, "I'd have to agree with you.
Certainly it's in accordance with their established policy where
control of termini of their wormhole junction is concerned. And
the economic possibilities this new terminus offers certainly aren't
anything to be sneered at." He chuckled suddenly, the sound
completely—and surprisingly, for some of his audience—genuine.
"Speaking from my own experience with the Committee of Public

Safety's treasury, I only wish our economy had access to something like the Junction! So, yes, Thomas. I'd have to agree that the
reasons they and their spokesmen have offered are completely
sufficient in their own right to justify their actions. I just don't
think they've made their full reasoning public."

"In what way?" Pritchart asked.

"I think a part of their private reasoning is that playing this
up as a major achievement is one way for them to distract their
public from the shift in our own negotiating posture and the
change in the balance of naval power."

"I'm sure I'd be thinking very much the same way in their place,"
Attorney General LePic said just a bit testily. Of all of the Cabinet secretaries, LePic was probably the poorest at concealing his
emotions, and all of them were aware of his fundamental antipathy
towards Giancola. And of his equally fundamental distrust of the
Secretary of State. "If they are aware of those possibilities, I hardly
think it represents any sort of Machiavellian secretiveness on their
parts."

"If all they were doing was trying to distract public attention
from the negotiations with us, then I probably wouldn't be particularly concerned myself," Giancola said calmly. "Unfortunately,
I think there's probably another strand to their reasoning."

"Which is?" Pritchart asked.

"I think they're laying the groundwork for a complete revision
of the traditional Manty foreign policy," Giancola said flatly.

"A complete revision?" Theisman regarded him narrowly. "Excuse
me, but I was under the impression that we'd just agreed it was
part of their long-standing policy—that very 'traditional' policy
you're talking about—to exploit the Junction thoroughly and to
secure control of its termini."

"Yes, we had. But I would point out to you that they decided
to annex Basilisk only after an extremely acrimonious and pro-
tracted domestic debate. A debate, I might add, in which the parties
which comprise the current Manty government were, almost
without exception, on the side arguing *against* annexation. Compare
that to how long it took them to decide to annex Trevor's Star.
That was the Cromarty Government, of course, but there was
amazingly little opposition to the decision, even on the part of
their Conservatives and Liberals. In other words, they made the
decision for Trevor's Star much more quickly than they did in

Basilisk's case . . . and did so on something much closer to a consensual basis.

"Now we're talking about Lynx and the rest of an entire cluster, and the very parties which were most strongly opposed to the annexation of Basilisk are the ones which have started coming out in favor of this new, larger annexation. And, I might add, they'd begun to do so within less than two weeks of discovering where this new terminus lies."

He shrugged.

"What all of that suggests to me, Thomas, is that the Star Kingdom of Manticore has become expansionist."

Several members of the Cabinet looked at him in exasperation. Others looked much more thoughtful, and Eloise Pritchart felt a sudden tingle of concern as she realized how many of them fell into the second category.

"In all fairness, Arnold," she said after a moment, "I have to say you've been, um, predisposed, if I may be permitted the word, to view the Star Kingdom as expansionist for some time now."

"And you wonder if my predisposition in that direction is causing me to view current events with undue alarm," Giancola agreed affably. He smiled at her, and Pritchart made herself smile back when what she really would have preferred would have been to punch him. But much as he infuriated her, she was forced to acknowledge that she couldn't simply dismiss his analysis out of hand, however much she might have wanted to. Just as she had to admit he truly did have a presence. One which she wished was far, far away from this meeting.

"To be honest, yes," she told him.

"Well, to be equally honest, I can't say positively that it isn't. On the other hand, that may be because there's a sound basis for my feelings. I agree that annexation of the terminus system itself would represent no more than a continuation of their long-term security policies. But we're not talking just about that star system. We're also talking about Lynx and, quite possibly, the other inhabited star systems of the Talbott Cluster. All seventeen of them. That's an enormous jump from annexing a single star system populated solely by primitive aliens like Basilisk, or even a strategically vital star system whose long-established population *asked* to be annexed, like Trevor's Star."

He shook his head.

"No, Madame President. I think that what this represents is an aggressive, arrogant expansionism. I think the Manty perception that they soundly defeated the Pierre Regime has fueled an imperialistic drive which was always latent in the Star Kingdom's foreign policy. I think you can see another manifestation of that same arrogance and imperialism in their attitude towards their current confrontation with the Andermani over Silesia. Obviously, they regard Silesia as their own private fishing pond, and no one else is welcome to drop a line into it. It's only a relatively small step from regarding a sovereign star nation as an economic dependency to embracing the outright annexation of individual star systems which aren't exactly in a position to resist."

"But according to Wilhelm's reports, the original impetus towards annexation apparently came from Lynx, not the Manties," Hanriot objected.

"How do we know that?" Secretary of the Interior Sanderson put in, and Pritchart's eyes narrowed. She'd thought Walter Sanderson was firmly in "her" camp, but suddenly she felt less confident of that. And she felt even less so as Sanderson continued. "The only contact anyone in Manticore has had with Lynx was via their own survey ship," he pointed out. "We have no way to know what they actually said; only what their survey ship crew allegedly *reported* they said. According to their government."

"You're suggesting they lied about it?" Theisman said, giving Sanderson exactly the same sort of look Pritchart was working so hard at not giving him.

"I'm suggesting that they certainly may have," Sanderson replied. "I don't know that they did. I also don't know that they didn't, and if they're thinking in the direction Arnold seems to be suggesting, then obviously the temptation to cast their own actions in the most favorable possible light would have to be strong. And a 'request' from Lynx would be a marvelous pretext."

"But why should they feel any need for pretexts?" LePic demanded.

"I can think of at least one reason," Giancola said reasonably. The Attorney General looked at him, and the Secretary of State shrugged. "Whatever we may think about what they're doing, I can guarantee you the Solarian League isn't going to be particularly pleased about this. And the Solarians are huge believers in 'self-determination.'"

"Sure they are!" Theisman snorted bitterly. "Until they're the ones doing the expanding, that is."

"I can't argue with you there," Giancola said. "In fact, I don't think anyone could. But what matters is that their public support for the concept would make it more difficult for them to object to the Manties' actions if the Star Kingdom can convince Solly public opinion Lynx really did ask to be annexed."

"That's all a bit too Machiavellian for me," LePic said.

"Maybe it is," Giancola said easily. "But any way you want to look at it, High Ridge and Descroix *are* pretty Machiavellian, you know. Or do you think they've been dragging out the negotiations on the occupied systems solely out of the goodness of their hearts, Denis?"

"Of course not," LePic growled.

"If they're willing to use those negotiations for domestic advantage, I see absolutely no reason to believe they'd be unwilling to think the way I've just described about expanding into the Talbott Cluster," Giancola pointed out.

"That would be bad enough," he said, "but I'd have to say that I wouldn't be enormously concerned if they were solely interested in Talbott. After all, that would be taking them directly away from our own territory and our own sphere of interest. Unfortunately, the way it looks to me is that their attitude towards Talbott is simply symptomatic of their attitude towards expansion in general. And if that's actually the case, then we're entirely too close to them for my peace of mind. Especially while they're still occupying Republican territory."

"Damn, but he's a smooth bastard," Theisman sighed. He and LePic sat in Pritchart's office several hours later. Beyond the huge windows, the glittering lights of night-struck Nouveau Paris blazed like multi-hued jewels, but none of them were particularly in the mood to appreciate their beauty.

"Yes, he is that," Pritchart agreed. She leaned back in her outsized chair and closed her eyes wearily. "And he's getting better at it," she told the ceiling beyond her lids.

"I know," LePic said. His tone was harsh, and he shrugged his shoulders irritably when Theisman looked a question at him. "He gives me the creeps," the Attorney General said. "I know he's smart, and a lot of what he says makes sense. Too damned much sense,

I sometimes think, especially when I'm feeling particularly pissed off at the Manties. But there's too much going on under the surface. He reminds me of Saint-Just."

"That may be going a little further than I'm prepared to," Theisman said after a moment. "I don't doubt that he's a lot less scrupulous than the image he likes to project, Denis. But compared to Saint-Just?" He shook his head. "I don't think he's even in the same league for sheer sociopathy."

"Not for lack of ambition, though!" LePic snorted.

"Unscrupulous, yes," Pritchart put in, opening her eyes and letting her chair come back outright. "But I think Tom has a point, Denis. Arnold is undoubtedly willing to do a great many things to further his ambitions, but I don't see him being willing to do something like detonating a nuclear device in the middle of Nouveau Paris."

"I only hope you're both right and I'm wrong," LePic told her. His phrasing didn't make her particularly happy, given who Walter Trajan and Kevin Usher both reported to, but she became even less happy when he continued. "In the meantime, though, did you two notice Sanderson?"

"Yes, I did," Theisman said, and grimaced. "I think we're in the process of suffering another defection."

"And unless I'm very much mistaken, he's gaining more ground in Congress, too," Pritchart observed. It was her turn to grimace. "So far, pushing High Ridge and Descroix in the treaty negotiations is still working more in our favor than against us where congressional support is concerned, but dear Arnold is proving more resilient than I'd like. The way he sees it, I stole his thunder by taking 'a firm hand' in the peace talks. So he's busy trying to return the compliment by viewing with even more alarm where the Manties are concerned. And do you know what the real hell of it is?"

She looked at both of her allies, who only shook their heads.

"The real hell of it," she told them softly, "is that he's so damned convincing that I'm not sure *I* don't agree with him sometimes."

"Thank you for the dinner invitation, Mr. Secretary. As always, the meal was delicious."

"And also as always, Mr. Ambassador, the company was excellent," Arnold Giancola said graciously.

Yinsheng Reinshagen, Graf von Kaiserfest, Andermani Ambassador to the Republic of Haven, smiled at his host. This wasn't the first private dinner he'd enjoyed with the Havenite Secretary of State, and he didn't expect it to be the last. Officially, it was a working dinner between two diplomats to discuss closer trade relations between the reborn Republic and the Empire. Kaiserfest rather admired that justification. Giancola's prior treasury experience made it even more believable . . . and also explained why he should feel no need to include representatives of the Commerce or Treasury Departments. It was an admirable cover to keep any potentially irritating witnesses away, and to make certain that it was maintained, Kaiserfest had actually agreed to quite a few trade concessions.

Giancola knew precisely what the Andermani was thinking, because he'd taken some pains to insure that Kaiserfest would think just that. But what the Ambassador didn't know was that the cover story they'd agreed upon was also the reason Eloise Pritchart thought Giancola was meeting with him.

"Well," Kaiserfest said now. "Excellent as dinner was, I'm afraid I'm due at the opera in two hours."

"Of course." Giancola picked up his brandy snifter and took an appreciative sip, then lowered the glass and smiled. "Basically, Mr. Ambassador, I only wanted to take the opportunity to reiterate my government's position that we share a certain commonality of interest with the Empire. Obviously, while our negotiations with the Manticorans are still in progress, we're not in a position to lend public support to your government's efforts to resolve your own . . . difficulties with them in Silesia. For that matter, until we've settled our own business with them, our official support for your interests would probably actually be counterproductive.

"Nonetheless, and without wishing to appear overly dramatic, my government is well aware that, in the words of the old cliché, our enemy's enemy is our friend. Both the Republic and the Empire would find it advantageous to . . . decrease the Manticorans' ability to meddle in our internal affairs and legitimate security interests. With that in mind, it seems to us that it would only be reasonable for us to coordinate our efforts in that direction. Discreetly, of course."

"Oh, of course," Kaiserfest agreed. He sipped his own brandy, letting the rich, fiery liquor roll around his mouth, then nodded. "I understand completely," he said then. "And I agree."

"You also understand, I trust," Giancola said seriously, "that although we intend to lend the Empire all the support we can, it will be necessary for our public stance to be somewhat different. Much as I've come to value our friendship, Mr. Ambassador, it would be naive for either of us to pretend that anything other than *realpolitik* is involved here."

"Of course not," Kaiserfest agreed once more.

"Unfortunately, my own star nation is still in the grip of a certain revolutionary fervor," Giancola observed. "That sort of enthusiasm is an uncomfortable fit for the pragmatic requirements of effective interstellar diplomacy. Which, of course, is the reason President Pritchart and I may find ourselves forced to make certain public statements which could be construed as criticisms of the Empire's Silesian policy. I trust that you and the Emperor will both understand why we find it necessary to cover our true policy with a certain degree of disinformation."

"Such a situation isn't completely unknown to us," Kaiserfest said with a thin smile. "And as you yourself have observed, our . . . pragmatic interests make us logical allies—for the moment, at least—whatever public rhetoric may be forced upon you."

"You're most understanding, Mr. Ambassador."

"Merely practical," Kaiserfest assured him. "I will, of course, inform His Majesty of our conversations."

"Of course," Arnold Giancola told him with a smile. "I wouldn't have it any other way."

CHAPTER THIRTY-SEVEN

"So, have you had any other thoughts about what they're likely to find?" Alistair McKeon asked.

He and Honor stood in the lift car, accompanied by Alfredo Yu, Warner Caslet, Captain Sampson Grant, Nimitz, Mercedes Brigham, Roslee Orndorff, Banshee, and—inevitably—Andrew LaFollet, while the light dot of the car sped across the schematic of HMS *Werewolf*. They were on their way to a meeting which Alice Truman really ought to have been attending, as well. At the moment, however, Alice was busy coordinating the redeployment of the system reconnaissance platforms . . . in no small part as a direct result of the events which had prompted the meeting.

"The reconnaissance platforms?" Honor asked.

"What?" McKeon blinked for a moment, then chuckled. "Sorry. I can see why you thought that was what I was asking about, under the circumstances. But I was actually referring to what we were talking about last night." She looked at him, and he shrugged. "Call it a way of distracting myself."

"A fairly futile one," she observed.

"The best distractions are," McKeon replied cheerfully. "If you can answer the question once and for all, it stops being a distraction, doesn't it?"

"Did I ever tell you that you're a peculiar person, Alistair?"

Orndorff, Grant, and Brigham grinned at each other behind their superiors' backs. Yu and Caslet, on the other hand, were sufficiently senior to chuckle openly, and Nimitz bleeked a laugh of his own.

"Actually, I don't believe you ever did," McKeon replied. "But all gratuitous insults aside, my question stands. What do you think they're likely to find?"

"I don't have the least idea," she said frankly. "On the other hand, whatever it is, they've undoubtedly found it by now. It's just going to take a while for the news to reach us."

"We are sort of on the backside of nowhere," McKeon agreed more sourly.

Which, Honor reflected, was certainly the truth in a lot of ways. McKeon's question had brought that back into clear relief, whether that was what he'd intended to do or not. They'd received word only two days ago that HMS *Harvest Joy* had been ordered to depart the Manticore System via the newly discovered Junction terminus, but that message had required over three standard weeks to reach them. It would take just as long for any report of what the survey ship discovered at the terminus' far end to make the same trip . . . which was also true of any *other* message it might occur to the Admiralty or High Ridge Government to send them.

Not that either of those august entities had so far evinced any interest in communicating with something as obviously unimportant as Sidemore Station.

"I don't have any idea what Zachary and Dr. Kare are likely to find," she told McKeon, "but I hope whatever it is doesn't distract the Government even more from our situation out here."

"Um." McKeon frowned. "I understand what you're saying, but I think it's a bit of six of one, half a dozen of another. We're not getting any support or guidance, but they're not screwing the situation up still worse, either."

Yu started to say something, then visibly changed his mind. Other people felt less constrained by tact, however.

"Admiral McKeon may have a point, Your Grace," Brigham offered diffidently from behind them. Honor looked over her shoulder at the chief of staff, and the commodore shrugged. "It's not fair for them to dump the responsibility for making policy, as well as executing it, on you," she continued. "But given the kind of policy they seem to delight in making, the Star Kingdom may be better off if something does distract them for the duration."

"I take your point—yours and Alistair's both," Honor said after a moment. "But I think this is probably something we shouldn't be discussing even 'in the family.'" She knew Yu and Caslet well enough to feel no discomfort at saying such a thing in front of them, and Grant, Yu's chief of staff, was an old-school Grayson; it was impossible to conceive of him ever telling tales out of school. Besides, the three of them were family themselves, by adoption, at least, and she gave the them a smile as she went on. "There's no point pretending we're not all concerned over the lack of new instructions, and I don't see any way to avoid speculating on why we're not receiving any. But I'd very much prefer for us to minimize discussion of how stupid we think our existing orders are. I don't expect either of you to tell yourselves to stop thinking about it, but, frankly, we've got more than enough distrust and resentment floating around the staff without our adding fuel to the fire."

She held Brigham's eye for a moment, then swept her gaze over Orndorff and McKeon, as well, waiting until each of them had nodded.

McKeon started to say something more, but then the lift car arrived at its destination. The door hissed open, and he shrugged, with a crooked grin for the distraction, and stood back to follow Honor out into the passageway.

Andrea Jaruwalski and George Reynolds were waiting in the briefing room when Andrew LaFollet poked his head through the hatch to give the compartment his customary once-over. A tallish, fair-haired senior-grade RMN captain and an unusually youthful Sidemorian lieutenant commander were waiting with the staffers, and LaFollet let his eyes linger on them for just a moment, as if committing their faces to memory. Then he withdrew into the passage once more, and permitted Honor to lead the rest of her small party through the hatch.

Her juniors came to their feet respectfully, and she waved them back into their chairs as she headed for her own place at the head of the table. McKeon seated himself to her right, with Orndorff to his own right, while Yu and Caslet sat to her left. Brigham found her own chair between Jaruwalski and Reynolds, and Honor waited a moment longer while the two treecats settled down on the tops of their people's chair backs, then turned her attention to Jaruwalski.

"Are you and George ready for us?" she asked.

"Yes, Your Grace," the operations officer replied.

"Then we might as well get started."

"Yes, Your Grace," Jaruwalski repeated, and nodded to Reynolds. "Go ahead, George."

"Certainly, Ma'am," the staff "spook" said, more formal than usual in the presence of outsiders. Then he cleared his throat. "First, allow me to present Captain Ackenheil."

"Of the *LaFroye*, I believe?" Honor said, raising one eyebrow at the captain.

"Yes, Your Grace," Ackenheil replied.

"That was a nice piece of work with *Wayfarer*," she complimented him. "Very nice. I could have wished we hadn't taken a slaver who was a namesake for one of my old ships," she grimaced, "but liberating almost two hundred slaves is more than enough to make up even for that. My report on the incident strongly commends you and your people for the job you did."

"Thank you, Your Grace. We couldn't have done it without the intelligence Commander Reynolds provided, though."

The captain was obviously extremely curious about just how that intelligence had been developed, but he showed no disappointment when Honor failed to enlighten him. He hadn't really expected her to . . . and she had absolutely no intention of telling him that she strongly suspected the information supporting Operation Wilberforce had come from a proscribed band of terrorists via a security firm on permanent retainer to a recently elected Member of Parliament.

"A successful operation is always the result of a lot of people pulling in the same direction at the same time, Captain," she told him instead, "and you and *LaFroye* were the ones at the sharp end of the stick. " *Not to mention being the ones whose careers would have gone down the toilet if our information had been wrong.* "In addition, your capture of the *Wayfarer* has given our intelligence on slaving operations in the Confederacy what may turn out to be an even bigger boost than any of us had expected. Under the circumstances, you and your people deserve the credit for a job very well done."

"Thank you, Your Grace," Ackenheil repeated, and then gestured to the young woman at his side. "Please allow me to introduce Lieutenant Commander Zahn, my tac officer."

"Commander." Honor nodded to the Sidemorian officer. "And

if I remember correctly, your husband is a civilian analyst attached to the Sidemore Navy."

"Yes. Yes, he is, Your Grace." Zahn seemed astonished that the station commander had made the link, and Honor hid a small smile at her reaction.

"Well, Captain," she said, returning her attention to Ackenheil, "I understand Commander Reynolds dragged the two of you aboard the flagship to tell us what the Andies have been up to."

"Actually, Your Grace," Reynolds told her, "it was Captain Ackenheil who came to us." Honor glanced at him, and the intelligence officer shrugged. "As soon as I heard what he had to say, though, I knew you'd want to hear it firsthand, without waiting for his report to wend its way through the normal channels."

"If your brief summary of it was as accurate as usual, then you were certainly right," she told him, and looked back at Ackenheil. "Captain?" she invited.

"If you don't mind, Your Grace, I'll let Commander Zahn describe what happened. She was on Tactical at the time."

"Fine." Honor nodded, and moved her gaze to Zahn. "Go ahead, Commander."

"Yes, Your Grace." Honor could taste the youthful Sidemorian's nervousness, but if she hadn't been able to sense the emotions of others directly, she would never have guessed that someone as outwardly calm and composed as Zahn felt at all uncomfortable.

"Thirteen days ago," Zahn began, "we were on station in the Brennan System. We'd been there for five days, and we were scheduled to depart in another three. It had been a thoroughly routine patrol up until that point, although we had picked up a few suspicious movements in-system."

"According to our sources," Reynolds put in for Honor's benefit, "Governor Heyerdahl may have a private arrangement with the Brennan System's domestic criminal element. So far as we can tell, it seems to be mainly fairly small-scale smuggling, not any sort of accommodation with hijackers or pirates . . . or slavers. *LaFroye* was tasked with tracking any 'black' shipping movements, mostly to confirm that smuggling is all Heyerdahl is up to."

"Understood." Honor nodded. If smuggling was all Heyerdahl was involved in, then he was a paragon of law-abiding virtue compared to most Silesian system governors. "Continue, Commander, please."

"Yes, Your Grace. As I say, we'd been on station for five days when our FTL recon platforms picked up the arrival of an Andermani battlecruiser. She wasn't squawking any transponder code, but we got a hard ID on her emissions signature from one of the platforms. Then we lost her completely."

"Lost her," Honor repeated.

"Yes, Your Grace. She just dropped right off the platforms' passives."

"What was the range to the closest platform?" Honor asked intently.

"Under eight light-minutes," Zahn replied, and Honor's eyes narrowed. She glanced expressionlessly at McKeon and Yu, and both of them returned her look with an equal absence of expression. Then all three of them returned their attention to Zahn.

"We were surprised to lose her at such a short range," the tac officer continued. "Our latest intelligence update had emphasized that their stealth systems had been substantially improved, but nothing in the briefing had suggested that much improvement. So as soon as we lost her, the Captain ordered me to find her again. Since the main recon platforms were fixed, I deployed a standard shell of Ghost Rider drones to blanket the volume around her last known locus with mobile platforms." The Sidemorian grimaced. "We didn't find her."

"How long did it take your drones to reach the locus, Commander?" Yu asked.

"Approximately sixty-two minutes, Sir," Zahn replied. "Given her observed velocity at the time we lost her and Intelligence's latest estimate on her probable maximum acceleration, she ought to have been within five-point-one light-minutes of her last observed position. She wasn't."

"Are you certain?" Honor asked. "She wasn't just coasting ballistic?"

"I think that's exactly what she was doing, Your Grace," Zahn replied. "But she wasn't doing it within five light-minutes of the last place we'd seen her. My drones covered that volume like a fine-toothed comb. If she'd been there, we would have found her."

"I see." Honor's voice was merely thoughtful, but inwardly she was impressed by the lieutenant commander's certitude. Young Zahn might be a bit nervous about finding herself face-to-face with so much seniority, but her confidence in her own competence was impressive. And, judging from the taste of Ackenheil's approving, almost paternal attitude towards her, that confidence was probably justified.

"So what do you think happened?" she asked after a moment.

"I think our estimates of their compensator efficiency are still low, Your Grace," Zahn told her. "And I think they may have a better feel for the capabilities of our standard surveillance systems than I'd like. I don't think they have an equally good feel for Ghost Rider's capabilities, but to be perfectly honest, I wouldn't like to make any bets even on that.

"If I'm right, then they were able to make a pretty decent estimate on exactly when and where they'd drop off of our orbital platforms' sensors using whatever improved stealth systems they were employing. I think that's exactly what they did, and that as soon as they were confident they'd pulled it off, they went to a higher acceleration than we thought they could pull on an evasion heading. And when they figured we might be getting drones into position to spot their emissions despite their stealth, they shut down and went ballistic, exactly as you just suggested they might have. But because they were able to pull a higher accel, they were outside the zone where even Ghost Rider's active systems could find them without an impeller signature."

"And how do you think they were able to make that close a time estimate?" Honor asked. In the wrong tone, her question might have suggested that she thought Zahn was inclined to believe in the improvement in the Andermani's capabilities she had just postulated as a way to excuse a less than stellar effort to find the elusive battlecruiser. The way it came out, it was clearly an honest information request, and she felt Zahn relax a bit more.

"I think there are two possibilities, Your Grace. We know from Captain Ferrero's report that the Andies clearly have an FTL com capability of their own. It's possible that they had stealthed platforms already in-system to observe us—or even a second stealthed starship doing the same thing—so that they knew when we deployed the drones. They're not particularly stealthy during the initial deployment phase," she pointed out.

"If they tracked the deployment, then they could have sent an FTL warning to the battlecruiser which would have given her at least a rough idea of when the drones might reach detection range of her. With that information, she would have had an equally rough idea of when she had to shut down her impellers to disappear from our passives."

"I don't much care for that scenario, Commander," Honor observed. "That, unfortunately, doesn't make it any less likely. But you said you saw two possibilities."

"Yes, Your Grace. Personally, I find the second one even more disturbing: they may have actually detected the Ghost Rider drones before the drones detected them."

"You're right," Honor said after a moment. "That *is* a more disturbing possibility." She glanced at Jaruwalski. "What do you think, Andrea?"

"At this point, Your Grace, I'm not prepared to rule anything out," Jaruwalski said frankly. "I realize it's always dangerous to overestimate a potential opponent's capabilities, but it's even more dangerous to *under*estimate them. Be that as it may, however, I'm strongly inclined to think that Commander Zahn's first hypothesis is the more likely. I know how hard it would be for us to detect an incoming Ghost Rider drone soon enough to shut down before it had us on passive, even if we were under stealth at the time. I don't see any way that anyone else could do it at all. Even making every possible allowance for improvements in their tech, I find it very difficult to believe that our local intelligence estimates could be far enough off for them to have developed the sort of capabilities which would let them manage a trick like that."

She had not, Honor noticed, said anything about the extent to which the *Admiralty's* intelligence estimates might be off.

"I'd have to concur with Captain Jaruwalski, Your Grace," Reynolds offered. "We could both be wrong, but I don't think we are. Not that far wrong."

"But the possibility that they had *LaFroye* under observation that close without her ever seeing them isn't all that much more palatable," Commander Orndorff pointed out.

"No, it isn't," Honor agreed with fairly massive understatement. She considered the implications for several silent seconds, then shook herself and returned her attention to Ackenheil and Zahn.

"I think we're going to have to accept, tentatively, at least, that one of your two hypotheses is correct, Commander. What happened after you failed to relocate her?"

"I ordered Commander Zahn to continue search operations," Ackenheil said before Zahn could reply. "I authorized the use of additional Ghost Rider drones, and I ordered a course change to take us towards the Andy's last known position."

"And?" Honor asked when he paused.

"And if the Andies had really planned on starting anything, Your Grace," Ackenheil said with unflinching honesty, "they probably would have blown my ship right out of space. And it would have been my fault, not Commander Zahn's."

"In what way?"

"Well, Your Grace, it's obvious in retrospect that the Andy made a depressingly accurate estimate of what I was likely to do. He was waiting for us. Still in stealth, and well on our side of where I estimated he could have gotten to in the elapsed time. The first thing that I knew, was when he locked us up."

"Locked you up," Honor repeated, and Ackenheil nodded.

"Yes, Your Grace. He didn't just have us on active sensors; he had us locked up with his fire control radar and lidar, and he kept us that way for over thirty seconds."

"I see." Honor sat back in her chair and exchanged another glance with McKeon and Yu. Then she gave her head a little toss, as if to clear her brain, and turned back to Ackenheil.

"And afterward?"

"And afterward, he just shut down his targeting systems and completely ignored us," Ackenheil replied. His voice was level, but Honor tasted the remembered echoes of white-hot rage. "I hailed him five times, Your Grace. He never responded once, never even identified himself."

"What the *hell* are those idiots playing at?" Alistair McKeon demanded rhetorically.

Captain Ackenheil and Lieutenant Commander Zahn had left the flagship to return to *LaFroye*. Honor had assured them both of her confidence in them, and that assurance had been genuine. It might not have been if Ackenheil had tried to minimize how completely the Andy battlecruiser had surprised him, but Honor had been surprised enough times herself to realize how easily it could have happened. And one thing she could be sure of was that if it was humanly possible, Jason Ackenheil would never let it happen again.

Which didn't make the fact that it could have happened once any more reassuring.

"It sounds like more of the same thing, to me," Alice Truman put in from the com screen above the conference table. She'd been brought thoroughly up to date when Honor summoned her to the electronic conference, and now she shook her head on the screen.

"But this incident is more pointed, Dame Alice," Warner Caslet pointed out. All eyes turned to him, and the commander of First Battle Squadron, Protector's Own, shrugged. "It was a lot more pointed. And there's not much question as to how directly it was pointed at us, either. Well, at the Star Kingdom, I suppose."

"There hasn't been much question about where most of their damned provocations were pointed," McKeon replied, and Caslet grimaced.

"That wasn't exactly what I meant. Or, rather, I've been wondering about something else, and I wish we had a way to answer the question that's been bothering me."

"What question?" Honor asked.

"Whether or not they've been prodding the Sillies as hard as they have us . . . or even harder." Honor looked at him, and he shrugged. "We know they've been giving us demonstrations of their capabilities, but have they been focusing solely on us? Or have they been making the same point to the Sillies?"

"Now that, Your Grace," Andrea Jaruwalski observed after a moment, "is an intriguing thought. And it would make sense."

"You think they're not just trying to convince us that they can handle our tech advantages?" Truman asked. "That they're making the point to the Sillies that the Confed Navy *can't* match the IAN's?"

"Something like that," Caslet agreed. "And that would make sense of how widely their anti-piracy forces are operating throughout Silly space, as well. If they're hoping to inspire us into backing off, then they may also be hoping to convince the Sillies that trying to resist any territorial demands they may press would be futile. Scattering their forces around in a way that shows how numerically powerful they are—and showing off their new toys to demonstrate how capable they are—could be part of both those strategies."

"Yes, they certainly could," Truman agreed. "Still, whoever that battlecruiser's skipper was, she took a big chance upping the ante that way. If Ackenheil had been feeling a bit more proddy, he might have been at battle stations and popped off a broadside before he realized he was only being harassed. Which could have ended up with us in a shooting war with the Empire."

"Yes, it could have," Honor agreed. "Unfortunately, this looks like more of the straight-line progression in provocation we've been seeing, whoever it is they intend to provoke. Or why. The question, of course, becomes where they intend to stop. *If* they intend to stop."

"Whatever they 'intend,' it seems to me that they're running a serious chance of pushing things over the edge," McKeon said. "Goddamned idiots! If they actually intend to make territorial demands on Silesia, why the hell don't they just go ahead and tell us so?"

"I don't know." Honor sighed. "If I were calling the shots from the other side, I certainly would have at least started laying the groundwork for some sort of negotiated settlement. I can't believe they really want a shooting war with us over something like this!"

"Under normal circumstances, I'd agree with you, My Lady," Caslet said. "But their new choice for their Silesian commander makes me wonder."

"Um." Honor gazed at him, eyes troubled, then nodded unhappily and looked at the rest of her officers. "In some ways, I agree with Warner," she admitted. "Alice met Chien-lu von Rabenstrange the last time all three of us were out here, too, but the rest of you may not realize just how significant the Emperor's announcement that he's going to be appointed to the Silesian command really is. Von Rabenstrange isn't just any old flag officer. Not only is he a *Gross Admiral*, he's the Emperor's own first cousin, and fifth in the succession to the throne to boot. And he also has a reputation as one of the best combat commanders they have.

"But by the same token, he's an honorable man. And unlike Admiral von Sternhafen, he's no anti-Manticoran chauvinist. I don't think he'd feel comfortable about accepting responsibility for executing a policy he *expected* to lead to war, and he wouldn't be the sort to enjoy picking a fight with us the way Sternhafen might. I'm not saying he wouldn't accept the slot and carry out his orders to do just that anyway if he were ordered to, because he takes his duties as an officer seriously. But unless I'm very mistaken, he'd do all he could to talk the Emperor out of deliberately starting something. And he and Gustav have always been close, ever since they were at the Andie naval academy together, so I'm sure he'd have spoken his mind about it. So maybe the fact that they're sending him out to relieve Sternhafen is an indication that they really don't plan on starting something."

"Maybe," McKeon agreed sourly. "But whatever they may be planning, the way they're actually behaving is going to push us into an exchange of fire whether or not either side wants one! If they'd just make their demands and let us respond, one way or the other, both sides would know what the options were. At least that way we wouldn't start killing each other because of some sheer, stupid accident!"

"They probably aren't making formal demands because they don't realize what gutless wonders are running the Star Kingdom," Honor said with a flash of sudden rage. "They think there may actually be someone in the High Ridge Government with a *spine*— someone who'd actually stand up to them! Someone—"

She chopped herself off abruptly as she realized just how much frustration she was revealing. And, for that matter, startled to realize how angry she actually was . . . and how clearly she was allowing it to show, despite the way she'd admonished McKeon, Orndorff, and Brigham in the lift car.

No one else said anything else for at least thirty seconds, but then McKeon cleared his throat and cocked an eyebrow at her.

"I take it," he said in a wry tone, "that your last comment indicates you haven't received any secret new orders from the Admiralty which we're not aware of?"

"No," Honor replied, then snorted. "Of course, if they were *secret* orders, I'd tell you I hadn't gotten any anyway, wouldn't I?"

"Sure," McKeon agreed. "But you're not a very good liar."

Honor chuckled, almost despite herself, and shook her head at him. But he'd succeeded in breaking her mood, exactly as he'd intended, and she gave him a smile of thanks, as well. Then she shook herself and turned resolutely back to the matter at hand.

"As a matter of fact," she said, "I wish I had received some sort of new instructions, secret or not. Even bad ones would be better than none . . . which is exactly what we've actually been sent. The Admiralty's acknowledged receipt of my last dispatches, including George's report on the pattern of increasing provocation and on the Empire's decision to send Rabenstrange out, but that's all. It's as if no one at the other end is even bothering to read our mail."

"So all you can do is continue under your existing orders," Alfredo Yu mused.

"Exactly. And they're even more out of date—and, to be blunt about it, irrelevant—than they were when they first sent us out here," Honor said, with a frankness she would have shown in front of very few non-Manticorans. "Worse, I'm beginning to think no one at Admiralty House or the Foreign Office is even thinking very much about Silesia or the Andermani right now."

"You think they're being distracted by the Peeps? I mean, by the *Republic*, of course," McKeon said.

Neither Yu nor Caslet so much as blinked, but Honor felt both of them wince internally. Not in anger, and certainly not because either of them suffered from mixed loyalties at this late date. It was more of a sense of loss, a bittersweet regret for the changes in Haven which they would never be a part of.

And a smoldering anger, worse even than that of most Graysons, over the policies of the High Ridge Government which seemed to be fanning the tensions between Haven and the Star Kingdom once again.

"I think that's exactly what's happening," she confirmed after a moment. In fact, she'd been afraid something like that was coming from the moment word that Benjamin Mayhew's concerns about the mysterious "Operation Bolthole" had been amply justified had finally reached Marsh.

"As a matter of fact," she went on, putting her fears into words openly for her staff, "I think the Government's confidence in its ability to 'manage' the Republic—" *and through it, the domestic situation*, she carefully didn't say "—is deteriorating. Thomas Theisman's announcement didn't help in that regard, but the most recent mail from home is full of op-ed pieces on President Pritchart's 'hardline' position in the treaty negotiations, too." She shook her head. "I don't know how whatever *Harvest Joy* discovers is going to affect the Government's thinking, but unless something changes radically, I think High Ridge is going to become more and more fixated on the Republic. I don't think he has the attention to spare for something as 'unimportant' as Silesia."

"So what do we do?" McKeon asked.

"We do the best we can," she said bleakly. "Our orders are still to protect Silesian territorial integrity—assuming that 'Silesia' and 'territorial integrity' aren't contradictions in terms. So we'll do our darnedest to somehow pull that off. But you're right about the way this latest incident ups the ante, Alice. And the more I think about it, the more I don't want any of our other captains left to dangle all alone the way Ackenheil found himself in Brennan."

She turned to Yu and Caslet.

"Alfredo, I want you and the Protector's Own to maintain an even lower profile. If the Andies already know you're here, well and good. But if they don't, I think it's suddenly become more important to have an extra pulser hidden up our sleeve than to try to discourage whatever they're up to." She snorted harshly. "Given Ackenheil's report, I'm very much afraid that it's too late to do any 'discouraging,' anyway."

"You think they've made up their mind to pull the trigger, My Lady?" Yu seemed relieved to be thinking about possible Andermani aggressiveness instead of the tension between the Star Kingdom and his ex-homeland.

"I think they've made up their mind what they're going to do," Honor corrected. "In fact, I think that's the reason Rabenstrange is coming out here. That may include pulling the trigger, or it may simply include a continuation of this escalation of incidents in hopes we—or the Government—will decide the game isn't worth the candle and get out of their way without the unpleasantness of a war. But whatever it is, I think I'm coming to the conclusion that I'd prefer to be able to administer a salutary shock to them at a moment of my choosing, if I can, and you and the Protector's Own are my best chance to do that."

Yu nodded, and Honor turned to Brigham and Jaruwalski.

"In the meantime, I want the two of you to lay out a new patrol schedule. With the Grayson units here to bolster our position in Marsh, I think we can free up more of our Manticoran screening units for detached service, so I want the patrols beefed up. Set it up so that none of our ships are operating as singletons. I want at least two units in any single star system, and I want them in regular communication. I want the Andies to know that if something goes wrong, we're going to have a witness on the spot to get the news to us as soon as it can get back to their own HQ. And for that matter, knowing that she has support handy ought to make any of our captains feel a bit less lonely and a bit more confident."

Chapter Thirty-Eight

The icon of the dispatch boat from Sidemore was still accelerating steadily away from *Jessica Epps* when Erica Ferrero assembled her senior officers in her briefing room.

They gathered there just a bit apprehensively, because the captain's temper had been uncertain of late, courtesy of IANS *Hellbarde*. They knew Ferrero had recently dispatched another formal report to Duchess Harrington, protesting *Kapitän zur Sternen* Gortz' provocative behavior. That report had been intended primarily for the duchess to use as the basis of a fresh protest to the Andermani Empire, but some might have thought its language a bit on the intemperate side. It was entirely possible that the dispatch boat had delivered an observation to that effect from the station commander.

One look at Ferrero's expression, however, swiftly disabused them of that concern. The captain's blue-green eyes glowed with an eagerness they hadn't seen in quite some time, and she waved briskly for them to take their seats so that they could get started.

"All right, People," she told them, once all of them had settled into place. "It seems we have a little job to do for the Duchess." She smiled thinly. "One I think we can all look forward to with a certain anticipation."

She entered a command into her terminal, and a holo schematic of a star system appeared above the briefing room table.

"The Zoraster System, Ladies and Gentlemen," she announced. "Not all that close to Sidemore, but not that far away, either." In fact, it was little more than twenty-four light-years from the Marsh System in the Posnan Sector. It was also one of the wealthier star systems in the sector.

"What, you may ask, is our interest in Zoraster?" the captain continued, and paused expectantly. Most of her officers had seen her in this mood at least once or twice before, and Lieutenant McClelland chirped up obediently.

"All right, Ma'am. What *is* our interest in Zoraster?"

"I'm glad you asked that question, James," she said with a chuckle. Then she sobered. "I'm sure all of you remember Captain Ackenheil's interception of that Solly slaver."

"Yes, Ma'am. The *Wayfarer*, wasn't it?" Commander Llewellyn asked.

"Exactly, Bob." Ferrero nodded. "Well, it seems some of *Wayfarer*'s crew decided that they preferred to assist the forces of goodness. I suspect that someone on the Duchess' staff took the opportunity to point out to them that turning Queen's evidence was one way to mitigate the penalty for slaving."

A nasty chuckle ran around the briefing room. Only Llewellyn and Ferrero herself had ever actually participated in the interception of a slaver, but all of them had seen reports, just as all of them knew the trade was particularly lucrative in places like Silesia. There was so much corruption, so many opportunities to operate under the protection of conveniently bribable officials, that the Confederation was a perfect transshipment point for someone like Mesa to make contact with its buyers. No one in *Jessica Epps*' company was going to waste much sympathy on anyone who chose to participate in the slave trade.

"At any rate, Lieutenant Commander Reynolds, the Duchess' staff spook, was able to generate a little more information for Operation Wilberforce, and that's what makes Zoraster of interest to us.

"It seems that Governor Chalmers has an understanding with certain individuals involved in the slave trade. As a matter of fact, the good governor, according to Commander Reynolds' source, is the majority owner of an orbital 'recreation' habitat in the New Hamburg System. One which apparently requires regular replenishment of its . . . staff."

All temptation towards humor disappeared when Ferrero

mentioned New Hamburg. Like Mesa itself, New Hamburg was an independent star system which had declined to sign any of the international accords which outlawed genetic slavery. Sixty-nine T-years before, New Hamburg had been forced—primarily by the missile tubes of the Royal Manticoran Navy—to "voluntarily" sign a treaty outlawing participation by its citizens and starships in the interstellar genetic slave *trade*, but the institution itself remained quite legal within its territory. Prior to the Havenite war, the RMN had made it its business to maintain sufficient patrol strength in New Hamburg's vicinity to make the importation of slaves a very risky business, indeed. Largely as a result of that pressure, the system's infamous "recreation habitats" had fallen upon hard times, but they'd made a substantial comeback when the demands of the war against Haven had diverted the anti-slavery patrols.

"According to Commander Reynolds' information," Ferrero went on in a flatter, harder voice, "Chalmers has recently taken receipt of approximately three hundred fresh slaves for delivery to New Hamburg. They arrived aboard a Solarian-flag freighter about two months ago, and they're due to be picked up by a New Hamburg-flag merchie sometime within the next couple of weeks. Under the terms of the treaty with New Hamburg, we have the authority to stop and search New Hamburg's vessels anywhere, and our instructions from the Duchess are to do just that."

"I would assume that under the circumstances we're not going to be able to expect any cooperation out of the local Silly authorities," Lieutenant Commander Harris observed.

"I think that's probably a safe assumption, Shawn," Ferrero agreed in a dust-dry tone.

"That's going to make intercepting the New Hamburger harder," the tac officer thought out loud. "Just spotting her is going to be hard enough."

"Might not be as difficult as you're thinking," Llewellyn pointed out. "Zoraster is better off than a lot of the star systems out here, but we're not talking about someplace like New Potsdam or Gregor. There shouldn't be more than three or four—half a dozen at the most—hyper-capable merchies in-system at any one time."

"Agreed, Sir," Harris replied. "On the other hand, though, there's only one of us."

"And we can only be in one place at a time," Ferrero agreed. "Fortunately, we have one more minor advantage, courtesy of

Commander Reynolds." They all looked at her expectantly, and she showed her teeth in an expression no one would have been likely ever to confuse with a pleasant smile. "It would appear that Governor Chalmers is also familiar with the terms of our treaty with New Hamburg. Which is why the ship he's expecting will arrive squawking the transponder code of an Andy merchant ship."

"That," Llewellyn said thoughtfully, "could be a bit of a problem, Ma'am, given how tense things are out here right now."

"I'm sure that's why Chalmers picked an Andy code." Ferrero nodded. "No Manticoran's skipper in her right mind is going to want to provoke any incidents by stopping Andy merchant shipping. Unfortunately for Governor Chalmers, if Commander Reynolds' information is correct, he's chosen the wrong ship this time."

"What do you mean, 'wrong ship,' Skipper?" Lieutenant McKee asked.

"Chalmers is going to be expecting a ship identifying herself as the Andermani merchant ship *Sittich*. There happens to be a ship of that name on the Andermani merchant registry. But that *Sittich* is a four-megaton *Spica*-class bulk carrier. The *Sittich* Chalmers is expecting is a two-megaton tramp. We don't have her class or any detailed sensor info on her, but we do have a complete fingerprint on the real *Sittich* from Gregor Astro Control, and it's less than six months old. So if we see someone squawking *Sittich*'s transponder code and she doesn't match our filed sensor data, then I think we can be fairly confident we've got the right target. And if Commander Reynolds' informant was telling him the truth, our *Sittich* is not only going to be outfitted as a slaver, she's going to have at least some slaves actually on board. Zoraster is her last stop before she heads back to New Hamburg, and she's supposed to have picked up consignments in at least two other star systems."

"What if this informant, whoever he is, is feeding us false information, Skipper?" McClelland asked. Ferrero looked at him, and he shrugged. "As you say, we're not exactly on the best terms with the Andies just now. What if someone's trying to set us up to stop one of their merchies expressly to create an incident?"

"I suppose the possibility exists," Ferrero acknowledged. "But if that's what someone's trying to do, whoever it is picked a particularly stupid way to go about it, James. First of all, they picked the name of an Andy ship we happen to have good sensor data on, which means we should at least be able to avoid stopping the real *Sittich* even if she should somehow happen to appear in this particular system at this particular time. Of course, there's no way a crewman on a Solly freighter could have known that would be the case. So it's at least remotely possible that he just picked a name out of a hat and dogged out on his choice. But think about it. *Wayfarer*'s entire crew was caught in the act of slaving. Every one of them is liable to execution. So whoever gave Commander Reynolds this information has to be aware that if it turns out to be bogus, and especially if it creates an incident between us and the Andies, any deal that might have saved him from the hangman goes right out the airlock."

McClelland considered that. After a moment, he nodded slowly, and Ferrero nodded back.

"All right, James. I want a course for Zoraster plotted soonest. Shawn, I want you and the exec to sit down and plan exactly how we're going to do this. Obviously, I don't want Chalmers to know we're in the system. The first thing he's going to do if he knows we're there will be to warn his accomplices. If he's smart, he'll also be doing his best to keep us tied up in official red tape or using his own system security ships to shadow and harass us, trying to keep us distracted. So we'll go in stealthy and stay that way."

"Aye, aye, Ma'am." Harris frowned thoughtfully. "Can I deploy perimeter platforms on the way in?"

"I'd prefer not to," Ferrero said after a moment. "We don't have any idea what kind of sensor suite our target may be carrying. It's remotely possible that they could spot the regular platforms, and unless we were in exactly the right place, we couldn't count on intercepting them before they broke back out across the limit and disappeared into hyper again. More to the point, Chalmers' system security units might spot them and warn our friends off."

"That's going to make things a little tougher, Skipper," Llewellyn pointed out for the tac officer.

"It is," Ferrero conceded. "But remember, we're hunting a merchie here, and there's only one habitable planet in the system. I don't think even Chalmers is going to want to risk parking that many slaves aboard one of the orbital refineries or fabrication platforms, and, by the same token, he's not going to want to try to hide them aboard one of the normal transient lodging habitats. That means our target is going to have to make contact with the planet, or at least one of the orbital warehouses where Chalmers can be confident of avoiding unwanted eyes, to pick up her 'cargo.'"

"So if we stay close enough to the planet, we should be able to get a good sensor look at anything coming close enough for a pickup." Harris nodded. "I can work with that, Skipper. Staying stealthed that close without being picked up ourselves won't be easy, even against Silly sensors, but I think we can hack it as long as we keep the wedge strength down."

"And if we catch her that deep into the system, there's no way she'll be able to outrun us back to the hyper limit," McClelland put in.

"Exactly," Ferrero agreed.

"Question, Skipper," Llewellyn said. "Do we want to intercept her inbound, or outbound?"

"Um." Ferrero rubbed her chin, frowning thoughtfully. "Outbound," she decided. "We could nail the ship on either leg, especially if Commander Reynolds' information about her already having slaves on board is accurate. But I want Chalmers, too, if we can get him. And our best shot at that is to intercept '*Sittich*' when she has slaves we know are bound for *his* 'recreation' habitat."

"Understood." Llewellyn gazed at the system schematic for a few seconds. "It's going to increase our exposure to the Sillies' sensor platforms, but not by all that much. And I hate to say it, but I'd really prefer to intercept her as far from whatever defensive systems Zoraster may have as we can. Chalmers would have to be a lunatic to fire on a Manticoran warship, but given the official penalties for slaving even here in Silesia, I'd just as soon not tempt him."

"I'm glad you're thinking that way, Bob," Ferrero told him. "On the other hand, you're talking about Silly weapon systems." She chuckled nastily. "I almost wish he *would* be stupid enough to try to nail us with that obsolescent crap. Shawn's missile crews could use the exercise!"

"Have you been informed as to the content of this note, Mr. Ambassador?" Elaine Descroix asked coolly.

"Only in the most general terms, Madame Secretary," Yves Grosclaude, the Havenite ambassador to the Star Kingdom, replied.

It might strike some that having any discussion with an ambassador from a nation with which one was officially still at war was . . . unusual, because it was. But Secretary of State Giancola had argued that more direct contact at a somewhat higher level than the teams deadlocked on the actual treaty negotiations would be helpful. In Descroix's opinion, there was some doubt as to just who it would be helpful for, but High Ridge had decided that it would be a fairly innocuous concession which would play well in the court of public opinion. Which was how Yves Grosclaude had become Haven's officially accredited "special envoy" (accorded the "courtesy" title of Ambassador solely as a gracious gesture towards the Republic, of course) to the Star Kingdom of Manticore.

As always, he and Descroix were punctiliously correct.

"And were you informed as to when Secretary Giancola anticipates a reply?"

"No, Madame Secretary. I was simply instructed to request a formal reply at the Star Kingdom's earliest convenience."

"I see." Descroix smiled. "Well, I assure you, Mr. Ambassador, that we will indeed reply at our earliest . . . convenience."

"We could ask no more," Grosclaude replied affably, with a smile as obviously false as her own. "And now," he continued, "since I've discharged my mission here, I will take up no more of your valuable time."

He rose with a slight, formal bow, and Descroix stood behind her desk to return it. She made no move, however, to escort him from her office, and he smiled again, this time as if in some obscure form of satisfaction at the deliberate slight.

She watched the door close behind him, then sat back down and turned her attention back to the text on her display. It was no more palatable on closer examination than it had been when she first glanced at it, and she allowed her anger to show now that she was once again alone in her office.

She read through the entire note, slowly, one phrase at a time, and her lips grew thinner and her eyes colder with each sentence.

"I don't believe I care for Pritchart's tone," Baron High Ridge observed coldly.

"And you think I do care for it?" Descroix demanded. Then she snorted. "At least you didn't have that jumped up Dolist Grosclaude in your office handing his frigging note to you."

"No," the Prime Minister agreed. "I've had to endure three interviews with him, and that's quite enough, thank you."

"I wish three interviews were all *I'd* had to put up with," Descroix replied. "But that's neither here nor there. What's important is the note itself. She's getting more and more hardline, Michael."

"So I see." High Ridge glanced back at his own copy of the note and grimaced. "I see that she's taken her offer of a plebiscite for Trevor's Star back off the table."

"That part doesn't really surprise me," Descroix admitted. "Especially with all of the talk here in the Star Kingdom about the annexation of the new terminus and the possibility of extending that to Lynx and the other Talbott systems. We're considering mass annexations, and she sees that as a bad precedent for her own occupied systems. And we've also been concentrating on Talbott to downplay the tension between us and the Republic, and she knows that, too. So she went looking for a way to slap us on the wrist hard enough to get our attention, and this is what she came up with. She figures that Trevor's Star is the most valuable counter on the board and that taking it back out of play—from her side, at least—at this particular moment will make the point that she's pissed off."

"I can understand that, I suppose. On the other hand, surely she's not so stupid as to think that whether she's willing to talk about Trevor's Star or not is going to make any difference to what happens there? We've formally annexed the system, for God's sake! Whatever she or those other idiots in Nouveau Paris may think, Trevor's Star and San Martin are definitely remaining under our control."

"Of course I don't think she's stupid enough to think any other outcome is possible," Descroix said. "But you've seen the analyses of their public discussion about Trevor's Star. At least a very large minority—possibly even a majority—of their public opinion has fastened on Trevor's Star as the symbol of all our 'evil' ways. That makes it an issue that would play well to her voters, and she knows we know that. Which, in turn, gives her threat at least a hint of credibility. And the fact that we may believe she'll have no choice but to concede the issue in the end doesn't mean we might not be willing to make concessions of our own elsewhere to have the Republic bless the annexation. It would defuse potential future disputes over possession of the system and knock any move by a later Havenite administration to regain it on the head. Maybe even more importantly, if the Republic were to formally concede that a legitimate San Martino planetary government had voluntarily asked to join the Star Kingdom, it would help to calm any fears among our allies—or the Sollies—that we might be planning on embarking on a career of conquest by force of arms. She knows that could be extremely valuable to us. So taking the plebiscite offer off the table is a way of warning us she has ways to punish us if we don't meet her demands.

"At the same time, she's actually opened the door to further concessions on her part."

"She has?"

"Of course she has! Didn't you notice the bit about recognizing our traditional concern for the security of termini of the Junction?" Descroix demanded. The Prime Minister nodded, and she shrugged. "That's very close to offering us the same arrangement we enjoy in Gregor. Admittedly, that sort of arrangement falls far short of anything we could finally accept, since we've already asserted outright sovereignty over the entire system, so I suppose it could be argued that it's actually a ploy to avoid recognizing that sovereignty. But it also moves at least one step towards us, and I think it's a way of signaling us that she's still open to a settlement on the system which we can accept. And the offer to cede those naval bases in the systems around Trevor's Star is probably another. She's showing us the carrot at the same time as she's trying to beat us with the stick, Michael."

"And this business about the possible recall of her negotiating team for 'consultations'? That's more of the stick?"

"Mostly. It's not as subtle a threat, though. Especially not coupled with their admission of their improved naval capabilities."

"You think they might seriously contemplate breaking off the negotiating process completely if we don't begin caving in?"

"Probably not permanently," Descroix said slowly. "I think Pritchart might consider doing that temporarily—long enough to make her point. But I doubt that she's any more eager to start shooting at us again than we are to start shooting at them."

"But you might be wrong," High Ridge said, unable to completely hide his anxiety.

"Of course I might," Descroix said testily. "Obviously, I don't think I am, however, or I wouldn't have said it in the first place!"

"I understand." High Ridge's fingers drummed lightly on his desktop, then he inhaled deeply.

"Clarence brought me the new poll figures this morning," he said. "Have you seen them?"

"Not today's, no. But I imagine the trend lines are pretty much what they've been being."

"By and large," the Prime Minister agreed. "The number of people who say they believe there's an immediate military threat from Haven has dropped almost another full percentage point. Approval for the annexation of Lynx is holding steady at almost eighty-five percent. For that matter, those who say they would approve the annexation of the entire Talbott Cluster are up above seventy percent. But those who anticipate the successful negotiation of a formal peace treaty with Haven have dropped another half percentage point. This—" he waved a hand at the note "—is only going to make that worse."

"Of course it is," Descroix said impatiently. "That's one of the things Pritchart is after. But if we let her stampede us into agreeing to her demands and signing that treaty, then we're going to have to call that general election none of us wants to call, Michael."

High Ridge's jaw muscles tightened angrily at her lecturing tone, but he forced himself not to snap at her.

"I am aware of that," he said, instead. The very calmness with which he replied rebuked her gently, but he didn't let the rebuke linger.

"My point," he went on, "was that I'm beginning to wonder if we might not want to make a few cosmetic concessions. Something to bring Pritchard back to the table and simultaneously bolster the public's faith in the negotiation process."

"If we were going to do that, we should already have done it," Descroix replied. "Something along those lines would probably be a good idea in the long run, but I'd really prefer not to do it right on the heels of this note. The language in this thing is pretty stiff, Michael. If we turn around and make concessions—any concessions—after the Republic's head of state has formally complained about our 'deceptive, intentionally obstructionist refusal to negotiate in good faith,' we give up our claim to the high ground. The momentum moves towards Pritchart's side of the table, and public opinion, both here and in the Republic, will probably see her as the positive force pushing the negotiations. Manticorans may not approve of her language, or even her methods, but if we give ground, we seem to be admitting that her basic accusations are accurate, after all. All of which will only make it harder for us to put the brakes back on later without provoking an even more negative reaction than the one you're worrying about right now."

"Um." High Ridge frowned. He considered her argument, then nodded slowly, but his frown remained.

"I see your logic. But it's going to be hard to convince Marisa of it."

"Marisa!" Descroix snorted contemptuously.

"Yes, Marisa. Whatever you may think, we still need the Liberals, and when Marisa sees this—" he indicated the text of the note again "—it's going to be very difficult to convince her that we can't make at least some concessions. You and I may understand the necessity of not giving in, but she has to consider the more . . . unruly members of her party. Especially now that Montaigne is making so many waves in the Commons."

"In that case, don't show it to her," Descroix shot back. "She's so good at closing her eyes to things it would be inconvenient for her to see. Why not take advantage of that with this?"

"Don't think I wouldn't like to do exactly that. But everyone in the Star Kingdom knows by now that Pritchart's sent us a fresh note. And if we don't make its contents public, in at least general terms, you can be certain that someone—Grosclaude himself, most probably—will see to it that a copy of the original gets leaked to the Opposition. And the 'faxes. But before we make anything public, we're going to have to share the original with the entire Cabinet. Which means Marisa."

"Let me think about that for a little while," Descroix said after a moment. "You're probably right. I don't much like the thought of listening to her piss and moan about her precious 'principles' and the potential danger of Theisman's new fleet. God knows she's been willing enough to share the advantages of stalling the talks! I just think it would be nice if she were willing to shoulder a little of the responsibility, maybe even risk getting her own lily-white hands just a tiny bit soiled doing the dirty work someone has to do. But that doesn't make you wrong about what would happen if we didn't brief her in on this."

The Foreign Secretary gazed off into the distance for several seconds, staring at something only she could see, then snorted softly.

"You know," she mused, "you and I are the only members of the Cabinet who have actually seen this thing."

"That's exactly what we've just been talking about, isn't it?" High Ridge's brow furrowed in confusion, and she chuckled.

"Of course it is. But it's just occurred to me that there's no reason I couldn't do a little judicious scissors work on Pritchart's more . . . objectionable turns of phrase before I handed it to someone like Marisa."

High Ridge looked at her in shock. She gazed back at him, then grimaced.

"Let's not start getting holier than thou, Michael!"

"But—I mean, falsifying diplomatic notes—"

"No one's talking about falsifying anything," she interrupted. "I wouldn't insert a single word. For that matter, I wouldn't even change any of them. I'd just . . . prune out a few passages completely."

"And if Pritchart publishes the text herself?" .

"I vote we cross that bridge when we come to it. If we release a paraphrase that conveys the same basic information but without using her hardline language, she'll probably let it go. My sense is that she'd cut us some face-saving slack in that regard. And if I'm wrong, I'm wrong." She shrugged. "Be honest, Michael. Do you really think we'd have a lot more trouble holding Marisa if Pritchart published the entire text later than if we showed it to her ourselves right now?"

"Probably not," he conceded finally. "But I don't like this, Elaine. Not a bit."

"I don't like it very much myself; I just like the alternatives less."

"Even if it works, it's only a temporary fix," he pointed out fretfully.

"As I see it, those poll trend lines you were just talking about suggest that if we can string Pritchart along for a few more months, long enough to actually push the Lynx annexation through, maybe even move beyond Lynx to the rest of the cluster, we should manage to cement enough public support behind us for even Marisa to be able to weather any concern over how we're handling negotiations with Haven. In the meantime, Edward will have time to get more of his new SD(P)s and CLACs out of the yards, which will go a long way towards offsetting Theisman's new ships. If we pull both of those off, then I think we may actually be able to move the polls far enough in our favor that we can afford to risk that damned election at last. And if we can get to that point, then we can go ahead and negotiate Pritchart's damned treaty because we won't need to string the talks out any further. And if we manage *that*, we could probably even call another election and increase our seats in the Commons even further."

"There's a lot of 'if's' in that," the Prime Minister observed.

"Of course there are. We're in a hell of a mess right now. There's no point pretending we're not. From where I sit, this gives us our best chance of getting out of it. So either we take it, or else we go ahead and resign the game. And when you come right down to it, whether we show Marisa the complete note now—and risk her withdrawal from the Coalition—or hold off on it until Pritchart sends us another, even nastier one a few months from now, the consequences are pretty much the same, aren't they? We win, or we lose . . . and I'm not all that interested in losing. So let's go for the whole nine meters."

CHAPTER THIRTY-NINE

"It's good to see you, Arnold," Eloise Pritchart lied as a member of the Presidential Security Detachment escorted Secretary of State Giancola into her office.

"Thank you, Madame President. It's always good to see you, too," Giancola replied equally smoothly for the benefit of the bodyguard. Not that anyone Kevin Usher had handpicked to protect the President of the Republic was going to be fooled by the surface exchange of pleasantries. Still, there were appearances to maintain.

The Secretary of State seated himself in the same chair Thomas Theisman preferred for his visits to Pritchart's office, and the PSD man withdrew.

"Would you care for some refreshments?" Pritchart inquired.

"No, thank you." Giancola grimaced. "I'm going straight from here to a dinner for the Ambassador from Erewhon. I'm afraid that means I'm going to have to tuck into that disgusting pickled fish dish they're all so proud of and pretend I like it. I'd just as soon not put anything down there that might surprise me by coming back up."

Pritchart laughed, and somewhat to her own surprise, her amusement was genuine. It was a real pity she couldn't trust Giancola as far as she could spit. Much as she disliked the man, and distrusted him, she wasn't unaware of the charm and magnetism he could exude whenever it suited his purposes.

"Well, in that case, I suppose we should get down to business," she said after a moment, and there was no more temptation to humor in her voice.

"Yes, I suppose we should," he agreed, and cocked his head at her. "May I assume you've already read my report?"

"I have." Pritchart frowned. "And I can't say I much cared for it, either."

"I don't much care for my conclusions myself," he told her, only partly truthfully.

"From the tone of Descroix's note, it sounds as if their position's actually hardening." Pritchart regarded him intently. "Is that your conclusion, as well?"

"It is," he replied. "Of course," he added in a voice which carried just a hint of satisfaction, "I may be a bit predisposed in that direction, given my earlier analysis of the Manties' foreign policy priorities."

"It's always good to be aware of the way expectations can sometimes lead us astray," Pritchart observed pleasantly.

Their eyes locked for just a moment. The challenge hovered there in the air between them, and the office seemed to hum with tension. But the moment was brief. Neither of them maintained any illusions about their relationship, but neither was quite ready for an open declaration of war, either.

"In the meantime," Pritchart resumed, "I'd have to agree that Descroix's note comes very close to rejecting our most recent proposals out of hand."

"Yes, it does," he agreed in a carefully neutral tone. In fact, the Manticoran Foreign Secretary's note had been the next best thing to perfect, from his perspective. The formal diplomatic language had been suitably opaque, but it was obvious Descroix was using it as a way to officially agree to "consider" Pritchart's initiatives while actually telling the Republic they were dead on arrival. Giancola could have kissed the woman when her note was couriered to the capital.

"Actually," he continued, "I'm inclined to believe that the Manties don't really appreciate the fundamental shift in the balance of military power which has occurred since negotiations began."

He'd been careful, Pritchart noted, not to suggest that announcing that shift earlier might have inspired the High Ridge Government with a more accurate appreciation of the military realities.

On the other hand, his failure to mention the possibility aloud was simply a more effective way of making the same statement.

"I really don't want this to turn into a matter of who has the bigger gun, Arnold," she said coolly.

"Neither do I," he said with apparent sincerity. "Unfortunately, in the end, effective diplomacy depends on a favorable balance of military strength more often than we'd like to admit." He shrugged. "It's an imperfect universe, Madame President."

"Admitted. I'd just prefer not to make it any less perfect that it already is."

"I've never advocated pushing things to the brink of an actual resumption of hostilities," he told her. "But star nations can stumble into wars neither of them want if they misread one another's strength and determination. And at the moment, the Manties seem to be busy underestimating both of those qualities where we're concerned."

"I don't believe our last note to them could have been much clearer in that regard," Pritchart observed, that edge of chill still frosting her voice.

"Not if they're actually bothering to listen to anything we say in the first place," Giancola replied.

And there, Pritchart was forced to admit, he might well have a point. She didn't like how hard it was for her to make that admission, because she knew why it was. Her personal antipathy towards Giancola was making it increasingly difficult for her to listen to anything he said without automatically rejecting it. It was one thing to maintain a healthy sense of suspicion where some-one who obviously had his own agenda was concerned. It was quite another to allow that suspicion to begin dictating an auto-response rejection of anything he ever said. Unfortunately, it was much easier for her to recognize that danger than it was to find a way around it.

In this instance, it was just a bit easier for her to concede that he might be correct, however. Previous experience with the Star Kingdom's diplomacy—as practiced by the current Government, at least—provided a more than sufficient counterirritant.

Her most recent set of proposals had been more than reason-able. She still hadn't actually offered formal recognition of the Star Kingdom's annexation of Trevor's Star. The Republic's permanent renunciation of all claims to San Martin was simply too valuable a bargaining chip to give up until she got at least something in return. And although she'd dropped her previous offer of a plebiscite in that system, her suggestion that she might accept the same sort of arrangement the Star Kingdom already enjoyed with the Andermani Empire in Gregor for the Trevor's Star Junction terminus had constituted a significant hint that she was at least open to the possibility of an eventual, formal recognition of the system's annexation. Moreover, she'd also conceded that legitimate Manticoran security concerns might well require at least some additional territorial adjustments, particularly in the area immediately around Trevor's Star. And she'd offered to cede the former Havenite naval bases in the systems of Samson, Owens, and Barnett outright, as permanent RMN bases to deepen the Manticoran Alliance's defensive frontier.

Of course, she admitted, the Star Kingdom was already in possession of all of those systems . . . not to mention all of the other systems currently in dispute, including the Tequila System, less than fifty-five light-years from the capital system itself. And Tequila was one of the systems she was *not* prepared to leave under Manticoran control.

The Manticoran Alliance actually controlled a total of twenty-seven star systems which were technically claimed by the Republic of Haven. Six of those twenty-seven were effectively uninhabited; most of them had boasted naval bases, which explained the Alliance's original interest in them, but possessed no habitable planets to attract civilian development. Another three had been sufficiently recent acquisitions of the People's Republic to leave the local inhabitants with an extreme dislike, even hatred, for anything coming out of the Haven System, regardless of any reforms which might have occurred there. Those three had already expressed their firm intention to seek annexation on the pattern of Trevor's Star, and Pritchart was prepared to let them go. The readopted Constitution gave them the right to do that, and even if they hadn't, she would have been perfectly willing to use them as bargaining chips. Assuming the Star Kingdom had shown any desire to bargain.

It was the other eighteen star systems under Manticoran occupation that created the stumbling block. Each of them, for its own reasons, was of special importance to the Republic. In most cases, those reasons were economic or industrial, but some of them were critically placed for military bases which would either protect the heartland of the Republic ... or provide a highway for its invasion. And most, though not all of them, had been member systems of the PRH long enough to think of themselves as Havenite territory, whether they were entirely delighted by the prospect or not.

The biggest problem was that at least three of them—Tahlman, Runciman, and Franconia—did not so regard themselves and had no desire to return to Havenite control. Two or three more were probably wavering, but the majority appeared to prefer the notion of being restored to the reformed Republic to ongoing occupation. In fact, a half dozen of them were obviously eager to rejoin the rest of the Republic before they missed out on the opportunities presented by the political and economic renaissance it was currently enjoying.

Those were the star systems Pritchart was unwilling to supinely yield to the Star Kingdom. She recognized that Tahlman, Runciman, and Franconia were going to require special handling, and it was entirely possible that in the end she would have to reluctantly allow them to go their own way. If it all possible, she preferred to do that by seeing them as independent single-system star nations in their own right rather than as additional Manticoran bastions so deep in Republican territory, but if she absolutely had to, she would agree to their voluntary annexation by the Star Kingdom. The return of the others to Republican sovereignty, however, was not negotiable.

A point Elaine Descroix and Baron High Ridge seemed determined to ignore.

"If they aren't listening to what we say," Pritchart told her Secretary of State, "then it's up to us to find a way to ... get their attention."

"That's precisely what I've been saying for some time now," Giancola observed mildly, while inside he savored the delicious pleasure of watching her move in the direction of his piping.

"At the same time, Madame President," he continued in a more somber tone, "I think we might want to exercise a little caution in precisely how we go about 'getting their attention.'"

"I thought you were in favor of finding ways to turn the screws on them," she said, eyes narrowed, and he shrugged. *That was before it became your policy*, he thought. And truth to tell, he was still perfectly willing to do just that, as long as it could be done on his own terms.

"In many ways, I still am in favor of being as firm as possible," he said aloud, choosing his words carefully while he wondered if Eloise Pritchart had ever heard of an ancient, obscure Old Earth folktale which had always been one of his own favorites as a child.

"However," he continued, "I believe our most recent offer was just about as explicit as it could possibly have been. Both in terms of what we were willing to concede, and in terms of what we clearly were *not* willing to concede. And in the clear implication that our patience isn't unlimited." He shrugged. "Speaking as the Republic's Secretary of State, I would be most hesitant to become even more openly confrontational."

Please, he thought, managing somehow not to smile. *Oh*, please, *don't throw me in that briar patch!*

"Firmness," Pritchart said, "isn't necessarily the same thing as being 'confrontational.'"

"I didn't mean to imply that it is," he lied. "I'm simply saying that I don't see any way to make our position clearer without explicitly telling the Manties we're prepared to resort to military action if our demands aren't met."

"I don't think we're so far along that our only options are to accept something like Descroix's meaningless response or go to war, Arnold," Pritchart said frostily, her eyes hard. It was interesting, she thought mordantly, the way that Giancola the firebrand had suddenly cooled off when the polls showed she was the one garnering public support for "standing up" to the Star Kingdom.

"I'm sorry if you think that was what I was saying," he replied, his expression a carefully crafted blend of frustration and mild disappointment even as a voice deep down inside was exulting *Gotcha!* "All I'm saying is that we've already made our feelings and our position amply clear. Obviously, the Manties haven't been impressed by that, however. So it seems to me that if we intend to continue to press them for concessions in the negotiations, we have to find some way other than still more diplomatic exchanges to increase the pressure on them. I probably overstated my position by mentioning military action, but let's be honest. What means do we have for exerting more pressure besides the potential threat of a resumption of hostilities?"

"I think we've already made them fully aware of that threat's potential," Pritchart said. "I see no reason to escalate tensions by waving the Navy in their direction even more explicitly. But I do intend to continue to press them on the diplomatic front. Do you have a problem with that?"

"Of course not," he said in a voice which implied exactly the opposite. "Even if I did, you're the President. However, if you— I mean, we—intend to maintain the diplomatic pressure, I believe we have to pursue all other avenues, as well. Which is why I would like to very strongly urge once again that we announce the existence of our CLACs, as well as the SD(P)s."

"Absolutely not," Pritchart said, then grimaced mentally. Her refusal had come out rather more forcefully than she'd intended. Partly, she suspected, that was because she was trapped between Thomas Theisman's position and Giancola's and resented it. The fact that Theisman was a friend while Giancola was something else entirely only made her resentment worse.

And, she reminded herself yet again, another part of it stemmed from her growing tendency to see anything Giancola suggested as a bad idea simply because it had come from him.

"No," she said in a calmer tone, and shook her head. "I'm not prepared to override Tom Theisman on that—not yet. But I do intend to reply to Descroix in no uncertain terms."

"It's your decision to make," Giancola conceded unhappily. Really, he reflected behind the cover of his frown, this was turning out to be even easier than he'd expected. It was like the old fables about "leading" a pig by tying a string to its hind leg and pulling in the opposite direction from the way you wanted it to go. The last thing he wanted at this point was for someone in the Star Kingdom to wake up too soon to the reality of the military threat it faced, and telling it about the CLACs was likely to accomplish just that.

"Yes," Pritchart told him, looking him straight in the eye, "it *is* my decision, isn't it?"

"The President is on the com, Sir."

Thomas Theisman looked up from the holo map floating above the conference table at Captain Borderwijk's announcement. His senior aide tapped her earbug lightly, indicating how she had received the information, and he managed not to frown. It wasn't easy. Normally, he was delighted to talk to Eloise Pritchart. Unfortunately, he knew who she'd been scheduled to meet with this afternoon.

"Thank you, Alenka," he said, instead, then glanced at the planners gathered around the map with him. "Ladies and Gentlemen, I'll leave you and Admiral Trenis to continue your discussions with Admiral Marquette. Arnaud," he turned to the Chief of Staff, "I'll go over your conclusions with you this evening."

"Yes, Sir," Marquette replied, and Theisman nodded to his subordinates, then turned and headed down the hall to his own office. Borderwijk followed him as far as the outer office, then peeled off to her own desk. His personal yeoman started to stand, but he waved the woman back into her chair and sailed on into his *sanctum sanctorum*. The attention light was blinking on his com terminal, and he drew a deep breath, then sat down in front of it and pressed the acceptance key.

"Hello, Eloise," he said when Pritchart appeared on the display. "Sorry it took me so long to take your call. I was down the hall with Marquette and the joint planning staff."

"Don't apologize," she told him. "After the conversation I've just endured waiting a few extra minutes is a small price to pay for the pleasure of talking to someone I *want* to talk to."

"That bad, was it?" he asked sympathetically.

"Worse," she assured him. "Much worse." Then she sighed. "But if I'm going to be honest, Tom, I suppose I have to admit part of it was how much I hate hearing Arnold say anything I might find myself forced to agree with."

"I don't see why that should bother you," Theisman said with a snort. "I haven't agreed with anything the son-of-a-bitch has said in the last two T-years!"

"I know you haven't. But you're the Secretary of War; I'm the President. I can't afford to indulge myself by rejecting the position of any Cabinet secretary out of hand just because I don't like—or trust—the person advocating it."

"No, I don't suppose you can," he said just a bit contritely, acknowledging the implicit rebuke.

"Sorry." She grimaced. "I didn't mean to take it out on you. But now Arnold is telling me that he thinks it would be . . . inadvisable to be any more 'adversarial' then we already have in our negotiations with the Manties."

"*Giancola* said that?" Theisman blinked.

"More or less. I don't know whether he's serious, or whether he's trying to talk me out of it because of the shift in my favor in the opinion polls. The problem is, that much as I'd like to, I don't think I can just dismiss his official concerns out of hand."

"Because you think he wants to make them part of the record in case you do dismiss them and it blows up in your face?"

"I'm sure that's part of it. But let's face it, Tom. Neither one of us may like him very much, but that doesn't make him an idiot. Basically, he's arguing that if we want to keep the pressure on the Manties, we have to be a bit more explicit about the steel fist inside our silk glove."

"If you're about to say he still wants to announce the existence of the CLACs," Theisman broke in, "I'm still firmly opposed. Shannon's people have managed to get nine more of them into commission, with complete LAC complements. The longer she has to get still more of them commissioned—and to work up the ones she has—before the Manties know they even exist, the better."

"I understand your position, Tom," she said patiently. "And I told him I wasn't going to override you. But that doesn't mean I can completely ignore what he was saying. I've done just about everything short of hitting Descroix over the head with a club, and she still doesn't seem to realize we're serious. It's going to take something fairly drastic to get through to her, I think. The sort of language diplomats don't usually use with one another."

"Is that really wise?" he asked.

"I don't know whether it is or not," she said snappishly. "I only know that if I'm going to continue to pursue any sort of diplomatic resolution with people so damned stupid they don't even recognize the kind of danger they're walking straight into—and taking the rest of us into with them, whether we want to go or not—then I need a big enough hammer to get their frigging attention!"

Theisman managed not to wince visibly, but it wasn't easy. Pritchart's growing exasperation with both Giancola and the Star Kingdom had worried him for months. Which, he admitted, had been just a little hypocritical of him when he'd been even more exasperated with both of them than she'd been. But as she'd just pointed out, she was the President. He wasn't. In the end, her anger was far more dangerous than his.

"If we're not going to announce the CLACs," he said carefully, "then just what sort of hammer did you have in mind?"

"I'm going to tell them it's time to fish or cut bait," she said flatly. "I want at least some concession, some forward movement, out of them. And if I don't get it, then I intend to recall our negotiators from the so-called peace talks for 'consultations' here in Nouveau Paris. And I'll keep them here for months, if I have to."

"That sounds just a little drastic," he observed. "I'm not saying it's unjustified, or even that it might not be a good idea, in the long run. But if you do it, especially in the wake of how recently we've admitted Bolthole exists, it's really going to ratchet up the pressure. Maybe further than anyone wants it ratcheted."

"I'm fully aware of that possibility," Pritchart assured him. "I don't think the situation is likely to get out of hand—not quickly, anyway. There's too much inertia on the other side. But it's possible I'm wrong about that. Which is the real reason I commed you."

She held his eyes for perhaps three heartbeats, then asked the question.

"How are your war plans coming?"

"I was afraid you were going to ask that." He sighed.

"I wouldn't if I had a choice."

"I know. I know." He drew a deep breath. "Actually," he admitted, "they're coming along better—if that isn't an obscene word to use, under the circumstances—than I'd anticipated."

"Oh?"

"The more we've looked at it, the more evident it's become that Case Red is our best option. I don't like that, in some ways, because of the mindset it engenders in my planners. And in myself, if I'm going to be honest." He frowned. "I'm happier thinking in offensive terms, of making an enemy respond to my actions, and I worry sometimes that it predisposes me towards the most aggressive solution to a problem."

"I don't think anyone who knows you is ever going to confuse you with a bloodthirsty maniac, Tom," Pritchart told him.

"As long as I don't do it myself," he replied wryly. She snorted, and he shrugged.

"With that said, though, I really believe our best chance would be an early, powerful offensive. It would give us our best opportunity to recover the occupied systems and to neutralize their ability to do anything about it, at least in the short term. Hopefully, that would provide a breather, during which diplomacy might actually accomplish something. And if that doesn't happen, at least we'd be as advantageously placed as possible if we're forced to fight it out to the end after all."

"How close are we to being ready to do that if we have to?"

He regarded her expressionlessly for several seconds.

"That depends," he said finally. "In the narrow technical sense, we could launch the operation tomorrow. And assuming our assumptions are valid and that the Manties didn't do anything drastic to change the operational parameters before we actually kicked off, I'd say we'd have at least a seventy or eighty percent chance of pulling it off."

"That good?" Pritchart sounded surprised, and he frowned.

"Let me point out that that's just another way of saying I estimate that even if all our assumptions are sound, there's still a twenty or thirty percent chance of getting our asses kicked."

"Hardly the resounding confidence of a committed militarist," the President observed with an almost-chuckle.

"If you wanted a committed militarist, you should have fired me," Theisman told her. "In my considered opinion anybody who actually wants to go to war is a lunatic, and that's especially true when we've just managed to somehow stave off complete military defeat as recently as four or five T-years ago. Eloise, I have to encourage aggressive thinking in my planners if I'm going to have any realistic prospect of winning a war with the Manties and their allies. But the truth is that even if we win, our problems won't be over unless we're willing to try to conquer the Star Kingdom outright. And even if we hurt them as badly in the opening stages as I think we could, any actual conquest is going to be bloody, expensive, and very, very ugly . . . while any sort of occupation on the old Legislaturalist model would be a whole lot uglier than that. Not to mention completely unworkable in the long run. I really cannot overemphasize my opposition to resuming active military operations if there's any possible alternative."

"I appreciate that, Tom," she told him quietly, impressed by his obvious sincerity. "And the fact that I know you feel that way is the exact reason—one of many—I would never dream of replacing you with someone else."

"It's my job to advise you on all the reasons not to go to war as well as to figure out how to fight the damned thing if it happens anyway," he replied. "And while I'm thinking about reasons not to do it, don't overlook the potential cost to our relations with other star nations."

"I haven't overlooked it," she assured him. "We've gone a long way towards recovering from the damage the Parnell Hearings did to our public image in the Solarian League. Their newsies have given full play to our domestic reforms, and I've exchanged several very friendly notes with the League's President. For that matter, we've been making ground steadily with our closer neighbors. They're no more blind to which side has been dragging its feet in our talks with the Star Kingdom than we are, and the fact that we've been willing to go on talking—especially since it's become common knowledge that we have the military potential to pursue other options if we chose to—has worked very strongly in our favor. I don't have any desire to throw all of that away. But we have *got* to get these talks off of dead center, and not just because Arnold is making himself such a pain. We have a moral responsibility to the people who want to return to our citizenship. And, for that matter, we have a moral responsibility to the people who don't want to do that—a responsibility to resolve their uncertainty once and for all."

"I understand that," he said. "But the plan that gives us our best chance under Case Red calls for an all-out offensive, Eloise. *All-out.* We'd hit Trevor's Star with a sufficiently powerful force to take out Kuzak's entire fleet. That would account for at least half of their SD(P)s and over a third of their entire CLAC strength. Simultaneously, we'd hit every occupied system in succession with sufficient strength to overwhelm any of their local system pickets and roll them up. At the same time, we'd direct strikes at their more important perimeter bases. In particular, they've been very careless with their security arrangements for Grendelsbane. We could hurt them badly there with a much lighter attack force than I'd assumed before we began really studying Case Red. And we've been looking at the distinct possibility that we could surprise their Sidemore Station task force, as well. In effect, if our operations succeeded completely, the Manties would be reduced to only their Home Fleet, and they couldn't commit that to offensive operations without uncovering their home system. Which, in theory at least, would leave them with no option but to negotiate peace on our terms.

"We have the ships and the weapons to do all of that . . . but our safety margin would be much narrower than anything I'd be comfortable with. And to make it all work, we'd have to hit them before they realized we were coming and redeployed."

"Redeployed how?" she asked.

"The most obvious thing for them to do would be to abandon the other occupied systems and concentrate on Trevor's Star. That's absolutely their most vital system, this side of the Manticore System itself. Next in priority would be Grayson. To be honest, the Grayson Navy scares me almost as much as the RMN, these days. All the intelligence indications are that High Ridge has managed to alienate Grayson pretty thoroughly, but I don't think it's bad enough that Grayson would refuse to come to Manticore's assistance. Some of my planners do think that, but they're wrong. Unfortunately, that's one more argument in favor of hitting the Manties hard, fast, and with as much surprise advantage as we can generate. Given the current tension between Grayson and the Star Kingdom, Mayhew would almost certainly have to stand fast, at least initially. Not only would he have his own system's security to worry about, but I doubt very much that Janacek and Chakrabarti have bothered with any of the preliminary planning that would be required to get the GSN effectively deployed quickly enough to hamper our operations. *If* those operations can be concluded on the timetable we're projecting."

"Can they be?"

"Obviously, I think it's possible or I wouldn't be pursuing the possibility. And I've tried to strike the best balance I can between allowing for the unavoidable friction that's going to slow us down and refusing to let concern over that paralyze the planning process.

"But as I say, all of this is predicated on our getting in the first punch, and that's the part that worries me the most."

Pritchart arched an eyebrow, inviting explanation, and he rubbed the scar on his cheek while he looked for exactly the right words.

"We can virtually guarantee ourselves the advantage of surprise," he said finally. "All that would be required would be for us to attack the Manties while we're still negotiating with them. The only problem is that if we did that, we might very well win all of the battles and still lose the war because of the long-term diplomatic and military consequences. The instant we did something like that, the galaxy at large would conclude that we've decided to go back to the same policy of expansion as the old People's Republic. And not just as far as foreign nations would be concerned. The very people right here at home we've been trying to convince to believe in the restored Republic would come to exactly the same conclusion. That could be an awful high price to pay for defeating the Star Kingdom."

"Yes, it could," she agreed quietly. She sat thinking for several seconds, her eyes distant, then refocused on him.

"What exactly are you trying to tell me, Tom? I know you're not just rehashing all of this to hear yourself talk."

"I guess what I'm saying is that, first, we need to do everything humanly possible to find a solution to our problems short of war. If it comes down to using force, though, our best chance is Case Red. But if we're going to execute Case Red, then we need to do it in a way that doesn't echo the old Duquesne Plan. Our diplomacy needs to make it clear that we've done more than merely go the extra kilometer trying to achieve a peaceful resolution. To make Case Red work, we're going to have to redeploy and preposition a lot of our fleet to execute an unexpected offensive ... but we can't execute that offensive until the Star Kingdom fires the first shot or at least breaks off negotiations. We just can't do it, Eloise. I *won't* do it. Not after how much blood you and I have shed to prove we're not the People's Republic."

"And when," she demanded angrily, "have I ever suggested to you that I *would* do that?"

"I—" he began, then closed his mouth with a click. Then he drew a deep breath and shook his head.

"I apologize," he said quietly. "I know you've never suggested anything of the sort. It's just ..." He inhaled deeply again. "It's just that we've come so far, Eloise. We've accomplished so much. If we go back to war with the Star Kingdom, we could lose all of that even if we win. I guess it just ... scares me. Not for myself, but for the Republic."

"I understand," she said, equally quietly, and her eyes held his levelly. "But at the same time, Tom, I can't simply ignore all of the other responsibilities of my job because discharging them *might* get us back into a war. Especially not when the Manties won't let me end the war we've already got. So I have to know. If I make it clear to Descroix and High Ridge that we mean business, that I'm prepared to break off negotiations—which could be construed as renouncing the existing truce—will you and the Navy support me?"

A moment of tension hovered between them as they faced one another, the man who'd made the restoration of the Republic possible, and the woman who'd overseen that restoration. And then Thomas Theisman nodded.

"Of course we will, Madame President," he said, and if his voice was sad, it was also unflinching. "That's what a Constitution is for."

CHAPTER FORTY

Shannon Foraker stood in *Sovereign of Space*'s boat bay once more and watched Lester Tourville's cutter settle into the docking arms. This time, however, she wasn't waiting for Thomas Theisman or Javier Giscard, as well. Theisman was back in Nouveau Paris . . . and Giscard stood beside her, behind Captain Reumann and Commander Lampert. She glanced sideways at the man who had become the second ranking officer of the Republican Navy and felt an undeniable pang of sorrow as she realized she was already an outsider in this boat bay.

The cutter finished docking, the pressure light blinked green, Tourville swung himself from the personnel tube into *Sovereign of Space*'s internal gravity, and the side party snapped to attention. Bosun's pipes twittered, and the lieutenant at the side party's head returned Tourville's salute.

"Permission to come aboard?" Tourville requested formally.

"Permission granted, Sir," the lieutenant replied, and stepped aside as Reumann moved forward to offer Tourville the traditional captain's handshake of greeting. Giscard stepped forward with him; Foraker did not, because Reumann was no longer *her* flag captain.

"Welcome aboard, Lester," Giscard greeted Tourville warmly, and the commander (designate) of Second Fleet smiled back at him.

"Thanks, Javier." He shook Giscard's hand, then looked past the other admiral and smiled at Foraker. "Hello, Shannon."

"Sir." She returned the greeting with an edge of formality which dismayed her when she recognized it. It wasn't his fault, or Giscard's. In fact, it wasn't anyone's fault. But as she looked at the two of them, she felt excluded, just as she'd felt when Theisman broke it to her that *Sovereign of Space* was about to become Giscard's flagship, instead of hers.

Tourville's expression showed momentary surprise at the brevity of her response. But the surprise vanished as quickly as it had come, and she saw a flicker of sympathy in his eyes. Of course he'd understand, she thought. She'd spent too much time on his staff for him not to realize exactly how she must be feeling at this moment.

She shook herself and gave herself a sharp mental scold for allowing her unhappiness to splash onto anyone else. Then she produced a smile for him. It might have been a tad lopsided, but it was also genuine, and she knew he recognized the unspoken apology for her terseness.

"Well," Giscard said, in a voice which was just hearty enough to show he, too, had caught the undertones, "we've got a lot to talk about. So I suppose we'd better get started."

He gestured at the waiting lift shaft, and his subordinates moved obediently towards it.

"So that's the bare bones of the current deployment plan," Captain Gozzi said, winding up the first stage of his briefing the better part of two and a half hours later. "With your permission, Admiral," he continued, turning to speak directly to Giscard, "I'd like to open the floor to general questions before we move on to the consideration of specific details."

"Of course, Marius," Giscard told his chief of staff, and glanced at the other two flag officers present in *Sovereign of Space*'s flag briefing room. "Lester? Shannon?"

"From what I seem to be hearing here," Tourville observed, frowning from behind a cloud of fragrant cigar smoke at the floating holo map of the region around Trevor's Star, "this is no longer a hypothetical deployment."

It wasn't precisely a question, but Gozzi nodded anyway.

"That's correct, Sir. The Octagon sent us the preparatory movement orders this morning."

"It sounds as if things are getting even dicier," Captain DeLaney said, her expression unhappy, and Tourville nodded in agreement with his own chief of staff.

"That's exactly what I was thinking," he said, and frowned.

"I know none of us are particularly happy about this situation," Giscard said with massive understatement, "but at least you're getting what you handle best, Lester—a detached, independent command."

"'Detached!'" Tourville snorted. "That's certainly accurate enough. Just who had this brainstorm, anyway?"

"That's not something I've been specifically told," Giscard replied with a wry smile. "Having said that, it has all the earmarks of something Linda Trenis would have come up with."

"Figures. Linda always was too smart for her own good."

"You don't think it will work?" Giscard asked, one eyebrow raised, and Tourville puffed on his cigar some more, then shrugged.

"I think it should do what it's supposed to do," he acknowledged. "I guess what bothers me about it is that sending Second Fleet clear to Silesia seems to indicate that someone is beginning to think a lot more seriously in terms of reopening a can of worms I don't think any of us want reopened."

"It sounds that way to me, too," Foraker put in. "That's one reason this whole deployment plan worries me."

Even as she spoke, Foraker reflected upon how insanely dangerous it would have been for any flag officer to express reservations about her orders under the Committee of Public Safety. But she didn't serve the Committee; that was the entire point.

"I don't think anyone in Nouveau Paris is taking the possibility of a resumption of hostilities lightly," Giscard said. "I know Secretary Theisman isn't, as I'm sure all of us are aware." He gazed at Tourville and Foraker until both of them nodded, then shrugged. "By the same token, it's his job—and ours—to be ready if worse comes to worst anyway. On that basis, do you have any reservations, Lester?"

"Other than those I think any of us would feel about going up against someone as good as Harrington that far from any of our own support bases, no," Tourville conceded. "I like the fact that I don't do a thing without positive orders from home. At least we don't have to worry about my starting a war because no one got me the orders *not* to in time!"

"Shannon?"

"Actually," Foraker said unhappily, "I do have a few reservations."

"Oh?" Giscard eyed her speculatively. "What sort of reservations?"

"I can't escape the feeling that we're running the risk of strategic overreach," she replied. "In most ways, I have to agree that Case Red is . . . well, for want of a better word, elegant. It requires a degree of coordination I'm not entirely happy about, but it avoids the mistake the Legislaturalists made by starting with detached forces which were too far apart to stay in communication with one another. Except, of course, for Second Fleet."

Giscard nodded. As soon as this conference ended, he and the newly designated First Fleet would depart the Haven System and head for his new station in the SXR-136-23 System. It had never received a name to replace its catalog designation because the thoroughly useless red giant had absolutely nothing, not even any planets, to attract anyone to it. It did, however, offer a handy anchor around which to park a fleet safely out of sight. And it just happened to be located less than forty light-years northwest of Trevor's Star.

The logistics ships to support First Fleet were already in place, orbiting SXR-136's dim central fires with sufficient supplies and spares to sustain the entire fleet on station for up to six months. If it turned out to be necessary to leave First Fleet there for longer than that, the fleet train would detach ships in relays to bring back what was needed. And if the balloon went up, every single task group (except Second Fleet) set up by the carefully orchestrated war plan known as Case Red Alpha would depart from SXR-136. Its components would sail at staggered intervals which would place each of them at its objective at precisely the same time, but they would all depart from the same place, under the same orders, without risking the strategic miscue which had sent Admiral Yuri Rollins to the Hancock System early. Of course, it helped that, with the exception of Grendelsbane, all of those objectives lay within no more than a hundred and twenty light-years of Trevor's Star.

"Unfortunately," Foraker continued, "the fact that this plan provides for better coordination doesn't change the fact that we're going to be attacking in a lot of places at once. Which means dispersing our forces to a much greater degree than I'd really prefer."

"That's a valid concern," Giscard agreed. "I think, though, that it's an element of risk we're just going to have to accept. And if we're going to be dispersed, at least the Manties are spread even thinner."

"There is that." It was Foraker's turn to nod.

"And," Captain Gozzi pointed out respectfully, "the ops plan does provide for us to hit our objectives in sequenced attacks, Ma'am. We'll be concentrating superior forces for each attack, and starting with their nodal positions to take out their response forces first."

"I know." Foraker frowned. "Given our resources and the mission objectives, this certainly looks like the most effective employment of our forces. I suppose when it comes right down to it, a lot of my concerns stem from the fact that I know how much of our planning is based on what we've been doing out at Bolthole."

She grimaced and glanced at her own chief of staff.

"Five and I—all our people—have tried to be as constructively critical of our own work as we could. But none of our conclusions have been tested in battle yet. Our simulations are solid . . . if the intelligence data on Manty hardware on which we based them is accurate. But we can't know for certain that it is. And even if the numbers are good, we're going to be committing an awful lot of ships, manned by people who're going to be going into battle using new hardware and new doctrine, both of which are completely untested where it really counts. I think we've all seen too much of Murphy not to realize how many things could go wrong, however well we've done our jobs at Bolthole. Under those circumstances, I'd really prefer a bigger numerical advantage at the critical points than it's going to be possible for us to achieve in light of how astrographically dispersed our ops area is."

"I can appreciate your concerns," Giscard said after a moment. "At the same time, I suspect at least a part of them stem from your own conscientiousness. And I think you may be underestimating the quality of the work you and your people have done. Oh, I don't doubt for a minute that we're going to hit at least some holes in the doctrine, or that we're going to find out some assumption about Manty capabilities wasn't sufficiently pessimistic. But Lester and I have gamed out a dozen battles in the simulators, using your new hardware and your new doctrine, and from what we've seen there, you've managed to increase our combat effectiveness by a factor of at least ten."

He shook his head.

"That's one hell of a lot better than we've ever had before going up against the Manties. If we manage to catch them still dispersed, then I think we're going to chew them up badly."

"I hope you're right, Sir. But I still think we ought to be throwing an even heavier punch at Trevor's Star. That's their strongest point . . . and they've been kind enough to concentrate virtually all of their modern ships there, outside of the ones assigned to Home Fleet, anyway. If we destroy that force, then we can spread out from Trevor's Star and gather in all of the other objectives easily, because they won't have anything in the area that could possibly stop us."

"But if we hit Trevor's Star concentrated," Tourville pointed out, "and they managed to get dispatch boats away—which they *would* do, Shannon, given the direct wormhole connection to Manticore— they might very well manage to redeploy their other covering forces before we could reach them with our own attacks. I don't see anything they could do that would actually stop us, but they could certainly concentrate sufficient forces on the more critical objectives to make it much more expensive for us to take them."

"I know. But by the same token, if they get dispatch boats away through the terminus, the *only* place they can go is the Manticore System. They're not going to be able to get from there to other systems inside our borders significantly before we can get to those same systems from Trevor's Star. The only dispatch boats we really legitimately need to worry about are the ones that won't be using the terminus in the first place."

"I appreciate your concerns," Giscard repeated. "But that aspect of the ops plan is effectively locked by this point. Unless someone presents a specific, demonstrable flaw, I don't see any real prospect of its being changed."

"And all I can offer are non-specific worries that may very well be based on my own concerns about where I could have dropped the ball out at Bolthole," Foraker conceded. She smiled crookedly. "I know. I guess I just had to be sure I got it said."

"Of course you did. That's part of your job." Giscard chuckled. Then he cocked his head at her. "And what about Second Fleet's assignment?"

"Obviously, the fact that I'd like to throw a heavier attack at Trevor's Star means I'd prefer to keep Second Fleet closer to home and commit it there. And the possibility that the Andermani might find Second Fleet's presence so close to their own doorstep objectionable doesn't exactly appeal to me, either. Left to my own devices, and given the fact that NavInt tells us Duchess Harrington has so few SD(P)s and CLACs, I think I'd probably choose to leave her entirely alone in the initial attacks. If we manage to pull off the rest of Red Alpha, then her task force shouldn't be enough to significantly improve the Manties' chances in a counteroffensive even after they recall her. But I have to admit that part of my desire to employ Second Fleet elsewhere may stem from the fact that, like Lester, I have a . . . lively respect for the Duchess' tactical talents. Something about letting sleeping dogs lie," she snorted. "Aside from that, the plan seems sound enough. At least, I don't see how we could come up with a better one to accomplish the same objective."

"If I may, Admiral Giscard," Captain Anders said quietly, "I do have one additional concern I haven't heard anyone address yet."

"What sort of concern, Captain?"

"Grayson, Sir." Several people glanced at one another, and Anders produced a brief smile. "I've been looking at NavInt's most recent estimates of their SD(P) strength," he continued. "I don't know if the Staff's planners are making sufficient allowance for what they might do with that strength."

"At the moment," Captain Gozzi replied before Giscard could speak, "they've sent a substantial chunk of that strength off on a training cruise, Five. And even if they hadn't, it's going to take them some time to figure out what's happening. Even assuming that their navy and the RMN were still on the same sort of terms they were before the cease-fire, there ought to be more than enough delay before they could respond for us to be in possession of Trevor's Star and all of the rest of our objectives."

"I know that's the analysts' conclusion," Anders acknowledged. "And they may well be right. But given the Graysons' performance to date, I'd prefer something a bit more definite than 'may well be right' where they're concerned. Admiral Foraker mentioned letting sleeping dogs lie in Silesia. My own preference would be to keep Second Fleet closer to home to cover against the possibility that the Graysons are quicker off the mark than we think they'll be."

"That thought certainly has merit," Giscard said, waving Gozzi off when his own chief of staff started to respond once again. "But

Grayson's possible reaction is another one of those risks we're simply going to have to accept. I think NavInt's analysts are almost certainly right about how quickly Grayson will be able to respond once they realize an attack is underway. I think they're also right about Janacek's attitude towards Grayson. He resents and loathes them as uppity neobarbs with no respect for their betters, so the last thing he's going to want to do is call them in to reinforce his own forces. Hell, he probably hasn't even done any contingency planning with them for how they might respond to an attack if we launched one! Which doesn't even consider the possibility that he and High Ridge have managed to alienate Grayson to an extent which would make Mayhew hesitate to respond in the first place."

"With all due respect for NavInt, Admiral, I don't think I'd put too much reliance on that last point. It's certainly legitimate to think in terms of the physical limitations on how quickly they can respond, but Grayson and the Manties have been through a lot together. I don't see Mayhew cutting his allies adrift. Especially if we're the aggressor."

Giscard gazed at Foraker's chief of staff thoughtfully for several seconds, then shrugged.

"I wasn't going to bring this up," he said. "And what I'm about to say doesn't leave this compartment."

He paused until all of them had nodded.

"All right. Captain Anders may very well be entirely correct in his estimate of the relationship between Grayson and the Star Kingdom. To be perfectly honest, Secretary Theisman tells me that the analysts at NavInt and ForInt are pretty badly divided over exactly how bad relations between the Protector and the High Ridge Government have actually become. However, there are at least some strong indications that the Manticoran Alliance is no longer as . . . solid as it was. Specifically," he continued as eyes narrowed speculatively around the conference table, "we've been in contact with the Republic of Erewhon. Obviously, no one has discussed Case Red Alpha with the Erewhonese, but last week the Erewhon Ambassador initialed an agreement in principle for a defensive military alliance with us."

"Erewhon is coming over to our side?" Lester Tourville asked in a very careful tone of voice, clearly unable to believe he'd heard correctly.

"So I've been assured," Giscard replied. "There's no way to

extrapolate from that to what Grayson might do, and no one's suggested to me that we've had any sort of direct diplomatic contact with Grayson, either. But if Erewhon is willing to make its own arrangements with us, I'd certainly call that an indication that High Ridge has managed to do a lot more damage to his alliance network than he probably realizes."

"That's one way to put it, Sir," Anders snorted. "Especially if you're given to understatement!" He paused, thinking hard, then shrugged. "All right, Sir. I'm still itchy about what Grayson might do, but I'll admit it looks like there's even more grit jamming the works of the Manty Alliance than I thought there was."

"Which is probably about the best we can hope for, realistically," Giscard replied with a shrug. "We're dealing with uncertainties no matter what we do. Anyone who thinks it could be any other way is dreaming. But my own feeling is that if we find ourselves forced to go back to war at all, this ops plan offers our best chance of winning."

Several hours later, Shannon Foraker watched through the viewport of her pinnace as *Sovereign of Space* broke orbit, accelerating away from the planet of Haven towards the rest of First Fleet.

It was hard to watch her go. Harder even than she'd expected it to be.

"Hate to see her go, don't you, Ma'am?" a quiet voice asked, and she turned her head to look at Captain Anders.

"Yes," she admitted. "Yes I do."

"Admiral Giscard will take good care of her," Anders reassured her, and she nodded.

"I know he will. And I know Pat will, too. But after so long, it just seems hard to see her as anyone else's flagship."

"I don't doubt it. But that's not all of it, Ma'am," Anders said almost gently, and she frowned.

"What do you mean?"

"Ma'am, you're not like me. I'm an engineer first, and a tac officer second; you're exactly the other way around. That's why you want to be out there, making Red Alpha work and executing the tactical doctrines *you* designed. That's the real reason you hate to see her go as much as you do."

"You know," Foraker said slowly, "for a wirehead, you're a

remarkably perceptive person, Five." She shook her head. "I hadn't considered it from that perspective, but you're right. Maybe I didn't think about it that way because I didn't want to admit how very right you are."

"You couldn't be who you are and feel any other way about it, Ma'am," he told her. "But the bottom line is that as good as you are as a tac officer, the Navy and the Republic need you worse at Bolthole than they need you with First or Second Fleet. It's not where you want to be, Ma'am; it's only where you need to be."

"Maybe you're right," she said softly, turning to look back out the port at the steadily accelerating superdreadnought. "Maybe you're right."

But as she watched *Sovereign of Space* dwindle in the distance, she knew she didn't want him to be.

Chapter Forty-One

The com attention signal chimed softly in the darkened cabin. It was a quiet sound, but decades of naval service had made Erica Ferrero a light sleeper. Her right hand shot out and hit the voice-only acceptance key before it could chime a second time, and her left hand raked sleep-tousled hair out of her eyes as she sat up in bed.

"Captain speaking." Her voice struck her as sounding much more awake than she actually felt.

"Captain, this is Lieutenant McKee. The Exec asked me to inform you that '*Sittich*' is breaking orbit."

"Understood." Ferrero came suddenly and fully awake at the announcement. She glanced at her bedside date/time display and grimaced. It was the middle of *Jessica Epps'* shipboard night. McKee had the bridge watch, and by rights, Llewellyn should have been in bed and as sound asleep as Ferrero herself. But her exec had always had a tendency to prowl around the ship at odd times, and it had become even more pronounced since their arrival in the Zoraster System.

"What's her accel, Mecia?" Ferrero asked the com officer.

"Just under two-point-five KPS squared," McKee replied.

"And her heading?"

"Just about what you'd predicted, Skipper. She's on a least-time heading from the planet to the hyper limit."

"Good. In that case, I don't see any reason to wake everybody else up this soon. I'll be up in about fifteen minutes. You and the Exec hold the fort until I get there."

"Aye, aye, Ma'am."

The red icon representing the ship masquerading as the Andermani merchant ship *Sittich* crawled across *Jessica Epps*' tactical display. She'd been accelerating steadily for over two hours now, and her velocity was up to just over 18,500 KPS. She'd traveled a hundred and thirty-nine million kilometers, taking her almost forty percent of the way to the G4 primary's hyper limit. And while she was doing that, *Jessica Epps* had crept stealthily closer to her, bending their vectors steadily together.

The tension on the heavy cruiser's bridge had climbed steadily. It wasn't the same sort of tension her officers might have felt if they'd been tracking another warship. No, this was the tension of a hunter as a long, careful stalk crept towards its successful conclusion, mingled with the vengeful anticipation of closing in on the sort of vermin any self-respecting naval officer recognized as his natural enemy.

Erica Ferrero glanced at her repeater plot. The range to the target was down to barely three million kilometers, and it was painfully evident that the false *Sittich* didn't have a clue *Jessica Epps* was even in the same star system with her. Ferrero supposed she shouldn't feel too much contempt for the slaver's crew. After all, they were deep in one of the better patrolled Silesian star systems, and as far as they knew, any armed vessels in that system were under the orders of the man whose illicit cargo they were carrying. Besides, Shawn Harris' carefully deployed Ghost Rider recon drones had gotten an excellent read on "*Sittich*'s" emissions, and the tramp's active sensors were exactly the sort of crap Ferrero would have anticipated from such a disreputable craft. They'd have been lucky to spot a medium-sized moon if they hadn't already known exactly where to look for it.

She smiled. Sneaking into someone else's star system, even when that someone else was limited to Silly sensor systems, was always a challenge. Of course, it was the sort of challenge Ferrero enjoyed, not to mention being an excellent training opportunity. That hadn't made it any easier, however, and she'd been just a bit surprised by how spoiled she'd become since FTL sensor arrays had become available. She missed the continually updated reports from the perimeter arrays she would normally have deployed. Their absence made her feel . . . exposed. As if someone who was supposed to be watching her back wasn't.

She wondered if she would have felt happier if the new patrol patterns Duchess Harrington was instituting had been fully in place and *Jessica Epps* had been paired off with another RMN vessel. She probably would have, she decided. And the availability of a consort would have given her much more flexibility in her stalk of the slaver. *Of the* probable *slaver*, she corrected herself conscientiously.

Of course, the presence of a second ship would have substantially increased the chances that at least one of them might have been spotted. Which made it one more example of the endless trade-offs imposed by an imperfect universe.

She snorted at the thought and looked up from the plot.

"I think we're just about ready, Bob," she said.

"Yes, Ma'am," Commander Llewellyn acknowledged. "Should we send the crew to quarters?"

"I don't see any reason to completely clear for action," Ferrero replied. "Not against a merchie who's still two and a half million klicks outside energy range! Go ahead and close up the missile crews and Missile Defense. We can always man the energy mounts if Mr. Slaver decides to be difficult and refuses to heave to before we close into graser range. Of course, he'd have to be particularly stupid for that to happen."

"Yes, Ma'am."

A true stickler might have detected a slight edge of disappointment in Llewellyn's reply. The exec, Ferrero knew, was a tactical officer's tactical officer. He hated to pass up any opportunity for comprehensive weapons drills, especially when Tactical had a live target—even one as unworthy as "*Sittich*"—to practice on.

"Patience, Bob," she said in a quieter voice, pitched for his ears alone, after he'd passed the necessary orders. "If you behave yourself, I'll let you take the first pinnace across."

"That obvious, was I, Skipper?" he asked wryly.

"Maybe not *that* obvious," she said with a grin. "But headed that way. Definitely headed that way."

"Missile batteries report manned and ready, Ma'am," Harris reported from Tactical.

"Very well, Shawn. I think we're just about ready. Remember, we can't afford to just blow this one out of space, whatever it does."

"Understood, Ma'am." Lieutenant Harris nodded soberly. Pirates were one thing; slavers, with potentially hundreds of innocent victims aboard, were something else entirely.

"If she refuses to stop when Mecia hails her," Ferrero went on, "we'll put a shot or two across her bows. But if she still refuses to stop, we'll have to get close enough to take out her nodes with energy fire. Or," she grinned at Llewellyn again, "let the exec take his pinnaces out and play Preston of the Spaceways shooting up her impeller rings with their lasers."

"Oh, frabjous day!" Llewellyn murmured.

"I see you're really looking forward to it," Ferrero observed, and Llewellyn chuckled. Then the captain turned to Communications. "Are you ready to transmit, Mecia?"

"Yes, Ma'am."

"Then go ahead. And just to be certain they get the point, Shawn, lock them up with your fire control lidar and stand ready to fire that warning shot."

"Aye, aye, Ma'am."

Lieutenant McKee leaned closer to her microphone. "*Sittich*, this is the Royal Manticoran Navy cruiser *Jessica Epps*. You are instructed to reduce acceleration to zero, cut your wedge, and stand by to be boarded for routine search and examination."

The crisp, uncompromising demand went out over a directional com laser. It was extremely unlikely that Governor Chalmers would fail to realize what was happening when *Jessica Epps* boarded the false *Sittich*, but it was remotely possible. Harris' fire control systems were more likely to be detected by the system sensor arrays than McKee's communications laser, and if Ferrero actually had to fire a warning shot, the detonation of its warhead would definitely give the game away. But if she could keep Chalmers from figuring out what was happening, he was much more likely to be sitting there, still all fat and happy, when the warrant for his arrest arrived from the Confed government.

And slaving is probably the one thing that will actually get a Silly governor arrested, she reflected. *Not that what passes for a government out here really has any particular moral objection to it. It's just that the Queen has made her own feelings on the trade abundantly, one might almost say painfully, clear. And no Silly in his right mind wants to cross her or her Navy on this one. Besides—*

"Incoming message!" McKee announced suddenly, and something about her tone snapped Ferrero's head up. She spun her command chair back towards the com officer.

"It's—" McKee broke off and looked up at her captain, eyes huge in surprise. "Skipper, it's *Hellbarde!*"

"*Hellbarde*?!" Ferrero stared at the lieutenant for perhaps three seconds, then darted an accusing look at her tactical plot. There was no sign of the Andermani cruiser on it.

"Shawn?" she snapped.

"I don't know, Skipper!" the tac officer replied. "But I'm on it."

His hands were already flying across his console as he, his ratings, and CIC went suddenly to a full-press sensor sweep. They were no longer trying to creep quietly up on an unsuspecting prey, and their active arrays lit up surrounding space like a beacon.

"Skipper, you'd better listen to this," McKee said urgently, pulling Ferrero's attention back from the tactical section.

"Put it on speaker," Ferrero instructed.

"Aye, aye, Ma'am."

There was a brief moment of silence, and then a familiar, harsh-accented voice banished it.

"*Jessica Epps*, this is *Hellbarde!* You are instructed to shut down your targeting systems and break off your approach immediately!"

"Shut down—?" Ferrero looked up at Llewellyn.

"Another incoming message," McKee broke in before the exec could reply. "This one's from '*Sittich.*'"

"Speaker," Ferrero snapped.

"*Jessica Epps*, this is the Andermani merchant ship *Sittich*! What seems to be the problem? *Sittich*, clear."

"Another from *Hellbarde*, Skipper," McKee said, and Ferrero gestured for her to put it on speaker, as well.

"*Jessica Epps*, this is *Hellbarde*. Shut down your targeting systems *now*!"

"Got her, Skipper!" Harris announced, and Ferrero looked back down at her plot as a bright red icon abruptly appeared. It was no more than ten million kilometers behind *Jessica Epps*, only a little over half a light-minute, and Ferrero swore mentally. No matter how good the Andies' new stealth systems might be, there was no way *Hellbarde* should have been able to get in that close without being detected on passives even with *Jessica Epps* under complete em-con!

"Skipper, *Sittich* is transmitting again," McKee reported.

"Her acceleration is climbing, too, Ma'am," Harris added. "She's up to three-point-two KPS squared."

"Instruct her to heave to immediately, Mecia!" Ferrero snapped.

"Aye, aye, Ma'am."

Ferrero rubbed her forehead, her brain racing. Obviously, *Hellbarde* had followed them to Zoraster—probably to continue her provocative harassment. And because *Jessica Epps* had been concentrating so hard on being unobtrusive while she lay in wait for the slaver, she hadn't realized *Hellbarde* was even there. But why was she interfering like this? Unless—

"Tell *Hellbarde* to stand clear!" she said sharply. "Inform her that we're stopping and investigating a suspected slaver!"

"Aye, aye, Ma'am."

McKee started speaking rapidly into her microphone once again, and Ferrero grimaced at Llewellyn.

"Gortz is looking for another opportunity to harass us, and I'm not in the mood for it this time," she half-snarled.

"Skipper," the exec said, "it's possible he thinks *we're* the ones doing the harassing."

"Give me a break, Bob! We're conducting a completely legitimate search of a suspected slaver using a false transponder code, and Gortz damned well knows it! Unless you want me to think we have better sensor data on Andie merchant ships than an Andie warship does!"

She snorted contemptuously at the notion.

"*Jessica Epps*, shut down your fire control! We will not warn you again!" the voice from *Hellbarde* snapped.

"Skipper," McKee said urgently, "we've just picked up another transmission from '*Sittich*'! *Hellbarde*'s transmitting omnidirectional, and they must have picked it up. They're hailing her and asking for protection."

"Well," Ferrero said, "they're nervy bastards, I'll give them that!"

"What if Gortz believes them?" Llewellyn asked.

"Ha!" Ferrero replied. Then she shook her head. "On the other hand, it would suit the Andies just fine to pretend they believed it. Long enough to twist our tails, anyway! Record for transmission to *Hellbarde*, Mecia."

"Recording, Ma'am."

"Captain Gortz, this is Captain Ferrero. I don't have time for your stupid games today. I've got a slaver to board; if you want to talk about it later, I'll consider it then. Now break off and get the hell out of my way!"

"Recorded, Ma'am," McKee said, and Ferrero hesitated for just an instant as she realized she was even angrier than she'd thought. It showed in both her choice of words and her tone, and a small voice in the back of her brain told her she should reconsider before she sent it. But it was a very small voice, and she decided to ignore it. It was about time *Kapitän zur Sterne* Gortz and the other arrogant pricks aboard IANS *Hellbarde* got a dose of their own enlightened communications technique! What were they going to do about it at this range, anyway? With *Jessica Epps'* overtake advantage, she'd have reached and boarded '*Sittich*' by the time *Hellbarde* could get into her missile range of Ferrero's ship.

"Ma'am, '*Sittich*' is transmitting to *Hellbarde* again. She says we've threatened to fire into her if she doesn't stop."

"Lying bastards, as well as nervy ones," Ferrero observed. In a way, she could almost admire the slaver's captain's nerve. Of course, given the penalties for slaving, he probably figured he didn't have a great deal to lose. But not even Gortz could be stupid enough to believe any Queen's ship would actually fire *missiles* into an unarmed merchant ship when that merchant ship couldn't possibly evade her, anyway.

"'*Sittich*' isn't slowing down, Skipper," Harris said. "Should I go ahead and fire the warning shot?"

"That might not be a very good idea, under the circumstances, Ma'am," Llewellyn said quietly.

"I am sick and tired of pussyfooting around the goddamned *Hellbarde*," Ferrero said sharply. "We are a Queen's ship, acting well within the letter of interstellar law, and I am *not* going to let Gortz turn this into one more opportunity to harass us!

"Mecia."

"Yes, Ma'am?"

"Record!"

"Recording, Ma'am."

"*Hellbarde*, this is *Jessica Epps*. We are acting within the established parameters and requirements of interstellar law and all applicable treaties. You have no jurisdiction here, and I instruct you to stand clear. Ferrero, clear."

"On the chip, Ma'am," McKee confirmed.

"Then transmit," Ferrero commanded, and looked back up at Llewellyn. "She's still a good two million klicks out of her powered missile range of us, Bob. But go ahead and send our people to quarters." She smiled thinly. "You wanted the extra drill anyway."

"Yes, Ma'am. I did. But I'm not too sure this is the best way to get it!"

"It may not be," Ferrero conceded. "But *Hellbarde* has pissed me off one time too many." She looked at Lieutenant McClelland. "James, I want a least-time intercept course for '*Sittich*' at her new accel."

"Already calculated, Ma'am," the astrogator replied.

"That's what I like to hear," Ferrero approved. "Put us on it."

"Aye, aye, Ma'am! Helm, come four degrees to port and go to eighty-five percent power!"

The helmsman acknowledged the order, and *Jessica Epps* surged suddenly forward after the fleeing slaver while the general quarters alarm began to shrill.

"Ma'am, *Hellbarde* is—"

"I don't really care what *Hellbarde* wants, Mecia," Ferrero said almost calmly. "Ignore her."

"Aye, aye, Ma'am."

Ferrero watched the range fall, as her speeding ship began to increase her overtake velocity. The slaver was continuing to yammer away at *Hellbarde* as she ran, and Ferrero smiled thinly. Satisfying as it would be to liberate the slaves aboard that ship, it would be almost more satisfying to rub *Kapitän zur Sternen* Gortz's nose in just who had been attempting to dupe him into saving them from *Jessica Epps*.

"Closed up at battle stations, Ma'am," Lieutenant Harris announced, and Ferrero blinked, astonished to discover that she'd been so lost in her thoughts she hadn't even noticed Llewellyn leaving the bridge to go to his own battle station in Auxiliary Control.

"Very good, Shawn," she acknowledged. "Is that warning shot ready?"

"Yes, Ma'am."

"Very well. Mecia, tell them one more time to cut their acceleration. And tell them this is their final warning."

"Aye, aye, Ma'am." Lieutenant McKee cleared her throat. "*Sittich*, this is *Jessica Epps*. You will cut your acceleration immediately. Repeat, immediately. This is your final warning. *Jessica Epps*, clear."

There was no response, and Ferrero glanced at Harris.

"Maintaining her accel, Skipper," the tac officer told her.

"Maybe she needs a more pointed warning," the captain observed. "Fire your warning shot, Shawn."

"Aye, aye, Ma'am. Firing now."

Harris pressed the firing key, and a single missile spat from *Jessica Epps'* Number One chase tube and went screaming off towards *Sittich*.

Ferrero watched the missile's icon slash across her repeater plot towards the fleeing slaver. No doubt Gortz was on the verge of apoplexy by now, she reflected cheerfully. Well, it served the bastard right. After all the times he'd—

"Missile launch!" Harris snapped suddenly. Ferrero jerked upright in her command chair in disbelief. Surely no one aboard *Sittich* was stupid enough to try to resist a heavy cruiser!

"Multiple missile launches from *Hellbarde*!" Harris barked. "Looks like a full broadside, Ma'am!"

For a fraction of a second, Ferrero stared at him. He couldn't be serious! *Hellbarde* was still well outside her effective missile envelope! There was no—

The thought chopped off. No, Erica Ferrero thought, her mind suddenly almost impossibly calm. *Hellbarde* wasn't still well outside her effective envelope; she was just outside what everyone had *thought* her envelope was.

What Erica Ferrero had thought her envelope was.

"Helm, go to evasion plan Gamma!" she snapped. "Tactical! Forget *Sittich*." She smiled thinly, forcing herself to radiate confidence even as her conscience flailed at her for the overconfident assumptions which had brought her command to this pass. But it was too late to worry about that, just as it was too late to try to talk any sort of sense into Gortz.

"It looks like we're going to have an even more interesting afternoon than we thought, People," she told her bridge crew, then nodded to Harris.

"Engage the enemy, Lieutenant," she said.

CHAPTER FORTY-TWO

"**Y**ou know," Mercedes Brigham said quietly as she, Nimitz, and Andrew LaFollet walked down the passage towards *Werewolf*'s flag briefing room with Honor yet again, "this couldn't have happened at a much worse time, Your Grace."

"You're right," Honor agreed, equally quietly. "Not that there could ever be a 'good' time for it."

"No, Ma'am."

The compartment hatch opened before them, and feet scuffed on the decksole as the waiting officers rose.

It was the first full-dress meeting of every single one of Honor's task group and squadron commanders, and it included an imposing array of rank and experience. It also included a lot of faces she knew very well indeed, beginning with Alistair McKeon and Alice Truman. Then there was Rear Admiral Samuel Webster, commanding the Sixteenth Battle Squadron; Rear Admiral George Astrides, CO of the Ninth Battle Squadron; Alfredo Yu, now a full admiral; Warner Caslet, commanding Yu's First Battle Squadron; Rear Admiral Harriet Benson-Dessouix, Commanding his First CLAC Squadron; Vice Admiral Mark Brentworth, commanding his Second Battle Squadron; and Rear Admiral Cynthia Gonsalves, commanding his First Battlecruiser Squadron. It was an impressive assembly of talent, backed up by a dozen more admirals she knew less well, beginning with Rear Admiral Anson Hewitt the previous station commander. And behind them were still more people she knew and trusted implicitly. Like Susan Phillips, Yu's flag captain aboard (embarrassing though Honor still found the name) GSNS *Honor Harrington*, and Captain Frederick Bagwell, once the operations officer on Honor's very first battle squadron staff and now Brentworth's flag captain. Her command team might not be quite the "band of brothers (or sisters)" so beloved of military hagiography, but as she looked at all of those waiting faces and tasted the emotions behind them, she knew it was a better one than most flag officers could ever expect in mundane reality. And at least she'd had time to get to know the ones she hadn't already known before arriving at Sidemore. A few of them would need closer attention, and some of the others were merely solid. But several of them were very good, indeed, and one or two probably deserved the label of brilliant. And every single one of them, however anxious he or she might be, was prepared to support whatever Honor decided.

But that was the difference between her and them, she thought as she crossed to her chair, nodded for all of them to resume their seats, arranged Nimitz on the back of her own chair, and sat herself. They were prepared to support *her* decisions; she was the one who had to make them.

"I'm glad we were all in range for a face-to-face meeting, Ladies and Gentlemen," she told them. "Of course, I would have been even happier if the subject of this meeting had never arisen. Mercedes," she looked at her chief of staff, "would you please summarize our latest information so we can be certain everyone is on the same page?"

"Yes, Your Grace," Brigham agreed, then paused and cleared her throat before she began in a deliberately dispassionate voice.

"Approximately three hours ago, the Manticoran-flag freighter *Chantilly* arrived here in Marsh from the Zoraster System. As many of you already knew, we had dispatched Captain Ferrero and the *Jessica Epps* to Zoraster to intercept a suspected slaver as part of Operation Wilberforce. According to our intelligence sources, the slaver in question was operating in the service of New Hamburg interests but squawking the false transponder code of an Andermani-flag merchie, the *Sittich*. Captain Ferrero was provided with a complete electronic fingerprint on the real *Sittich* in order to ensure that she could be positive the ship she stopped was not, in fact, the Andy to whom that code legitimately belonged.

"Apparently, *Jessica Epps* successfully intercepted the false *Sittich*. In the process, however, there was an . . . incident with the Andermani heavy cruiser *Hellbarde*. *Chantilly* didn't have complete details, but Captain Nazari, her skipper—who holds a Reserve naval commission as a full commander—decided that it was more important for her to reach us with the information she did have than to delay in the hopes that she might somehow obtain still more. Fortunately, Captain Nazari herself was close enough to the scene of the incident for her sensors to provide us with at least some firsthand observational data. Unfortunately, *Chantilly* is a merchant ship. As such, her sensor suite is scarcely up to military standards, and the data available to us leave much to be desired."

Brigham paused again, as if to be sure her listeners were still with her, then continued.

"Nonetheless, despite any shortcomings of the raw data, Commander Reynolds, Captain Jaruwalski, and myself have been able to reach certain conclusions. I stress that these are *only* conclusions, although the three of us believe them to be valid.

"Apparently, while *Jessica Epps* was in the process of challenging the suspected slaver, *Hellbarde* challenged *Jessica Epps*, in turn. I say 'apparently,' because *Chantilly*'s sensors showed absolutely no trace of *Hellbarde* at that time. This leads us to conclude that *Hellbarde* was operating under stealth, and from the course of events, we strongly suspect that *Jessica Epps* was unaware of her presence when she began the interception of the '*Sittich*.'

"Without access to the message logs of the ships involved, there's no way for us even to guess at this point about what communications passed between *Jessica Epps*, *Hellbarde*, and '*Sittich*.' All that *Chantilly* and Captain Nazari can tell us for certain, is that Captain Ferrero apparently fired a single warning shot across '*Sittich*'s' bows. Almost immediately, *Hellbarde* fired a full missile broadside at *Jessica Epps*."

Something like a sigh ran around the compartment as Brigham said the words at last. They were hardly a surprise; all of them knew why they had been summoned to this meeting. But somehow, that foreknowledge hadn't robbed them of their impact, and Honor tasted the internal tightening, the sense of foreboding, that came with them.

"*Chantilly*, given the limitations of her sensor suite and the capabilities of Andermani EW, was completely unaware of

Hellbarde's presence until she opened fire. Nonetheless, the sequence of shots, and their firing bearings, can be unambiguously determined from her sensor records. Clearly, *Jessica Epps* fired the first shot, but it was a single missile, fired almost directly away from *Hellbarde*. *Hellbarde*'s broadside, on the other hand, was clearly targeted on *Jessica Epps* and was not intended in any way as a 'warning shot.' Moreover, although it isn't really germane to the cause of this incident, it would appear from *Chantilly*'s sensors that Hellbarde opened fire from a range in excess of ten million klicks from *Jessica Epps*."

This time, Honor did taste a ripple of true surprise . . . and dismay. That was still much shorter than Ghost Rider's maximum effective range, but it was also much greater than even their most pessimistic estimates had assigned to Andermani missiles.

And, she reminded herself, *that's only the range at which we know they fired. We don't have any real reason to conclude that it was the maximum range at which they* could *have fired.*

"*Jessica Epps* returned fire," Brigham continued. "The ensuing engagement lasted for approximately thirty-seven minutes. Casualties on both sides were extremely heavy. Captain Nazari herself headed for the scene of the action as soon as firing had ceased in order to render such assistance as she could. There wasn't a great deal she could do. *Jessica Epps* was destroyed with all hands." The chief of staff's voice level never changed, but it sounded suddenly very, very loud in the hush her words produced. "*Hellbarde* was apparently in little better condition. Her captain, her executive officer, and most of her bridge officers were apparently killed in the engagement. Captain Nazari's rescue efforts were quickly superseded by those of local Confed security units, but her estimate is that no more than a hundred of *Hellbarde*'s ship's company survived. From the visual imagery of *Hellbarde*'s wreck which *Chantilly* was able to obtain, I would be very surprised if Nazari's estimate isn't high. One thing on which Commander Reynolds, Captain Jaruwalski, and I all agree strongly is that *Hellbarde* will never fight again.

"For what it matters, *Chantilly*'s sensor data clearly indicate that *Jessica Epps* was winning the engagement handily when a hit from one of *Hellbarde*'s last laser heads apparently caused one of her fusion plants to lose containment."

The chief of staff paused once more, then turned to look at Honor.

"Those are the bare bones of Captain Nazari's report, Your Grace. The full raw take from *Chantilly*'s sensors, plus the recording of Captain Nazari's verbal report, will be made available to all of the Station's flag officers and their staffs. Captain Nazari herself is still available, and *Chantilly* will remain in-system, in order to ensure the availability of any potential witnesses from her ship's company, until such time as we authorize her to continue her voyage."

"Thank you, Mercedes," Honor acknowledged, and it was her turn to meet the eyes of her assembled subordinates.

"Obviously," she said, her soprano voice much calmer than she felt, "this is precisely the sort of incident we've all been afraid of. The most important question, and one we can't possibly answer definitively at this point, is whether or not this represents deliberate Andermani policy."

"My initial reaction is that it probably does, Your Grace," Anson Hewitt said. Then he shrugged. "On the other hand, I may well be prejudiced by my own experiences out here."

"If you are, Anson, you certainly have more than enough reason to be," Honor told Sidemore Station's former commanding officer.

"At the same time, My Lady," Cynthia Gonsalves observed, "this would appear to be a rather abrupt break with the Andies' policy of gradually increasing the level of their provocations. Particularly in light of the fact that *Hellbarde* fired on *Jessica Epps* first, without being threatened herself. And that she did so from a range which clearly revealed the fact that her missiles were substantially longer ranged than we'd previously been given any cause to suspect."

"Those are excellent points," Honor agreed.

"With all due respect, Your Grace," Alistair McKeon pointed out, "as important as the question of intent obviously is, it may also, unfortunately, be completely beside the point. Shots have been fired, casualties have been suffered, and we've lost a Queen's ship with all hands. Whatever these clever-assed bastards may have been planning on doing, what they've actually accomplished is to present us with an act of war."

The sudden, brief silence which greeted his blunt observation was profound.

"Yes, they have," Honor said into that silence after a moment. "But the reason they did may still be of critical importance. My own initial read is that this entire incident represents a mistake."

"Mistake?" Alice Truman shook her head. Unlike many of the other flag officers in the briefing room, Truman had had the opportunity to look over the sensor data from *Chantilly* before joining the rest of them. "Your Grace, *Hellbarde* was clearly not threatened in any way when she opened fire on Captain Ferrero's vessel. Given how long and how assiduously *Hellbarde* had been harassing *Jessica Epps* for months prior to this, there's not very much chance *Hellbarde* didn't know exactly who she was dealing with, either. Which means that whatever else may have happened, an Andermani warship, deliberately, without provocation, and *knowingly* attacked a Queen's ship."

"I don't disagree with your analysis of what happened, Alice," Honor said. "I'm not at all certain, however, that 'deliberately and without provocation' is the best way to describe it."

She felt more than a little incredulity from her subordinate officers, astonishment at both the thrust of her argument and that "the Salamander" should be the one to voice it.

"As Captain Gonsalves has already pointed out," she continued calmly, "this represents an enormous break with the level of harassment we've seen out of the Andermani in the past. Moreover, we know Herzog von Rabenstrange is expected at Sachsen to relieve Sternhafen within the next few weeks. I find it very difficult to believe that the Andermani Navy would deliberately kick off an offensive against the Star Kingdom before their new station commander—widely regarded as perhaps the best flag officer in the IAN—even arrived."

"There is that," Truman agreed.

"True," Alfredo Yu said. "But it's also remotely possible that the timing represents a form of disinformation. By timing it to occur shortly before Rabenstrange's arrival in Sachsen, they may have intended to give him a degree of plausible deniability. He can always lay the blame for the attack on Sternhafen."

Honor felt a strain of bitter amusement under his words and had to suppress an ironic snort of her own as she remembered how Yu himself had been disavowed by his government during the operations which had first brought him to Yeltsin's Star all those years ago.

"Why would he want to blame Sternhafen?" Hewitt asked.

"I don't say I agree that it's what they were trying to do," Harriet Benson-Dessouix replied. "But it's possible that they might see this as a way to hit us with a really painful provocation, a demonstration of the fact that people can get hurt out here if they don't get out of the Andies' way, while leaving themselves room to retreat from actually starting a war. They may think that if they blame it on Sternhafen, or even on *Hellbarde*'s captain and simply officially fault Sternhafen for not having reined in *Hellbarde*'s previous aggressiveness—which certainly wouldn't have been the result of any official Andermani policy, under this interpretation—and possibly offer some form of reparations, we'd choose to absorb the attack without retaliating. Especially if they've interpreted the position of the Star Kingdom's present government as indicating an . . . unwillingness to embrace a confrontational policy here in Silesia."

"And the purpose of hitting *Jessica Epps* would have been to demonstrate their own willingness to fight while simultaneously hitting the Government between the eyes with how much standing in their way in Silesia could end up costing," McKeon mused. "All without their having done a single thing to us deliberately . . . officially."

"*If* they did it on purpose," Benson-Dessouix pointed out. "And even though I'm the one suggesting the hypothesis, that's an awful big 'if,' Alistair."

"It's certainly one possible scenario," Honor agreed. "But, as you say, Harry, it's all entirely speculative and highly problematical. It would also impute more subtlety to the Andermani than they normally demonstrate. Also, I think it may be overlooking the fact that the slaver *Jessica Epps* was intercepting was squawking an Andermani merchant transponder code at the time."

"That's true enough, Your Grace," Lieutenant Commander Reynolds said. "At the same time, *Chantilly*—with merchant-grade sensors and from almost as far away as *Hellbarde*—was able to clearly identify the '*Sittich*' Captain Ferrero was intercepting as at least two m-tons smaller than the ship that transponder code actually belongs to. Surely *Hellbarde*'s ship list for the Empire's merchant marine is at least as up to date as ours is! I find it very difficult to believe that a merchant ship would be more capable of identifying her correctly than an IAN heavy cruiser."

"Assuming that *Hellbarde* attempted to identify her in the first place," Warner Caslet said quietly. "That's where you're going, isn't it, My Lady?"

"Yes." Honor nodded. "Remember the history between *Hellbarde* and *Jessica Epps*. Mercedes, you and Andrea and George and I have all read Ferrero's previous reports. It's obvious *Hellbarde* was specifically assigned to shadow and harass *Jessica Epps*, not just any of our ships. As Alice just pointed out, it's been going on for months now, and Captain Ferrero's increasing frustration and anger were clearly evident from her reports. I see no reason to believe that the confrontation between them wasn't becoming equally personal for *Kapitän zur Sternen* Gortz, *Hellbarde*'s CO. It's entirely possible that both of them found their judgment less than completely clear and impartial where the other one was concerned."

"You're saying that this Gortz character may have been sufficiently pissed off with *Jessica Epps* to jump her without trying to determine '*Sittich*'s' real identity one way or the other?" McKeon asked skeptically. He shook his head. "Again, with all due respect, what would a yahoo like that be doing commanding an IAN heavy cruiser?"

"Are you sure you want to ask that question, given some of the people you and I have seen commanding Manticoran heavy cruisers?" Honor replied with a more crooked than usual smile. "Especially in backwater systems like . . . oh, Basilisk, say?"

"*Touché*," McKeon murmured after a moment, nodding slowly, almost as if against his will.

"It could have happened that way," Truman conceded. "But if it did, there must have been some pretty serious lapses on both sides. Ferrero certainly should have informed Gortz of her intentions. And from *Chantilly*'s sensor log, *Jessica Epps* had plenty of overtake on '*Sittich*.' There was no way a merchie was going to evade her at that point, so there was no compelling need for Ferrero to be firing warning shots if there was any confusion or uncertainty in her communications with *Hellbarde*."

"I'm not prepared to condemn one of my captains' actions without a lot more information than we currently have," Honor said. "On the other hand, from the very limited data actually available to us, it would certainly appear that that may have been true. In the final analysis, it was Gortz who first fired on *Jessica Epps*, which certainly seems—from our perspective, at least—to have been a much more serious 'lapse' than anything of which Ferrero may have been guilty. That doesn't mean both COs didn't contribute to what happened, and I think we all need to be aware of the fact that we're automatically prejudiced against the captain who killed one of our own ship's entire company. Not to mention the depth of the anger and resentment we all feel because of the Andermani's previous, deliberately provocative policy.

"But the two key points at this moment, as I see it, are that we have a very serious shooting incident between our own forces and the Andermani Navy, and that we don't have any way of knowing precisely what led up to it. The fact that it occurred in the territorial space of a third, neutral power complicates things even further, of course, but it doesn't change those two considerations."

She paused once more, surveying the faces and tasting the emotions about her, and behind her own calm façade she felt her own tension, her own anxiety. Her own sense of responsibility.

"I intend," she said, "to send *Chantilly*'s sensor log to Sachsen for review by Admiral Sternhafen. I will point out to him that according to that log, his commander clearly fired on our vessel before *Jessica Epps* returned fire. I will suggest to him that it would be . . . appropriate for him to determine whether or not the ship identifying itself as *Sittich* was the ship which ought to have been squawking that transponder code, and I will share with him the intelligence we developed suggesting that the ship in question was in fact both a slaver and illegally squawking a fraudulent code. I will request that he thoroughly investigate these events, and offer to conduct such an investigation jointly with him. In particular, I will request access to *Hellbarde*'s surviving personnel—under Andermani supervision, of course—in an effort to obtain firsthand testimony from the only survivors."

"Your Grace," Reynolds said, "all of our information on Graf von Sternhafen suggests that he's not going to pay you a great deal of attention. According to everything we have, he's a card-carrying member of the anti-Manticore faction within the IAN. Not to put too fine a point on it, he hates the Star Kingdom's guts."

"I'm well aware of that, George. That's one reason why I've been looking forward to Herzog von Rabenstrange's arrival to replace him. And why I think the timing on this episode is particularly tragic. Nonetheless, I don't see any way to justify not at least attempting to defuse this situation before it careens entirely out of control. If, in fact, this was an accident—if the Andies didn't intend from the beginning to pull the trigger on a general war between the Empire and the Star Kingdom—then I have an absolute responsibility to do all I can to pull us back from the brink instead of simply plunging over it because I don't expect my efforts to succeed."

Several heads nodded unconsciously in agreement around the conference table, but she tasted *dis*agreement from several of her subordinates, as well. And, in all fairness, she couldn't really blame them for it. For all of her effort to remain analytical and detached, she felt a bright, searing flicker of rage whenever she thought of what had happened to Erica Ferrero's ship and all of her crew. Alice was undoubtedly correct that there'd been lapses on both sides, but if the Andermani hadn't been deliberately provoking incidents for so long, those lapses probably wouldn't have occurred . . . and would never have had such fatal consequences if they had.

She wanted vengeance. She wanted to avenge her dead and simultaneously pay back all of the premeditated slights the Andermani had given the Royal Manticoran Navy. And she wanted, God help her, an enemy she could face openly, across the broadsides of her warships, without all of this endless hiding in shadows and groping with uncertainty even as she looked over her shoulder at a Government she neither agreed with nor trusted. She wanted that so badly she could taste it, like fire on her tongue.

Which was precisely the reason she dared not leap to any conclusions or foreclose any options. However much she wanted to.

"In addition to the messages I'll be sending to Sachsen," she went on, "I will, of course, dispatch a complete report to the Admiralty."

Who probably won't bother to read even this *one,* she thought bitterly.

"Unfortunately," she went on in that same calm, even tone, "even our fastest dispatch boat will take over two weeks to reach the Star Kingdom. And, of course, any reply will take equally long to get back to us. That means we're going to have to respond without fresh instructions for a minimum of more than a full standard month."

She didn't really need her ability to taste emotions directly to sense her subordinates' response to her use of the plural pronoun. As good as these people were, they would have been superhuman not to feel a flash of intense relief at the realization that someone other than they was ultimately responsible for deciding just how "we" were going to respond.

Her lips quirked ever so briefly at the thought, then she shook it aside and continued.

"Until—and if—we receive instructions to the contrary, I have no choice but to continue to enforce existing policy and directives in our operational area. Accordingly, we'll continue to patrol the star systems to which we've regularly assigned priority. I'm willing to pull in a bit from the periphery of our ops area, but we're going to maintain a definite presence in the core systems. In fact, I want our patrols beefed up even further. We can't afford to disperse our screening elements too broadly, and I have no desire to dilute our combat power. Nonetheless, I want our present plans to assign our vessels to operate at least in tandem to be expedited. In fact, where at all possible, I want ships operating in at least divisional strength, and pulling in a bit should free up the strength for that.

"We've already dispatched warnings to all of our units currently on station in other star systems, and I've instructed them to minimize potential additional incidents. Hopefully, all of them will receive our dispatches before they find themselves face-to-face with Andermani units which have already been informed of events in Zoraster. We certainly can't rely on that, however, which means we have to face the conclusion that it's entirely possible that we'll have additional incidents before we get everyone warned. In fact, it's possible we've already had one or more of those additional incidents.

"At the same time I've instructed them to minimize potential incidents, I've also made it very clear to them that their first and overriding responsibility is to safeguard their commands and their personnel. They're to take whatever measures they believe are required to that end. Which is why," she drew a deep breath, "I have instructed them to go to rules of engagement Alpha Two."

Something like a shiver went through the compartment, and she smiled bleakly. ROE Alpha Two specifically authorized a captain to open fire preemptively if she believed her command was under threat of attack. It specifically did not require her to allow a potential opponent to get in the first shot, although even under Alpha Two she was expected to do all she could to avoid shooting before she pressed the button herself.

Despite that, Honor was fully aware of the danger of escalation her change in the rules of engagement constituted. She would have preferred to avoid it, but her conscience would never have permitted her to. Not nowadays, when the massive salvos ships armed with missile pods could throw were capable of completely swamping and overwhelming an opponent's point defense. Allowing the enemy to fire first in order to clearly establish responsibility for a hostile act was no longer a survivable option.

"Understand me clearly on this, People," she said very quietly. "It's our responsibility to maintain the peace if that's at all possible. But if it *isn't* possible for us to do that, then we have an even more overriding responsibility to enforce Her Majesty's Government's policy in Silesia and to protect the Marsh System and Sidemore. If that brings us into open conflict with the Andermani Empire, then so be it.

"I don't look forward to a war with the Andies. I don't want one. No one in her right mind does. But," Lady Dame Honor Harrington told her admirals softly, "if *they* want one, I intend to make them regret their choice.

"Seriously."

CHAPTER FORTY-THREE

"I'm afraid we have another one, Your Grace."

Honor looked up from the report on her display, and her mouth tightened as she tasted Mercedes Brigham's emotions. The chief of staff's mood wasn't dark enough for a report of heavy casualties, but if there was no death in it, there was something else. Something which had provoked a fresh anxiety in her.

"How bad this time?" Honor asked quietly.

"Not as bad as the last one," Brigham reassured her quickly. "And a hell of a lot better than what happened to *Jessica Epps*. The dispatch is from Captain Ellis—"

"He has *Royalist*, doesn't he?" Honor interrupted.

"Yes, Your Grace," Brigham confirmed, and Honor nodded. *Royalist* was a *Reliant*-class ship, like Honor's own one and only battlecruiser command, HMS *Nike*. The *Reliants* were no longer the latest, most modern ships in the Royal Navy's inventory, but they remained large and powerful units, capable of taking on anything below the wall, and they'd had priority for refits and upgrades.

"He and his division were picketing the Walther System, over in the Breslau Sector. They'd been on station there for just under five days when an Andermani cruiser squadron entered the system. As per your orders, Ellis transmitted a warning to the Andies to stay clear of his ships."

Honor nodded again. Her standing instructions to all of her units now required them to instruct any Andermani warships they might encounter to maintain a minimum separation of twenty million klicks between themselves and any Manticoran or Side-morian vessel or be fired upon. The same warning carried a brief summary, outlined as dispassionately as possible, of what had happened in Zoraster from the Manticoran viewpoint. She had no doubt that any Andermani skipper who received that warning and had already made up her mind about who'd fired the first shot in Zoraster would be less than impressed by the Manticoran ver-sion. In fact, in some cases that summary would probably only inflame tempers which were already running high. But she couldn't afford to assume that every Andermani ship already knew what was happening, and she wanted it firmly on the record that the Andies had not only been warned to stand clear of her ships but told why they were to do it, as well.

Not that it will do all that much good if one of my units does *open fire*, she thought. *But at least my skippers will be covered, whatever Janacek and his geniuses back home decide about* my *judgment.*

"Apparently," Brigham continued, "the Andies weren't impressed by his warning. They split up into two four-ship divisions and started maneuvering to sandwich Ellis between them. According to his report, he was inclined to play tag with them in order to maintain our position on freedom of navigation, but he'd deployed his long-range recon drones, and one of them got close enough to pull a clear visual up the kilt of one Andie wedge. It saw this, Your Grace."

The chief of staff handed over a memo board, and Honor keyed the flatscreen display alive. Unfortunately, its image was too tiny for her to make out any details, so she pressed another control and activated the holographic display, instead. The much larger "light sculpture" version of the imagery appeared above the board, and she frowned. There was something odd about it. . . .

"What *are* those things?" she murmured, mostly to herself, and felt Nimitz raising his head on the back of her chair to gaze at the imagery with her as he tasted her intent curiosity. Then her lips tightened.

"Those are missile pods," she answered herself, and looked up at Brigham with arched eyebrows.

"More precisely, Your Grace, according to Ellis—and George's first run at the data agrees with him—those are *half* missile pods. It looks like they sawed a conventional pod in half lengthwise and bolted the resulting abortion onto the ship right at the upper turn of the hull."

"My God." Honor looked back at the imagery and did a quick mental estimate. Assuming that the spacing of the handful of undersized pods she could see was maintained uniformly for the length of the ship between its hammerheads, then the cruiser floating before her had to have mounted at least thirty-five or forty of them. "What about the lower turn?" she asked.

"We don't know, Your Grace. Let's face it, *Royalist* was dead lucky to get as much as she did. If I had to guess, though, I'd guess they probably mounted them top and bottom both. If it were me, that's certainly what I would have done, and I think we have to assume the Andies are at least as smart as I am." She smiled with absolutely no humor. "Assuming they are top and bottom, George and I estimate they probably have between sixty and eighty of them in each broadside. That gives them a maximum salvo throw weight of between three hundred and four hundred birds."

Honor's lips pursed in a silent whistle of dismay. No non-pod ship in her order of battle could even come close to that heavy a broadside. And mounting the pods directly onto the hull of the ship also put them inside the cruiser's impeller wedge and sidewalls, protecting them from the proximity "soft kills" which threatened pods deployed behind ships on tractors. Which meant the ship would be much freer of the "use them or lose them" constraints which normally affected pods deployed by light and medium combatants.

"Unless they've upgraded their fire control suites massively," she thought out loud, "no ship this size could manage a salvo that heavy."

"No, Your Grace," Brigham agreed. "They wouldn't have the telemetry links, even if they could see past the wedge interference of that many missiles to guide them in the first place. But if they use them right, they can probably fire broadsides of up to fifty, maybe even sixty, missiles each. Assuming that there's some way for them to see around the pods themselves, that it is."

"I see your point." Honor rubbed the tip of her nose in thought. The long row of pods was mounted well clear of the cruiser's standard weapon decks. As Mercedes had observed, they were carried at the turn of the hull, where the central spindle of a warship curled over into the relatively flat top and bottom of her hull. Those areas, protected by the impenetrable roof and floor of her wedge, were effectively unarmored. And they were also where most warships mounted additional active sensor arrays for their missile defenses and offensive fire control. The main arrays would be clear, but not the supporting ones used to manage individual missile telemetry links or for dedicated laser cluster fire control. Which meant that the Andie's pods almost certainly had to be interfering with her ability to see her targets . . . not to mention incoming fire.

"I'll bet you these things are designed to jettison," she told Brigham. "Probably mounted on some sort of external hard point."

"That's what's George and I think," Brigham said with a nod. "For that matter, that was Ellis' conclusion, as well."

"Yes, Ellis." Honor shook herself and turned off the holo display, then leaned back in her chair and frowned at the chief of staff. "You say he got this visual using his long-range drones?"

"Yes, Your Grace. And he doesn't think the Andies spotted them, either. Which is a little reassuring. At least they haven't broken all of Ghost Rider's advantages!"

"Let's not fret ourselves into assigning them superhuman powers, Mercedes," Honor said with a small, crooked smile. "I'm sure they have some additional surprises for us, but by the same token, I'm sure we have some for them. And everything we've seen out of them so far is still effectively a case of their playing catch-up with where we already are. Which inclines me to think that whether they want us to realize it or not, they have to be at least as nervous about what we might be able to do to them as we are about what they might be able to do to us."

"No doubt that's true," Brigham replied with a dry chuckle. "On the other hand, Your Grace, my sympathy for what *they* may be worrying about is decidedly limited just now."

"Yours and mine both," Honor assured her. "But getting back to Walther. What did Ellis do when he got the visual?"

"Well, it took him a few minutes to recognize what he was looking at," Brigham told her. "When he did, he realized his two battlecruisers would be on the extremely short end of the stick if missiles started flying. By the same token, he was determined not to be driven out of the system. So he deployed close-in drones, and the mid-range EW platforms, and accelerated to meet one of the two Andie forces."

"He took on four cruisers armed like this one—" Honor tapped the deactivated memo board "—with just two *Reliants*?"

"Well, according to his report, he figured he'd probably gotten a better look at them than they could have gotten at him," Brigham said. "So in addition to the decoys he'd put out to duplicate his ships' emissions signatures for the bad guys' fire control, he also deployed an additional two dozen decoys behind each battlecruiser."

She paused, and Honor looked at her suspiciously.

"What sort of decoys?" she asked.

"He had them set to look like missile pods, Your Grace," Brigham told her, and chuckled at Honor's expression. "And he was careful to hold his accel down to something he could have managed with that many pods on tow, too."

"He was running a bluff on them?"

"Precisely, Your Grace. And it looks like he pulled it off, too. Apparently, however aggressive the Andies might be feeling, they didn't want to take on a pair of battlecruisers, each of whom were prepared to put two hundred and fifty missiles into space in a single broadside."

"I wouldn't have wanted to either," Honor agreed. Then she frowned. "Still, if your estimate of their own broadsides is accurate, then theoretically four of them could have put out three times the weight of fire they figured both of Ellis's ships together could have laid down."

"That's why I said this incident wasn't as bad as the last one, Your Grace. No shots were fired, and the Andies backed off. They didn't maintain the full twenty million-klick separation Ellis had demanded, but they were careful to stay well outside anything approaching standard missile range. And eventually, they cleared Walther and went on about their business. Ellis had a couple of fairly anxious days first, but we got out of this one without any shooting. Which, given the disparity in the weight of fire, might indicate that they had orders not to pick a fight."

"Um." Honor rubbed her nose in more, then shook her head unhappily. "Actually, I think, Mercedes, we just lucked out this time. I think we had an Andermani squadron commander who wasn't particularly eager to die for her Emperor and figured that at least some of her ships were going to catch it right along with Ellis' battlecruisers if it came down to it. And if *these* people had orders not to pick a fight, what about those idiots at Schiller?"

It was Brigham's turn to look unhappy, and she nodded slowly. The confrontation in the Schiller System had ended far less happily than the one at Walther. The Andermani senior officer in that case had seen fit to ignore the senior Manticoran officer's warning to maintain separation when he caught the Manticoran patrol separated. Instead, the understrength three-ship Andermani division of light cruisers had continued to bore in on the single Manticoran heavy cruiser which had been operating in a detached role.

Fortunately, in that instance the Andies obviously hadn't had any of their handy-dandy strap-on missile pods. The three light cruisers had continued to close, and the Manticoran cruiser *Ephraim Tudor* had opened fire when they approached to within fifteen million kilometers.

The brief engagement which followed had not gone well for the Andermani. Apparently, the best powered attack range for missiles carried by their medium combatants was no more than twelve million kilometers, for they'd closed to that range before launching their first birds. It also seemed obvious that *Ephraim Tudor*'s electronic warfare capabilities had been better than theirs. They'd scored three hits on the Manticoran cruiser, inflicting damage that was surprisingly light . . . and killing nine of her crew. Another seven members of her company had been wounded, but in return for that damage, one of the Andermani light cruisers had been battered into an air-leaking, powerless wreck. One of the others had also suffered serious damage to her impeller ring, judging by the drop in her wedge strength and acceleration, and whoever was in command on the other side had decided it was time to exercise discretion. Both of the light cruisers still capable of combat had rolled up on their sides, interposing the roofs of their wedges against additional incoming fire from *Ephraim Tudor,* and maneuvered to cover their crippled sister in their impeller shadows.

In compliance with Honor's orders to minimize tensions as much as possible, *Ephraim Tudor* had broken off the engagement when it became obvious the Andies were maneuvering to avoid further action. Honor had no reports on exactly how bad Andermani casualties had been, but she knew they had to have been much heavier than her own. Not that the thought was going to offer much comfort to the families of her dead.

"Maybe the Andie SO in Walther had heard about what happened in Schiller," Brigham suggested. "It's obvious that they haven't been able to match the defensive side of Ghost Rider—or, at least, to find a way around that side. Maybe what *Ephraim Tudor* managed to do to them is making them more cautious."

"It's possible," Honor conceded. "But given the time interval, any courier from Schiller would have had to cut it pretty tight to pass that word to the second force before it headed out for Walther. And whatever was going through their heads when Ellis decided to run his bluff, it certainly looks like they'd been planning to crowd him, at the very least, before he managed to convince them he had so much firepower in reserve."

"Well," Brigham said, "at least we've gotten all of our units warned by now. And unless someone's managed to ambush one of our people even after we'd warned them, we shouldn't lose any more ships without making the Andies pay the ferryman."

"I know." Honor smiled again, more crookedly than before. "I know, Mercedes. The only problem is that I'd just as soon not kill anyone. Vengeance won't bring back anyone we lose, and the more shooting incidents we have, even if we 'win' all of them, the tenser things are going to get out here. If there's any chance of containing this thing, we've got to get a handle on it before it spins entirely out of control."

"You're right, of course," Brigham agreed. "But Sternhafen's response to your message doesn't strike me as a good sign. If he's so unwilling to consider even the possibility that his man could have made a mistake that he's officially rejected any board of inquiry, it doesn't sound like he's very interested in containing the situation, does it?"

"No," Honor agreed somberly, remembering the uncompromising communique Admiral Sternhafen had released to the Silesian and interstellar media in response to her message to him.

"No, it doesn't sound like it," she admitted.

"Perhaps, *Herr Graf,* you would be so kind as to explain this to me?" Chien-lu Anderman, Herzog von Rabenstrange, requested in tones of icy courtesy as he tapped the message chip. It was in the color-keyed folio which identified an official naval press release, and it lay on the corner of the desk which belonged—so far, at least—to Admiral Xiaohu Pausch, Graf von Sternhafen.

That, of course, was subject to change.

"There is nothing to explain, *Gross Admiral*," Sternhafen replied in a flat, politely defiant voice. "A Manticoran heavy cruiser fired upon one of our merchant ships after *Kapitän der Sternen* Gortz had repeatedly instructed it to break off its attack run. Under the circumstances, *Kapitän der Sternen* Gortz had no option but to engage the Manticoran to protect the safety of our own nationals. In the ensuing engagement, provoked by the Manticorans, there was very heavy loss of life on both sides. Given those self-evident facts I saw no reason to subject the Emperor's dignity to the humiliation of a Manticoran-directed 'investigation' into the actions of a navy of a sovereign power. Not only would submission to such a thinly veiled demand on Harrington's part have been insulting and demeaning to both His Imperial Majesty and the Navy, but the obvious prejudice of the Manticorans would have made any 'impartial' verdict's conclusion that *we* were at fault inevitable. I had no desire to participate in such a farce for the benefit of exonerating the officer actually responsible for this atrocity, and as His Imperial Majesty's representative in Silesia, I so informed the Manticoran commander at Sidemore in no uncertain terms. And in order to foreclose the possibility of allowing her to score any sort of propaganda triumph out of this, I acted to get the true version of events into the media's hands as rapidly as possible, as was my obvious duty."

"I see. And you have *Kapitän der Sternen* Gortz' own sworn testimony as to precisely what events occurred in Zoraster, I suppose?"

"Of course not, *Gross Admiral*," Sternhafen half-snapped, his outward courtesy fraying noticeably under the lash of Rabenstrange's frigid sarcasm.

"Ah, yes. I'd forgotten. *Kapitän der Sternen* Gortz is dead, is he not, Admiral?" The smallish *gross admiral* smiled coldly at the considerably taller Sternhafen and watched the other man visibly bite his tongue. There were advantages, Rabenstrange reflected, to being the Emperor's first cousin.

"And because Gortz is dead," he continued after a moment, "it's impossible for you to ascertain with complete certainty precisely what he did or didn't do, is that not correct?"

"We have the testimony of the three surviving bridge personnel," Sternhafen replied hotly. "All of them agree that—"

"I've viewed their statements, *Herr Graf*," Rabenstrange interrupted him. "None of them were communication ratings, however. They were concentrating on other duties at the time, and their memory of precisely what Gortz said to this Captain Ferrero is extremely vague and scarcely reliable. Moreover, what little they can tell us, vague as it is, pertains only to Gortz' side of the conversation, because none of them actually heard Ferrero's transmissions to him. So the fact that they agree that their captain reacted nobly and selflessly to a totally unprovoked Manticoran attack upon an innocent merchant ship might be just the slightest bit suspect, don't you suppose, *Herr Graf*?"

"I protest your tone, *Gross Admiral*," Sternhafen said curtly. "I'm fully aware of your rank, and of your position in the Imperial Family. However, I am still His Imperial Majesty's commander in Silesia until you formally relieve me of my duties. And while I am the Silesian commander, I am not required to submit to your verbal abuse of myself or of the personnel—especially of the personnel who have given their lives in the Emperor's service—under my command!"

"You're quite correct," Rabenstrange told him after a brief, taut moment of silence. "Of course, the question of precisely what command you'll ever hold again remains open." He smiled thinly as Sternhafen's eyes flinched ever so slightly away from his own. Then he drew a deep breath, folded his hands behind him, and made himself take a quick turn around Sternhafen's ground-side Sachsen office.

"Very well, *Herr Graf*," he said finally, turning back to face the taller man once more. "I'll attempt to amend my manner. But you, *Graf*, will answer my questions. And I warn you now, I am not interested in defensive temporizations. Is that understood?"

"Of course, Your Grace," Sternhafen replied stiffly.

"Very well," Rabenstrange repeated. "The point I was attempting to make was that so far as I've been able to determine from your reports, neither you nor anyone in your command made any attempt to discover whether or not Duchess Harrington's hypothesis as to what transpired in Zoraster might be accurate before you summarily rejected her offer of a joint investigation."

"Your Grace," Sternhafen sounded dangerously patient, but

Rabenstrange decided to let it pass . . . for now, "Harrington will naturally attempt to put the best possible face upon her captain's actions. No doubt you'll argue that I must feel the same temptation in Gortz's case, and you may well be right. However, this particular Manticoran ship had established a clear pattern of arrogance and confrontation in previous encounters with *Hellbarde*. I believe any fair reading of the Fleet base's file copies of *Hellbarde*'s communication log of Captain Ferrero's previous messages will bear out *Kapitän* Gortz' view of Ferrero as a dangerously provocative woman.

"When the final encounter between these two ships occurred—in, may I point out, the sovereign territory of a third star nation and definitely *not* Manticoran territory—Ferrero was clearly maneuvering with the intention of stopping and, at the very least, searching an Imperial-flag merchant vessel proceeding about its lawful concerns. That, at least, was the completely reasonable conclusion of *Kapitän der Sternen* Gortz. While the testimony of the surviving fire control ratings as to the precise content of the message traffic exchanged between *Jessica Epps* and *Hellbarde* may not be conclusive, all three of them agree messages *were* exchanged. Moreover, all three agree that *Kapitän der Sternen* Gortz's demand that Ferrero break off her harassment of the vessel in question was not only rejected by her but clearly preceded her decision to open fire upon that vessel.

"Under the circumstances, I repeat, I fail to see what other option Gortz had. In my opinion, Ferrero acted in typical Manticoran fashion, arrogantly assuming—and *demanding*—that an Imperial warship stand by with its hat literally in its hands while she violated the sovereignty of the Empire's flag. It's my belief that we ought to be discussing posthumous decorations for *Kapitän der Sternen* Gortz and his crew, not trying to fasten blame for this . . . episode upon them as any so-called 'joint' investigation under Manticoran authority would certainly do."

Rabenstrange stared at him for a long moment, and then the herzog's nostrils flared.

"*Graf* von Sternhafen," he said, enunciating each word with extreme precision, "while I intend to make all due effort to address you with the courtesy you've reminded me a station commander in His Imperial Majesty's service deserves, you make that extremely difficult. I am interested in getting to the bottom of what happened;

as nearly as I can tell, *you* are primarily interested in justifying *Kapitän der Sternen* Gortz's actions in their totality. And, I repeat, you apparently made no effort whatsoever to investigate Duchess Harrington's statements or to consider the possibility that, however patriotic and noble he may have been, *Kapitän zur Sternen* Gortz might—*might*, I say!—have committed an error in this instance."

"Errors were certainly made, *Gross Admiral*," Sternhafen replied. "They were not, however, made by *Kapitän der Sternen* Gortz."

Rabenstrange forced himself not to shout in the other man's face. It was difficult. And not least because the herzog found himself in fundamental disagreement with his imperial cousin's Silesian policy. Despite his own lofty birth and accomplishments, Chien-lu Anderman was not an especially vain man. He saw no point in pretending to be any more modest than he was, either, but he wasn't one of those individuals who worried particularly about what others might think of him or about matters of reputation and "face."

Despite that, he was aware that the Emperor regarded him more as a favored brother than as a mere cousin, and that very few individuals in the Andermani Empire had as much influence with Gustav as he did. But there were limits in all things, and try though he might, he'd been unable to dissuade Gustav from embarking upon his grand adventure in the Confederacy.

Truth to tell, Rabenstrange found it impossible to fault Gustav's basic determination to secure the Empire's legitimate frontiers in Silesia. Unlike the Star Kingdom of Manticore, the Andermani Empire was physically close enough to Silesia to suffer occasional border violations by Silesian pirates and freebooters. That situation had become even worse (although, he admittedly, not enormously so) in the wake of the steady trickle into the Confederacy of outlaw warships which had once belonged to the People's Navy. Which, if one wanted to look at it that way, was at least partly the fault of the Manticorans, since it was their war with the People's Republic which had ultimately created the situation. And whatever implications Silesian instability might have had for the Star Kingdom's merchant marine, that instability offered no direct, immediate threat to the security of Manticore's territory or citizenry at large. The fact that Manticore had presumed for so long to dictate Andermani behavior in Silesia under those circumstances certainly explained the long-standing, deep-seated anti-Manticoran prejudices of old-line wardogs like Sternhafen. For that matter, Rabenstrange himself was far from immune to the same sort of burning anger when some fresh example of Manticoran high-handedness fanned the flames.

But this was the wrong way to go about seeking redress. Rabenstrange had argued strenuously against the policy of gradually increasing the pressure on Manticore. Not because he disagreed with Imperial Intelligence's estimates of the fundamental gutlessness of the High Ridge Government, but because of the dangerous potential for provocations to get out of hand and spill over into acts of war. Far better, he'd argued, for the Ministry of State to formally inform the Star Kingdom that the Emperor proposed to press his legitimate security interests in Silesia. Get it all out in the open. Give High Ridge his options and call in the debt the Star Kingdom owed the Empire for the way in which Andermani "neutrality" had favored it in its confrontation with the People's Republic of Haven. And if Manticore persisted in refusing to concede the Empire its just due, *then* pursue the military option, openly and straightforwardly.

But other counsel had prevailed. Other advisers had convinced Gustav that the application of sufficient pressure would not only inspire a spineless leader like High Ridge to withdraw unilaterally from Silesia but also remind the Confederacy government that resisting his eventual demands might be . . . unwise. And if no explicit demands upon or threats to Manticore were made, then the possibility of accidentally backing someone like High Ridge into a position in which public opinion might force him into a hardline response would be substantially reduced. The belated offer of covert Havenite support which Ambassador Kaiserfest had reported after his conversations with Secretary of State Giancola had been the clinching factor in the triumph of the faction which favored gradually ratcheting up the pressure in Silesia. Rabenstrange's own argument that such a policy offered far more fertile ground for misunderstandings and accidents had been rejected.

And so they had all come to this—to precisely the sort of incident Rabenstrange had feared from the outset might occur. And it was his responsibility to drive the policy he'd argued against through to a successful conclusion.

Which he would. Whether he agreed with it or not was

immaterial at this point. But that didn't mean he was prepared to plunge blindly ahead into open warfare with the Star Kingdom if there were any way he could avoid it.

Unfortunately, it was looking more and more as if he might not have that choice. And it was people like Sternhafen, and the recently deceased Gortz, who had made that true.

"Allow me to explain to you, *Graf* von Sternhafen," he said finally, "that, in the delightfully pithy Manticoran phrase, *Kapitän der Sternen* Gortz 'screwed the pooch' in a truly spectacular display of stupidity." Sternhafen swelled angrily, but Rabenstrange continued in that same level, biting tone.

"Unlike you, I did conduct a certain amount of research. And I found it trivially simple to confirm that the vessel squawking *Sittich*'s transponder code was not *Sittich*." Sternhafen stared at him, and Rabenstrange smiled thinly. "I base that statement not simply on the data in Duchess Harrington's message to you, *Herr Graf*, but also on the data your own vessels secured from the local Silesian security LACs who were in sensor range of the incident. Based upon its observed tonnage alone, the vessel *Jessica Epps* was moving to intercept was *not* an Andermani-flag merchant—or, at least, not the one it claimed to be. And since I assume that as a conscientious servant of His Imperial Majesty you've seen to it that all units under your command have current, updated copies of the Registry of Merchant Vessels, I must also assume that it would have been possible for *Hellbarde*'s sensors to establish that that same vessel was squawking a false transponder code . . . and thus violating the sovereignty of our flag in contravention of solemn interstellar law. Given those facts and deductions, I see no reason to doubt the remainder of Duchess Harrington's analysis and explanation. In short, *Herr Graf*, your 'heroic' *Kapitän der Sternen* Gortz managed to kill virtually his entire crew and the complete company of a Manticoran heavy cruiser out of sheer, incompetent stupidity, and all in the name of allowing a vessel engaged in the filth and perversion of the interstellar genetic slave trade to escape interception and capture!"

"There's no proof of any such thing!" Sternhafen snapped, but something flickered in his eyes, and Rabenstrange snorted.

"The problem is that there's no proof *at all*," the herzog shot back. "And because you—you, *Herr Graf*, and no one else—refused even to consider the possibility that Gortz might have been in error, this entire situation is in the process of spiraling completely out of control."

"I did no more than exercise my legitimate authority as the Empire's representative in Silesia, and I'm prepared to face whatever inquiry His Imperial Majesty may feel appropriate," Sternhafen replied. His effort at noble defiance fell considerably short of total success, and Rabenstrange's lip curled.

"That's very courageous of you, *Herr Graf.* Unfortunately, His Majesty isn't prepared to have your incredible incompetence aired for all the galaxy to see. Obviously, I've had no time to confer with him on this matter, but the instructions I was given before being sent out here leave me in no doubt as to what the Imperial policy will be in the wake of this incident. By issuing your formal statement 'explaining' the Zoraster Incident, you've committed us to a policy of denying that the Star Kingdom might have acted properly in this case. I can do nothing else, no matter how much I might wish to, because to admit anything else at this late date would look like an act of weakness, rather than the act of strength an immediate and thorough investigation would have been."

"Caving in to the Manticoran version of events would have been the act of weakness!" Sternhafen protested.

"That conclusion," Rabenstrange said coldly and precisely, "is the product of your own stupidity and prejudice against the Star Kingdom. It would have been a simple matter for us to investigate from a position of strength. For us to move in and secure temporary control of the entire Zoraster System in order to be certain all relevant evidence still in the system was preserved. We could have asserted our authority to conduct the investigation ourselves, and I have no doubt whatsoever that High Ridge would have instructed Duchess Harrington to give us a free hand in that investigation . . . which she would have been inclined to do in the first place because, unlike you, she is a decent and open-minded individual. But that concession from High Ridge would have established his government's acceptance of *our* primacy as the interstellar police force with paramount jurisdiction in this instance, thus granting us equality with the Star Kingdom in dealing with Silesian lawlessness. And when, at the end of our investigation, our report to the galaxy at large didn't attempt to whitewash the actions of our commander on the spot, we would have emerged from the incident as a mature, responsible force in Silesia. Our willingness to admit when we ourselves were the ones at fault would have made us a voice of reason in a region whose anarchy and lack of effective central authority promote outrages like the slave trade which provoked the entire tragic incident. Which, you idiot, would have given us the moral highroad for our annexation of critical territory here as the means of putting an end to that same anarchy!"

Despite himself, his voice rose to a shout with the final sentence, and he clenched his fists behind him, glaring at Sternhafen. The other admiral seemed to wilt inside his spotless white uniform tunic, and Rabenstrange made himself close his eyes and draw another deep, cleansing breath.

"Now, after you've chosen to reject Harrington's proposal and rushed to proclaim the official verdict of the Empire without any investigation whatsoever, *I* have no choice but to maintain the farce to which you've committed His Imperial Majesty. An opportunity which would have allowed us to turn this entire wretched incident decisively to our advantage has been totally foreclosed by your narrowminded, knee-jerk need to announce to the galaxy at large that the Manticorans were at fault. And because I can't repudiate your official announcement without revealing to the entire universe just how stupid our policy has been, I'm probably going to find myself faced with fighting the war against the Star Kingdom which His Imperial Majesty so earnestly wished to avoid."

The herzog smiled very coldly at Sternhafen.

"I suspect, *Herr Graf*, that the Emperor may have just a little to say to you upon this subject himself."

"I did warn you they were becoming increasingly hardline," Arnold Giancola said in an artfully regretful tone.

Eloise Pritchart glared at him, too angry, for once, to maintain the sort of carefully crafted mask which had preserved her from detection by StateSec's minions. Giancola settled back in his chair, presenting a properly submissive mien while deep inside he savored her obvious fury.

"Yes, Arnold, you did warn me," she told him with savage, icy precision. "Which isn't particularly useful, just at the moment."

"Sorry," he replied as sincerely as possible. "I didn't mean to sound as if I were saying 'I told you so.' It's just that I've been seeing them moving in this direction for so long without being able to do anything about it that—"

He shrugged helplessly, and the President turned her back to stare out the window of her office at downtown Nouveau Paris while she fought to control her own temper.

The traditional, archaic hardcopy of Elaine Descroix's response to the Republic's most recent note lay on her desk, and a corner of her mind was a bit surprised that the sheer, white-hot fury which had filled her as she read it hadn't ignited the paper on which it was printed. Descroix had finally abandoned the platitudes and vague, generalized nothings with which the Star Kingdom's negotiators had strung out negotiations for so long. Her new note was a combination of an arrogant lecture on the People's Republic's long history of interstellar misbehavior coupled with curt observations that "confrontational, antagonistic expressions of anger and impatience do not contribute to the mature resolution of differences between interstellar powers." It also included a flat refusal to acknowledge that the Republic, as the direct successor of the "brutally oppressive prior regimes of the People's Republic," had any right "at this late date to wrap itself in a supposed mantle of moral authority" and demand the return of its territory to its sovereignty. Apparently, Pritchart noted furiously, that was true even if the citizens living in the territory in question requested in a freely voted upon plebiscite to do exactly that! In essence, Descroix's note represented a thinly veiled ultimatum demanding that the Republic of Haven submit completely to the total package of the Star Kingdom's diplomatic demands as the price for a formal treaty.

"Obviously," she told the crystoplast of the window, never turning to look at Giancola, "High Ridge and Descroix aren't impressed by the reasonableness of our proposals."

"If they were interested in reasonable proposals," Giancola pointed out diffidently, "we could have had a peace treaty years ago. And while I argued before our last note that adopting a still more . . . assertive stance might be counterproductive, I have to admit that at least it's had the effect of openly crystallizing their position. Madame President, much as we may dislike admitting it, the demands contained in their response are, in my opinion, precisely where they've been headed from the beginning of this process. I know you haven't wanted to hear that. I know we've disagreed at many times during these negotiations. I even know you have certain concerns about my loyalty and commitment to the official positions of this administration's diplomacy. But whatever our differences in the past may have been, surely the entire tenor of this response represents an admission by the High Ridge Government at last of its intention to forcibly annex the Republican star systems its naval forces currently occupy."

Something inside Eloise Pritchart tied itself into a knot as his respectful, reasonable tone washed over her. The fact that she still didn't trust him didn't necessarily invalidate his observations or his conclusions, she reminded herself yet again. And whatever she might have thought about his motivations, he wasn't the one who'd drafted the infuriating, arrogant, dismissive note lying on her blotter.

She gazed out at Nouveau Paris, and as her eyes rested on the gleaming walls of the New Octagon, a sudden sense of decision flowed through her. She gazed at the Navy's central HQ for a moment longer, then turned at last to face Giancola once more.

"All right," she said flatly. "If they want to play hardball, then we'll damned well *play* hardball."

"Excuse me, Madame President?" he asked, and the sudden edge of concern in his voice wasn't entirely assumed. He'd never seen Pritchart quite this angry before—never realized she could *be* this angry—and he felt a brief, uncharacteristic uncertainty about his ability to continue to manage events properly.

"I said I'll play the game just as hard as they want to play it," she told him, and crossed to her desk to punch a combination into her com. The connection went through almost instantly, and she nodded briskly as Thomas Theisman's face appeared on her display.

"Madame President," Theisman said. He seemed unsurprised to see her, but then, only eleven people in the entire Republic of Haven had the combination to his personal New Octagon com.

"Arnold Giancola is in my office with me, Tom," she told him without preamble. "He's brought Descroix's official response to our last note, and it isn't good. Not good at all. They're clearly refusing to give a single centimeter."

"I see," Theisman said cautiously.

"I think," she continued in that same, flat voice, "that it's time to convince them of the error of their ways."

✧   ✧   ✧

"I wish I weren't telling you this," Thomas Theisman said into the visual pickup as he recorded the "Eyes-Only" message for Javier Giscard. "Unfortunately, I am."

He drew a deep breath.

"This letter is for your personal information, but the official dispatch accompanying it should be considered a war warning. At the present time, Eloise has informed me that she has no intention of firing the first shot, but in my opinion the risk that *someone* will fire it has just gone up considerably."

He paused, reflecting upon the fact that he was speaking to the man who loved Eloise Pritchart and probably knew her better than anyone else in the universe, with the possible exception of Kevin Usher. But Giscard was aboard his flagship, orbiting SXR-136, not in Nouveau Paris.

"Eloise and Giancola are drafting a new note for the Manties. It will no longer request that they consider our new proposals. Instead, it will insist that they accept our demands. She's assured me that she doesn't intend—at this time—to specify the potential consequences if they fail to accept them, but it's obvious to me that her language is going to be more than merely 'stiff.'

"We've discussed the operational assumptions and concepts of Case Red Alpha in some detail. She understands that for it to succeed, we need to maintain the advantage of surprise. She also agrees that it's essential for us not to launch an offensive without clearly demonstrating to both domestic and foreign public opinion that we had no choice, however. And, frankly, I hope and believe she continues to agree that renewed hostilities against the Star Kingdom are a disaster to be avoided at almost any cost."

At least the first verb in that final sentence, he reflected, was still accurate. Unfortunately, he was no longer as confident as he would have liked to be that the second one was.

"This is not an order to commence operations," he said firmly. "It is, however, a heads-up. Eloise's new note will be dispatched to Manticore within thirty-six standard hours. I don't think anyone in the capital—not even Giancola—claims to have any idea how High Ridge will respond to it. But it looks like we're going to find out."

Arnold Giancola sat in his private office. It was very late, and he smiled in amusement burnished by an undeniable touch of anxiety as he contemplated the text of the document on his reader. The hour was entirely appropriate, he reflected. By long and venerable tradition, conspiracies were supposed to be executed by dark of night.

Not that he would have admitted to anyone else that what he was doing constituted anything conspiratorial, of course, but whatever he might have said to others, there was no point trying to deceive himself. Some might even argue that what he was about to do was illegal, but he'd researched the question with some care, and he rather doubted that a court would have agreed. He might be wrong, but his own judgment was that his actions represented at best a gray area. After all, he *was* the Secretary of State. Any communication with a foreign government was his responsibility, and the exact way in which that communication was delivered was arguably a matter for his judgment.

Still, the fact was that Eloise Pritchart and he had discussed this particular note at length and agonized over its phrasing. The President obviously expected him to send it in the exact form to which they'd both finally agreed. Unfortunately, she hadn't given him any formal instruction to that effect, and—upon more mature consideration, based solely on his extensive experience with the Department of State and the Manticoran government and acting on his own authority as Secretary of State—he had identified a few small modifications which would make it far more effective.

Although, he admitted with a thin smile as he studied the revised text, the effect towards which it was directed might not be exactly the one the President had had in mind. . . .

CHAPTER FORTY-FOUR

Sir Edward Janacek had discovered that he no longer enjoyed going to work in the morning. He would never have believed that might come to pass when Michael Janvier first invited him to return to Admiralty House, but things had changed since that heady day of triumph.

He nodded to his yeoman and strode on into his inner office. His desk was waiting, and there in the middle of the blotter sat the locked dispatch case containing chips of the overnight communications. Like the trip to his office itself, that box had become something he dreaded, especially in light of the arrival of Eloise Pritchart's most recent missive the day before. He didn't really want to admit its existence, but he glanced at it as he started to walk past the desk towards the coffee carafe sitting in its accustomed place on the credenza. Then he stopped dead. A crimson light blinked on top of the dispatch case, and his stomach muscles tightened as it flashed at him.

Given the inevitable lags in communication time for units deployed over interstellar distances, there wasn't a great deal of sense in awakening senior members of the Admiralty when dispatches arrived in the middle of the night. Even if their contents were desperately important, getting them into the hands of their recipients an hour or two sooner wasn't going to have any significant effect on the turnaround time for a decision loop a dozen

629

light-years or so across. There were, of course, exceptions to that rule, especially for star nations which possessed wormhole junctions, and senior communications staffers were expected to recognize when those exceptions occurred. Except in those very special circumstances, however, the Admiralty's most senior echelons could anticipate a night's sleep unflawed by the precipitate delivery of bad news.

But that flashing light indicated that Simon Chakrabarti, as First Space Lord, had already read the overnight dispatches . . . and that in his opinion one of them was of special importance.

The First Space Lord had been becoming steadily more unhappy for months now. Janacek was prepared to accept his in-house expression of a certain degree of concern, of course. It was the First Space Lord's job to warn his civilian superiors of any worries he might entertain, after all. But Chakrabarti had gone beyond private discussions of concern or even verbal expressions of those same concerns in face-to-face meetings. He'd actually begun drafting formal memos whose arguments were becoming steadily more pointed, and he'd been following the message traffic—especially from Silesia—with what Janacek privately considered obsessive attentiveness.

As part of that attentiveness, he'd taken to recording marginal notes on the dispatches he found of particular concern. Which, Janacek thought as he watched the malignant, blinking red eye with a sort of dread fascination, was not something he wanted to deal with just now.

Unfortunately, as Pritchart's response to Elaine Descroix's most recent note had reminded the entire High Ridge Government, what he wanted didn't always bear a great deal of resemblance to what he was going to get.

He squared his shoulders, inhaled deeply, and marched across to the desk. He sank into his chair, scarcely noticing its comfort, and reached out to key the combination into the dispatch case lock plate. The combination of fingerprints, proper numerical code, and DNA tracers convinced it to open for him, and he pulled out the chip on top of the pile.

For just a moment, he felt an undeniable sense of relief, because it was in a Fleet message folio, not one with the flashings of the ONI. So at least it wasn't a fresh admission from Francis Jurgensen that that insufferable son-of-a-bitch Theisman had managed to deceive them as to his navy's combat capabilities after all. But that fleeting relief vanished as he read the header that identified it as a message from Sidemore Station.

Oh my God, he thought around the fresh sinking sensation in the pit of his stomach. *What's that lunatic done now?*

He drew another deep breath, slipped the chip into his desktop reader, and called up the message header.

"Just how bad is it, Edward?"

The Prime Minister's anxiety showed far more clearly than he wanted it to. Indeed, Janacek thought, it undoubtedly showed far more clearly than High Ridge thought it did. Not that the baron was alone in that, and the First Lord felt the echo of his own tension and strain coming back from the other members of the working cabinet. Aside from Janacek and High Ridge himself, that working cabinet currently consisted of Elaine Descroix, Countess New Kiev, Earl North Hollow, and Sir Harrison MacIntosh.

"That's very difficult to say," the First Lord replied. "I'm not trying to dodge the question, but all we have right now is Harrington's initial report about the Zoraster System incident itself. It will be at least a few days before we get anything more than that, I'd imagine. It would have taken at least that long for the Andies to respond to the incident—or to Harrington's message to their station commander in Sachsen. So any later report from her is going to be delayed at least that long before reaching here."

"But when those messages do get here," Marisa Turner pointed out anxiously, "the events in them will be over two weeks old. There's absolutely no way for us to tell how far Harrington may have pushed the Andies even as we sit here."

"Now, just a moment, Marisa," Janacek replied strongly. "Everyone in this room knows my opinion of 'the Salamander.' I'm not about to change it at this late date, either. But, much as I may distrust her judgment, in this instance she's certainly showed far more restraint than I would ever have anticipated."

He tapped the hardcopy of Harrington's report, where it lay on the conference table in front of him. An identical copy lay in front of each of them, and he wondered for a moment if New Kiev had even bothered to read hers.

"To be perfectly honest, my initial fear when I read her account of the incident was that she was likely to head for Sachsen cleared for action to demand satisfaction from Admiral Sternhafen. Instead, to my considerable surprise, she actually seems to be working actively to reduce tensions. Of course, there's no way to tell how Sternhafen reacted to her suggestion of a joint investigation, but the fact that she came up with the idea at all has to be taken as a good sign, I think."

"On the surface," she agreed. Then she shook her head and made a face. "No, you're right," she admitted. "It's just that I worry about her temper. Her first reaction has always seemed to be to resort to force immediately—or, at least, to meet force with greater force. I suppose it's just . . . difficult for me to conceive of her in the role of peacemaker."

"For you and me both," Janacek admitted. "Nonetheless, that does seem to have been her initial response, at least, in this case."

"If so," North Hollow observed acidly, "it's undoubtedly for the first time in her entire life!"

"I won't disagree with you there, Stefan," Janacek replied.

"But you say there's no way to predict how Sternhafen reacted to her proposal," High Ridge pressed, and Janacek shrugged.

"Obviously not. If this really was an accident, an unintended confrontation, then the man would have to be a bigger lunatic even than Harrington not to seize this opportunity to back off and cool things down. Of course, given the provocative behavior the Andies have been evincing out there, it's impossible to say whether or not it really was accidental. Admiral Jurgensen, Admiral Chakrabarti, and I, are currently inclined towards the view that it was unintended. If the Andies had intended to begin a war with us, then surely they would have done it by attacking more than a single, isolated heavy cruiser. Moreover, it seems fairly evident that their ship took *Jessica Epps* by surprise. Whether that's the case or not, they'd at least managed to get into attack range well before *Jessica Epps* initially ordered this suspected slave ship to heave to. What that suggests to us, is that the Andies didn't go into this looking for a fight. If that had been their objective, then it's virtually certain that they would have fired sooner—probably before *Jessica Epps* even knew they were there."

"So you think they were responding to our effort to intercept this slaver, this *Sittich*," Elaine Descroix said.

"It certainly looks that way," Janacek agreed. "Precisely why they responded the way they did is more than we can say at this point.

If Harrington's report's conclusions about the ship and the tonnage discrepancy our shipping list information indicated are correct, then I have to say I'm baffled by the Andy captain's actions. We may not get along with the Andermani all that well, but as far as we've been able to tell, they don't especially care for the slave trade, either. They don't have the long-term standing commitment to its suppression which the Star Kingdom's had, but they've certainly acted promptly to stamp on it whenever it's reared its head in their backyard."

"And very properly so," New Kiev put in. "But as you say, Edward, given that history of theirs, then surely their captain should have acted to assist *Jessica Epps*, not fired on her!"

"I believe that's approximately what I just said, Marisa," Janacek observed.

"I realize that," she said a bit snippily. "My point was that perhaps his reaction suggests that Harrington's suspicions about this particular ship weren't as well founded as she believes. Or, at least, as her report suggests."

"The same thought had occurred to me," Janacek replied. "But Admiral Jurgensen pulled the central file copy of the real *Sittich*'s emissions fingerprint and compared it to the sensor data from *Chantilly*." He shook his head. "There's no question, Marisa—the ship squawking *Sittich*'s transponder code wasn't *Sittich*. I can't say for certain who she was, but she wasn't who she claimed to be."

"I must say," Descroix observed, "that I'm afraid Harrington may have put us all in a false position with this quixotic crusade of hers."

"What 'quixotic crusade'?" New Kiev asked.

"This 'Operation Wilberforce' of hers," Descroix said.

"I may question her judgment and temper, and even at times her motivation," New Kiev said sharply, "but I hardly think it's appropriate to call the Star Kingdom's long-standing commitment to the suppression of the interstellar genetic slave trade a 'quixotic crusade.'"

Descroix glared at her and opened her mouth to fire back, but High Ridge interrupted before she could.

"Marisa, no one is suggesting that we ought to abandon that policy. For that matter, no one is suggesting that it was inappropriate for Harrington to act in accordance with it."

And we're especially not going to suggest it, he reflected, *with that maniac Montaigne holding our feet—and yours—to the fire over the entire slavery issue in the Commons!*

"Nonetheless, Elaine may have a point. Obviously, this entire incident only occurred because Harrington decided to act on the basis of testimony from a criminal caught in the act of committing an offense punishable by death. I think one might arguably call it a 'quixotic' decision to act so precipitously on the basis of such legitimately questionable 'evidence.'"

Janacek started to point out that, questionable or not, the fact that the suspected ship obviously had been squawking exactly the false transponder code Harrington's informant had told her it would seemed to suggest the evidence had been sound. But he didn't. Whether she'd acted precipitously or not was really beside the point, after all.

"So, Edward," High Ridge said after a moment, when it became apparent that neither New Kiev nor Descroix was prepared to continue their confrontation, however sullen they might be about it, "what does the Admiralty suggest we do?"

"Nothing," Janacek said with a promptness which caused the others to look at him sharply.

"Nothing?" High Ridge repeated.

"Until we know more, there's no point trying to formulate a response," Janacek said. "We could respond by immediately scraping up additional reinforcements and rushing them off to Sidemore. Unfortunately, we don't know that those reinforcements are going to be required. My current feeling is that Sternhafen is very likely to take the out Harrington has offered him and agree to a joint investigation. If that is his decision—or, more probably, given the time lag in our communications, *was* his decision—then it's probable that this particular crisis is well along the way towards being defused.

"If, on the other hand, he's decided not to take her suggestion, then all of the data ONI has amassed on Andermani deployment patterns suggests that it will take some time, probably at least a couple of months, for the IAN to redeploy for offensive operations against Sidemore. They can probably push her back from the systems we've been patrolling in the Confederacy itself, but the Fleet base is a much tougher nut than that. Even with the delay in communications between here and there, we should know within no more than another week or so whether or not he decided to go along with her. At that point, we can think seriously about sending additional forces to Sidemore."

Assuming, he carefully didn't add, *that we haven't found out we need them much worse closer to home.*

"So you think we'd have enough time to respond?" High Ridge pressed.

"That's the consensus at Admiralty House," Janacek assured him . . . almost accurately. In fact, Admiral Chakrabarti was far from agreeing. His steadily growing concern over how thinly spread the Navy's assets had become in the face of its commitments had only been made sharper by Harrington's news. But there was no point bringing that up just now.

"In that case," the Prime Minister decided, "I think we should draft fresh instructions for her to restrain her martial instincts and continue her efforts to keep a lid on the situation. To be completely honest, I must confess that at this moment the situation in Silesia is clearly of secondary concern. In the end, we could afford to simply let the Andermani have the entire Confederacy without suffering any irreparable damage to our interests. Even our commercial interests would survive with only minor losses, especially in light of the offsetting access we've just gained to the Talbott Cluster and the shipping lanes on that side of the League."

"I agree," Descroix said decisively. "And if that's settled, I suggest we turn our attention to a matter of *primary* concern."

No one needed to ask which matter she had in mind.

"Very well," High Ridge agreed. "Would you care to open the discussion, then, Elaine?"

"If you want." Descroix folded her hands on the document holder in front of her and looked around the conference room.

"My staff has completed its analysis of Pritchart's latest note," she announced. "Needless to say, the distracting effect of Harrington's report from Silesia has scarcely helped, but I set up three separate teams to evaluate it. After they'd finished their initial work, I had all three reports combined for final analysis by a fourth study group.

"The conclusion those analysts have reached is that this note represents an effort to set up the moral justification to support its threat to break off negotiations if we don't accede immediately to their demands."

Complete silence greeted her announcement. It was the heavy silence of gloom, not the silence of shock, because everyone in that conference room had already guessed what the "experts" were going to tell them.

"What do you think they'll do after they break off negotiations—assuming, of course, that that's what they actually intend to do?" New Kiev asked.

"If they break off negotiations for a peace treaty, Marisa," Descroix replied with an edge of exasperation, "they really only have one choice, don't they?"

"You think they'd actually resume operations," New Kiev said, sufficiently focused in her anxiety that she failed to take umbrage at the Foreign Secretary's tone.

"I think that's the only alternative to talking to us they really have," Descroix responded in an unwontedly serious tone, forgetting, however briefly, her antipathy for the Chancellor of the Exchequer in light of her own worries.

"But you've assured us that they don't have the technical capability to fight us, Edward," New Kiev said, turning to Janacek.

"What I've said," the First Lord said, cursing mentally as the countess put her finger on what, whether he'd cared to admit it or not, had always been the most problematical aspect of ONI's estimates of the Havenite navy's capabilities, "was that all available intelligence data suggested to us that their technology remains significantly inferior to our own. In fact, that's what our latest information still indicates. Unfortunately, the fact that we believe that to be true—or even the fact that it actually *is* true—doesn't necessarily mean Theisman and his advisers agree with us. It could be that they're overestimating their own capabilities, or *under*estimating ours. In either of those cases, they may be advising their civilian authorities that they do have the capacity to successfully resume operations against us."

"And if they do?" New Kiev pressed.

"If they do," Janacek admitted unwillingly, "they'll hurt us. Mind you, Admiral Chakrabarti and ONI remain confident that we would defeat them in the end, whatever they may believe they might accomplish. But defeating them won't be as easy as it was during Operation Buttercup, and the casualties and ship losses will almost certainly be significantly higher."

"That's terrible," New Kiev said softly. Which, Janacek reflected, was probably one of the most superfluous things even she'd ever said.

"It certainly is," Descroix said. "If they're stupid enough to do something that suicidal, public opinion here at home will never understand that it's not our fault they chose to commit suicide. All the public will see it is that the war has started all over again. The Centrists and Crown Loyalists will eat it up with a spoon!"

"I hardly think public opinion should be our greatest concern just now, Elaine!" New Kiev half-snapped. "From what Edward's just said, we can anticipate heavy casualties—thousands of them!"

"I'm scarcely overlooking that aspect of it, Marisa," Descroix shot back. "But if Pritchart and her advisers choose to attack us, the blood of every one of those casualties will be on her hands, not ours! In the end, I'm sure history will bear out that verdict. But in the meantime, we have to be concerned with our ability to continue to govern effectively in the face of such a crisis."

She glared at New Kiev, who returned her fiery stare with interest, and High Ridge frowned thunderously. The last thing he needed was for the members of his Cabinet to turn on one another. As Descroix said, the ability of the Government to continue to function effectively in the face of a possible Havenite attack was crucial. And, in the longer run, none of the members of his coalition could afford to quarrel with one another if they were to have any hope of surviving the disastrous political consequences of such an attack.

"Please, Marisa, Elaine!" He shook his head. "Both of you have voiced perfectly legitimate concerns. Marisa, all of us feel horrible over the possibility of heavy loss of life among our naval personnel. Of course we do! And we'll do everything we can to minimize casualties. But if we suffer them anyway, it will be because someone else forced military action upon us, not because *we* chose to go back to war. And that means Elaine is also correct that our primary responsibility as the leaders of Her Majesty's Government in the face of such an attack must be to insure the smooth continuation of our ability to govern."

And, he decided not to add, *to somehow salvage our domestic position out of the wreckage a Havenite attack would leave.*

"There is one possibility we haven't considered," Janacek said slowly.

"What sort of possibility?" New Kiev asked, eyeing him suspiciously.

"Before I answer that," the First Lord replied, "let me ask you a question, Marisa. Given the tone and the content of Pritchart's note, do you personally think she's seriously contemplating breaking off negotiations and not just running some sort of bluff?"

"I'm not Foreign Secretary anymore," New Kiev pointed out, sparing Descroix a poisonous glance from the corners of her eyes. "I don't have the sort of sources which might allow me to form any sort of independent judgment of the analysis Elaine's staff has prepared."

"Please, Marisa," Janacek said with a patience he maintained only with difficulty. "The situation is obviously too serious for us to dance around the point. You've read Pritchart's note. And, as you just pointed out, you used to be Foreign Secretary yourself. On that basis, how would *you* have evaluated this note?"

New Kiev frowned, clearly unhappy at being put on the spot. But then, slowly, she shook her head.

"I'm afraid I do think this is nothing more than a step to justify her actions in the eyes of her own public—and, probably, interstellar public opinion—when she chooses to break off negotiations," she admitted.

"The language is far more uncompromising than anything she's said yet," the countess continued, still blissfully ignorant of the exact wording of the preceding communication from the Republic's president, "and the flat, unqualified assertion that the Republic retains unimpaired sovereignty over *all* 'occupied systems' could be read to include Trevor's Star. If it does, that represents an enormous escalation in their bargaining position, especially after her earlier apparent willingness to concede that system's loss. And the fact that she's seen fit to recite an entire catalog of allegations that we've been the ones obstructing the talks is a clear bid to convince her own voters that she's been driven to take such an adamant position by our own unreasonableness."

She gave Descroix another smoldering glance, but obviously restrained herself from adding an "I told you so" to her analysis. Then she looked back at Janacek.

"Was that what you wanted to hear?" she asked harshly.

"Not what I wanted to hear, no," Janacek replied. "But that doesn't mean it isn't what I expected. And the reason I asked you is that I agree with Elaine; if they choose to break off negotiations, that decision is tantamount to a decision to resume active operations. In other words, if they've decided to stop talking to us, they've also decided to start shooting at us again. Would you agree that that's a reasonable conclusion?"

"I don't think I'd apply the word 'reasonable' to anything that's going to unnecessarily cost so many lives," New Kiev said unhappily.

"I understand your position, but you're still avoiding my point. Technically, we're still at war with them, you know. Pritchart wouldn't even need a declaration of war. All she'd need would be to decide, as commander in chief of their military, to resume operations. Wouldn't you agree that it looks very much as if that's what she's decided to do here?"

"I don't—" New Kiev began, then stopped and visibly bit her tongue. "All right, Edward," she sighed. "I don't like your conclusions, but, yes. I'm afraid I'd have to agree that that's precisely what a decision to terminate negotiations *could* amount to in practical terms."

"I see we're in agreement, then," Janacek said. "I won't say I'm happy we are, because I'd rather not be faced with the situation at all. But since we are in agreement, I would further submit to you that if they've decided to resume operations, it's our responsibility to prevent those operations from succeeding."

He raised an eyebrow and held New Kiev with his eyes until she nodded, then shrugged.

"Well, the only way to do that is to . . . remove their ability to attack us."

"And exactly what sort of black magic do you intend to use to do that?" New Kiev asked skeptically.

"Not black magic," Janacek demurred. "Just Her Majesty's Navy."

"What do you mean?" High Ridge asked, leaning forward across the table and regarding the First Lord through narrowed eyes.

"I mean exactly what you think I do, Michael," Janacek said flatly. "I've pointed out once before that if we know they're going to attack us, the logical thing for us to do is attack them first. If ONI's right, the bulk of their new fleet is still concentrated in the Haven System. If we act quickly and decisively, a preemptive strike by our own SD(P)s and CLACs would destroy or at least decisively cripple their modern combat capability. In which case, they'd have no choice but to return to the negotiating table whether they want to or not."

New Kiev stared at him in horror, which was hardly unexpected.

Descroix looked suddenly thoughtful, as did Stefan Young, but MacIntosh's expression had gone completely blank. Janacek felt the consternation his proposal had generated, but he'd anticipated exactly that reaction, and so he simply sat there, looking reasonable and confident.

"You're actually suggesting," the Prime Minister said slowly, "that we break off negotiations ourselves and attack the Haven System?"

"Not precisely, no," Janacek disagreed. "First, I'm certainly not proposing that we formally break off negotiations. It's obvious they intend to do that anyway, and our formal withdrawal from the conference would only alert them to our own plans. I believe the tone and wording of Pritchart's note should make it clear to any impartial reader that she intends to withdraw from the talks and attack *us*, so I believe we would be completely justified in carrying out the strike without formally terminating negotiations first. Afterward, we could publish the diplomatic correspondence in order to show the voters the fashion in which our hand was forced.

"Second," he continued, rolling forward over the increasing horror on New Kiev's face, "I'm not suggesting that we attack 'the Haven System' at all. I'm suggesting we attack Theisman's new fleet, which simply happens to be located in the Haven System at this time. Our objective would be the destruction of the ships which have destabilized the negotiating process, and we would scrupulously avoid any other targets in the course of our attack." He shrugged. "Given the circumstances, I hardly see how any fairminded observer could question the propriety of our actions."

It was obvious that New Kiev wanted to protest his reasoning, but she seemed temporarily bereft of speech. She could only stare at him, as if even now she couldn't quite believe what she'd heard. Then she turned a look of raw appeal on High Ridge, and the Prime Minister cleared his throat.

"I'm not certain the public—or the galaxy at-large—would appreciate the fine distinction between attacking the Haven System and attacking a fleet which 'simply happens' to be located there, Edward," he said carefully. "Leaving that aside, however, I think your suggestion may overestimate the . . . sophistication of the average voter's appreciation for the realities of interstellar diplomacy. While it's obvious to us that Pritchart is the one determined to derail the negotiating process if we don't supinely concede her completely unreasonable demands, it may be a bit difficult to convince the man in the street of that."

"Michael," Janacek replied patiently, "look at her note."

He opened the document folder before him and turned to the final page of Pritchart's note.

"It says, and I quote, 'In light of the Star Kingdom of Manticore's persistent refusal to accept even in principle the legitimacy of a single one of the Republic of Haven's attempts to formulate some basis for agreement, and in light of the Manticoran government's complete and unreasonable rejection of all assertions of the Republic's legitimate sovereignty over its occupied territory and its responsibilities to its citizens living under Manticoran occupation, these so-called peace negotiations have become not simply a farce but the laughingstock of an entire sector. Under the circumstances, the Republic of Haven seriously doubts that there remains any point in attempting the futile task of breathing life back into a negotiating process which the Star Kingdom of Manticore has systematically throttled from the outset.' "

He looked back up from the sheet of paper and shrugged.

"That seems explicit enough to me," he observed mildly.

"Expressing doubt about the viability of negotiations is scarcely the same as actively withdrawing from them," High Ridge pointed out. "Or that, at least, is the position someone like William Alexander or his brother will certainly take. And let's face it, Edward—when they make that argument, the typical voter is going to agree with them."

"Then the typical voter will be wrong," Janacek said flatly.

"Wrong or right doesn't really come into it," High Ridge said patiently. "Public perceptions do. No, Edward. I appreciate the courage it took to make your recommendation, but this Government can't possibly contemplate such a preemptive strike at this time."

"You're the Prime Minister," Janacek said after a moment of pregnant silence. "If that's your decision, then, of course, I have no option but to abide by it. I'd like to state once again for the record, however, that I believe the strategy I've just outlined represents the Star Kingdom's best opportunity of nipping this new war in the bud."

And you've gotten that viewpoint on record to cover yourself if that war breaks out after all, High Ridge reflected. *That's a bit more sophisticated than I expected out of you, Edward.*

"Your position will certainly be noted," he said aloud.

"But in the meantime," New Kiev said, making no effort to keep her enormous relief out of her voice, "we still have to decide what sort of response we're going to make to Pritchart."

"My initial reaction," Descroix growled, "is to tell her we refuse to negotiate at all in the face of such a blatantly implicit threat!"

"If we tell them that, we only confirm their accusations that we're the ones who have sabotaged the peace process!" New Kiev snapped.

"And if we don't, then we cave in," Descroix shot back. "Do you think there'd be any serious chance of ever resuming talks successfully if we just roll over and let them get away with talking to us this way?"

"Talking is always preferable to killing people," New Kiev said icily.

"That depends on who you're talking about killing, doesn't it?" Descroix snarled, glaring at the Chancellor of the Exchequer in a way which left very little doubt about who she would have preferred to nominate for victim. New Kiev's face darkened with fury, but once again High Ridge hastily pushed himself between the two of them.

"We're not achieving anything by snapping at each other!" he pointed out sharply.

Descroix and New Kiev clamped their jaws and looked away from one another in almost perfect unison, and the temperature in the conference room slipped back a notch or two from the point of explosion.

"Thank you," the Prime Minister said into the ringing silence. "Now, I agree with you, Elaine, that we can't allow the provocative language of this note to pass unremarked. But I also agree with Marisa that breaking off the negotiations ourselves is unacceptable. Not only is talking preferable to shooting, but we cannot afford to be labeled with responsibility as the party which finally withdrew from the peace process, no matter what provocation was offered by the other side.

"I see no way we could possibly agree to meet all of Pritchart's demands, particularly her outrageous insistence at this late date that the Republic retains unimpaired sovereignty over Trevor's Star, and that we're obligated to return it to Republican control. In light of that, and coupled with the fact that it would be completely politically unacceptable for us to be the first party to withdraw from the talks, I suggest that our best response is to rebuke her for her language, adamantly refuse to negotiate under pressure, but suggest that it's clearly time for some new initiative to break the logjam of frustration and ill will which has grown up between our two governments. Rather than attempting to specify just what that initiative might be, I think it would be wiser to leave it essentially undefined so as not to foreclose any possibilities."

New Kiev sat back in her chair, visibly unhappy. Had her mood been light enough to allow for such observations, she might have reflected that at least Descroix looked almost as unhappy as she was.

"I don't really like it," the countess said finally. "I can't avoid the feeling that we're still being too confrontational. I've argued from the beginning that we've been overly cavalier in rejecting Republican proposals that—"

She cut herself off and shook her head sharply.

"I'm sorry," she said almost curtly. "I didn't mean to rehash old arguments. What I *meant* to say, Michael, is that while I don't like it, I also don't see that we really have any other choice. As you say, it would be impossible to give her everything she's insisting upon. I feel we'll have to make that very clear in our response. But by the same token, leaving the door open will exert pressure on her to return to the table with a more reasonable attitude. And if she refuses to do so, then the onus will have been placed firmly where it belongs—on the Republic."

Despite his own anxiety, his sense that the situation was spinning further and further out of control, High Ridge felt a brief, bleak amusement at the countess' ability to evade what had to be evaded in the name of political expediency.

For himself, he conceded, his proposal was uncomfortably close to a council of despair. He doubted very much that the woman who'd composed that belligerent, exasperated note was prepared to put up with still more diplomatic sleight of hand. But for the backing of the naval strength Theisman had somehow managed to assemble without that idiot Jurgensen realizing he was doing it, she would have had no option but to continue to dance to his and Descroix's piping. Now, unfortunately, she thought she did have an option, and even if Janacek was right about the miscalculations on which she based that belief, she seemed oblivious to the possibility. Which meant she was just likely to rely upon it.

No. Whatever face he chose to put upon it for the rest of the Cabinet, High Ridge was well aware that his proposed response was actually a concession of weakness. All he could realistically hope to do at this point was to spin things out just a little longer. Long enough for Janacek's belated resumption of the Navy's building programs to produce a few new ships. Or, failing that, at least long enough for Pritchart to clearly and obviously become the aggressor in the wake of his own offers of "reasonable" compromise.

Neither of those things, he admitted to himself behind the mask of his outwardly confident features, was really likely. But his only alternatives were to play for the possibility, however remote, that he could pull one of them off or else to simply surrender everything he'd spent the last forty-six T-months trying to achieve.

He couldn't do that. Even running the very real risk of slipping back over into a brief, bloody clash with the Republic was better than that. Nor could he allow anything to divert his attention or his resources from the looming confrontation with Pritchart. Everything must be focused at the critical point, including the full resources of the Navy. Which meant all other problems, including whatever was happening in Silesia, must be relegated to a secondary or even tertiary level of priority. So people like Duchess Harrington were simply going to have to get by as best they could with the resources they already possessed, because Michael Janvier, Baron High Ridge, Prime Minister of the Star Kingdom of Manticore, refused to surrender without a fight.

CHAPTER FORTY-FIVE

"**T**he exec needs you on the bridge, Skipper."

Thomas Bachfisch laid his cards facedown on the card table and swung his chair to face the rating who'd just poked his head through the hatch into the officers' lounge.

"Did he say why?" the captain asked.

"Yes, Sir. One of those Peep destroyers is up to something."

"Is it?" Bachfisch made his voice sound completely calm and glanced back at his partner and their opponents.

"I'd better go take a look," he told them, and nodded to Lieutenant Hairston. "Make sure they don't cheat when they add up the score, Roberta. We'll finish trouncing them later."

"If you say so, Skip," Hairston said, looking dubiously at the score sheet.

"I do," he assured her firmly, then stood and headed for the hatch.

Jinchu Gruber looked up from *Pirate's Bane*'s main tactical display as Bachfisch arrived on the armed freighter's bridge. The plot was less detailed than it might have been, since the *Bane* had no interest in advertising her full capabilities. All of the data displayed on it had been collected using solely passive sensors, but that was quite adequate for Bachfisch's purposes. Especially this close to the object of his interest.

"What's happening, Jinchu?" he asked quietly as he crossed to the exec's side.

"I'm not really sure, Skipper," Gruber replied in a tone which made the simple statement answer at least half a dozen questions. Like "Why do you think we're so interested in a pair of Havenite destroyers?" or "Why do you think we've sat here in orbit for the last four days, piling up penalty fees for late delivery?" or "What in the galaxy do you think is going on in your captain's putative mind?"

Bachfisch's lips hovered on the edge of a smile as the thought passed through his brain, but it was a fleeting one.

"One of them is staying exactly where she's been ever since we got here," Gruber continued. "But the other one is headed out-system."

"She is, is she?" Bachfisch moved a bit closer to the exec and gazed down at the tac plot himself. The bright icon representing one of the Havenite tin cans was, indeed, headed for the hyper limit at a leisurely hundred gravities of acceleration. He watched it for a few seconds, then looked up and met Gruber's eye.

"I think it's time we were getting underway, Jinchu," he said calmly. "Take us out of orbit and put us on a heading of—" he glanced back down at the plot again "—one-zero-seven two-three-niner at one hundred gees."

Gruber looked back at him for perhaps three seconds, then nodded.

"Yes, Sir," he said, and turned from the tactical section towards the helmsman.

Bachfisch tipped back comfortably in his command chair, crossed his legs, and contemplated the spectacular beauty of the main visual display. *Pirate's Bane* rode the tangled force lines of a grav wave, sliding through hyper-space on the wings of her Warshawski sails. The huge disks of focused gravity stress radiated outward for the better part of three hundred kilometers at either end of her hull. They glowed and flickered with an ever-shifting pattern of gorgeous radiance in an almost hypnotic rhythm which never ceased to amaze and humble him.

This time, however, his attention wasn't on the vision before him. It was on something else entirely, something he couldn't see at all . . . unless he looked back at his tactical repeater.

The Havenite destroyer loped steadily onward with the lean, greyhound grace of her breed, apparently oblivious to the cart horse of a freighter rumbling stolidly along behind her. It was unlikely that she was genuinely unaware of *Pirate's Bane*'s presence. On the other hand, grav waves were the broad, gleaming highways of the ships which plied the depths of hyper-space. Given the sheer immensity of the universe, it was unusual for two ships not actively in company to find themselves within sensor range of one another even in a grav wave, but it was scarcely unheard of. After all, if two ships were headed in the same direction, they were bound to chart their courses to use the same grav waves. And some freighter skippers made it a point to ride the coattails of a transiting warship, whatever navy it belonged to, as a way to acquire a sort of jury-rigged escort through dangerous space.

If the destroyer had noticed *Pirate's Bane* behind her, she might be wondering where the freighter was bound. Which was fair enough, since Bachfisch was busy wondering where *she* might be bound. For that matter, he'd felt a lively curiosity about her and her sistership from the moment the *Bane* made port in the Horus System. Havenite warships had always been rare in Silesia. Most of those currently in the Confederacy, unfortunately, were crewed by fugitives who had turned to an unauthorized life of crime now that the officially approved brigandage which StateSec had waged against the People's Republic's own citizens had come to a screeching halt.

But those outlawed vessels wouldn't normally have been found in a system like Horus. Unlike altogether too many other star systems in the Saginaw Sector, Horus had that rarest of Silesian phenomena: an honest system governor. The sector had enjoyed more than its share (even for Silesia) of corrupt and venal sector governors, and the current holder of that office was no exception to the rule. But Horus had lucked out somehow in the man sent to administer its internal affairs. Pirates, smugglers, and slavers found a most unpleasant welcome in Governor Zelazney's jurisdiction. Besides, these two ships—obviously operating in company—were much too new to be pirates. Neither of them could have been more than one or two T-years old, at most, which meant they'd been launched and commissioned only after Thomas Theisman overthrew the Committee of Public Safety.

So what were a pair of brand spanking new destroyers of the

Republican Navy doing in a parking orbit around the planet of Osiris?

Fortunately, Bachfisch had excellent contacts in Horus. None of them had been able to answer his question for him, but they'd been able to tell him that the Havenite tin cans had arrived less than three days before *Pirate's Bane*. And they'd also been able to point out to him that because of its reputation as a law-abiding star system, Horus was one of the handful of Confed systems which boasted a Havenite trade legation and diplomatic mission.

To Bachfisch's naturally suspicious mind, there had to be a connection between the existence of that diplomatic mission and the presence of the two destroyers. Given the fact that the destroyers in question seemed to be doing absolutely nothing beyond orbiting the planet, he'd come to the conclusion that he must be looking at some sort of communications rendezvous. But that raised another interesting question. Why in the world would the Republican Navy, which everyone knew was girding for a possible confrontation with the RMN closer to home, be wasting a pair of modern destroyers as courier vessels rather than using a normal, unarmed, and much cheaper dispatch boat?

He hadn't been able to come up with an answer for that question, but he'd had an unpleasant suspicion that if he had been able to, he wouldn't have liked the explanation. Still, that hadn't meant he wasn't determined to discover what was going on if he possibly could, which was why *Pirate's Bane* had diverted from her planned course and schedule.

Thomas Bachfisch was fully aware that Gruber wasn't the only member of *Pirate's Bane*'s company who wondered what in hell their captain was playing at. All of them knew where the ship was supposed to be by now, just as they were aware of the astronomical late delivery penalties Bachfisch was busy piling up for himself. And most of them had to be at least a little leery of getting themselves involved with warships of foreign powers—especially of foreign powers so recently at war with their captain's birth nation.

Yet not a one of them had questioned him. They might not have a clue about what he was up to, but they were obviously prepared to go along with him even in the absence of any explanation.

He looked up as someone walked by his command chair. It was Gruber, and Bachfisch smiled and beckoned for his executive officer to step a little closer.

"Yes, Skipper?" Gruber said quietly.

"Where do you think this fellow is headed?" Bachfisch asked, waving a hand at the single icon glowing on the tactical repeater plot.

"I haven't got the faintest idea," Gruber admitted. "There are a lot of places he could be headed to out this way. The only problem is that I can't think of a single reason for a Peep to be going to any of them. Or not any reasons I'd like, anyway."

"Um." Bachfisch rubbed his chin for a few moments, then reached out and punched a command into the touchpad on the arm of his chair. The tactical repeater reconfigured to a navigational display, and he punched another key, shifting it from maneuvering to astrographic mode.

"Look here," he invited, and his index finger tapped the bright green line of the Havenite destroyer's projected course. Gruber leaned over the plot, and Bachfisch tapped the course line again.

"You pointed out that there were a lot of places he could be headed," the captain said. "But he started changing course about an hour ago, and on his new heading, there don't seem to be any."

"Skipper, he's got to be going somewhere," Gruber objected.

"Oh, he's going somewhere, all right. Only I don't think it's to any of the settled systems out here."

"What?" Gruber blinked, then looked up from the plot to meet his CO's eyes. "Why not? And where *do* you think he's headed?"

"First," Bachfisch said reasonably, "like you, I can't think of a single reason for a Havenite warship to be headed for any of the inhabited systems out this way. Second, he's angling steadily across this grav wave, heading roughly southwest. If he maintains his present course, he's going to separate from the wave in the middle of nowhere, Jinchu. He's not headed to pick up another wave, and according to our charts, there's not an inhabited system within a good seven or eight light-years of where he'll leave this one. Which suggests to me that he's probably headed right about here."

He tapped another light code on the display. It was the small red-orange starburst that indicated a K-class main sequence star, but it lacked the green circle which denoted an inhabited system, and no name appeared beside it. Instead, there was only a catalog number.

"Why do you think he should be headed there, Skipper?" Gruber asked intently.

"I could say it's because it lies within less than a light-year and a half of the point at which his projected course leaves the wave. But that's not really the question you're asking, is it Jinchu?"

He cocked an eyebrow at the exec, and, after a moment, Gruber nodded slowly.

"What I'm afraid of," Bachfisch said then, "is that he's headed there because he has friends waiting for him. Probably quite a lot of them."

"Peep naval units in the middle of Silesia camped out in an uninhabited star system?" Gruber shook his head. "I'm not quite ready to call you crazy, Skipper, but I'm damned if I can think of any reason for them to be doing something like that."

"I can think of one," Bachfisch said, and his voice was suddenly grim. "Horus is the only star system in the Saginaw Sector which has an official Havenite diplomatic mission. It also happens to lie on an almost direct line from the Basilisk terminus of the Wormhole Junction to the Sachsen Sector. And if you extend our destroyer's course from Horus to this star," he tapped the icon on his display yet again, "you'll see that it also forms a straight line . . . from Horus towards Marsh."

Gruber dropped his eyes to the plot and stared at it for several seconds, then looked back up at his captain.

"With all due respect, Skipper, that's crazy," he said. "You're suggesting that the Peeps have sent some sort of naval force clear from the Republic to the Confederacy and parked it in a star system in the middle of nowhere so they can attack Sidemore. Unless you're suggesting that they're out here to attack the *Andies* for some reason!"

"I can't see any reason for them to be picking a fight with the Andies right now, no," Bachfisch said. "And I admit that sending a big enough force out here to mount a credible attack on Duchess Harrington's forces at Sidemore would be a fairly lunatic act under any normal set of circumstances. But you've heard just as many rumors about the tension between the Star Kingdom and the Republic as I have, Jinchu. It's possible the new ships Theisman has been talking about really do exist. In fact, it's possible that there are more of them than he's chosen to tell us about.

"Now, if I were the Havenite Secretary of War, and I knew my government was getting sick and tired of being put continually on hold in its so-called peace negotiations with the Star Kingdom,

I might be thinking very seriously about my war plans. And if the Admiralty had been kind enough to send one of the Star Kingdom's better admirals out to a distant station, with only a handful of modern ships and a lot of obsolescent ones, then I might figure that it would be worth my while to send a much larger force of my own modern capital ships out here to pounce on her as part of a coordinated offensive against the Star Kingdom and the Manticoran Alliance."

"Skipper, are you seriously suggesting that the Peeps are not only planning to restart the war but looking to kick it off with some sort of sneak attack?" Gruber asked very quietly.

"Frankly," Bachfisch said grimly, "I've been surprised they didn't do it months ago. If I were President Pritchart or Thomas Theisman, I'd have been thinking about it very seriously for at least a T-year now."

Gruber's surprise showed, and Bachfisch chuckled harshly.

"Of course I would have, Jinchu! It's been obvious from the beginning that the High Ridge Government had no intention of negotiating seriously or fairly with them. Why in the world should they feel any compunction about kicking someone who totally ignores their own efforts to actually end this damned war and normalize relations in the ass? *I'd* do it in a heartbeat, assuming I had the capability, under the same circumstances, and I think they've been trying to get the Star Kingdom's attention in hopes that someone would listen without their resorting to brute force. Hell, when you come right down to it, they've done everything short of handing a copy of their war plans to High Ridge and Janacek! Why do you think Theisman announced their new fleet units?"

"To bring pressure to bear on the Star Kingdom," Gruber replied.

"Of course. But the kind of pressure they brought to bear is significant, too. I think in a lot of ways it amounted to a deliberate warning that they've developed the capacity to stand up to the Royal Navy. A warning they delivered in the forlorn hope that someone in Landing would be able to rub at least two brain cells together and realize the Star Kingdom has to start treating the Republic as a legitimate government and begin negotiating in good faith.

"Neither of which High Ridge has done."

"You sound almost as if you're on the Republic's side, Skipper," Gruber said slowly.

"I'm not. But that doesn't mean I can't recognize that they have a perfect right to be angry at having their legitimate concerns so persistently ignored."

"So what, exactly, do you think we're doing out here, Skipper?" Gruber asked after a moment.

"At the moment, all I'm really after is confirming the point at which this fellow is going to leave the grav wave. If we can get away with it, I'd really like to see the point at which he begins translating back down to n-space. That would confirm whether or not he's headed where I think he's headed. But I don't cherish any illusions about how likely they are to let an unidentified freighter go traipsing through the middle of their fleet if they really are out here. And given that the system I think this destroyer is bound for is officially uninhabited, I can't think of any possible way to come up with a convincing story for why we might 'just happen' to be dropping in on them."

"And if we manage to confirm all of that?"

"If we manage to confirm all of that—or even half of it— then we immediately make tracks for Sidemore," Bachfisch said. "I know the people who are expecting us to deliver their cargoes are going to be more than a little pissed off when we don't show. And I know we're going to be looking at some pretty stiff penalties. But I strongly suspect that Duchess Harrington will defray any of our losses out of her discretionary funds when she hears what we have to tell her. And she and her intelligence people can probably help us concoct some sort of explanation for our customers' benefit."

"I see." Gruber looked back down at the plot.

"I realize I'm taking a chance shadowing a destroyer," Bachfisch said softly. "And I suppose it's not fair to our people for me to be doing it in the interests of my own kingdom. None of them signed on to be Preston of the Spaceways. But I can't just sit there and watch something like this happen."

"I wouldn't worry about the people, Skipper," Gruber told him after a moment. "I don't say they're looking forward to any possible confrontations with the Peeps, but most of them have already figured out at least part of what you're up to. And the truth is, Skip, that if you figure this is what we need to be doing, we're all prepared to trust your judgment. You've gotten us into trouble a time or two, but you've always gotten us out the other side again."

He looked up, and Bachfisch nodded in satisfaction at what he saw in the exec's face.

"That bogey is closing up on us a little, Sir."

Lieutenant Commander Dumais, captain of the *Trojan*-class destroyer RHNS *Hecate*, cocked his head in an invitation for his tac officer to continue.

"I still can't tell you exactly what it is," Lieutenant Singleterry admitted. "Local h-space conditions are particularly bad just now. But it still looks like a merchie."

"A merchie," Dumais repeated, then shook his head. "I don't question your judgment, Stephanie, but just what in Hell do you think a merchie would be doing following us around this way? Using us for cover against pirates, sure. But following us out into the middle of nowhere?"

"If I could tell you that, Skipper, then I'd be wasting my time in the Navy compared to the fortune I could be making choosing winning lottery numbers." Singleterry shook her own head in turn. "All I can tell you for sure is that whoever this is, she's been following along behind us ever since we left Horus. Well, that and the fact that she's closed up by almost half a light-minute in the last six hours."

"Hmmm." Dumais frowned in thought. "You did say local sensor conditions are bad?"

"Yes, Sir. In fact, they pretty much suck, and they're getting worse. Particle count is way up, and that grav eddy at three o'clock is funneling them straight over us."

"In that case, I can think of two possible explanations for her behavior," Dumais said. "The one I like better is that she *is* riding our heels as cover against pirates and she wants to stay close enough to be sure we'll notice if anyone hits her."

"And the other one is that she's closing up to hold us on her own sensors?" Singleterry asked, then tugged at the lobe of her left ear as Dumais nodded. "I guess that might make sense. But that would suggest she really has been deliberately shadowing us."

"Yes, it would," Dumais agreed.

"Which brings me back to the question of why a merchant ship would be doing anything of the sort," Singleterry said.

"I suppose that one possibility is that she *isn't* a merchant ship, whatever she may look like," Dumais suggested.

"You think she might be a warship?"

"It's certainly possible. Play a few games with your nodes, and you can make a warship's impeller wedge or Warshawski sails look like a merchie's."

"A Manty?" Singleterry suggested unhappily.

"Possibly. On the other hand, it's more likely to be an Andie out here. For that matter, it could actually be a Silly. This is officially their territorial space, after all, even if everyone else seems inclined to forget that. One of them could have noticed us hanging around in Horus and gotten curious."

"I guess an Andie or a Silly would at least be better than a Manty," Singleterry said. "But either way, I don't think the Admiral is going to be very happy if there's anything to your suspicions."

"Tell me about it!" Dumais snorted. He gazed at his plot for several more seconds, frowning in thought.

Hecate would be transitioning from Warshawski sail to impeller wedge when she left the fringes of the grav wave in another three hours. At that point, she'd be within less than five and a half hours' flight time of her destination. And if that was a shadowing warship back there, then whoever she belonged to would have a very shrewd notion of where Dumais' ship was headed. Which meant that they'd have a very shrewd notion of where Second Fleet lay awaiting its orders from Nouveau Paris.

The lieutenant commander growled a silent mental curse. He'd worried about the decision to use his ship and her squadron mate *Hector* as Second Fleet's communications link with Ambassador Jackson in Horus from the moment he was assigned the duty. He understood the absolute necessity of making sure that link was secure, but it would have been a lot smarter to use a regular dispatch boat for the job. Unfortunately, whatever New Octagon genius had thought this one up had neglected to consider that possibility, and apparently no one there—or on Admiral Tourville's staff—had realized until Second Fleet reached Silesia that Ambassador Jackson didn't already have a dispatch vessel assigned to him.

Under the circumstances, the Admiral hadn't had any choice about making his own arrangements to cover the final leg of the communications link. And because he didn't have any dispatch boats of his own, he'd had to detach a couple of destroyers for the job.

The worst part of it was that Second Fleet had to be positive its communications were functioning properly. If the order to attack was sent from home, it *had* to get through. So Admiral Tourville had left not one, but two destroyers behind to ensure the maintenance of his communications with Ambassador Jackson. Two destroyers weren't going to be all that much more noticeable than one, and at least this way, the ambassador could use one ship to shuttle back and forth between Horus and Second Fleet, maintaining constant contact while keeping the other on station in Osiris orbit in case the actual attack order should come in.

Dumais wasn't at all sure what was in the sealed dispatches Jackson had instructed him to deliver to Admiral Tourville this time. Nothing the ambassador had said had given him any impression that they were truly vital, and he would really have preferred not to be sent off to play postman with some routine message. On the other hand, he supposed it did make sense to use his ship rather than risk hiring a commercially available dispatch boat and giving it the coordinates for Second Fleet's hiding place.

Which was how he found himself out here with that incredibly irritating sensor ghost dogging his heels.

"We don't have any idea of what his sensor capabilities might be, do we?" he asked Singleterry after a moment.

"Assuming he's hanging back at the very edge of his ability to hold us on his scanners," the tac officer replied, "I'd say that they aren't quite as good as ours are."

"Which would seem to suggest that there's a better chance it's a Silly than an Andy," Dumais mused aloud.

"Or," Singleterry countered, "that it's a merchie with a really good commercial-grade sensor suite. Given how risky a neighborhood this can be, a lot of the merchant ships that spend time out here have much better sensor packages than anything we'd see closer to home."

"Definitely a point to bear in mind," Dumais acknowledged. He thought for a few more moments, then grimaced.

"I don't think we can risk making any assumptions where this bird is concerned, Stephanie. I suppose it is still possible that it's pure coincidence that he's back there, but it strikes me as unlikely. And the one thing we can't do is lead anybody straight to the Fleet. Unfortunately, we're already close enough to the Fleet rendezvous that anyone with half a brain should be able to narrow the volume down without much difficulty. So we'd better go see who it is."

"What do we do if it turns out it is a warship?" Singleterry asked.

"If it's a warship, then it's a warship." Dumais sighed. "There's provision in the ops order for the Admiral to shift to another star system if he has to. We don't want to do it, because it's always possible that the jump off order could reach Horus before we got Ambassador Jackson and *Hector* informed as to the new rendezvous point. Unfortunately, if this is a warship, we won't have much choice, unless I want to risk creating a fresh interstellar incident by opening fire."

"Even if it's a Manty?" Singleterry asked in a deliberately expressionless voice, and Dumais grinned crookedly.

"*Especially* if it's a Manty," he replied. "Not that the Admiral would thank us if we shot up an Andie or a Silly, either. And," he added conscientiously, "let's not forget that we don't know what size this fellow is. If he's a heavy cruiser, or a battlecruiser, then it might just be a bit . . . foolhardy of us to cross swords with him, don't you think?"

"Oh, yes," Singleterry said fervently. "Foolhardy is exactly the word I'd choose, Sir, and I can't begin to tell you how happy I am to hear you using it under the circumstances!"

"I thought you might approve," Dumais said dryly.

"And if it turns out this really is a merchie?" Singleterry asked.

"In that case, our options are a little broader," Dumais pointed out. "First of all, a merchie isn't going to argue with a warship if it tells him to heave to and be boarded. Secondly, we could put a prize crew aboard her and hand her over to Admiral Tourville. He could hold her at the fleet rendezvous indefinitely, if he had to, and the assumption when she didn't turn up at her destination as scheduled would simply be that one of the pirates operating out here had picked her off. If we're ordered to carry out the attack, he can release her after the fact with an apology and probably a fairly stiff reparations payment from the Government."

"And if we're never ordered to attack?" Singleterry asked very quietly, and Dumais grimaced again. He knew what she was really asking, because their orders had made it crystal clear that if no attack was ever launched, then Second Fleet had never been here. Exactly what the Republican Navy might be expected to do with a merchant ship full of people who knew Second Fleet *had* been here wasn't something he really wanted to consider. Even so, he knew it would be far better for that to be a merchantman rather than a warship.

"We'll just have to cross that bridge when we come to it," he told his tac officer after a moment. "For right now, we have to concentrate on the matter at hand. If this turns out to be a merchie, we'll put enough of our people aboard to make sure everything stays under control and leave her right where she is while we take *Hecate* on to the rendezvous and report in to the Admiral. If he wants her brought the rest of the way in to him, we'll come back and get her. If he decides to shift the rendezvous, we'll come back, take our people off, apologize politely, and decamp." He shrugged. "It's not perfect, but it's the most flexible option we have, and the Admiral would expect us to show some initiative."

"It sounds to me like it should work, Skipper," Singleterry said thoughtfully.

"I hope so," Dumais said cheerfully. "Because if it doesn't, we're going to have a hell of a time explaining to the Admiral why we couldn't handle a single merchie!"

CHAPTER FORTY-SIX

Honor stepped back and allowed Commander Denby to climb to his feet. The commanding officer of *Werewolf*'s third LAC squadron was a little slower than he might have been under other conditions, and he shook his head like a man listening to a ringing sound no one else could hear.

He dropped back into a ready position, but Honor shook her own head and removed her mouth protector.

"Sorry about that, Commander," she said contritely. "Are you all right?"

Denby removed his own mouth protector and then rotated his right shoulder cautiously and gave her a lopsided grin.

"I think so, Your Grace," he replied. "I'll tell you for sure when that damned bird stops singing in my ear!"

Honor chuckled. She and the commander both wore traditional *gis*. Although Denby's belt showed only five rank knots, he was really very good . . . and like quite a few officers who followed the *coup*—perhaps somewhat disproportionately represented among the LAC portion of *Werewolf*'s complement—he was always available for a sparring match with the station commander.

Unfortunately, he'd forgotten about Honor's artificial arm. The move he'd just attempted had depended upon its victim's reaction to leverage against her elbow joint. Which hadn't worked out quite the way his reflexes had assumed it would in this particular case. Honor's counter had caught him out of position and completely by surprise, and he'd hit the mat hard. In fact, he'd hit it rather harder than she'd intended, because her reflexes hadn't assumed that he'd be left quite as open as he had by her left arm's failure to flex properly.

"Well," she said now, "we've got enough time for you to finish listening. Take your time."

"Thank you, Your Grace, but I think he's coming to the end of his selection."

Denby gave her another grin and reinserted his mouth protector, and she smiled back before she did the same thing. The two of them stepped back towards the center of the mat and dropped back into the ready position. Honor watched him warily. They'd sparred enough over the course of this deployment for her to have a very good feel for his personality. Even without her ability to sense his emotions, she would have known that his recent misadventure had inspired him to dump her on her very senior posterior. On the other hand, inspiration and success weren't necessarily the same thing, and—

"Excuse me, My Lady."

Andrew LaFollet's voice interrupted, and she stepped back from Denby and turned towards her senior armsman.

"I'm sorry to interrupt, My Lady," LaFollet said from where he'd stood watching her back, even here in *Werewolf*'s gym, and she removed the mouth protector once again.

"What is it, Andrew?" she asked.

"I don't know," he replied. "Lieutenant Meares just commed. He says you're needed on Flag Bridge."

"On Flag Bridge?" Honor repeated. "He didn't say why?"

"No, My Lady." LaFollet half-raised his wrist-mounted com. "I can com him back and ask, if you'd like?"

"Please do. And ask him how urgent it is." She waved one gloved hand at her *gi*. "Unless it's earth-shattering, I'd like to at least shower and change before I report for duty!"

"Yes, My Lady," LaFollet acknowledged with a small smile, and spoke into the wrist com. Then he looked up with the slightly absent expression of a man listening to a reply from her flag lieutenant over his unobtrusive earbug.

It was an expression which changed abruptly, and Honor's head snapped up as she tasted the surprise and apprehension in his emotions.

"What?" she asked sharply.

"Tim says *Pirate's Bane* just passed the perimeter patrols, My Lady," the armsman replied, using the flag lieutenant's first name instead of the more formal rank titles he was usually careful to employ out of deference to a young man's dignity. Now he met his Steadholder's eyes, and his expression was taut. "He says she's damaged—badly."

Honor stared at him for perhaps two breaths, her thoughts completely frozen. Then they jerked back into motion with an almost physical shock.

"*How* badly damaged?" The question came out crisply, but even as she asked it she was aware of how much a lie that calmness was. "And what about Captain Bachfisch?"

"Tim doesn't know exactly how bad it is, My Lady. But from what he said, it doesn't sound good." The armsman inhaled. "And it was her executive officer who answered the patrol's challenge. He says Captain Bachfisch has been wounded."

Honor held herself in her seat in the pinnace by sheer force of will. Nimitz was curled in her lap, and she felt the physical tension in his muscles as the pinnace cut its drive and *Pirate's Bane*'s boat bay tractors reached out for it.

She looked out through the armorplast viewport, and her jaw muscles clenched as she saw the ugly holes blown in the *Bane*'s skin. "Badly," she supposed was one way to describe what had happened to the armed merchantman. Personally, she considered it to be grossly inadequate.

The pinnace rolled on its internal gyros, aligning itself so the tractors could deposit it gently in the docking buffers. At least the bay gallery was still vacuum tight, she thought grimly as she watched the personnel tube run out to the pinnace's airlock. Bleak anger and anxiety roiled within her, and then she looked down as a hand-foot patted her on the knee.

<They said he'll be all right,> Nimitz's true-hands signed.

"No," she replied. "They told me that *he* said he'll be all right. There's a difference."

<He wouldn't lie. Not to you. Not about this.>

"Stinker," Honor sighed, "sometimes I think 'cats still have a lot to learn about humans. There may not be any point in empaths or telepaths trying to lie to each other, but we two-foots always think we get away with it. And when we don't want someone to worry . . ."

<I know. But still say wouldn't lie to you. Besides,> even through the 'cat's own anxiety, she tasted a sudden flicker of amusement, <he knows what you'd do to him when he got better if did.>

Honor looked down at him, and then, to her own amazement, she actually chuckled.

"You may have a point," she conceded. "On the other hand," she sobered again, "the fact that it was his exec who reported in doesn't sound good."

<Will know soon,> Nimitz signed back. <Green light.>

Honor flicked her eyes to the telltale above the airlock. Nimitz was right, and she scooped the 'cat into her arms and rose as the pinnace's flight engineer reached for the hatch button.

Others pushed up out of their seats behind her, and she glanced over her shoulder. LaFollet and Spencer Hawke sat in the row directly behind her, but there were enough others to make the pinnace's spacious passenger compartment seem almost crowded. Mercedes Brigham, George Reynolds, Andrea Jaruwalski, and Timothy Meares were all present . . . and so were Surgeon Captain Fritz Montoya and a full twenty-person medical team.

A second pinnace, this one loaded with two platoons of *Werewolf*'s Marines, settled into the docking buffers beside Honor's pinnace, and her expression tightened once more. Then she moved forward as the inner hatch of the airlock opened.

It wasn't the first time Honor had seen Thomas Bachfisch wounded. But this time was worse. Much worse. She felt the physical pain radiating from him as she stood beside his bed in *Pirate's Bane*'s spartan sick bay, and it took every ounce of self-discipline she possessed to keep her own nonphysical pain out of her expression.

"Your Grace," Jinchu Gruber said, "will you *please* convince him to let Doctor Montoya get him out of here?"

Pirate's Bane's executive officer stood on the other side of Bachfisch's bed. Gruber wasn't exactly in pristine condition himself, Honor noted. His left arm was in a sling, he walked with a noticeable limp, and the left side of his face was badly bruised.

"Stop fussing, Jinchu." Bachfisch's voice was hoarse with pain, but he managed a tight smile. There was a different sort of pain in that smile, and something inside Honor winced as she tasted his emotions. "I'm better off than a lot of people."

"Yes, you are, Skipper." Gruber's voice was harsh, hard-edged with exasperation. "Now stop feeling guilty about it, damn it!"

"My fault," Bachfisch replied, shaking his head doggedly on the pillow.

"I didn't see you holding a pulser on anyone to make us sign on," the exec shot back.

"No, but—"

"Excuse me, Your Grace," Fritz Montoya put in, "but I'd appreciate it if the three of you could argue about this later." Honor turned to crook one eyebrow at the doctor, and Montoya shrugged. "I've already sent the worst half dozen cases across to *Werewolf*. Or, perhaps I should say, the worst half dozen other cases. I'd really like to get Captain Bachfisch over there sometime this week, too."

"I'm not leaving the *Bane*," Bachfisch said stubbornly.

"Oh yes you are, Captain," the blond-haired surgeon captain told him with an implacable calm Honor knew altogether too well from personal experience. "We can argue about it for a while first, if you really want to. But you are leaving."

Bachfisch opened his mouth, but before he could speak, Honor put one hand gently on his shoulder.

"Don't argue," she told him, resolutely not looking at the space where his legs ought to have tented the sheets. "You'll lose. For that matter, you'd lose even if Fritz was the only person who was going to be arguing with you. And he isn't."

Bachfisch looked back up at her for a moment, and then smiled crookedly.

"You always were a stubborn woman," he murmured. "All right, I'll go. But since you're here now . . ." He looked past her, indicating her staff officers with his eyes, and she nodded.

"I gathered from Commander Gruber's message that you were going to insist on a bedside debrief," she said serenely. "Now, if I were inclined to indulge in calling any kettles black, I might comment on the stubbornness involved in that. Since I'm far too broad-minded to do anything of the sort, however, why don't we just get started?"

Bachfisch's chuckle might have been tight with pain, but it was also genuine, and she tasted his gratitude for her manner.

"Commander Gruber," she waved at the exec, "already told us

about your decision to shadow the Peep—*Hecate*, wasn't it?" She glanced up at Gruber, who nodded, and Honor looked back down at her old captain. "He told us you'd decided to, but what he couldn't tell us was what the *hell* you thought you were doing?"

Bachfisch's eyebrows flew up, and Honor tasted the surprise of all of her officers at hearing even that mild an oath out of her, but she never took her own eyes from Bachfisch's. She was willing to be calm and collected about his state, but she wanted him to cherish no illusions about her opinion of the sanity involved in getting himself and his ship mixed up in something like this.

"What I thought I was doing," he told her after a moment, "was trying to figure out what a Havenite fleet might be doing in your bailiwick, young lady. And I might point out that I've been old enough to make decisions for myself for quite some time. Why, just last week I picked out which shirt I wanted to wear without any help at all."

Their eyes held, and then, almost against her will, she smiled.

"Point taken," she told him. "On the other hand, I'd appreciate it if you wouldn't try quite so hard to get yourself killed next time. You think we could compromise on that?"

"I'm certainly willing to take it under advisement," he assured her.

"Thank you. Now, getting back to business. You followed *Hecate* until she left the grav wave."

"Yes." Bachfisch leaned back against his pillow. "We hit a bad patch. Particle densities went way up, and I had to close up on her if I wanted to hold her on sensors. From what her survivors say, that was probably what drew her attention to us. At any rate, she was waiting when we transitioned to wedge."

"And she ordered you to stand by for boarding?"

"Yes." Bachfisch grimaced. "I wouldn't have been too crazy about that under the best of conditions, but out in the middle of nowhere, dealing with a Havenite warship, I *really* didn't want an armed boarding party to discover that the 'merchie' who'd been shadowing them was armed to the teeth. Besides, there wouldn't have been much point in following her if we'd just let ourselves be hauled off and incarcerated."

"Assuming they'd been willing to simply incarcerate you, Captain," Lieutenant Commander Reynolds put in quietly.

"That thought did occur to me, Commander." Bachfisch

grimaced again. "I know there's been a change of government in the People's Republic, but I'm inclined to take that with a grain of salt where the safety of my own people is concerned. Besides, if they're here covertly, it might be . . . inconvenient for them if witnesses to their presence ever turned up."

"I understand your concerns, Captain," Honor said. "And, in your place, I would have felt exactly the same way. But I strongly suspect that you and George are both doing whoever Thomas Theisman sent out here a disservice. Theisman isn't the sort of man to countenance atrocities or to send anyone who would countenance them off to an independent command. I speak from a certain degree of personal experience."

"You may be right," Bachfisch agreed. "But either way, I didn't want a Havenite boarding party aboard the *Bane.* If *Hecate* had been a pirate, it would have been easy enough. Just let them come in close to drop their pinnace, then run out the grasers and blow her to hell." He shrugged. "We've done that often enough.

"But this *wasn't* a pirate, and I didn't want to kill anyone I didn't have to. Maybe I was too squeamish. Or maybe I was just stupid. Anyway, I refused to be boarded."

"Was that when she opened fire?" Honor asked quietly when he paused.

"Yes and no," Bachfisch replied. Then he sighed. "She certainly did fire," he said. "The only problem is that I'm still not sure it wasn't intended solely as a warning shot to encourage us to cooperate. We were so close by that point that her captain may simply have chosen to use an energy mount instead of a missile, and the shot did miss. But it didn't miss by very much, and I didn't feel I could take a chance—not with a regular warship already in energy range. And besides," he admitted, "I was nervous as a cat." He shook his head. "At any rate, I jumped. I didn't pull the trigger, perhaps, but I did stop requesting him to stand clear and *ordered* him to. And I also ordered the plating over our weapons bays jettisoned."

"At which point," Gruber put in harshly, "they *definitely* opened the ball."

"Yes," Bachfisch agreed heavily. "Yes, they certainly did."

Honor gazed down at him and nodded slowly while her always excellent imagination showed her what must have happened in the instant that *Pirate's Bane* trained out her own grasers. There'd been no way the destroyer's captain could have guessed that he was accosting a ship which was actually more heavily armed than his own. He'd fired his warning shot—which, as Bachfisch had just suggested, was almost certainly what he'd done—in the belief that he was dealing with a typical, unarmed merchantman. The shock when he realized what he was actually facing, coupled with the way Bachfisch had followed him, must have been . . . profound.

"The entire 'engagement' lasted about twenty-seven seconds," Bachfisch said. "As nearly as I can determine, *Hecate* hadn't even cleared completely for action. Her people weren't even in skinsuits, and only four of their broadside laser mounts appear to have been manned. As soon as they saw our weapons, they opened fire with those four and blew the ever-living hell out of two of our main cargo holds, three of our starboard graser mounts, and our backup enviro plant. They also killed eleven of my people and wounded eighteen more."

"Nineteen," Gruber corrected grimly. Honor glanced at him, and he jabbed a finger at Bachfisch.

"Nineteen," Bachfisch conceded. Honor looked back towards him, and he twitched his shoulders. "Compared to some of the rest of my crew, I got off easy."

"We're not going to have that particular conversation, Captain," Honor told him firmly. "You and I have both been there before, and I'm not going to help you beat yourself up over it. Even," she added with a wry smile, "if this does seem to happen to both of us quite a bit out here in Silesia!"

Bachfisch blinked at her, then laughed out loud, and she smiled more naturally as she felt the cold, bleak knot of his guilt ease . . . for the moment, at least.

"At any rate," he went on more briskly, "they blew the crap out of us. But a destroyer isn't much better armored than a merchie, and they were wide open. I didn't even suspect just how wide open they were, but it was like pushing baby chicks into a pond, Honor. We fired a single broadside and—"

He broke off, shaking his head, and Honor tasted a brief, intense layer of a completely different sort of guilt. This time she didn't try to do anything about it. No one could have, anyway.

"We took her survivors aboard afterward," he said heavily. "There were only forty-three of them, and we lost two of them to wounds despite everything we could do. Then we came here."

"We have all forty-one of the remaining survivors in custody, Admiral," Gruber put in. Honor looked back up at him, and the exec shrugged. "The Captain told me to get to Marsh as quickly as we could to report to you, but it occurred to me on the way here that with everything else you already have going on, you don't need to be officially involved in an attack on a Havenite warship."

"I'd hardly call what you and the Captain have described an 'attack' on a warship," Honor observed.

"No, Your Grace," Gruber agreed. "But you're not the government that warship belonged to. At any rate, we're prepared to present the evidence of our own sensor logs before any admiralty court and to stand by an impartial verdict on our actions. At the moment, however, any court would be considering the actions of a Silesian-flag vessel holding a warrant as a Silesian Navy auxiliary merchant cruiser. As such, we could argue that we had a legitimate *Silesian* security interest in investigating *Hecate*'s actions and intentions. If we hand them over to the Manticoran authorities, however, we bring the Star Kingdom officially into all of this. From all we've heard out here about the current relations between the Star Kingdom and the Republic, I wasn't at all sure that would be a good idea."

"So he has them confined in the secure quarters I had fitted up for pirates," Bachfisch said, smiling approvingly at his executive officer. "They don't know where we are at the moment. In fact, they don't even know we're not still underway. So if you prefer, we can continue on to a Silly naval base and turn them over to 'proper authorities' there."

"I'm impressed, Commander Gruber," Honor said. "And I appreciate your forethought." She didn't add that she felt confident his forethought had been exercised more because of what he knew his captain would want than because he really cared all that much himself about relations between Manticore and Haven.

"All the same," she said thoughtfully, "I think handing them over to us would probably be the best course. We're the closest naval base to the point at which this action actually occurred. It would make sense for a ship as badly damaged as the *Bane* to head for the closest authorities, particularly since you have wounded from both ships' companies who need medical attention."

"But if we hand them over to you," Bachfisch pointed out, "then you have to take official cognizance of their presence, and you have enough hand grenades to juggle just now without that."

"Yes, I have to take 'official cognizance,'" she agreed. "On the other hand, the way I do that is up to me. I think I'll just hold these people here until my own medical people are willing to sign off on their release from hospital, then send them home by way of the Star Kingdom aboard one of our regularly scheduled supply runs." She smiled thinly. "Right off the cuff, I'd estimate that it will probably take at least a couple of months to get them as far as Manticore. By which time, hopefully, things will have settled down."

"And if they haven't?" Bachfisch asked.

"And if they haven't," Honor said much more bleakly, "then things are probably going to be so bad that throwing this into the mix won't matter at all."

"Fritz says Captain Bachfisch will recover fully," Honor told her assembled staff and senior flag officers two hours later in the briefing room aboard *Werewolf*. "Unlike some of us," she added wryly, "the captain responds quite well to regeneration. It will take him a while to grow new legs, but he should be fine. And under the circumstances, I believe he and all the rest of his wounded personnel are definitely entitled to have the Navy pick up the tab on their medical bills."

"You can say that again," Alistair McKeon agreed.

His expression was grim, and he shook his head. The handful of survivors from *Hecate* were still in a state of semi-shock, but they'd been remarkably and uniformly reticent about precisely what their ship had been doing. Some of that was probably inevitable, given the history between the RMN and the Havenite navy, but this went beyond traditional dislike or antipathy. These people were clearly maintaining operational security, and like everyone else in the briefing room, McKeon could think of only one star nation against which any Havenite operation in Silesia could possibly be directed.

"We certainly owe *Pirate's Bane* and her crew an enormous debt for alerting us to the Peeps' presence," Mercedes Brigham added.

"Agreed." Honor nodded. "Which is why I instructed the Fleet repair base here in Sidemore to see to all of her damages *gratis*. If anyone back at Admiralty House has a problem with that, they can take it up with me."

Her tone and expression alike suggested that anyone who did fault her decision probably would not enjoy her response.

"In the meantime, however," she went on briskly, "the question is how we respond to this information."

"I agree fully," Alfredo Yu said. "The problem is that we're still not entirely sure what information we have."

"Captain Bachfisch's people did get a few more facts out of *Hecate*'s database," Lieutenant Commander Reynolds pointed out.

"But not very many," Alice Truman objected. Reynolds looked at her, and she shrugged. "We know she was assigned to their 'Second Fleet,'" she said. "But nothing in our intelligence files even shows that fleet's existence. We have no idea how powerful it is, who's in command of it, or precisely what its mission out here may be!"

"With all due respect, Dame Alice," Reynolds replied, "we do know at least a little. For one thing, there's a fragment of a report which refers to the fact that *Hecate* was assigned to this Second Fleet's third task group. If it's organized into at least three task groups, then it's obviously a fairly good-sized force. And since *Hecate*'s survivors are being so intensely uncooperative with us, I think we have to assume that whatever reason it was sent out here for has something directly to do with us. And I'm very much afraid that I can think of only one scenario which would send a large Havenite fleet to an uninhabited star system this close to Marsh in complete secrecy."

"You're suggesting that they're planning to attack us," Anson Hewitt said flatly.

"I'm suggesting that they *may* be planning to attack us, Sir," Reynolds corrected. Then he sighed. "No," he admitted. "That's being wishy-washy." He faced Hewitt squarely. "The truth is, Sir, that I can't really believe they'd send a heavy force out here under these conditions if they weren't planning to jump us."

Silence hovered in the conference room, bleak and bitter as the implications of the intelligence officer's analysis sank into the brains of officers already confronting the early stages of a shooting war with the Andermani Empire.

"You may well be right, George," Honor said after several seconds. "On the other hand, there's one point that confuses me."

"Only one?" McKeon laughed harshly. "There are dozens of them confusing me right now!"

"Only one main point of confusion," Honor told him, then let her gaze sweep over the other officers in the compartment. "If all they wanted to do was to attack us, then the logical way for them to proceed would have been to move straight into the attack as soon as they reached Silesia, before some freak accident—like this one—betrayed their presence. But they didn't do that. Instead, we've got this Second Fleet of theirs hiding out in an out-of-the-way star system close enough to use as a jump-off point while one or two of their destroyers play postman back and forth between them and their closest diplomatic mission."

"You think they're waiting for orders to attack?" Truman mused aloud.

"Or for orders to turn around and go home and pretend they were never here," Honor replied.

"There may something to that," Yu said slowly. Of all the officers in the compartment, he was probably the least happy. "On the other hand," he continued with stubborn integrity, "much as I would prefer for my old homeland not to be the heavy of the piece, there's no way they would sent a force as heavy as the one Commander Reynolds is postulating this far if they didn't seriously intend to use it. They may be waiting for orders from home to kick off the attack, and they may actually be hoping they'll get recall orders, instead. But the mere fact that they've sent an attack force into a region where they know the Star Kingdom is already confronting a possible war scenario indicates all sorts of things I'd really rather not think about."

"Things none of us would like to think about, Alfredo," Honor agreed grimly. "Nonetheless, I think we do have to consider them. And whatever may be going on closer to home, we still have to respond to our own situation out here."

"What did you have in mind, Your Grace?" Jaruwalski asked, regarding her intensely. Honor glanced at her, and the ops officer shrugged. "I've known you for a while now, Your Grace," she said, "and I've heard that tone of voice before. So since you've already made up your mind about what it is you're planning to do, perhaps you'd care to share it with the rest of us?"

A rumble of laughter rolled around the compartment as Jaruwalski's wry tone punctured the tension, and Honor smiled at her. Any number of flag officers would have stamped on an operations officer who semi-twitted them that way in front of the rest of the staff, but no one thought twice about it on *this* staff.

"Actually," she said, "I have made up my mind. Alice," she turned to Truman, "I'm going to pull *Werewolf* out of your task group to hold her here. I'll swap you the *Glory* from the Protector's Own to replace her; she's a little bigger, but her emissions signature is close enough that I doubt anyone who sees her will realize she's Grayson and not Manticoran. Then I want you to take your entire group and run a LAC sweep through the star system *Hecate* was headed for. And I want you to be obvious about it."

There was a moment of silence, then Truman cleared her throat.

"May I ask why you want me to be obvious, Your Grace?" she asked quietly and a bit more formally than usual.

"First," Honor told her with a tight smile, "I don't want any more accidents. If we seem to be sneaking LACs into the middle of their fleet under stealth, then there's entirely too much chance that they might mistake it for a serious attack. We don't need that when things are already this tense with the Andies." Several heads nodded, and she went on. "Second, I want them to know that we know they're here."

"What if they have orders to attack if they're discovered, My Lady?" Yu asked.

"I doubt very much that they do. I could be wrong, of course, but we can't afford to paralyze ourselves trying to second-guess what they may or may not be planning to do. My feeling is that this entire operation was set up to be as covert as possible. Under the circumstances, I think it's more likely they have orders to withdraw if their presence becomes known. If nothing else, I'd think that they'd have to be unhappy about how the Andies may react to their having sent a major fleet presence this close to their borders. At any rate, I think it's worth the gamble. We'll drop in on them, let them know we've realized they're here, and see how they respond."

She looked back at Truman.

"So, as I say, I want you to be obvious, Alice. But I also want you to emphasize the need to be cautious when you brief your COLACs. I don't want anyone crowding the Peeps—I mean, Havenites—closely enough to provoke them into defensive fire. Clear?"

"Clear," Truman agreed, and Honor was pleased to taste her

intense satisfaction at having been handed the assignment. Some task group commanders would have been wondering if they were being sent out as a way for the station commander to put a convenient scapegoat into the line of fire in case something went wrong. Other station commanders would have been completely unable to delegate the authority, which might have suggested a certain distrust of their subordinate's capabilities. There was no need, she thought, for Alice to know just how hard she really did find it to delegate in this instance. Not because she had any qualms whatsoever about Alice's abilities, but because the responsibility for what she'd just ordered done was hers, not Alice's.

Unfortunately, with everything else that was going on, she needed to be right here, just in case it all hit the fan while Alice was away. Speaking of which . . .

"In the meantime, Alfredo," she continued, turning back to Yu, "we'll keep your other people here with Alistair's at Sidemore to cover it during Alice's absence. I think it's at least possible that no one in Nouveau Paris knew Benjamin had sent you out here when they dispatched this Second Fleet. I'd just as soon keep it that way in case things go south on us."

"Understood," Yu agreed.

"In that case, People, let's be about it."

"*Hecate* is over two days overdue, Sir," Captain DeLaney pointed out quietly.

"I know, Molly. I know."

Lester Tourville frowned as he contemplated the unhappy implications of DeLaney's reminder. There could be any number of reasons for *Hecate*'s failure to arrive as scheduled. Unfortunately, he couldn't think of one of them that he liked. And whatever it might have been, his orders were clear. It seemed extremely unlikely that anything could have given away Second Fleet's presence, but extremely unlikely wasn't the same thing as impossible. Nor was it impossible, however unlikely, that *Hecate*'s nonarrival was the result of something besides the normal hazards of navigation.

"All right, Molly," he sighed. "Pass the movement instructions. I want to pull out for the alternate rendezvous within the hour."

Chapter Forty-Seven

"**N**othing, Ma'am."

"Nothing at all, Wraith?" Dame Alice Truman asked.

"No, Ma'am." Captain Goodrick shook his head. "We've swept the system pretty thoroughly. I suppose it's remotely possible that there could be one or two stealthed pickets hiding out there somewhere. After all, any star system is a mighty big haystack. But there's no way there's anything I'd call a fleet inside the system hyper limit."

"Damn," Truman said softly. She and her chief of staff stood on HMS *Cockatrice*'s flag bridge looking at an astrographic display of a completely empty star system. Truman knew how badly Honor had wanted to either confirm or deny the presence of a Havenite fleet. And how badly she'd wanted for any Havenite admiral to know he'd been spotted. Unfortunately, an empty star system accomplished neither of those objectives. The mere fact that there was no one here *now* didn't indicate a thing about who might have been here when *Hecate* and *Pirate's Bane* fought their brief, bloody battle. Indeed, it was entirely possible that the destroyer's failure to arrive with their mail had inspired the people waiting for her to move to another address.

And the fact that there was no one here to note Truman's own arrival prevented her from delivering Honor's message.

"All right, Wraith," she said finally. "We've swept the system

672

without finding anyone; now all we can do is get back to Sidemore ASAP. Her Grace needs to know what we found—or didn't, depending on how you want to look at it—and if there was a fleet here, it's not here now. Which suggests it's somewhere else. I'd just as soon not have it turn out that 'somewhere else' is launching an attack on Sidemore while we're out looking for it here!"

Honor regarded Truman's report with profound dissatisfaction. Not with Truman or her LAC crews, but with the elusiveness of the Republic's "Second Fleet."

George Reynolds had finished his systematic dissection of every fragment Captain Bachfisch's people had been able to extract from *Hecate*'s mangled computers. It was unpleasantly evident from those fragments that Thomas Theisman's navy was extremely good at maintaining operational security. No one aboard *Hecate* had been in a position to initiate any sort of data purge—not while *Pirate's Bane* was blowing their ship apart around them. And Reynolds had confided to Honor that it was fairly evident that Lieutenant Ferguson, the "civilian" electronics specialist Gruber had sent across to *Hecate*'s wreck to tackle her computers, was not merely military in background but extremely familiar with Peep naval hardware and software for some reason. Despite the catastrophic damage the destroyer had suffered, it seemed evident that Ferguson had gotten everything that was left in her computers, and there was actually a great deal of background information.

But there was very, very little about the organization and nature of this "Second Fleet" . . . and none at all about its purpose in Silesia.

That lack of information made Truman's failure to find the Havenites even more frustrating. No one on Sidemore Station doubted Second Fleet's existence, but without more information on it, her options for preparing against whatever it intended to do were limited, to say the very least.

She growled something under her breath that made Nimitz raise his head and look at her disapprovingly from his bulkhead perch. She felt him considering something a bit more demonstrative, but he decided to settle for sighing with exaggerated patience, instead.

She looked up from the report long enough to stick her tongue out at him, then returned to her contemplation of unpalatable reality.

At least there hadn't been any fresh shooting incidents with the Andermani while she tried to figure out what to do about this live grenade. Not that she expected that to last much longer. She'd hoped the arrival of Herzog von Rabenstrange might have brought about some easing of the tensions between their forces, but it hadn't happened. At least, unlike Sternhafen, he appeared to have no interest in actively fanning the fire, but he also hadn't renounced Sternhafen's obviously self-serving—and grossly inaccurate—official verdict on the Zoraster Incident.

Chien-lu Anderman was far too smart to believe Sternhafen's version. More than that, he was too good an officer not to have investigated what had happened on his own. So if he was signing off on Sternhafen's obstruction of the truth, it was a very bad sign. Worse still, she couldn't believe he would have been a party to any such action without very specific policy directives from the Emperor. And if his directives precluded the minimization of tensions, then the chances of avoiding a more direct and vastly more dangerous confrontation were slight. Indeed, her greatest fear was that this relative quiet represented the lull before the storm while the Andies finished deploying their assets.

However she looked at it, she was caught between two threats. She would have felt reasonably confident about dealing with either of them alone, at least long enough to be reinforced from home, with the backing of Alfredo and the rest of the Protector's Own. But even with that welcome reinforcement, she lacked the resources to protect her area of responsibility from two totally separate threats. And so far, the High Ridge Government had declined to provide her with any additional support.

But that wasn't the worst of it—not by a long chalk.

She sighed heavily, her face creased with a worry she was careful never to allow anyone else to see, and faced the most unpalatable conclusion of all. If the Republic of Haven was prepared to launch an attack clear out here, then they must be simultaneously prepared to do the same thing much closer to home. Committing an isolated act of war on the scale represented by an attack on Sidemore Station in a region so far away from the front line between them and the Manticoran Alliance would be an act of lunacy. This *had* to represent only a single aspect of a far larger operations plan . . . and the ships committed to it, however many of them there were, likewise had to represent a force Thomas

Theisman felt he could afford to divert from the truly critical theatre of operations.

That was what worried her most. She knew Thomas Theisman personally, something only two other Manticoran admirals could say. Both of those flag officers were right here with her, and all three of them had the utmost respect for him. More, she knew that both Hamish Alexander, who'd also fought him, and Alfredo Yu, who'd been his one-time mentor, shared that respect. So if Thomas Theisman felt he had sufficient naval strength to open a war on what amounted to two totally separated fronts, then it was painfully obvious to Honor that ONI had catastrophically underestimated the new Republican Navy. Theisman might be wrong in his force estimate, but she found it very difficult to believe his calculations could be that far off . . . especially given that the strength of the Royal Manticoran Navy, unlike that of the Republic, was a matter of public record following the bitter budget debates. Unlike Jurgenson, Chakrabarti, and Janacek, he knew exactly what his opponents had.

But there was nothing she could do about that from here. She'd made every defensive adjustment within her own command area that she could think of in the absence of any fresh instructions from home. All she could do now was to report the scraps of information they'd managed to recover from *Hecate* to the Admiralty and hope someone back home drew the appropriate conclusions.

And not just that Sidemore Station was urgently in need of additional reinforcements, either.

She contemplated Truman's report one more time, mental teeth gnawing at the rocky shell of her dilemma while she felt the impending collision sliding towards her like ground cars on glaze ice. If only Alice had found Second Fleet! At least then she'd have proof for Janacek and Jurgenson. As it was, all she had was circumstantial evidence, and she knew the mere fact that that evidence came from her would make it suspect in Janacek's eyes. Had Patricia Givens or Thomas Caparelli still been at the Admiralty, she wouldn't have worried about that, but Janacek was backed by Chakrabarti and Jurgenson, neither of whom was likely to stand up to his prejudices, and that meant—

Her dreary mental recitation of all the disasters looming on the horizon paused, and her eyes narrowed as a new thought thrust itself suddenly into her mind.

Wait, she thought. *Wait just a minute, Honor. Janacek and his cronies don't operate in a pure vacuum . . . and the Royal Navy isn't the only one caught in the middle of all this. For that matter, the Manticoran Alliance treaty partners aren't the only people who have a stake in it! Of course, if you do it, and if you're wrong . . .*

Nimitz's head snapped up, and she tasted his sudden spike of emotions as he sensed her inner turbulence. Then his ears flattened as he felt her reach a decision, and she looked up to meet his gaze. He looked back at her, the very tip of his tail twitching ever so slowly while he sampled the resolution flowering suddenly at her core. Then his ears came up and his whiskers quivered as he radiated the unmistakable image of a huge smile.

She smiled back fiercely and nodded.

After all, it wasn't as if she wouldn't have another career to fall back on if it didn't work.

"So I'm afraid," Arnold Giancola said regretfully, "that Foreign Secretary Descroix's response is scarcely what I could call forthcoming."

The Cabinet room's oppressive silence underscored the massive understatement in which he'd just indulged himself. The actual text of Descroix's note had been made available to all of them in electronic format before this meeting, which had given all of them plenty of time to reach the same conclusion.

Of course, the text they'd received wasn't exactly the same as the one Descroix had transmitted.

Giancola hid a smile of satisfaction behind his studiously concerned expression. Placing Yves Grosclaude in the ambassador's slot on Manticore had paid off even more handsomely than he'd anticipated. He and Grosclaude had served together in Rob Pierre's State Department before Giancola was recalled to Treasury for the Turner Reforms. They'd become friends along the way, and they understood one another, just as they shared a genuine, implacable distrust of the Star Kingdom of Manticore. Despite their history, Giancola had been very cautious about feeling Grosclaude out, but their old friendship and mutual trust had still been there. Which meant no one in Nouveau Paris was going to be aware of any tiny discrepancies between the note Grosclaude had been handed on Manticore and the one Giancola had delivered in Nouveau Paris.

And the discrepancies truly were tiny, he reflected. High Ridge and Descroix had reacted almost precisely as he'd anticipated. All he'd had to do was to remove a half dozen minor connective words to make their response sound even more uncompromising. Best of all was the way they'd reacted to the one critically ambiguous sentence he'd managed to get included in the Pritchart-approved draft of the Republic's own communique.

"I don't understand," Rachel Hanriot said finally. "I know they've been deliberately stringing these talks out. But if that's what they want to continue to do, then why should they be so flatly confrontational?"

"I agree that they're being confrontational," Eloise Pritchart said. "On the other hand, I suppose it's only fair to point out that our last note to them was pretty stiff, too. Frankly, I lost my temper with them." She smiled thinly, topaz eyes bleak. "I'm not saying I wasn't justified when I did, but the language Arnold and I addressed them in certainly could have put their noses sufficiently out of joint to explain some of this."

"In all fairness, Madame President," Giancola said, "I doubt very much that our last note was really needed to 'put their noses out of joint.' Their assumption from the beginning has been that they held the whip hand. Their belief that we would ultimately have no choice but to accept whatever terms they were graciously prepared to grant us has been fundamental to their attitude throughout. I may have had my doubts about the immediate tactical consequences of sending such a stiff note to them, but in a strategic sense, I doubt it's had any significant effect on their posture. All its really done, I suspect, is bring their fundamental arrogance and intransigence out into the open."

"Maybe it has." Thomas Theisman's tone was sharp, and the look he bestowed upon the Secretary of State was not one of unalloyed friendliness. "At the same time, however, there's one point in this note of theirs which strikes me as particularly significant."

"The question about Trevor's Star?" Pritchart asked.

"Exactly." Theisman nodded. "They're specifically asking whether or not we intended to include Trevor's Star in our demand that they acknowledge in principle our sovereignty over the occupied star systems. It seems obvious to me that we didn't, but I suppose, looking back at our own note, that I can see how its wording might have been misconstrued. If they believe we're upping the ante by demanding the return of a star system which they've formally annexed, then I'd have to call that a fairly ominous development."

"In the greater scheme of things, it's only one of several strands that worry me," Pritchart told him. "And if they'd ever actually sit down to talk with us in good faith, we could tie up all of the confusion in a day or two. On the other hand, I see your point."

"But there's another side to it, too," Denis LePic said. The Attorney General tapped the hardcopy of Descroix's note where it lay on the conference table in front of him. "They're asking for clarification," he pointed out. "I think that's significant. Especially when you couple it with this part at the end where they're talking about the need to 'break the logjam of mutually antagonistic positions.'"

"That last part is nothing more than self-serving eyewash!" Tony Nesbitt retorted. The Secretary of Commerce snorted disdainfully. "It sounds good, and they probably expect it to play well to the 'faxes and their own public opinion, but it doesn't really *mean* anything. If it did, then they would have offered to give at least a little ground in response to our last note."

"You may be right," LePic replied, although it was fairly obvious from his tone that he didn't think anything of the sort. "On the other hand, their request for clarification could be a sort of backhanded way of suggesting both that they have a genuine concern over the issue and that there's some room for movement. If all they wanted to do was to prepare their own public opinion for some sort of resumption of hostilities, then they wouldn't have asked the question. They'd simply have deliberately assumed that we intended to demand the return of Trevor's Star and rejected our 'presumption' indignantly."

"That's certainly possible," Pritchart said thoughtfully.

"Well, *anything's* possible," Nesbitt conceded. "I just think some things are more likely than others."

"As we're all well aware," LePic shot back. Nesbitt glared at him, but that was as far as he was prepared to go under Pritchart's cold eye.

"All right," the President said. "We can sit here and argue over exactly what they meant all day, but I don't really think that's going to get us anywhere. I think we're all generally in agreement that this isn't precisely a forthcoming response to our last note to them?"

She looked around the conference table and saw nothing but agreement. Indeed, the secretaries who'd most strongly backed her against Giancola from the beginning seemed even angrier than the Secretary of State's supporters. She wondered how much of that was genuine exasperation with the Manties, and how much of it was frustration at seeing Giancola's predictions of the Star Kingdom's intransigence being borne out.

She made herself pause for a few seconds to acknowledge the danger of so much anger. Angry people didn't think clearly. They were vulnerable to the making of overly hasty decisions.

"On the other hand," she made herself say, "Tom and Denis are right to point out that there's at least a potential opening in their question about Trevor's Star. So I propose that we send them a reply specifically and definitively ceding sovereignty over that single system to them."

Several of Giancola's longest-term supporters looked rebellious, but the Secretary of State himself nodded with every appearance of approval.

"What about their closing section?" LePic asked. "Should we take some notice of it and express our own desire to break this 'log-jam' of theirs?"

"I'd advise against that, actually," Giancola said thoughtfully. LePic looked at him suspiciously, and the Secretary of State shrugged. "I don't know that it would be a bad idea, Denis; I'm just not sure it would be a good one. We've been to some lengths to establish our impatience with the way they've been fobbing us off for so long. If we send them a very brief note, possibly one which responds only to a single point from this one, " he tapped his own hardcopy of the Descroix note, "and does so in a way which makes it obvious that we're attempting to address their legitimate concerns—their *legitimate* concerns, Denis—but ignoring what Tony just called 'eyewash,' then we make it clear we're willing to be reasonable but not to retreat from our insistence that they negotiate seriously. In fact, the briefer the note, the more likely it is to make those points for us, particularly after how lengthy our previous notes have grown."

Pritchart regarded him with carefully concealed surprise. Much as she might distrust his ultimate ambitions, she couldn't fault his logic at the moment.

"I think it might be wiser to make at least some

acknowledgment of their comments," LePic argued. "I don't see any harm in making an explicit connection between our assurances about Trevor's Star and their expressed desire to find some way to move forward."

"I understand your position, Denis," Giancola assured him. "You may well even be right. I just think we've used up so many millions of words talking to these people that it might be time to resort to a certain brutal brevity to make our point. Especially when the one we're making is our willingness to concede one of *their* demands. At the very least, the change of pace should be like letting a breath of fresh air into the negotiations."

"I think Arnold may have a point, Denis," Pritchart said. LePic looked at her for a moment, then shrugged.

"Maybe he does," the Attorney General conceded. "I suppose a part of it is how much time I spend wrestling with legal briefs and law codes. You don't want to risk any possibility of ambiguity in those, so you nail everything down in duplicate or triplicate."

"Very well, then," Pritchart said. "Let's see just how brief and concise—in a pleasant way, of course—we can be."

Arnold Giancola leaned back in the comfortable chair and gazed at the short, to the point message on his display. It was, indeed, brief and concise, and he felt a cold, unaccustomed tingle of something very like dread as he looked at it.

He'd made only one, very small change in it—deleted a single three-letter word—and for the first time, he felt a definite flicker of uncertainty. He'd known from the moment he'd set out to engineer Pritchart's foreign policy failure that this moment or one very like it would come, just as he'd always recognized the fire with which he was playing. But now the moment was here. By transmitting his version of this note to Grosclaude, he would finally and irretrievably commit himself. Despite the smallness of the change, this was no minor alteration, nothing anyone could possible explain away as a mere effort to clarify or emphasize. There would be no going back after it, and if the fact that he'd deliberately altered the President's language ever came out, his own political career would be over forever.

It was odd, he reflected, that he should come to this point . . . and that even now, he'd broken no laws. Perhaps there ought to be a law specifically requiring a secretary of state not to make any further adjustments to the agreed-upon language of a diplomatic note. Unfortunately, there wasn't. His quiet but detailed examination of the relevant law had made certain of that point. He'd broken at least a dozen State Department regulations dealing with the filing of true copies, but a good defense attorney could argue that they were only regulations, without statutory authority from Congress, and that as the Secretary of State, his own department's regulations were subject to his own revision. He'd need a sympathetic judge to make it stand up in court, but he happened to know where he could find one of those.

Not that technical questions of legality would make any significant difference to what would happen to him if his maneuver failed. Pritchart's fury would know no bounds, and his betrayal of his responsibility to her—and he was too self-honest to use any word besides 'betrayal,' even in the privacy of his own thoughts—would raise a firestorm of congressional support for her decision to fire him. Even those who would have agreed with his objectives would turn on him like starving wolves.

Yet even as he thought that, he knew he wasn't going to allow any doubts, any uncertainty, to deflect him. Not now. He'd come too far, risked too much. Besides, whatever Pritchart might think, it was obvious to him that the High Ridge Government would never agree to negotiate in good faith. He was in the process of educating the rest of the Cabinet to recognize that. In fact, he thought with grim amusement, he was actually educating Pritchart. But the truth hadn't gone fully home.

No. He needed one more lesson. One more Manticoran provocation. Hanriot, LePic, Gregory, and Theisman remained committed to the idea that somehow, some way, there had to be an accommodation which could be reached if only the Republic looked hard enough, waited long enough, possessed its soul in sufficient patience. The rest of the Cabinet was coming steadily around to Giancola's own position . . . and so, for that matter, was Eloise Pritchart, unless he missed his guess. But her present frustration was no substitute for the strength of will to look the Royal Manticoran Navy in the eye with the defiance that would make High Ridge recoil. She would still flinch if that happened, still fumble the chance to achieve her own goals. All he needed was one more push to generate the proper sense of crisis, reveal

her weakness, and consolidate the Cabinet behind *his* solution
to it.

He took one more look at the text of the note, inhaled deeply,
and pressed the key authorizing its dispatch to Ambassador
Grosclaude.

CHAPTER FORTY-EIGHT

"**E**xcuse me, Sir."

Sir Edward Janacek looked up with an expression of intense irritation. His personal yeoman stood in the open door of his office, and the First Lord's irate expression headed rapidly towards thunderous. The man had been with him long enough to know better than to physically intrude into his office unannounced, especially when he was grappling with something like the latest report from a lunatic like Harrington.

"What?" he barked harshly enough to make the yeoman flinch. But it wasn't enough to send him scurrying in retreat, and Janacek's brows knit in a cumulonimbus frown.

"I'm very sorry to intrude, Sir," the yeoman said quickly, "but . . . That is, you . . . I mean, you have a visitor, Sir!"

"What in God's name are you babbling about?" Janacek demanded furiously. There was no one on his schedule this afternoon until his meeting at four o'clock with Simon Chakrabarti, and the yeoman knew it. He was the fumble-fingered idiot responsible for maintaining the First Lord's schedule!

"Sir," the yeoman said almost desperately, "Earl White Haven is here!"

Janacek's jaw dropped in disbelief as the yeoman vanished back out of the door like a Sphinxian chipmunk, darting into its burrow with a treecat in hot pursuit. The First Lord had just put his hands on his desk to shove himself up out of his chair when the office door opened again, and a tall, blue-eyed man in dress uniform, tunic ablaze with medal ribbons, stepped through it.

Janacek's dropped jaw closed with a beartrap-click, and the disbelief in his eyes turned into something much hotter as he took in the newcomer's appearance. White Haven had every right to appear at Admiralty House in uniform, and Janacek had no doubt at all that the sight of the four gold stars on the earl's collar and that glittering galaxy of ribbons explained his yeoman's failure to simply send the intruder about his business. Much as he wanted to, the First Lord really couldn't fault the man for that, and his jaw clenched even tighter as that same uniform's impact washed over him. It was a somewhat different emotion in his own case, because had they both been in uniform, his collar would have borne only three stars. And when last he'd been on active duty, it would have borne only two.

But that didn't matter in this office, he reminded himself, and instead of pushing himself fully to his feet, he dropped back into his chair. It was a deliberate refusal to give White Haven the courtesy of standing to greet him, and felt a stir of satisfaction as anger flickered in those ice-blue eyes.

"What do you want?" he half-snapped.

"Still wasting no courtesy on visitors, I see," White Haven observed.

"Visitors who want courtesy should know enough to go through my appointments yeoman," Janacek replied in that same, harsh voice.

"Who undoubtedly would have found all manner of reasons why you couldn't have squeezed in the time to meet with me."

"Maybe he would have," Janacek growled. "But if you think I would deliberately have refused to see you, maybe that should have suggested that you stay the hell away."

Hamish Alexander started to snap back, then made himself pause and draw a deep breath, instead. He wondered if Janacek even began to suspect what a childish, petulant appearance he presented. But it had always been that way where the two of them were concerned, so he could hardly pretend the First Lord's attitude was unexpected. And if he was going to be honest, Janacek had always brought out the very worst in him, as well. It was as if simply walking into the other man's presence was enough to transport them both back to a confrontation on a grammar school playground somewhere.

But at least White Haven was aware of that. That gave him a certain responsibility to at least try to act like an adult. And even though he felt deep in his bones that any sort of rational discussion of what brought him here was unlikely—to say the very least—it was also far too important for him to allow Janacek's temper to provoke his own.

"Look," he said after a moment in a reasonable tone, "we don't like each other. We never have, and we never will. I don't see any point in pretending otherwise, especially when there aren't any witnesses." He smiled thinly. "But I assure you, I wouldn't be here unless I thought it was sufficiently important to justify the sort of scene you and I usually seem to end up a part of whenever we meet."

"I'm sure a man of your well-known brilliance and intellect must have all sorts of things that need doing," Janacek replied sarcastically. "What could possibly make *me* important enough for you to waste time in my office?"

Again, White Haven began a hot retort, only to bite it off.

"I do have any number of things I could be doing instead," he agreed. "None of them, however, are quite as important as the reason I'm here. If you'll give me ten minutes of your time without the two of us snarling at each other like a pair of playground bullies, perhaps we can deal with that particular concern and I can be on my way."

"I'm certainly in favor of anything which would produce that effect," Janacek snorted. He cocked back his chair, deliberately drawing attention to his failure to invite his "guest" to be seated. "What seems to be on your mind, My Lord?"

"Silesia," White Haven said shortly, eyes hard as Janacek kept him standing in front of his desk like some junior officer who'd been called on the carpet. The earl considered sitting down anyway and daring Janacek to respond, but instead he reminded himself yet again that one of them had to at least pretend to be an adult.

"Ah, yes, Silesia." Janacek smiled nastily. "Admiral Harrington's command."

His implication was crystal clear, and White Haven felt a fresh, white-hot spurt of anger. It was harder to strangle this one at birth, but he managed—barely—and simply stood there, cold eyes boring into the First Lord.

"Well," Janacek said finally, his tone irritable under the icy weight of the fabled Alexander glare, "what about Silesia?"

"I'm concerned about what the Republic may be up to out there," White Haven said flatly, and Janacek's face darkened in fury.

"And what, if I may ask, My Lord," he grated, "leads you to believe that the Republic is up to *anything* in Silesia?"

"Private correspondence," White Haven said briefly.

"'Private correspondence' from Admiral Harrington, I presume." Janacek's eyes were hard as flint. "Correspondence divulging sensitive information to an officer who not only had no compelling security need to know but isn't even currently on active duty!"

"Security considerations don't come into it," White Haven retorted. "The information Duchess Harrington shared with me isn't classified and never has been. Even if it were, My Lord, I believe you would discover that all of my security clearances are still in effect. And that as a member of the Naval Affairs Committee of the House of Lords, I have a 'need to know' which transcends the normal uniformed structure of Her Majesty's Navy."

"Don't you split technical hairs with me, 'My Lord'!" Janacek glared.

"I'm not splitting hairs with you. Nor, as we're both well aware, does it really matter at this point whether or not the Duchess technically violated any security regulation. If you believe she did, the appropriate thing for you to do would be to file charges against her. I wouldn't recommend it, because you and I both know how that would end, but that decision is up to you. What matters right this instant, however, is what response you intend to make to her report."

"That's not your affair, My Lord," Janacek replied.

"You're in error," White Haven said flatly. "I realize you report to the Prime Minister, not directly to the Queen. But Her Majesty is also in possession of this information." Janacek's eyes went wide, and the earl continued in that same flat, almost robotic tone. "I'm here at her behest, as well as my own. If you doubt that, My Lord, I invite you to com Mount Royal Palace and ask her about it."

"How dare you?" Janacek rose at last, planting both knuckled fists on his desk and leaning over it. "How *dare* you attempt to blackmail me?!"

"Who said anything about blackmail?" White Haven demanded. "I simply informed you that the Queen also wishes to know what her Admiralty is prepared to do about the situation in Silesia."

"If she wants to know, there are proper channels through which she may inquire," Janacek snapped. "This isn't one of them!"

"Unfortunately," White Haven said icily, "'proper channels' seem to be somewhat . . . constricted these days." He smiled again, his eyes cold. "Think of this as the Gordian knot and me as another Alexander, My Lord."

"Fuck you!" Janacek snarled. "Don't you dare come walking into *my* office and demand information from me! You may think you're God's gift to the fucking Navy, but to me you're just one more pissant admiral without a command!"

"I find myself singularly unimpressed by your view of me," White Haven replied contemptuously. "And I'm still waiting for an answer I can deliver to the Queen."

"Go to Hell," Janacek growled.

"Very well," White Haven said with deadly precision. "If that's your final word, I'll go and deliver it to Her Majesty. Who will then, I feel certain, call a news conference in which she will inform the press of precisely how forthcoming her First Lord of the Admiralty was." His smile was colder than ever. "Somehow, My Lord, I doubt the Prime Minister will thank you."

He turned away, striding towards the door, and Janacek felt a sudden stab of panic. It wasn't enough to overcome his fury, but it was sharp enough to penetrate it.

"Wait," he said flatly, and White Haven paused and turned back to face him. "You have no right at all to demand an accounting from me, and Her Majesty is fully aware of the constitutional channels through which *she* should request any accounting. If, however, you're truly prepared to spew such sensitive matters into the media, regardless of their potential effect on the military security and diplomatic posture of the Star Kingdom, I suppose I have no alternative but to tell you what you want to know."

"We may differ on just what would be affected if I spoke to the newsies," White Haven said coldly. "However, other than that, I find myself unusually in agreement with you, My Lord."

"What, specifically, do you want to know?" Janacek grated.

"Her Majesty," White Haven stressed, "would like to know the Admiralty's official reaction to Duchess Harrington's report of Havenite Naval activity in Silesia?"

"At the moment, the Admiralty's official reaction is that the Sidemore Station commander's report contains far too little detail for any definitive conclusions to be drawn."

"Excuse me?" White Haven's eyebrows rose.

"All that we—or Admiral Harrington—know," Janacek retorted, "is that a single Republican destroyer engaged—or was engaged by—an armed merchant auxiliary of the Silesian Navy commanded by a half-pay Manticoran officer who was dismissed his ship for cause forty T-years ago. That virtually the entire crew of the destroyer was massacred in the ensuing action. And that the captain of the armed auxiliary in question handed over fragmentary records which he claimed to have obtained from the wrecked destroyer's computers."

White Haven stared at him, as if momentarily bereft of words. Then he shook himself almost visibly.

"Are you suggesting that Admiral Bachfisch fabricated this entire affair for some unknown Machiavellian reason of his own?" he demanded.

"I'm suggesting that at this moment we know absolutely nothing for certain," Janacek shot back. "I can't think of any reason why Bachfisch might have fabricated anything, but that doesn't mean I'm prepared to dismiss the possibility out of hand. The man's been out of Manticoran uniform for forty years, and he didn't exactly leave it voluntarily, did he? He fucked up by the numbers when he wore the Queen's uniform—under remarkably similar circumstances, I might add—and I see no reason to assume he didn't do the same thing here. And even if he didn't, he's undoubtedly still bitter over what happened to his career. That might make him an ideal conduit if someone wanted to deliberately plant disinformation on us."

"That's preposterous," White Haven snorted. "And even if he was inclined to do anything of the sort—even to the extent of voluntarily allowing both of his own legs to be shot off to lend authenticity to his efforts—Duchess Harrington and her staff evaluated the records and interviewed the surviving crew members independently."

"Yes, and sent a task group off to examine the star where this hypothetical 'Second Fleet' was supposedly stationed," Janacek retorted. "But she didn't find anything there, did she?"

"Which proves absolutely nothing," White Haven pointed out. "There are any number of reasons why a fleet ordered to remain covert might have shifted its base."

"Of course there are. And that's precisely what Theisman wants us to think."

"Theisman? Are you suggesting now that the Republic's Secretary of War deliberately sacrificed a destroyer and its entire crew just to convince us he was prepared to contemplate an act of war against us?"

"Of course not!" Janacek snapped. "He never intended for the destroyer to be damaged. But he did expect it to be spotted and followed—why else would he have openly sent two fleet destroyers to ostentatiously orbit the one planet in the entire sector where there was a Havenite diplomatic mission? In a star system where our patrol units call regularly?" The First Lord sneered. "If they were so damned determined to remain 'covert,' don't you think they could have found something just a bit less obtrusive than *that*?"

"And the purpose of allowing themselves to be spotted and followed?" White Haven asked, fascinated despite himself and despite his scalding anger.

"To convince us of exactly what Admiral Harrington was convinced of," Janacek said with the patience of someone speaking to a very small child. "Our relations with the Republic are deteriorating steadily. You know that as well as I do. And despite all of his public statements of confidence in his navy's abilities, Theisman isn't at all certain of his ability to stand up to us. So he sent his two destroyers off to Silesia with orders to draw our attention there in order to convince us he was sending forces to threaten Sidemore. Obviously what he wants is for us to divert still more of our strength to Silesia, thus weakening ourselves at the decisive point if the cease-fire should fail."

"I see." White Haven considered the First Lord in silence for several seconds, then shook his head. "Exactly how were his destroyers supposed to suggest all of this to us?"

"By being followed to an appropriate star somewhere—exactly as this *Hecate* was. Undoubtedly, they hoped to be picked up by one of our warships. If one of them had been, she would have 'suddenly' realized she was being trailed and broken away from the star she'd been to such trouble to bring to our attention. Our ship would have followed her until she either lost us or else returned to the Horus System 'for new orders.' In either case, when the incident was reported to Sidemore, Admiral Harrington and her staff could be relied upon to draw the proper conclusions.

"As it turned out, they were spotted and shadowed by what they thought was a typical Silesian merchant ship, and they thought they saw an even better way to get their disinformation into our hands. Obviously, they intended to board Bachfisch's ship, drop a few hints, and then turn her loose with stern orders not to go anywhere near the Marsh System. Of course any Silly merchant crew would immediately see the possibility of selling such information to us, which would have sent them straight off to Admiral Harrington!"

"And the data Admiral Bachfisch recovered from her computers?" White Haven asked.

"Strictly a fallback position," Janacek said confidently. "*Hecate* was never intended to be captured or destroyed, but it must have been apparent to their planners that their ship might be unfortunate enough to attract the attention of a cruiser or even a battlecruiser. With our compensator efficiency advantages, *Hecate*'s ability to pull away would have been far from assured, so they briefed her crew with a cover story and planted a few ambiguous references to this 'Second Fleet' of theirs in her computers. They probably had it set up to look as if the crew had attempted to purge their database and failed to get everything dumped." He shrugged. "When they screwed up and misidentified Bachfisch's ship as a regular merchie, someone had time to go back to the fallback plan before he was killed."

"Do you seriously believe any of that?" White Haven asked almost conversationally, and Janacek swelled with fury.

"Of course I do!" He shook his head angrily. "Oh, I'm sure we have some of the details wrong, but there's no way—no way in the universe—Theisman would even contemplate genuinely sending a force as powerful as the one Harrington is postulating that far away from the decisive theater at a time like this! I don't doubt that their ops plan came apart on them. Certainly I don't believe they deliberately sacrificed an entire destroyer crew just to convince us their information was genuine! But the only thing that makes any sense is that this was intended as some elaborate diversionary effort."

"And you don't intend to be diverted by it, do you?"

"No, My Lord, I do not," Janacek said flatly, staring unyieldingly into White Haven's eyes.

"My Lord," White Haven said quietly, "haven't you even considered the other implications of this supposed diversionary effort of yours?"

"What 'other implications'?" Janacek demanded.

"If Duchess Harrington's belief that sizable Havenite forces have been sent to Silesia is, in fact, correct, then they can only be there for one purpose: to attack Sidemore Station and destroy her task force. If they did such a thing, it would be a clear act of war, and we would respond to it as such—everywhere, not just in Silesia. The implication is clearly that they're actively contemplating resuming hostilities, and if they're willing to do so in an area as far from our strategic center as Silesia, then they're certainly willing to do it somewhere closer to home, as well.

"Even if you assume this was no more than an effort to draw us into dispersing our forces, it certainly suggests they're planning active operations against us *somewhere*. Any dispersal we were drawn into as a result of this disinformation attempt you've postulated would be only temporary. If we found no other sign of their 'Second Fleet' within a few weeks—or, at most, a few months—then we'd begin recalling any reinforcements we'd sent. Once we did that, the balance of forces would revert to what it had been, and Theisman would know that as well as we did. Trust me, the man is an excellent strategist.

"So if the dispersal would be only temporary, I have to wonder why he should bother. Unless, during that temporary window of dispersal, he intended to attack us here."

"Make up your mind," Janacek said nastily. "You came in here prepared to demand that we send reinforcements to Sidemore. Now you're saying that if we did that, we'd be playing directly into Theisman's hands."

"I'm saying nothing of the sort," White Haven snapped. "I'm simply pointing out that even if your analysis were correct—which I don't for a moment believe it is—it only underscores the danger of a Havenite attack. If Duchess Harrington is correct, on the other hand, the danger isn't underscored; it's confirmed!"

"Tensions are undoubtedly running high," Janacek told him, biting off each word as if he were chewing an iron bar. "The danger of a resumption of hostilities is greater than it's been in quite some time. If you want me to concede that the interruption of our building programs was a mistake, then off the record, I will. However, nothing ONI has turned up convinces me that the Republican Navy is capable of meeting us in combat successfully."

"And if they don't agree with your analysis?"

"Then they may be stupid enough to find out the hard way."

"Will you at least put our system pickets and station commanders on a higher state of readiness and reinforce Trevor's Star?" White Haven demanded.

"Our system pickets and station commanders are always at a high state of readiness," Janacek shot back. "As for Trevor's Star, the system picket—as you're perfectly well aware—is already extremely powerful, and the terminus forts are online and fully ammunitioned. To further reinforce Third Fleet at this particular moment would only increase tensions between the Republic and the Star Kingdom without providing any practical increase in the system's security."

"So you're telling me that alerting our commanders and reinforcing Third Fleet are politically unacceptable options?"

"In essence, yes," Janacek said unflinchingly, and White Haven gazed at him for several silent seconds. It was obvious that the First Lord had no intention of being swayed, and, finally, the earl shook his head.

"Do you know," he said in a conversational, almost pleasant tone, "if I hadn't heard it with my own ears I wouldn't have believed it was possible for you to get even stupider."

Janacek's already rage-darkened face turned an alarming shade of purple and his jaw worked, as if his mouth were independently trying to get out the words his infuriated brain couldn't quite wrap itself around. White Haven simply looked at him for two or three breaths, then shook his head again.

"Obviously, there's no point trying to talk sense into you," he said, his voice flat with cold contempt. "Good day."

And he strode out the office door before Janacek ever managed to find his voice once more.

✧   ✧   ✧

"Edward, I think we need to seriously consider further reinforcing Sidemore."

"Out of the question!" Janacek snapped, and glowered at Admiral Chakrabarti, wondering just what the First Space Lord had heard about his "interview" with White Haven.

Chakrabarti only looked back at him levelly, and Janacek threw his hands up.

"Just where do you propose we find those reinforcements?" he demanded. "Especially after the note we just sent off to Pritchart? If she and Theisman are stupid enough to break off negotiations after they get it, we're going to need every hull we've got a lot closer to home than Silesia!"

"In that case," Chakrabarti said, "I think we need to draft new instructions for Duchess Harrington."

"What sort of 'new instructions'?" Janacek growled.

"Instructions to give the Andermani whatever the hell they want!" Chakrabarti shot back with highly unusual asperity.

"What?" Janacek stared at him in disbelief.

"I've been rereading Sternhafen's version of what happened in Zoraster," Chakrabarti told him. "It's obvious that it's a total fabrication. And his official rejection of Harrington's offer of the joint investigation is more of the same. In my opinion, the Empire's clearly setting the stage for it to demand major territorial concessions in Silesia. I believe the Emperor is prepared to go so far as risking open conflict with the Star Kingdom in order to get those concessions and that he's using this incident to bludgeon us into acquiescing rather than risk still further escalations in the level of confrontation. In fact, I wouldn't be a bit surprised if the rising tensions between us and the Republic are leading him to deduce—correctly, as it happens—that we're not in a position to reinforce Sidemore."

"But according to everything Francis has been able to dig up, the Andies are still redeploying," Janacek protested.

"With all due respect for Francis," Chakrabarti said in a not particularly respectful tone, "I think he's wrong. Or, rather, I think the Andies are probably a lot further along in their redeployment than he's been assuming. It's the only explanation I can see for the way Sternhafen jumped on this Zoraster Incident. And then there's this entire *Hecate* affair. I know," he waved a hand in the air, "Francis believes the whole thing was intended as a diversionary effort. Maybe it was, but maybe it wasn't, either. Whatever the Republic might be up to, however, doesn't change the situation where the Andies are concerned. Except, of course, that if Harrington's right, and there is a Havenite fleet screwing around out there, then the threat situation is even worse.

"I reiterate, Edward. In my opinion as First Space Lord, we either have to reinforce Sidemore significantly, or else we have to draft new instructions for the station commander, reducing the scope of what we expect her to do with the forces she has."

"I don't think that's politically possible," Janacek said slowly. "Not right now. Not when we're already in such a delicate position with the Republic. Even if it's not exactly what Theisman has been trying to convince us to do, it would be too great a concession of weakness."

"It would be an admission of reality," Chakrabarti replied crisply.

"No, it's out of the question," Janacek said firmly.

"In that case," Chakrabarti said, "I see no option but to tender my resignation as First Space Lord."

Janacek stared at him in utter disbelief.

"You can't be serious!"

"I'm afraid I can, Edward." Chakrabarti shook his head. "I won't pretend I'm happy about it, because I'm not. But I've been telling you for months that we've got too many forest fires. In my opinion, we have got to reduce our obligations and consolidate our forces. In fact, I deeply regret having earlier supported such deep reductions in our naval strength."

"It's a bit late to be bringing up that particular piece of after-the-fact wisdom!" Janacek snapped.

"Yes, it is," Chakrabarti agreed. "And given what we knew at the time we decided to make them, I'd probably have made the same decision today. What I meant was simply that because of those reductions we lack the strength to even contemplate a two-front war. And that's precisely what we're going to be looking at if the Andies have decided to push and we simultaneously stumble back into hostilities with the Republic. I don't know about you, but I am not going to bear the responsibility for finding ourselves in that position. So either the Government is going to have to decide to alter Duchess Harrington's instructions so we can actually bring some of her strength home, or else I'm very much afraid that you're going to have to find a new First Space Lord."

"But—"

"No, Edward," Chakrabarti interrupted firmly. "We need to consolidate our strength. Either we call the bulk of Task Force Thirty-Four home from Sidemore, or else we find the strength to reinforce our system pickets somewhere else. Or else I resign."

"But there *isn't* anywhere else!"

"There's always Grayson," Chakrabarti said flatly.

"No! No, I refuse to beg those neobarb bastards for help!"

"I know you don't trust them, and I know you don't like them. Hell, I don't *like* them myself!" Chakrabarti barked a laugh. "But they've got the naval strength to reinforce our pickets in the occupied systems sufficiently to give the Republic pause . . . if they'll do it."

Janacek's jaw clamped, and he glared furiously at the First Space Lord. The confrontation with White Haven had left his emotions lacerated and raw. It had also left him determined to prove once and for all to that superior, sanctimonious, supercilious son-of-a-bitch that he wasn't fucking infallible after all. And that he and his precious "Salamander" weren't going to call the tune for the Admiralty's piping the way the two of them had when Mourncreek was First Lord.

And now this. All very well for Chakrabarti to suggest at this late date that they go crawling to Benjamin Mayhew and his precious High Admiral Matthews. He wasn't the one who'd had to deal with the insufferable, arrogant, religious fanatic barbarians and put them in their places! No, that had been Janacek's job. So of course it was easy for Chakrabarti to propose that the First Lord eat dirt and beg Grayson to save their bacon now!

"Just where did this particular brainstorm come from all of a sudden?" he demanded icily.

"It's not 'all of a sudden,'" Chakrabarti replied. "I admit that I haven't broached the possibility of calling on Grayson with you before this, but you've certainly been aware of my concern over how thinly we're spread. Harrington's report may have galvanized my concerns, but I've been thinking about this particular possible solution for two or three months now, particularly in light of my correspondence with Admiral Kuzak."

"*Kuzak!*" Janacek spat out the name like a fishbone. Theodosia Kuzak was the one senior fleet commander he'd been unable to get rid of. He'd had to choose between her or White Haven, given the way the citizens of San Martin worshiped the pair of them. White Haven might have liberated the system, but Kuzak had commanded the fleet which protected Trevor's Star for almost ten T-years. He'd wanted desperately to fire her right along with her precious friend White Haven, but High Ridge had overruled him. The Prime Minister had been unwilling to expend the political capital involved in firing both of the flag officers the San Martinos held in such high regard.

"Yes, Kuzak," Chakrabarti acknowledged. "That's one reason I haven't discussed the possibility with you. I knew anything she approved of would automatically . . . irritate you. But she's got a point, Edward. We're in trouble. How we got there is really immaterial at the moment in practical terms. Getting out of it is what matters, and if the Graysons are prepared to reinforce us, then I think we need to very seriously consider asking them to do just that."

"No," Janacek repeated in a somewhat calmer tone. "And not just because I don't trust the Graysons or Kuzak. I don't," he admitted, "and for good reason, I think. But leaving that completely aside, asking Grayson to send additional units to back up our pickets at this point could only be seen by the Republic as a provocative move."

"Provocative?"

"Of course it would be provocative! You're talking about strengthening our naval presence in the very systems whose possession is under dispute. How could that not be seen as a provocative gesture at this time?"

"Unless I'm very much mistaken, the diplomatic note we've just sent them could certainly be considered provocative, Edward!"

"Not in the same fashion. One is only a matter of diplomacy; the other is a matter of actual military movements. I think there's a very distinct difference between the two, myself."

"I don't think you and I are going to agree on this," Chakrabarti said after a moment. "So let me ask you one more time. Will you agree to ask the Prime Minister to modify our Silesian policy so that we can bring sizable portions of Task Force Thirty-Four home, or else to explore the possibility of seeking Grayson reinforcements for our system pickets?"

"No," Janacek said flatly.

"Very well." Chakrabarti stood. "In that case, I submit my resignation, effective immediately."

"You can't do this!"

"Yes, I can, Edward."

"You'll be ruined!"

"Perhaps I will. It's certainly possible. But in my judgment, it's far more likely that I'd be 'ruined' if I simply sat by and watched the shuttle crash."

"Oh?" Janacek looked scornfully at the taller man. "And have you discussed this with your brother-in-law and your cousin?"

"As a matter of fact, I have," Chakrabarti said, and Janacek blinked at him in astonishment. "Akahito made more or less the same arguments you've just made. In fact, his advice was that I just keep my mouth shut and do whatever I was told to do. I can't say I was too surprised by that. But Adam had a somewhat different viewpoint."

Janacek realized he was gaping at the First Space Lord and commanded his mouth to close. It wasn't easy. Like Chakrabarti, he was hardly surprised that Akahito Fitzpatrick had advised his cousin not to rock the boat. The Duke of Gray Water had been one of High Ridge's closest political allies for decades, after all. But Chakrabarti's brother-in-law, Adam Damakos, was another matter entirely.

"And just what did Mr. Damakos have to say about it?" The First Lord asked warily.

"I'm not sure it would be appropriate for me to discuss that with you," Chakrabarti replied. "I'll simply say that Adam is . . . increasingly less enamored of the current Government, despite New Kiev and MacIntosh's presence in it."

"What?" Janacek laughed scornfully. "He prefers that bleeding-heart, mealy-mouthed, babbling idiot Montaigne?"

"As a matter of fact, I believe he does," Chakrabarti said. "In fact, he's not the only Liberal MP who seems to me to be leaning in that direction. But what matters in this instance is that he's the ranking Liberal member of the Naval Affairs Committee in the Commons. That means he's considerably better informed on the realities of our naval posture than Akahito is, and his judgment is much the same as mine. We have too many responsibilities and too few hulls to meet them all. Either we find the extra hulls, or we reduce the responsibilities. Those are our only two options,

Edward. And if you can't agree with me on that, then you and I have no business working together."

"Very well," Janacek grated. "Your resignation will be accepted before the end of the day. I trust that I need not remind you of the provisions of the Official Secrets Act."

"No, you most certainly don't," Chakrabarti replied stiffly. "I'll keep my mouth shut about the privileged aspects of my knowledge. When the newsies ask me why I've resigned, I'll use that old standby about personalities that just don't mesh smoothly. But trust me, Edward. If you don't do something about this, I'm very much afraid that your concerns about why people may think I resigned are going to be the least of your problems."

CHAPTER FORTY-NINE

"**S**o much for suggesting that there might be some way to move *forward* with negotiations!" Elaine Descroix snarled.

For once, not even Marisa Turner seemed inclined to argue with her. The latest communique from Eloise Pritchart had arrived less than six hours earlier, and the entire Cabinet had been stunned by its terse, brutal rejection of any possibility of compromise.

"I can't believe this," New Kiev said softly, shaking her head with a stunned expression. "What in God's name could possess them to send us something like this?"

"At the risk of sounding like I'm saying I told you so," Janacek grated, "I'd say it's pretty clear. Theisman has miscalculated the military equation. They actually think they could win a new war with us, and they're willing to court one rather than make any reasonable concession."

"Surely that's too pessimistic a reading!" New Kiev protested, but it was obvious she was protesting against Fate, not dismissing Janacek's analysis.

"Whatever they may or may not be willing to court," High Ridge said finally into the silence New Kiev's protest had spawned, "we have no choice but to respond to this. And I don't see any way we can possibly allow this position to pass unchallenged. Even if it wouldn't be political suicide for this Government, *no* Manticoran government could possibly concede what Pritchart is obviously demanding. I think it's imperative that we tell them that as clearly as possible."

"This whole thing is sliding out of control," New Kiev objected. "Someone has to show at least some vestige of restraint, Michael!"

"Maybe someone does, but it's not us!" Descroix snapped, and thumped her fist on the hardcopy of the note Grosclaude had delivered. "We can't, Marisa! You and I have had our differences in the past, and I'm sure we'll have them in the future. But Pritchart has to know that what she's done is to reject the absolute minimum we would have to demand under any peace agreement. If we allow it to stand, it renders the final conclusion of any treaty absolutely impossible. As Michael says, *no* government—not even one led by Allen Summervale's resurrected ghost!—could concede this point and survive."

"No, it couldn't," High Ridge said heavily. "And even if it could, the Crown would refuse to ratify any treaty which accepted Pritchart's position." He didn't elaborate upon that particular point. There was no need to . . . and not one of his listeners doubted that Elizabeth would do just that, and constitutional crisis be damned. Her fury with "her" government had assumed proportions which were rapidly approaching a self-sustaining fusion reaction, and more than one of "her" ministers was astounded that she hadn't already vented her rage in public condemnation of the Government's naval policy. The only thing which could possibly explain her restraint was that she recognized such an attack would only make the interstellar situation worse and materially increase the risk of war.

"We will not only not accept this demand," the Prime Minister told them, "but reject it in no uncertain terms."

Elaine Descroix's eyes narrowed, and she gazed at him intently.

"Exactly what 'no uncertain terms' did you have in mind, Michael?"

"Given the present . . . uncertainty as to the actual naval balance of power," the Prime Minister said, bestowing a moderately venomous look upon Sir Edward Janacek, "it's essential that we not be responsible for initiating any sort of military confrontation."

"That's certainly true enough," Descroix agreed, joining him in glaring at Janacek. The First Lord glared back like a beleaguered bear besieged by too many hounds. True to his word, Chakrabarti had kept his mouth shut about the reasons for his resignation, but his departure hadn't helped a bit. In fact, as Janacek was becoming increasingly well aware, his own position at the Admiralty hung by a thread.

"The Admiralty has no intention of provoking any confrontations," he said flatly. "At the same time, I'd like to ask all of you to remember that before we ever sent our last note to Pritchart, I put forward a proposal for preventing this very situation from arising. Had the rest of the Cabinet supported me and Admiral Chakrabarti at that time," he continued, ruthlessly attaching the departed First Space Lord's name to a plan he'd never supported with any warmth, "our current problems might have been avoided. And Admiralty Chakrabarti might still be serving at the Admiralty."

No one else in the Cabinet knew what had actually passed between him and Chakrabarti, and he saw one or two eyes flicker away from his own as he stared at them defiantly.

"Well, that's all very well," Descroix said after a moment, "and no doubt you have a point, Edward. But Michael has one, too. And the preemptive strike you wanted to launch certainly would have represented 'initiating' a military confrontation!"

"I'm very well aware of that point," Janacek replied. "And I'm not disputing Michael's authority to rule against my proposal. But I want it firmly understood that it was a political decision, however well justified it may have been, to reject a military resolution of our difficulties."

"Are you saying you still want to pursue that option?" Descroix demanded.

"I'm not certain we still could, even if the Cabinet reversed itself and authorized us to. Given the fact that tensions are even higher now than they were then, it's entirely possible—even probable—that some or all of Theisman's modern vessels have been deployed away from Haven."

"Then what would you propose doing?" Stefan Young asked.

"Frankly, our purely military options are limited at this point," Janacek said. "There are several things we could do, but most of them would be purely cosmetic, in my opinion."

For just an instant, he considered purposing a further reinforcement of Trevor's Star. But only for an instant. Without calling on Grayson—which he would never do—the only place reinforcements could have come from would be Home Fleet. Diverting forces from the Star Kingdom's home system would have been an unthinkable admission of weakness and fear. Besides, there was no real need to. If necessary, Home Fleet in its entirety could be deployed to Trevor's Star in considerably less than a single standard day.

"So you recommend against shifting our deployments?" High Ridge asked.

"Any changes we made at this point would have a purely marginal effect. It would take weeks, at least, for news of them to reach Nouveau Paris, which would effectively prevent them from exercising any deterrent effect on Pritchart and Theisman in the interim. It's possible that when Theisman did learn of them, he might very well misinterpret them as responses generated out of panic. And even leaving all of that aside, if we start juggling our forces and the Republic does try something, we run the risk of being caught off balance. We could very easily find ourselves with units in transit from one star system to another instead of available at their current stations in the event of an attack.

"I'm not saying I might not change my opinion as the situation continues to develop and more information on Theisman's deployments becomes available. All I'm saying is that on the basis of what we now know, any redeployment we might attempt would be based on guesswork, at best. As a result, the chance of accomplishing anything worthwhile in military terms would be slight, especially in light of any such move's potentially escalating effect on the political situation."

The Prime Minister gazed at him for several long moments, then shrugged.

"You're the best informed on our military posture, Edward. If that's your advice, I'm inclined to take it. But at the same time, something more than a business-as-usual response is required in this case. Since the Republic has seen fit to be so terse and explicit in its latest communique to us, I propose that we be equally terse in response."

"Do you believe they're actually prepared—willing, I mean—to go back to war?" New Kiev asked unhappily.

"I don't know," High Ridge admitted with unwonted honesty. "I doubt that they would have been this confrontational without considering the possibility, at least. At the same time, they did stop short of formally breaking off talks. That suggests they're not prepared yet to simply walk away from the conference table. So it's time for us to point out to them that that's precisely the corner their intransigence is painting both sides into."

"Do you suppose," New Kiev suggested hesitantly, "that it might be worthwhile to suggest the possibility of a direct ministerial level conference? If we were to invite Secretary of State Giancola to personally visit the Star Kingdom, then perhaps it might be possible to put the brakes on even at this late date."

"I can't fault your motives for suggesting the possibility, Marisa," High Ridge replied heavily. "But I think that before we issue any such invitations, we have to make it plain we're not prepared to be dictated to. The first step is to make it absolutely clear to Pritchart and her administration that this outrageous escalation of her demands is completely unacceptable. Once we've pruned their expectations back to something which might conceivably be acceptable to us, it would make an enormous amount of sense to invite Giancola—or possibly even Pritchart herself—to visit Manticore in a bid to restart the peace process on a new basis."

Descroix gazed at him again. For just a moment she hesitated on the brink of asking him openly if what he'd just said represented the complete abandonment of their entire domestic political strategy. But she didn't. She couldn't, not in front of New Kiev. That was something she and the Prime Minister would have to discuss privately. In the meantime, however . . .

"So what you're saying," she said, "is that our first priority is to smack Pritchart down, after which we'll offer her a hand to stand back up."

"Perhaps a bit more bluntly phrased than I might have preferred, but, essentially, yes," High Ridge agreed.

"All right then. In that case, I think we need to consider exactly how we want to go about smacking her."

Swathes of brown could still be seen amidst the startling silver hair of the hazel-eyed man waiting in the shuttle pad's VIP lounge as Hamish Alexander debarked from the Grayson Space Navy pinnace which had collected him from the *Paul Tankersley*.

The earl had felt more than a little uncomfortable using Honor's private starship for this trip, even though he'd known it was silly of him. Honor herself had suggested that he do so in her letter to him, because the *Tankersley* was a very fast ship indeed. The fact that it enjoyed diplomatic immunity these days as Steadholder

Harrington's personal ship was another reason. But White Haven was honest enough with himself to admit that the true reason for his discomfort was the ship's name. He'd been aboard her several times before, but never since he had admitted his feelings for Honor to her. Now he felt vaguely as if using the ship named for her murdered lover was somehow an act of infidelity.

Which, he reflected with a wry mental grin, was not only silly of him but an example of the sorts of inconsequential things a man's mind could find to fasten upon when the potential for cataclysm threatened to overwhelm him.

"My Lord," the man waiting in the lounge greeted him.

"High Admiral," White Haven replied with equal formality, then smiled as he held out his hand.

"Welcome back to Grayson, Hamish," High Admiral Wesley Matthews said warmly, gripping the proffered hand and squeezing firmly.

"Thank you, Wesley," White Haven said, but then his own smile faded. "I only wish I were here under happier conditions," he said.

"So do we all," Matthews assured him, releasing his hand. The high admiral stepped back and waved towards a waiting air car. "Under the circumstances," he said, "I suspected that you'd prefer to go straight to Protector's Palace."

Protector Benjamin rose behind his desk and held out his hand as an armsman in Mayhew maroon and gold ushered White Haven and Matthews into his office. Major Rice, Benjamin's personal armsman, stood unobtrusively behind him, and Gregory Paxton was already present in his position as the director of Sword Intelligence. Honor's onetime intelligence officer had aged noticeably. He walked with a cane these days, and he made no effort to hoist himself to his feet, but his eyes were still bright and alert, and he nodded a welcome to the newcomers.

"Hamish." Benjamin's greeting was warm, but it was also subdued and dark with anxiety.

"Your Grace," White Haven replied as they shook hands. "Thank you for agreeing to see me on such short notice."

"There's no need to thank me," Benjamin said, shaking his head. "I'd have made room in my schedule even if you'd turned up totally unannounced. As it was, Honor's letter had warned me you'd probably be coming."

"Well," White Haven acknowledged with a grimace, "she certainly predicted Janacek's reaction accurately enough, so I don't suppose I should be surprised she predicted mine, as well!"

"Under the circumstances," Matthews said grimly, "it didn't really require very much clairvoyance on her part, I'm afraid."

"Probably not," White Haven agreed. Benjamin waved him into a chair, and the earl sat obediently. An armsman appeared beside him, and White Haven grinned, despite the seriousness of the moment, as a bottle of Old Tillman materialized on the small table at his elbow.

"Now," Benjamin said briskly as the earl reached for his beer, "according to the letter Honor sent me, she believes Eloise Pritchart is seriously contemplating resuming active operations against the Star Kingdom. I have to admit that even now that surprises me just a bit. Do you think she's right, Hamish?"

"I'm afraid I do," White Haven said somberly. He set the beer bottle back down, and leaned forward in the chair, resting his elbows on his knees. "I'm not privy to the details of the diplomatic exchanges between High Ridge and Pritchart, Your Grace. I don't think anyone outside the High Ridge Cabinet is—not in the Star Kingdom, anyway. From what I do know, though, it seems fairly obvious that the treaty negotiations have been deteriorating steadily for months now."

"Actually," Paxton said quietly, "the deterioration you refer to started well over a T-year and a half ago, My Lord." White Haven looked at him, and the intelligence director shrugged. "There was never any real hope of a treaty, but it's only been in the past eighteen T-months or so that Pritchart began really pushing the Star Kingdom for some sort of significant progress."

"All right," White Haven agreed. "A year and a half, then. At any rate, the truce talks have been shuddering towards a breakdown for quite some time. Now, if my brother's sources in the Foreign Office are correct, they're on the brink of a complete collapse. In the middle of all this, we have Theisman announcing the existence of his new navy, and then this 'Second Fleet' they've run in on Honor in Silesia."

He shook his head.

"Like Honor, the only explanation I can come up with is that they're actively planning to attack us," he sighed, still shaking his head. "And I wish to Hell I could blame them for it!"

"I'm afraid we agree with Lady Harrington and Earl White Haven, Your Grace," Matthews put in. "Naval Intelligence has shared everything we had with Sword Intelligence, and Greg's analysts agree with ours. We can't say for certain that the Republic has definitely made up its mind to launch an attack, but it's obviously putting its assets in place with that possibility in mind. We've known that for quite some time. Lady Harrington's discovery that they're actually going so far as to deploy forces all the way to Silesia confirms our existing suspicions."

"Worse than that," Paxton added, "the presence of Havenite forces in Silesian space may be an indication that their war plans are not only already in place but have already been activated."

All eyes turned to him, and he shrugged.

"I'm not saying that's what's happened. I'm saying that we have to be aware that it *may* be what's happened. If it is, we may have very little time to respond—assuming we have any time at all."

"What do you want us to do, Hamish?" Benjamin asked, gazing at his guest intently.

"I don't know exactly what was in Honor's letter to you," White Haven replied. "I know what she said to me, and Elizabeth allowed me to view her letter." He smiled suddenly. "I think it's probably a very good thing Janacek didn't get to see either of them. Although it might have simplified our problem a bit when he dropped dead of pure apoplexy!"

"Now there's an image I'll treasure," Matthews observed almost dreamily, and he and White Haven grinned at each other.

"Anyway," the earl resumed, turning back to Benjamin, "as I say, I don't know exactly what she said to you. What she suggested to us was that we needed to confer with you if Janacek proved . . . unresponsive. And she pointed out that Trevor's Star is the absolute linchpin of our position within Republican territory."

"How did Elizabeth react to Janacek's response?" Benjamin asked quietly, and White Haven winced mentally in memory.

"Not . . . well," he admitted. "She wanted to call a news conference, lay Honor's letters in front of the 'faxes, and publicly charge her Prime Minister and her First Lord of the Admiralty with everything short of outright treason."

"I'd call that reacting 'not well,'" Benjamin agreed judiciously. "On the other hand, it might actually have worked, you know."

"Certainly it might have," White Haven agreed, "but Willie sat on her long enough to talk her out of it—for now, at least. As he pointed out, what we do know about Pritchart's notes indicate that they've become increasingly belligerent. That her frustration and anger is what's driving the negotiations now, if you will. And as we've just acknowledged, it's entirely possible that the Republic has already decided to commit to military action. That leaves us with the choice between trying to bring High Ridge down—which might not be as easy as we'd like to think, given how public awareness of our deteriorating relations with Haven is lagging behind events—or leaving it in place at least until we get through the present crisis.

"If they haven't decided to attack us, then drop-kicking High Ridge and Janacek, assuming we could do it, might be the best thing we could possibly do. Especially if we got it done in time to repair the worst of Janacek's blunders. But we don't think they'd go quietly, and if the Star Kingdom suddenly finds itself embroiled in a major domestic political crisis, it could be the final straw needed to push Pritchart into attacking if she *hasn't* already committed."

The earl shrugged.

"Willie managed to convince Elizabeth that, under the circumstances, her best bet is to just file all of this away for now and concentrate on what we can do to prepare for a possible attack despite 'her' government. The best possible outcome would be for all of this to blow over with no shots fired, even if High Ridge got credit for that outcome. If shots are fired, then she'll have the information of the way they screwed the pooch on file when it comes time to form a new government. And by doing what we can quietly, behind the scenes and without any public fanfare, we may actually accomplish some good without striking the final spark a domestic political dogfight might provide."

"Um." Benjamin frowned, then leaned back and tugged at an earlobe.

"I follow the logic. I'm not sure I agree with it, but your domestic situation is different from ours. And I do agree that the best possible outcome would be no shots fired . . . however unlikely I think that might be."

"I agree, Your Grace," Matthews said. "Both that it would be the best outcome and that it's unlikely at this point. And Lady Harrington's analysis of the Peeps' possible opening gambits certainly makes sense to me. If the Republic really intends to attack the Star Kingdom anywhere, it's going to hit Trevor's Star as one of its primary objectives—if not *the* primary objective."

"And knowing Thomas Theisman," White Haven said grimly, "it's going to hit Third Fleet with enough strength to smash it to bits."

"Absolutely." Matthews nodded. "Not just to take the terminus away from you, either. That would be important enough, given the logistics advantages it offers, of course. But their real objective would be Third Fleet's SD(P)s and CLACs."

"Agreed. But I can't get Janacek to agree to reinforce. He flatly refuses to do it."

"In all fairness to Janacek," Matthews said in the voice of a man who manifestly found it very difficult to be anything of the sort, "he doesn't have a great deal he could reinforce *with*. I'd imagine that he's hoping desperately that everything will blow over without ever coming to actual fighting. If the Republic does attack, he probably figures he can do a repeat of your relief of Basilisk from Trevor's Star using units of Home Fleet direct from Manticore."

"Then he's dreaming," White Haven said flatly. "Even if he had Home Fleet sitting out on the Junction, which would leave Manticore and Sphinx effectively unprotected, he couldn't get them through the Junction and into support range of Theodosia's fleet before an attacking force could pin her against San Martin and force her into action." He laughed harshly, the sound cold and ugly. "I found that out when I couldn't stop Giscard from blowing the entire Basilisk infrastructure to Hell!"

"Oh, I know that," Matthews snorted. "The problem is that I don't think Janacek does."

"Neither do I," Benjamin said. He tipped back in his own chair, gazing at White Haven thoughtfully. "Do you think Janacek would accept a squadron or two of our SD(P)s to support Third Fleet?"

"I doubt it very much, Your Grace," Paxton said before White Haven could respond. Everyone looked at him, and he shrugged again. "Janacek has made his attitude towards Grayson abundantly and unfortunately clear. He doesn't like us, he doesn't trust us, and he finds the very thought of asking us for help humiliating and demeaning. I'm sure he'll find some other justification for turning the offer down. He'll probably convince himself that moving Grayson warships into the disputed area would constitute a provocative escalation. But if that's not his reason, he'll find another one."

"Even if he wouldn't," Matthews said with a troubled expression, "I'm not certain how much exposure we could accept here at home, Your Grace. With the Protector's Own away, we're already short sixteen SD(P)s and six carriers. That's a sizable chunk of the entire Navy. Allowing for units down for repair or overhaul, we've got approximately sixty available modern ships of the wall and only eleven carriers. That's enough for me to feel completely confident about holding Grayson against anything our intelligence people estimate the Republic could throw at us. But with every ship we divert to someplace like Trevor's Star, our margin of security drops. And if I were the Republic of Haven and I intended to go back to war against the Manticoran Alliance, then I'd certainly make taking out Grayson a high early priority."

"He's right there," White Haven said unhappily.

"I don't doubt he is," Benjamin acknowledged. "But at the same time, I don't really expect an early attack on us here."

"Why not, Your Grace?" Matthews asked. It wasn't a challenge, only a question.

"Because they've been trolling diplomatic bait in front of us for the last six months in an effort to get us to withdraw from the Alliance," Benjamin said.

White Haven jerked upright in his chair, and even Matthews looked astonished, but Paxton only sat there looking inscrutable.

"Their efforts haven't succeeded, Hamish," Benjamin told the earl with just a hint of a smile. "And they certainly never suggested that military operations were imminent. But it's fairly evident to me that they've been attempting to split the Alliance for some time, and I really couldn't tell you how successful they may have been elsewhere. We've been politely noncommittal, but you may have noticed that we didn't exactly blow the whistle on them to the rest of the Alliance and the galaxy at large, either. Hopefully, they think that's because we're covering our bets by keeping the door open for a possible future agreement. That there's at least the possibility that we're pissed off enough with High Ridge to cut our losses and sign up with them—or at least agree to stay out of their way—if the austen drops.

"That's all problematical, of course. But what matters just now is that I read their diplomacy as implying that they're very tightly focused on the Star Kingdom. Unless I'm very mistaken, they see Manticore's defeat as the only means by which they're going to be able to reclaim their occupied territory. They don't want to fight anyone else. For that matter, I don't think they *want* to fight the Star Kingdom; they just don't think they have any other option.

"If I'm right, then they'll probably want to give anybody who might decide to become neutral—and let's face it, Hamish; quite a few members of the Alliance would have to find that tempting after the way High Ridge has treated us all—the chance to do just that. Besides, however much Theisman may have accomplished in building up the Navy, he doesn't have an infinite supply of hulls. If Honor is correct and he's already diverted a sizable force to Silesia, that's going to restrict the numbers available to him here even more. We've just agreed that Trevor's Star has to be their primary objective. I don't think Thomas Theisman is likely to risk an attack on Grayson until and unless he believes he can launch it in overwhelming force."

"And if he doesn't know we've diverted forces to reinforce Trevor's Star, then he won't believe he can," Matthews said slowly.

"That's what I'm thinking," Benjamin agreed.

"But if High Ridge won't ask for help in the first place, what makes you think he'll accept it if you offer it?" White Haven asked.

"Who says I'm going to 'offer' anything?" Benjamin countered, and snorted when White Haven looked at him. "First of all, there's no time to waste pussyfooting around while High Ridge and Janacek figure out which is their ass and which is their elbow. Secondly, if I made any sort of formal offer to send even more of our Navy off to pull Manticore's chestnuts out of the fire at this point, even the Conclave of Steaders would pitch a fit. You don't even want to think about how the Keys would respond!

"No. If I commit forces to Trevor's Star at all, I'm not going to ask anyone if I can send them. I'm just going to send them."

White Haven blinked as Benjamin's statement drove home to him once again the difference between the personal authority the Protector wielded and that which the Constitution allowed to Elizabeth.

"But how could we get them there?" Matthews sat back in his chair and rubbed his chin. "It's going to take us at least a few days—probably a week, minimum—to organize and plan the kind of movement it sounds like we're talking about. And it's over a hundred and fifty light-years from Grayson to Trevor's Star. That's over three weeks' voyage time. Do we have an entire month to get into position?"

"I don't know," White Haven replied, "but I don't think we can assume we do. Not if they've already deployed forces to Silesia."

"In that case, we won't assume it," Benjamin said. "And we won't spend three weeks getting there, either. We'll use the Junction."

"The *Junction*?" White Haven looked at the Protector. "How are you going to do that, Your Grace? If Janacek and High Ridge won't request your assistance, what makes you think they'll let you go sailing through the Junction in front of God and everybody? At the very least they'd be deeply humiliated, and if they've convinced themselves that strengthening Trevor's Star with Manticoran units would be 'provocative,' they certainly won't want you reinforcing it with Graysons!"

"Actually," Benjamin said grimly, "I don't much care what the two of them would like, Hamish. And as for their trying to prevent us from using the Junction, I don't think that would be very wise of them. Under Article XII of the Manticoran Alliance Charter, any treaty partner has free and unlimited access to the Junction for its warships. If I decide I want to send the entire damned Navy through the Manticoran Wormhole Junction, I have the legal right to do so and be damned to anyone who tries to stop me."

He smiled at his guest, and it was not a pleasant expression.

"Under the circumstances," he said softly, "I rather hope they do try."

"I cannot *believe* this!" Eloise Pritchart spat, glaring at the hardcopy in front of her. "Of all the unmitigated, lying gall! How *dare* they hand us something like this?!"

"Well, I certainly didn't expect it either," Giancola began, "but—"

"'But' nothing!" Pritchart snarled. "They've flat out lied to their own people and to ours!"

Thomas Theisman sat in his own chair at the conference table, as shocked and almost as furious as Pritchart herself as he looked back down at the critical passage of the latest note from Manticore.

"I don't understand it," LePic muttered. "Why would they do this? We told them our territorial demands didn't include Trevor's Star. We told them that in so many words."

Theisman nodded almost unconsciously, for he shared his friend's confusion fully. Why, when the Republic had outright announced its willingness to renounce all claim of sovereignty over Trevor's Star had the Manties effectively threatened to unilaterally withdraw from the peace negotiations on the grounds that the Republic had demanded that sovereignty be returned to it?

"Could they possibly have misunderstood somehow?" Walter Sanderson asked slowly.

"How?" Pritchart demanded furiously. "How could even an idiot like High Ridge have misunderstood something this simple!" She pawed angrily through the folder in front of her until she found her copy of the Republic's most recent note to the Star Kingdom.

"'In response to the Star Kingdom's request for clarification as to the Republic's view of the status of the Trevor's Star system,'" she read aloud in a hard, tight voice, "'the Republic specifically does not claim sovereignty over that star system.'" She slammed the note back down on the tabletop. "*Not* claim sovereignty, Walter! I fail to see how we could possibly have been any clearer than that!"

Sanderson shook his head slowly, clearly bemused.

"I'm afraid there's one very simple possible explanation," Tony Nesbitt said. All eyes swung to him, and he shrugged. "This is about as bald-faced a misrepresentation of the truth as anyone could possibly have presented. It's not a misunderstanding; it's a *lie*. It's an effort to shift the full responsibility for the failure of the negotiations onto us. The only reason I can see for them to do that is because they intend to break off those negotiations, and they want their people and the rest of the galaxy to believe it was our fault."

"And what do they hope to accomplish?" Hanriot asked, but she no longer sounded as skeptical as she once had where Nesbitt's long-standing suspicions about the Star Kingdom's motives were concerned.

"I think that's clear enough, Rachel," the Secretary of Commerce said in a flat voice. "They don't want just Trevor's Star. They plan to keep *all* of the occupied systems. They're just using Trevor's Star as the wedge."

"I think it's possible we're all overreacting just a bit," Giancola said. The eyes which had focused on Nesbitt traversed back to him, and he waved one hand. "I'm not trying to minimize the huge conflict between what we told them and what they seem to be trying to say that we told them. And obviously I've always been suspicious about their ultimate intentions myself. But let's all back off for a moment and try to catch our breaths."

"It's a little late to be playing Mr. Reasonable, Arnold," Pritchart told him a bit spitefully. "Especially after this." She thumped the text of the most recent Manticoran note yet again.

"There's always time to let reason have its say, Madame President," Giancola replied. "That's the most important single fundamental principle of diplomacy. And it's not as if we have to respond to this immediately. No one outside the Cabinet, with the exception of Ambassador Grosclaude, knows anything about the specific content of this note. If we keep a lid on this, at least to the extent of not waxing publicly furious over it, then we've got a chance to cool tempers down and work our way through it."

"No, we don't," Pritchart said flatly, and Giancola felt his smile congeal ever so slightly as something about the President's iron tone sounded warning bells.

"Madame President—"

"I know all about the gentleman's agreement about respecting the confidentiality of official diplomatic communications," Pritchart grated. "But as far as I'm concerned, it no longer applies."

"Madame President—!"

"I said it no longer applies, Arnold!" She shook her head. "The only reason they could possibly have drafted this piece of crap," she said, "was to justify exactly the scenario Tony's just described. Which means that at some point, probably after they attack us, they're going to publish their version of our diplomatic correspondence. And judging from this," she thumped the Manticoran note again, "their version of it isn't going to bear very much resemblance to reality. Well, if that's what they have in mind, I'll damned well see the truth released to the newsies and the galaxy at large first!"

Giancola swallowed hard. Things were moving much more quickly than he'd anticipated. Pritchart's decision to go public with the text of Descroix's most recent note was hardly unexpected, but he hadn't planned on her reaching it this quickly. He was a little nervous about what might happen when the Republic and the Star Kingdom published their versions of their official diplomatic correspondence and the discrepancies between them came to light, but he wasn't too concerned about it. Or, he hadn't been, at any rate. He'd calculated that by the time the two star nations reached that point, each of them would be completely prepared to believe the other was editing the actual notes in order to support its own territorial ambitions. Certainly he and Grosclaude had been very careful to insure that all of the official archived copies of the Republic's correspondence agreed with the versions approved by Eloise Pritchart.

But he hadn't counted on the sheer, fiery passion of Pritchart's anger. And that, he suddenly realized, had been remarkably stupid of him. She'd fooled him. She'd insisted on being so calm, so magisterial. On thinking things through and 'giving peace a chance.' And because she'd been and done those things, he'd expected her to go on doing them. He'd counted on at least one more round of notes in which he would magically soothe away the tension over Trevor's Star. But that was because he'd forgotten that before she was ever President Pritchart, before she was ever People's Commissioner Pritchart, Eloise Pritchart had been "Brigade Commander Delta" . . . one of the three top field commanders in the most effective single guerrilla movement to have fought against the Legislaturalists before the Pierre Coup.

Arnold Giancola felt a sudden, icy sinking sensation as he realized just how completely he'd misread her probable response to his carefully engineered Manticoran "provocation."

"As far as I am concerned," she said in a voice of hammered iron, "this travesty, this . . . farrago of lies, constitutes a unilateral decision to break off negotiations with us. I intend to lay it before a joint session of Congress, and on the basis of its obvious dishonesty and transparently disguised justification for the Star Kingdom to permanently annex planets occupied by our citizens regardless of those citizens' desires, announce my intention to resume active military operations!"

CHAPTER FIFTY

"**G**ood evening, Lady North Hollow. I'm so happy you could come!"

"Why, thank you! I was delighted to be invited," Georgia Young replied as the butler ushered her into the palatial sitting room. It was a very large sitting room, for an apartment, even in the City of Landing, where space was hardly at the premium it was on more populous planets. It might be smaller than, say, the Green Sitting Room in the Landing residence of the Earl of the Tor, but not by all that much. Not surprisingly, perhaps, given that the luxurious "apartment" to which it belonged easily ran to at least three thousand square meters. In, needless to say, one of the most expensive residential towers in the entire capital.

Not bad for a commoner, Georgia thought as she handed her stylish jacket to the butler with a gracious smile. He smiled back at her, and one of her eyebrows tried to quirk in surprise. Mostly because it was unusual for any well-trained, professional servant to return the smile—or frown—of one of his employer's guests. But also because there was something . . . odd about that smile. Something she couldn't quite put a finger on.

The butler bowed slightly, and withdrew from the sitting room, and Georgia gave herself a mental shake. Perhaps there had been something unusual about his smile. But equally perhaps she was imagining things. Not that she was in the habit of doing something that silly, but this afternoon was shaping up to be unusual enough to put any self-respecting troubleshooter for the Conservative Association on edge. She wondered again if she should have mentioned the invitation to High Ridge before she accepted it. And decided once more that she'd been right not to do so. It would be a mistake to let him believe that she felt she required his permission for anything she chose to do, and an even bigger mistake to allow *herself* to believe it.

"Please," her hostess invited. "Sit down. May I offer you some form of refreshment? Tea, perhaps? Or something a bit stronger?"

"No, thank you," Georgia said as she seated herself in a powered armchair that was almost appallingly comfortable. "While I was delighted when you asked me to stop by this afternoon, My Lady, I was also very surprised. And I'm afraid that my schedule was already pretty fully booked before this unanticipated pleasure presented itself. I can only stay a short time, because the Earl and I are due to join the Prime Minister for a fund-raising dinner tonight." She smiled. "And while I appreciate your having thought to ask me to drop by, I'm sure you'll forgive me if I'm blunt enough to say that I rather doubted it was for a social occasion."

"Of course I'll forgive you." Her hostess chuckled. "In fact, I'm sure you've heard that I tend to be on the blunt side myself. I'm afraid my own social graces are less than polished, which always caused my parents quite a bit of distress. Still, I suppose I should point out that, socially speaking, of course, you really don't have to address me as 'My Lady' any longer, My Lady. I'm afraid I'm just plain Cathy Montaigne these days."

"And before my marriage to Stefan," Georgia responded with another gracious smile, "I was 'just plain' Georgia Sakristos, so perhaps we could simply dispense with any 'My Ladies' from either side?"

"That would be perfectly fine—and so diplomatic!" Montaigne chuckled again, in high good humor, and Georgia wondered what she felt so cheerful about. She also wondered whether or not Montaigne's obvious good cheer was a good sign or a bad one. According to the ex-countess' dossier, she was at her most dangerous when she smiled.

"While I'm being diplomatic," Georgia said, "allow me to congratulate you both on your election to the House of Commons and on the power base you seem to be building there. I trust you'll forgive me if I don't repeat those congratulations in public, since Stefan and the Prime Minister would never speak to me again if they caught me exchanging pleasantries with the enemy. And, of course, Countess New Kiev would probably do something far worse than that."

"I'm sure she would," Montaigne said with a blinding smile. "Indeed, I spend the occasional evening contemplating the degree of irritation I must be causing both of them. Well, all three, I suppose, counting your husband. Of course, I have to wonder if anyone *does* count him. Including yourself."

"I beg your pardon?" Georgia stiffened, coming upright as abruptly as the luxuriously enfolding chair allowed. Her voice projected both surprise and an edge of anger, but there was another emotion behind those she'd deliberately allowed herself to show. A sudden, abrupt tingle of anxiety. A suspicion that perhaps Montaigne's cheerfulness might turn out to have been a very bad sign indeed.

"Oh, I am sorry!" Montaigne said, with every appearance of sincerity. "I did say my social graces leave something to be desired, didn't I? I certainly didn't mean to denigrate your husband. I simply meant that it's fairly well known in political circles that the Earl depends heavily on your . . . advice, shall we say? I wouldn't want to be tacky enough to go about using phrases like 'the power behind the throne' or anything equally cliché-ish, but surely you know that no one in Landing doubts that Earl North Hollow follows your guidance very closely."

"Stefan does confide in me," Georgia said, her tone stiffly proper. "And I do advise him, from time to time, when he does. Nor do I think it's inappropriate for me to do so, particularly given my position with the Conservative Association."

"Oh, I never meant to suggest that *that* was improper, in any way!" Montaigne smiled again. "I simply wanted to establish that whatever your official place in the hierarchy of the High Ridge Government, your actual niche is somewhat higher."

"Very well," Georgia agreed, eyeing her hostess narrowly. "I'll concede that I have somewhat more influence behind the scenes than may be apparent to the public eye. I suppose in that regard I'm rather similar to, say, Captain Zilwicki."

"Oh, *touché*!" Montaigne's green eyes glowed, and she clapped her hands in delight. "That was very well done," she congratulated her guest. "I scarcely felt the knife slipping between my ribs!"

"I hope you'll forgive me for saying this, Ms. Montaigne," Georgia observed, "but the Conservative Association has amassed a fairly extensive file on you. Especially since your election to the Commons. And when you invited me over, I reviewed that file, of course. It said, among other things, that you enjoy being disconcertingly direct. An observation whose accuracy I'm rapidly coming to appreciate."

"Well, it would never do to disappoint all of the astute analysts, yourself included, who labor so diligently on the CA's behalf, now would it?"

"Indeed not. On the other hand, perhaps you and I could agree to put up our foils and get to the real purpose of my visit . . . whatever it is?"

"Certainly. You do have that fund-raiser to attend." Montaigne smiled yet again, and pressed a button on the wrist com disguised as an extremely expensive antique wristwatch. "I'm afraid the jig is up, Anton," she said into it. "Would you care to join us?"

Georgia crooked an elegant eyebrow but said nothing. Then a door concealed behind a tasteful light sculpture slid open, and Anton Zilwicki stepped through the sculpture into the room.

Georgia studied him with carefully concealed interest. She'd been preparing a dossier on him since his and Montaigne's return from Old Terra, and especially since Montaigne had decided to stand for election as an MP. The more she'd discovered, the more impressed she'd become. She strongly suspected that Montaigne's surprising decision to stand for a seat in the Commons had been Zilwicki's inspiration. The man had a positive talent for "thinking outside the box," and it was obvious to Georgia that he and Montaigne made a potent and potentially dangerous team. She was just as happy that her marriage to Stefan placed her firmly in the ranks of the Conservative Association. At least the team of Montaigne–Zilwicki was unlikely to become a direct threat to her own power base . . . unlike what she strongly suspected was going to happen to New Kiev in the next two or three T-years.

This was her first opportunity to see Zilwicki in the flesh, as it were, and she was forced to admit that he was an impressive specimen. No one was ever going to call him handsome, but neither was anyone ever going to call him anything uncomplimentary if they were within arm's reach of him. She felt an almost overwhelming desire to chuckle at the thought of her husband's expression if he should happen to find himself trapped in a small room with an irate Zilwicki, but that didn't keep her instincts from twanging. She was far too experienced not to realize that they were rapidly coming to the true reason Montaigne had invited her to "drop by." Not that they were making any particular effort to pretend otherwise.

"Lady North Hollow, allow me to introduce Captain Anton Zilwicki," Montaigne said cheerfully.

"Captain." Georgia gave him a small, seated half-bow of greeting and allowed the frankly measuring edge of her glance to show clearly. "Your reputation precedes you," she added.

"As does yours," Zilwicki acknowledged in his deep, rumbling voice.

"Well!" Georgia continued, returning her attention to her hostess. "I presume that the Captain's presence indicates that you have some startling bit of political intelligence to bestow upon me? That, after all, would have been the reason that the Prime Minister, for example, might have seen fit to invite me into a similar meeting."

"There are certain advantages to dealing with a fellow professional," Zilwicki observed. "Efficiency and directness, if nothing else."

"I do try not to waste time when there's no tactical advantage in doing so," Georgia conceded.

"In that case," Montaigne put in, "I suppose I owe you five dollars, Anton." Georgia glanced at her questioningly, and the ex-countess shrugged. "He bet me that you wouldn't spend any time beating around the bush." She smiled at Georgia for a moment, then turned back to her towering, slab-sided lover. "Should I ask Isaac to step back in for a moment, Anton?"

"I doubt that will be necessary," Zilwicki told her. He smiled, but the smile, Georgia noticed, never touched his eyes at all. Nor did he look at Montaigne. His attention was completely focused upon their guest, and it was difficult for Georgia not to shiver under its weight.

"The reason we invited you here," he told her after a moment, "was to offer you a certain opportunity. One I think you'd probably be wise to accept."

"Opportunity?" Georgia repeated calmly. "What sort of opportunity?"

"The opportunity," Montaigne replied in a voice which was suddenly calm, almost cold, and very, very focused, "to withdraw from politics and leave the Star Kingdom."

"Excuse me?" Georgia managed not to blink in surprise, but it wasn't easy.

"It's really a very good opportunity," Montaigne told her in that same chill voice. "Especially the bit about leaving the Star Kingdom. I'd recommend that you do it as tracelessly as possible, too. If you agree with us, we're prepared to give you up to three days' headstart . . . Elaine."

Georgia had opened her mouth to snap an angry retort, but it closed with a snap, retort unspoken, as the name "Elaine" sent a sudden icy chill through her. Her eyes clung to Montaigne for perhaps two heartbeats, then snapped to Zilwicki. Deadly as the ex-countess might be in the purely political arena, there was no question in Georgia's mind as to which half of the partnership had turned up the information that name implied.

She considered trying to brazen it out, but only for an instant. Zilwicki's reputation for competence and thoroughness had become very well established in certain rarefied circles over the past four T-years.

"I see," she said instead, forcing her voice to come out sounding calm and collected. "I haven't heard that name in quite a few years. I congratulate you on making the connection between it and me. But I'm afraid I don't quite understand why the fact that you have leads you to believe that you can . . . convince me to leave the Star Kingdom at all, much less 'tracelessly.' "

"My dear Lady Young," Montaigne cooed, "I very much doubt that the Prime Minister would be at all happy to hear about Elaine Komandorski's career before she went to work for the late, unlamented Dmitri Young. Such sordid stuff! And, you know, that little affair of yours with the badger game and the industrial intelligence you extorted from that *unfortunate* gentleman. You remember— the one who committed suicide?" She shook her head. "I'm positive the Prime Minister's delicate sensibilities and exquisite sense of justice would be completely shocked by that one."

"I see that your reputation is well deserved, Captain," Georgia said, gazing steadily at Zilwicki. "On the other hand, I doubt very much that you have any proof of Ms. Montaigne's . . . accusation. If, and please note that I did say *if*," she added for the benefit of the inevitable recorders, "I had indeed had anything to do with an affair such as she's just described, I feel confident that someone in my position would have spent the intervening time making certain there was no proof of the fact that I had."

"I'm sure you would have," Zilwicki rumbled. "Unfortunately, as accomplished as you are, you're also merely mortal. I'm afraid you missed the odd witness along the way. I have three very interesting depositions, actually."

"Depositions which, I feel sure," Georgia said, still much more calmly than she felt, "must amount to no more than hearsay. Partly, of course, because I never had anything to do with the events Ms. Montaigne is describing. But also because if I *had* had anything to do with them, I would have been certain that I had no accomplices who might have been able to testify against me of their own first-hand knowledge."

"I'm sure you would have," Zilwicki conceded, and in someone else, Georgia might have thought she'd seen a twinkle in his eyes. Of course, the thought of "twinkle" and Anton Zilwicki were two concepts which were mutually contradictory, especially at a moment like this. There was too much Gryphon bedrock in the man. "Of course, as Duchess Harrington and Earl White Haven discovered not so very long ago," he continued, "hearsay testimony can be quite devastating in the court of public opinion."

No, definitely *not* a twinkle, Georgia thought. At best a gleam . . . and an ugly one, at that.

"But as the Duchess and the Earl also demonstrated," she replied, "false hearsay evidence used in an effort to discredit someone has a tendency to rebound against the accuser. And given the many connections my husband's family has, I feel sure we would be able to weather any such accusation. Why, you might be astonished by the people who would come forward to testify to the uprightness of my character!"

She smiled sweetly, but her confidence took another blow when neither Montaigne nor Zilwicki even flinched at her oblique reference to the power of the North Hollow Files.

"On the contrary, I wouldn't be surprised at all," Zilwicki told her. "No doubt it would be embarrassing for them when a DNA scan demonstrated that you were indeed Elaine Komandorski. You were quite efficient in obliterating Elaine's public record, but you missed at least one copy of your dossier with the Landing City Police." He smiled at the flinch she couldn't quite conceal. "I'll concede that there are no convictions in Elaine's LCPD file, but it's truly amazing how many times she was investigated. And the two times that charges were dropped because the key witness suddenly and mysteriously—and permanently—vanished would make fascinating reading. Under those circumstances, I suppose it would only be natural for your friends and allies to attempt to convince the public that such a sterling and upright individual as yourself could never have been guilty of all the terrible things the police thought you'd done. Unless, of course, the Prime Minister decided that, just as with certain individuals accused of trafficking in genetic slaves, it would be more politically expedient to throw you to the wolves."

"I think," she said, in a flatter, harder voice, "that you may be underestimating my . . . influence with the Prime Minister."

"Ah! So he *is* in the files," Montaigne observed. "I always suspected he was. Still, Elaine, you'd have to have a very strong hold on him to convince him to stand loyally by you. Especially now, with the diplomatic situation deteriorating the way it is." She shook her head mournfully. "I'm afraid my reading of Baron High Ridge's character suggests that, under the circumstances, he'd be inclined to do the right thing and, however regretfully, disassociate himself from anyone who might once have been involved in such improper acts, however peripherally. After all, whatever you might want to do with the information on him in the files, there'd be any number of powerful people who'd feel compelled to stop you. I mean, think of how many people's careers and political agendas depend on his remaining in power. Unless, of course, you have enough on all of them to convince the entire Government to commit *seppuku* to save your own neck. Because—just between us—I don't think I'd count on them to do it out of loyalty and the goodness of their hearts."

"Perhaps not. But even if they didn't choose to speak out in my behalf, I'm scarcely without a power base of my own from which to defend myself against such libelous accusations."

"Well, 'libelous' is a very value-laden term," Zilwicki said. "For example, if someone were to go to the LCPD and provide them with evidence that a certain Elaine Komandorski, shortly before she vanished and one Georgia Sakristos appeared on the scene, was involved in the murder of one of the PD's own criminal fraud investigators, I'm sure they wouldn't consider that libel. Not until they'd investigated very thoroughly, at any rate."

"I see." There was nothing at all pleasant about her voice now, but it was warmer than her eyes as she glared at him. "On the other hand, when it turned out that it was impossible to prove those allegations—because, of course, they would be completely false—I'm sure the courts would be inclined to consider it libel, given that the allegations would have originated with a political opponent. The Crown looks with a certain disfavor on people who attempt to use the courts as a political weapon, Captain."

"They certainly do," he agreed. "And while it pains me to admit it, it's entirely possible that there are enough judges in your famous files for you to survive even with the interesting odds and ends of evidence I've already managed to assemble. On the other hand, it doesn't really matter. I don't need to go anywhere near the police. Or the courts."

"Meaning what?" she demanded tautly.

"Meaning that once I discovered Elaine's existence," Zilwicki said, "I found myself wondering where she'd come from? I mean, she just . . . appeared one day, didn't she? And with such a substantial store of initial operating capital."

"What do you mean?" Georgia heard the quaver in her own voice, and cursed herself for it. But there was nothing she could do about it, any more than there was any way to prevent herself from paling.

"Meaning that I found your first biosculpt technician," Zilwicki told her very, very softly. "The one who rekeyed the genetic sequence on your tongue."

Georgia Young sat absolutely still, stunned into a realm far beyond mere disbelief. How? How could even someone with Anton Zilwicki's reputation have dug that deep? She'd buried that. Buried it where it would never see the light of day again. Buried it behind Elaine, willing even for someone to find her original criminal record because they would stop there, without going still deeper into who she'd been before Elaine.

"Of course," Zilwicki went on, "there's no law against having the number removed, is there? Most freed slaves don't have the resources to pay for it, but having it removed certainly isn't a crime.

But he kept the record of the original number, Elaine. The number of a slave the Ballroom has been looking for for years. The slave who sold out an entire freighter full of escaped slaves in return for her own freedom and a half-million Solarian credits. Do you know what they intend to do with that slave when they find her?"

Georgia stared at him, her vocal cords frozen, and he smiled thinly.

"I've never been a slave. I don't pretend to understand what someone who has been one would be willing to do to gain her own freedom. And, by the same token, I don't pretend to stand in judgment on those who want to . . . discuss her actions with her. But I think, Elaine, that if I were her, I'd be far more concerned about the Ballroom than about anything the Star Kingdom's courts might want to discuss with her."

"What . . . what are you offering?" she asked hoarsely.

"Seventy-two standard-hours' headstart," he said bluntly. "I won't promise not to hand the evidence I've assembled over to the Ballroom. Cathy's 'butler' would never forgive us if I did. But Isaac will give me those three days, as well. He and Jeremy are reasonable men. They'll be unhappy with me, but they recognize the realities of horse-trading, and they know what sort of political stakes we're playing for here in the Star Kingdom. They'll settle for knowing where to start looking for you again."

"So you want me to just vanish?" She stared at him for a moment, then shook her head. "No. You want something more than that. I'm not important enough for you to risk the possibility that the Ballroom might not be as 'reasonable' as you hope it will. Besides, you'd do much more damage to High Ridge and his government if you just told Jeremy where to find me." She shook her head again. "You want the files for yourself, don't you?"

"No." It wasn't Zilwicki. It was Montaigne, and her level voice was like liquid helium. Georgia looked at her in disbelief, and the ex-countess shrugged. "I won't pretend that a part of me isn't tempted. But those files have done enough damage already. Oh, I could probably convince myself that the real criminals, the bastards who've broken the law and gotten away with it, deserve to be turned in and brought down in public, as spectacularly as possible. But the other temptation . . . the temptation *not* to turn them in." She shook her head. "It would be too easy to turn into another New Kiev and convince myself that the nobility of my purpose justified whatever tool I chose to use."

"Not to mention," Zilwicki rumbled, "the fact that a good third of the 'evidence' contained in those files was probably manufactured in the first place."

"Not to mention that," Montaigne agreed.

"So what *do* you want?" Georgia asked flatly.

"We want the files destroyed," Zilwicki told her. "And we want it done in a way which proves they've been destroyed."

"How am I supposed to do that?" she demanded.

"You've already demonstrated that you're a very inventive and capable woman, Elaine," Montaigne told her. "And it's common knowledge that the files are stored in a high-security vault under the Youngs' townhouse here in Landing. I'm sure that you could arrange for that vault—and the house, for that matter—to suffer some spectacular mischief. Without, I hasten to add, any loss of life."

"You expect me to arrange all of that and get off the planet within three standard days?" She shook her head. "Even if I wanted to, I couldn't pull something like that off that quickly. Not, at least, and leave myself enough time to run to make any difference in the end."

"Your three days would begin the day after the files are destroyed," Zilwicki told her. "Unless, of course, you tried to leave the planet *before* they were destroyed."

"And if I refuse, you'd really hand me over to the Ballroom? Even knowing what they'd do to me?"

"Yes, I would," Zilwicki said flatly.

"I don't think I believe you," she said softly, then looked at Montaigne. "And despite everything I've heard about you and your relationship with the Ballroom, I don't think you'd let him. I don't think you'd care to live with what they'd do."

"Maybe I wouldn't," Montaigne replied. "No. I'll go further than that. I *wouldn't* like to live with it. But don't you think for one fucking minute that I wouldn't do it anyway. Unlike Anton, I've spent decades working with the Ballroom and with escaped slaves. Like him, I can't really put myself in their places. The living Hell any slave experiences—even you—is something I can only attempt to imagine. But I've seen what slaves have done to gain their freedom. And I've heard them tell about the other slaves—the ones who helped someone else gain her freedom, and what it cost them. I'm not going to sit here and tell you that I require any slave to be that heroic, that self-sacrificing. But I have by God known slaves who *were* that heroic, and I know the tales of the ones who *were* that self-sacrificing. And I know that you were directly responsible for sending almost five hundred escaped slaves back into that Hell to save yourself . . . and for a tidy little profit, as well. So, yes, 'Elaine.' If Jeremy catches up with you, I'll live with whatever he does."

Georgia felt something shrivel deep within her as she gazed into those implacable green eyes.

"And think about this," Zilwicki told her. Her eyes snapped helplessly back to him, and the smile he gave her would have suited any shark. "Even if I didn't have the stomach in the end to turn you in to the Ballroom, I don't have to. I found the middleman you used to contact Denver Summervale. I have his deposition, too. I doubt very much that it would stand up in a court of law, but it wouldn't have to. I'd simply send it to Duchess Harrington."

What had already begun to shrivel crumpled completely at the icy promise in Anton Zilwicki's eyes. Georgia Young, Lady North Hollow, looked back and forth between those two very different yet equally unyielding faces, and knew both of them had meant every word they'd said.

"So, 'Elaine,'" Montaigne asked softly, "what's it going to be?"

CHAPTER FIFTY-ONE

"**I** wish we had some damned idea where they've gone," Alistair McKeon growled. He reclined in a deplorably unmilitary sprawl in his chair, tipped back with one heel resting on the beaten copper coffee table in Honor's day cabin. His uniform tunic hung untidily across the back of his chair, which constituted a substantial concession on James MacGuiness' part. He didn't allow just anyone to clutter up his admiral's quarters.

Alice Truman, on the other hand, was her neat, tidy self as she sat in the chair facing McKeon across the coffee table. Where McKeon nursed a stein of Honor's beer, Truman contented herself with a steaming cup of coffee and a small plate of flaky croissants.

Alfredo Yu, for his part, had seated himself at the writing desk and was idly doodling on a sheet of paper with an old-fashioned stylus, while Honor sat sideways on her comfortable couch. Her long legs were stretched out before her, lengthwise across its cushions, with Nimitz curled comfortably across her thighs, while she leaned her back against the armrest. A plate on the coffee table, within easy reach for a treecat, still held two uneaten stalks of celery, and Honor stroked the half-asleep treecat gently with her right hand while her left managed her cocoa mug.

It was all a very comfortable, domestic scene, she thought, regarding her three senior subordinates. Unfortunately, there was a decided air of the lull before the storm about it, and Alistair's question underscored that sense of tense anticipation altogether too well.

"We all wish we knew where they were, Alistair," Truman told him. "But we don't."

"We may not know where they are," Yu put in, "but I'm afraid we know where they're *going* to be once they get their orders."

The ex-Peep obviously didn't care a great deal for his own conclusion, but that didn't invalidate it, Honor thought moodily.

"Do you think the Andies know Haven is sticking a thumb into the Silesian pie?" McKeon asked.

"I don't see how they could," Honor replied after a moment. "We only know about them because Captain Bachfisch told us. Unless they've been a lot sloppier somewhere else, I can't quite imagine their letting the Andies get a peek at them."

"I don't know," McKeon half-argued. "*Pirates' Bane* spotted their destroyers in Zoraster, and we know Andie naval intelligence is pretty damned good. I'd think there was at least a chance that they'd notice a pair of brand-new Peep destroyers hanging around here in Silesia."

"If they can pick them out of the clutter of all of the older Havenite designs that've gone rogue out here," Yu responded sourly. "Remember, Admiral Bachfisch only noticed them because he realized they were new-build ships."

"Even if they noticed them," Truman observed, "they probably wouldn't guess the reason they were there. I mean, on the face of it, the whole idea is pretty absurd. I doubt that something so preposterous would occur to any rational analyst."

"Not 'preposterous,'" Honor corrected. "'Audacious' would be closer to it."

"'*Lunacy*' would be even better!" Yu shot back. "Or maybe it would be even more accurate to call it 'delusions of grandeur.'" He shook his head. "I hate thinking that Tom Theisman could become as guilty of strategic overreach as this looks like."

"It's only overreach if they don't actually have the combat power to pull it off," Truman pointed out.

"Alice is right, Alfredo," Honor said. "In fact, that's what worries me the most about it. I don't know Theisman as well as you do, of course, but what I do know of him suggests that he's not very likely to succumb to the temptations of overreaching. That's what I keep coming back to. He wouldn't have sent this force all the way out here if he hadn't thought he was retaining sufficient strength closer to home when he did."

"I know," Yu agreed. "Maybe I'm just trying to give myself some sort of false courage by convincing myself that Tom has screwed up by the numbers this time. But I guess what really bothers me the most about it is that Tom Theisman is the last person in the galaxy I would have expected to want to go back to war with the Star Kingdom. My God! Look at what the man's accomplished. Why in Heaven's name would he risk throwing that away when the diplomats are still talking?"

"It may not have been his idea," Honor said almost soothingly. "There are other decision-makers involved, you know. And, I hate to say it, but the situation may very well look different from his side of the line. As you say, the diplomats are still talking, but how long has it been since they actually *said* anything to one another? Or, at least," she corrected herself bitterly, "since High Ridge and Descroix have shown any sign of really wanting a treaty?"

"I hope you and Alfredo won't take this wrongly," McKeon said, "but the bottom line from our perspective out here is that it doesn't really matter why Theisman might have decided to send his 'Second Fleet' out to Silesia. Other than the fact that it's obviously here to attack someone, I mean." Honor and Yu looked at him, and he shrugged without straightening up in his chair. "I liked Theisman when I met him at Yeltsin's Star, too. And I wouldn't have picked him for the heavy in this piece, either. But whatever his motives, and however justified they may have been by the admitted stupidity of our own beloved Prime Minister, what we really need to consider right now are the consequences. And the consequences are that there's a Havenite fleet, of unknown size and strength, at a currently unknown position, for the purposes of carrying out a mission whose objectives I think we can all guess with a fair degree of accuracy. Which brings me back to my original point. I wish we had some damned idea where the hell they are!"

"Well, at least we know where they aren't," Truman said sourly. "Or, at least we know one star system where they aren't anymore."

"Yes, we do," Honor said, and Truman looked at her. So did Yu, and McKeon turned his head to give her a very sharp glance indeed as the thoughtful edge to her tone registered. The three of them gazed at her for several seconds, then looked at one another.

"And?" McKeon prompted after a moment.

"Um?" Honor shook herself. "I mean, what did you say, Alistair?"

"We all know that tone, Honor," he told her. "There's something going on inside your head, and I just wondered if you'd care to share it with the rest of us mere mortals."

He grinned impudently at her, and she shook her head.

"There will come a time, Alistair McKeon, when *lese majesty* will come home to haunt you. And if there is any justice in the universe, I'll be there to see it!"

"No doubt. In the meantime, you're still not sharing."

"All right," she conceded. "I was thinking about something— something you brought up earlier, in fact."

"Something I brought up?"

"When you were wondering whether or not the Andies knew the Republic was fooling around out here."

"What about it?" McKeon asked, cocking his head and frowning in thought.

"Well, it's just that if I were the Andies, I wouldn't be very happy about their presence. Especially not given how unhappy the Empire already seems to be about *our* presence out here."

"Forgive me, My Lady," Yu objected mildly, "but if I were the Andies, I might not be very upset at all by the prospect of having the Republic attack the people I'm already trying to squeeze out of Silesia. Worst-case scenario, either we beat them, or they beat us, and the winner is much weaker than he was before the engagement. Which means the Andies can basically either simply order the 'victor' out of the region, or move in with the virtual certainty that they can take whatever he has left."

"That's all true enough," Honor agreed. "But hasn't it occurred to you, Alfredo, that whatever the Andies are up to in Silesia may be the result of an error on their part?"

"What error?" Truman asked. Honor looked at her, and the golden-haired admiral shrugged. "I can think of several errors they could have made. Which one did you have in mind?"

"The same mistake High Ridge and Descroix have been making for years, in a sense," Honor told her. "Maybe they've been assuming the war between us and the Republic was effectively over, as well."

"If they ever thought that in the first place, surely they realized when Theisman announced the existence of his new navy that all bets were off," McKeon protested.

"Maybe not," Honor said. "We keep thinking about how good Andie naval intelligence is, but there are limits in all things. And even if their intelligence people got all the available information straight, it doesn't necessarily follow that the Emperor and his advisors drew the right conclusions."

"With all due respect, why should they care whether or not the war is over?" Truman inquired. "The new management in Nouveau Paris doesn't seem especially interested in conquering the known galaxy, and the Empire is all the way on the far side of the Manticoran Alliance from Haven. Under the circumstances, I don't see Gustav and his advisors considering the Republic much of a threat to the Empire, whatever happens to the Star Kingdom. In fact, they'd probably be just as happy to see us involved in a shooting war with Haven again, because it would prevent us from reinforcing against *them* out here. For that matter, that's what the mere threat of renewed hostilities with Haven is already doing!"

"I understand all of that," Honor said. "And you may very well be right, Alice. But if Thomas Theisman is prepared to go back to war with the Star Kingdom under any circumstances, or for any reason, then he and Shannon Foraker between them must have done a lot more to equalize our technology advantage than anybody in Jurgensen's ONI is prepared to admit they could have. And if that's the case, then whatever balance of power equation Gustav may have been contemplating is probably pretty badly out of date. And whatever the new management in the Republic might really want, Gustav Anderman is *not* the sort of ruler to rely on the good intentions of a powerful neighbor. Especially not a powerful neighbor which, up to four or five T-years ago was into the conquest game in a really big way."

"And," Yu observed in a suddenly thoughtful tone, "a powerful neighbor he can't be certain will remain under the present management."

"Exactly," Honor agreed. "Historically, the Andermani haven't been big believers in the value of republican forms of government. They don't like them, and they don't really trust them. They were probably more comfortable with the Legislaturalists than with the Committee of Public Safety, but I wouldn't be very surprised if they were more comfortable with the Committee than they are with the Republic. They regard elective forms of government as dangerously changeable and unpredictable at the best of times."

"So what you're suggesting," McKeon said slowly, "is that if they thought that the Republic was really powerful enough to have a realistic chance of defeating the Star Kingdom, they wouldn't care for it very much."

"The Empire is a great believer in playing the balance of power game as the best long-term way to promote its own security," Honor said. "But if the Republic, which is already so much larger than the Star Kingdom, succeeds in destroying or at least seriously crippling the Manticoran Alliance, there *is* no balance of power. And the star nation which would suddenly emerge—or reemerge, perhaps—as the premier military power in this entire region would be governed by a system an Andermani monarch would be naturally inclined to distrust and fear."

"And one which had yet to demonstrate that it has the legs to last," Yu agreed.

"You may be onto something," Truman said. "But even if you are, I'm afraid it's too late for your insight to change anything. Whatever Theisman and Pritchart may be up to, Gustav is obviously planning on devouring the choicer bits and pieces of Silesia. And our own brilliant leaders haven't done a thing to seriously dissuade him. Except, of course, for hanging this task force out to dry. It's a bit late in the day to expect the current government to do anything more serious than that, however accurate your analysis may be. Assuming, of course, that anyone in Landing was inclined to listen to anything that came from you or Earl White Haven, anyway."

"Yeah, sure!" McKeon grimaced. "I can just see High Ridge or Descroix changing their foreign policy on the basis of anything *you* suggested, Honor!"

"I wasn't necessarily thinking about them," Honor said very slowly.

"What?" McKeon set up straight so that he could swivel his chair to face her directly, and his expression could only have been called a scowl. "Just who *were* you thinking about, then?" he inquired in tones of profound suspicion.

"Come, now, Alistair!" she chided. "If I'm not thinking about anyone on our side, then who else could I be thinking about?"

"And what makes you think Admiral Rabenstrange would believe any message you sent him about this putative 'Second Fleet' we've never even been able to find?" McKeon demanded. "Hell, for that matter what makes you even think he'd read it?!"

"Who said anything about sending him a message?" Honor asked, and suddenly all three of her subordinates were staring at her in disbelief.

"It's *what?*"

Chien-lu von Rabenstrange looked at his chief of staff in complete and total disbelief.

"According to Perimeter Security, Sir," *Kapitän der Sternen* Isenhoffer said in the tone of a man who wasn't quite certain he believed his own report, "it's a single Manticoran ship of the wall. She's identified herself as HMS *Troubadour*, one of their *Medusa*-class SD(P)s. According to our current Intelligence appreciations, *Troubadour* is the flagship of their Rear Admiral McKeon."

"And this ship has arrived here at Sachsen all by herself?"

"As nearly as Perimeter Security can tell," Isenhoffer confirmed, and Rabenstrange frowned in thought. Sachsen's passive sensor arrays might not be as exquisitely sensitive as those which protected a system like New Berlin, but they would certainly have detected the transit footprints of any other ships which might have accompanied *Troubadour* out of hyper.

"And has this ship said anything beyond identifying herself?" he asked after a moment.

"As a matter of fact, *Herr Herzog*, she has," Isenhoffer said.

"Well, please don't make me drag each word out of you one at a time," Rabenstrange said tartly.

"Forgive me, Sir," Isenhoffer said. "It's just that, on the face of it, it's so absurd that—" He stopped and seemed to give himself a mental shake. "Sir," he said, "according to *Troubadour*, she has Duchess Harrington aboard. And the Duchess has formally requested to speak personally to you."

"To me?" Rabenstrange repeated carefully. "Duchess Harrington herself?"

"That's what *Troubadour* says, Sir," Isenhoffer replied.

"I see."

"With all due respect, Sir," Isenhoffer said, "I would advise against allowing *Troubadour* to come any further in-system." Rabenstrange looked a question at him, and the chief of staff shrugged. "Duchess

Harrington's request, even if it's sincere, is ridiculous. There are proper channels for one fleet commander to contact another through."

"And why do you think the Duchess failed to avail herself of those other channels?"

"I suppose it's possible that this represents some dramatic attempt on her part to find a peaceful resolution to the tension between her command and yours," Isenhoffer said carefully. As Rabenstrange's chief of staff, he knew how strongly the herzog had argued against the Empire's current policy in Silesia. He also knew exactly what Rabenstrange had said to Sternhafen before that admiral had been sent home in disgrace. Perhaps even more significantly at this particular moment, Isenhoffer was also aware of the respect in which Rabenstrange held Honor Harrington.

"From your tone," the herzog observed now, "although you may suppose it's possible, you don't find it very likely."

"Frankly, Sir, I don't," Isenhoffer acknowledged. "And, again with all due respect, even if that's what this is, surely she must realize that by now it's too late."

"I don't recall having issued any orders to attack Sidemore Station," Rabenstrange said in a suddenly chill voice.

"Of course not, Sir!" Isenhoffer spoke quickly, yet there was an edge of diffident stubbornness in his reply. Chien-lu Rabenstrange hadn't picked a chief of staff he expected to be a yes-man or a weakling. "I didn't mean to imply that you had. But Duchess Harrington must be aware by this time that His Imperial Majesty fully intends to secure our strategic frontiers here in Silesia. I would submit to you, Sir, that, that being the case, the only thing she could say to you which would resolve the tension between our two forces would be a concession on her part of our territorial demands. And if she were prepared to make such a concession, it would undoubtedly represent instructions from her government at home, which would have been communicated to us through normal channels."

"Which brings us back to the question of why she didn't use those channels in the first place, does it not?" Rabenstrange asked, and Isenhoffer nodded. "Well, if you don't believe she's here to propose some sort of diplomatic resolution, then why *do* you think she's here?"

"I think, perhaps, for two reasons, Sir," Isenhoffer replied. "First,

I would not be surprised to discover that she's here on her own authority in an effort to at least delay the inevitable. She may propose some sort of stand-down while she requests additional instructions from her government, but I would be somewhat suspicious of any such proposal. The delay involved might well permit the Star Kingdom to transfer additional reinforcements to Sidemore.

"Secondly, Sir, I can think of very few ways in which she could acquire a more precise estimate of our current strength here in Sachsen than by bringing a ship of the wall, with its sensor suite, right into the heart of the star system. I don't say that that would be her primary ●bjective, but it would almost certainly be an inevitable consequence if we permit her to enter the system."

"You may be correct," Rabenstrange said after a moment. "On the other hand, unlike you, I've met the lady. When she speaks, it's usually worth taking the time to listen. And the one thing she doesn't do—or, at least, will never do well—is lie.

"As for what *Troubadour*'s sensors might be able to tell her about our strength, my concerns are strictly limited. In fact, in some respects, I'd prefer for her to have an accurate appreciation of our strength. The sorts of 'mistakes' which have plagued us since that idiot Gortz got himself killed in Zoraster are dangerous, Zhenting. And more than just in terms of the additional people they've already killed.

"The Emperor may fully intend to secure our frontiers, and he may even be willing to go to war with the Star Kingdom in order to accomplish that if he must, but that doesn't mean he wouldn't prefer to do it without any more bloodshed. Nor do I care to be responsible for any more deaths that can possibly be avoided. Let her deliver whatever message she wishes me to have. And let her see what strength we have. If there is some way we can prevent further loss of life, then by all means let us explore the possibilities. And if knowing how powerful our forces are makes her more cautious or encourages her to press her own superiors for authority to concede the Emperor's demands, so much the better."

"But, *Herr Herzog*," Isenhoffer protested, "she's a Grayson steadholder. She'll insist upon bringing her armsmen to any meeting, and you know what the Emperor's feelings about anything like that have been since the Hofschulte affair."

"I do, indeed." Rabenstrange frowned again. Then he shrugged. "Explain the Emperor's conditions to her, Zhenting. If she can't accept them, then we'll be limited to an electronic meeting."

"I don't like it, My Lady," Andrew LaFollet said stubbornly.

"And I'm afraid I don't recall asking you if you liked it," Honor replied, and her voice was considerably tarter than usual.

"But especially now," LaFollet began, "with tensions so high, it's—"

"Especially now," Honor said implacably, "it's particularly important that there not be any incidents. *Or* any indication that I distrust Herzog von Rabenstrange in any way. This subject is no longer open to debate, Andrew."

LaFollet had opened his mouth. Now, he shut it. His expression hovered somewhere between mulish and profoundly disapproving, but he recognized the end of the discussion. He and Spencer Hawke exchanged glances, and then he turned back to Honor.

"All right, My Lady," he half-sighed. "We'll do it your way."

"I know we will," she replied serenely.

The *fregatten kapitän* escorting Honor from the superdreadnought *Campenhausen*'s boat bay was perfectly courteous, but he clearly had his reservations about this entire business. The fact that the holsters of her three accompanying armsmen were conspicuously empty had apparently reconciled him somewhat, but from the look he'd given Nimitz, the 'cat's reputation had preceded him. Apparently the *fregatten kapitän* wasn't any too certain that he shouldn't have been considered as much a weapon as the armsmen's pulsers. On the other hand, he obviously wasn't prepared to argue the point on his own authority.

The lift car delivered Honor's small party to the passage just outside *Campenhausen*'s main flag briefing room. Two Andermani Marines stood guard at the hatch, accompanied by a full *kapitän der sternen* with the shoulder aiguillette of a staff officer.

"Duchess Harrington," the staffer said in precise, accented Standard English, with a small, formal bow.

"Yes," Honor acknowledged, and cocked an eyebrow. "And you are?"

"*Kapitän der Sternen* Zhenting Isenhoffer, Herzog Rabenstrange's chief of staff," the captain replied. "I am honored to meet you, My Lady."

"And I you," Honor said.

Isenhoffer glanced past her at her armsmen, and something suspiciously like a twinkle glimmered in his eye as he took in their expressions.

"Your Grace," he said, returning his attention fully to Honor, "I apologize for any unintended insult in our insistence that no weapons be brought into the Herzog's presence. The stipulation was not his to make. The Emperor has made himself most specific on this particular issue in the wake of the Hofschulte Incident. I am afraid that his instructions are nondiscretionary."

"I see." Honor considered him thoughtfully. Gustav Anderman had never been noted for his warm and trusting nature, but it was difficult to blame him for being even less so in this instance. Gregor Hofschulte had risen to the rank of lieutenant colonel in the Andermani Marines. A man of impeccable loyalty, who had served his Emperor well for almost thirty T-years. And a man who had, with absolutely no warning, drawn his sidearm and opened fire on Prince Huang, the Emperor's younger brother, and his family. The Prince and his wife had survived; one of their children had not.

Precisely why and how Hofschulte had done such a thing remained unknown, because the lieutenant colonel hadn't survived the attack. Prince Huang's bodyguards had reacted almost instantly, and Hofschulte's body had been very badly mangled by the fire that killed him. According to ONI, at least some members of the Andermani security services believed Hofschulte had been "adjusted" to carry out the attack. Which, in a way, worried them much more than the possibility that a man who had been considered completely loyal might have snapped "naturally" and gone berserk with no warning at all. The Andermani military, like the Manticoran military, was supposed to be protected against things like adjustment. If someone had managed to crack those safeguards once, there was no guarantee they couldn't do it twice. Which, in turn, undoubtedly explained Gustav's draconian, across-the-board prohibition on arms in the presence of any member of the Imperial Family.

"I assure you, *Kapitän* Isenhoffer, that I don't feel insulted in the least," she reassured the Andermani officer. "However, there is one small additional item I should deal with before meeting with the Herzog. Excuse me a moment."

Isenhoffer looked puzzled, but the confusion in his expression was nothing compared to LaFollet's expression as she urged Nimitz down from her shoulder and passed him to Simon Mattingly. Then she unsealed her uniform tunic and handed it to LaFollet. Her personal armsman gave her a very old-fashioned look, indeed, as he took the garment from her, and his look became even more old-fashioned as she rolled up the left cuff of her uniform blouse. The smile she gave him mingled impishness with just a hint of apology, and then she told her prosthetic hand to flex in a movement which should have brought the tip of her index finger into contact with the tip of her little finger. But the neural impulses which would have moved the fingers of her original hand in that pattern did something completely different now, and a rectangular patch of skin on the inside of her forearm, perhaps two centimeters long and one and a half across, suddenly folded back. A small compartment in the artificial limb opened, and as she closed her fist, a thirty-round pulser magazine ejected itself.

She caught it in midair with her right hand while LaFollet stared at her in disbelief, then smiled at Isenhoffer—who, if possible, looked even more astonished than her armsman.

"Forgive me, *Kapitän*," she said. "As you may know, I've experienced more than one assassination attempt of my own. When my father helped me design my prosthesis, he suggested a few small . . . improvements. This," she handed Isenhoffer the magazine, "was one of them."

She raised her hand between them and sent its artificial muscles another command. In response, her left index finger snapped abruptly and rigidly straight, and the hand's other fingers folded under, almost as if they were gripping the butt of a nonexistent pulser.

"I'm afraid I'd have to have the tip of the finger rebuilt if I ever used it," she told him with a whimsical smile. "But Daddy insisted that it would be worthwhile."

"I see," Isenhoffer said a bit blankly. Then he gave himself a shake. "I see," he repeated in more normal tones. "Your father would appear to be a man of rare foresight, Your Grace."

"I've always thought so," Honor replied, studiously ignoring the fulminating look Andrew LaFollet was busy sending in her direction.

"Yes. Well, if you're ready," the Andermani officer continued, sliding the pulser magazine into a pocket as Honor reclaimed her tunic and slipped back into it, "the Herzog is waiting."

"Of course," Honor murmured, and held out her arms to Nimitz. The treecat leapt lightly into them, and she followed Isenhoffer through the hatch into the briefing room. She had no doubt that surveillance systems had been watching her in the passage, and she hoped they would draw the proper conclusion from her surrender of the pulser magazine. She doubted very much that even Imperial Andermani security agents would have been able to spot the weapon built into her arm. She'd certainly paid enough to be certain no one could, at any rate! And she'd had Palace Security test it for her back on Manticore. So she'd just demonstrated that she could have brought a weapon into Rabenstrange's presence if she'd really wanted to . . . and that she took her solemn promise not to do any such thing seriously. And that she wanted Rabenstrange to know she'd done both of those things.

It was a small thing, perhaps. But small things were what trust and confidence were built upon, and she badly needed Chien-lu von Rabenstrange to trust her this afternoon as he never had before.

Her armsmen came with her, and she watched the eyes of the two bodyguards standing behind Rabenstrange. The woman she suspected was the senior of the two gave her a very sharp look, and Honor smiled mentally at the proof that she had indeed been under surveillance in the passage. But the woman only looked at her for a moment before her eyes joined her companion's in carefully examining LaFollet, Hawk, and Mattingly. The three Graysons returned the examination with equal professionalism, and Honor hid a bigger smile as she tasted the wary emotions on either side. But the stillborn smile was fleeting, and she turned her attention to the small man seated at the head of the briefing room table.

"Welcome aboard *Campenhausen*, Your Grace," Chien-lu Rabenstrange said.

"Thank you, Your Grace," Honor replied, and Rabenstrange smiled ever so slightly. She could taste the caution of his emotions, but she also tasted curiosity. And, even more important, she did taste something very like trust. She'd hoped she would, but she hadn't allowed herself to count on it. Still, she and

Rabenstrange had established a certain personal empathy which extended beyond their purely professional relationship during her last assignment to Silesia. Apparently, it was still there. He was obviously aware of the tension inherent in their meeting, under the circumstances, but he trusted her personal integrity. At least far enough for him to have agreed to meet with her in the first place, at least.

"I must confess," he told her, "to being somewhat . . . surprised by your presence here, Your Grace. Under the circumstances, given the tension and recent unfortunate events between our two commands, I would not have anticipated a direct contact at this level."

"I'll confess that I was rather counting on that, actually, Your Grace," she responded. He cocked his head questioningly, and she smiled. "I have something a bit unusual to discuss with you," she told him, "and I felt that this might be the most effective way to get your attention."

"Did you?" he murmured, and it was his turn to smile. "Well, Your Grace, I certainly can't guarantee that I'll find myself in agreement with whatever brings you here. But I will confess, that you have piqued my curiosity! So, why don't you begin?"

He waved gracefully at the chair at the foot of the conference table, and Honor seated herself in it and collected Nimitz in her lap.

"Certainly, Your Grace," she told him. "Now, I realize that tensions between the Empire and the Star Kingdom are running high at the moment. And I don't propose attempting to magically sort things out between the two of us. That, obviously, is something which ultimately will have to be accomplished at a higher level. In the meantime, however, I've recently become aware of certain information which I believe ought properly to be shared with a representative of the Empire. Information which might have a certain bearing on the deployment of both of our forces."

"Information?"

"Yes, Your Grace. You see . . ."

CHAPTER FIFTY-TWO

"**S**o, Zhenting, what did you think?"

Herzog von Rabenstrange and his chief of staff stood on *Campenhausen*'s flag bridge, watching the glittering icon of HMS *Troubadour* as the Manticoran superdreadnought accelerated steadily towards the hyper limit.

"I thought—" *Kapitän der Sternen* Isenhoffer paused, then shrugged ever so slightly. "I thought that in many ways it all sounded very . . . convenient for Duchess Harrington, Sir."

" 'Convenient'?" Rabenstrange rolled the word across his tongue and cocked his head at the taller Isenhoffer. "An interesting choice of words, Zhenting. Not entirely without applicability, I suppose, but still . . ." He shook his head. "However 'convenient' it might be for her under some circumstances, it remains most *in*convenient under most of them. I believe the old cliché about rocks and hard places comes to mind."

"Unless she can convince us not to be the rock . . . or the hard place, Sir," Isenhoffer pointed out in tones of respectfully stubborn skepticism.

"Perhaps," Rabenstrange conceded, but his own voice was dubious. "Still, I suspect His Imperial Majesty would be quite impressed by the logic of her analysis. Assuming, of course, that the data upon which it's based has some basis in reality."

"I would certainly agree that the accuracy—or lack of it—of

her basic information is the crux of the matter," Isenhoffer said. He started to say something else, then paused, and clearly reconsidered.

"Yes?" Rabenstrange prompted.

"I was only going to say, Sir," the chief of staff said after a moment, "that while I continue to cherish my own suspicions about Duchess Harrington's motives, I honestly don't believe she lied to you."

Isenhoffer was clearly uncomfortable saying that, and Rabenstrange smiled without humor. The *kapitän der sternen*, he knew, must have hated admitting that. It would have suited his purposes much better if he'd been able to argue that Honor Harrington had been less than truthful about what she had discovered about the Republic of Haven's activities in Silesia. Unfortunately, he had too much integrity for that. Which, the herzog admitted, only gave his suspicions of her motives even greater weight in some ways.

"I think," the small admiral said slowly, "that it would be as well to remember that hers are not the only suspect motives in this instance. For example, if we assume that the Duchess has, in fact, been truthful with us, and also that her intelligence officer's analysis is accurate, we must ask ourselves precisely what the Republic is actually up to."

"Forgive me, Sir," Isenhoffer said, "but in my opinion, the Republic's objectives are relatively clear and straightforward. If I were President Pritchart or Admiral Theisman, I would almost certainly have resorted to military operations in order to force a resolution of the negotiations long before this. Assuming, of course, that I had the capability to do so." He shrugged. "In that regard, I believe Duchess Harrington was probably completely correct as to the Republic's intentions, both in regard to its own occupied systems and in regard to Sidemore."

"Perhaps so," Rabenstrange replied. "But consider this, Zhenting. The Republic has encouraged us to pursue our objectives in Silesia. True, they've done so only in private conversations, not publicly, but you and I have both read the Foreign Ministry's synopses of Ambassador Kaiserfest's discussions with their Secretary of State. Even allowing for a certain degree of corruption in transmission, Secretary Giancola was remarkably specific. And very encouraging."

He paused for a long moment, watching *Troubadour*'s icon, then looked back up at Isenhoffer.

"Yet for all his specificity, Zhenting, he never once mentioned the possibility of Havenite operations in the Confederacy. Even more to the point, he specifically informed Kaiserfest that it would be impossible for the Republic to offer us even verbal support openly because of the Republic's internal public opinion."

"You think that he was attempting to maneuver us into a false position?" Isenhoffer frowned.

"I think it's certainly possible. At the very least, he obviously hoped to use us as a cat's paw, yet another way to distract the Star Kingdom while his own navy prepared its offensive. That much, of course, I'm sure the Foreign Ministry had already considered. But the fact that he never so much as hinted—as far as I can tell from the synopses, at least—that Haven was preparing to resume active operations strikes me as significant. Indeed, I would judge that he went out of his way to avoid even the least suggestion that such operations were being contemplated. Some, at least, of that could be no more than the maintenance of operational security. But the decision to send their own naval forces into the Confederacy without so much as mentioning it to us at the same time as they were encouraging us to embark upon an adventure here was at best . . . reckless."

"What possible motive could they have?" Isenhoffer wondered aloud.

"I can think of at least one," Rabenstrange said grimly. "Suppose their intention—or, their hope, at least—was that we and the Manties would indeed go to war, and that one of us would defeat the other. I believe that their strategists could confidently assume that whichever of us won, we would be severely damaged, possibly crippled, in the process. And if it were to happen that the Republic just coincidentally had a fresh, unbloodied fleet of its own in the vicinity . . ."

His voice trailed off, and Isenhoffer's frown deepened.

"Sir, do you actually believe that the Republic of Haven would seriously contemplate going to war with the Star Kingdom and the Empire simultaneously?"

"On the face of it, it would seem ridiculous," Rabenstrange admitted. "But you've seen the same intelligence reports I have. For all of our inability to penetrate 'Bolthole's' security, it's perfectly obvious that Theisman and Pritchart have been able to build a substantially larger and more modern fleet even than the one they've admitted to possessing. Perhaps they've accomplished even more than we believe they have. Don't forget that for decades the Legislaturalists' foreign policy was based on a timetable of first the Star Kingdom, then Silesia, and then the Empire. If Pritchart and Theisman feel they have sufficient naval power, might they not be tempted to revert to that policy now?"

"Nothing any of the analysts have reported would suggest that President Pritchart's mind works that way, Sir," Isenhoffer pointed out.

"Analysts can be wrong. Perhaps more importantly, Pritchart doesn't operate in a vacuum. I've never felt comfortable with our grasp of the internal dynamics of her government. It's impossible for us to know all of the factions and counter-factions she might find herself forced to cope with. And even if she was as reluctant to resort to active operations against Manticore as our analysts and her own public statements would seem to suggest, she certainly seems to have decided to do so anyway. And if she feels herself compelled to go back to war, then perhaps she also sees an opportunity to accomplish the traditional Havenite goal in this sector once and for all."

"The possibility no doubt exists, Sir," Isenhoffer said slowly. "It just strikes me as rather more Machiavellian than I would have expected out of her."

"Me also," Rabenstrange admitted. "To be honest, I don't like considering the possibility even now. But it's possible that her public concentration on domestic reform has, in fact, been something of a mask all along." He shook his head with a grimace. "Even now, when I hear myself saying it, it's hard for me to believe that of her. But what I keep coming back to, Zhenting, is that her Secretary of State approached us with the offer of an informal, behind-the-scenes understanding. Almost an undeclared alliance against Manticore. He came to Kaiserfest, not the reverse. And the entire time that he and Kaiserfest were building their 'working relationship' he never even broached the possibility of Havenite naval forces in Silesia. Not once, Zhenting. Clearly Pritchart is working to some sort of carefully orchestrated plan, and equally clearly the Empire will eventually become aware of the presence of her military forces in the Confederacy. This is not a stupid woman, because a stupid woman couldn't have achieved all that she has. So why would she deliberately approach us with this informal alliance, and then turn around and intrude militarily into the very area she's had her Secretary of State encouraging us to annex? Unless her entire plan was to keep us ignorant of her ships' presence for as long as she could. Until it was too late for us to do anything about them."

"But that way, it sounds . . . plausible," Isenhoffer said finally. "Insanely reckless, unless they have indeed managed to build their naval forces to a level far in excess of Intelligence's estimates, but plausible. Yet, with all due respect, Sir, every bit of it is completely speculative. At this point, we don't have any proof even that the Republic is contemplating attacking the Star Kingdom at all. Duchess Harrington's hypothesis is the only indication that they might be, to be perfectly honest. And whatever suspicions you might have, His Imperial Majesty's instructions are explicit."

"I realize that. But the ultimate responsibility is mine as the Sachsen fleet commander. And our timetable isn't all that time-critical. Even if my suspicions are completely unfounded, we would lose little by waiting a few more weeks, or even months. If, on the other hand, there is any substance to them, we might court disaster by *not* waiting."

Troubadour's data code reached the hyper limit and vanished, and Chien-lu Rabenstrange inhaled deeply.

"Inform Communications that I will require a dispatch boat," he said quietly.

"Do you think it did any good, Your Grace?" Mercedes Brigham asked.

"I don't know," Honor replied honestly. "I can tell you that Herzog von Rabenstrange believed I was telling him the truth. Or, at least, that nothing I told him was a lie. But precisely how he'll react . . . ?" She shrugged.

"Well," her chief of staff observed, "whatever comes of that part of it, at least we managed to nail down a little more definite information on Andy capabilities. Unfortunately."

"Ah?" Honor glanced at Brigham, and the commodore nodded.

"I don't think they even suspected Captain Conagher had deployed the drones, Ma'am." She smiled thinly. "Whatever else they've done, it doesn't look like they've solved our EW capabilities just yet."

"I'm glad . . . I think," Honor said. "I almost wish I hadn't let you and Alistair talk me into deploying them in the first place. If we'd been caught at it, it could have convinced Rabenstrange that my entire visit was only an intelligence ploy."

Brigham started to reply, then decided not to. She still believed that even if the drones had been detected, a bunch as pragmatic as the Andermani Imperial Navy would have accepted it as no more than the way the game was played. In fact, she suspected, Honor probably believed the same thing, deep down inside. But if fretting about it represented her sole concession to the anxiety Brigham knew she must be feeling, then the chief of staff was perfectly willing to put up with it.

"At any rate," she continued after a moment, "we got good visuals on several of their ships. Admiral Bachfisch was right about their new battlecruisers, too. They have at least one pod-based design in service; we got confirming visual imagery on three of them."

"I wish I could say it was a surprise," Honor observed.

"You and I both, Your Grace," Brigham agreed. "But after seeing those strap-on pods of theirs, a surprise is one thing it isn't. As a matter of fact, I'd have been delighted if that were the only thing the drones had confirmed."

Honor crooked an eyebrow at her, and the chief of staff shrugged.

"They definitely have at least one SD(P) class in commission, Ma'am. We're not positive how many of them they have in Sachsen. For that matter, neither Captain Conagher's tac people nor George and I are prepared to give you any definitive estimate on their total ship strength in Sachsen. They'd clearly dispersed their units and gone to emissions control before we got far enough in-system to spot them all. But we picked up at least twenty superdreadnoughts, and the drones say that at least five of the twenty were SD(P)s."

"Darn," Honor said with a mildness which deceived neither Brigham nor herself.

"We didn't pick up any sign of CLACs," Brigham told her. "That doesn't prove anything, of course. And we did see an awfully high number of LAC drive signatures scattered around the system." She shrugged. "Call me paranoid, but to my suspicious mind, the existence of pod-based main combatants suggests that they have to have solved the problems of building something as simple as a LAC carrier."

"You're probably right," Honor agreed. "And if you are, then they're going to be a lot more dangerous. You know," she went on slowly, "I wonder if they really failed to spot the drones at all."

"You think they may have *wanted* us to know about their new hardware?" Brigham sounded skeptical, and it was Honor's turn to shrug.

"I think it's possible," she said. "Think about it. If they're still hoping to convince us to pull out without a fight, letting us know that they're going to be tougher opponents than we might have assumed would make sense. And they could kill two birds with one stone, in a way, if they deliberately failed to respond to our drones. First, they let us 'steal' the data they wanted us to have anyway. And second, by 'not noticing us' when we did, they lead us to assume that they can't crack our electronic warfare capabilities. Which could come as a very nasty surprise down the road if we didn't take the hint and withdraw from Silesia completely."

"You know, Your Grace, I'd just *hate* double- and triple-think situations like this."

"And you think I don't?" Honor smiled crookedly, then gave her head a little toss. "But at least we know a bit more than we did, whether the Andies wanted us to know it or not. And *they* know a bit more about what's going on than they did before we went to call on them. I'm sure that someone back at Admiralty House is going to be upset with me for 'consorting with the enemy,' but I can't help thinking that this is the first *positive* contact between us and the Andermani since the entire escalation in tensions began."

"I'd have to agree with that," Brigham said. "But even so, that just brings me back to my original question, I'm afraid. *Do* you think it did any good?"

CHAPTER FIFTY-THREE

"*Starlight*, you are Alpha-One for transit at the inner beacon."

"Astro Control, *Starlight* copies Alpha-One for transit. Beginning final approach to insertion now."

"*Starlight*, Astro Control shows you on nominal approach. Enjoy your trip. Astro Control, clear."

"Thank you, Astro Control. *Starlight*, clear."

Lieutenant Commander Sybil Dalipagic watched the data code of the Silesian Confederacy diplomatic courier blink out of existence as it disappeared into the Junction's central terminus on its way to Basilisk. As she'd informed *Starlight*'s astrogator, the dispatch boat's flight path had been nominal, but that hadn't kept her from sweating the transit, anyway. Diplomatic couriers were the one type of vessel with which Astro Control could not establish direct telemetry links. Dalipagic shuddered to think what would have happened if she'd even suggested to *Starlight* that she could have handled the entire transit much more safely and efficiently from her own console. The very idea would have violated at least half a dozen solemn interstellar accords, although in Dalipagic's professional opinion, those solemn accords were pretty damned stupid. It wasn't as if establishing an interface and an override with the ship's maneuvering computers would have in any way compromised the sacred integrity of its diplomatic files. Or, not at least if the people the dispatch boat belonged to had an IQ recorded in double digits.

She snorted in familiar amusement at the thought. Her brother-in-law had served for almost forty T-years aboard the ships of the Royal Manticoran Mail Service. The RMMS was never used for secure diplomatic dispatches, but there were plenty of other people who wanted to be sure their mail was transmitted in complete security. Which was why the mail ships' secure data banks were completely separated—physically, not just by electronic firewalls—from any other computer they carried. Somehow, Dalipagic thought, it was . . . unlikely that a diplomatic courier wouldn't have built in security measures at least that good. Which would just happen to have obviated any possibility that she could have hacked into *Starlight*'s dispatches simply by interfacing with the dispatch boat's astrogation systems. Hell, not even a hacker as celebrated as the Navy's Sir Horace Harkness could have managed that!

Not that any properly paranoid diplomat was likely to let her do any interfacing anytime soon. For that matter, even *Manticoran* couriers were often picky as hell about the degree of remote access they granted Astro Control. Of course—

The comfortable, well-worn rhythm of Dalipagic's thoughts faltered abruptly as the master plot suddenly altered. She stared at the thick rash of icons which had dropped unannounced out of hyper and begun decelerating towards the Junction. There were at least forty of them, and alarms began to whoop and wail as the ACS sensor platforms identified them as warships.

There was a brief, breathless pause—a break in the quiet background chatter of controllers in contact with transiting merchantmen—as the crimson-banded light codes of potentially hostile superdreadnoughts and battlecruisers headed directly for the terminus. The icons of the standby forts, far less numerous than they once had been, changed color, flashing almost instantly from amber to the blood-red of combat readiness, and the two battle squadrons assigned to support them changed color almost as rapidly.

It couldn't be an attack, Dalipagic's brain insisted. No one would be stupid enough to try something like this! But even as a part of her mind insisted on that, another part reminded her that there were no military transits at all scheduled for today.

The transitory instant of silence vanished as suddenly as it had come. Urgent, priority directions went flashing out over the communications and telemetry links as Astro Control reacted to the sudden, unanticipated threat. Merchantmen already on final held their courses, but anyone more than fifteen or twenty minutes back in the transit queue was already being diverted. Not without massive confusion and protests, of course. The last thing any merchant skipper wanted was to find herself stuck in the middle of a shooting confrontation between a fleet that size and the Junction's active forts. And the way that every one of them wanted to avoid that possibility was by making her own transit through the Junction. They could always take refuge from whatever might be about to happen in the Junction's vicinity by retreating into hyper-space, but if they didn't make their transits now, they might be delayed for weeks, or even months, with catastrophic consequences for shipping schedules.

Their protests at being diverted were vocal, imaginative, and frequently profane. Intellectually, Dalipagic understood and even sympathized with them. Emotionally, all she wanted was for them to get the hell out of the way.

She was explaining that, in a tone of complete, courteous professionalism, to a particularly irate and vituperative Solly, when the master plot changed yet again. The crimson bands disappeared from around the incoming warships, replaced by the friendly green of allied units.

Well, Dalipagic thought as she recognized the data codes of units of the Grayson Space Navy, *this should be interesting*.

"I don't care about that!" Admiral Stokes snapped into his com. "You can't just come barging through my Junction and screw my traffic profiles all to hell!"

"I'm afraid we can," Admiral Niall MacDonnell replied calmly. His expression, as his tone, was politely courteous, but it was also implacable. "Under the terms of our alliance with the Star Kingdom, units of the Grayson Navy have unlimited and unrestricted access to the Junction. I intend to exercise those options, and my message to you constitutes formal notification of that intention as per Article XII, Section 7, paragraph (c)."

"Not without clearing it ahead of time, you won't!" Stokes shot back. The Astro Control CO glared at the image on his com screen.

"On the contrary," MacDonnell corrected in that same, calm voice. "The treaty of alliance specifically provides for unannounced, emergency transits which take absolute priority over all routine traffic."

"*Emergency* transits," Stokes grated, "are one thing. Just turning up unannounced, sashaying into the middle of my transit patterns, and screwing an entire day's work all to hell is another. I'm not about to interrupt the normal traffic through the Junction just to allow you to carry out some sort of training exercise, Admiral!"

"Yes, you are, Allen," another voice said. Stokes' mouth froze in the open position, then closed with an almost audible click as another officer leaned forward into the field of MacDonnell's pickup. The newcomer wore the black-and-gold of the Royal Manticoran Navy, not the GSN's blue-on-blue. His ice-blue eyes were hard, and he smiled thinly as he saw the stunned recognition in Stokes' expression.

"Admiral MacDonnell," Hamish Alexander said coldly and precisely, "is acting under the direct orders of High Admiral Matthews and Protector Benjamin, himself. He is requesting transit instructions in strict accordance with Article V of the treaty of alliance between the Star Kingdom of Manticore and the Grayson Protectorate. If you require it, I'm sure he will be most happy to transmit the relevant section of the treaty for your perusal. In the meantime, however, the first elements of his task force will be arriving at the Junction threshold in approximately twelve minutes. They will be anticipating an immediate departure, via the Junction, for Trevor's Star. If they aren't assigned priority transit vectors upon arrival, I suspect that the repercussions will be . . . interesting."

Stokes' face turned an intriguing shade of puce. His assignment to command Manticore Astro Control coincided with Baron High Ridge's assumption of the premiership. ACS was a civil service organization, despite its military ranks, but it came under the authority of the Ministry of Trade. Like his colleague Janacek, at the Admiralty, the Earl of North Hollow had wielded a clean broom when he took over at Trade, and Stokes had been his handpicked choice for the Junction. Like many of North Hollow's allies, he was not held in particularly high esteem by Earl White Haven. Nor had White Haven ever made any effort to conceal that fact.

"Look," Stokes half-snarled, "I don't really give a good goddamn about all of that crap! If you want to use the Junction, fine. But you'll damned well take your own slot in the transit queue instead of coming through here and bumping anybody in your way!"

"We'll make transit as we arrive," White Haven replied coldly, "or there will be a formal protest from Protector Benjamin on Foreign Secretary Descroix's desk by this time tomorrow." He showed his teeth briefly. "Admiral MacDonnell brought it with him in case it might be needed. And that protest will be accompanied by a report from Admiral MacDonnell specifically listing the names of the Manticoran officers who refused to honor the Star Kingdom's solemn obligations under interstellar covenant. A covenant from which the Protectorate will offer to withdraw if the Star Kingdom finds its reciprocal obligations under it odious. Somehow, Allen, I don't think you want to be named in Admiral MacDonnell's report."

Stokes' expression seemed to congeal like cold gravy. Its angry flush faded abruptly into something much paler and tinged with green. The Junction lay four hundred and twelve light-minutes from Manticore-A. At the moment, the capital planet itself was on the far side of the primary, which added another twelve light-minutes. Of course, ACS had been provided with grav-pulse communicators as soon as they became available. Although the capital planet lay beyond direct transmission range of even the latest generation FTL systems, repeater stations had been emplaced to cover the gap, which meant that the sheer distance between Stokes and the city of Landing no longer imposed the delays of simple light-speed transmission lags. At the moment, however, that was of scant comfort to Admiral Allen Stokes.

However quickly his message could reach the capital, there was still going to be an inevitable period of confusion and consternation at the far end of the com link. Nobody was going to want to stick *his* neck out until he'd had time to consult a copy of the treaty, his own immediate superiors, at least three attorneys, and probably a justice of the Queen's Bench. As White Haven had just observed, however, the first Grayson warships would reach the transit threshold in little more than ten minutes. Which meant that no one on Manticore was going to take the heat off of Stokes in time to do him any good.

The Astro Control commander was quite certain that both Stefan Young and Sir Edward Janacek were going to be livid the instant they heard about this. And he was equally certain that the two of them would relieve some of their frustration by taking it out on whatever unfortunate officer gave the Graysons permission to make transit. But if he didn't give them transit authority, and if White Haven was telling him the truth about the strength of protest Benjamin was prepared to lodge, the consequences for one Allen Stokes' career would probably be even worse. Whatever Janacek's view of the value of the alliance with Grayson might be, neither he nor North Hollow was about to court responsibility for wrecking it. And especially not at a moment when diplomatic tensions with the Republic of Haven were at their highest level since the war. So if Stokes defied MacDonnell—and White Haven—and his refusal to let the damned Graysons trample all over his traffic patterns blew up into a major diplomatic incident, he would almost certainly become the sacrificial victim offered up in its wake.

He drew a deep breath and glowered at White Haven, but even he knew that his expression lacked the voltage of true defiance.

"I feel certain," he said, with all the dignity he could muster, "that the high-handedness of this arrogant disruption of the Junction's normal civilian transit patterns will be protested at the highest level of government. There are, after all, proper procedures—procedures allies observe as a matter of simple, minimal courtesy. I, however, am not prepared to compound the diplomatic exchanges which this . . . incident will inevitably generate. I continue to protest in the strongest possible terms, but we will clear your units for immediate transit upon their arrival. Stokes, clear."

The com screen blanked, and Hamish Alexander looked at Niall MacDonnell and grinned.

"I don't think he likes us very much," the Earl of White Haven observed. "What a pity."

"Well," Commander Lampert said quietly, his eyes on the date-time display, "that's that."

"What?" Captain Reumann looked up from the message board in his lap. He let his command chair come fully upright, and swiveled it to face his executive officer. Lampert waved one hand wordlessly at the time display, and Reumann followed the gesture, frowned in brief thought, and then chuckled humorlessly.

"You know, Doug, the die was actually cast, if I may be permitted a somewhat purple phrase, when the Admiral sent *Starlight* on her way. It's not like we could have called anything back once she headed off into hyper, you know."

"Oh, I realize that, Sir." Lampert shook his head with a lopsided grin. "I suppose it's just that I'm a compulsive stage watcher."

"'Stage watcher'?" Reumann shook his head. "I'm afraid I am not familiar with that one."

"We're the ones who insist on chopping complex operations up into discrete stages so that we can check them off, one at a time." Lampert shrugged. "I know it doesn't make a lot of sense, but it's how I keep things organized."

"Well, I certainly can't complain, then," Reumann told him. "Without you to keep the *Sovereign* organized, God knows where we'd be. But somehow I don't think the Admiral would be very happy about the results."

"Executive officer's job, Sir," Lampert replied with another shrug. "All the same, I'll feel better this time day after tomorrow."

"You'll feel better this time day after tomorrow if the ops plan works," Reumann corrected, and Lampert grimaced.

"I seem to recall having heard somewhere that it was an officer's job to project cheerful confidence, Sir."

"Indeed it is. And it's also an officer's job to remain constantly aware of potential difficulties which may interfere with the successful completion of the tasks assigned to him. Like, for example, the Manty navy." Reumann chuckled again at Lampert's expression.

"Sorry," he said after a moment, with an edge of contrition. "I don't really mean to give you a hard time, Doug. Just put it down to the peculiar way I deal with defusing my own tensions."

"'S another thing execs are there for, Skipper." Lampert shrugged. "If the Master after God can relieve his tension, thereby improving his own efficiency, just by abusing his hapless executive officer, then said hapless executive officer is only too pleased to suffer for the good of the Service."

"Yeah. Sure he is." Captain and first officer grinned at one another, but then, as if by unspoken agreement, their eyes slid once more to the time display on the bulkhead, and their grins faded.

When it came down to it, Reumann reflected, Lampert was right. Maybe they couldn't have changed the schedule, and no doubt they truly had been committed from the moment Admiral Giscard activated Operation Thunderbolt on the instructions of President Pritchart and the Congress. But there was something more than merely symbolic about *Starlight*'s departure from

Trevor's Star to Basilisk via Manticore. Battle divisions and squadrons had been departing First Fleet's rendezvous for several days, each force heading off for its own individual objective. In fact, all of First Fleet had dispersed in accordance with Thunderbolt's minutely organized timetable, and no one could possibly have called any of them back. So the Rubicon had actually been crossed well before *Starlight* reached Trevor's Star. But there was still a special significance to the dispatch boat's mission, even if Reumann couldn't possibly have offered a logical explanation for why that was true.

Maybe it was simply the scale of the operations. Or perhaps it was knowing how many megatons of warships and how many thousands of Navy personnel were waiting with Second Fleet in Silesia for the arrival of that single, small vessel. Or perhaps it was even simpler than that. Perhaps it was just fear that something would still go wrong. That the Silesian Ambassador's crew would screw up their mission, or let something slip . . . or even intentionally betray the Republic whose monumental bribe had convinced the Ambassador to make his ship available to it. So much coordination depended on such a tiny ship. Somehow, the universe hadn't seemed quite so vast—or the dispatch boat quite so minute—when Thunderbolt had simply been an ops plan. Now it was reality, and Patrick Reumann had discovered that he was only too well aware of the fragility of their communication link to Second Fleet.

He gave himself a stern mental shake. What was really happening, he told himself firmly, was that he had opening night jitters. That, and the fact that despite all of the upgrades in the Republican Navy's weapons and hardware, despite all of the doctrine and tactical development Shannon Foraker and her team had carried out at Bolthole, and despite all of the simulation runs, all of the training exercises, which Javier Giscard had put First Fleet through, there was still that edge of dread. That sense of challenging Fate itself by going up against the enemy fleet which had shattered the Republic's Navy like so much glass in the final months before the cease-fire. Intellectually, Reumann knew that the Manties were far from superhuman. He only had to glance through the intelligence reports and the analyses of the incredibly stupid policies Janacek and High Ridge had instigated since assuming power to know that. But what his brain knew and his emotions expected weren't necessarily the same thing, and he felt a familiar flutter somewhere deep inside as he, too, looked at the time display and realized that, in barely thirty-two hours, the Republic of Haven would once again be openly at war with the Star Kingdom of Manticore.

Chapter Fifty-Four

"So why isn't the Minister of Trade here?" Sir Edward Janacek demanded in a voice which only too accurately reflected his outrage.

"Be reasonable, Edward," Michael Janvier replied with more than a trace of answering impatience. "The man's wife has disappeared, his home has just been blown up—possibly with her in it—and even if he's not ready to admit it, all of the 'North Hollow Files' went with the house. And if you believe that the entire disaster was the result of a 'leaking air car hydrogen cylinder in the parking basement,' then you probably believe in the tooth fairy, too!"

Janacek started to snap back sharply, then visibly made himself pause. The ferocious explosion which had rocked one of Landing's most luxurious suburbs had left a smoking crater where the Young's capital residence had once been and administered an equally savage shock to the political establishment. The existence of the North Hollow Files had been one of the open dirty little secrets of Manticoran politics for so long that even those who'd most detested the tactics they reflected were temporarily disoriented. Of course, just as the Earls of North Hollow had never officially admitted to their files' existence, Stefan Young wasn't about to admit that his enormous behind-the-scenes political leverage had blown up along with his mansion. And it was going to take some time—and a lot of cautious probes and tests—before the

Star Kingdom's political leadership was prepared to believe it truly had been. Especially for the people who had been the subjects of that leverage over the years.

The First Lord of the Admiralty knew that the implications of the North Hollow explosion were only just beginning to ripple through the establishment. As those implications went more and more fully home, the consequences for the High Ridge Government might well prove profound. Janacek wasn't really certain exactly how many of High Ridge's "allies" had been coerced into giving him their support, but he had no doubt that some of them—like Sir Harrison MacIntosh—were in extremely important, if not vital, positions. What might happen once they realized the evidence of their past misdeeds no longer existed was anyone's guess, but he didn't expect it to be good. Apparently, the Prime Minister shared his expectations, which probably helped to account for his waspish tone.

Of course, there were other factors which undoubtedly helped to account for it, as well.

"All right," Janacek said finally. "Personally, I suspect that the disappearance of his wife and his house are pretty directly connected. And no, I *don't* think her limo just happened to blow up because of a fuel leak, whatever he wants to believe. I don't know what anyone could have offered her, but given the LCPD's failure so far to find any human remains at all in the rubble, much less hers—" He shrugged angrily. "Still, I can understand that he's . . . distracted just now. Which doesn't change the fact that his precious ACS appointee just let the fucking Graysons stomp all over us!"

"Yes, he did," High Ridge said coldly. "And I can understand that you're irritated, Edward. At the same time, however, I have to say that angry as I am over the Graysons' high-handed actions—yes, and over White Haven's involvement in them—it may not be all bad."

"What?" Janacek stared at him in disbelief. "Benjamin and his precious Navy have just openly defied us in our own space, and you say 'it may not be all bad'?! My God, Michael! Those neobarb bastards have just put their thumb right in our eye in front of the entire galaxy!"

"Indeed they have," High Ridge agreed with a dangerous calm. "On the other hand, Edward, your refusal to *invite* Grayson to do precisely what it's just done unilaterally was called to my attention during my visit yesterday to Mount Royal Palace." He smiled thinly. "Her Majesty was not amused by it."

"Now, wait a minute, Michael," Janacek said sharply. "That decision was endorsed by you and by a majority of the entire Cabinet!"

"Only after you'd already rejected White Haven's arguments in favor of seeking their assistance," High Ridge pointed out icily. "And only, or so I hear, after Admiral Chakrabarti had made essentially the same argument to you. That was before he resigned, of course."

"Who told you something like that?" Janacek demanded around the sudden sinking sensation in the pit of his stomach.

"It wasn't Chakrabarti, if that's what you're wondering," High Ridge replied. "Not that the source changes the implications."

"Are you telling me that you disapproved of the decision not to ask Grayson for help?" Janacek shot back. "Because it certainly didn't sound that way to me at the time. And I don't think the minutes of our meeting or the memoranda in the files sound that way, either."

The two of them glared at one another, and then High Ridge inhaled sharply.

"You're right," he admitted, although he clearly didn't enjoy doing it. "I may not have thought it was the best decision possible, but I'll concede that I didn't protest it at the time. Partly that was because you'd already effectively committed us to it, but if I'm going to be honest, it was also because I don't much care for Graysons—or for the thought of owing them some sort of debt of gratitude—either.

"Still," he continued in a stronger voice, "the fact that they've seen fit entirely on their own to send such a substantial reinforcement to Trevor's Star may not be entirely a bad thing. At the very least, the fact that they did so so openly is going to have to give Pritchart and her war party pause. And God knows anything that does that can't be all bad!"

Janacek made an irate, wordless sound of angry agreement. He might enormously resent Benjamin Mayhew's actions, and Hamish Alexander's part in them might only add fresh fuel to the First Lord's smoldering hatred. But with the diplomatic situation so rapidly going to hell in a handbasket, any factor which might slap Pritchart and Theisman across the face with a dose of reality had to be a good thing. Of course, it would take a while for news of the . . . call it 'redeployment' to reach Nouveau Paris. Once it did, however, even a lunatic like Pritchart would be forced to recognize that the Manticoran Alliance remained far too dangerous to casually piss off. A reminder, judging by the recent exchanges of diplomatic correspondence, of which she stood in serious need.

"Whatever good it may do us with the Peeps," he said after a moment, "it's going to have unfortunate domestic consequences, though." High Ridge just looked at him, and he shrugged. "At the very least, this is going to embolden Alexander and his crowd. They're going to argue that we were too stupid or too stubborn to take 'prudent precautions' ourselves, so our allies were forced to do it for us."

"If they do, then whose—?" High Ridge cut himself off before he reopened the blame game, but the flash of fresh anger in Janacek's eyes was proof enough that the First Lord knew what he'd been about to say.

"If they do, they do," he said instead. "There isn't a great deal we can do about that just now, Edward. And to be brutally frank about it, the domestic political situation is so . . . confused at the moment that I don't really know how much of an impact it will have even if they do."

Again, Janacek found himself forced to concede the Prime Minister's point. The Government's official decision to grant the Talbott Cluster's request to be annexed to the Star Kingdom— contingent, of course, upon the approval of the full Parliament— had proven immensely popular. The worsening diplomatic situation with the Republic of Haven, on the other hand, had produced an almost equally powerful negative response. The current parlous state of the Navy was another factor on the negative side of the balance of public opinion. Still, a significant proportion of the public remained uncertain whether to take the Government or the Opposition view of the Navy's effective strength, and the somewhat belated resumption of construction on the suspended SD(P)s had blunted much of that criticism. By the same token, the Government's spending programs remained extremely popular with those who had benefitted from them . . . which meant their partisans resented the diversion of funds back to construction budgets. And, finally, the news accounts of the clashes with the Andermani in Silesian space had refocused public opinion on the precious

"Salamander" and her supposedly glorious record in combat . . . not to mention fanning the fire for those concerned over the Star Kingdom's disintegrating interstellar relations.

The only good thing about Silesia, so far as Janacek could tell, was that the average voter really didn't consider the Confederacy a priority issue. Mister Average Voter was irritated and offended by the Andermani "insult" to the Star Kingdom, and extremely angry over the loss of Manticoran lives which had so far occurred. But he was also aware that there had been Andermani fatalities, as well, and for once Harrington's grossly inflated reputation was a plus. The man in the street had been told she had ample forces to restrain the Andermani, and he trusted her to do just that. It galled Janacek down to the very depths of his soul to admit that, but he knew it was true and that however much he resented it, he ought to be grateful for it.

"What do the polls look like now?" he asked.

"Not good," High Ridge admitted more candidly than he probably would have to almost anyone else. "The base trend lines are pretty firmly against us, at the moment. We score fairly high on several issues, but the increasing concern over the Peeps' belligerence is undercutting that badly. The fact that the Queen is scarcely even speaking to the Government at the moment is another serious problem for our public approval rating. And I suppose if we're going to be completely honest about it, the backlash from our campaign against Harrington and White Haven is still another negative factor. Especially now, when so many of the poll respondents are expressing their confidence in her ability to handle the Silesian situation if anyone can." He shrugged. "Assuming that we can hold the Cabinet together and weather the storm on the Peep front—without, of course, getting into a major shooting war in Silesia at the same time—we'll probably survive. Whether or not we'll be able to complete our domestic program, unfortunately, is another question entirely."

Janacek felt an icicle run lightly down his spine. Despite the steadily rising anxiety level of every member of the High Ridge Government, this was the first time the Prime Minister had sounded so openly pessimistic. No, not pessimistic. There'd been moments of that before. This was simply the first time Janacek had heard him admitting his pessimism in an almost resigned tone. As if a part of him had finally come to *expect* disaster.

"Do you think the Cabinet *won't* hold together?" the First Lord asked somberly.

"I can't really say," High Ridge admitted. He shrugged. "Without the proper . . . leverage, MacIntosh is likely to prove much less controllable, and New Kiev is already very uncomfortable. Worse, that madwoman Montaigne is steadily eroding Marisa's authority within her own party, and she's doing it mainly by attacking her for 'prostituting' herself by joining our Cabinet. Marisa may decide that she has no option but to withdraw from the Government over some carefully chosen 'matter of principle' if she's going to fight effectively to retain control of her own Party Conference. If she does, she'll almost have to 'denounce' us in the process . . . and if we lose the Liberals, we lose the Commons completely. Not to mention our clear majority in the Lords." He shrugged again. "Unless the Liberals go completely over to the Centrists—which I think is unlikely, even if Marisa feels a need to clearly separate herself from us—then no one would have a clear majority in the Upper House, and I can't begin to predict what sort of power-sharing agreement might have to be worked out in that case."

The two of them looked at one another for several seconds in silence. There was one more question Janacek badly wanted to ask, but he couldn't quite bring himself to. *"Can we at least make sure that any 'power-sharing agreement' contains a guarantee that none of us will be prosecuted?"* wasn't exactly the sort of thing one asked the Prime Minister of the Star Kingdom of Manticore even in private. No matter how burningly it presented itself to one's own mind.

"So," he said instead, "should I assume that no formal protest of MacDonnell's actions will be addressed to Grayson?"

"You should," High Ridge replied. He, too, seemed almost grateful for the change of subject. "That's not to say that we won't be speaking to Protector Benjamin about the high-handedness with which he exercised his undoubted rights under his treaty with us. There are, as Admiral Stokes pointed out, proper procedural channels through which such a transit should have been arranged without causing such mammoth dislocation of normal Junction operations. But that, I'm afraid, is as far as we're going to be able to go under the current circumstances."

"I don't like it," Janacek grumbled. "And I'm especially not going to like having to pretend to be civil to their precious High Admiral

Matthews after this, either. But if we don't have a choice, then I suppose we don't have a choice."

"If we survive in power, we may be able to find a way to make our displeasure felt at a later date," High Ridge told him. "But to be completely honest, Edward, even that's unlikely. I think this is just one of those insults we're going to have to swallow in the name of political expediency. Not," the Prime Minister assured the First Lord grimly, "that I intend to forget it, I assure you."

Secretary of State Arnold Giancola sat in his office and stared at his chrono. Another nine hours. That was all.

He closed his eyes and leaned back in his comfortable chair while a complex storm of emotions whirled and battered against the back of his bland expression.

He'd never planned on this. He admitted that to himself, although it wasn't easy for him to concede the collapse of his plans. He remained convinced that he'd read the Manties correctly; it was Eloise Pritchart he had catastrophically underestimated. Her, and her control over Thomas Theisman. Or perhaps he'd been wrong there, too. He'd never expected her to be able to drag Theisman into supporting any open act of war even if she'd had the nerve to contemplate one—not after how hard the Secretary of War had fought against even admitting Bolthole existed. But perhaps all along, Theisman had possessed the intestinal fortitude to unflinchingly contemplate a resumption of military operations and Giancola, deceived by his insistence on concealing his new fleet until it was ready, simply hadn't recognized it.

But wherever Giancola's error had lain, it was too late to undo it now. Even if he commed the President this instant, confessed all he'd done, and showed her the originals of the Manties' diplomatic notes, it was still too late. The Navy was in motion, and no one in the Haven System could possibly recall it in time to stop the Thunderbolt from striking.

He *could* have stopped it, he admitted to himself. He could have stopped it before it ever began. Could have stopped it before Pritchart ever appeared before Congress in the blazing majesty of her righteous indignation, laid the Manties' "duplicity" before it, and carried her request for what amounted to a declaration of war by a majority of over ninety-five percent. Could have stopped it even after that, if he'd been prepared to confess his actions and accept the consequences before the final activation order had been sent to Javier Giscard.

But he hadn't been, and he still wasn't. A huge part of that, he knew with bleak honesty, was simple self-preservation and ambition. Disgrace and a total, irrevocable fall from power would be the very least he could expect. Trial and imprisonment were far from unlikely, however strongly he might argue that he'd actually violated no laws. Neither of those was a fate he was prepared to embrace.

Yet there was more to it than that. He hadn't planned on this, no; but that didn't necessarily make what was happening a disaster. Certainly he'd manipulated the Manties' diplomatic correspondence, but the fact that he might have changed their words didn't mean he'd misrepresented their ultimate goals. Weak and unprincipled High Ridge and his associates might be, but the expansionist trend of Manticoran policy remained, and another Manty regime—one with a spine and the will to make its policies effective—would inevitably have embraced those same goals in time. And so, perhaps, this was in fact the best of all possible outcomes. To strike now, when the Navy's advantage over the Manties was at its strongest . . . and when the current Manticoran government was at its weakest.

And, he acknowledged, when Thomas Theisman had displayed a degree of strategic imagination and willingness to take the war to the enemy which Giancola had never imagined for a moment he might possess.

The Secretary of State opened his eyes, looked at the chrono once again, and felt the decision make itself, once and forever.

It was too late to stop what was going to happen. Confessing his true part in the events which had set Operation Thunderbolt in motion could only destroy him without stopping anything. And so he would not admit it.

He turned to his private computer station and brought it online. Half a dozen keystrokes were all it took to erase the record of the original Manticoran notes he had stored "just in case." Another three keystrokes and that portion of the Department of State's molycirc memory core where those notes had been stored was reformatted with a "document shredding" program guaranteed to make the data permanently non-recoverable.

Grosclaude, he knew, had already destroyed all of his records on Manticore, as well as every other sensitive file which might fall into enemy hands, in anticipation of Thunderbolt. The thought held a certain ironic satisfaction, even now, because no one—not even the Manties, when the discrepancy in the diplomatic record became public knowledge—could accuse Grosclaude of destroying incriminating records in the name of self-preservation. Not when he'd had specific orders to do so from the President of the Republic herself.

And that's that, he thought. *No tracks, no fingerprints. No proof. Now, if only the Navy gets it done.*

Javier Giscard looked at the bulkhead date-time display, and his bony face was expressionless.

It was very quiet in his day cabin, but that was going to change in little more than three hours. That was when *Sovereign of Space*'s general quarters alarm would sound and First Fleet would clear for battle.

But the war, Giscard thought, would start even sooner than that. In approximately ninety-eight minutes, assuming Admiral Evans met his ops schedule at Tequila the way Giscard expected him to.

The admiral laid out his own thoughts before his mind's eye and tried to decide—again—what he truly felt.

Wary, he thought. And yet, if he was honest, confident, as well. No one in the history of interstellar warfare had ever attempted to coordinate a campaign on such a scale. The operational plan Theisman and the Naval Staff had worked out included literally dozens of minutely coordinated operations. The timing was tight, yet they had avoided situations in which it was truly critical. There was plenty of room for slippage, for schedules to be readjusted on the fly. And the strategic audacity at its core was almost literally breathtaking for an officer who had survived the desperate, uncoordinated defensive efforts of the People's Navy following the Legislaturalist purges.

Dozens of operations, each with its own objectives, its own place in the overall strategy. And each—even Giscard's own attack on Trevor's Star—independent of one another. Any one, or two, or even three, of them could fail completely without spelling the defeat of Operation Thunderbolt as a whole. To be sure, the destruction of Third Fleet at Trevor's Star was the most important single objective, but even if Giscard failed there, the other operations would inflict a defeat upon the Star Kingdom which would utterly surpass even the one Esther McQueen had delivered in Operation Icarus.

The objective of Thunderbolt, Giscard knew, was to convince the Manties that they must negotiate in good faith and compel them to begin the process. Eloise had no ambitions beyond that point, as she had made crystal clear in her address to the Congress. But much as Giscard loved her, he wasn't blind to the blind spots in her own judgment. By and large, they were so minor, especially compared to her strengths, as to be completely negligible. But sometimes . . . sometimes her faith in the rationality of others betrayed her.

It seemed so obvious to her that all the Republic wanted was to be treated fairly, for the Star Kingdom to negotiate in good faith, that some essential part of her couldn't quite believe anyone else could fail to see that. She didn't want to conquer the Star Kingdom. She didn't want to reconquer Trevor's Star. All she wanted was for the Star Kingdom to *talk* to her. To once and for all negotiate an end to this ugly, festering, endless conflict. And so, because that was all she wanted and because it was so obvious to her that it was all she *could* want, she truly believed that the Manties would recognize both the justice of her demands and the realities of their hopelessly weakened position and allow her to achieve the equitable diplomatic solution she craved.

But Javier Giscard, as both the lover who knew her better than anyone else in the galaxy and as the senior field commander of her Navy, suspected she was wrong. Not in what she wanted, but in how likely she was to get it. Even if the High Ridge Government fell, no Manticoran successor government was going to simply roll over and quit—not without additional proof of how Thunderbolt had crippled them. Nor were the Manties likely to believe that peace was truly all she wanted. Especially not if Thunderbolt secured the level of advantage Giscard expected it to. The Star Kingdom would have no choice but to expect the opportunities Thunderbolt would offer to tempt the Republic into exploiting them. Into imposing a peace on its own terms, not negotiating for one equitable to both sides. And just as Eloise had been unwilling to accept such an imposition for the Republic, so any new Manty government would be unwilling to accept one for the Star Kingdom. Which meant the war that Eloise hoped would be both begun and ended with a single campaign wouldn't be.

Giscard knew that. Thomas Theisman knew that, and both of them had explained it to Eloise. More operations would be required, more people would be killed—on both sides. And, intellectually, Eloise had admitted the possibility that they were correct. It was a possibility she was prepared to face as unflinchingly as she had been prepared to defy the Committee of Public Safety as Giscard's people's commissioner. But it wasn't one she'd truly accepted on an emotional level, and he was frightened for her. Not because he expected Thunderbolt to fail, because he didn't. And not because he expected defeat after Thunderbolt, because he didn't expect that, either. Theisman's plan was too good, its objectives too shrewdly chosen, for that. If additional operations became necessary, the Republican Navy would be well-positioned, with the strategic momentum on its side and an ever-increasing stream of powerful new warships coming forward from Bolthole to replace any losses.

But even now he doubted that Eloise was truly prepared for the casualties. Not for loss of money, or loss of hardware—of lives. The deaths of men and women, Manticoran as well as Havenite, which would stem directly from her decision to go back to war. The deaths Javier Giscard firmly expected to continue for months, possibly even years, beyond the end of Operation Thunderbolt.

And if they did, he told himself grimly, then it was his job— his and Thomas Theisman's and Lester Tourville's and Shannon Foraker's—to see to it that in the end those people did not die for nothing.

He looked back at the date-time display, and as he did his com terminal beeped softly. He looked down at it and pressed the acceptance key, and Captain Gozzi's face appeared upon it. The chief of staff's expression combined tension and confidence, and he smiled at his admiral.

"Sir, you wanted me to remind you at X-minus three. The staff is assembling in your flag briefing room now."

"Thank you, Marius," Giscard said. "I'll be there in a moment. Go ahead and distribute the briefing packets so people can be looking over them. We don't have much time, so if anyone sees any last-minute detail we need to address, we'd better get on it quickly."

"Yes, Sir. I'll get right on it."

"Thank you," Giscard said again. "I'm on my way."

CHAPTER FIFTY-FIVE

Lieutenant Commander Sarah Flanagan finished the current report, affixed her electronic signature, and dumped it back into the station's communications system. No doubt, she thought sourly, she'd be seeing it again soon. After all, there had to be some section she'd forgotten to initial, some signature block she'd forgotten to check, or—all else failing—some arcane routing number she'd somehow managed to delete from the header. Something. Right off the top of her head, she couldn't think of a single report which Captain Louis al-Salil hadn't bounced back to her for one obscure reason or another.

Now if he'd only spent half as much effort on keeping his LAC group's training up to standard. . . .

Unfortunately, al-Salil had better things to do with his time than to waste it on boring, "routine" training ops. And if the group absolutely had to train, it made so much more sense to him to rely on the simulators. The fact that no more than a quarter of the group could fit into the available simulators at any one time (which made exercises in things like full-group coordination impossible) was not, in his opinion, a particularly significant drawback.

Sarah Flanagan disagreed. Her last posting had been to HMS *Mephisto*, a CLAC assigned to Home Fleet. Even there, the LAC training tempo had slackened noticeably from the pace Eighth Fleet had maintained under Admiral Truman during Operation Buttercup, but it remained far more demanding than anything al-Salil seemed to feel was necessary. Flanagan had been only a lieutenant during Buttercup, working her way up to command her own LAC, but she'd had her eye on a squadron command slot even then. She'd absorbed everything she could under Truman's tutelage and applied it with an aggressive efficiency which had carried her to that goal in something close to record time. Although, she admitted to herself, if she'd known they were going to assign her to a bare-bones space station in a podunk frontier system when they gave it to her, she might have had second thoughts about her ambition.

She supposed it made at least some sense to economize on starships, especially given the way the Admiralty and Government had built down the Navy's strength. And certainly a LAC group could cover far more space, and do it more efficiently, than a like tonnage of light cruisers or destroyers could. But that wasn't a great deal of consolation to the unfortunate souls assigned to crew the LACs in question. Especially not when among the starships being economized upon was the carrier they ought to have been operating from.

Her Majesty's Space Station T-001 had never even attained the dignity of a formal name. Known to its denizens as "the Tamale" for reasons Flanagan had never been able to divine, T-001 offered absolutely no amenities. About the only good thing anyone could say about it was that an ex-Peep cargo transfer space station modified to play orbital mothership to a standard group of a hundred and eight LACs was big enough that at least there was ample personnel space. Of course, that personnel space had been carved out of the previous owners' temporary cargo stowage decks, and no one had bothered to do much to make it particularly pleasurable to inhabit. Still, Flanagan had to admit that her cabin gave her at least twice the cubage she'd enjoyed aboard *Mephisto*, and she didn't even have to share it with anyone.

It would have been nice if the increase in living space had been accompanied by an improvement in the quality of that space. On the other hand, perhaps the amenities they had were actually better suited to the quality of the LAC group living in it. Not that the problem was with the basic quality of the personnel assigned to the 1007th LAC Group (Temporary). One had to look a bit higher up the military feeding chain to find the reason for that.

Flanagan had been stunned and dismayed by the standard of readiness which appeared to satisfy al-Salil and Vice Admiral Schumacher, the system CO. She'd heard that Schumacher was considered one of the Navy's golden boys by the Admiralty, despite purely limited combat experience, but no one could have proved it by Flanagan. His operational standards would never have satisfied Admiral Truman, at any rate. They didn't particularly satisfy Sarah Flanagan, either. Unfortunately, as al-Salil's most junior squadron commander, there wasn't very much she could do about it.

She muttered a weary, heartfelt curse at the familiar thought, then punched up the next report in her queue and grimaced as she read the header. Lovely. Now The Powers That Were wanted her squadron's crews to run a complete inventory of all emergency survival stores. She wondered why that was. The group's maintenance personnel were fully capable of performing such inventories. In fact, it was part of their job description. So why exactly were the LAC flight crews supposed to do exactly the same job behind them? Had someone been pilfering e-rats? Was this somehow supposed to catch the arch thief at her work? It seemed unlikely that anyone so incredibly capable that she could actually make a profit selling emergency survival stores was likely to be trapped by any merely mortal agency.

But whether it made sense or not wasn't Flanagan's problem, so she drew a deep breath, settled down in her chair, and prepared to dive into yet another exhilarating adventure in creative paperwork.

That was the moment the entire universe changed.

The sudden, raucous, atonal howl took her utterly by surprise, but her instincts knew what they were doing. She was already out of her chair and halfway out of her small office before she even realized she'd moved. She was up to a full run within five meters, dashing through a bedlam of startled exclamations, other chairs skidding across decksoles, hatches cycling madly open, feet thundering down passages towards lift shafts, and over all of it that bone-crawling, brain-piercing alarm shrieking its warning.

As a squadron skipper, Flanagan's office cubicle was on the same deck as her squadron's LAC bays. She didn't need a lift shaft to reach her command ship, and only one member of her crew—Ensign Giuliani—had managed to beat her there. Of course, a corner of her brain reflected with something very like shell-shocked detachment, Giuliani practically lived aboard *Switchblade*. He was the command LAC's coxswain, and he'd discovered that he could seduce the flight computers into providing what amounted to his own, private simulator. As far as al-Salil was concerned, of course, Giuliani's solo excursions in training were completely unauthorized, but Flanagan had somehow failed to mention them to T-001's COLAC.

"What's happening, Cal?" she demanded pantingly as she skidded to a halt just inside *Switchblade*'s boarding tube.

"I'm not sure, Skipper," Giuliani replied flatly, never looking up from the tactical plot he'd brought online as soon as the alarm began to sound. "But from the looks of things, we're fucked."

Flanagan felt her eyebrows try to crawl up into her hairline. She'd never heard quite that note in the brash young ensign's voice. Nor, now that she thought about it, had she ever heard even the mildest profanity from him in her own august presence.

"Can you be more specific?" she asked tartly, and this time Giuliani raised his head and gave her a half-apologetic smile.

"Sorry, Skip," he said contritely. "I should've said that it looks like the system is under attack by unknown forces operating in overwhelming strength. Except that unless I'm completely wrong, they're not 'unknown' at all. I think they're Peeps."

"Peeps?" Flanagan wanted the word to come out as a question, or perhaps a protest, but it didn't. After all, who else would be attacking a Manticoran picket here in the Tequila System? Elves? Yet despite that, she felt an underlying sense of disbelief. Everyone had heard the rumors about the Peeps' new fleet, but no one had suggested to her that any sort of attack was imminent.

"Can't think of anyone else they'd be," Giuliani told her as the other members of *Switchblade*'s crew began to arrive. Flanagan heard them opening equipment lockers and dragging out their skinsuits. Suits weren't usually stored aboard LACs, but "the Tamale's" conversion had been a bit on the crude side. It worked—most of it, usually—but no one had bothered with any frills. And since the flight crews' battle stations were aboard the LACs, the decision had been made to keep the skinsuits there, as well. It had led to a few problems with personnel with more extreme nudity taboos, but it worked better than a lot of T-001's arrangements, and, besides, Flanagan had other things on her mind just then.

She stepped up beside Giuliani and leaned over the tactical plot with him.

Whoever it was, they'd come loaded for bear, she thought. T-001 and her sister station T-002 were all the defenders the Tequila System had. Which was pretty frigging stupid, she reflected grimly, given its status as the furthest advanced system Eighth Fleet had occupied during the final offensive of the war. Or maybe it wasn't. What they had was big enough to deter casual intrusions, and if it wasn't powerful enough to mount a defense against an all-out attack, at least it was sufficient to act as a credible tripwire. Anyone who wanted Tequila was going to have to pay cash for it. Unfortunately, it looked like the Peeps had brought plenty of spare change.

At least Vice Admiral Schumacher had decent in-system FTL sensor capability. The big passive arrays which had once been planned to cover the system perimeter and watch for hyper footprints far beyond it had never been emplaced . . . of course. Too expensive in this era of austere naval budgets. That probably didn't matter in this case, though. It didn't look as if the intruders were attempting anything particularly subtle. They'd simply sent in a squadron of superdreadnoughts with cruiser escorts. Given the power of the *Shrike-B*'s graser armament, they were going to take damage even on superdreadnoughts, but nothing to compare to the damage the LACs were going to take. Even Peep SDs were going to tear unsupported light attack craft apart when they closed to energy range.

Which meant Cal was correct; "fucked" was exactly what they were.

"Launch instructions are coming up now, Skip," Lieutenant Benedict announced. Flanagan turned away from the plot and looked a question at her exec.

"It looks like we're going with Delta-Three, at least initially," Benedict told her.

"Time till launch?" she asked, and he checked the launch clock on his console.

"Thirty-one minutes," he said. "Station Engineering started bringing the nodes up on remote as soon as GQ sounded. They'll be optimal in another twenty-eight minutes."

"What about missile loadout?"

"Nothing on my screen, Skip," Benedict replied with a shrug. "Looks like we're going to launch with a standard package."

Flanagan managed not to stare at him in disbelief, which would undoubtedly have been terrible for morale, but it wasn't easy. The standard missile package consisted of a little bit of everything and not enough of anything. It was intended as a standby weapons load, one that gave at least limited capability under almost any circumstances. But it was effectively an *emergency* load. Standard tactical doctrine assumed that any COLAC would tailor his missile loads to the tactical mission—deleting the ordnance he wouldn't need to make room for the weapons he did—unless he found himself forced to launch under emergency conditions at minimal range. That wasn't the case here. Even if the Peeps had been able to match the extended range of the RMN's capital ship missiles, it would have taken them the better part of three hours to get into effective attack range of "the Tamale." That was plenty of time for the 1007th to strip the standby packages off of its LACs and replace them with a load that made sense, especially since the high-speed magazine tubes were the one part of T-001's conversion which had always worked perfectly.

But apparently al-Salil and Schumacher didn't see things that way.

Sarah Flanagan hovered on the brink of comming the COLAC to suggest that it might be time for a little sanity. She had no doubt that most of the group's personnel were about to die, although that lingering sense of disbelief mingled with trained professionalism had managed to so far hold that realization at arm's length. Still, she knew, the odds were very good that she would be among the ones who did, and it offended that same professionalism deeply to think that al-Salil would just throw them away this way without even attempting to maximize the damage they might inflict before they were destroyed.

She almost did it. She *ought* to have done it, and she knew it. But she was the most junior squadron commander of the group, and she knew precisely how al-Salil would react. Given the circumstances, she had no particular desire to spend any of the time she had left in fruitless debate with a feckless incompetent. Or to be stripped of command and left behind when her people went off to die.

"Override Group's ammunitioning instructions," she told Benedict flatly. The exec looked at her, and she shrugged. "We've got time if you get right on it," she said. "Use the squadron interlinks to the station magazine queue. I want a Lima-Roger-Two package loaded to all ships ASAP. Anybody in the station crew asks any questions, refer them to me."

"Aye, aye, Ma'am!" Benedict said sharply, and she nodded and reached for her own skinsuit.

She peeled out of her uniform and started climbing into the skinsuit with the lack of body modesty which was part and parcel of LAC operations here in Tequila. While she did, she heard Benedict working at his console, and she bared her teeth in an almost-smile.

Lima-Roger-Two—or "Standard Missile Load, Long-Ranged Intercept, Mod Two"—was hardly a tailor-made armament package, but it would give Flanagan's LACs at least some chance of penetrating the envelope of a superdreadnought's defensive fire. It was designed to help LACs which had to go out and meet heavy combatants from outside the supporting missile range of their own wall of battle. As such, it was EW-heavy, with emphasis on counter missiles, jammers, and decoys.

It wasn't much, she thought harshly as she sealed the skinsuit. It was simply all she could offer her people under the circumstances.

"Missile reload complete in approximately nine minutes, Ma'am," Benedict reported formally. "Time to launch now eleven-point-three minutes." He looked up from his displays. "It'll be tight, Skip," he said much more informally, "but we'll make it."

"Good," Flanagan said, picturing the high-speed missile pallets and robotic arms blurring and flashing as they rearranged *Switchblade*'s missile loads. "Any reaction from Captain al-Salil?" she asked after a moment.

"No, Ma'am," Benedict replied in a painfully neutral tone, and Flanagan snorted mentally.

Of course there wasn't anything from al-Salil. And there'd probably be precious little in the way of any sort of briefing on the battle plan he undoubtedly didn't have. This was not only going to be an ugly battle, it was also going to the most fucked up one since Elvis Santino got his entire task group wiped out at Seaford.

And there was absolutely nothing Sarah Flanagan could do to change that.

✧   ✧   ✧

Vice Admiral Agnes de Groot studied the flag deck master plot in a mood of pronounced satisfaction.

De Groot had approached Operation Thunderbolt with less than total enthusiasm. Not because she didn't want to get some of the Navy's own back from the Manties. And not because she didn't agree with President Pritchart that the Star Kingdom of Manticore damned well deserved to have its ass kicked up between its ears over its diplomatic doubledealing and chicanery. Not even because she disagreed with the ops plan's underlying assumptions or strategy.

No, de Groot's reservations had stemmed from the fact that the Staff had expressly ruled out any pre-attack reconnaissance of Tequila.

Agnes de Groot had risen to flag rank in a fleet which had experienced a seemingly unending series of drubbings—interrupted only occasionally by something like Operation Icarus—at the hands of the Manticoran Alliance. In light of that experience, she'd found it . . . difficult to accept NavInt's estimates of the enormous decline in the efficiency of the Royal Manticoran Navy. She'd been certain that the spooks had to be overestimating the degree to which the Manties had lost their edge. Or thrown it away, if there was a difference. Which meant that she had also found it difficult to accept that they could have been stupid enough to reduce their picket in Tequila to the levels NavInt insisted they had.

She knew all about the reports the intelligence types had generated. But she also knew that the data on which those reports were based had come solely from the civilian-grade sensors of merchantmen passing through the system. It wouldn't have been hard for any navy, and especially not for one with the Manties' EW capabilities, to hide an entire fleet from a merchie's sensor suite, and de Groot had been privately certain that that must be what had happened.

It seemed she'd been wrong.

Her own recon drones were twelve million klicks—over forty light-seconds—ahead of her screen, with a secondary shell thrown out to cover her flanks and rear. While she was always prepared to recognize the Manticorans' supremacy in the field of electronic warfare, she found it difficult to believe that she wouldn't have gotten at least a sniff of any heavy units closing to missile range of her own command. Of course, there was missile range, and then

there was missile range. Judging from their performance immediately before the cease-fire, Manty multi-drive missiles had a powered attack range of somewhere around sixty-five million klicks,
which was at least eight million more than the RHN's new weapons
could manage. But not even Manties were going to score many
hits against alert targets at ranges of better than three and a half
light-minutes. To be effective, they were going to have to come a
lot closer than that, and her platforms should have started getting a sniff of them well before they got within five light-minutes
of the outer shell, much less her actual starships.

A part of her still insisted that they had to be out there somewhere, but she told herself that was just the last gasp effort of her
own paranoia. If they'd really had heavy ships, those vessels would
be where her drones could see them. They'd have to be if they
were going to offer any support at all to the two hundred and
eleven LACs sweeping to meet her.

*And if the Manties really hadn't shot themselves in both feet and
one kneecap where their readiness states and training are concerned,*
she thought with grim satisfaction, *those LACs would be doing
something a hell of a lot smarter than what they're doing now.*

She supposed whoever was in command over there was being
brave enough, but Lord God was she *stupid!* What NavInt's estimates insisted was the entire LAC strength based on the system,
allowing for four or five down for routine maintenance, was coming
straight at the invaders with absolutely no attempt to maneuver
for advantage. It looked like the Manty CO intended to charge
straight down de Groot's throat, possibly in an effort to avoid the
Republican broadsides and sidewalls. Of course, that would also
expose her LACs to the fire of de Groot's entire squadron's chase
armament as she closed, but maybe she figured she could survive
that long enough to get into range. If so, she was an idiot . . . or
even more unaware of the improvements in the Republic's naval
hardware—including the new classes' bow walls—than de Groot
would have believed was possible.

Of course, she probably thought she was facing only ships of
the wall, too.

"Another message from the COLAC, Skipper," Chief Petty Officer
Lawrence announced. Flanagan turned her command chair to face
Switchblade's com officer and waved one hand in an unspoken "tell

me" command. She tried very hard not to let the gesture radiate her disgust, but she knew she'd failed.

"Captain al-Salil instructs all *Shrike* commanders to remember to close to minimum range before firing," Lawrence said as expressionlessly as possible.

"Acknowledge," Flanagan replied, and this time she didn't bother with concealing her emotions. It wasn't as if it was going to matter very much longer, and she knew her entire squadron must be as disgusted as she was. Both LAC groups had been accelerating steadily to meet the oncoming Peeps for over two hours. They were less than forty minutes from intercept, and the idiot was still sending fatuous, *stupid* "reminders" instead of anything approaching useful attack orders.

She supposed, in fairness (although she had very little interest in being fair to al-Salil under the circumstances), that he *had* specified an attack plan ... of sorts. Unfortunately, like the missile loads his LACs were carrying, Attack Plan Delta-Three, was purely generic, little more than a vague set of objectives and procedures. It had been obvious to Flanagan for months that neither al-Salil nor Schumacher had believed, even as the diplomatic situation worsened, that the Peeps would dare to attack Tequila. So neither of them had spent much time or effort thinking about serious defensive plans. All of their thinking had been directed towards maintaining "system security" against any purely local disorder or some sort of scouting foray or harassment the Peeps might have attempted with light forces. Delta-Three would probably have worked fairly well against a destroyer sweep, or a few flotillas of light cruisers. Even a battlecruiser squadron or two. Against what they actually faced, it was about as useful as a screen door on an airlock.

At least it looked as if the Peep commander must have missed almost as many classes in tactics as Flanagan's superiors had, because her formation might have been purposely designed to actually let Delta-Three hurt her. Flanagan wasn't certain what the Peep was thinking of, but the attack commander wasn't making any effort to deploy her escorting units in the sort of anti-LAC defensive shell the RMN had devised in its own wargames. She was keeping all of her cruisers tucked in unreasonably tight. They'd be able to mass their energy fire effectively against the *Shrikes* as the LAC groups closed in for point-blank energy attacks, but they were interfering with one another's long-range sensor envelopes, and they were going to offer extremely vulnerable targets to the massed missile fire the *Ferrets* would be pumping out any minute now.

She watched the Peep icons change color on her own tactical repeater as al-Salil's tactical officer designated missile targets. The escorting cruisers turned crimson, one by one, as the COLAC assigned a massive overkill to them. In some respects, it was an admission of despair, a concession that the cruisers were the only ships they had the firepower to kill, although Flanagan doubted that al-Salil would have admitted it. Delta-Three called for a converging attack, taking out the flank guards first, to clear a path for the graser-armed *Shrikes* to execute a minimum-range attack on the core of any enemy force. Which would have been all well and good if their targets had been battlecruisers, or even battle-ships. Against superdreadnoughts with their sidewalls up and their weapons online, the *Shrikes* would be impossibly lucky to inflict damage that was more than merely cosmetic.

Still, she told herself grimly, the Peeps would at least know they'd been nudged. And she owed it to her own people not to let her own crushing sense of despair affect her own effectiveness. If they were going to die anyway, then it was her job to keep her own head clear and make their deaths mean at least something by expending them as effectively as possible. And, who knew, maybe—

The plot changed suddenly, and Sarah Flanagan's heart seemed to stop.

Apparently the Peep commander wasn't quite the idiot she'd thought.

Agnes de Groot smiled like a hungry wolf as the master plot changed.

The incoming Manty strike was a confusing mass of red light dots. That was their infernally effective onboard ECM, coupled with the capability of their decoys and jammers. Still, as far as de Groot could tell, there were fewer EW birds covering them than had been projected, and CIC seemed to be getting a better count on the hostiles than she'd hoped for. It was always possible, of course, that they were being allowed to get "a better count" by Manty electronics officers with their ECM in deception mode, but she didn't think so. It looked to her as if she had genuinely caught the Manties completely unprepared and with very little idea of how to respond to the unanticipated threat.

Which, she thought ferociously, had just become an even greater threat than they'd imagined.

The large green beads of three of her "superdreadnoughts" were suddenly surrounded by clouds of smaller green fireflies, dashing away from them, as they launched full groups of *Cimeterre*-class LACs. NavInt's sources all confirmed that the Manties had stuck with their original, basically dreadnought-sized CLACs. Given the compensator advantages which the Manticoran Alliance had enjoyed for years, it gave them the best combination of LAC capacity and acceleration. But the Republican Navy had adopted a different philosophy. Its CLACs were visualized as primarily *defensive* platforms, mobile bases for the LACs intended to protect the wall of battle from long-range Manty LAC strikes. As such, there was no reason to make them any faster than the superdreadnoughts they would be protecting, and all of that lovely tonnage advantage could be put into additional LAC bays.

Which meant that whereas a Manty CLAC could pack approximately one hundred and twelve LACs into its bays, a Republican *Aviary*-class carried well over two hundred.

Now seven hundred-plus *Cimeterres* went charging outward to meet less than a third that many Manty LACs which were far too close at far too high a closing speed to even hope to evade them.

They were all dead . . . and for *nothing*.

The thought stabbed through Sarah Flanagan's mind with cold, unspeakable bitterness as she realized how utterly the Royal Navy had failed in its most basic responsibilities to its Queen and to its own people. It wasn't just al-Salil and Schumacher after all. It was the entire Navy, from ONI to Flanagan herself, and something deep inside her—the something which had sent her into her Queen's uniform in the first place—shriveled in shame.

The Peeps had CLACs . . . and no one had even suspected it. Or, even worse, if anyone had, they'd kept their suspicions to themselves. And this was the result. Disaster unmitigated.

Even as the huge cloud of LACs flashed towards her, some detached observer in her brain was visualizing all of the other system pickets. Most of them, unlike Tequila, had at least a division of capital ships, or a battlecruiser squadron, or a dozen cruisers or so, to back up the LACs expected to bear the brunt of system defense. But it wasn't going to matter. If the Peeps had committed three CLACs to Tequila, where they had to know the picket was so understrength, then they'd committed more to the systems where they expected something approaching respectable resistance. And no one in any of those systems knew what was headed for them any more than al-Salil and Schumacher had.

It would be like an avalanche. Not one of snow and tumbling boulders, but of laser heads and grasers. Waves of LACs and thundering broadsides. Of broken Manticoran starships and shattered light attack craft. And there was nothing at all that anyone could do to stop it. Not now.

She heard her own voice issuing orders, overriding the COLAC's targeting designations. Her own *Shrikes'* tac officers responded quickly, almost as if they didn't realize how complete the catastrophe was. She heard al-Salil frantically issuing commands of his own, but she paid them little heed. They were half incoherent to begin with, and even if they hadn't been, it was too late.

Her squadron launched even while al-Salil was still gibbering away. She launched on her own authority, with no orders, and at the oncoming enemy LACs rather than the starships whose defenses her *Shrikes'* light missile loads could never have penetrated.

Then she hunkered down in her command chair, braced her forearms on the armrests, and watched the holocaust come.

De Groot grimaced as a single Manty LAC squadron launched every bird it had. The rotary launchers which were the central feature of modern LAC design couldn't be "flushed" in a single salvo the way the old-style box launchers could be. But they could come close, and that single squadron got every offensive missile away before her own squadrons reached launch range.

That fire reached deep into her LACs' formation. Eighteen of them were destroyed outright. Seven more were crippled, five so badly that there wouldn't be any point in repairing them. Another eight took lighter damage.

But then it was the turn of the remaining seven hundred and sixty *Cimeterres*.

Commander Clapp's "triple ripple" roared outward. The magazines of two hundred of the Republican vessels fed that onrushing wave of missiles. The other five hundred and sixty held their fire, waiting.

Agnes de Groot watched the first wave of ferocious detonations sweeping away Manty EW drones like a broom of brimstone. Even from here, she could almost feel the despair enveloping the enemy as they realized what was happening, but it was far too late for them to do anything about it.

The second wave of explosions lashed at the Manties, hashing their sensors, crippling their onboard electronics ever so briefly. And then, exactly as Clapp had predicted, the *third* wave of missiles swept through the hopelessly disorganized Manticoran defensive envelope.

Thirty-three Manticoran LACs survived the triple ripple.

None of them survived the single massive salvo which followed it up.

De Groot's total losses were less than forty.

CHAPTER FIFTY-SIX

"We're coming up on translation in five minutes, Sir," Lieutenant Commander Akimoto said.

"Thank you, Joyce." Admiral Wilson Kirkegard thanked his staff astrogator as gravely as if he hadn't been watching the translation clock for the last hour.

"You're welcome, Sir," Akimoto replied, and the grin she gave him told him that she knew perfectly well that her formal announcement had been superfluous, to say the very least.

Kirkegard smiled back, then turned to Captain Janina Auderska, his chief of staff.

"Any last-minute details waiting to bite us on the ass, Janina?" he asked quietly.

"Can't think of any, Sir," she said, wrinkling her nose in thought. "Of course, if I could think of them ahead of time, they wouldn't be waiting to bite us on the ass, I suppose."

"As profound an analysis as I've ever heard," Kirkegard approved, and she chuckled.

"Sorry. Bad habit of mine to indulge myself in the obvious when I'm nervous."

"Well, you're not alone in that," Kirkegard assured her, and turned his attention back to the maneuvering plot as his over-strength task group headed towards the alpha wall. He spared the visual display a brief glance, struck even now by the familiar, flickering beauty of his flagship's Warshawski sails. He could pick out the sails of at least another half-dozen of his starships, but he had other things on his mind and the maneuvering plot gave him a far more accurate idea of their positions.

He had less carrier support than some of the other attack forces set up by Operation Thunderbolt, but he shouldn't need it, either. Maastricht, according to NavInt, was picketed by a single reinforced division of pre-pod superdreadnoughts, supported by one CLAC and a battlecruiser squadron. Given the draw-down in Manticoran naval units, that was a fairly hefty picket for a single system which was far less important to the Manticoran Alliance than it was to the Republic of Haven. And by the standards of the earlier war years, it should have been able to give an excellent account of itself even against a task group as large as Kirkegard's.

But those standards no longer obtained . . . as Kirkegard was about to teach the Manties.

"Admiral Kirkegard should be hitting Maastricht just about now, Sir," Commander Francis Tibolt, chief of staff for Task Force Eleven observed, and Admiral Chong Chin-ri nodded.

"I'm sure Wilson has the situation well in hand," the tall, dark-haired admiral agreed. "Do we?"

"Unless the Manties have run substantial reinforcements into Thetis on us at the last minute without NavInt catching them at it," Tibolt replied.

"I suppose there's nothing anyone can do about that possibility," Chong agreed. "Not that a proper chief of staff wouldn't be busy reassuring me that they couldn't possibly have done that."

"Believe me, Sir. If I'd observed any signs of pre-battle jitters, I'd be reassuring the hell out of you."

"They're there," Chong told him. "I'm just better at concealing them than most."

"That's one way to put it, I guess," Tibolt said with a smile, and Chong chuckled, then glanced at the date/time display.

"Well, we'll probably be finding out whether or not they're justified in about forty minutes," he said.

"That's funny."

"What?" Lieutenant Jack Vojonovic looked up from the solitaire game on his hand comp.

"Did I miss something important on the shipping schedule?" Ensign Eldridge Beale replied, turning his head to look at his training officer.

"What are you talking about?" Vojonovic set the hand comp aside and swiveled his chair to face his own display. "We don't have anything big on the ship sched until tomorrow, Eldridge. Why? Did you—"

Vojonovic's question chopped off, and his eyes widened as he stared at the preposterous icons on his display. One or two merchantmen or transports arriving unannounced would have been almost routine. No one ever managed to get everything onto the shipping schedules, however hard they tried. But this was no singleton turning up without warning. It wasn't even a convoy, and Vojonovic felt his stomach disappearing somewhere south of the soles of his shoes as he saw what had just come over the Grendelsbane alpha wall.

He couldn't get a count yet. The point sources were too jumbled together. But he didn't need a count to know there were a hell of a lot more of whoever they were than there was of Admiral Higgins' task force.

That thought was still racing through his brain as his thumb came down on the big red button.

"We're gonna get reamed," Lieutenant Stevens said flatly, watching the oncoming Peep task force on his tactical display as it swept steadily deeper into Maastricht.

"We're outnumbered, sure," Lieutenant Commander Jeffers replied in a distinctly reproving tone. The tac officer turned his head to look at HMS *Starcrest*'s CO.

"Sorry, Skipper," he apologized. "It's just—"

He gestured at the display, and Jeffers nodded grudgingly, because he knew his tac officer had a point.

"It doesn't look good," he conceded quietly, leaning towards Stevens to keep their conversation as private as possible on the destroyer's relatively small bridge. "But at least we've got LACs and they don't."

"I know," Stevens said, still apologetically. "But *Incubus*' group is at least two squadrons understrength."

"That bad?" Jeffers knew he hadn't quite managed to keep the surprise out of his voice and went on quickly. "I mean, I knew they were short a few LACs, but two whole squadrons?"

"At least, Skipper," Stevens told him. "A buddy of mine is *Incubus'* assistant logistics officer. He says Captain Fulbright has been pestering the Admiralty for a couple of months, trying to get his group back up to strength. But—"

He shrugged, and Jeffers nodded unhappily. Maastricht had been at the back edge of nowhere as far as replacements and reinforcements were concerned for as long as *Starcrest* had been here. The rumor mill said the situation was tight everywhere, but Jeffers' ship wasn't "everywhere." She was right here, and he didn't much care what "everywhere" else had to put up with.

"Well," he said with perhaps a bit more confidence than he actually felt, "Admiral Maitland's good. And if *Incubus* is understrength, that's still better than no LACs at all."

"You're right," Stevens agreed, but his eyes drifted back to the display and the oncoming icons of eight superdreadnoughts. Assuming what the sensor platforms were seeing was what was really there, Rear Admiral Sir Ronald Maitland's short superdreadnought division was outnumbered by almost three-to-one. "I just wish we had an SD(P) or two to even things up."

"So do I," Jeffers admitted. "But at least we've got the range advantage for the pods we have."

"Which is a darned good thing," Stevens acknowledged. His eyes were still on the display, where the diamond dust icons of *Incubus'* LACs were fifteen minutes from contact with the Peeps. The LACs' FTL reports accounted for the detailed accuracy of *Starcrest's* tactical plot, and Stevens didn't envy their crews a bit. It was bad enough for *Starcrest*, attached to the superdreadnoughts' screen, but at least *Starcrest* was the better part of thirteen million kilometers from any enemy missile launchers. The LACs weren't.

He looked at the light codes of Maitland's superdreadnoughts and his single CLAC and visualized the long, ungainly trail of missile pods towing astern of them. As Jeffers had suggested, Sir Ronald had a reputation as a canny tactician—one which in the humble opinion of Lieutenant Henry Stevens was well deserved. Unlike all too many system picket commanders, Maitland believed in hard, frequent drills and battle maneuvers, and he had kept his "task group" at a far higher state of readiness than some of the other pickets could boast. His announced battle plan had made it obvious that he recognized the weight of metal the Peeps had sent his way, too, but he planned to fight smart to offset the discrepancy in tonnages.

According to ONI's analysts, his missiles had an enormous range advantage over anything the Peeps could have produced. Stevens tended to take those reports with a grain of salt, and it was evident to him that Sir Ronald did, too. ONI had assured them that the maximum powered range the Peeps might have managed to get their missiles up to was on the order of seven or eight million kilometers. Sir Ronald had added a twenty-five percent "fudge factor" to the spooks' estimate just to be on the safe side, which brought their theoretical max range up to somewhere around twelve million klicks. That was well within the effective range of the RMN's multi-drive capital missiles which, in theory, had a maximum range at burnout more than five times that great. Of course, that could hardly be considered "effective" range, since not even Manticoran fire control was going to be able to hit a powered, evading target at that distance.

But Rear Admiral Maitland wasn't going to try to accomplish anything that preposterous. He intended to allow the range to drop to thirteen million kilometers, then start pumping missiles out of the pods on tow behind all of his capital ships and cruisers. Given his range advantage, he'd elected to tow maximum loads, which reduced his acceleration to a crawl but would allow him to throw at least a half-dozen heavy salvos from outside any range at which the enemy could reply. Accuracy wouldn't be anything to write home about, but at least some of them would get through. And if he timed things properly, they would come in in conjunction with his LACs. The combined attack would put a considerable strain on the Peeps' defensive systems, which should increase the effectiveness of LACs and missiles alike.

And if it all hits the crapper anyway, Stevens thought, *we'll be far enough away that at least we can break off and run for it. Which the LAC jockeys can't—not from three-quarters of the way down the kodiak max's throat! So we can at least bleed them and run if we—*

"Missile launch! Multiple missile launches!"

Stevens' head snapped around at the sound of PO Landow's voice. The veteran noncom was a key member of Stevens' own tac team, yet for a moment the lieutenant was convinced Landow must have lost her mind.

But only for a moment. Only until he looked back at his own plot and realized that Sir Ronald's battle plan had just come apart.

"God, I almost feel sorry for them," Janina Auderska said so quietly no one but her admiral could possibly hear.

"Don't," Kirkegard said, his eyes glued to the display showing the storm front of his missiles as they scorched towards the Manticoran system picket. The chief of staff glanced at him, surprised by the almost savage edge of harshness in the admiral's usually pleasant voice, and Kirkegard glanced sideways at her.

"This is exactly what they did to us in their damned 'Operation Buttercup,'" he reminded her coldly. "Exactly. I read an interview with their Admiral White Haven. NavInt clipped it from one of their newsfaxes. He said he felt almost guilty—that it was too much 'like pushing baby chicks into a pond.'" Kirkegard gave a harsh crow caw of a chuckle. "He was right, too. Well, now it's our turn. Let's see how *they* like it."

Sir Ronald Maitland watched the hurricane of missiles thundering towards him.

"How good are our targeting setups?" he asked his staff ops officer flatly.

"Uh, they're—" The ops officer shook himself physically. "I mean, they're about as good as we could hope for at this range, Sir," he said more crisply.

"Well, in that case I suppose we'd better use them before we lose them," Maitland replied. "Reprioritize the firing sequence. Flush them all—now."

"Aye, aye, Sir."

"Here they come," Auderska murmured.

"Had to get them off before our birds got close enough for proximity kills," Kirkegard agreed, watching the sidebars of his plot as CIC assigned threat values to the incoming warheads. "More of them than I expected, too," he acknowledged.

"Yes, Sir. We're going to get hurt," Auderska said.

"Price of doing business," Kirkegard replied with a shrug. "And at this range, not even Manty targeting systems are going to be able to score a very high percentage of hits. Neither are ours, of course, but—" his smile was thin and hungry "—we can fire heavy follow-on salvos . . . and they can't."

"Tracking reports that their missile ECM is much better than it's supposed to be, Sir," Maitland's chief of staff said very quietly into his ear. Sir Ronald looked at him, and he grimaced unhappily. "They're estimating that our point defense is going to be at least twenty-five percent less effective than we'd projected. At least."

Maitland grunted and turned his gaze back to the master plot while his brain raced. It was obvious from the weight of fire coming at him that the Peep superdreadnoughts on that plot were a pod design. But the situation wasn't completely hopeless, he told himself. Everything the LACs' sensors had reported so far indicated that the Peeps' EW capabilities, while substantially better than anticipated—as CIC's new estimate of their missile ECM confirmed—were still far below Manticoran standards. That would give Maitland an enormous advantage in a long-range missile duel like this. Or it would have, if he'd been able to shoot back at all.

He gritted his teeth as bitter memory replayed his repeated requests for at least one SD(P). But the Admiralty had not seen fit to assign such scarce, valuable units to a secondary system like Maastricht. At least the launchers aboard two of the three older ships he did have had been refitted to handle multi-drive missiles. Which meant that once his pods were exhausted, he wouldn't be completely unable to return fire. It only meant that he could respond with less than twenty percent of the Peeps' weight of fire until he somehow managed to close to within six million klicks of them.

Which none of his starships could possibly survive long enough to do.

"Are those new acceleration figures for their superdreadnoughts confirmed?" he asked his ops officer.

"Yes, Sir," the commander confirmed unhappily. "They're still lower than ours, but the difference is almost thirty percent less than ONI's estimates."

"That figures," Sir Ronald half-snarled before he could stop himself. Then he closed his mouth, drew a deep breath, and looked back at the chief of staff.

"Transmit an immediate message to Commodore Rontved," he said. "Instruct her to activate Case Omega immediately."

"Yes, Sir." The complete absence of surprise in the chief of staff's voice showed that he'd already reached the same conclusion Maitland had. Rontved commanded the small, three-unit squadron of maintenance and support ships the Admiralty had deployed to support Maitland's picket. They were effectively unarmed, aside from a strictly limited point defense capability, and under Case Omega their job was simply to be sure that as much as possible of the infrastructure which had been built up to support the system picket was destroyed before they themselves ran for it.

"Warn her not to waste any time about it," Maitland emphasized. "We know they have multi-drive missiles now. If ONI can be that completely wrong about one thing, they can be wrong about another. So I wouldn't be surprised if a CLAC or two turned up in their order of battle."

"Yes, Sir." The chief of staff paused for just a moment, then nodded his head sideways at the master plot. "Speaking of LACs, Sir, what about ours?"

"They'll continue the attack. After all, they can't run if we lose *Incubus*," Maitland said harshly. Then he grunted again. "Just in case Rontved doesn't make it out, though, detach one of the tin cans. We need to be certain someone gets home with a warning."

Lieutenant Commander Jeffers stood at Henry Stevens' shoulder, staring down the tactical display while *Starcrest* continued to accelerate towards the hyper limit at maximum military power. The fact that their inertial compensator might fail at any moment and turn all of them into so much strawberry jam was completely beside the point as they stared at the chaos and devastation behind them.

Two of Rear Admiral Maitland's superdreadnoughts were already gone, and the flagship was dying. *Incubus* was still in action, but her acceleration had fallen by over fifty percent as the damage to her beta nodes mounted. The only reason she hadn't been destroyed outright, Jeffers thought grimly, was that her ship-to-ship combat capability was so limited. The Peeps had concentrated on anyone who might hurt them first; they could always finish *Incubus* off any time they chose.

It hadn't been entirely one-sided—only almost.

Maitland's single pod-spawned wave of missiles had hammered one Peep superdreadnought into an air-bleeding wreck and damaged two more of them. His internal launchers had concentrated on one of the two wounded SD(P)s and inflicted substantially more damage on her, and one Peep battlecruiser had been destroyed outright, while another seemed to be in little better condition.

But that was it. The LACs had done their best, and their efforts had helped to account for the one destroyed battlecruiser and inflicted damage on most of her consorts. But the Peeps aboard those starships were no longer confused and panicked by the mere sight of an impossible "super LAC." They'd had time to think and analyze, and they recognized the weaknesses of such small, relatively fragile attackers. The LAC crews had bored in with all the guts and gallantry in the universe, and they'd actually managed to inflict at least a little damage in the process. But these superdreadnoughts' sidewalls were intact, the vulnerable throats of their wedges were protected by bow walls almost as good as the RMN's own, their point defense and energy gunners were waiting, and the massive armor protecting their flanks was fully capable of withstanding the pounding of even a *Shrike-B*'s graser long enough for their defensive fire to kill the LAC.

Incubus' group had gotten in one good firing pass on the ships of the wall. After that, the survivors had been swatted almost negligently when they tried for a second one.

Jeffers tried not to let his own sense of shocked disbelief show. It was obvious that the Peeps still hadn't quite equalized the gap between Manticoran hardware and their own. Their ECM was still nowhere near as good. Their missile pods seemed to carry fewer birds per pod, which suggested that they'd had to accept a more massive design. That meant lighter broadsides from the same tonnage of capital ships and a bigger squeeze on magazine space. And that might prove significant in the long run, for although their seeker systems seemed to have been improved almost as much as their missiles' range had, they still weren't quite up to Manticoran standards, either. Given the RMN's remaining edge in electronic warfare, long-range missile accuracy was going to favor Manticore by a probably substantial edge, but it wasn't going to be spectacular even for the RMN. So the number of missiles an SD(P) could carry was about to become extremely important. Which probably meant it was a damned good thing BuShips had pushed ahead with the new *Invictus* design.

Now if only that fucking idiot Janacek had let the Navy build some of them!

Jeffers felt his jaw muscle ache from how fiercely he was gritting his teeth and made himself turn away from the plot. He was a bit surprised that *Starcrest* had been able to make good her escape when Maitland ordered her to run for it. Probably it was simply a case of the Peeps having bigger fish to fry, he thought bitterly. But it could also have something to do with the amount of damage Maitland's superdreadnoughts and LACs had managed to inflict, as well.

Alan Jeffers was too honest with himself to pretend that he wasn't intensely grateful that Maitland's orders meant he and his crew would live. But neither could he absolve himself from a crushing sense of guilt. It was a burden, he suspected, which would cling to him for a long, long time.

"I wonder how Admiral Kirkegard did at Maastricht, Sir," Commander Tibolt murmured. He and Admiral Chong stood side-by-side on RHNS *New Republic*'s flag bridge as TF 11 settled into orbit around the Thetis System's sole habitable planet.

"No telling," Chong replied. He watched the blue-and-white beauty of the planet on the visual display for several moments, then squared his shoulders and turned away. Another display attracted his eyes. The one that listed his task force's losses.

Only a single ship's name glowed in the blood-red color that indicated a total loss, and his lips curved in a smile of grim satisfaction. No one liked to lose any ship, or the people who crewed that ship. But after the savage losses the old People's Navy had taken at the hands of the Manties again and again, a single heavy cruiser and seventy LACs actually destroyed was a paltry price to pay for an entire star system. Not to mention the fact that the Manties had lost over two hundred of their own LACs, four heavy cruisers, and a pair of superdreadnoughts, as well.

"Actually," he told Tibolt after a moment, "I'm more curious about what's happening at Grendelsbane and Trevor's Star."

CHAPTER FIFTY-SEVEN

"**M**ay I ask what you think of Prime Minister High Ridge's message, My Lord?" Niall MacDonnell asked politely.

"I think that making himself sound civil probably increased his blood pressure enough to take two or three decades off his life expectancy," Hamish Alexander replied cheerfully. "One could certainly hope so, at least."

MacDonnell smiled. A native-born Grayson, himself, he was sometimes bemused in many ways by the Manticoran officers who had taken service with the GSN. The Earl of White Haven was scarcely in that category, of course, although he'd fought enough battles side-by-side with Grayson units to make him one of their own by adoption, at least. But what bemused MacDonnell the most was that the Manticorans seemed so outspoken in their criticism of the High Ridge Government. Of course, they were talking about their prime minister, not their monarch, but it was difficult for MacDonnell to conceive of a serving Grayson officer expressing himself so frankly—and contemptuously—about the Protector's Chancellor.

Not that any of his fellow Grayson citizens disagreed where High Ridge was concerned. It was just that Graysons as a group were more . . . deferential than most Manticorans. It confused MacDonnell sometimes. The crux of the Star Kingdom's entire current political dilemma lay in the aristocracy's control of who formed the executive branch of their government. That same condition, in an even more virulent form, had afflicted Grayson before the Mayhew Restoration had returned the authority which had eroded away from several generations of protectors. But the profound deference which the steaders of Grayson had always extended to their steadholders seemed oddly lacking in Manticorans where their own nobility was concerned.

Of course, White Haven himself was a member of that very aristocracy, which probably accounted for his own lack of automatic respect for it.

"I won't pretend that I don't share your hopes, My Lord," the admiral said after a moment. "But it looks as if he's decided to put the best face he can on the situation."

"He doesn't have a lot of choice," White Haven pointed out. "To be honest, I'm quite certain that was a part of Protector Benjamin's calculus when he hatched this entire notion. And while it would never do for me to accuse the Protector of meddling in the internal political affairs of an ally, I think he put High Ridge into his current position with malice aforethought."

MacDonnell looked a question at him, and the earl shrugged.

"High Ridge's only option is to pretend he's in favor of Benjamin's actions. Anything else would make him look at best weak and ineffectual, since he couldn't keep Benjamin from doing it anyway. At worst, if it turns out we're right and he's wrong about the Peeps' intentions, he'd look like a complete and total idiot if he'd sat around protesting the fact that we're saving him from his own stupidity. Not," White Haven added with a particularly nasty smile, "that we're not going to make him look stupid anyway, if the ball does go up."

MacDonnell cocked his head. White Haven sounded almost as if he *wanted* the Peeps to attack because of the damage it would do the High Ridge Government. The Grayson knew he was being unfair. That the earl most certainly didn't want the Republic of Haven to go back to war with the Star Kingdom. But White Haven had clearly passed beyond the point of hoping that that wouldn't happen. Unlike MacDonnell, who continued to cherish his doubts, despite the fact that the original warning had come from Lady Harrington, the earl had completely accepted the proposition that a Havenite attack was imminent. And since he'd done all he could to prepare for that looming catastrophe, he was ready to look for whatever silver lining he might be able to find.

And, MacDonnell conceded, anything that offered to remove Baron High Ridge from power had to be considered a silver lining.

The Grayson returned his attention to *Benjamin the Great*'s flag plot. It was appropriate that he and White Haven should be standing on that ship's bridge at this particular moment, he thought. The "*Benjie*," as the Navy affectionately referred to *Benjamin the Great*, had been White Haven's flagship from the day she commissioned until the conclusion of Operation Buttercup. But although the ship was still less than eight T-years old, *Benjie* belonged to a class of only three ships. Her design had been superseded by the *Harrington*-class SD(P)s, and MacDonnell knew that some of those in the Office of Shipbuilding wanted to designate his flagship for disposal. He hated the very thought of sending her to the breakers for reclamation, although he had to admit that there was a certain cold-blooded logic to it. Grayson was straining every sinew to build and maintain the fleet it had. It couldn't afford to retain ships, however new, or however beloved, whose design had been rendered obsolescent.

Personally, MacDonnell hoped Shipbuilding would adopt one of the alternate proposals, instead, and refit the *Benjie*'s shipboard launchers to handle the latest generation of multi-drive missiles. But that was someone else's decision. For right now, *Benjamin the Great* was exactly where she needed to be. Designed from the keel out as a fleet command ship, she had arguably the finest flag deck and fleet information center of any ship in commission anywhere.

"Whatever High Ridge might think of all this," White Haven said, stepping closer to MacDonnell and gazing into the plot with him, "Admiral Kuzak doesn't seem to have any reservations, does she?"

"No, she doesn't," MacDonnell agreed. His eyes moved from the plot which showed his own command to the secondary display set for astrographic mode. The Trevor's Star terminus of the Manticoran Wormhole Junction lay much closer to the system primary than the Junction itself lay to Manticore-A. Still, there was the better part of three light-hours between it and Trevor's Star itself. Even with the powerful forts which had been built to cover it, the sheer distance between the system's inhabited planet and the terminus had created an almost insuperable difficulty for Admiral Theodosia Kuzak.

Her Third Fleet could be in only one place at a time, unless she wanted to accept an extremely dangerous dispersion of its strength. In theory, the forts could deal with most attacks on the terminus itself. Actually, calling them "forts" was something of a misnomer. To most people, the term "fort" implied a fixed fortification, something ponderous and immobile. But while the terminus forts were certainly ponderous, they were not—quite—immobile. Instead, they might be better thought of as enormous sublight superdreadnoughts. Ships so huge that their low acceleration made them totally unsuited to mobile operations, but which remained capable of at least minimal combat maneuvers ... and which could generate the impeller wedges which were the first line of defense for any warship.

But for all their massive size, thick armor, and potent weaponry, they—like *Benjamin the Great*—were an obsolescent design. Their rate of fire in a missile engagement was only a fraction of that which a *Harrington*-class ship could produce. If they had time to deploy missile pods before a battle, they could throw stupendous salvos as long as the pods lasted, of course. But that was another way of saying they could fire for as long as no one could get warheads close enough to take out their pods with proximity kills.

When only the Manticoran Alliance had possessed SD(P)s, no one had worried particularly about pod vulnerability. First, because no other navy in space could produce the weight of fire an SD(P) was capable of, and, second, because no other navy in space could match the range of the Alliance's multi-drive missiles. Which meant that the forts' pods would be able to wreak havoc on any attacker before that attacker could possibly get close enough to kill their remaining pods. But the navy Thomas Theisman had built did have SD(P)s. And it was just possible that those SD(P)s had multi-drive missiles of their own.

And under those circumstances, pod vulnerability became a very serious concern, indeed.

All of which helped to explain why a conscientious system commander like Theodosia Kuzak had been so unhappy about her mutually contradictory defense obligations. The official Admiralty view, that there was no evidence that the forts could no longer look after themselves against anything the Peeps might bring to bear against them, was cold comfort for the officer on the spot. Completely ignoring the potential consequences for her career if the Peeps managed to get in and destroy the forts, the sheer loss of life such attack would entail had undoubtedly been enough to give her nightmares. So it was with enormous relief that she had turned responsibility for supporting the forts over to MacDonnell's task force while she concentrated her own SD(P)s and supporting CLACs to cover San Martin and the inner system.

"If you were the Peeps, and you were planning to attack this system, My Lord," he asked White Haven now, "which would you concentrate on? The terminus, or San Martin? Or would you go for both simultaneously?"

"I asked myself those same questions a lot when I was trying to take the system away from the Peeps," White Haven replied. "The biggest problem is that the terminus and the inner system are close enough to offer each other a degree of mutual support that just isn't possible at the Manticore end. It's not the easiest thing in the galaxy for the defense to arrange, you understand, but an attacker going after one objective can never afford to forget about what can come up his backside from the other while he's doing it. That was bad enough for us when the Peeps held the system. For the Peeps, who can never be absolutely certain that a sizable chunk of Home Fleet isn't in range for an emergency transit direct from Manticore, it's even worse."

"Granted," MacDonnell agreed. "But if you're going to attack this system at all, you have to pick one objective."

"Oh, certainly!" White Haven grinned wryly. "In my case, I chose to concentrate on their fleet, squeezing it to defend the inner system. After all, San Martin was a lot more important to them than the terminus of a wormhole junction they couldn't use anyway! And they didn't have anywhere near the terminus fortifications we've put into place since we took the system away from them. Even so, I had to be pretty cautious."

"That's not exactly the way I heard it, My Lord," MacDonnell told him with a smile. "I heard that in the end you threw an assault straight through the Junction."

"Well, yes," the earl said with a slightly uncomfortable expression. "It was something close to a council of despair, you understand. Esther McQueen was commanding here at the time, and she was a holy terror. Just between you and me, I've often thought that she may well have been a better tactician than I was, and she was a devilishly good strategist, as well. She'd forted up here with battleships and superdreadnoughts in a defense in depth, and however I maneuvered, she managed to stay close enough to keep me from having a free hand for either objective. So I settled in to convince her that I was prepared for what amounted to a siege of the inner system, and when I'd convinced her—or, rather, her replacement, after Pierre and Saint-Just pulled her out for Octagon duty—to redeploy to face it, well—"

"So basically, you forced the Peeps to commit to protecting one objective, then hit the other one with a surprise attack," MacDonnell observed.

"Yes. But I had certain advantages Theisman and his people wouldn't have in attacking the system. Despite the disadvantages a fleet faces in using a junction as an avenue of attack, the element of surprise tends to offset them to a considerable degree. But Theisman won't have a friendly fleet sitting at the other end of the terminus. So he can't really threaten it from two directions at once, the way I did. That would have given Theodosia the opportunity to repeat McQueen's defensive deployments against him.

"In the end, I suspect he could probably have taken her anyway. If our more pessimistic assumptions about what he may have added to his fleet mix without mentioning it to anyone are accurate, the odds swing even further in his favor. But in answer to your question, if I were him, I'd concentrate on the inner system."

"But as long as the Star Kingdom continues to hold the terminus, it can always reinforce or counterattack," MacDonnell pointed out.

"That assumes it has something to counterattack *with*," White Haven said in a much grimmer tone, and waved a hand at the gleaming icons of the inner system. At this range and on such a scale, all of Third Fleet's ships of the wall formed a single green bead. "Third Fleet has almost a hundred ships of the wall in its order of battle, including forty-eight of our SD(P)s, Niall, and two SD(P)s are down for local refit. We have exactly two—count them; two—more squadrons of them with Home Fleet. We have another squadron of them assigned to Sidemore Station. We have a fourth squadron assigned to Grendelsbane. And we have, at the moment,

four more of them in various stages of overhaul and working up
back home but not assigned to Home Fleet. That's it, even with
the dribs and drabs Janacek has managed to add to his order of
battle. If Theisman could take out Third Fleet, he'd destroy around
a third of our pre-pod wall and *two-thirds* of our total modern
wall. That makes Theodosia's ships his true objective, and if he
can pin them against the star, force her to defend San Martin, he
has an opportunity to destroy them.

"If he pulled that off, he could deal with anything we had left
with relative ease. To be perfectly honest, the only remaining
counterweight the Alliance would have would be your own fleet,
and Grayson would find itself facing much the same quandary the
Manticore System faces. How much of your home fleet can you
afford to commit to offensive operations?"

"To be honest?" MacDonnell shook his head. "We've probably
actually exceeded that limit by what we've deployed here. Not that
I think it was a mistake to send us," he added hastily. "I think Lady
Harrington and Mr. Paxton are correct in arguing that the Peeps
are unlikely to make Grayson one of their priority objectives. That
could change, of course, especially once word gets back to them
that a sizable portion of our Navy is reinforcing here at Trevor's
Star. But at the moment, they almost have to be assuming the GSN
is still concentrated at Yeltsin, and they aren't going to want to
provoke us until after they've dealt with your SD(P)s."

"Exactly," White Haven agreed, hiding any trace of the instinctive
irritation he felt. It wasn't anything MacDonnell had actually said.
Nor was it anything White Haven could have disagreed with, even
if the Grayson had put it into so many words. But it was unut-
terably galling for any senior Manticoran admiral to hear a Grayson
calmly assessing the RMN as only the *second* ranking navy of the
Alliance.

Especially given the fact that, at the moment, that assessment
was entirely accurate.

"Actually," he went on, "the best-case scenario would be for
Theisman to realize that you've reinforced us here before he kicks
off any attack. The realization that the GSN is prepared to reinforce us this promptly, despite any . . . difficulties you may be
experiencing working with our present deplorable Prime Minister, would almost have to give him pause. He'd also have to rethink
any ops plan he'd already drawn up on the assumption that you

wouldn't be. And if we can win that jackass Janacek just another four or five months, the ships he's finally resumed construction on will begin to come into commission in something like genuinely useful numbers. Especially the ones in the Grendelsbane shadow yards. They were further along in construction when they were suspended, and the first of *them* will be ready for acceptance trials in just a couple of weeks."

"From your lips to the Tester's ears," MacDonnell said fervently.

"It's confirmed, Sir. All of them."

Admiral of the Red Allen Higgins was a man of only middling height, with a round, almost chubby face that was usually a faithful mirror of his affable nature. At the moment, that face was the color of old oatmeal and the eyes were haunted.

He stared down at the pitiless display and felt like a fly in the path of Juggernaut as the Peep attack force rumbled down upon him. Thirty-two superdreadnoughts, an unknown number of them SD(P)s. There were also at least some CLACs in that oncoming freight train of destruction. There had to be, because the four-hundred-strong LAC strike he'd sent out to meet them had been ripped apart by an even stronger LAC counterattack.

And to oppose it, once his LACs had been effectively destroyed, he'd had seven SD(P)s, sixteen pre-pod SDs, four CLACs with less than thirty LACs between them, and nineteen battlecruisers and cruisers. He'd thought he might still be able to accomplish something, given his outnumbered SD(P)s' range advantage. But he'd been wrong. As the Peeps had just demonstrated by destroying all seven of them from a range in excess of forty million kilometers.

His remaining twenty capital ships were hopelessly outclassed. The incredible missile storm which had wiped away his SD(P)s was proof enough of that. Thank God that at least he'd held them back when he sent in the SD(P)s! Thousands of RMN personnel were still alive because of that simple decision on his part. A decision he'd tossed off almost casually at the time.

But that was the only mercy which had been vouchsafed to him.

"We can't stop them," he said softly and looked up to meet his chief of staff's equally shocked eyes at last. "Anything we send out to meet them will only end up giving them extra target practice," he grated. "And the same thing is true of the shipyards. Hell, we always depended on the mobile force for the system's real security.

Why bother to upgrade the forts to fire MDMs? That's what the frigging Fleet was for! God*damn* that bastard Janacek."

"Sir, how—I mean, what do we do now?" the chief of staff asked almost desperately.

"There's only one thing we can do," Higgins ground out. "I am *not* going to be another Elvis Santino, or even another Silas Markham. No more of my people are going to be killed in a battle we can't win anyway."

"But, Sir, if you just abandon the yards, the Admiralty will—"

"Fuck the Admiralty!" Higgins snarled. "If they want to court-martial me, so much the better. I'd love to have an opportunity to discuss their excuse for a naval policy in front of a formal court! But right now what matters is saving everyone and everything we can . . . and we can't save the yards."

The chief of staff swallowed hard, but he couldn't disagree.

"We don't have time to set scuttling charges," Higgins went on in a harsh, flat voice. "Get every work crew back to the main facility. I want all secure data wiped now. Once you've done that, set the charges and blow the entire computer core, as well. I don't want the bastards getting squat from our records. We've got about a ninety-minute window to evacuate anyone we're going to get out, and we wouldn't have the personnel lift to take more than twenty percent of the total base personnel even if we had time to embark them all. Grab the priority list and find everyone on it that you can. We're not going to be able to get all of them to a pickup point in time, but I want to pull out every tech with critical knowledge that we can."

"Yes, Sir!" The chief of staff turned away and started barking orders, obviously grateful for something—anything—to do, and Higgins rounded on his ops officer.

"While Chet handles that, I've got another job for you, Juliet." His corpse-like smile held no humor at all. "We may not have enough missiles with the legs to take those bastards on," he said, waving a hand at the tactical display. "But there's one target we can reach."

"Sir?" The ops officer looked as confused as her voice sounded, and Higgins barked a travesty of a laugh.

"We don't have time to set demolition charges, Juliet. So I want you to lay in a fire plan. As we pull out, I want an old-fashioned nuke on top of every building slip, every immobile ship, every fabrication center. *Everything.* The only thing you don't hit are the personnel platforms. You understand me?"

"Aye, aye, Sir," she got out, her expression aghast at the thought of the trillions upon trillions of dollars of irreplaceable hardware and half-completed hulls she was about to destroy.

"Then do it," he grated, and turned back to the pitiless display once more.

Javier Giscard checked the time again. It was odd. Nothing could be calmer or more orderly than *Sovereign of Space*'s flag bridge. There were no raised voices, no excitement. No one rushed from console to console or conferred in urgent, anxious tones.

And yet for all of the order and serenity, the tension was palpable. Task Force Ten had yet to fire a shot, but the war had already begun. Or resumed. Or whatever future historians would agree it had done.

The exact verb didn't matter all that much to the men and women who would do the killing and the dying, and as he sat in his command chair and listened to the quiet, efficient murmur of his staff, he felt the cold wind of all that mortality blowing through the chinks in his soul. He was about to do something he'd already done once before, in a star system named Basilisk. He'd had no choice then, and he had even less of one now, but that didn't mean he looked forward to it.

He checked the time again.

Fifteen minutes.

"Perimeter Security has bogeys, Admiral!"

Niall MacDonnell turned quickly from his conversation with Earl White Haven at his ops officer's announcement.

"They just made their alpha translations," Commander William Tatnall continued. "We're still getting a preliminary count on their transit signatures, but there are a lot of them."

MacDonnell felt White Haven standing behind him and sensed how difficult it was for the earl to keep his mouth shut. But White Haven had assured him before they ever departed from Yeltsin's Star that despite any questions of relative seniority, he had no intention of backseat driving. This was MacDonnell's command, not his, he'd said, and he was as good as his word now.

"Locus and vector?" MacDonnell asked.

"They made translation right on the hyper limit for a least-time course to San Martin," Commander David Clairdon, his chief of staff, amplified quickly.

"Any sign of anything headed for the terminus?" the admiral pressed.

"Not at this time, Sir," Clairdon replied carefully, and MacDonnell smiled thinly at the unspoken "yet" everyone on the flag bridge heard in Clairdon's tone.

The admiral turned back to the main plot as the glittering light codes of the bogeys' hyper footprints appeared upon it. Clairdon was certainly right about their position and course. And Tatnall was right, too—there *were* "a lot of them."

"CIC makes it over eighty of the wall, Sir," Tatnall announced a moment later, as if he couldn't quite believe the numbers himself. "Uh, they say that's a minimal estimate," he added.

"Sweet Tester," MacDonnell heard someone mutter. Which, he decided, reflected his own reaction quite well.

There was no way to tell how many of those ships were SD(P)s and how many were pre-pod designs. If he were Thomas Theisman, there'd be as many of the former and as few of the latter as he could possibly arrange. Either way, it sounded as if the Peeps had sent a force twice as powerful as the one they had expected to face. And it sounded very much as if they were doing what White Haven had said he would do in their place.

But MacDonnell couldn't be certain of that, and his brain raced as he considered possibilities and options. It seemed to him as if he stood there, staring at the plot, for at least a decade, but when he looked at the date/time display again, less than ninety seconds had passed.

"Alpha One, David," he told his chief of staff calmly. Clairdon looked at him for just a moment, then nodded briskly.

"Alpha One. Aye, aye, Sir," he said, and MacDonnell looked back at White Haven as Clairdon headed for the com section to pass the necessary movement orders.

"I think they're doing exactly what you said you'd do, My Lord," MacDonnell told the Manticoran. Then he smiled mirthlessly. "Of course, I suppose half of those ships could be EW drones and it could all be a huge ruse designed to draw the terminus picket force they didn't know was here out of position."

"It does seem unlikely," White Haven agreed with a slightly

warmer smile of his own. "And I doubt they'd be foolish enough to repeat their Basilisk pattern. They know this terminus' forts are completely online. They could still have it—the force they seem to be sending towards San Martin could take all of the forts without too much trouble. But I find it difficult to believe that even Thomas Theisman and Shannon Foraker between them could have given them enough ships to let them hit Trevor's Star with *two* task forces that size. Especially not if Duchess Harrington was right and they have sent an attack force all the way to Silesia. Or, at least, if they *can* attack Silesia and still hit Trevor's Star with a hundred and sixty ships of the wall, we'd better start working on our surrender terms now!"

Admiral Higgins stood like a statue of acid-etched iron on HMS *Indomitable*'s flag bridge, waiting, as his task force's remaining units accelerated towards the Grendelsbane hyper limit. No one spoke to him. No one approached him. There was an invisible perimeter around him, a circle of pain and self-loathing none dared enter.

Intellectually, he knew as well as anyone else on that bridge that what had happened here wasn't his fault. No one with his assigned order of battle could possibly have stopped the force the Peeps had thrown at him. That didn't guarantee that he wouldn't be scapegoated for it, of course—especially not by the Janacek Admiralty—but at least he'd had the sanity and moral courage to refuse to throw away any more of the lives and ships under his command.

None of which was any comfort to him at all at this moment.

His eyes were on the visual display, not the tactical display or the maneuvering plot. He was staring at the huge naval yard, its individual structures long invisible as they fell away astern, and his eyes were cold and empty as space itself.

And then his mouth tightened and pain flickered in those empty eyes as the first small, intolerably bright sun flashed behind his ships. Then another. Another, and another, and yet another as a tidal wave of flame marched through the huge, sprawling naval base Manticore had spent almost two decades building up from literally nothing.

Those silent pinpricks looked tiny and harmless from this range, but Higgins' mind's eyes saw them perfectly, knew their reality. It watched the forest fire of old-fashioned nukes—his own missiles' warheads, not even the enemy's—consuming fabrication centers, orbital smelters, reclamation yards, stores stations, orbital magazines, the huge hydrogen farm, sensor platforms and relays, and System Control's ultra-modern command station. And the ships. The handful of ships in the repair yards. The ones who'd had the misfortune to choose this particular moment to be immobilized in yard hands because they required some minor repair, or to be undergoing refit. And worse—far worse—the magnificent new ships. Twenty-seven more *Medusa*-class SD(P)s, nineteen CLACs, and no less than forty-six of the new *Invictus*-class superdreadnoughts. Ninety-two capital ships—almost six hundred and seventy *million* tons of new construction. Not just a fleet, but an entire *navy's* worth of the most modern designs in space, helpless as they lay beside fitting-out stations or half-finished, cocooned in their building slips and dispersed yards. The fifty-three additional lighter types being built alongside them hardly mattered, but Higgins could no more spare them from the fiery sword of fusion than he could the superdreadnoughts.

The fireballs marched, hobnailed with fire, ripping the heart out of Grendelsbane Station. A tidal wave of flame and fury carrying disaster on its crest. And behind that wave were the personnel platforms and the yard personnel he hadn't been able to withdraw. Over forty thousand of them—the entire workforce for a complex the size Grendelsbane once had been, just as lost to the Star Kingdom as the ships they had come here to work upon.

In one catastrophic act of self-inflicted devastation, Allen Higgins had just destroyed more tonnage and *far* more fighting power than the Royal Manticoran Navy had ever lost in the entire four T-centuries of its previous existence, and the fact that he'd had no choice was no consolation at all.

"Sir," Marius Gozzi said urgently, "I'm sorry to interrupt, but we've just picked up a second task force."

Giscard turned quickly to his chief of staff, raising one hand to stop his ops officer in mid-conversation.

"Where?" he asked.

"It looks like its coming in from the terminus," Gozzi said. "And we're very lucky that we saw it at all."

"Coming from the terminus?" Giscard shook his head. "It's not 'luck' we saw it, Marius. You were the one who insisted that we needed to scout it to cover our backs while we dealt with the inner system."

The chief of staff shrugged. Giscard's statement was accurate enough, but Gozzi still suspected that the admiral had subtly prompted him to make the suggestion. Giscard had a tendency to build a staff's internal confidence by drawing contributions out of each of them . . . and then seeing to it that whoever finally offered the contribution he'd wanted all along got full credit for it.

"Even with the drones and the LACs, we were still dead lucky to pick them up, Sir. They're coming in heavily stealthed. But they're also pushing hard. One or two impeller signatures burned through the stealth, and once the drones got a sniff, the recon LACs knew where to look. The numbers are still tentative, but CIC is estimating it as between twenty and fifty ships of the wall. Possibly with carrier support."

"That many?"

"CIC stresses that the numbers are extremely tentative," Gozzi replied. "And we're not getting the take directly from the drones."

Giscard nodded in understanding. The recon LACs were heavily modified *Cimeterres*, with greatly reduced magazine space in order to free up the volume for the most capable LAC-sized sensor suite Shannon Foraker and her techies had been able to build. Their main function, however, if the truth be known, was to serve as drone tenders. Foraker and her wizards still hadn't figured out how to fit a grav pulse transmitter with any sort of bandwidth into something as small as a drone. But they could put a LAC in range for the drone to hit with a whisker laser, and a LAC could carry an FTL com. They still couldn't real-time the raw drone data to *Sovereign of Space*, but they could get enough summarized information through to give Giscard a far better picture of what was happening than any previous Havenite fleet commander could have hoped for.

The question, he reflected wryly, was whether that was a good thing, or a bad one. There was such a thing as knowing too much and allowing yourself to double-think your way into ineffectualness.

He walked across to a smaller repeater plot and punched in a command. Moments later, CIC had displayed its best guess of the new force's composition and numbers. He frowned slightly.

Apparently, CIC had managed to firm up its estimate at least a little while Marius was reporting to him. They were showing a minimum of thirty of the wall now, although some of the impeller signatures were still a bit tentative.

He folded his hands behind him and squared his shoulders while he considered the display.

It was always possible, perhaps even probable, that what looked like Third Fleet in the inner system was something else entirely. Or, for that matter, that it was actually only a portion of Third Fleet. In fact, that was the more likely probability. If Kuzak had been as completely surprised as Thunderbolt's planners had hoped, then she might very well have been caught with her fleet divided between the inner system and the wormhole terminus. In that case, she might be employing ECM to convince his sensors that she was actually fully concentrated near San Martin in an effort to keep them from noticing the second half of her force sneaking in to join her.

The only real problem with that neat little theory was that there seemed to be too many ships in that second force. Giscard had studied Kuzak's record, and he had a lively respect for her strategic judgment. If she'd split her forces to cover two objectives in the first place, she would have placed the larger force to cover the more important one. And in this instance, there was no comparison between the value—politically and morally, as well as economically—of defending San Martin's citizens as opposed to a wormhole terminus. So if one force was going to be more powerful than the other, then the one in front of him ought to be substantially more numerous than the one behind him, yet CIC's estimate suggested that the trailer was damned nearly the size of Kuzak's entire fleet.

But if it wasn't the second half of Third Fleet, then what was it, and what was it doing here? Could it be a detachment from their Home Fleet that had simply happened to be in range for a crash Junction transit? That was certainly possible, although a part of him rejected the possibility. It would have been too much like history repeating itself. That was exactly how White Haven had reached Basilisk in time to keep Giscard from taking out the terminus there when he'd raided that system. But the possibility of a coincidence like that happening a second time was remote, to say the least.

No. If there really was a second force out there, then it had been deliberately placed there ahead of time. Only that didn't make a lot of sense, either . . . unless he assumed that they'd somehow guessed what was coming. Which should have been impossible. On the other hand, he couldn't even begin to count the number of "top secret" plans which had somehow been compromised in the long history of military operations.

But even if it were a force from their Home Fleet, how bad could that be? They didn't have enough SD(P)s in Home Fleet to significantly affect the odds here, and rushing in pre-pod SDs would be suicidal. But they'd know that, too. So where—?

"I wonder," he murmured, and turned back to Gozzi. "We need to nail this down, Marius. Send the LACs in closer."

"Sir, if they get any closer and this is what it looks like, they're going to be awfully vulnerable," the chief of staff reminded him quietly.

"I realize that," Giscard acknowledged. "And I don't like it a whole lot more than you do. But we have to know. This is the largest single task force of Operation Thunderbolt. If the Manties have somehow figured out what we're up to, this would be the one place they'd try hardest to set a trap for us. Don't forget what they did to Admiral Parnell at Yeltsin's Star at the beginning of the war. And whether they deliberately set it up as a trap or not, we can't afford to get ourselves enveloped by a superior force. If we take heavy losses here, we could be in serious trouble until Admiral Tourville gets back from Silesia. Or, at least, until Admiral Foraker and Bolthole can make up our losses. If we have to risk some LACs, or even deliberately sacrifice them, to ensure that doesn't happen, then I'm afraid we'll simply have to do it."

"Yes, Sir."

"They know we're here," Commander Tatnall said positively, and MacDonnell nodded.

He'd hoped that the Peeps wouldn't spot them until it was too late. Although it had become evident that there were actually at least a hundred capital ships in the Havenite task force, he remained confident that his task force and Third Fleet, with almost a hundred SD(P)s and fifty pre-pod SDs between them, could take them. The small, fast impeller signatures which proved that the Peeps did have CLACs, after all, had caused him to raise his estimate of the losses he and Kuzak would probably suffer, but that hadn't affected his fundamental confidence. Not with the hundreds of planet-based LACs the Janacek Admiralty had deployed to back up Third Fleet as relations with the Republic worsened steadily. He knew they could take them . . . and that White Haven shared his confidence.

But in order to defeat them, he and Kuzak had to be able to get at them in the first place, and if they cut and ran for it, the chances of catching up to them would be poor at best.

He glowered at the display, where the steadily, if cautiously, advancing impeller signatures of scouting LACs crept ever closer to his own stealthed units. The question wasn't whether or not they knew he was here—it was whether or not they knew what he had. If they did realize that he was coming in behind them with another forty SD(P)s, plus carriers, anyone but idiots would disengage in a moment, and those probing LACs were going to provide their commander with that information before very much longer. However good his own EW and however poor Peep sensor suites might be, he couldn't hide from them if the range fell much further. Of course, it was always possible that they already had him. There was no way for anyone to be certain how much Shannon Foraker might have managed to improve their sensors in the last three or four years. But if they hadn't managed to lock up his units yet they might not know just how powerful his force was.

"Contact *Ararat*," he told Clairdon. "Tell Captain Davis that I want him to . . . discourage those LACs."

The chief of staff looked at him for a moment, then nodded, and MacDonnell turned back to his plot. *Ararat* was one of the *Covington*-class CLACs. Somewhat larger than the RMN's carriers, the *Covingtons* carried twenty-five percent more LACs, and unlike the RMN, the GSN had developed the *Katana*-class LAC, specifically designed for the "dogfighting" role. The Graysons had begun from the assumption that eventually someone else was going to produce their own LACs and carriers for them. When that time came, the GSN intended to be ready . . . especially since the RMN's "space superiority LAC" project had been one of the casualties of the Janacek cuts.

He heard Clairdon passing on his instructions, and then he nodded in satisfaction as the green diamond chips of *Ararat*'s LACs suddenly blinked into existence less than eight minutes after he'd given the initial order.

Javier Giscard's scouting LACs realized they were doomed the instant *Ararat* launched. There were only fifteen of the recon platforms, each of them only lightly armed, and there were over a hundred and twenty LACs coming at them. Worse, their own vectors were almost directly *towards* the enemy vessels.

There was no way they could possibly escape, and so they pressed on, accelerating directly towards the Graysons in an effort to at least get close enough to see the enemy clearly before they died.

Giscard knew exactly what they were doing, and a knife seemed to turn in his heart as he watched them do it. Nothing he could do at this point would affect what was about to happen to them. But he was the man who'd deliberately sent them out to die, and even though he knew he'd been right—that he would do the same thing again under the same circumstances, even knowing the outcome—that didn't make it hurt any less.

He watched his people accelerate, rushing to meet their deaths rather than fight for every instant of life they could cling to. He watched the red icons of their killers sweep towards them even as their sensors reached out and confirmed one capital impeller signature after another. He saw the missile storm that blotted them from the heavens. And then, finally, he turned away and made himself meet Captain Gozzi's eyes.

"What does CIC say now?" he asked quietly.

"We've confirmed thirty-seven positive superdreadnought impeller signatures, with another three probables and one possible," Gozzi said, equally quietly. "There are also at least eight other ships out there. They're a shade too small for SDs but too big for anything else on the Manty ship lists."

"Judging by what we just saw," Giscard said dryly, "I suspect that they must be CLACs."

"Yes, Sir. But our recon crews were quite definite. They're bigger than Manty carriers."

"Graysons, then," Giscard murmured.

"That would certainly be my guess, Sir," Gozzi agreed, and Giscard snorted softly.

The confirmation of the presence of the GSN in strength put

an entirely different complexion on the tactical situation. The sheer numbers coming up behind him would have been bad enough under any circumstances. The fact that they were Graysons made it even worse. Not just because of the profound respect with which the Republican Navy had learned to regard the GSN, but because of what their presence implied.

"Do you think they knew we were coming, Sir?" Gozzi asked, speaking softly enough to avoid other ears, and Giscard snorted again as his chief of staff followed his own thoughts.

"I think they must have figured out that *something* was coming, at any rate," he replied. "I doubt they managed to penetrate Thunderbolt, if that's what you're asking. But they wouldn't have needed to do that to set up an ambush here. All they would really have needed was one analyst with enough IQ to seal his own shoes and they could have guessed what would happen if the negotiations collapsed. And if they did that, even Janacek could figure out this would be the best spot to use for a counterstroke. After all, when you combine the concentration of most of their modern ships with the political significance of San Martin, this is undoubtedly the most valuable target we could have hit. That's precisely why this is our strongest task force. Which means that if they wanted a place to arrange for us to suffer a mischief, this would certainly have been a logical choice for it.

"If that's what they had in mind, though, it looks like they've come up a little short on the execution end. We know they're out there now, and they haven't gotten us quite deeply enough in-system to pin us between their two forces."

He fell silent once more, studying the displays and pondering options and alternatives. He could try turning on either one of the enemy task forces with his entire force. He'd have an excellent chance of defeating either one of them in isolation, if he could intercept it before its allies could come to its assistance. But if they chose to avoid action with one force while pursuing with the other, they might manage to prevent the interception he wanted. Or, even worse, let him have it but with too tight a time window to defeat the force he'd "caught" before the other one caught him from behind, in turn.

If the Committee of Public Safety had still been in power, the decision ultimately wouldn't have been his. It would have belonged to his people's commissioner, and if he'd dared to argue about it he would have found himself shot for his temerity. But the Republic had no commissioners, and he drew a deep breath and committed himself to the decision no admiral of the People's Navy would ever have dared to make.

"Go to evasion Tango-Baker-Three-One," he told Gozzi.

"Are you sure about this, Sir?" Gozzi asked in a painstakingly neutral tone.

"I am, Marius," Giscard replied with a small smile. "Trevor's Star was a primary objective, I know. And I know why Admiral Theisman wanted Third Fleet destroyed. But if they've managed to assemble this much firepower here, then they have to be buck naked on all of Thunderbolt's other objectives. That means we've kicked their ass everywhere else. I realize that we've got a chance here to carry through and cripple or destroy three-quarters of the combined Manty–Grayson SD(P) force. But we've got too many pre-pod ships of our own, and we'd be risking over half of our own SD(P)s. Not to mention the fact that there's too good chance of their catching us between them instead of us catching them separated." He shook his head. "No. There's always tomorrow, and if we've gotten out as lightly as I think we have elsewhere, the comparative loss figures are going to hit Manticoran public morale right in the belly. I don't want to give them a victory here to offset that effect. Nor do I want them to think that they hurt us badly enough we can't continue to take the war to them."

"Yes, Sir," Gozzi acknowledged and headed for the com section yet again.

Giscard watched him go, and then returned his attention to the master plot. He knew that Gozzi's question had reflected the chief of staff's concern over the possible repercussions the decision might have on Giscard's career. His own concern, hidden behind a confidently serene expression, had nothing to do with his career prospects. He knew Tom Theisman would expect him to exercise both judgment and discretion in the case like this, nor was he afraid that Theisman would see his decision to withdraw as an act of cowardice. For that matter, he snorted in genuine amusement, he could probably count on the President to intervene if things got too grim.

No, his concern was that he might be wrong. He didn't think he was. But he could be. And if he was, if he was throwing away a genuine opportunity to gut the Manticoran Alliance's wall of battle, the implications of that would dwarf anything that might ever have happened to anyone's career.

Michael Janvier, Baron High Ridge, was also thinking about careers as he paused, some hours later, in the hallway outside the polished wooden door. An armed sentry—a captain in the uniform of the Queen's Own—stood stiffly at attention before that door, and the immaculately uniformed woman didn't even glance at the Prime Minister.

High Ridge knew that the traditions and training of the Queen's Own required that ramrod stiffness, that apparent obliviousness to anything even as the sentry saw and noted everything that happened about her. But there was more to it than mere tradition or training. Something no one could ever have put a finger upon or isolated, but nonetheless there.

An edge of contempt, High Ridge thought as he made certain the mask of his own expression was firmly in place. The hostility that all of Elizabeth III's partisans reflected, each in his or her own way.

The Prime Minister drew an unobtrusive breath, squared mental shoulders, and moved the two meters closer which brought him within the sentry's designated official field of view.

The captain reacted then. Her head snapped to the side, her eyes focused on High Ridge, and her right hand flicked to the butt of the holstered pulser at her side with mechanical precision. It was all meticulously choreographed. Only an idiot would have thought the captain was anything less than a deadly serious professional, yet her response was also a display of formal military theater. One which required an equally formal response from him.

"The Prime Minister," he informed her, as if she didn't already know perfectly well who he was. "I crave a few minutes of Her Majesty's time to attend to affairs of government."

"Yes, Sir," the captain said, never removing her right hand from her pulser, and her left hand moved in a precisely metered arc to activate her com.

"The Prime Minister is here to see Her Majesty," she announced, and High Ridge's jaw muscles clenched. Usually, he rather enjoyed the formalities, the time-polished procedures and protocols which underscored the dignity and gravity of the office he held and the Star Kingdom he served. Today, each of them was a fresh grain of salt rubbed into the wound which brought him here, and he wished they could just get on with it. It wasn't as if his secretary hadn't scheduled the appointment before he ever came, or as if sophisticated security systems hadn't identified him and kept him under direct observation from the instant he entered Mount Royal Palace's grounds.

The sentry's eyes held him with unwavering, impersonal concentration—still flawed by that cold little core of contempt—as she listened to her earbug. Then she took her hand from her pulser and pressed the door activation button.

"Her Majesty will receive you, Sir," she said crisply, and snapped back into her original guard position, gazing once more down the hall as if he no longer existed.

He inhaled again and stepped through the door.

Queen Elizabeth waited for him, and his jaw tightened further. She'd received him in this same formal office many times over the past four T-years. Not happily, but with at least a pretense of respect for his office, however poorly she'd concealed the fact that she despised the man who held it. In those same four years, she'd never seen him a single time except for the unavoidable requirements of government and her constitutional duties, yet both of them, by mutual unspoken assent, had used the mask of formal courtesy when she had.

Today was different. She sat behind her desk, but unlike any other time he'd entered this office, she did not invite him to be seated. In fact, there was no chair in which he might have sat. The coffee table, the small couch which had faced it, and the conversational nook of comfortable armchairs, had all vanished. He had no doubt at all that she'd ordered their removal the instant his secretary screened the Palace for an appointment, and he knew his fury—and dismay—showed through his own masklike expression as the unspoken, coldly intentional insult went home.

Even if his own emotions hadn't shown, and even if the Queen had greeted him with smiling affability rather than the cold-eyed silence in which she watched him cross the office, the treecat on the back of her chair would have been a sure and certain barometer of the hostility coiled in that office. Ariel's tufted ears were more than half flattened and his bone-white claws sank deep into the upholstery of the Queen's chair as his green eyes watched High Ridge.

The baron came to a halt before her desk, standing there—like, he thought from a lava field of resentment, an errant schoolboy and not the Prime Minister of Manticore—and she regarded him as coldly as her treecat did.

"Your Majesty," he managed to get out in very nearly normal tones. "Thank you for agreeing to see me so promptly."

"I could hardly refuse to see my own Prime Minister," she replied. The words could have been courteous, even pleasant. Delivered with the tonelessness of a computer they were something else entirely.

"Your secretary indicated that the matter had some urgency," she continued in that same chill voice which pretended that she didn't know precisely what had brought him here.

"I'm afraid it does, Your Majesty," he agreed, wishing passionately that the unwritten portion of the Star Kingdom's Constitution didn't require the formality of a face-to-face meeting between a prime minister and the monarch at a time like this. Unfortunately, there was no way to avoid it, although he'd toyed—briefly, at least—with the thought that since this was technically only a violation of a truce and not a formal declaration of war he might have evaded it.

"I regret," he told her, "that it is my unhappy duty to inform you that your realm is at war, Your Majesty."

"It is?" she asked, and he heard his own teeth grinding together at the proof that she intended to spare him no smallest fraction of his humiliation. She knew precisely what had happened at Trevor's Star, but...

"Yes, unfortunately," he replied, forced by her question to formally explain the circumstances. "Although we've received no notification that the Republic of Haven intended to resume active military operations, their Navy violated Manticoran space this morning at Trevor's Star. Their task force was engaged by our own forces and driven off after suffering relatively light casualties. Our own forces suffered no damage, but the Republic's action in violating the Trevor's Star territorial limit can only be construed as an act of war."

"I see." She folded her hands on her desk and looked at him steadily. "Did I understand you to say, My Lord, that our own forces drove the intruders off?"

The emphasis on the possessive pronoun was subtle but

unmistakable, and High Ridge's eyes flickered with rage. But, again, still trapped by the prison of formality and constitutional precedent, he had no choice but to reply.

"Yes, Your Majesty. Although, to be more precise, they were driven off as a result of the joint action of our forces and those of the Protectorate of Grayson."

"Those Grayson forces being the ones which made unauthorized transit through the Junction yesterday?" she pressed in those same, chill tones.

"Yes, Your Majesty," he made himself say yet again. "Although, it would be more accurate to call their transit unscheduled rather than unauthorized."

"Ah. I see." She sat there for several seconds, regarding him levelly. Then smiled with absolutely no trace of warmth or humor. "And how do my ministers recommend that we proceed in this moment of crisis, My Lord?"

"Under the circumstances, Your Majesty, I see no option but to formally denounce our own truce with the Republic of Haven and resume unrestricted military operations against it."

"And are my military forces in a fit state to pursue that policy in the wake of this attack, My Lord?"

"They are, Your Majesty," he replied a bit more sharply, despite everything he could do to control his tone, as her question flicked him unerringly on the raw. He saw her satisfaction—not in any flicker of an expression on her own face, but in the treecat's ears and body language—and fought to reimpose the armor of his formality. "Despite the Republic's incursion into our space, we suffered no losses," he amplified. "Effectively, the military position remains unchanged by this incident."

"And is it the opinion of my Admiralty that this incident was an isolated one?"

"Probably not, Your Majesty," High Ridge admitted. "The Office of Naval Intelligence's estimate of the enemy's current order of battle strongly suggests, however, that the forces which violated the Trevor's Star limit constituted virtually the entirety of their modern naval units. That clearly implies that any other operations they may have carried out, or attempted to carry out, must have been on a much smaller scale."

"I see," the Queen repeated. "Very well, My Lord. I will be guided by the views of my Prime Minister and my First Lord of the

Admiralty in this matter. Are there other measures which you wish to propose?"

"Yes, there are, Your Majesty," he replied formally. "In particular, it's necessary that we inform our treaty partners of the state of affairs and notify them that we intend to formally reinvoke the mutual defense clauses of our alliance." He managed to get that out without even gagging, despite the gall and bile of suggesting any such thing. Then he drew a deep breath.

"In addition, Your Majesty," he continued, "given the significance and extreme gravity of the Republic's actions, and the fact that the entire Star Kingdom is now forced, however unwillingly, to take up arms once again, it is my considered opinion as your Prime Minister that your Government must represent the broadest possible spectrum of your subjects. An expression of unity at this critical moment must give our allies encouragement and our enemies pause. With your sovereign consent, I believe that it would be in the Star Kingdom's best interests to form a government of all parties, working together to guide your subjects in this moment of crisis."

"I see," the Queen said yet again.

"In time of war, such a suggestion often has merit," she continued after a brief pause, her eyes deadly as her sentence reminded him of another meeting in this same office four years before. "Yet in this instance, I think it may be . . . premature." High Ridge's eyes widened, and the merest hint of a smile touched her lips. "While I am, of course, deeply gratified by your willingness to reach out to your political opponents in what you've so correctly described as a moment of crisis, I feel that it would be most unfair to burden you with possible partisan disputes within your Cabinet at a moment when you must be free to concentrate on critical decisions. In addition, it would be unjust to create a situation in which you did not feel completely free to continue to make those decisions for which you, as Prime Minister, must bear ultimate responsibility."

He stared at her, unable to believe what she'd just said. The Constitution required him to inform her and obtain her formal consent to any proposal to form a new government, but no monarch in the entire history of the Star Kingdom had ever *refused* that consent once it was sought. It was unheard of—preposterous! But as he gazed into Elizabeth Winton's unflinching, flint-hard eyes, he knew it was happening anyway.

She gazed back at him, her face carved from mahogany steel, and he recognized her refusal to countersign his bid for political survival. There would be no "coalition government," no inclusion of the Centrists and Crown Loyalists to broaden his basis of support . . . or share in the guilt by association if additional reports of disaster rolled in. Nor would she even permit him to extend in her name the invitation William Alexander would almost certainly have refused, thus giving High Ridge at least the threadbare cover of being able to accuse the Centrists of refusing to support the Crown at this moment of need.

She had limited him to just two options: to continue without the cover of a joint government with the Opposition, or to resign. And if he resigned, it would be no more and no less than a formal admission of full responsibility on his part.

The moment stretched out between them, shivering with unspoken tension, and he hovered on the brink of threatening to resign if she did not endorse a coalition. But that was what she wanted. That was precisely the politically suicidal misstep into which she strove to drive him, and he felt a flowering of indignant outrage that the Crown should resort to such blatant political maneuvering at such a moment.

"Were there any further measures you wish to propose or discuss?" she asked into the ringing silence, and he recognized the question's message. Whatever he might propose, whatever he might recommend, she would saddle him unmistakably, personally, and permanently with responsibility for it.

"No, Your Majesty," he heard himself say. "Not at this time."

"Very well, My Lord." She inclined her head in a slight bow. "I thank you for your solicitous discharge of your responsibilities in bringing this news to me. I'm sure it must have been a most unpleasant task. And since there are undoubtedly many matters which require your urgent attention in the wake of this unprovoked aggression, I won't keep you longer."

"Thank you, Your Majesty," he got out in a strangled voice. "With your permission?"

He bowed considerably more deeply to her, and she watched with pitiless, unflinching eyes as he withdrew.

CHAPTER FIFTY-EIGHT

"How do you think we did back home, Sir?" Captain DeLaney asked quietly as she and Lester Tourville rode the lift car towards RHNS *Majestic*'s flag briefing room.

"Well, that's the million-credit question, isn't it, Molly?" the admiral responded with a tight grin. His chief of staff gave a small grimace of agreement, and he chuckled. "I admit I've done the odd bit of speculating myself," he confessed. "And despite my irritating conclusion that there's absolutely no way to be certain, I also have to admit that I feel fairly confident. Assuming that the NavInt estimates in the sitrep *Starlight* brought out with her are as accurate as they've tended to be for the last couple of years, First Fleet should have pinned the Manties' ears back. Now," his expression sobered, "whether or not all of this was a good idea or a bad one is another question, of course."

DeLaney looked sideways at him, faintly surprised even after all these months by his pensive tone. It was easy for even Lester Tourville's own staff to sometimes confuse the always aggressive public persona with the reality, but she'd been with him for the better part of three T-years now, and she knew him better than most.

"Did we really have a choice, Sir?" she asked after a moment, and he shrugged.

"I don't know. I feel certain President Pritchart did her

818

damnedest to find an alternative short of this one, and from *Starlight*'s dispatches, it's obvious the diplomatic situation got even worse after we'd been sent out. And I feel as confident as I imagine anyone could that Operation Thunderbolt is going to—has already, I suppose I should say—succeed in its immediate objectives. And if we're going to be completely honest, I suppose I want revenge on the Manties as much as the next man.

"I'm a little more doubtful about our whole end of the operation," he admitted, not really to DeLaney's surprise, "but if our estimates of Sidemore's strength are accurate, we should be able to pull it off. And I have to agree that the potential advantages of doing that, from a political and a morale standard, as well as a purely military one, make it worth the risk. I can't quite avoid the suspicion that we're being just a little too cute, a little too clever, about it all, but as some ancient wet-navy type from Old Earth said a long time ago, it's a natural law that those who refuse to run risks can never win. On the other hand," he smiled again, tightly, "there's always the fact that we're talking about attacking Honor Harrington."

"I know she's good, Sir," DeLaney said with an ever so slightly pronounced air of patience, "but she's really not a reincarnated war goddess. She's good, granted, but I've never quite understood why the newsies—theirs, as well as ours—fixate on her the way they do. It's not as if she'd ever commanded in a real fleet engagement, even at Yeltsin's Star, after all. I mean, compare her actual battlefield accomplishments to what someone like White Haven has done to us, and he doesn't get anywhere near the press she does!"

"I never said the lady was a 'war goddess,'" Tourville replied, then chuckled out loud. "On the other hand, that might not actually be all that bad a description of her, now that I think about it. And I know she's not invincible, although the only time anyone on our side has ever actually beaten her, she was just a tad outnumbered, you know."

DeLaney nodded, and actually felt herself blush a bit at the reminder that Lester Tourville was, in fact, the only Havenite admiral ever to defeat Honor Harrington.

"The truth is, though," Tourville went on more seriously, "that she's very probably the best—or, at the very least, one of the two or three best—tacticians the Manty navy has. Nobody on our side has ever come close to taking her in an even fight. Just between the two of us, I think from some of the things Admiral Theisman has said that he probably could have beaten her at Yeltsin's Star after Operation Stalking Horse fell apart. But even if he'd destroyed her entire force, it still would have been a strategic victory for her. She hasn't had a chance yet to show what she can do in 'a real fleet engagement,' and, frankly, that's one reason I feel a little nervous about this whole thing. I don't want to be the one who lets her notch up her first win on that scale. As to why the newsies 'fixate' on her, I guess it has to do with her way of always beating the odds. The fact that she looks damned good doesn't hurt any, of course. But the truth is, I think even the newsies sense something about her. Something you have to meet her in person to really understand . . . as much as anyone can."

DeLaney looked a question at him, and he shrugged.

"She has the touch, Molly," he said simply.

"The touch, Sir?"

"The touch," Tourville repeated, then shrugged again. "Maybe I'm an incurable romantic, but it's always seemed to me that there are just some officers who have that little bit extra. Sometimes it's just charisma, but usually it's a combination of that and something else. Esther McQueen had it, in a way. Everyone always knew she was ambitious, and no one who wasn't on her side ever really trusted her, but I think every officer who ever served directly under her would have followed her anywhere . . . until her luck ran out, at least. McQueen could convince you that she could do anything, and that you wanted to help her do it. But Harrington . . . Harrington makes you believe that *you* can do anything, because *she* believes it . . . and then dares you to do it with her. McQueen convinced people to follow her; Harrington just leads them, and they follow her on their own."

"You admire her, don't you, Sir?" DeLaney's question was really a statement, and Tourville nodded.

"Yes," he said. "Yes, if I'm going to be honest about it, I do. Probably of all of the officers on our side, Admiral Theisman comes closest to matching her ability to lead, and to draw the best possible performance out of her personnel. And I think he's probably as good a tactician as she is. But much as I respect and admire him, I think she still has that little bit more than he does. The touch. I can't think of anything else to call it.

"And the other thing she's had has been a positive gift for being in the right place at the right time—or the wrong place, at the wrong time, from our perspective. As you just observed, most of her actions have been on a fairly small scale, compared to something like White Haven's offensive just before the cease-fire. But they've had an impact all out of proportion to their size. Which undoubtedly accounts for a huge part of her reputation. If you want to put it that way, she's been lucky, although to some extent it's been a case of making her own luck. Which is one reason why I personally think that sending us out here was the right idea, despite any reservations I may feel."

"It was, Sir?" DeLaney looked at him again, and he snorted.

"Molly," he said, and it was his turn to sound patient, "I'm perfectly well aware that you think I've been a bit Cassandra-like about this entire operation. That, however, is known as the determined but sober attitude of a responsible military commander." The chief of staff's blush was considerably darker this time, and he smiled at her. "I'd be more than human—and an idiot, to boot—if I didn't have huge reservations about taking a fleet this size this far away from any of our bases or support structure to attack an officer with Harrington's reputation. Even assuming that we completely defeat her, which I happen to think we will, we're going to take losses and damage, and it's a hell of a long voyage home from here. Having said all of that, the very fact that Harrington enjoys the reputation and stature that she does makes her a sort of military objective in her own right. Defeating her, hopefully decisively, at the same time Thunderbolt is crunching up the Manties' frontier systems, will be a body blow to the Manty public's confidence and willingness to fight. And depriving the Manties of her services if they don't decide to start negotiating with us in good faith wouldn't be anything to sneeze at, either. Although at least this time, if we manage to capture her again, I can damned well guarantee there won't be any trumped-up charges or plans for executions!"

DeLaney started to reply, but the lift car reached its destination before she could, and she stood aside to allow her admiral to precede her into the flag deck passage.

The rest of the staff was waiting, along with Captain Caroline Hughes, *Majestic*'s CO, and Commander Pablo Blanchard, her exec. Second Fleet's task force and squadron commanders attended the meeting electronically, their faces floating in the quadrants of a holo display above the briefing room conference table. DeLaney knew that Tourville would really have preferred to have them aboard *Majestic* in the flesh for this final meeting, but that hadn't been practical. The fleet was squarely in the heart of a grav wave, bearing down on Sidemore, which made it impossible for any impeller-drive small craft to transport personnel back and forth between its units. For her own part, DeLaney was perfectly satisfied with the electronic substitute for an old-fashioned face-to-face meeting, but her boss was more of a traditionalist in that respect.

Those physically present stood as Tourville entered the compartment, then seated themselves once again after he'd settled into the chair at the head of the table. He tipped that chair back while he slowly and carefully prepared a cigar, stuck it into his mouth, lit it, and produced a cloud of fragrant smoke. He grinned through the fog bank of his own making, like a mischievous little boy, as the overhead air return sucked it away, and DeLaney hid a smile of her own. He was back on stage again, once more the hard-charging complete naval officer, ready, as the old cliché put it, to kick ass and take names.

"All right," he said briskly. "In about five hours, we're going to be dropping in on Sidemore without calling ahead for reservations." Several people chuckled, and his mischievous grin grew fierce. "When we do, there are going to be some people who won't be especially happy to see us. Which is going to be unfortunate . . . for them." A louder chuckle responded, and he nodded at his operations officer. "And now," he said, "Commander Marston is going to answer any last-minute questions you may have about exactly how we're going to make sure that it's unfortunate for them. Jeff?"

"Thank you, Sir," Commander Marston replied, and turned to face both the others present in the briefing room and the camera which connected the compartment to the holographic faces above the conference table. "I know all of you are familiar with our basic operational plan," he began. "Several of you, however, have expressed some concerns, particularly about the points covered in Annex Seventeen, so I thought, with your permission, Admiral, that we might start there."

He glanced at Tourville, who waved his cigar in an airy gesture of approval.

"Very well, then. First, Admiral Zrubek has raised a very interesting point in regard to the proper employment of our long-range recon platforms." He nodded respectfully to the holo quadrant filled by the recently promoted commander of Battle Squadron Twenty-One, which included eight of Second Fleet's twelve SD(P)s. "I've discussed the same point with Captain deCastries and Commander Hindemith," Marston continued, "and we've come to the conclusion that . . ."

Lester Tourville leaned back comfortably in his chair, listening with both ears, and half of his attention, to Marston's brisk, competent exposition. He would have paid more attention to the actual explanation if he'd had less confidence in the ops officer's ability and thoroughness. As it was, he was free to spend his time doing what, as far as he was concerned, was the true purpose of this meeting—taking the pulse of his command team's state of mind.

What he saw pleased him. One or two of them were obviously a bit on the anxious side, but he didn't blame them for that. Indeed, a certain edge of nervousness was probably a good thing, and there were enough others—like Zrubek and DeLaney—whose supreme confidence in the ops plan and, he supposed, in his own leadership, more than offset it. Yet however anxious or however confident any one of them might be, there was no hesitation. These people were as ready as anyone could possibly be for the task before them.

"Talk to me, Andrea," Honor said briskly but calmly as she arrived on *Werewolf*'s flag bridge. Nimitz rode in her arms, once more in his own custom-designed skinsuit, and she paused to park him on the back of her command chair. She gave his tufted ears a caress, then turned back to face her operations officer while the 'cat's nimble true-hands fastened the harness straps between his skinsuit and the chair.

"We still don't have positive confirmation, Your Grace," Captain Jaruwalski replied, "but I don't think there's much question. It's the Peeps."

"I tend to agree with Andrea, Your Grace," Mercedes Brigham put in from her own console, "but at the same time, I don't think we should positively rule out the possibility that this could be the Andies, instead." Honor looked at her, and the chief of staff shrugged. "I'm not saying that I believe it's the Andies, Ma'am. But until we know for certain, one way or the other, I think we'd better keep an open mind on the subject."

"That's a valid point," Honor acknowledged. "But whoever it is," she turned to consider the huge holo sphere of the master plot, "they look like they mean business."

"They certainly do that," Brigham agreed, and stood to join Honor beside the plot.

The unknown units were headed in-system on a course which would bring them to a zero-zero intercept with Marsh in just over six hours, assuming that they made turnover in three. And there were quite a few of them. In fact, it looked very much as if her "official" order of battle would have been outnumbered by at least fifty percent.

"We're getting light-speed emissions signatures now, Your Grace," George Reynolds reported. Honor turned towards them, and the intelligence officer looked up to meet her gaze. "They're not Andies," he said quietly. "We don't recognize some of them, but we've positively IDed at least eight Havenite battlecruisers."

Something like a not quite audible sigh seemed to run around the flag bridge, and Honor smiled thinly. She couldn't say she was glad to have her worst fears confirmed, but at least the uncertainty was over. She closed her mind resolutely to speculation about what might have happened closer to home, and nodded as serenely as she could.

"Thank you, George," she said, and glanced at Jaruwalski.

"CIC is trying to break them down by type, Your Grace," the ops officer said. "It's a bit difficult without better intelligence on whatever new types they've been building, especially since, as George just said, we don't recognize some of them at all. At the moment though, it looks as though they've brought along fifty or sixty superdreadnoughts, with twenty or thirty battlecruisers in support."

"Time of response to our sublight challenge, Harper?" Honor asked her com officer.

"If they respond to it immediately, we should be hearing something from them in another four or five minutes, Your Grace," Lieutenant Brantley told her.

"Thank you." Honor frowned thoughtfully for a moment, then returned her attention to Jaruwalski. "Any indications of CLACs?"

"No, Your Grace," the ops officer replied. "Which doesn't necessarily mean there aren't any."

"Your Grace, we're getting IDs on at least some of their superdreadnoughts from the remote platforms," Reynolds put in. "They're
confirmed Peeps. We've got nine of them so far. All pre-pod designs
ONI has good recorded emissions signatures on."

"That's about twenty percent of their total SDs," Brigham
observed.

"True," Jaruwalski agreed. "On the other hand, it still leaves over
fifty which could be SD(P)s."

Honor nodded once more, accepting Jaruwalski's caveat, then
gave the plot another glance and reached her decision.

"It doesn't look like we're going to get a better chance for
Suriago," she said, and looked at the com screen connecting her
to *Werewolf*'s command deck. "Get us underway, Rafe."

"Aye, aye, Your Grace," Captain Rafe Cardones replied crisply,
and began passing orders.

"They're not trying to be very stealthy about it, are they, Sir?"
Molly DeLaney remarked.

"No, they're not," Tourville agreed. He sat in his command chair,
legs crossed, expression calm, while his right hand's fingers
drummed very slowly and gently on its armrest. His eyes were
equally calm but intent as he studied the repeater plot deployed
from his chair.

The defending Manticoran task force was headed to meet him.
The range remained too long for real-time reports from light-speed
sensors, but impeller signatures were FTL, and they blazed clear
and strong in the plot, confirming what the first wave of recon
drones had already reported. Thirty-one Manty superdreadnoughts,
eleven dreadnoughts, four LAC carriers, and sixteen battlecruisers,
covered by two destroyer flotillas and at least three cruiser squadrons accelerated steadily on almost a direct reciprocal of his own
course. A cloud of LACs spread out to cover the axis of their
advance and its flanks. It was much more difficult to get a drive
count on units that small, but NavInt had reported that somewhere around four hundred and fifty LACs had been permanently
based on Sidemore. It looked like Harrington had brought all of
them with her, since CIC estimated her main combatants were
accompanied by somewhere around eight hundred of them. Taking

NavInt's highest figure and combining it with the six CLACs she was supposed to have gave her a maximum LAC strength of right on a thousand. She might have left a couple of hundred of them to cover the inner system against the possibility that the main attack was actually a feint to pull her out of position around Marsh, especially if she believed the Republican Navy still lacked any CLACs of its own.

And she was continuing to transmit her sublight challenges and demands that he identify himself as she came.

DeLaney's comment on Harrington's lack of stealth was a definite understatement, he reflected. And that made him a little nervous. One thing no one had ever accused Honor Harrington of was tactical obviousness. She had demonstrated repeatedly her willingness and ability to use the traditional Manticoran advantage in electronic warfare to deadly effect. Yet in the face of CIC's definite identification of her units, it seemed that this time, at least, she had disdained such tactics. She wasn't hiding or concealing a thing . . . which was the reason for his nervousness. "The Salamander" was at her most dangerous when an opponent was most certain he knew what she had in mind.

Let's not double-think ourselves into a panic, there, Lester, he told himself dryly. *Yeah, she's sneaky. And smart. But she doesn't really have a lot of options here. And besides . . .*

"It may just be that she's still hoping to get out of this without anyone shooting at anybody," he murmured aloud, and DeLaney's eyebrows rose.

"That seems . . . unlikely, Sir," she said, and Tourville grinned at her tone of massive restraint.

"I didn't say it was likely, Molly. I said it was *possible.* And it is, you know. She has to have IDed at least some of our emissions signatures by now, so she knows we're Republican. And she'd have to be a hell of a lot stupider than I know she is if she didn't suspect exactly why we're here. But at the same time, she can't know what's going on back home—not yet. So there's probably at least an edge of caution in her thinking right now. She's not going to shirk her responsibilities, but she's not going to want to start a war out here that could spill over on the Star Kingdom's own territory unless she absolutely has to, either. I'd guess that's why they're continuing to challenge us despite the fact that we haven't answered them."

"Do you think she'll actually let us into range because she doesn't want to fire the first shot, Sir?"

"I doubt very much that she's going to be that obliging," Tourville said dryly. "We are in violation of the territorial space of a Manticoran ally at the moment, you know. That means she's in a very strong position under interstellar law if she decides to shoot some dumb son-of-a-bitch who's too much of an idiot to even reply to her communications attempts!"

He flashed his teeth in a white smile under his bristling mustache, and DeLaney heard someone chuckle.

"On the other hand, if NavInt is right and the Manties still haven't confirmed that we have MDMs of our own, she may let us get in a lot closer before she gets around to opening fire. She knows we have SD(P)s, but she also knows by now that at least some of the SDs we brought with us are pre-pod designs. On top of that, she has to suspect from our acceleration rates that our older ships are towing heavy pod loads. She, on the other hand, isn't, even though NavInt says that she has only six SD(P)s of her own. She may have some pods tractored inside her other superdreadnoughts' wedges, but she can't have as many of them there as we're towing. Combined with how openly she's coming to meet us, that suggests to me that she still believes she has a decisive range advantage. That she can open fire at a range of her own choosing, from outside our effective reach, and hold it there."

"Do you think she knows about the new compensators, Sir?"

"I wouldn't be a bit surprised if she's figured out that we've improved our performance, whatever her ONI reports might be telling her," Tourville said. "She's certainly smart enough to realize that we must have made overcoming their acceleration advantage a very high priority. Unfortunately, for all their improvements, our compensators still aren't anywhere near as efficient as theirs are ... and she's smart enough she's probably figured that out, too. So if she thinks she has the range advantage, she'll expect to be able to prevent us from closing with her."

"So you think she's basically hoping to bluff us into breaking off," DeLaney said.

"I suppose you might put it that way," Tourville conceded. "I wouldn't express it quite that strongly, myself. I think she intends to continue to give us the opportunity to decide this was a bad idea, break off, and go home right up to the last minute. It's not a 'bluff,' Molly, because I don't think she actually expects us to break off for a moment. But knowing Harrington, she figures that it's her responsibility to give us the option, and she's determined to do it. Which," he added almost regretfully, "probably also means that she'll hold her fire until the range drops to what she believes is just outside the maximum at which we could engage her effectively."

"The range is down to three light-minutes, Your Grace," Mercedes Brigham said in the tone of voice of someone politely reminding someone else of something she might have forgotten.

"So I see," Honor replied with a slight smile, despite the tension coiling inside her. At fifty-four million kilometers, they were well inside her own maximum powered-attack missile range.

"Still no response to our challenges, either, Ma'am," Brigham pointed out, and Honor nodded.

"How good is your targeting information now, Andrea?" she asked.

"It's still not anything I'd call satisfactory, Your Grace," Jaruwalski responded promptly in a slightly sour tone. "Whatever else they may have managed, they've improved their ECM significantly. It's still not as good as ours is—or, for that matter, quite as good as what we've seen out of the Andies over the last few months. But it's a lot better than it was during Operation Buttercup. I'd estimate that we should expect at least a fifty or sixty percent degradation in accuracy at this range. Possibly a little bit more."

"And even without worrying about ECM, accuracy against a target under power isn't anything to write home about at this range," Brigham observed.

"No, but theirs is probably worse," Honor said, and Brigham nodded in unhappy agreement.

Honor knew that Mercedes still thought that her own insistence that they operate on the assumption that the Republic's new SD(P)s' missiles could match the full range of their own MDMs was unduly pessimistic. On the other hand, Honor would far rather find out that she had, in fact, been overly pessimistic than suddenly find herself under fire at a range which she had assumed would give her ships immunity from attack.

"And whatever their base accuracy might be, Your Grace," Jaruwalski put in, "from everything I've seen so far, our ECM is going to degrade their accuracy a lot more than theirs is going to do to us. That's even assuming that they've managed to improve their missile seekers as much as they have their EW capabilities."

"Well, given that it looks like they have at least twice as many SD(P)s as Admiral McKeon does, that's probably a good thing," Honor replied with another smile, and Jaruwalski chuckled in appreciation as Honor turned to Lieutenant Kgari.

"How far are they from Suriago's point of no return, Theophile?" she asked.

"They've been inbound for about two and a half hours at two hundred and seventy gravities, Your Grace. Their base velocity is up to two-six-point-seven thousand KPS. Assuming they maintain heading and acceleration, they'll hit no return in another eleven-point-five minutes, Your Grace," her staff astrogator told her.

"Then I suppose it's about time," Honor said almost regretfully. "Harper, pass the word to *Borderer* to stand by to execute Paul Revere in twelve minutes."

"Aye, aye, Your Grace."

Twelve more minutes passed. Second Fleet's base velocity rose to just over 28,530 KPS and Task Force 34's velocity reached 19,600 KPS. The range continued to fall, gnawed away by a closing velocity of almost sixteen percent of light-speed. It dropped from fifty-three million kilometers to barely thirty-seven and a half million, and then HMS *Werewolf* transmitted a brief FTL message to HMS *Borderer*. The destroyer, almost ten full light-minutes outside the system hyper limit received the transmission, acknowledged receipt, and translated up into hyper . . . where it sent a second transmission.

Twenty-six seconds later, the Protector's Own, Grayson Space Navy, made its alpha translation out of hyper, directly behind Second Fleet, and began accelerating furiously in-system in its wake.

"Hyper footprint!" Commander Marston announced. "Multiple hyper footprints, bearing one-eight-zero, zero-two-niner, range approximately one light-minute!"

Lester Tourville snapped upright in his chair and spun to face the ops officer. Marston stared at his readouts for a few more seconds, then looked up to meet his admiral's eyes.

"They're more Manties, Sir," he said in a tone of disbelief. "Either that . . . or Graysons."

"They can't be," DeLaney protested almost automatically and waved one hand at the plot. "We've got positive IDs on all of Harrington's ships. They can't have fooled the RDs at such close range—not even with their EW!"

Tourville's mind fought to grapple with Marston's impossible announcement. DeLaney was right. The range to Harrington's ships was less than two light-minutes. It might have been possible for Manticoran electronic warfare systems to fool shipboard sensors even at that short a range, but Second Fleet's recon drones had closed to within less than three light-seconds. At that range, they could make *visual* identification on a superdreadnought or a LAC carrier, and they'd accounted for every single ship Harrington had.

Or, his mind told him coldly, *for every ship NavInt said she had, anyway*.

For just an instant, Lester Tourville was five years in the past, when no admiral had been able to trust the intelligence appreciations produced by Oscar Saint-Just's StateSec analysts. A dreadful sense of betrayal flashed through him at the thought that Thomas Theisman's NavInt had just proven itself equally unreliable. But then he shook himself. Whatever had happened here, NavInt had proven its fundamental reliability too often over the last four T-years. There had to be an explanation, but what?

"We have hard IDs on the new bogeys' types," Marston said flatly. "CIC makes it twelve *Medusa*-class SD(P)s, six *Covington*-class CLACs, and six battlecruisers. CIC isn't positive, but it thinks the battlecruisers are probably *Courvoisier*-class ships."

"*Covingtons? Courvoisiers?*" DeLaney shook her head. "Those *are* Grayson types!" She turned to face Tourville. "What are *Graysons* doing out here in the middle of Silesia?" she demanded almost plaintively.

Tourville stared back at her for perhaps four seconds, then muttered a short, pungent obscenity.

"It's the Protector's Own," he said flatly. "Damn! NavInt *told* us they were off on some long-ranged deployment training mission. Why didn't it even occur to us that that sneaky bastard Benjamin might have sent them *here*?"

"But why here?" DeLaney protested.

"I don't know," Tourville replied, but his mind continued to race even as he spoke, and he grimaced. "Best guess? Benjamin and Harrington discussed it before she ever came out here. Damn! I'll guarantee you that's what happened. She knew High Ridge wasn't going to give her what she needed to do her job, so she borrowed it from her *other* navy without even telling anyone she was doing it!"

He shook his head in brief, heartfelt admiration. Obviously, he thought, NavInt needed to update its estimate of Harrington as a brilliant military technician to include a degree of political sophistication no one had expected from her. But then he brushed the thought aside. There was no time for it—not when his entire fleet had just been mousetrapped with consummate professionalism.

He pushed himself up out of his chair and crossed to the main plot, staring into it as data sidebars updated and acceleration vectors established themselves. The numbers flashed and danced, then settled, and Admiral Lester Tourville felt a ball of ice congeal in his belly.

"The Graysons are launching LACs," Marston reported. "Tracking reports over six hundred impeller signatures already."

Tourville only grunted. Of course they were launching their LACs, but that wasn't what was going to do most of their killing. Not today. Both Harrington and the Protector's Own were well within MDM range of Second Fleet, and his own twelve SD(P)s, which had been supposed to give him a two-to-one advantage over Harrington's *Medusas* were suddenly outnumbered by two-to-one, instead. And if NavInt was right about the Graysons new *Courvoisier II* battlecruisers, Harrington had an additional six pod-launcher types. Given the Manticoran and Grayson advantages in electronic warfare and missile defense, that gave them a devastating edge in the pounding match about to begin. And Harrington had timed things perfectly. Second Fleet was too far inside the hyper limit, sandwiched between two forces, both of which had higher fleet acceleration rates than it did.

"Alter course one-two-zero to starboard," he said. "Maximum military power for the SDs. Shift formation to Mike-Delta-Three and prepare to launch LACs."

Acknowledgments came back to him, and he could almost taste the sense of relief that flooded through his staff as they heard a trusted voice giving crisp, clear orders. It was, he thought bitterly, a reaction that was going to be repeated over and over again on the ships of his fleet. Repeated because he had taught his people that they *could* trust him. Because they had faith in him.

But this time, that faith was going to be disappointed. Even on his new course, his units were going to continue to slide into the arms of Harrington's Manticoran units. His new vector would start generating lateral separation quickly, and it was the fastest possible course back to the system's hyper limit. But it wouldn't kill velocity quickly enough to prevent the range between him and the Manties from closing by at least another thirty light-seconds. And by the time he could kill an appreciable fraction of his closing velocity, the Graysons would be on a direct course for the point at which he would hit the hyper limit out-bound. If he could maintain his present acceleration, they wouldn't—quite—catch him from their much lower base velocity, but they'd sure as hell overrun any cripples who fell behind. And the entire time he was trying to run away, they were going to be pounding him with a hurricane of missile fire precisely to produce as many cripples as they possible could. Not to mention LAC strikes.

Which meant that his fleet, and his people, were about to be destroyed.

"So, they do have CLACs," Honor said quietly as the display blossomed with hundreds upon hundreds of fresh impeller signatures.

"Yes, Ma'am," Jaruwalski confirmed. The ops officer stood beside Lieutenant Commander Reynolds where they'd been studying the latest reports from the system surveillance platforms. Now she turned to face Honor and gestured at the LAC drives blazing in the plot.

"It looks like at least eight of their 'superdreadnoughts' are actually CLACs, Your Grace," she said. "That makes them a hell of a lot bigger than anything we have, and it looks like each of their groups is at least a third again the size of a *Covington*'s. CIC estimates that they have right on two thousand of them."

"Then they're screwed," Rafe Cardones said confidently from Honor's com screen. "Two thousand gives them less than two hundred more than we have," he went on, lumping the Manticoran and Grayson LAC groups together. "I can't believe they could possibly have managed to improve their tech enough to keep us from tearing them apart when we're that close to parity with them numerically."

"You're probably right," Honor replied. "But let's not get over-confident. ONI never even guessed they had CLACs, so we don't have any meter stick at all for evaluating their LAC effectiveness."

"You're right, Your Grace," Cardones admitted.

"Should we commit our own LACs, Your Grace?" Jaruwalski asked.

"Not yet," Honor said. "Before we do that, I want to whittle down their shipboard defenses. I'm not going to throw away our LAC groups by committing them against an unshaken wall that knows they're coming."

"If we don't commit them soon, we may not have an opportunity to use them at all, Your Grace," Jaruwalski warned, gesturing at CIC's projection of the Peeps' new course. "If we hold them back more than another fifteen or twenty minutes, they won't have the accel to overcome the Peeps' base velocity advantage and overhaul short of the alpha wall."

"Granted," Honor conceded. "But I'm not prepared to accept massive casualties if we don't have to. Especially when we don't know for certain what the Andies will do if we take heavy losses against the Republic. If we can beat these people without getting our LACs chewed up, so much the better."

Jaruwalski nodded in understanding, if not total agreement, and Honor looked at Lieutenant Brantley.

"My compliments to Admiral McKeon and Admiral Yu, and instruct them to open fire."

"Missile separation!" Marston announced. "I have hostile launches—*many* hostile launches!"

"Return fire," Tourville said almost calmly.

"Aye, Sir! Returning fire—*now*."

Multidrive missiles howled out across the endless light-seconds of emptiness. No fleets in history had ever engaged one another at such a preposterous range. More than two full light-minutes lay between TF 34 and Second Fleet, and it would take almost seven minutes for even Manticore's missiles to cross that stupendous gulf of vacuum. Second Fleet's missiles, with their marginally lower accelerations, would take even longer to reach TF 34. But the

Protector's Own was closer than that. The flight time for Alfredo Yu's missiles was little more than three minutes.

Both sides' starships had extra missile pods on tow, and both sides flushed them all in the initial salvo. Second Fleet had seventy-eight capital ships: forty-six superdreadnoughts, eight CLACs, and twenty-four battlecruisers, but its planned margin of superiority had been more than erased by the presence of Alfredo Yu's command. TF 34 and the Protector's Own between them had a hundred and six capital ships: forty-three superdreadnoughts, ten CLACs, eleven dreadnoughts, and forty-two battlecruisers. Still, eleven of Honor's ships of the wall were only dreadnoughts and forty-four percent of her other "capital ships" were mere battlecruisers, and although the Allies' weapon systems remained superior to those of the Republic, the margin of superiority was thinner than it had ever been before.

The Havenite missile pods contained fewer missiles because those missiles had to be thirty percent larger than Manticoran missiles to approximate the same performance. But since she'd had no choice but to build enormous missiles because of the mass requirements of their drive elements and power plants, anyway, Shannon Foraker had been able to give them larger payloads than their Manticoran counterparts, as well. She'd used some of that volume to increase the destructive power of their warheads, but most of it had gone into additional sensor capability. The result was a weapon with eighty-eight percent as much range, very nearly eighty percent as much accuracy, and greater hitting power than anything Manticore had.

But that accuracy still had to get through Manticore's superior ECM, and decoys and jammers went to work on both sides as the deadly tides of destruction swept down upon them. False targets offered themselves, singing to targeting systems, beckoning and seducing them away from the actual starships they sought to destroy. Jammers howled, threshing space with active interference to blind sensitive seeking systems, and as the range fell still further, counter missiles went screaming out to meet the incoming fire with kamikaze devotion.

The Manticoran systems were far more effective, especially with the remote Ghost Rider platforms to spread the EW envelope wider and deeper. Despite the increases in accuracy Foraker had managed to engineer into the Republic's MDMs, the Allies'

targeting systems were at least fifty percent more effective simply because of the difference in the two sides' electronic warfare capabilities.

Active defenses engaged the weapons which slashed their way
through the screen of electronic protection. The latest generation
Manticoran counter missiles had increased their effective intercept
range to just over two million kilometers, although the probability
of a kill in excess of one and a half million was low. Shannon
Foraker's best efforts, even with reverse-engineered Solarian technology, had a *maximum* intercept range of little more than one
and a half million. That meant Honor's missile defenses had
sufficient depth for two counter missile launches to engage each
incoming missile before the attacking birds could reach effective
laserhead range. Foraker could get off only a single launch at each
incoming wave of Allied missiles, but she'd compensated by
increasing the number of launchers by more than thirty percent.
Her missiles were individually less effective, but there were many
more of them per launch, and Second Fleet threw up a wall of
them in the path of the incoming warheads.

Impeller wedge met impeller wedge, obliterating counter missile and MDM alike in blinding flashes as impeller nodes and
capacitors vaporized one another. Both sides were using layered
defenses, ripple-fired, multiple waves of counter missiles backed
by point defense laser clusters in the innermost interception zones,
and Foraker and Commander Clapp had integrated the *Cimeterres*
into the Republican Navy's missile defense doctrine, as well. Even
a LAC's laser clusters could kill an incoming missile if it could
hit it, and very few of those missiles would deign to attack something as insignificant as a LAC.

Space was a blinding, roiling cauldron of energy around Second Fleet as counter missiles, shipboard lasers and grasers, and
LACs poured fire into the phalanx of destruction sweeping down
upon it. At least sixty percent of the Allies' fire was defeated by
ECM or picked off by active defenses. But that meant that forty
percent wasn't, and Lester Tourville's ships spun and twisted like
dervishes, fighting to interpose wedges and sidewalls against the
ravening fury of bomb-pumped lasers as the Manticoran warheads
began to detonate.

At least half of those lasers wasted themselves harmlessly against
the impenetrable stress bands of superdreadnought impeller wedges,

or found themselves bent and twisted wide of their targets by sidewalls. But some of them got through.

Lester Tourville clung to the arms of his command chair as RHNS *Majestic* staggered and bucked. No one sent damage reports to the flag bridge. Those were the concern of Captain Hughes on her own command deck, but Tourville could feel the big ship's wounds as laser after laser crashed into her. Even her massive armor yielded to that savage pounding, and he knew Manticoran fire was smashing away sensors, energy weapons, missile tubes . . . and the human beings who crewed them.

He felt that wave of destruction in the back of his brain, but he made himself ignore it. If it was Hughes' job to deal with *Majestic*'s wounds it was Tourville's job to save what he could of Second Fleet.

It didn't look as if he would be able to save very much of it.

Both the Manticoran and the Grayson fire had concentrated mercilessly upon his own SD(P)s and CLACs. Quite a few missiles—like the ones targeting *Majestic*—had lost track and gone after other victims, yet it was obvious that they amounted to little more than errant shots which had initially been intended for the newer types. He wondered, at first, how the Manties could have targeted them so accurately, picked them out of his formation so unerringly, when the Allies had no emissions signatures or targeting profiles on file for them. But then he realized how absurdly easy it actually was. They hadn't picked the new ships out; they'd simply chosen *not* to fire at the ships they could positively identify as pre-pod designs. By process of elimination, that concentrated their fire on the newer, more dangerous designs.

They were tough, superdreadnoughts. The most massively armored and protected mobile structures ever built by man. They could soak up almost inconceivable amounts of punishment and survive. More than survive, continue to strike back from the heart of a holocaust which would have vaporized any lesser ship. But there were limits to all things, including the toughness of super-dreadnoughts, and he watched the damage report sidebars flicker and change as incoming missiles sledgehammered his own SD(P)s again and again and again.

He felt a moment of bitter shame leavened by relief as he realized most of the Manties were virtually ignoring his own flagship. He'd chosen *Majestic* because she'd been designed as a command ship, with the best communications and battle management systems available. But she was a pre-pod design, and so, for all her damage, she was largely spared as that first, deadly exchange of fire completely gutted a third of Tourville's SD(P)s. Two more were damaged almost as badly, and a seventh lost two alpha nodes. Only one of them escaped totally undamaged . . . and fresh Manticoran missiles were already howling in upon her in follow-on salvos.

Honor watched the return Havenite fire rip into her own formation. Her wall of battle was too far from its enemies for shipboard sensors to resolve what was happening to Second Fleet in any detail, but the Ghost Rider sensor platforms she'd had deployed were another matter entirely. Not even Manticore had yet been able to find a way for the platforms to send targeting information directly to MDMs, and even an MDM was too small for BuWeaps to cram in an FTL receiver which would have allowed real-time targeting telemetry to be relayed through the ships who'd launched them. But she could at least evaluate what happened when those missiles reached their targets, and her eyes narrowed in respectful surprise at the sheer toughness of that multilayered, tightly coordinated defensive envelope.

It was obvious that the Republic recognized the technical inferiority of its defensive systems. But Shannon Foraker's touch was equally obvious in the way in which those individually inferior systems had been carefully coordinated. The same approach would have been redundantly wasteful of capabilities given Manticoran system efficiencies. Given Republican hardware, it represented a brilliant adaptation of existing capabilities. An answer in mass to the individual superiority of Allied weapons.

And it worked.

Like Tourville, Honor had chosen her flagship for the effectiveness of its command systems more than its ship-to-ship offensive power. And even more than Second Fleet's commander, she found that flagship virtually ignored by the incoming Republican missiles. It made sense, she supposed, although she hadn't really considered it when she made her choice. After all, a carrier which had already launched its LACs automatically had a lower priority than superdreadnoughts which were busy launching missiles of their own or providing fire control to pods laid by another SD(P).

Werewolf was miraculously and completely untouched in that first, crushing exchange of fire. Other ships were less fortunate. Alistair McKeon's *Troubadour* was a priority target. Almost a dozen missiles broke through every electronic and active defense, and the SD(P)'s icon flashed and flickered on Honor's plot as she took damage. Her sistership *Hancock* was hit equally hard, and *Trevor's Star* took at least ten hits from individual lasers. The pre-pod ships *Horatius*, *Romulus*, and *Yawata* took their share of the punishment, as well, and the battlecruiser *Retaliation* strayed into the path of a full broadside intended for the dreadnought *King Michael*. All of the ships of the wall survived; *Retaliation* didn't.

Honor watched the battlecruiser's data code disappear from her plot and wondered how many hundreds—or thousands—of her people were wounded or dying aboard the other ships of her task force. She felt those fresh deaths pressing upon her, joining their weight to all the rest of her dead, but even as the toll mounted among her own ships, she knew the enemy was being hammered even harder.

Lester Tourville watched the mounting tide of destruction swelling up in the plot's sidebars and fought to keep his despair out of his expression and voice.

Despite the incredible range, despite the MDMs' long flight times, the Manties' deadly concentration on his SD(P)s had crippled his offensive firepower in the first two salvos . . . and, for all intents and purposes, destroyed it completely in less than thirty minutes. Only one of his long-range missile ships, Battle Squadron 21's flagship, RHNS *Hero*, remained in action. Two of her sisters had been totally destroyed, four had been abandoned, with scuttling charges set, three more would have to be abandoned very quickly if their nodes could not be brought back online, and if she herself was still in action, she was also heavily damaged. Her fire control had been gutted by the same missile salvo which had destroyed her flag bridge . . . and killed Rear Admiral Zrubek instantly. She was effectively blind and deaf, yet she continued to roll pods at her maximum possible rate, turning them over to her older sisters' fire control. It let Second Fleet continue to spit defiance at the Manties, but *Hero* was the only ship he had which could still deploy pods at all, and she had only a finite number of them.

Nor had the SD(P)s been his only fatalities. Five more superdreadnoughts had been destroyed or so badly damaged that he'd had no option but to leave them behind while his survivors continued to run. At least one more had taken critical impeller damage; like the lamed SD(P)s, he'd be forced to leave her behind when he made translation into hyper if she couldn't get the missing alpha node back. One of his CLACs had also been destroyed, and two more were little more than air-bleeding wrecks, which meant that at least seven hundred of his two thousand LACs were going to have to be written off, whatever happened to the rest of his fleet.

He checked the maneuvering plot again, and his face clenched with pain. He was still two hours from the hyper limit, and if Harrington's task force had begun losing ground as the geometry of his vector change crabbed away from her, the Graysons were closing in steadily. Not that it mattered. He might be slowly, painfully opening the range from her launchers, but he was still over two light-minutes inside their reach.

At least some of Harrington's ships had been sufficiently battered to fall astern in the chase, he thought grimly. Some of them, judging from the recon drone's' reports, had taken serious damage. Two of her battlecruisers had been completely destroyed, as had at least three destroyers or light cruisers. CIC wasn't certain which at this range—especially when they hadn't been targeted in the first place. But MDMs were proving as indiscriminate in their targeting at long-range as Shannon had predicted. Most of them went after their programmed victims; a significant percentage wound up going after whatever targets they could see at the ends of their runs.

Even as he watched his fleet being pounded towards destruction, he felt a fresh flicker of admiration for Shannon and her staff. Second Fleet could not have found itself in a more disastrous tactical situation than trapped between two separate enemy forces with more long-range firepower than it could muster. No tactical doctrine could have nullified those disadvantages, but although Second Fleet's offensive firepower had been all but destroyed, he was astonished by how many of its ships still survived. They could no longer realistically hope to damage the enemy, but as long as they held together, they could continue to defend one another against the storm of destruction beating upon them. And if his single remaining SD(P) was running low on ammunition, then surely Harrington's SD(P)s had to be doing the same thing. Maybe he could outlast her firepower after all.

"Our magazines are down to twenty percent," Alistair McKeon told Honor from her com screen. His face was grim, and Honor knew from the sidebars in her plot that *Troubadour* had taken serious damage and heavy casualties. But McKeon's flagship was still in action, still rolling pods, and whatever had happened to Honor's command, what had happened to the Havenites was worse.

"The older SDs are in better shape on a percentage basis," he went on, "but they can't pump the kinds of broadsides the SD(P)s can. We've got maybe another fifteen minutes. After that, we'll be down to salvos too light to penetrate that damned defense of theirs from this range."

"Alistair's right, Honor," Alice Truman said from her own screen. "And my LACs can't catch them from here. Not before they make it across the limit. Alfredo's could intercept, but we can't support them."

Honor nodded—not in agreement, but in acknowledgment of unpalatable reality. She'd sprung her trap perfectly and savaged the Havenites brutally. Her own losses were painful, but only a fraction of what she'd done to them, and she knew it. But even so, almost half of the enemy fleet was going to escape. They'd held together with too much discipline, and their missile defense doctrine had proven too hard a nut to crack without more MDM firepower then she had. And even if her LACs had been able to intercept, she knew what would happen if she committed them against the close-in defenses which had so badly blunted her missile attack.

Which was the reason she couldn't possibly commit Alfredo's LACs to an unsupported attack.

"You're right—both of you," she said after a moment. She looked back at her plot, where only a handful of missiles continued to launch from the shattered ranks of the Havenite fleet. The enemy was decisively routed and broken, but even though every bone in her body longed to run the survivors down and complete their destruction, she knew she couldn't do it.

"We'll continue the pursuit." Her soprano was calm, giving no more hint of her intense frustration than it did of the pain of her own losses. "Alistair, I want you to reprioritize our missile fire. We're not going to be able to hammer our way through those defenses by saturating them, so I want you to slow your rate of fire and pick your targets carefully. Use delayed activation launches to thicken your broadsides while the pods last and try to concentrate on SDs with undamaged impellers. If we can slow some more of them down, our older ships of the wall can take them out as we overhaul, or else we can commit Alice's LACs to deal with them as we go by."

"Yes, Ma'am," McKeon acknowledged.

"Alice, I know you're frustrated by not getting your LACs into this yet," Honor went on, "but at least half a dozen of those Havenite ships are going to be too slow and too beat up to get away from you. When you're free to commit to go in after them, I want you to be sure to offer them the chance to surrender first. They're a long way from home and badly hurt, and I don't want to kill anyone who wants to give up."

"Of course," Truman agreed.

"Very well then." Honor sat back in her command chair and nodded to both of her senior subordinates. "Harper will pass similar instructions to Alfredo. In the meantime, we have a battle to finish up. So let's be about it, People."

CHAPTER FIFTY-NINE

The planet of Manticore was a blue-and-white-swirled beauty as the pinnace from GSNS *Seneca Gilmore* swooped into its outermost atmosphere. Admiral Lady Dame Honor Harrington, Duchess and Steadholder Harrington, sat in its large passenger compartment, alone but for her three-man security team, and watched the seas of featureless white turn into fluffy, wind-textured billows of cloud as the pinnace swept lower and lower towards the City of Landing.

It was a short flight, the last leg of the journey home from Sidemore which had begun two weeks earlier when the Protectors' Own was finally recalled to Grayson by way of Manticore, and she sat very still, feeling the emptiness and the tension within her as the pinnace banked gracefully onto its final heading and settled towards the private landing pad behind Mount Royal Palace.

Queen Elizabeth had wanted to welcome Honor home in the manner in which she insisted Honor deserved to be welcomed, but Honor had managed to avoid that ordeal, at least. It was already obvious to her that there would be other ordeals, just as public and just as exhausting, which she would not be able to avoid. She'd seen the HD of the cheering crowds, celebrating wildly in the capital's streets when news of the Second Battle of Sidemore was announced, and she dreaded what would happen when those same crowds learned "the Salamander" was home. But in this instance, her monarch—well, one of her monarchs, she supposed—had agreed to relent, and so there was no huge honor guard, no crowd of newsies, to observe her arrival once again upon the soil of her birth-kingdom's capital planet.

There was a greeting party, however. One that consisted of four humans and three treecats. Queen Elizabeth herself and her consort, Prince Justin, headed the small group of two-footed people awaiting her. Ariel rode on Elizabeth's left shoulder, while Monroe rode on Justin's right shoulder. Behind them stood Lord William Alexander and his brother, the Earl of White Haven, with Samantha standing high and proud on his shoulder, eyes glowing as she tasted the mind-glow of her mate for the first time in far too long. Colonel Ellen Shemais stood alertly to one side, overseeing the small squad of Palace Security and Queen's Own personnel guarding the perimeter of the landing pad, but that was their only function here. There were no bands, no flourishes and salutes. There were only seven people, friends all of them, waiting for her as she came home once more.

"Honor." Elizabeth held out a hand to her, and Honor took it, only to find herself enveloped in a fierce hug. Five or six T-years before, she wouldn't have had a clue how to respond to her Queen's embrace. Now she simply returned it, tasting the equally fierce welcome which came with it.

Other emotions washed over her, flooding through her as she, too, sampled the mind-glows of those about her. Samantha's spiraling joy and delight as she rose still higher on White Haven's shoulder and began signing to Nimitz in joyous welcome. Prince Justin, as glad to see her, in his own way, as Elizabeth, and William Alexander, her friend, political mentor, and ally.

And then there was Hamish. Hamish, standing there, looking at her with his soul in those ice-blue eyes from the heart of a firestorm of welcome and joy that turned even Elizabeth's into a candle's glow by comparison. She felt herself reaching out to him—not physically, not moving as much as a centimeter in his direction, yet with all of the irresistible power of a stellar gravity well. And as she looked into his eyes over the Queen of Manticore's shoulder, she saw the echo of that same reaching out. Not with the same sharpness or acuity as her own empathy. Not even with any conscious recognition of what it was he felt. It was . . . blinder than that, and she suddenly realized it must be what treecats saw when they looked at their mind-blind people. A sense of a presence that was asleep. Unaware yet immensely powerful and somehow linked to them. Yet not totally unaware. He had no idea what he was feeling, yet he felt it anyway, and a part of him knew he did. She tasted that confused, groping sensitivity in the sudden flare of his mind-glow, and saw Samantha stop signing to Nimitz and turn to stare in wonder at her person.

Honor had never felt anything quite like it. In some ways, it was like her link to Nimitz, but weaker, without the strength anchored by a treecat's full-blown empathic sense. And yet, it was also far stronger, for its other end was not a treecat, but another human mind. One that matched her own. That . . . fitted on levels that hers and Nimitz's would never be able to fully share. There was no "telepathy," no sharing of thoughts. Yet she felt him there, in the back of her brain as he had already been in her heart. The other part of her. The welcoming fire ready to warm her on the coldest night.

And with it the knowledge that whatever else might have happened, the impassable barriers which held them apart still stood.

"It's good to see you home," Elizabeth told her, her voice slightly husky, as she stood back, still holding Honor's upper arms, and looked up into her face. "It's very good."

"It's good to be here," Honor replied simply, still tasting Hamish, still feeling his amazement as the echo of her awareness flowed through him, however faintly, as well.

"Come inside," Elizabeth urged. "We have a lot to talk about."

"—so as soon as word came in about Grendelsbane, High Ridge had no choice but to resign," Elizabeth said grimly.

Honor nodded, her own expression equally grim. She, her hostess, and Elizabeth's other guests all sat in deep, old-fashioned, comfortable chairs in Elizabeth's private retreat in King Michael's Tower. It was a welcoming, cheerful room, but Honor could taste the tangled flow of conflicting emotions deep inside Elizabeth. Emotions which stood in stark contrast to their surroundings.

Horror and dismay over the disastrous defeat the Navy had suffered at Grendelsbane. An awareness of how brutally the Fleet's strength had been wounded that terrified even the woman treecats called "Soul of Steel," especially in light of what the new Director of the Office of Naval Intelligence had reported about the probable strength of the Republican Navy. And mingled with all of that, the savage, vengeful joy she'd felt when the merciless requirements of formal protocol ground High Ridge's face into the totality of his ruin and disgrace as he surrendered his office.

"Is it true about Janacek?" she asked quietly, and it was White Haven's turn to nod.

"According to the Landing Police, there's no question but that it was suicide," he confirmed.

"Not that very many people were prepared to accept that in the immediate aftermath," his brother added with a harsh snort. "He knew where an awful lot of the bodies were buried, and quite a few people found it suspiciously . . . convenient that he should decide to blow his own brains out."

"Descroix?" Honor asked.

"We're not sure," Elizabeth admitted. "She tendered her resignation along with High Ridge, of course. And then, a couple of days later, she headed out to Beowulf on one of the day excursion ships . . . and didn't come back. From the looks of things, there was no foul play involved, unless it was her own. I think she planned on not coming back, although at this point no one has the least idea where she may have headed. All we know for sure it is that she transferred about twenty million dollars through a numbered DNA account on Beowulf to another account in the Stotterman System." The Queen grimaced. "You know what the Stotterman banking laws are like. It's going to take us at least ten or twelve T-years to get access to their records."

"Where did the money come from?" Honor wondered.

"We're working on that one from our end, Your Grace," Colonel Shemais put in diffidently. "So far, we don't have any definite leads, but there are a couple of at least slightly promising avenues for us to follow up. If we find what I expect to, we may be able to break Stotterman open a little sooner. They are part of the Solarian League, after all, and Sollie banking regulations are pretty specific about cooperating with embezzlement and malfeasance investigations."

"And New Kiev?" Honor asked, and blinked in surprise as Elizabeth laughed out loud.

"Countess New Kiev," the Queen said after a moment, "has . . . retired from politics. It might be more appropriate to say that she was fired, actually. Your friend Cathy Montaigne led something of a *coup d'état* within the Liberal Party leadership."

"She did?" Honor couldn't keep the delight out of her response, even though she hadn't been aware that Elizabeth even suspected that she herself had been in contact with Montaigne and Anton Zilwicki.

"She certainly did," William Alexander replied with a grin. "Actually, the Liberal Party as we've known it doesn't really exist anymore. Things are still in the process of working their way out, but when the dust settles, it looks like there are going to be two separate political parties, each calling themselves the Liberal some-things. One is going to be a substantial majority of the old Liberal Party, centered in the Commons behind Montaigne's leadership. The other's going to be a rump of diehard ideologists who refuse to admit how completely they were used by High Ridge. They're probably going to be concentrated in the Lords . . . since the only way someone that out of touch with reality could possibly survive as a political figure is by inheriting his seat."

"North Hollow is also lying conspicuously low just now," White Haven put in, and Shemais chuckled nastily. Honor cocked an eyebrow at her, and the colonel smiled.

"One of the more interesting consequences of the destruction of the 'North Hollow Files'—I mean, one of the consequences of the ridiculous assertion that something which never existed, like the *so-called* 'North Hollow Files,' had been theoretically destroyed—is that quite a few people seem to want to discuss certain concerns with Earl North Hollow. It's almost as if he'd had some sort of hold over them and now that it's gone, well . . ." She shrugged, and Honor found it very difficult not to smile as she tasted the colonel's vengeful delight. A delight, she admitted, which she shared to the full.

"So now that High Ridge and his cronies are gone, who's running the Star Kingdom?" she asked after a moment. "Besides Willie, I mean." She grinned. "The dispatch boat that delivered my recall orders also brought the 'fax stories about High Ridge's resignation and the fact that you'd asked Willie to form a government, Elizabeth. But they were short on details."

"Well," Elizabeth replied, leaning back in her armchair, "Willie's Prime Minister, of course. And we've brought back Baroness Mourncreek—except that I've decided to create a new peerage for her and make her a countess—as Chancellor of the Exchequer. We've brought in Abraham Spencer to run the Ministry of Trade for us, and I've convinced Dame Estelle Matsuko to take over the Home Office. Given the state High Ridge and that idiot Descroix managed to let the entire Manticoran Alliance get into—it's confirmed, by the way, that Erewhon has definitely signed a mutual defense treaty with the Peeps—Willie and I figured we needed someone the smaller members of the Alliance would trust as Foreign Secretary, so we asked Sir Anthony Langtry to take over there."

"I see." Honor cocked her head to one side and frowned at the Queen. "Excuse me, Elizabeth, but if you've asked Francine to take over at the Exchequer, who's going to be running the Admiralty?"

"Interesting that you should ask," Elizabeth said around a bubble of treecat-like delight. "I knew I'd need someone particularly reliable to dig out the unholy mess Janacek and those idiots Houseman and Jurgensen left in their wake. So I turned to the one person I knew Willie and I could absolutely rely on." She nodded at Hamish. "Allow me to introduce you to First Lord of the Admiralty White Haven."

Honor's head whipped around in astonishment, and White Haven smiled crookedly. It was a very ambivalent smile, and it matched the taste of his emotions perfectly.

"Actually," Elizabeth said much more seriously, "it was a hard call to make. God knows that taking Hamish out of a fleet command position at a time like this wasn't anything that I wanted to do. But it would be impossible to exaggerate the gravity of the wreckage Janacek left behind." She shook her head, her eyes now completely grim. "That son-of-a-bitch is damned lucky he committed suicide before I got my hands on him. I could probably have made a case for treason out of the way he mishandled his responsibilities and duties. ONI was the worst, and at the very least Jurgensen is going to be dismissed from the service as unfit to wear the Queen's uniform. There may well be criminal charges, as well, once the full story comes out, although I hope we can avoid witch hunts for the 'guilty men.' I fully intend to see those responsible for the unmitigated disaster of our present position punished, one way or another, but Justin—and Willie, not to mention Aunt Caitrin—have lectured me very firmly on the absolute necessity of administering justice evenhandedly and fairly. No star chambers, and no twisting of the law. Anything I can nail them for legitimately, yes, damned straight I will. But if I can't, then the bastards walk."

She brooded darkly for a moment, then shook herself.

"At any rate," she went on more briskly, "just as Willie and I agreed that we needed someone we could trust at the Exchequer and someone our alliance partners could trust at the Foreign Office, we desperately needed someone at the Admiralty who both the governments and navies of all our alliance partners could trust. As a matter of fact, we decided that was especially important because we're both confident that we're only just beginning to fully understand the damage Janacek managed to do. There are going to be still more public revelations that won't do a thing for public confidence in the integrity of the Navy—or its war-fighting ability, for that matter—and that made it absolutely imperative to put a face people could feel comfortable trusting on the Admiralty. Since *you* weren't available," the Queen smiled wickedly at Honor's expression, "we drafted Hamish."

"And working on the same principle that it's vital to restore confidence in the Admiralty," White Haven put in, "I've brought Tom Caparelli back as First Space Lord as well as bringing Pat Givens back in as Second Space Lord. And," his wry grin became absolutely astringent, "Sonja Hemphill to run BuWeaps."

Honor was hard put not to goggle at his last sentence, and he chuckled.

"I expect there to be the occasional, um . . . clash of personalities," he acknowledged. "But I think it's time Sonja and I put our silly feuds behind us. As you pointed out to me once, the mere fact that she's the one who had an idea doesn't automatically mean it's a bad one. And one thing we're going to need badly in the immediate future is as many good ideas as we can get."

"I'm afraid that's true," Honor admitted sadly. She leaned further back in her chair and sighed. "I'm still trying to come to grips with it all. It's like that old Pre Diaspora children's book—the one about wonderland. I can understand, in a way, what happened to us here, domestically. But the rest of it . . ." She shook her head. "I've *met* Thomas Theisman. I just can't understand how this all happened!"

"It happened because they're Peeps," Elizabeth said, and Honor felt a sudden stab of alarm at the cold, bottomless hatred that flowed through the Queen in the wake of her bleak reply.

"Elizabeth," Honor began, "I understand how you feel. But—"

"Don't, Honor!" Elizabeth said sharply. She started to say something else, quickly and angrily, then made herself stop. She drew a deep breath, and when she spoke again, Honor didn't need her own empathic sense to recognize the effort the Queen made to keep her voice calm and reasonable.

"I know that you personally admire Thomas Theisman, Honor," Elizabeth said. "In an intellectual way, I can even understand that. And I fully realize that you have certain . . . advantages when it comes to assessing someone's motivations and sincerity. But in this instance, you're wrong."

She met Honor's eyes levelly, and her own eyes were like flint. In that instant, Honor recognized how completely accurate her treecat name truly was, for she tasted the unyielding steel in the Queen of Manticore's soul.

"I will go as far as acknowledging that Theisman, as an individual, may be an honest and an upright human being. I will certainly acknowledge his personal courage, and his dedication to his own star nation. But the fact remains that the so-called 'Republic of Haven' has cold-bloodedly, systematically lied with a cynical audacity that not even Oscar Saint-Just could have matched. From Pritchart and Giancola on down—*including* your friend Theisman—without a single voice raised in dissent, their entire government has presented the same distorted, deceitful face to the entire galaxy. They've *lied*, Honor. Lied to their own people, to our people, and to the Solarian League. God knows that I could sympathize with *anyone* who was as systematically used and abused as the Peeps were by High Ridge and Descroix! I don't *blame* them for being angry and wanting revenge. But this 'diplomatic correspondence' they've published—!"

Elizabeth made herself stop and draw another deep breath.

"We have the originals of their correspondence in our own files, Honor. I can show you exactly where they made deletions and alterations—not just in their own notes, but in ours. It's too consistent, too all pervasive, to have been anything but a deliberate plot. Something they spent literally months putting into place to justify the attack they launched against us. They're busy telling the rest of the galaxy that we *forced* them to do this. That they had no intention of using this new navy they've built up in some sort of war of revenge until we left them no choice. But not even

High Ridge did the things they say he did. They invented the entire crisis out of whole cloth. And what that tells me is that Peeps . . . don't . . . change."

She gritted her teeth and shook her head fiercely, like a wounded animal.

"They murdered my father," she said flatly. "Their agents here in the Star Kingdom tried to murder Justin. They murdered my uncle, my cousin, my Prime Minister, and Grayson's Chancellor. They tried to murder me, my aunt, and Benjamin Mayhew. God only knows how many men and women in *my* Navy they've butchered in this new war already, not to mention all the people they killed in the last one. It doesn't seem to matter how good or honest or well-intentioned anyone who comes to power in that cesspool of a nation may be. Once they do, something about the way power works in Haven turns them into exactly what came before them. Peeps. They can call themselves whatever they want, Honor, but they're still *Peeps*. And there's only one way in the universe that there will ever finally be peace between this Star Kingdom and them."

Later that same evening, Honor found herself once again in the dining room of the White Haven family seat. In some respects, it was even harder on her than her first visit had been.

There were no pretenses now, and she was grateful for that, at least. The painful truths had been spoken. There were no more masks, no more attempts at self-deception or refusal to face reality. And there was no anger, for this had gone beyond anger. But the jagged edges remained. She had yet to even begin to explore the new bond, her new awareness of Hamish, nor had she had any opportunity to discuss it with him. But, wonderful as it was, she already recognized its potential to make the pain infinitely worse. She knew herself well enough to know she could not feel what she felt and refuse to act upon it. Not for very long. And with a new certainty, and ability to see even more deeply and clearly into Hamish Alexander's soul, she knew that he couldn't, either.

If there had been any way in the world to refuse tonight's dinner invitation without wounding Emily, Honor would have done it. She couldn't be here. She didn't know where she *could* be, but she knew it wasn't here. Yet she'd had no choice but to come, and she and Hamish had done their level best to act completely normally.

She was quite certain she'd failed, but for the first time in years, however hard she tried, her own empathic sense had failed her. She couldn't sample Emily Alexander's emotions for the simple reason that she could not separate herself from those of Emily's *husband*. Not yet. It would take time, she knew—lots of time, and matching amounts of effort—for her to learn to tune down and control this new awareness. She could do it. If she had enough time, enough peace to work at it, she could learn to control its "volume" just as she had finally learned to control the sensitivity of her original empathic awareness. But for now, the blinding power of her bond to Hamish was still growing, still gaining in power, and until she could learn to control it, its power and vibrancy would drown out the mind-glow of anyone else as long as he was present. And she couldn't do it yet. She couldn't disengage herself from the glowing background hum of Hamish, and she felt oddly blinded, almost maimed, by her inability to reach out to Emily.

"—so, yes, Honor," Emily was saying in response to Honor's last attempt to keep something like a normal dinner table conversation moving, "I'm afraid Elizabeth is entirely serious. And to be honest, I don't know if I blame her for her attitude."

"Willie certainly doesn't," Hamish put in. He handed Samantha another stick of celery, and she took it with dainty, delicate grace. Even without that maddeningly glorious link with Hamish, Honor would have recognized the ease and familiarity into which their adoption bond had blossomed.

"I suppose I can understand it, myself," Honor admitted with a troubled expression. "It's just that she's painting with such a broad brush. She's lumping Sidney Harris, Rob Pierre, Oscar Saint-Just, and Thomas Theisman into the same group, and I'm telling you, there is no way in the universe that Theisman belongs in that same category."

"But what about this Pritchart?" Hamish asked in a tone of reasonable challenge. "You've never met her, and she *is* their President. Not to mention having been some sort of terrorist before the Pierre Coup. What if she's the one driving it all and Theisman is just going along? From all you told me about him, he sounds like someone who would do his duty and obey duly constituted authority whatever his personal feelings."

"Hamish," Honor said, "this is the man who overthrew State

Security, probably shot Saint-Just personally, single-handedly convinced Capital Fleet to support him, called a constitutional convention, turned power over to the first duly elected President of the star nation whose constitution he had personally rescued from the dust bin, and then spent the better part of four T-years fighting a six or seven-cornered civil war in order to defend that constitution." She shook her head. "That's not the description of a man who's a weakling. And a man who would do all of that because he believes in the principles the old Republic of Haven's constitution enshrined, is not a man who's going to stand by and watch someone else grossly abuse power."

"Put that way, Hamish," Emily said slowly, "Honor certainly seems to have a point."

"Of course she does," White Haven said a bit testily. "And as far as I'm aware, she's the only person in the 'inner circle,' as it were, who's ever personally met the man. Not to mention the . . . special insight she has into people. I'm not trying to discount anything she's said. But the central, unpalatable fact remains. Why ever he did it, he's publicly signed off on the Pritchart version of the negotiating process." He shrugged. "Honor, he hasn't simply said that he's 'following orders' because Pritchart is his President, or even because he believes what she's told him. He's publicly on record as having *seen* diplomatic correspondence which we know for a fact didn't exist."

He shook his head, and Honor sighed and nodded in unhappy acknowledgment of his point. She still couldn't believe it, not of the Thomas Theisman she'd met. And yet, there it was. Whether she could believe it or not, it had happened. And God knew people often changed. It was just that she couldn't imagine what sort of process could have so completely warped the internal steel of the man she'd known in so short of time.

"Well, whatever is going on there," she said, "how bad is it, really, on the military front? And can we really afford to have you sitting in a dirtside office as First Lord instead of in a fleet command? I'm supposed to visit the Admiralty tomorrow afternoon for a formal briefing from Admiral Givens, but the bits and pieces I've already heard aren't very encouraging."

"I suppose that's one way to put it," White Haven said grimly. He reached for his wineglass and sipped deeply, then put it down and leaned back in his chair.

"As far as where we can 'afford' for me to be, I don't see any alternative to my taking on the Admiralty. I don't want to, but someone has to do it, and Elizabeth and Willy are right about how important is it for that someone to be a person the entire Alliance trusts. Which, for our sins, means either me or you. And, to be perfectly honest about it, it makes a lot more sense for it to be me. So I suppose—" he smiled crookedly at her "—that this war is going to be yours, Honor. Not mine.

"As for how bad the situation is, High Ridge and Janacek between them, with more than a little help from Reginald Houseman, managed to do even more damage than we'd guessed. Of course, what happened when the Peeps hit us made it far worse, but if they hadn't set us up for the blow, our backs wouldn't be so firmly against the wall.

"Basically, we've lost in excess of twenty-six hundred LACs, seventy cruisers and light cruisers, forty-one battlecruisers, and sixty-one superdreadnoughts." Honor inhaled sharply as he listed the figures. "None of which includes all of the ships which were currently under construction at Grendelsbane, or the construction personnel we lost there and in half a dozen minor repair facilities scattered around what were occupied Peep star systems. And we've lost," he finished in a granite voice, "every single system we'd taken away from them—with the sole exception of Trevor's Star—since the war started. We're back where we were strategically on Day One, aside from controlling all of the Junction termini, and proportionately, we're much weaker now compared to the Peep navy than we were before the Battle of Hancock."

Honor gazed at him in dismay, and he shrugged.

"It's not *all* doom and gloom, Honor," he told her. "First of all, thank God for Grayson! Not only did they save our asses at Trevor's Star and help bail you out at Sidemore, but they constitute the only true strategic reserve the Alliance has. Especially now that Erewhon has effectively gone over to the Peeps." He glowered again. "Erewhon didn't have the full Ghost Rider tech package, or the beta-squared nodes, or the LAC fission plants, but they had just about everything else . . . including the newest compensator version *and* the latest grav-pulse transmitters. When Foraker gets her hands on that and starts reverse-engineering it, we're going to be in an even worse mess than we are now.

"Maybe even worse than that, though, Pat has been engaged in a massive reevaluation of ONI's files, cross-indexed with information Greg Paxton has made available, and she's come up with some possible ballpark figures for what the Peeps may still have in reserve. I'm inclined to think that she's probably overestimating their capabilities, which would be a natural enough reaction to how badly we were surprised by what they hit us with. On the other hand, I've seen her basic analysis, and it certainly doesn't seem to me that she's being alarmist in the way she approaches it. So it may be that she's right. But if she is, then the Peeps have a minimum of another three hundred of the wall currently under construction. A *minimum*, Honor. That's at a time when Grayson has just under a hundred SD(P)s, and we're all the way up to seventy-three. Since we seem to have observed damned close to two hundred of them in action *exclusive* of the ones they sent to Sidemore, we're looking at what might conservatively be called an unfavorable balance of forces."

Honor had felt her face become stiff and drawn as the figures rolled over her. She'd already had first-hand experience of how effectively the Republic was using its new ships and hardware. Now she had a sense for the sheer size and mass of the juggernaut which had been assembled to smash the Alliance.

"We're not dead yet, Honor," Hamish told her almost gently, and she shook her head as if she could physically banish her sense of doom.

"What do you mean?" she asked after a moment.

"First of all, what you managed to accomplish at Sidemore seems to have had a profound impact on their thinking. Obviously, they don't know exactly what happened yet—it's going to take their commander on the spot a lot longer to get home, since he can't use the Junction. But they know they got reamed, if only from news reports of what we've already announced. Willie and I have discussed it with Elizabeth, and we're going to go ahead and announce their loss figures officially tomorrow morning, as well. I doubt that we're going to really astonish anyone, after the rumors have already been flying for so long. But when we confirm that you managed to destroy well over half of their attack force and damage most of the rest of it, I think it will give them even more pause. Not to mention what it's already done for our own civilian— hell, not just civilian!—for our civilian *and* military morale. What you pulled off out there is the only really bright spot in this entire disaster."

"What about what you and Niall managed at Trevor's Star?" she challenged.

"What we managed there was a negative event," he replied. She started to say something else, and he shook his head. "I'm not trying to be falsely modest, Honor. And I'm not trying to downplay what we accomplished, or to pretend that the public as a whole and the San Martinos in particular don't realize that what we staved off would have turned the Peep offensive into a total and complete disaster for the Alliance. But the fact remains that the fleet *we* had a shot at escaped intact, with nothing worse than the loss of a few LACs. The fleet that *you* had a shot at didn't just retreat—it was *destroyed*. I'm prepared to admit that in a strategic sense Sidemore is infinitely less vital to the Star Kingdom than Trevor's Star, and even that the ships they committed to the attack there seem to have included a higher percentage of obsolescent types which, in the final analysis, they could afford to lose much more readily than they could have afforded to lose the ships they committed to Trevor's Star. All of that may be true, but it's also beside the point.

"Given the increases in their technical capabilities, especially now that Erewhon is on their side of the line, the moral ascendancy we established before the cease-fire is even more vitally important. Frankly, they've just demonstrated that we don't have a right to that ascendancy any longer, but they may not realize it. For that matter, *our* people may not realize it . . . if we're lucky. The fact that you defeated them so decisively in the one place where effectively equal forces stood and fought is what we want them to remember. It's what we want our own people to remember, too, but it's even more important where the Peeps are concerned.

"The fact that they refused to engage at roughly equal odds at Trevor's Star is also going to loom in their thinking, I hope, of course. But that refusal takes on an entirely new light in the wake of what happened at Sidemore. Now it could be seen not simply as prudence—which, between you and me, is precisely what it actually was—so much as cowardice. Or, at least, an admission of their continued inability to meet us on equal terms."

"I suppose I can follow your argument," Honor said a bit dubiously. "It all seems very thin to me, though."

"Oh, it's certainly that," White Haven agreed with feeling. "But there's a second string to our bow, as well. And, to be honest, you created the preconditions for it, as well."

"I did? And what sort of 'second string' are you talking about?"

"Sir Anthony has already been in touch with the Andermani," White Haven told her. "Given the Gregor terminus, we can communicate back and forth with New Berlin faster than the Havenite fleet could retreat from Trevor's Star to the Haven System, and Willie and Elizabeth didn't lose any time taking advantage of that.

"The Andermani are as shocked by what happened as we were. No one outside the Republic of Haven so much as guessed this was coming, or would have believed how completely their initial offensive would succeed even if they'd seen it coming. The Andermani certainly never anticipated anything like it. And, to be honest, I think it frightened them. Badly, in fact. You know how little Emperor Gustav trusts 'Republican' forms of government in the first place. I think that predisposed him to believe our side when we explained that Pritchart and Giancola manufactured the diplomatic correspondence they're busy publishing to the galaxy. In addition, he's admitted to us that Pritchart deliberately encouraged them to pursue an aggressive policy in Silesia at the same time she was turning up the heat on us at the truce negotiations. My impression from what Willie's said is that the Peeps' obvious willingness to use the Empire as one more cat's paw in what was obviously a very carefully planned policy of deception has had a profound effect on the Emperor's view of the galactic balance of power.

"At any rate, it looks very much as if the Andermani Navy is about to come in on our side."

Honor stared at him in disbelief.

"Hamish, we were *shooting* at each other less than two months ago!" she protested.

"And your point is?" he asked, and chortled at her expression. Then he sobered. "Honor, 'realpolitik' is the guiding deity of the Anderman Dynasty. What Gustav Anderman is seeing right this minute is that the Peeps are unpredictable, that they attempted to use him, and that they're lying to the entire galaxy. Oh, and that they once again have the biggest Navy this side of the Solarian League." He shrugged. "On that basis, they're obviously a much greater danger to him than we are. Remember, the Andermani never really thought of us as a threat to their own security. What they resented was our interference in their efforts to secure what they regarded as their 'natural frontiers' in Silesia. *Everybody*, on the other hand, regarded the old People's Republic as a threat. And now that the new Republic has demonstrated that it has the same leopard spots as the old one, the Andermani see it in very much the same light.

"So since they never had anything personally against us in the first place, they're suddenly much more receptive to the notion that their enemy's enemy is their friend. Especially when Willie and Elizabeth agreed to sweeten the pot just a bit."

"How?" Honor asked, regarding him suspiciously now, rather than disbelievingly.

"With a little *realpolitik* of our own," White Haven told her. "The Conservative Association and the Liberal Party are effectively nonexistent at the moment. You haven't been to the Lords recently, so you can't begin to appreciate just how completely the entire Parliament is supporting Willie's new government right now. To give you some idea, the Lords have already agreed to take up a bill to transfer the power of the purse to the Commons over a five-T-year transition period. Unless something very drastic happens, it will be passed on third reading next week."

Honor was too astonished even to speak, and he shrugged.

"I know. Stupid, isn't it? The very issue that High Ridge was able to ride into power. The huge political bogeyman the entire peerage was so terrified of that a majority of them actually signed off on High Ridge's manipulations and dirty little deals. And now, in less than a month from the time shooting resumes, something on the order of an eighty percent majority is prepared to give it all up. If the stupid bastards had just been willing to consider making the same concession three years ago, *none* of this would've happened. Or, at least, if it had, it would've happened in a way which would have deprived Pritchart of the fig leaf of justification she's manufactured.

"But as far as the Andermani are concerned, the Lords' support for domestic finance reform is beside the point. What's going to bring the Empire in on our side is the fact that all of that ideological resistance to anything smacking of 'imperialism' went down the toilet along with High Ridge and New Kiev. Something like it would probably have materialized again soon enough, except for the fact that it's not going to have the chance to. Because later this week, Willie is going to propose to a joint session of Parliament that the Star Kingdom and the Andermani Empire finally bring an end to the incessant bloodletting and atrocities in Silesia."

"Oh, my God. You can't be serious!"

"Of course I can. I don't say it would have been my first choice of how to proceed, but I certainly understand the logic. And the Peeps haven't left us very much choice, either. We *need* the Andies to survive, Honor, and their price is the extension of their frontier into Silesia." He shrugged. "Well, if we're going to be in for a penny, we may as well be in for a dollar."

"And if the Confederacy government objects to being partitioned between two foreign powers?" Honor demanded.

"You've been to Silesia more than most of our officers," White Haven said. "Do you really think the average Silly wouldn't actively prefer to be a Manticoran subject?"

Honor started to reply quickly, then stopped. He had a point. All the average Silesian really wanted was safety, order, and a government that actually considered her wishes and well-being rather than seeing her as one more potential source of graft and corruption.

"Whatever the average Silly wants, the Confed government may not see things quite the same way," she pointed out.

"The Confed government consists of a bunch of corrupt, self-seeking, moneygrubbing grifters, thieves, and conmen whose concerns begin and end with their own bank accounts," White Haven said flatly. "For God's sake, Honor! You know perfectly well that the government of the Silesian Confederacy is probably the only bunch of crooks who could actually make High Ridge and Descroix look good by comparison."

Despite her grave reservations, Honor's lips quivered in appreciation of White Haven's comparison.

"Willie and Sir Anthony are already in the process of coming up with what's going to amount to a massive bribe," he went on with an expression of distaste. "Together with Gustav, they're going to buy the existing government off. Most of its members will do very well out of the deal. But the hook they don't know about is that we're going to be serious about requiring them to obey the law afterward. We may pay them off now and effectively amnesty them for past crimes, but we'll come down on them like the

Hammer of God the first time they try to go back to business as usual under new management." He shrugged. "I'm not too sure how I feel about the methodology, but the final outcome is going to be that we get an ally we desperately need, a problem which has been a source of tension between us and the Empire for the last sixty or seventy T-years gets resolved once and for all, and—maybe most important of all—we finally bring an end to a situation which has been costing literally hundreds of thousands of lives every single year in Silesia."

"And along the way, we become the Star *Empire* of Manticore," Honor replied with a troubled expression.

"I don't see that we have any choice," White Haven said. "And what with Trevor's Star and the Talbott Cluster, we're already moving in that direction."

"I suppose so," Honor said pensively. "I guess maybe what worries me the most about it is that it could be seen as validating the Republic's charges that we were already expansionist. That that's the reason High Ridge never had any intention of negotiating with them in good faith for the return of the occupied systems."

"That's my greatest concern, too," Emily put in, then moved her right hand in the gesture she used for a shrug as Honor and White Haven both looked at her. "Interstellar relations are so often a matter of perceptions rather than realities," she said. "If the Republic is trying to convince someone else—like the Sollies—that we're the villains of the piece, then this could play straight into their hands. They'll treat it as proof that we were expansionist all along, exactly as Honor has just suggested they will, and that in effect they had no choice but to attack us in self-defense."

"You may be right," her husband said after a few moments' thought. "Unfortunately, I don't think it changes the imperatives Willie and Elizabeth have to deal with. The bottom line, again, is that we have to have the Andie fleet if we're going to survive. There's not much point in worrying about anything else if we don't do that, after all. If we do," he shrugged, "then we can worry about other PR problems then."

Honor sat back in her chair, gazing at him intently, and then, finally, nodded. Her reservations hadn't disappeared, but as Hamish said, the imperatives of survival trumped them.

"Well," Emily said into the brief silence which followed, "I think that's quite enough politics for tonight."

"More than enough, as far as I'm concerned," White Haven agreed with a sour chuckle. "Your autocratic, aristocratic, stiff-necked, politics-hating husband is going to be up to his neck in them for the foreseeable future. I'm sure we'll be spending all too many nights discussing the entire depressing topic over dinner."

"That's as may be," she replied serenely, then smiled ever so slightly. "Actually, it should be rather interesting. You may not like politics, but that doesn't mean I don't, my dear!"

"I know," he said glumly. "In fact, that's about the only con-solation I see."

"Oh, come now!" she scolded. "There's always Samantha, you know. I'm sure she'll be happy to bring her perspective to bear on your political problems."

"That's all we'd need!" Honor laughed. "I've spent decades trying to explain two-leg-style politics to Stinker here." She reached out and tugged on one of Nimitz's ears, and he swatted her wrist with a true-hand. "I can hardly wait to see what Her Nibs would have to say about them!"

"You might be pleasantly surprised, my dear," Emily told her. "In fact, Samantha and I have been having long and fascinating con-versations about the differences between the People and us two-legs."

"You have?" Honor looked at her with interest.

"Oh, yes." Emily laughed quietly. "Fortunately, I only had to learn how to read her signs. She understood me just fine when I spoke to her, which was a good thing, since it would be just a little difficult to sign with only one hand. But poor Hamish has been so busy, what with one thing and another, that Samantha and I have had an opportunity for some uninterrupted 'girl talk' behind his back. It's amazing what . . . acute observations she had to make about him."

" 'Observations,' is it?" Hamish regarded her suspiciously.

"No one's telling tales out of school, dear," Emily reassured him. "On the other hand, Samantha did have several interesting pithy observations on the thickheadedness of humans in general."

"What sort of observations?" Honor asked.

"Largely on the inevitable differences between a race of empathic telepaths and a race which is 'mind-blind,' " Emily replied in a voice which was suddenly considerably more serious. "In fact," she went on quietly, "one of her most telling comments, I thought, was that by treecat standards, it's insane for two people not to admit what they feel for one another."

Honor froze in her chair, stunned by the totally unanticipated direction Emily had abruptly taken the conversation. She wanted to dart a glance at Hamish, but she couldn't. All she could do was stare at Emily.

"The societies are quite different, of course," Emily continued, "so it's inevitable that there shouldn't be a direct point-to-point correspondence between them. But the more she and I spoke about it, the more I came to see why a race of empaths would feel that way. They're right, you know. It's worse than just senseless for two people who love each other deeply, and who have no desire or intention to hurt anyone else, to condemn themselves to so much suffering and such bitter unhappiness just because two-leg society is mind-blind. That's not just foolish, it's insane. And the fact that the two people involved are doing it to themselves because they're such splendid and responsible human beings that they would rather suffer themselves than risk the possibility of hurting someone else doesn't make it any less insane. It may make them both people to be deeply admired... and trusted. But if they really thought about it, perhaps they would realize that the person whose pain they're trying to spare knows how much pain they're causing themselves. And perhaps, you know, she wouldn't want them to be hurt any more than they want *her* to be. And so, if they were treecats instead of humans, all three of them would know what each of them felt. And that no one was betraying anyone by being a loving, caring individual... and expressing that love."

She sat there in her life-support chair, looking at Honor and Hamish with a small, gentle smile, and then she waved her right hand in that same shrug-equivalent gesture.

"I've given it quite a lot of thought, you know," she said, "and I've come to the conclusion, my dears, that treecats are really most remarkably sane individuals. I suspect that if you spent some time talking with them, or possibly even with each other, you might come to the same conclusion."

She smiled at them again, and then her life-support chair moved silently back from the table.

"You might want to think about that," she told them as her chair floated towards the door. "But for now, *I'm* going to bed."

GLOSSARY

Alpha nodes—The impeller nodes of a starship which both generate its normal-space impeller wedge and reconfigure
to generate Warshawski sails in hyper-space.

Alpha translation—The translation into or out of the alpha (lowest)
bands of hyper-space.

Andermani Empire—Empire founded by mercenary Gustav Anderman. The Empire lies to the "west" of the Star Kingdom,
has an excellent navy, and is the Star Kingdom's primary
competitor for trade and influence in the Silesian Confederacy.

Andies—Slang term for citizens and (especially) the military
personnel and forces of the Andermani Empire.

BB—Battleship. At one time, the heaviest capital ship but now
considered too small to "lie in the wall." Average tonnage is from 2,000,000 to 4,000,000 tons. Employed by
some navies for rear area system security but no longer
considered an effective warship type.

BC—Battlecruiser. The lightest unit considered a "capital ship."
Designed to destroy anything it can catch and to outrun anything that can catch it. Average tonnage is from
500,000–1,200,000 tons.

Beta node—Secondary generating nodes of a spacecraft's impeller wedge. They contribute only to the impeller wedge

used for normal-space movement. Less powerful and less expensive than alpha nodes.

BLS—Basic Living Stipend. The welfare payment from the PRH government to its permanent underclass. Essentially, the BLS was a straight exchange of government services for a permanent block vote supporting the Legislaturalists who controlled the government.

DD—Destroyer. The smallest hyper-capable warship currently being built by most navies. Average tonnage is from 65,000–80,000 tons.

"Down the throat shot"—An attack launched from directly ahead of an impeller-drive spacecraft in order to fire lengthwise down its impeller wedge. Due to the geometry of the impeller wedge, this is a warship's most vulnerable single aspect.

DN—Dreadnought. A class of warship lying midway between battleships and superdreadnoughts. No major navy is currently building this type. Average tonnage is from 4,000,000 to 6,000,000 tons.

CA—Heavy cruiser (from Cruiser, Armored). Designed for commerce protection and long—endurance system pickets. Designed to stand in for capital ships against moderate level threats. Average tonnage is from 160,000–350,000 tons, although that has begun to creep upward towards traditional battlecruiser tonnage ranges in some navies.

Centrists—A Manticoran political party typified by pragmatism and moderation on most issues but very tightly focused on the Havenite threat and how to defeat it. The party supported by Honor Harrington.

CIC—Combat Information Center. The "nerve center" of a warship, responsible for gathering and organizing sensor data and the tactical situation.

CL—Light cruiser. The primary scouting unit of most navies. Also used for both commerce protection and raiding. Average tonnage is from 90,000–150,000 tons.

CLAC—LAC carrier. A starship of dreadnought or superdreadnought size configured to transport LACs through hyperspace and to service and arm them for combat.

COLAC—Commanding Officer, Light Attack Craft. The commander of the entire group of LACs carried by a CLAC.

Committee of Public Safety—The committee established by Rob
S. Pierre after his overthrow of the Legislaturalists to control the PRH. It instituted a reign of terror and systematic purges of surviving Legislaturalists and prosecuted
the war against the Star Kingdom.

Confederation Navy—Organized naval forces of the Silesian Confederacy.

Confeds—Slang term for citizens of the Silesian Confederacy and
(especially) for members of the Confederation Navy.

Conservative Association—A generally reactionary Manticoran
political party whose primary constituency is the
extremely conservative aristocracy.

Coup de Vitesse—A primarily offensive, "hard style" martial art
preferred by the RMN and RMMC. Main emphasis is
on weaponless combat.

Crown Loyalists—A Manticoran political party united around the
concept that the Star Kingdom requires a strong mon-
archy, largely as a counter balance to the power of the
conservative element in the aristocracy. Despite this, the
Star Kingdom's more progressive aristocracy is heavily
represented in the Crown Loyalists.

Dolist—One of a class of Havenite citizens totally dependent on
the government-provided Basic Living Stipend. As a
group, undereducated and underskilled.

ECM—Electronic counter measures.

EW—Electronic warfare.

FIA—Federal Investigative Agency. The national police force of the
restored Republic of Haven.

FIS—Federal Intelligence Service. The primary espionage agency
of the restored Republic of Haven.

Ghostrider, Project—A Manticoran research project dedicated to
the development of the multi-drive missile and associated technology. The original Ghostrider blossomed into
a large number of sub-projects which emphasized electronic warfare and decoys as well as offensive missiles.

Gravity waves—A naturally occurring phenomenon in hyper-space
consisting of permanent, very powerful regions of
focused gravitic stress which remain motionless but for
a (relatively) slow side-slipping or drifting. Vessels with
Warshawski sails are capable of using such waves to

attain very high levels of acceleration; vessels under
impeller drive are destroyed upon entering them.

Grav pulse com—A communication device using gravitic pulses
to achieve FTL communications over intrasystem ranges.

Grayson—Habitable planet of Yeltsin's Star. Star Kingdom of
Manticore's most important single ally.

Hyper limit The critical distance from a given star at which
starships may enter or leave hyper-space. The limit varies
with the mass of the star. Very large planets have hyper
limits of their own.

Hyper-space—Multiple layers of associated but discrete dimensions
which bring points in normal-space into closer congru-
ence, thus permitting effectively faster than light travel
between them. Layers are divided into "bands" of closely
associated dimensions. The barriers between such bands
are the sites of turbulence and instability which become
increasingly powerful and dangerous as a vessel moves
"higher" in hyper-space.

IAN—Imperial Andermani Navy.

Impeller drive—The standard reactionless normal-space drive of
the Honor Harrington universe, employing artificially
generated bands (or "wedges") of gravitic energy to
provide very high rates of acceleration. It is also used
in hyper-space outside gravity waves.

Impeller wedge—The inclined planes of gravitic stress formed above
and below a spacecraft by its impeller drive. A military
impeller wedge's "floor" and "roof" are impenetrable by
any known weapon.

Inertial compensator—A device which creates an "inertial sump,"
diverting the inertial forces associated with acceleration
into a starship's impeller wedge or a naturally occurring
gravity wave, thus negating the g-force the ship's crew
would otherwise experience. Smaller vessels enjoy a
higher compensator efficiency for a given strength of
wedge or gravity wave and thus can achieve higher
accelerations than larger vessels.

InSec—Internal Security. The secret police and espionage service
of the PRH under the Legislaturalists. Charged with
security functions and suppression of dissent.

LAC—Light Attack Craft. A sublight warship type, incapable of entering hyper, which masses between 40,000 and 60,000 tons. Until recently, considered an obsolete and ineffective warship good for little but customs duty and light patrol work. Advances in technology have changed that view of it.

Laser clusters—Last-ditch, close-range anti-missile point defense systems.

Liberal Party—A Manticoran political party typified by a belief in isolationism and the need for social intervention and the use of the power of the state to "level" economic and political inequities within the Star Kingdom.

Legislaturalists—The hereditary ruling class of the PRH. The descendants of the politicians who created the Dolist System more than two hundred years before the beginning of the current war.

Manties—Slang term for citizens of and (especially) military personnel/forces of the Star Kingdom of Manticore.

MDM—Multi-drive missile. A new Manticoran weapon development which enormously enhances the range of missile combat by providing additional drive endurance.

NavInt—Shortened version of Naval Intelligence. The naval intelligence agency of the Republic of Haven.

New Men—A Manticoran political party headed by Sheridan Wallace. Small and opportunistic.

Office of Naval Intelligence (ONI)—The RMN's naval intelligence service, directed by the Second Space Lord.

Peeps—Slang term for citizens and (especially) military personnel of the Peoples' Republic of Haven.

Penaids—Electronic systems carried by missiles to assist them in penetrating their targets' active and passive defenses.

Pinnace—A general purpose military small craft capable of lifting approximately 100 personnel. Equipped with its own impeller wedge, capable of high acceleration, and normally armed. May be configured for ground support.

Powered Armor—Battle armor combining a vac suit with protection proof against most man-portable projectile weapons, very powerful exoskeletal "muscles," sophisticated on-board sensors, and maneuvering thrusters for use in vacuum.

Progressive Party—A Manticoran political party typified by what it considers a pragmatic acceptance of real politik. It is somewhat more socially liberal than the Centrists but has traditionally considered a war against Haven as unwinnable and believed that the Star Kingdom's interests would be best served by cutting some sort of "deal" with the PRH.

Protector—Title of ruler of Grayson. Equivalent to "emperor." The current protector is Benjamin Mayhew.

PubIn—Office of Public Information. Propaganda arm of the PRH under both the Legislaturalists and the Committee of Public Safety.

PRH—Peoples' Republic of Haven. The name applied to the Republic of Haven during the period when it was controlled by the Legislaturalists and/or the Committee of Public Safety. It was the PRH which began the current war by attacking the Star Kingdom of Manticore and the Manticoran Alliance.

Republic of Erewhon—Government of the Erewhon System. A single-system unit which controls the Erewhon Wormhole Junction connecting the Solarian League and the Phoenix Wormhole Junction. A member of the Manticoran Alliance since before the start of the current war.

Republic of Haven—The largest human interstellar political unit after the Solarian League itself. Until recently it was known as the Peoples' Republic of Haven, ruled by an hereditary governing class known as the Legislaturalists until they were overthrown by Rob S. Pierre. Thereafter controlled by Pierre through the Committee of Public Safety until it, too, was overthrown in turn and the original constitution of the Republic was reinstated.

RHN—Republic of Haven Navy. Navy of the Republic of Haven as reorganized by Thomas Theisman.

RMAIA—Royal Manticoran Astrography Investigation Agency. Agency created by High Ridge Government to explore the Manticoran Wormhole Junction searching for additional termini.

RMN—Royal Manticoran Navy.

RMMC—Royal Manticoran Marine Corps

SD—Superdreadnought. The largest and most powerful

hyper-capable warship. Average tonnage is from 6,000,000–8,500,000 tons.

Shuttles—Small craft employed by starships for personnel and cargo movement from ship to ship or ship to surface. Cargo shuttles are configured primarily as freight haulers, with limited personnel capacity. Assault shuttles are heavily armed and armored and typically are capable of lifting at least a full company of ground troops.

Sidewalls—Protective barriers of gravitic stress projected to either side of a warship to protect its flanks from hostile fire. Not as difficult to penetrate as an impeller wedge, but still a very powerful defense.

Silesian Confederacy—A large, chaotic political entity lying between the Star Kingdom of Manticore and the Andermani Empire. Its central government is both weak and extremely corrupt and the region is plagued by pirates. Despite this, the Confederacy is a large and very important foreign market for the Star Kingdom.

Sillies—Slang term for Silesian citizens and/or military personnel.

Solarian League—Largest, wealthiest star nation of the explored galaxy, with decentralized government managed by extremely powerful bureaucracies.

Sollies—Slang term for citizens or military personnel of the Solarian League.

StateSec—Also "SS." Office of State Security. The successor to Internal Security under the Committee of Public Safety. Even more powerful than InSec. Headed by Oscar Saint-Just, originally second-in-command of InSec, who betrayed the Legislaturalists to aid Rob Pierre in overthrowing them.

Star Kingdom of Manticore—A small, wealthy star nation consisting of two star systems: the Manticore System and the Basilisk System.

Treecats—The native sentient species of the planet Sphinx. Six-limbed, telempathic arboreal predators which average between 1.5 and 2 meters in length (including prehensile tail). A small percentage of them bond with "adopted" humans in a near symbiotic relationship. Although incapable of speech, treecats have recently learned to communicate with humans using sign language.

"Up the kilt shot"—An attack launched from directly astern of a starship in order to fire down the length of its impeller wedge. Due to the geometry of the impeller drive, this is a warship's second most vulnerable aspect.

Warshawski—Name applied to all gravitic detectors in honor of the inventor of the first such device.

Warshawski, Adrienne—The greatest hyper-physicist in human history.

Warshawski sail—The circular gravity "grab fields" devised by Adrienne Warshawski to permit starships to "sail" along gravity waves in hyper-space.

Wormhole junction—A gravitic anomaly. Effectively, a frozen flaw in normal space providing access via hyper-space as an instantaneous link between widely separated points. The largest known junction is the Manticoran Wormhole Junction with six known termini as of the beginning of *War of Honor*.